Derail this Train Wreck

By Daniel Forbes

For Herself, a True Gift Beyond all Others

Disclaimer

This is a work of fiction, book and website alike. References to real people, events, establishments, organizations or locales are used fictitiously. All other characters, and incidents, and dialogue are drawn from the author's imagination and not to be construed as real.

Cover Design by Julie Forbes

ISBN 9780983608714

DerailthisTrainWreck.com

Derail this Train Wreck

Every apathetic citizen is a silent enlistee in the cause of inverted totalitarianism.

– Sheldon S. Wolin

Philosophy should always know that indifference is a militant thing. It batters down the walls of cities and murders the women and children amid the flames and the purloining of altar vessels. When it goes away it leaves smoking ruins, where lie citizens bayoneted through the throat. It is not a children's pastime like mere highway robbery.

– Stephen Crane

Chapter One

Behind the Mesh

The early Saturday evening train slowed approaching Jamaica, the big station in Queens where the Long Island Rail Road sorts out who's going where. Then, for some reason over the intercom riders hear, someone told the engineer to radio for an emergency police response to the third car.

"What are you talking about? You sure a *4-7G* is necessary? What do we got here, anyway?"

Offended, the first guy's voice rose. "It's all there: failure to comply, threat undetermined, outcome unknown. I'm not taking it from these people anymore."

"Come on, Jamie. You sure you want to do this, or is this just another one of your little scrapes? You even know they have platform-ready cops at Jamaica on a Saturday night?"

"They got cops, MTA or state troopers, at Jamaica 24/7. So just radio him to the third car. It's on me."

"Roger, Jamie. But after what happened last month, this is definitely on you."

"I'm authorized, BEI, and I'm doing it."

Threat undetermined. Outcome unknown – hell, just more of the standard daily static since HeadMan burrowed his way to the top. No big deal, I told myself.

Soon enough, a woman conductor treated us to the usual verbiage about Track 7 for the train to Hempstead, etc., followed by the pro forma, oft-ignored instructions not to bellow into your micro-zap, keep your feet off the seats, and take your trash. Plus, "Ladies and gentlemen, please be advised that backpacks and other large containers are subject to random – repeat, random – search by police." That seemed a bit much pulling *into* a station, but….

The warning that you might get searched had quickly become more of the background noise of travel, like the drone about emergency exits by the wings. Never mind that in a different age populated by a less timorous sort, it might've led to marching in the streets.

Despite my prior fumbling, I pondered trying to build on the alliance forged with the woman across the aisle during her confrontation with the tin-pot conductor as we left Manhattan a half-hour before. Wasting the extra legroom in the seat by the door – the only one where I wasn't scrunched knees by ears – she was cute enough, sure. And in her mid-thirties, Cat Wrangler was the right age. Plus she had stood up to that conductor in fine fashion. But with her Sally Striver blonde dye-job and high-heeled sandals she couldn't walk six blocks in, she was regrettably not my type. I couldn't see her tramping by the water in some far corner of Brooklyn or the Bronx just for the hell of it as the Wife and I once did in happier days.

Aside from the priss and podiatric aspects, Cat Wrangler looked a little shaky, with her lipstick fudged, a far-off stare and a cut-up white sock secured with red duct tape bandaging the back of her hand. Right: never date anyone with more problems than you.

Still, propinquity staked its claim. Deciding to wing it, I peeked over to see that only her sister's cat was awake. Imprisoned in his mesh-walled little rolling suitcase by her feet and making his usual threatening moans deep in his throat, it probably wouldn't be much of a conversation with that troublemaker either.

The mob switching trains pushed on and off at Jamaica, one guy dropping a big suitcase by the door to join the monstrous one left there unsupervised since Manhattan. The train jerked to a start, and again the announcement: hush with the micro-zap, feet, trash, and kiss your rights good-bye locked on a moving train, this last particularly asserted.

Then a large, don't-mess state trooper came striding through the short end of the car looking neither left nor right. In his early forties, tall, dark and handsome, he moved stiffly and held his head like it'd been removed for servicing and just recently stuck back on his neck. He wasn't quite used to having the muck cleaned out of the grooves yet. Yup, he stopped and looked down at my snoozing new friend, her bandaged hand clenching the handle of the cat's odd case.

"Miss, Miss! You're capable of waking? I need you to open that bag – now! There's been an official report of a concealed threat – type, outcome unknown – capable of impacting the riding public. As a designated first-tier responder, I need to clear that bag."

On thin ice already, she cracked quick. "I can't. It's just a cat, but he'll escape – I can't control it. And then he'll run somewhere and my sister will kill me."

The cop started to say something, but she plunged on. "You don't understand. My mother's sick, and I have to take this stupid cat out to Huntington. Why do you have to look in my bag anyway, all these suitcases and stuff all around? We're not bothering anyone, the cat was finally quiet."

Not anymore. Apparently finding pants of State Police gray no more appealing than he'd previously found LIRR blue, the cat again launched himself at the black mesh with a cry from deep in the jungle. I couldn't decide which turned my blood to water more, the moan or the hiss from what I clocked as a 19-pounder. Not flinching a whit, the cop said, "Miss – shut it. You say it's a cat? Procedurally, that's of no significance." He'd looked bored approaching us, but now confronting someone, however slight, with the temerity to refuse, he kicked into full stentorian gear.

"There's been an incident response request over official channel 12/41, a transmission logged by state, local and federal dispatchers at Jamaica, Albany and at Fort Meade, Maryland. Whether it rises to the Data Minders' concern is up to you, but I cannot dismiss it without making a ruling. Now, do I delay this train, and all the hundreds of Homelanders and others properly traveling home, to have a Crisis Disposal Team equipped with a mechanized arm – which will take an hour to assemble on a Saturday night – meet us at the next station? Or will you submit to lawful authority?"

"Maryland? What are you talking about? What's happened to this country? It's a *pussycat*! But it's not mine, and I can't control it. And neither can you or that stupid team of yours."

Furtive whispering wafted forward from the rest of the car, and I peered back to see folks standing and staring, grinning or appalled. Grab 'em and pound 'em the norm since HeadMan's installation, everyone was riveted by her hen's-tooth refusal. I'd done all of nothing a half-hour back to help my comely new friend with that clown conductor. So I decided to toss a little pacifying fat on the fire.

Painful personal experience having taught it's best to approach crazed authority types man-to-man, I hauled myself up and ended up standing closer to a cop than I should, especially being as big myself as one this big. A gun accessible on their hip, cops are skittish, like horses. It went with being hated and feared these days. Regretting my heat-wave scruffiness, my mollifying tone was meant for a cranky three-year-old past due for a nap. "Officer, perhaps I can be of assistance: She and I were just talking and, well, that's a Siamese cat. I happen to know a little about cats, and the Siamese is a particularly temperamental breed. Just look at her hand. You see – "

Without word or warning, he stepped back, drew his nightstick from his belt and jabbed me hard in the collarbone, knocking me back down in my seat. I yelped, and was almost as pissed at myself for giving him that small victory as I was at a MoFo going ape for no reason. Astonishment lagging pain, it hurt nothing like it would the next morning. Somebody back there yelled, "Hey, watch it!" But that was the extent of all those folks' outrage – well, that and more yowling and spitting at our feet.

The trooper stared down and said, "Maintain a seated position at all times, mister. Or you'll be taken in for interfering with government administration, obstructing a T investigation, assaulting a sworn Protector and resisting arrest. I'll let you think about that last one, BEI."

BEI my fat red ass. As when lecturing Cat Wrangler, he puffed up for these pronouncements plucked from air. Stepping back, he almost tripped over one of the big suitcases by the door. He kicked it aside, put his nightstick under his arm and struggled into the too-tight, black leather gloves that cops favored. Thus fortified, he launched in again. "Now, Miss. According to the new Regs, during the Current Permanent Crisis, any hand wound elevates the need for a formal case ruling. Which means I have to determine the cause of your wound."

Great. I'd managed to work my usual turd-touch magic pointing out her cat scratch. Not daring to actually speak, some blessed provocateur behind us let loose a note-perfect yowl. Particularly affronted by mimicry, the cat's response nearly drowned out some of the laughter sprinkled through the car. The cop continued, "Your fresh wound was possibly caused by something sharp. Homeland Control refers to a machined edge. Be aware that I will examine your person shortly, focusing on coagulation."

The whispering grew louder as people wondered what he meant with talk of a machined edge and focusing on – what? He looked up and addressed the car at large. "As Citizens and others should know, Homeland Control has issued Regs – equal to legislation – that require an immediate ruling on all T incidents. The bandage, which looks to be an improvised field dressing, will be removed to rule out concealed weapons, explosives or toxins."

She and I turned to each other, torn between horror and protest.

"Now, the statements regarding a cat have not been proven. Irregardless, your baggage is strange, Miss. All these little holes in its sides, are they possibly a bio/chem passive-delivery device?"

She jumped up and turned to face the longer portion of the car. "People, do you hear that? He's trying to turn a cat carrying case into a weapon. I'm starting to think I really need to document all this because" – her voice broke – "I don't, I don't know where it's headed. Is there anyone here with a licensed whole-vid who's willing to film this? I know that's a risk. Or maybe even someone good at old-fashioned taking notes?" No reply from the mostly bent heads to a very dicey request, she wavered to a stop, barely as tall as the fourth button on the cop's shirt. "People – nobody?" She turned and crumpled back into her seat.

Taking notes, un-huh. A resurrected art since HeadMan banned whole-vid-capable micro-zaps once it became apparent people would risk lengthy jail time to video police acting ugly on the street. Savvy observers cut through the pretext that cops – that MoFos of all stripes – were 'endangered' by people recording their brutalities. Such observers branded the edict as a boon to an over-saturated, decidedly mature micro-zap industry. That's because everyone but a few, onerously licensed individuals was forced en masse to buy retro personal pacifiers that couldn't take whole-vids. But it was common knowledge that even note-taking branded you worth a second look. Might as well have print-outs from the wrong website littering your coffee table when the cable guy showed.

Feeling left out, but butt parked firmly in seat, I ventured to inquire, "Hey, pal, what is this 'ruling' you keep talking about – that you're going to *rule* on things? Is it some kind of special state-cop thing? Or somebody die and make you king?"

Was his talk more than mere blowhardism run wild? They promulgated anew on a monthly basis, so who knew. He turned, and I steeled myself not to flinch. But he just curled his lip like a dog you're foolishly trying to pet tied up outside a store. "You're asking for a Boosting with that kind of talk, mister, the Data Minders with a spot for you right up top."

Damn right I shut the hell up at that, but he had more intriguing prey. "Now, Miss, you've yet to prove that the noise from your portable storage device – loud enough to mask a threat or act as a diversion itself – comes from a live animal. Such masking could have been generated for strategic use at this time."

Never mind that the cat at that moment was bashing its brains out against the mesh, mere facts didn't deflect him from his appointed path. Six-foot-four, broad of beam and in his prime, he was rarely interrupted once he got it in gear. But she made him pause by *laughing*, then saying, "You don't have a leg to stand on, do you? And you know it. That's why all you guys yell and bully and manufacture all this empty authority so no one will look behind the curtain. BEI and everything, it's all crap, isn't it?"

That elicited a gasp from some lady as the trooper plowed on. "If all you have is a cat as you claim, I have the training, experience and equipment on my person to handle such a threat. You, Miss, need to produce this alleged cat's license. Therefore, you will open this bag or – "

"Go ahead, you big jerk. You open it! I hope you have a net or something on your 'person.' Do they teach you to talk like that, or do they just put a tape in your big head and turn you loose? And this guy is right: since when do cops make 'rulings?' Is that *more* new HeadMan nonsense we're supposed to bow down to?"

Both of them a bit taken aback by her outburst, she finally said, "I hope he bites your fucking head off!"

The earth not parting at her feet, swearing at a cop who richly deserves it can be massively liberating. As I well knew. Short, dyed hair just so and wearing those horrible Capri pants, I'd pretty much written her off. But talking like that to a sworn MoFo – hotdiggity!

Daring actual speech rather than cat-mimicry, a well appointed old dame not far behind us started in about being good with cats and maybe she could help. The trooper said, "Button your mouth, Ma'am. Not a word during this T investigation. This operation is being monitored by federal authorities. Do I make myself clear?"

The old lady's mild offer cracking the dam, some guy yelled,

"Officer – you're bugging. You gonna make the old lady go stand in the corner with her gum on her nose?"

Someone else chimed in, "Yo, that cat's from a foreign country, so they're watching this on the Big Board in the White House."

"Dude, that cat's from Asia," called a third jackal behind us. "That's what we got coming up next, invading them countries. All them people – watch out!"

Any and all dissent was helpful, everyone stoning the dike with the rock they found at their feet. But no one but the pair seated right beneath him seemed willing to challenge the cop on substance.

He put up his nightstick and leered down at my new hero. "Now, Miss. You're already in enough trouble as it is without directing a foul tongue at a duly sworn Protector. If you are transporting an uncontrollable animal, I cannot be held responsible liability-wise. Any resulting damages and/or injuries are the responsibility of you, your guardian or your heirs. That stated, Homeland Control's current alert status requires me to clear your baggage."

"What makes you think a woman my age has a guardian? Forget that – what's your name? And how come you're not wearing a badge? What the hell kind of cop are you anyway in that gray uniform?"

"My name, Miss, is Officer Schiakoczyk of the New York State Police. As to my badge, know that my Commander cleared me for patrol at roll call today."

"Schia – what? How the hell do you spell that?"

"Treat my parents' name properly, Miss, or HateCime defamation of a sworn Protector will be added to your charges."

Marveling at the practiced nonsense he spun so not to spell his name, I told her I thought I had it pretty close written on my hand.

"Young man, Officer!" It was the old lady again. "Actually, I was reading in the paper – I have it right here somewhere – that, despite the Current Permanent Crisis, they've temporarily lowered the alert status for mass transit all the way down to 87. I imagine that covers the searching of cats on the Long Island Rail Road. I'm sure they can micro-zap you the memo if you haven't gotten it already."

Given the general pusillanimity, the cop was probably met with more resistance in ten minutes than in the past month. He worked his jaw, gave an involuntary shudder, adjusted his gloves and bent to the cat. Out of nowhere, a conductor almost as tall and a lot heavier than the cop rushed up the aisle from behind. "Hey, Statie! I'm still running this train, no matter what you guys think. So let's talk about this a minute, cause I am not having a *cat* loose on my train!"

And moving quicker than he had a right to, the tall, barrel-chested conductor, pushing sixty and with a full shock of white hair, nudged the cop away from the bag. Caught by surprise and off-balance from bending over, the cop fell back into the vestibule, stumbled on that same giant suitcase, righted himself and half-drew his nightstick.

Chapter Two

Assault-by-Proxy

A whole fine mess from a popinjay's pique. Leaving Manhattan a half-hour before – back when worrying about cops was mere background static – a conductor had come flapping in from the short end of the car, chirping about tickets, all tickets, please. The LIRR's among the world's least flattering uniforms, he was styling nonetheless with a shiny pompadour, clunky bracelet, several rings and glittery, big-frame Vegas glasses on a gold chain resting just above his little belly roll.

As he turned to the woman, the cat, who'd momentarily stilled his steady complaint, launched himself at the thin mesh by the conductor's leg, yowling and hissing like some sort of woozle getting skinned alive. The conductor dropped his ticket punch, squeaked out an oath, stepped back and splayed his hand to his chest, breathing heavily.

To recapture the dignity that accrued to his station in life, one way or another, cat and owner would pay. Drawing himself up to his full five-foot-eight, he demanded she put the permeable, wheeled case up on the luggage rack where it belonged. She mildly replied that she had to keep an eye on the cat. He persisted, and she finally agreed. But she couldn't lift it, not without grabbing it in a bear hug and thus exposing herself to the cat's claws through the mesh. If he wanted to put it up there....

No, that wasn't part of his job, he said.

Technically not, but he was at least equally afraid of the spitting monster. She offered to move the case to the other side of her legs, where it'd be up against the bulkhead and no trouble to anyone. This a summer weekend train, there were quite a few backpacks and suitcases scattered about, and she wondered why hers was being singled out.

"Not that it's any concern of yours, but I may well get to those other bags. They are a passenger hazard in case of T. Things have gotten a little slipshod. But that's going to change, starting now with your bag, Miss, a bag with a vicious animal in it. I'm warning you, I have issued a Direct Request."

"Oh come on. Look, this is my sister's cat and, you're right, he probably is vicious. But he's secure in his case, and I've been working to calm him down. If you'd just let us be, I'm sure he won't be any more trouble."

"It's already been far too much trouble, and you have a lot of nerve bringing an animal you can't control onto public transportation. Considering your attitude, I'm tempted to have you charged with assault-by-proxy once we reach Jamaica. No, don't laugh, Miss. Assault-by-proxy is a federal crime, a *Homeland Control* crime. Assaulting a conductor in uniform – or a ferry crewman or any transport official – would, I imagine, lead to a Boosting."

The cat didn't buy it either, launching into his full repertoire at twice his prior volume. Jesus, a Boosting over this nonsense. Things had spun out of control awfully damn quick, even by the hair-trigger standards of the day.

I clutched for some way to derail this train wreck, loath though I was to step in it yet again.

She gave a tense little laugh and then smiled up at him, trying to slow things down. With one of those quirky ferret faces, she did have a fetching smile despite the bollixed lipstick. "Let me ask you, do you really think a pussycat constitutes a proxy? That hissing at you is an assault? Come on, you deal with the public every day. I see the drunk-fests these kids have, waving bottles of vodka around heading into the City every Saturday night. So is this *cat* really something you need to have a cow about? Stop for just a minute, Big Boy, and ask yourself. And what does that mean, anyway, 'assault-by-proxy'? Every time you turn around, there's some new way to get in trouble – or 'Boosted,' whatever that might really mean. All the beggars since the Plunge, give one a quarter and you risk a ticket. You can't even ride a bicycle with a couple of friends without getting some sort of ridiculous permit."

"Hey, don't forget all the biometric scans everywhere."

They ignored my little contribution. The conductor stepped

back and put his glasses on and then off to remove an offending speck. Only then could he study her properly. He got out a pad, wrote a moment and made a big production of checking his watch and jotting down the car's serial number.

"Miss, you have refused my Direct Request regarding passenger safety in a time of T. Therefore, you will have to bear the consequences. And believe me, there will be consequences. Now, I have tickets to punch." He dismissed her to a rattling good hiss from her ten-foot python. Aside from naturally opposing this martinet – staying rooted when they barked *Move!* – that was the other reason I didn't just put the case up on the rack myself.

He turned for my ticket with a slightly tremulous hand. I said, "Feeling all better now, Big Boy?"

"Sir, your comment is not helpful. Please do not interfere in a private matter."

Yeah, private, him a government employee talking of Boostings. My echoing her tag for him earned a smile as he moved on down the car. So, "I don't trust that jerk talking about consequences. Not these days, MoFos lurking under every rock. How far you going? … Huntington, huh. Too bad you're not changing trains at Jamaica, cause he sounded serious."

Not able to see through the dark mesh, I asked if it was a Siamese. She said yes, and how did I know? "No other kind of cat makes a noise quite like that, moaning and gurgling like some soldier shot through the throat, trapped in a World War One no-man's land bleeding to death." Stolen from something I'd read the day before, I was pleased to regurgitate it right on cue. She, however, was almost as cute looking horrified as when smiling up at Big Boy before that all went south. Since she wasn't, I laughed for us both and asked why a Siamese.

"Ask my sister, not me. I'm just taking him cause my mother's sick, and she's staying with Mom out in Huntington a few days. I thought this type of cat was supposed to be pretty refined, but he fought like a tiger getting put in his case. Just look at my hand." She held it up, the red duct tape over the sock the same as was wrapped crazily all around the top flap of the case.

"Homemade bandage, huh?"

"My sister'll be furious I cut up one of her socks, but I don't care. Eating out and taking taxis everywhere she goes, I don't think she ever cuts herself, so that's all I could find. I wonder how much blood I lost, cause I really don't feel well."

"Eat some cookies when you get to Huntington. That's what they give us donating blood at school." Boy, a regular Florence Nightingale was I. At least we were talking, but – years of rust or no – that was lame. Walking the mile from the subway to my hovel in her idiot sandals would prove a challenge, but maybe that's why God invented her place.

A pale soul, she studied her hand, then admitted, "I guess it wasn't right sliding those books at him under the bed. But what could I do after he cut my hand so bad when I reached under there? I'll probably get reported to some *new* authority."

"Minders Turn Elsewhere!" I intoned, just to be polite.

She looked up surprised and asked, "You don't really believe all that crap about Data Minders and Boostings, do you? I mean, no offense, but a guy like you."

Aside from the baggy cutoffs, work boots and a newer tee shirt on yet another in a long string of sulfurous, woolly-headed days, whatever could she mean? "You mean, is the Data more than just rhetorical underbrush to trip us up? I don't know and don't want to find out."

"Mostly I try to ignore it. Just another one of HeadFuck's" – she shot a little sidelong glance to check that I was onboard with that – "idiocies."

I nodded my concurrence, and she mused about a tetanus shot cause her hand sure hurt. I said only if the cat's claws were rusty. And despite that tripe earning her first real laugh, there things stalled. She soon closed her eyes, so I fished an old *Book Review* out of my back pocket to sneer at anyone with the gall to get published. And shortly before we hit Jamaica, Big Boy sicced a state trooper on her.

****

The cop put up his nightstick and kicked the entangling suitcase aside. But he remained trapped in the vestibule by the doors, the ample conductor blocking his way, his hands locked on the bars that edged the walls framing the aisle, Cat Wrangler and I seated right behind. The conductor had felt the need to intervene only as cat was about to be loosed from bag. Otherwise a state trooper had free reign on 'his' train. Both men in uniform unaccustomed to challenge in their domain – the conductor's being the train and the cop's wherever he found himself – they soon threw down loud.

Bags everywhere, the conductor asked why he had to search this particular one. The trooper said he'd gotten a Homeland Control 4-7G Emergency Response Order at Jamaica initiated by conductor badge number 37-946, who then directed him to this specific bag. "So, Conductor, with only four years until my earned retirement, I'm making no negatory career decision here tonight. As God made me, Conductor, I will not still be clocking in at your age, BEI."

"Oh nuts."

"I now order you to remove your person before this becomes a career decision of your own."

As the cop moved to bull his way past, the conductor said, "But emergency response for what? That's what I don't get. Why this girl and this stupid cat?"

Confronting a worthy adversary, with institutional backing, not just the Jane and Joe Q. Public he'd been bullying, the cop got his radio out. Kicking the suitcase that kept tangling him up, he moved back by the train door but still couldn't make it work.

"Go ahead, call a whole bunch of cops. Just make sure one of them's a sergeant with some sense," said the boss conductor. "In the meantime, somebody get Jamie up here now."

A third conductor moved up the aisle and said that Jamie had had some static with the woman. He'd told him to leave it alone, but Jamie had insisted it was his right to call it in at Jamaica. Get Jamie now, Boss Conductor barked, and forty people who'd been holding their breath listening started whispering again. Following recent brown-out Regs on saving power during the weekend, the train rolled slowly through eastern Queens as dusk fell.

Soon dragged up by the ear, Jamie (AKA Big Boy) started

blubbering that Cat Wrangler had refused his appropriate, lawful request regarding placement of her bag. That she had brought a vicious animal out to menace the public in a camouflaged bag. And that –

She erupted, it getting easier every time. "That's called mesh, you idiot. So he can get some oxygen to his brain – something you might try." Then she really started yelling. "I can't believe calling this ridiculous cop, getting this guy attacked and everything else was just because you almost wet your pants when the cat jumped at you – jumped while still in his case! Now why don't you apologize to everyone for this nonsense, including Mr. State Kook over there trying to call in the 82nd Airborne, and let us get where we're going?"

Big Boy pointed to the bandage on her hand and asked how did they know the cat's claws hadn't been treated with anthrax. The new Homeland Control Regs about suspicious injuries to the hand meant they couldn't be too careful.

"Jamie, never mind that she wouldn't be infecting herself. If you ever – ever –" and Boss Conductor made like to swat him, "mention that Homeland Reg on Wounds to the Hand again, I will write you up so bad for any one of maybe eleven things I got on you, you'll be working Christmas and Thanksgiving *both* for the rest of your very short LIRR career."

I laughed out loud, partly for real at Big Boy's comeuppance and partly to bolster Boss Conductor, and tried to think what to say to nail the carcass to the wall. Then, somebody, a black guy by the sound of him, started bellowing in a voice that'd shake a brick from a wall. "Leave her alone, you turkeys. Anthrax my ass! This is bullshit and you know it, picking on that lady cause she's small. Why don't you pick on someone your own damn size."

A chorus of boos failed to shut him up. "I'm a sergeant major in the United States Army with twenty-four years serving his country, Fomenting Democracy all over Asia, and I got the medals to prove it. I don't take no shit from anybody under a major, so I sure ain't taking any from some lame-ass state cop. And, oh Lord, I really, truly would like to see him hit me with that little stick of his I'll shove up his hole for him. You heard me, a damn police worrying about a cat on a train, ain't got nothing better to do. Is that the deal under HeadFuck now? Cause all you people but Jack and Jill up there are sitting here taking it."

A woman from somewhere back there – ah, democracy in our rolling town square, one of its few remaining face-to-face venues – objected to the sergeant major's outburst, each plummy word pried from very tight lips. "Young man, that's a Protector standing there, one of the true-blue heroes putting his life on the line *daily* to keep us safe during the Current Permanent Crisis. As to your despicable term for your commander-in-chief: *Bold, Extolled, Impregnable!*"

"You forgot your BEI-stiff-arm salute, lady. You people out here on Long Island don't have a clue what's going down in this world, driving around in vehicles so big you can't fit past each other on the street. I didn't fight all them warlords and maniacs – six tours in four different countries – to come back to this shit here at home. And now I'm hearing rumors about going somewhere new for tour number *seven*! Me just trying to go visit my kid cause his fool mother thinks it's better to raise him out here with you jackasses. Try this shit in Brooklyn, it'd be another story."

A bunch of ugly hubbub followed. But I focused on what was happening right in front of me. The trooper put his silent radio away and, slapping one fist, leather on leather, into the palm of his other hand, tried to push past Boss Conductor as Big Boy fled the car. Re-anchoring his hold on the walls separating the vestibule from the aisle, the conductor snarled, "Look, Statie! We are not having a riot over a cat on my train! This is *my* train, Goddamnit, and *you're* the one talking about a career decision here. You never had anyone swear at you before, you with sixteen years in?"

"Get out of my way, Conductor – now! That's a lawful ruling."

"Yeah, get out of that big bastard's way. I'd like to see if he really does come back here. Probably have to call his momma on that radio first." This from a soldier with way too many Sands under his belt.

Holding his ground against the cop with an absolute minimum of effort, the conductor said, "Look, *Officer*, you want me out of your way, just say the word."

The cop said nothing. Eight tortuously long, silent beats later, Boss Conductor laughed. "I didn't think so. It's always the same when somebody calls your bluff, guys like you, isn't it?"

I grinned over at Cat Wrangler, incredulous that our tormentor had been exposed as such a paper tiger by a smart old man and a voice of doom from in back. The conductor now made some pronouncements of his own. "Statie – it's a cat. You got that? We've already determined that radioing you here was bogus, and my conductor is in more trouble than he'll know what to do with. Now, this lady here is no more a T-Fiend than I am."

The cop started sputtering, so the trainman reached for the hole card he'd been fingering all along. "Mister, I don't want to hear it. Not with you assaulting this passenger here for nothing. That's right, I saw it. Now we both know he could make your vacation go up in smoke. Those new, 'Protect-the-Protector' Regs haven't been issued yet, right, cause the cops don't want EMTs included in the bonus pool."

It hadn't occurred to me in the heat of battle to try to discipline this cop during the Current P. Crisis. I just wanted to make him go away.

"Conductor, that was clearly self-defense. Everyone here saw that man charge me."

"Charge you! I just stood up right here in my seat, and you went bat-shit cause someone had the nerve to try to talk to you. I should – " But he shouted me down.

"Only concern for passenger safety kept me from drawing my service weapon in self-defense in response to this Suspect's assault. I will affirm that with all the power of the uniform I wear."

Their uniforms had special powers now?

"I will also run the Perpetrator's ID through several national T Sets as soon as my radio clears. Unless he's adopted an uncommon alias, a match will be found. The same goes for the female Suspect. The Data Minders will be notified, of course. But first: her baggage can serve as a 'passive-porous dissemination device,' a threat outlined by Homeland Control. She says it's a cat, yet remains unwilling to prove it."

Cat Wrangler jumped up, protest and invective tumbling out all over. But the conductor bodied her back in her seat.

It was like watching the ventriloquist's evil dummy spring free to reveal his true nature. "In fact, Conductor, iris profiles, along with facial-recognition templates, will be obtained on both Subversives. Finally, the female's fresh wound will be examined by the senior first-tier responder present here tonight before she can cauterize it, negating key evidence along its … *unstable* edges."

I tried to figure how to get the hell off the train without this guy scratching me to capture flaked-off-skin under his nails. Or would he just yank out some hair I could ill afford? He turned ingratiating. "As to my vacation, from your vantage, Conductor, you could not see I drew my field baton to ward off an attack for the Perpetrator's own safety. Should his touch have fouled this uniform, I am honor-bound to respond."

" 'Honor-bound.' What is that, sacred cloth? That's all you can do, lie and try to get away with it, thicker and deeper as you go." I jumped up, safely behind the conductor's broad back. "Look at my damn chest." I pulled my tee shirt down below a nasty circular abrasion the diameter of his club. "This is gonna look a whole lot worse by the time I get to a licensed whole-vid parlor, Officer Rumpelstiltskin. And how come you're not wearing a badge – what's that all about? How do we know your name is whatever the hell you said anyway?"

The drama queen turned around to the longer section of the car, pulled down his shirt and – a pipe dream, sure – demanded, "Anyone got a whole-vid to take a picture of this? Hell, to take a picture of the maniac who attacked me? You don't have to worry about the vid – I'll put my name on top."

The old lady gasped and someone yelled for me to shut up and sit down, that I got what I deserved. Someone else called for informing the Minders I was trying to whole-vid a sworn Protector. But Boss Conductor's voice rose above the clamor. "You can 'affirm' from here to next week if you want to, Statie, but I know what I saw, and his chest proves it. Meanwhile, and this isn't even your fault I'm sorry to say, I got a damn 4-7G to make disappear. Now – no, mister, it's my turn to talk – it's gonna take an extra hour that I don't need tonight, especially because it's going to be for free. Neither one of us is calling attention to this … incident by putting in for any OT. You got that?"

The trooper barely nodded.

"We write it up so that we just throw her off at the next stop. But the Regs are mandatory that it has to be the next stop. 'Exigent circumstances: refusal to comply with search' it's called. We determine she's not an imminent threat – in her case, that'll last a couple of decades – throw her off the train and everything's fine. You got that?"

He nodded more emphatically.

"You write it up exactly like I say, and you're covered too. But I am not having a *cat* loose on my train! The last time was four years ago, and I'm not over it yet."

Chapter Three

You'll Stop Twitching Soon Enough

The cop crossed his arms and looked at us all in turn – conductor, Cat Wrangler, feline, then me – leveling his harsh gaze on me the longest. "Conductor, this field operation does contain exigentness. We must first de-escalate the threat posed by the female Suspect and then neutralize the obviously unbalanced male who is ruled a Person of Concern. I will now determine the origin of the female's wound before the next stop, which is what?"

"New Hyde Park. But wait a – "

"Now, Miss!" the cop barked as he tried to edge past the conductor. "Home Front defense requires you to present your hand undressed for inspection, or duly sworn authority will remove the bandage."

The conductor remained a wall as she rocketed back up. "You're out of your mind. This is my body – mine! You're deranged if you think I'm letting you touch me. You don't even have a badge on. All you have is a gun and a twisted little mind." She leaped and tried to claw his face over the conductor's shoulder, and for a moment, he shielded cop from citizen. He stepped back and rest his hand on the butt of his gun.

A woman started chanting, "Shame! Shame! Shame!" Another woman weakly joined in before they were hollered down by first one, then several leather-lunged louts bellowing "USA! USA! USA!" I loved when prideful dudes did that, lowering their voices by two octaves. The Lake Placid hockey team that beat the Russians must've gotten on at Jamaica without me noticing.

The conductor told the cop they were getting her off the train momentarily, so he could forget about examining anyone's hand. They sparred some and finally had another of their little stare-downs. But having exposed the cop's bullying as hollow, like he kept saying, it was his train.

"Conductor, my report will note your refusal to follow Homeland Control Regs on wounds made by a sharp edge."

"Look, mister, until I go out one way or the other, those idiot hand-wound Regs do not apply on my Goddamn train! I'm third-generation railroad. My father was an LIRR conductor for 39 years till he finished his run at Ronkonkoma one night and dropped dead on the platform, his totals done."

Not unkindly, Cat Wrangler said that was horrible. Busy laying down the law, I don't think he heard. "So nobody, no matter what they got strapped on their hip, is messing with my passengers' bandages. Now that's the train slowing for New Hyde Park, and that's where she's getting off! And what do you mean, anyway: cut with a 'sharp edge?' We got to make sure she didn't cut herself eating soup with a spoon?"

Cat Wrangler seized on a good point. "Conductor, maybe you didn't hear this. But I already gave that big jerk permission to search my bag. As any number of people here can verify, I told him to go ahead. That I hoped the cat bites his head off. So this is all nonsense. Go ahead, look in the cat's bag if it gets you off *and* you think you can control him. I don't care anymore. Believe it or not, people have problems and lives and stuff that have nothing to do with the Long Island Rail Road. So just let me get where I'm going and leave me the fuck alone!"

Man, she packed a wallop, not to mention she was right. Everyone had forgotten she'd told the cop to go ahead and fool with the cat if he dared, and he was about to when the conductor stomached him away. This was all a bunch of hooey. But, haunted by cats loose on his train, the conductor had way too much invested, particularly his mastery of the cop, in throwing her off at New Hyde Park.

Sparking the cat's paroxysms by grabbing his carrier's long handle, the conductor said rules are rules. She had, for reasons of her own, delayed a *timely* search, and – passenger safety his main concern – really, his hands were tied. What's more, she certainly didn't want her cat getting loose, now did she? Another train would be along in an hour, he said and, pulling a voucher from his shirt pocket, he told her to just give it to the conductor on the next train for a free ride.

He was about to grab her by the arm and tug her up when the old lady – who I wanted by my side my next back-alley brawl – piped up. "Just a minute, Conductor. If she and her kitty are such a danger they have to be removed from this train, what about the passengers on the next train? How can you put them at risk?"

This bull's-eye roused some scattered applause as the cop drew his stick again and pointed it at the old lady over the conductor's shoulder. "Ma'am, I have previously warned you about interfering in this federally mandated T-Operation. I will not warn you or any other Subversive again."

Boss Conductor bent to grab her, and Cat Wrangler hissed and hopelessly tried to wrench her arm free. She started swinging with her free hand, but he easily held her at arm's length. An enormous guy, quite a specimen remained beneath the fat and the years. As the train pulled to a stop and the doors opened, a chorus of boos and leave-her-alone and throw-her-off underlay a rich stream of invective from the foghorn of a sergeant major and a veritable catophony from the enmeshed.

I jumped up and shouted, "Dudes – gentlemen! You can't throw her off here. It's not safe, this deserted stop on the weekend. Make it Mineola."

"Can't? Watch me!" Again moving quicker than you'd think, he lifted the hissing, spitting case, dragged the girl by her arm, bodied them past the cop and flung her, who he outweighed by 170 pounds, onto the platform and out of my life. Snarling and spitting herself, she had about as much effect as did the cat.

I sprang for the closing door, but the cop blindsided me and pushed me back down in my seat. "Not you! We're not finished with you yet."

Yelling at his minion at the far end of the car to close the doors, Boss Conductor got out his flashlight, pushed the sputtering girl back and signaled the engineer to go.

Three guys who'd been watching in back started yelling, hey wait, this was their stop too, but that was lost in the general uproar. One man kept proclaiming he'd been riding these trains for 37 years and had never seen a conductor put his hands on a passenger. Some said it wasn't right putting her off at a lonely stop like that near dark. Others argued that the girl should have just let them look in her case, mangling that she'd given her permission long before. As in any shout-fest, the facts quickly grew obscure. But the talk leaned heavily against her, people on the train having been inculcated over the fractious months and years like everyone else, the flame under our kettle ever higher. What was she trying to hide, and what exactly was that vicious cat guarding in that weird case?

Damn, never came close to even her name. So, comrade, with your spunk standing up to Statie like that, I don't care what kind of shoes you wear. Let fortune smile and throw us together again to go spend a week in Philadelphia some weekend.

****

I shrank in my seat as the cop approached, my broad LIRR shield no longer between us. His interest in the girl, if he'd ever had any aside from subjecting her wound to his lawful authority, vanished with her off the train. He now focused on the mope posing a threat to his vacation, not that little old me had made a peep about it.

"Alright, Subversive. Produce your ID for determination of your record and outstanding warrants. Now!"

"You know, Officer, I don't think I will. Cause legally I've done nothing to require I show you ID." A stretch, but I was pissed about Cat Wrangler. "Or how 'bout some spit? I thought all you needed was DNA." This last didn't cut much ice, me cowering in my seat.

He put away his stick, reached down – to turn me upside down and shake my wallet out? – but then straightened and got out his radio. He didn't care if Joe was in the john – "Get him *now*!" Nice to know he used his favorite word with colleagues too. His combat-ready black gloves as scary as intended, I needled him while he waited. "Hey man, why don't you take those gloves off? That mean old pussycat is off the train."

"That's right," came the sergeant major's unmistakable boom. "Take those damn gloves off, Robocop. Skin on skin, baby!"

Ms. Locust Valley Lockjaw, who'd plummily instructed us to shut up and support the cops, chimed in. "You say you're a soldier, but I'm sure they didn't teach you to disrespect sworn Protectors like that in the military that serves *my* United States. Now, if you can't conduct yourself properly in public, I suggest you return to wherever it is you said you're from. Furthermore – "

"What do you mean, get back to Brooklyn with the rest of my kind? Hell, why am I even dealing with you. You're about as dumb as the end-of-the-world cow-lovers running the Army if you think men under arms talk like your fat, comb-over husband there when he's asking for another cup of tea. Go ahead, tell me again where I'm supposed to go. You better hope Chicken-Shit's boots ain't glued to the floor up there by the doors, cause you notice he ain't come nowhere near back here."

The cop sneered down at me. "You hear all the trouble you and your little girlfriend have caused? Well, don't you worry, punk. None of it's going to stop our little tango. The gloves mean: no marks – no marks on me. Sitting on a beach on my vacation, I wouldn't want my hands scratched up by you clawing like a girl, now would I?"

Wow, he could talk like a real person when he wanted. Somebody squawked on his radio, and he stepped back and said, "Joe, that you? This the private channel? Now listen, Joe. Harry and Dennis working tonight? No? Shit. OK, Joe, I need two troopers for a job. Call it a 39-19, eastbound at Mineola."

Joe squawked something, and he said, "Damn right with a taser, and I need them now. Mineola's my next stop, an ETA of about four minutes. But Joe, two *good* cops, BEI, and tell 'em to fix their badges. And don't – do not – radio anything about an officer needing assistance. I don't need any Mineola cops getting pushy on their home turf…. Yeah, a real wiseass. But he's not close to being the hard case he thinks he is. No – he's poor. Right. Nothing a little juice won't fix. What? … Shit no, no National Guard! You out of your mind after what happened in Hempstead? Those soldiers are not – negatory – not team players. That nigger soldier may still drag me to court unless somebody wakes him up."

Drooling at the thought of kicking my ass, the bastard didn't care who heard what. But this second time confirmed that he talked like any other jerk at the end of the bar when he wasn't blowing smoke. I had to escape and quick, cause I sure didn't like his talk of tasers. That's how large dudes end up dead at the feet of cops bent on punishment zapping them with 50,000 volts. The four cops present couldn't just sit on him like in the old days. They don't like to get their hands dirty anymore, so old ladies and guys already cuffed or in wheelchairs get the juice.

Mineola wasn't actually the next stop, but we'd hit it in a few minutes. My only hope was to raise a ruckus there on the snowball chance that, rather than scurrying from the train, folks might throw off their blinders and rise to my defense against three cops in uniform. Un-huh. Why the hell had Cat Wrangler sat across from the one seat I fit? I made blindly to get up, but he moved quick to stand painfully on my foot, pin me with his shin on my knee and keep talking.

"Joe, listen. You work this out quick and quiet, it clears that marker you owe me. And you know that's no small deal. All right. Affirmative, the next stop – Mineola."

He then addressed the car at large. "Suspect, you will be charged with obstructing a T Investigation, assault on a sworn Protector, disorderly conduct and resisting arrest. Already ruled a Person of Concern, your refusal to supply identification also rules you an imminent T Threat. You will be taken off this train at Mineola for a full and immediate search of your person for any papers, marks or wounds."

"You really dig wounds, don't you cop?"

Even louder, "Citizens of this train, I – "

"All right, cop. That's enough of you spewing your shit. I hear you had a problem with a 'nigger soldier' in Hempstead. Well, you got a problem with a natural-born, nigger soldier in your face right here, right now."

Indeed, he was standing in the aisle about six feet behind us.

"I ain't seen thirty-four of my own over the years – that's right, thirty-four *nigger soldiers!* – blown up or shot by them maniacs over there to hear talk like that of any kind from a man in uniform and on-duty. A man ain't fit to shine them boys' boots. They're not here anymore. They left me behind. So I guess I'll just have to take care of this white boy instead. Both of us know damn well you're planning on jacking the shit out of him you get him off this train."

The cop futilely worked his mouth.

"Come on, coward. I ain't slammed anybody in the whole two months I been home. You like messing with civilians never been in a real fight their whole lives. But you're about to commence a real fight now – no taser, just skin on skin – with a fighting machine from the Third ID!"

"Soldier, back up and produce identification now! Your interference in my lawful detention of this Subversive will not prevent your redeployment to either Mesopotamia, the Central Front, Operation Enduring Struggle or any other Sand. Your incarceration stateside is merely delayed for the duration of the Current Permanent Crisis."

"Come on, man. Make the first move, cause then it's self-defense from the jump. Come on, ofay-man, there's a 'nigger soldier' in your face calling you a coward in front of all these rich white people paying you to keep people like me down. Ain't no backup on this train – just you and me. So what you gonna do about it? And I do hope you make a move for that little cap gun you're wearing. Nothing'd give me more pleasure than you try to shoot me for calling you a name – pussy!"

The ensuing pandemonium washed over me as things both sped up and slowed way down. The sergeant major wasn't terribly tall, but he stretched his tight black shirt everywhere you looked, and his flat boulder of a head rested on a girder of a neck. The venom pouring off him, sheer mass was the least of it.

The cop stood dumbfounded as the train started slowing. He looked around, then down at me. I had eyes for nothing but his hand by his gun. He kicked my foot, got me to look up and said quite aloud, "Sixteen years in, you believe it, and in the last month I got two shines – I don't care if they're soldiers or lawn jockeys – questioning a sworn Protector's lawful Home-Front authority. And you wonder why we're losing so many Sands with personnel like that."

Crouched down in a fighting stance, the sergeant major had moved back a couple of steps in the aisle to, what, commence festivities with a flying kick? A couple of women were screaming,

32

and some louts were again bellowing in that exaggerated bass, "Yo, break his face!" and "Kick his ass!" A white man in uniform versus a menacing black man, little mystery whose face these Long Islanders wanted broken, whose ass kicked.

The cop drew his club. "All right, Bosco! I've given you too much rope already, let's see how you swing." His baton sniffing the air between them, he moved slowly forward, finally freeing my path to the door. I darted up and turned to watch, amazed he hadn't drawn his gun. Further back, a young black guy was struggling to break free of the woman begging him to sit down. The old lady was praying loudly, and her husband looked like he'd fainted. Ms. Lockjaw started in on "God Bless America" in her shrillest Ethel Merman, interrupting herself to demand that those physically able should support the Hero manning the front lines of Homeland defense, with the elderly and infirm joining her in song.

The train shuddered to a stop at Merillon Avenue, a little jerkwater station in ritzy Garden City before you hit Mineola, a stop unknown to the cop, who probably patrolled all over Long Island. Shit, what about the conductor? There'd be no clean getaway with him throwing his 290 pounds my way. But he leaned on the partition studying his nails. I thought it, but he said it, the great-minds-think-alike exact same phrase as I bolted for the door and out to the platform: "Happy now, asshole?"

People piling out of our car's doors, I ran back up the platform, bent and saw through a window the cop raise his club and pose nicely for a righteous blow as the soldier lashed out and hit him hard in the throat. Down went the cop and up came the soldier's foot for the first stomp. Three or four people scuffled in the aisle, including the young black guy who'd escaped his woman and a hefty, redheaded broad in a yellow polo shirt wildly swinging her purse. Did the combatants care about anything beyond getting within range of any assemblage of bone and flesh of any color? The soldier's piston of a leg drove down again, then he turned and nodded straight at me before grinning and raising it again. Not knowing I could still do such a thing, I grabbed the rail at the platform's edge and vaulted up and over, down a lot further below than it looked.

Chapter Four

Tighter Still to Cut the Pain

Christ, I could only hope that soldier was wearing sneakers rather than his no doubt highly polished Army boots. I clawed my way upright to make tracks, just *gone*, a cop looking to arrest me getting stomped. I could almost feel the damn do-gooder throwing himself at my heels, but only us chicken-shits had fled the car, the high-testosterone types fighting in the aisle.

The doors whooshed shut, and the train took off faster than I knew an LIRR could go, its horn blaring as the engineer raced for help at the big Mineola station, the passengers abandoned on the platform yelling all the louder.

Thrilled to escape a Data Boosting (I'd recently learned I was already way too high) and too freaked to notice the ankle damaged by my leap, I ran … where? OK, my folks' place in Mineola, that being the quickest route off the streets. Yup, this whole grim farce, my part in it anyway, arose from being so newly, miserably alone that my Saturday-night plan was to seek succor from those that bred me (and their fridge) rather than moping around the Hovel or out lurking and staring at dudettes who stared right back somewhere over my right shoulder.

Garden City nice and dark – such a rich, lily-white town didn't worry about lighting its streets – I jogged the long way less traveled and scurried across the couple of busier streets only when the coast was clear. My throbbing ankle finally forced a halt to tie my shoe tighter to cut the swelling and pain.

Crouching there proved all the excuse a dog needed to steal up and leap, his jaws snapping shut a couple of feet from my head, the shock wave bowling me over. Awash in his foul, kibbly breath, I scuttled away on all fours like a beached crab, mangling the ankle more. But rather than advancing the few feet to finish the job, he snapped and slavered and growled, hopping up and down right at the edge of his lawn, a brute with a remarkably well defined sense of territory. I braced to fend off a Doberman with my bare hands.

… Ah-ha, Can't Touch Me! I remembered the canine electronic fence I'd been so appalled by visiting an old friend who'd married well and moved to Connecticut. (My stretch of Queens, anybody with a yard also had a real fence.) No flip-flops for this beefaroni, I hurried to tie my ankle boot extra tight. I didn't need the paranoid lord of the manor – paranoid, or why a guard dog in Garden City – calling some MoFo public or private over a man squatting on his sidewalk.

The dog quieted and finally lay down nose on paws, twitching and growling with my every move. Suddenly the whole house and lawn were flooded in light, and I forced a gimpy trot. Intent on never acknowledging the whole painful episode to my parents, I braved a bright gas station to call and cancel, hunched over at the exposed phone booth. I'd deliberately left my micro-zap home, the better not to hear it silent on a Saturday night, no one caring to inform me they'd just arrived at the corner of 22nd Street, having stopped for a slice on 19th. Pop answered and affirmed he'd cope with my absence. "I didn't get why somebody newly single was wasting a Saturday night coming out here anyway. But no big deal either way." Great, Pop.

I gimped along familiar blocks and eventually snuck into my parents' garage and collapsed on some tarps in the back around ten. Scared and depleted, I fell into a fitful swoon, but kept jerking awake jarring my ankle. Once I woke to see by the dim light over the back door the name, Schiakoczyk, scribbled on my hand and scrubbed furiously with spit to erase the incriminating mark. Amidst dreams of car headlights shining on me and sketchy people of dubious intent flitting about, I later woke without a clue where I was or what I was lying on. It was a bad moment until I pieced it all together, my rising panic made worse by apprehending that I hadn't been drinking, and so how in blazes had I ended up sleeping rough in some dark, musty little building?

I got up sometime after five, judging by the murk, my chest aching where that bastard clubbed me and starving from having squirreled myself away the night before, not willing to risk a bite somewhere public. As the night dragged, I'd had to stifle the urge to raid my parents' own damn fridge. Not that my folks would ever turn me in – Pop would rather take a dump on the Mineola cop-shop's lawn. Consumed by the rigors of age, they just didn't need another worry heaped on their own growing pile. From vague ribbing from his two older brothers, I was dimly aware that Pop had had his own dealings with the boys in blue. Not that he'd shared many tales of his days as a youthful reprobate and then a union man out at the airport with his only kid.

Turn me in for what, damnit? But such was the calculus in HeadFuck's America. After all, I'd been declared a Prosecutorial Prospect or whatever the verbiage hiding the truncheon. Another man fighting in my stead, shame dripped from my heels as I fell to sneaking through town and a night of nightmares on a cement floor, unwilling to ask my own mother for a crust or enjoy the sleep of innocents in my teen-age bed.

It didn't feel like anything was broken, but man, the bruise on my chest had spread I saw in a coffee-shop's bathroom mirror. The bull's-eye still an angry red, a lot of purple, blue and yellow had splotched all around. Should I have turned to the train's window and sucked my thumb as the trooper strode down the car – aped the fashion of the day? Fearful of hungry cops, I grabbed coffee and an egg sandwich and skedaddled. But as the first food in many an hour kicked in, I almost convinced myself there was no way to trace me from the train.

I'd had a ticket stashed in my wallet. So, despite the ambient taping galore at New York's Penn Station where I'd started my trip, no video camera could link me to the purchase of a Mineola ticket. Nor had I fumbled away a library book or a print-out of an e-mailed article sporting my name. I doubted one of those white-bread, "break his face!" thug-wannabes sitting behind me had defied HeadMan's confiscation of whole-vid capable micro-zaps to capture me displaying my wound. Still, a dumb move, my on-the-fly impulse to parade my victimhood *and* offer up my biometrics cause I neither rallied the groundlings against Statie, nor pressured him to back off. And there were always the Merillon Avenue platform cameras, the cops databasing my eyes, ears and full, sensitive lips. Hell, maybe they'd deputize the entire city, splashing a Merillon image all over a front page or two.

Or, if my luck held and I didn't venture to Long Island any time soon, maybe I wouldn't get nailed. Entirely more sinned against than sinner, there I went skulking down a back alley rather than standing up on my hind feet, filing assault charges, and suing Statie for a cool quarter-mil. Yeah, just what I needed, *another* freaking interminable law suit against the police, even assuming I lucked into an old-school judge like the one the Wife and I had.

Stopping to tie my shoe ever tighter, I stewed about not throwing my injured shoulder to the wheel. No, I wasn't just turning and leaping on his back. I wasn't the sort to do that to unarmed civilians let alone to MoFos with guns. But I could've vaulted some seats, gotten, yeah, *behind* the sergeant major and … and screamed at that cop. Called him a liar, that impermissible word.

Yeah, and how long had I known that vicious, deranged soldier anyway? A stranger, huh? Then why did he risk getting shot to protect me? And why did we arrange to travel together but sit apart? What's more, what was my relationship with the woman who'd disappeared so precipitously into the night? The woman whose criminal recalcitrance triggered the whole spate of anti-state violence. Exactly how many thousands of dollars did I have spirited away for a good defense lawyer for the T they'd conjure with a snap? Nope, just suck this one up.

Such was snuffling victimhood during the Current P. Crisis. No spine, no resistance – and yeah, no potentially fatal taser. I tempered my shame with the thought that I was better suited to assist damsels in distress with logic, my winning personality and little knowledge of cats beyond which end to pet. Battle-shaky Sands vets looking for any excuse to slam somebody – well thanks, Sergeant Major, but I'll offer my encouragement while tumbling far over an LIRR railing.

I limped down my old hometown's quiet, Sunday-morning streets, pushing through gauze already hot and thick at dawn to grab a bus to Queens and then the subway home. The … set of my jaw indicating I wasn't a bum though I was *walking* on Long

Island, men my age up early with their dogs failed to meet my nod. Guys with wives along with dogs, and houses and kids and a spewer or two crowding driveways built for smaller vehicles. And the thought flickered yet again that maybe the Wife was right.

Chapter Five

Scrambling Rats, Shrinking Cheese

Plodding home to the Hovel from the subway, swimming against the tide streaming early to lousy jobs they were glad of in the City, the occasional odd bright flash darted across my field of vision. That was normally a sure sign of getting toasted. But it only felt like I'd been drug through the late-night wringer since I'd actually crawled onto that tarp far too early and sober.

Eight on a Sunday morning and no one with a badge or a licensed whole-vid banging on my door, nothing for it but to get horizontal again, wiped as I was. But of course I couldn't shut it down. No, not about the riot on the train, so new it wasn't implanted in my brain quite that way yet. Instead, there I lay fending off thoughts of the Wife, which, pending the arrival of Monday's mail, I was still *legally* entitled to call Nicki.

Hell, I only called her a hack maybe twice, both times when she was hassling about money. Besides, I never said she couldn't write, even if she sometimes spent a week on a few lines of copy. Her ad agency, Fornix & Foyst, paid her by the week – not my by-the-word servitude – so who cared.

"Let Others Worry," the brand line for the giant SUV from India that won such applause for raw honesty was Nicki's, though, truth be told, at least half the ads' impact came from the unaccustomed shots of the monster maneuvering over dense city traffic rather than the usual bounding unfettered by some waterfall. (Never mind how much it flipped.) Then, of course, the sticky-glue mousetrap, "Feet in the Trash: The Lazy Cat's Way to Save on Cat Food."

Also Nicki's, for the woman raising the bushel on her dimming light, the $399 do-me shoe, "Enervation: The Heels for a Taut Calf." People loved the obscure name with its possibly louche undercurrent. Then came the golden PR of some feminist website stringing up a baby cow (taut indeed) in homage to the crippling four-inch heels.

And my favorite, her tag for CheeseSpray, the genetically modified goop that came in a can but didn't clog you up: "Deracinated, So It Binds to Your Taste Buds, Not Your Bowels." Again, the odd word no one knew to rarify the brand. Her bosses always freaked, then the focus groups would endorse it, and after much anguish, they'd go with Nicki's gut. That it made no sense became something of her trademark, adding to her growing mystique.

Still, I'd like to get my hands on a little of whatever the client was on when they OKed mention of bound bowels. At the CheeseSpray launch party high atop some garish Midtown hotel, not a soul, not even some client-services lackey told that afternoon to throw his stomach on a sword, touched a single can of the stuff so lovingly arrayed on silver platters around the room. Except me, who discovered that one reason no one sprayed 'cheese' was the cans were glued to the platters.

A tall, very pointy number in an orange cashmere dress sidled by just then, every sculpted inch of her shrieking Client Manager for Morons. That being appropriately dazzled me, I picked up the can with the platter still attached and *sotte voce* (sure) asked her what the deal was. Nicki flew across the room before the woman could say a word, draped herself smotheringly on me like she hadn't done in public in ages and said, "Melanie, I see you've chanced upon my husband. Dear, you must remember meeting Melanie Artenunotte of *The New York Slimes*. She's one of their main advertising writers now, a real up-and-comer."

"Oh, the gentlelady of the NYS. Nicki, you've been derelict in not introducing us sooner. As colleagues, I'm sure we have much to speak of." That nonsense at least turned us from the canned cheese whose purveyors had bought the drinks in our hands not to mention, ultimately, Nicki's own tight dress new for the occasion. I had no particular desire to mess with her job.

How so, Artenunotte barely managed to inquire. She stopped listening to my not brief enough reply long before she fled. But I spread the butter with a generous enough knife that Nicki was merely miffed, not furious. I hid behind how was I supposed to know her until Nicki reminded me I'd met her in that very room less than two years before. Like I was supposed to remember every *gosh*-but-ain't-getting-slippery-with-her-either encounter at one of these things.

Nonetheless, the room's general acclaim for "Deracinated," etc. left Nick in a sterling mood. Verbally mauling her from the podium, a client top-dog left so many paw prints, if I was any kind of man I'd have socked him one mid-slobber. So sterling and giddy, we actually fell into it when, deliberately snooping stumbling out of the hotel two hours later, we ended up in a deserted banquet room with a nifty little outdoor balcony. Much of Manhattan sparkling before us, Central Park dense and dark at our entangled feet, the hem of her fabulous dress shimmied up her back as I pulled Nicki hard by the shoulders for some ooh-baby right *there*!

There were beaucoup giant shrimp at these affairs up amidst the Midtown rooftops, always a new one more gaudily bathed in light to try to penetrate the murk. I've had worse than fifteen-year-old whiskey pleasantly redolent of coal with a touch of freeze-dried cat urine thrown in for nose, each snoggerful on someone else's dime a bit smoother than the one before.

At least at Nicki's ad parties a good portion of the room clutched at a good time. Sometimes there was music, however techno-disco lousy, and dancing. But at the publishing snoot-fests I wrangled my way into for about six minutes – my dollop of Warhol's standard fifteen – guests fled from fun. All the rats in attendance were too busy clawing and scrambling for an ever-shrinking chunk of cheese. Deciding whether to come along, Nicki would ask if it was going to be just another "boring, rat-chasing-cheese party." I'd approach a grizzled, in his case, actually famous digger-of-dirt, or perhaps some trust-funded meta-fantabulist. Droll as all get-out, I'd gesture around the lush, dark or maybe bright, shiny room, everyone clutching and gabbing, and lob my standard proffer over the net: "So, whadiya think of all this wretched excess?"

And his incomprehension as he looked around and saw nothing excessive and certainly nothing wretched, everyone glossed and starched and sheened, would turn to disgust at my stab at fun. Humor? When I'd presumed to a precious moment of his time, he with not another invite in hand till Thursday? Humor, when there'd been a momentary gap in the fierce scrum round the Chief Assistant to the Assistant Chief of Engulf & Devour hobnobbing with the Senior Enervationist at Crutchem and Baggit – a gap he'd foolishly failed to exploit thinking I might actually be somebody.

A particularly scrawny rat at these publishing parties (yet like all the rest thinking *I* was the one with the squirrel's transformatively bushy tail), I'd claw my way towards the morsel of cheddar always just beyond reach. Far better to be a mere spouse at Nicki's shindigs, my heavy but sole obligation not to embarrass her. A minor guest, I was free for leering conversation with all sexes. Ensconced in a hedonistic cocoon, awash in money and its *ostensibly* apolitical pursuit, it was easy to imagine the nearest Data Minder miles away. At my publishing parties, on the other hand, people were wary lest they let slip to the wrong ear.

Nine years together, and I kept rolling the conviction uphill that Nicki didn't take her ad-drivel seriously despite the increasing pay and recognition. That everything was and would forever remain jake between us as long as we went dancing once in a while, marched against the Sands of the moment and wandered around Throg's Neck, Bay Ridge or Jamaica Bay for kicks, the sun setting over some body of water. We had mediocre pizza over the years, or spicy shredded meat, in every part of the City even remotely near the water. Then, as my freelance work dried up, its cloth ill-cut for the times, she got the big promotion to VP that sparked her move to Manhattan by herself.

Though we'd been dating only a year way back when, we were both old enough for me to drop to one knee, ring in hand, when that kid unexpectedly elbowed his or her way on stage. Sure, we got married three years later – malingering on my part for at least half of that – but, despite lots of fine, fun times traipsing all over creation, we never quite recaptured our full groove. There's a well-worn path for a couple to maybe recover. But despite always saying sure, she'd think about it next month, she never mustered the faith to deliberately harbor my seed.

Chapter Six

Nipped

Sleep finally came that Sunday morning in the midst of recalling our oddball outing to Bayonne some years back to gaze at big ships and their attendant big cranes before plopping down in a park, a pair of decaying bridges soaring off over to the right. Nicki and I sat and sipped and watched the planes land at Freedom's Watch International across the big bay – never mind the interminable trek home to Queens. I felt better after a couple of hours sleep – that is, rested and in pain. Neither the two "all-tripe, all-the-time" radio stations nor any local news sites had anything on any LIRR fracas. Cops doing the boogaloo on my ass actually tired old ground, I was more freaked by the fight on the train, its outcome unknown, than by getting assaulted. Monday would be the test, whether there was any grainy Merillon-platform photo under the headline, "Protectors Ask Help Finding this 'Prosecutorial Prospect.' "

I wolfed down a quantity of grub over brown rice, the spicy mush I'd cook by the gallon and live on for days. Mooning around that afternoon, I risked getting downgraded from a hurricane to a tropical depression. Riskcd pacing, sweating and swearing, followed by beering and staring, my ankle precluding a jaunt.

A sure route to waking up feeling lousy come Monday morning. Lousy about having a violent state trooper maybe stalking me. And lousy knowing I wasn't storming the barricades alongside whoever was standing up to some lout with a gun. Nope, I was scramming pretty damn quick, cops with Tazers part of the mix.

Far better to stick to the weeks-old plan for that Sunday: Shenanigans by the Sea, the free, two-stage throw-down they had every summer out at Coney Island. The Furred Tongues, of all people, were promised on the second stage. A *current* band whose music I actually owned, its purchase spurred by their monster hit the summer before, "Residue Remains." Presumably a couple of the other bands, nothing more than names on a list to me, also funneled a groove.

But the prowl more to the point, I dispensed with my fine new East German Army backpack in favor of a little satchel crammed with a book, underwear, towel and yet another stupid PBJ club sandwich, the third slice for extra heft – then and later. Still with Nicki, I probably would've skipped the swim and just gone to the music. But then, still with her, I wouldn't be spending Saturday night with the parents and so wouldn't be wincing every time I forgot and took a deep breath. As it was, along with the concert and its attendant, scintillating disappointments, Mother Ocean's soothing embrace beckoned, a reliable Rita Moreno to Jack Nicholson's diminished scoundrel at the end of *Carnal Knowledge*.

Sweating in my bathing suit under my shorts, I got off the train with a bunch of kids – Don't Trust Anyone Under Thirty! – looking to get sloppy in the heat. We trooped through a spruced up station, meant to be a catalyst plopped down amidst the general squalor. With its soaring glass walls and huge glass roof, it looked like some crystal-palace European train shed. Gazillions for glitz, part of the mayor's never met a developer he didn't like campaign to get Hiltons and Hyatts lining the boardwalk. Though the surrounding grime was little changed, should Coney Island ever shake off the Plunge, bye-bye, old and in the way – two-legged included. One of New York's last down-at-heels good times slated for the heap.

The throng shuffled down a long ramp, pushed through the turnstiles and swung left around a wall. Ambushed, we fell into the clutches of a mess of cops not just standing around like usual, but steering people one way or the other. They looked to be plucking out some of the freakier dudes with packs and sending them over to a table with two cops behind it.

Godfreakingdamnit, there was no escape even way out here by the sea, even having *left* the subway though still on City property. I'd apparently been moping round my little corner of stumblebum Queens too much to know what the heck was going on. None of the kids transporting any Siamese cats, the chosen plunked down their stuff for the paw-through. Some looked pissed, but most had these idiot grins pasted on like they were glad of the chance or would at least get in less trouble the less trouble they made. Pretty disturbing to see some of the more macho psuedo-punks holding their bags out eagerly as if for scoops of ice cream. Aside from not wanting to risk a Data Boosting, maybe they had something problematical secreted away somewhere and were hoping for a pass.

Not carrying (more's the pity) and old by this crowd's standards, they weren't gonna mess with someone limping along staring at the heels of the guy in front. Could they possibly pop me for the underwear in my bag for conspiracy to disrobe on the beach? Nah, I'd paid my hassled-by-cops dues for some considerable time. So good luck, dudes (oddly, not a single girl), but get me out of this sweaty crowd and into that salt water.

I made it past the cops but against my better judgment stopped to watch. I heard not a peep as they chose a steady stream of the more outre males for the privilege. Were they just punishing the types they didn't like? In any event, so much for a *random* search cause, with a dozen bands on two stages, there was enough music to appeal to almost anyone. Yet the cops chose not a single one of the clean-cut prepsters in polo shirts and the flip-flops that made no sense heading into the scrum before the stage.

(Why the rage to be effete around the feet? Not that gays wear 'em, they know about being able to run. How you gonna cope with a zombie crisis in flip-flops? Fleeing down an alley in shower slippers, how kick down a side door to escape come the next robot uprising? How leap over an LIRR railing and then tie it tight for a gimpy forced march?)

A kid at the table exploded: "What the hell – you're gonna arrest me for an open nip bottle? You gotta be kidding me. There's exactly two swallows in that thing. You going nuts or what?"

Looking like a circus strong man with his big pink slabs of arm disappearing into the same too-small black gloves that Statie favored, the cop doing the honors was beefy, buzz-cut and wired way too tight. The kid with the wispy beard and flower-power shirt was heading for a fall with that kind of talk. The sergeant on the scene advanced to state primly that an open container,

45

no matter the size, was in violation of this, that and the other, including the rank nonsense of endangering the welfare of any minors on the train.

Make a bad left turn, you get drug-tested, and your DNA is harvested on the spot. Everybody knew that. But now you had to be like new-driven snow *exiting* the train? How long before you're at risk a foot from your own front door? They brought up the hand-held to iris-scan him for any priors or warrants – yeah, and arrange for a Boosting, he made any more cracks about "going nuts."

Buzz-cut asked his sergeant, "So you want him with the potheads we got waiting for the van?"

I hadn't noticed the five guys off in a corner being watched by yet another cop costing a whopping $120K a year, maybe, you throw in pension and benefits, plus all the T overtime. The downtrodden mix of hippies and punks wore those mass-arrest plastic cuffs around their wrists. Imagine: a joint at a big outdoor concert. Not worth a Boosting, it'd just screw up finding a job or an apartment. And holding on to their driver's license might end up costing thousands for months of coerced 'treatment,' not to mention years of vastly inflated car insurance. They presumably knew giving the preps a pass side-stepped a lot of reefer, so were the cops just afraid of popping some rich kid whose dad would make a stink?

Possessed of a weary grandeur, the sergeant weighed Buzz-cut's question on adding the nip offender. Not caring who heard, he said, "Callaghan, we're already pushing it. Some captain starts running stats and sees a cop got OT processing a nip-bottle arrest along with all the marijuana, we're screwed – and that means me."

"Come on, Sarge, what's the odds on that? Besides, this fruit really needs to learn some manners, know what I mean?"

"He does. But we still can't get greedy. The lieutenant takes that guy with the roach, with the van showing up late like I told them, we only need one more doper for everybody here to get OT. So focus on the fucking golden goose however long it keeps laying. And hope for another … *incident* down the road. Just give him an open-container ticket, but seventy-five, not fifty.

Maybe that'll teach him some manners."

Sarge went back to gleaning hopheads from the invading hoards seeking a beachhead at Coney Island. Processing the arrests, his men would get maybe $175 each in piece-of-pie OT, more if they had some years under their belt.

I'd never been angry immersed in Mother Ocean before, the salt's sting on my roughed-up chest not helping.

****

I threw my sweaty sheet off and barked my ankle. And it welled up from somewhere that blue Monday mourn that I'd messed up worse than a night's foolishness that left me with gravel in my mouth and shredded, wet wool in my head. Finding myself in the Hovel's vertical coffin of a bedroom rather than a cell and only my chest and foot sore, there'd apparently been no new insult visited upon me. Despite that accomplishment, disgust at some unspecified pigheadedness gripped me, and the aspirin and water were five long steps away.

Emily! was her name it came to me as I gulped, she of the delectable cutoffs. I'd already seen my glasses unbroken on the bathroom floor, so I held my palm close to search for some remnant of the phone number I knew wasn't there. She'd been shucking and jiving along by herself by the second stage, old enough – mostly – tall and with the requisite long dark hair, though she didn't look *too* much like Nicki. (A carbon copy just made your friends snicker and you crazy with unwarranted hopes of duplicating the memory currently plaguing you.)

Emily laughed at my japes, and we even danced when the Furred Tongues kicked it their last couple of songs – face-to-face and responding to the other person's moves, an ancient courtship ritual otherwise unseen among thousands of music lovers. Blasé youth apparently falling into bed with no preliminaries, we looked to be the only ones flirting at all.

No guarantee, even (especially) with someone so nifty, I had to get greedy and write her number on a piece of paper rather than on my hand – unforgivable but understandable since I hadn't been at such a scene in years. Not unattached. Ever the strategist,

I figured a number smeared on my hand would only complicate getting a second. Safety in numbers, diversifying one's assets – all clown-talk.

I guarded the paper fine until the unsurprising tussle a few sodden hours later with some overly entitled big meathead in flip-flops and a rugby shirt trying to cut in line at the bodega. Boxing him out to keep him behind me, I fumbled in my pocket for change and *half*-sensed the paper falling to the floor. He even more soused, in the midst of fending him off, I certainly couldn't let my guard down by bending to the floor. So I paid quick for that crucial last beer and, heading out, silently dared him into throwing the first punch cause then it was self-defense from the get-go, like the Sergeant Major said. And nary a thought for that shot at happiness lying trampled on the floor.

I should have written Emily's number on my forehead to see it the next morning, cause her laughing eyes as we gyrated to the Tongues promised a generous soul in a fabulous package. There improbably alone, she was no doubt newly unencumbered like myself. Remembering the 718 area code, I needed to start dialing till I found her. Fingers don't fail me, cause women like her un-unencumber quick.

PART TWO

Chapter Seven

Inching Ahead Bowed and Barefoot

"Get up! Move! You think this is a game? You think this is funny?" Trying to get away, I rolled over on my bad side that Wednesday morning, the residual pain from Statie's clubbing waking me up and away from the oversized brute in a weird grey uniform. I was in someone else's seat, my ticket apparently good for the night before, and I wasn't moving fast enough. It took a moment to grasp who was what, and that my heart was racing from a dream. My sore chest waking me throughout the night, I lay there exhausted. Though my ankle had become tolerable mincing around in a black work boot tied tight, I slept on my back as if pregnant, my dreams lousy with menace.

Hell, turn the page, not that I was justified in closing the book on Statie, his and my pages still all gummed up who knew how.

Languishing, I worked visions of women – shoot, some of them barely more than girls they were from so long ago – Nicki way too painful as she promised to be for a long time. I visited some highlights, a clothes-optional, all-night car trip and that storied evening at Jones Beach, inattentively climbing well-worn trails till I could fling myself over the cliff for a brief flight. Men sleeker, richer or younger (or easily all three) scaling the higher peaks, was I to be relegated to hills flattened by time?

Bored, I kept losing the thread. Soldiers littered the streets, snoops were everywhere, the Data Minders remained amorphous, their capabilities veiled and, on increasingly rare occasions, HeadMan hurled odd, stunted bolts from on high. New York City and State both beyond broke, I would've thought things had eased in the realm of stop and search. Finally catching hold of a pedestrian memory not dulled by overuse – Lord, what was that good-time hussy's name? – I dusted myself off at the bottom of the cliff and swung my feet to the floor. Damn, more sleep would've shortened another stifling day before I could thankfully cross it off my allotment.

I deserved a snooze. Monday and Tuesday were pretty frantic churning out a two-day article for a very eventual two-hundred bucks on the mass disinterment, cremation and co-mingled re-burial of many hundreds of skeletons to clear land for the New Jersey Devils hockey arena in Newark some years back. The dead, including forty-seven veterans of the American Revolution, were accorded little of the ceremony or – my article argued – respect normally accompanying the disposition of human remains.

Given the skeletons' surprise discovery and overwhelming number, haste decreed they end up as co-mingled ashes, an outrage driven by the time-value of the $310-million (in pre-Plunge dollars) that particular hockey palace cost. The indignity heaped upon them contrasts poorly with the fate of 3,500 human remains found in a potter's field during construction of a nearby N.J. Turnpike exit in Secaucus. Those folks – "the poor, the insane and criminals" a plaque read – were afforded the costly and time-consuming dignity of individual reburial that was denied Newark's high and mighty.

The cemetery's owners, Newark's First Presbyterian Church – which dates to the theocratic founding of Newark in 1666 and whose pastors helped found both Princeton and Yale – were adding insult to injury. They had originally paved over a big section of their cemetery for a 400-space parking lot in the 1950s. They removed a number of bodies then and perhaps considered the issue resolved. But laying asphalt for a parking lot and digging an arena's deep foundation are endeavors of a different stripe. When the backhoes started digging, hundreds and hundreds of bodies were discovered. And so a small army of archaeologists was eventually deployed, working seven-day weeks and sworn to secrecy. As it was, each body was dug up following archaeological procedure before being shipped to the ovens.

As British Prime Minister William Gladstone observed, "Show

me the manner in which a nation cares for its dead, and I will measure with mathematical exactness the tender mercies of its people, their loyalty to high ideals, and their regard for the laws of the land." Or, as one of the participants I interviewed told me somewhat less grandly, "These people were people at one point in their lives."

Staring out my one window and pondering another hopefully two-day article, the radio (channeled clearly to listless rock the night before) caught my ear. "And the news overnight from the Central Front, Bob?"

"There is no Affiliation news from that particular Sands, Phil. Well, actually just this: Endorsed Proscription News has learned of a previously unseen combination of T-Fiends – comprised of ethnic groups traditionally hostile to each other – confronting Affiliation Heroes on the main road just a quarter-mile south of the Exclusion Zone. Surrounded, our Boots tried heroically to – "

"Bob, I think EPN has made it clear what's suited for the breakfast hour. In other news, the recently transmogrified Jacquine was spotted tonguing – "

Yikes! I silenced the claptrap to carve some space to think. Snarling cretins haunting my dreams, I had to do something. Something more than fiddling and piddling, clicking and calling, searching for a story idea not already done to death till a couple of tallboys lubricated the evening's baseball unaccountably on real TV. And thus another day done, praise be.

Heck, like all but a few in a nation mired in a string of wars, I'd leaned on a soldier whose name I didn't know. Then I fled, taking up arms with the throngs fighting over the biggest piece of crumb cake. Had I slip-slid my way into Auden's vast kennel "where the dogs go on with their doggy life"? Nicki pulling the plug on our life together, had I joined the ranks clutching at booze, sugar, pills, Enhancements, a remote, borrowed money or a mouse – whatever combo it took to tolerate outrage with a shrug in what some might call our Empire of Illusion.

A heaping helping of outrage, what with a helicopter lurking overhead, no way to pierce the murk to see if it had any markings. Stationary over *your* building way too long, the staccato beat soon the thumping of your heart. Pray God it was that dude down the hall with the stringy hair who always wore those baggy, disgusting shorts. Your license plate Data-enshrined just for driving into Manhattan – no problem. Snatching folks off the sidewalk? Wasn't happening to anyone you knew, except for maybe that Null who worked with your cousin. He fell off the ferry, or a woozle got him or…. No one knew.

Acquitted but still imprisoned? What the times demanded. Arrested, or maybe just foolish enough to travel abroad – cough up your micro-zap and laptop for *copying*. Write the wrong letter to the editor and join the millions (tens of thousands more each month) on the proctological flying list.

Sure, you can show up at some caged, 'free-speech' zone and march in all the damn circles you want under a bridge at the edge of town, hemmed in by hundreds in helmets glad of the easy OT. Just make sure to smile for their biometric cameras. Ignored by every TV station in town, such *permitted*, official marching was a wisp in the willows an hour after completion. The press, from the little scratch-and-claw news sites my byline graced on up, was also showered with malign neglect. HeadMan found it easier to ignore its pillowy output than to shut down the dwarfed, dispirited and depoliticized fourth estate, especially since a new Reg outlawed anonymous content. Enforcement was somewhat slipshod on the more self-infatuated margins of the Net. But any text and certainly any video that resembled 'news' demanded a supposedly real name up top.

Forget all that and line up quick, the very first on your block to get the new Enhancement! *"Guaranteed non-communicable when used as directed."* Thankfully, I couldn't afford one. Nope, cops pawing through your stuff cried out for a stick in the spokes. No longer could you just huddle behind the wall with the other mice bemoaning the existence of the cat. A fool's errand, probably, in a fearful nation groped by strangers. Laden with false bravado and enslaving labor-saving devices (how did they ever build the Empire State Building in a year without them?), knuckles rapped, without compass, glad to be permitted a magazine on board, we inched ahead bowed and barefoot.

Anyone call for a fool?

****

They shredded the tattered last remnants of the Fourth Amendment after a bombing in Manila shortly after HeadMan's installation, New York police commissioner Walk-on-Water Ted issuing the edict that the cops could randomly search anyone dicey enough to venture onto public transportation. His dictate applied, apparently, to any cop in any jurisdiction within range of his well-broadcast voice, never mind that their ostensible civilian overseers didn't answer to Ted. He pronounced and everyone fell in line.

Ted's astonishing admission that he'd wanted to do this for years and had just been waiting for the excuse of an attack anywhere in the world to bludgeon the public into acceptance, got no play beyond a single story deep in the paper. This one guy, however square-jawed, rectitudinous and all that piffle he might be, burned the aged parchment in full view of the cameras, the mayor shouting muffled encouragement from his locked trunk. Where were the screaming headlines, 'Top Cop Proclaims: Leave Your Rights at Home'?

The press gave space to a smidgen of mute distress, some of the scant mention deteriorating to comments like this witticism in *The Weakly Glossy* about pot dealers wary of subways now charging a taxi surcharge: "Call it the anti-T tax." And thus dismiss with a hoot the nutters fixated on centuries-old, civ-lib abstractions.

The media preferred social marketing like the Mercedes radio ad – no joke – that "Homeland Security" will immediately taze any dumb bunny who raises the slightest objection to them looking in his car's trunk. A twofer: model acquiescence to getting searched and normalize tasers as punishment for noncompliance.

The apparent indifference was fueled in part by the notion, back when people were paying attention, that you could feel free to refuse a search and turn on your heel – forget getting to work on time, the next station ten blocks away. Of course that threw any results-based rationale out the window, anyone with

53

ill intent just going to another station. Also, what was the point of doing bags unless they actually frisked the tens of thousands of subway-riding home-boys of any race in clothes four sizes too big? Mere security theater to cow folks into accepting the next outrage on tap. Not for nothing had the civ-lib trampling Brits rejected the scheme as useless.

But after an initial flurry, the cops had retreated to setting up occasional show searches. They far preferred to amuse themselves racing around the city in caravans of fifty, lights flashing and sirens blaring, supposedly causing nearby Bad Guys to melt, overawed, onto the sidewalk, but merely proving that's the only way to cut through Manhattan traffic. (Bad Guy: like T, a term justifying any excess, reminiscent of a little kid's cry chasing playmates around the backyard, his finger a pistol.) Then they'd sit in their cars for a spell, these cops making time-and-a-half whose vehicle precinct numbers pegged them from all over the city, sit in their AC, reading the paper and spewing exhaust, until time came thirty minutes later to race somewhere else to sit and read and spew some more.

Soon, the Current Permanent Crisis sweeping mute objection aside, teams of cops with dogs and submachine guns began patrolling mass transit. More security theater and not a peep in the papers on whether machine guns on packed subway platforms might not be such a swell idea.

The random searches were forgotten by all but the stoutest civil libertarians until, some weeks back as July melted into August, the papers blew up a tiny commercial dispute into a full-scale emergency. And cable news, the macro-transmitters, shout radio and Walk-on-Water Ted (the earnest little prig who pretended to be Ted's boss jumping up and down in back) all buffaloed us along for the ride.

The sky began to fall when two Sikh newsstand operators in Midtown got into a scuffle over one constantly stealing the other's morning bundles of newspapers. This had apparently occurred sporadically for months, escalating from words to blows until finally the victim snapped before dawn one morning and burned down the thief's stand right across the street from the big Herald Square Macy's. But he did it before his tormentor got to work, a nice clean arson. When someone walking by sold a very picture of the flames to *The Daily Chirp* for the next day's front page, *The New York Toast* tripped all over itself trying to play catch-up.

Its second-day story unfurled its usual jingoistic and, in this case, nonexistent Fright flag, pulling from the ether any number of possible attackers on this commercial landmark. It rustled up anonymous deputy assistants and junior commissioners from a big bowl of alphabet-soup agencies to muse quite aloud to the seven *Toast* reporters on the story about vague plots originating in the Hindu Kush, or in Leeds, or South Flushing or somewhere. Cause there was *chatter* out there, chatter galore – shake it on your cereal for regularity. The arsonist had somehow mistakenly poured gasoline on the newsstand across wide 34th Street instead of the giant store.

Down this hoary, stinking rock tumbled into the slow summer news hole. Thus did the searches return worse than ever on any vehicle that took a ticket in three states, all on some uber-cop's decree. And then they spread nationwide, including Boston, Los Angeles and DC. Not from any particular threat, the LA cops actually said, but just to keep pace with New York, all that T money at stake.

As with any police power, it spread like water seeping into a basement, migrating to dumb public gatherings like movie night in Bryant Park. A friend had his stuff rifled exercising his patriotic duty going to watch the 4th of July fireworks. The lines entering ballparks so long, you were lucky to get to your seat by the third inning, though the only effect was to discourage folks from bringing their own sandwiches. Baseball even prohibited bottles of sun-screen for a while, cheering dermatologists in three states. On the PATH trains (the 'subways' from Manhattan to New Jersey) regular announcements "strongly encouraged" passengers not to carry anything they couldn't fit in their pockets. Or they'd face a search. (Then PATH started testing body scanners at one of their stations.)

And I'd heard of not a single teeny-tiny arrest over the principle of the thing, not a soul in three states gripped by sufficient umbrage to risk a Boosting.

High time to take a Goddamn stand, block that kick, an army of one, sis boom bah and Fourth Amendment fame. A nice, neat civ-lib arrest if I dared, a Boosting likely – screw it – but hopefully no pounding. A grandiose comparison, sure, but why not sit down at the local Woolworth's lunch counter and demand service? Some old-fashioned, one-man street theater, a bit of agitprop, a *contribution*. You have draw a line somewhere, otherwise it's ain't worth chewing through the leather straps to start your day. Like the Mahatma said, "Whatever you do will be insignificant, but you gotta do something." Or, as somebody put it, "Don't burn the flag, wash it."

Seeing the cops in place, what would happen if I didn't offer my knapsack for the paw-through or flee to another station, assuming that was still allowed? Simply refused, started proclaiming loudly about the Constitution and continued towards the turnstile brandishing my Metrocard? Hard to predict the outcome messing with jittery cops who saw obeisance as their due. It wasn't like any article ever mentioned the official, "critical head shot" policy accompanying the searches – a rather severe form of criticism. What if some cop was a battle-scarred vet or had the hangover shakes?

Bereft, bothered and bedraggled, cast adrift by the Wife and responsible to no one, maybe I plain didn't care. Should something, like, *tragic* ensue, the parents would assimilate their grief somehow – buoyed by a healthy dose of I-told-you-so, Pop probably before they finished shoveling dirt. And Nicki? Let her feel real bad real long.

Christ, was *that* – yeah, that dirt-shoveling solution to all my problems – behind this oh-so-principled plan? Nicki had kicked me out and then immediately joined the flies buzzing round that gilded pile across the East River. (Melt glaciers, melt!) I didn't even know her new address in one of those anthill-stirred-by-a-stick towers in Manhattan's soulless East 80s. Why the secrecy, Nicki? I wasn't a stalker. Got a little more self-respect than that.

I'd washed up on the decidedly less gilded opposite bank of that same river in Bumfuckville, Queens at a crumbling, carved-up old mansion that stank of frying onions. Kids from the projects a block away brought their dogs to crap on the sidewalk out front, none of the rabble of single men from all over the world who occupied the many cells inside caring to echo the crabby old landlord's objections.

I paced my kitchen one-and-a-half strides in each direction (hell to pay some day, all those footprints on the wall). Would refusing a search be just another dumb tree falling in the forest on deaf ears, or did he howl most poignantly who howls alone? Shoot, somebody had to do it, write about it, then put his freaking name on top to pass the new Regs – why not this lonely lone wolf? Weren't no spineless politicians or media big-foots objecting.

Chapter Eight

HeadMan

A Statement – yeah me, cause what did I care. Damn few of them since HeadMan's ascendency. The last presidential election had featured the usual prolonged and excessive vitriol – only more. Much, much more given all the unleashed new 'citizens.' Benefiting from a splintered opposition (the delusional vs. the merely rapacious), the incumbent squeaked out a narrow victory. But, though he'd already served four years, three weeks later a federal court declared him "illegitimate."

The capper: upholding empty principle all the way to the grave, the two self-righteous mooncalves he'd appointed to the Supreme Court in his first term recused themselves when it hit their desk, something inconceivable to the other side's judges. So, in an entirely unsurprising four-to-three verdict, the president's 'illegitimacy' – and therefore his new running mate's as well – was upheld. He slunk away as, shockingly, did she, amidst fervid whispers of threat and inducement.

Then the real shocker: though he'd run a racist, fire-in-the-belly campaign, the challenger refused to serve under such tainted circumstances. Was he plain bought off, or had Gov. Frank Marlmon been threatened with exposure? Were there indeed some very curious old whole-vids lurking about? Nonsense. He just had too much … respect for the country to be rammed into office in such partisan judicial fashion, Marlmon asserted. Astoundingly, he made that weak cheese stick. Despite the uproar, despite the growing contention in the streets, neither plea nor threat could force him to stand on the Capitol steps and solemnly swear.

So…. Third in line to the presidency, the Speaker of the House was a back-bench thug whose election to that august office following the previous Speaker's sudden demise was the prior political shock of the day. His elevation to the Speakership apparently had something to do with a zealous, eschatological claque rumored to be sweeping Capitol Hill. Something about *constructing* the proper catalyst to usher in End Times, it wasn't much discussed.

In any event, after a confused and sporadically violent interregnum following Gov. Marlmon's refusal – the whole country up in arms except, mystifyingly, the two party standard-bearers with greatest claim to the presidency – the buffoonish Speaker was invested as a caretaker of sorts. The Plunge still plummeting, millions of folks were distracted by the little matter of getting food in their kids' bellies. Besides, though nary a Brooks-Brothers 'rioter' in sight, it wasn't much more of a coup than the last one. Not really.

Half-pregnant politesse, the Speaker wasn't immediately given the title of president, so HeadMan stuck – not surprising given his own loopy, third-person usage pounding the podium. Giddy after years of deserved obscurity in the House, the snarling bastard probably even liked the HeadFuck it morphed to in most circles.

Very soon, the Disruption broke out – was engineered, *happened*, at any rate – and he revealed our future. The economy Plunging for years by then, everything crabbed and cramped, the first food riot broke out in Chevy Chase, Maryland, of all places, its hazy spark much debated. The governor of Virginia in his pocket, HeadMan precipitously deployed the Virginia National Guard across the river against the vocal opposition of the governor of Maryland. A youngish distance swimmer, Maryland's governor suffered a bizarre 'stroke' at a raucous states' rights rally. Railing against troops crossing borders unbidden, parts of him crumpled and parts went ramrod stiff. For twenty months he lay in a coma doctors couldn't explain before his wife finally won the right to pull the plug. Some say that the viral video of the guv struggling to denounce HeadFuck with only half his face working was a main reason whole-vid capable devices were banned.

Or maybe it was all the videos of folks getting run over or shot. (That brave fool in Pittsburgh should've known that tank wouldn't stop.) Because things fractured badly as the Disruption gained steam. The remarkably *non*-spontaneous smashing of supermarket windows spread to a dozen states in ever hazier fashion. (Bricks for the purpose trucked in on pallets were discovered in Hartford and Cincinnati). And increasingly lethal Guardsmen ranged far from home.

Sure there were voices in the wilderness – a lot of them at first. But the 'illegitimate' incumbent's party had already SOP-folded like a cardboard suitcase. Most Americans were struck dumb in fear and amazement at such images as tanks ringing the Capitol building and rolling through Times Square. Twenty-seven cops, sixteen soldiers and 912 civilians were slain the fearsome ten days it took the clamp-down to clamp down. After two scary forays to Manhattan to sidle wide-eyed along the edge of protest, following the bloody Battle of 45th Street, Nicki and I joined the majority hiding under the covers.

Some media reported courageously during the Disruption's worst days, but the loudest and slickest went along for the ride. And why not, HeadMan not messing with *them* much. Blaring from your screens, he was initially hard to escape. Unlike most politicians, he wasn't afraid to be hated, which really freed his hand. But it went to his shaved head and, proving too hot for TV, he was dialed way back by his handlers. He still speechified on occasion, but like some of his predecessors, only in strictly managed, limited doses. No more thrusting that giant turtle head at roaring crowds. Of late, he'd just *appear*, seated stiffly behind his Oval Office desk or, once in a great while, behind a freakishly large podium addressing a select military audience in stilted fashion. No rope line handshakes, the audience was always ushered out first beneath his vacant gaze.

As he faded from view, more and more of the government's authority seemed to rest on HeadMan's personal motto: *Bold, Extolled, Impregnable*. Often shortened to a muttered *BEI*, it became a conversational touchstone, at least for the burgeoning numbers professionally or emotionally nourished by T.

Yup, HeadFucked. All the forms and much of the rhetoric, the empty observances and staunch words, the enabling courts, impotent press and institutional shells – heck, the grand marble buildings and the Easter Bunny – all remained in place. Peering through a telescope from Mars, much would look the same.

But, especially with elections bought and sold in newly naked fashion, the centuries-old Great Experiment fizzled out, and the Hammer rained down on short and tall alike. To think that a great many Americans initially embraced HeadMan as a needed strong hand.

****

Whether HeadMan personally orchestrated the Data or just acquiesced to the Data Minders' brute inevitability was kicked around some back when such was still discussed. Americans' heads-down response to this whole new infringement helped speed our political demobilization as a furtive populace – cutthroat conservatives and laptop liberals alike – largely disassociated itself from much beyond gossip and scandal. Tough enough steering the wolf to someone else's door, just recite: *Minders Turn Elsewhere!* as we learned to do, and time for a snack and a screen. Had the latest *Beach Blanket Smackdown* streamed yet?

The Data assigned Americans to one of four inelegantly named surveillance Levels. Those few at the top, in the Mirror, suffered the most intense scrutiny. Next came RoundUp; the third Level had the ham-handed name of Middling Severity; and the largely ignored mass at the bottom comprised the Null Set. The middle two Levels – RoundUp and Middling Severity – were further sliced into eleven Tiers. Neither the sparsely populated Mirror at the top nor the vast Null Set at the bottom were split into Tiers. Finally, getting kicked up a Tier for some transgression was referred to as a Boosting; scrutiny was said to increase incrementally as you rose from Tier to Tier.

So, from the top: The Mirror, RoundUp (11 Tiers), Middling Severity (11 Tiers), and the Null Set.

The taxonomy, clunky names and all, soon became second nature. Late of an evening in a bar, you might silently wonder your new friend's Tier, all the flirting leading you to assume she was in Middling Severity like you and everyone you knew. Poor form to ask too quick, like asking about HIV, it was best done delicately. (Also like HIV status, by no means did everyone know.)

In descending order: the Mirror, RoundUp (11 Tiers), Middling Severity (11 Tiers), and the Null Set.

The highest Level was called the Mirror because at that height, basically any endeavor was mirrored in the Data *in real time*. Rather than a passive recording mechanism, someone with eyeballs – a human – was into your shit. The Mirror was almost a status crime in and of itself: you were headed for trouble, it just remained to be seen for what. Not that anyone knew anyone in the Mirror.

The Mirror's intense, present-tense shadowing of every jot and tickle (electronic, commercial, romantic or political) was reserved for roughly half-a-million Americans. That was the estimate you'd find – should you dare such a problematical search. None but the adept knew for certain, and no one knew any of them to ask. Tiers weren't necessary in the Mirror, for how fine could you slice a walking colonoscopy?

The second Level, RoundUp, captured some five percent of us, or 17 million Americans, in its eleven Tiers; the lower the Tier, the less intrusion. Though with far less intensity than in the Mirror, actual human beings poured over RoundUps' Data in real time too. (For the 95 percent of us below the top two Levels, the surveillance was almost entirely automated.)

Which of the eleven Tiers RoundUps found themselves in determined how global and draconian the real-time human monitoring of their phone and Net use, their micro-zapping and e-mail, their health care, love lives, friendships, consumer purchases, (legal) vices, charitable contributions, travel and porn. At RoundUp's bottom, some semblance of a normal life was thought possible.

Also eleven Tiers, Middling Severity was a stupendous maw of automated Data, said to be discarded every thirty days, unseen by human eye unless the subject did something dumb. There was always the hope that this third Level was just a big, impenetrable jumble of 120-million people. Self-censorship became a way of life for this thirty-five percent of the country, people instinctively knowing what malodorous phrases shouldn't slip from thumb or lip. It was like back when the simple term, *liar*, a powerful judgment on any playground, became verboten in regard to our leaders.

The fourth Level, the vast Null Set, anchored the bottom. The Minders hadn't bothered to slice this apolitical sixty-odd percent of us into Tiers. No need to mess with subsets for the over 200-million who did the cleaning, the picking and packing, the heaving and hoeing, the post-Plunge begging and staring and – along with all the foreign Boots seeking Homelander status – the fighting and dying. The roofers, the loafers, the shop-girls and the clerks, the security guards covering the land like dandelions, the pothole fillers and the bus drivers, all had to throw a bomb (of some sort) to attract real notice.

Of course, the Data did track the Nulls with a basic, passively collected file: over the course of time it would presumably come to note that he or she lived here, worked there, stole that content online, moved, married her or him, had that one DWI along with the two kids, one foreclosure and three bouts of illness. Divorced him or her, had this, that and the other micro-zap, messed up on his or her taxes those two years, moved and remarried and then moved again. The Data's automatic overlay of the Null's passage through life would presumably accumulate as the years fell one upon another.

But otherwise the Minders weren't that interested in the back-bowed souls who propped things up for the rest of us. By definition, the Nulls didn't participate much in politics, or they'd be Middling Severity or higher. They typically needed three or more jobs per couple – and damn lucky to get 'em – to survive. They'd totter home at an odd hour from one of their grueling jobs and collapse in front of a screen, hoping the kids were asleep or, better yet, out playing in traffic.

Finally, speaking of kids, were the Newbies, sort of a place-holder Level for children under ten, also with no Tiers far as anyone knew. It got them registered in the Data and helped grout their minds right. Kids would get properly assigned once they started generating their own Data, especially once the ongoing mental health tests to mandate pharmaceutical 'correction' kicked in in fourth grade.

Since the bleak day HeadMan announced the Data, no one actually knew where it was 'located,' who ran it, the untold scores of billions it cost, or how many multitudes toiled away in its bowels. Forget that no one had ever met a Minder, no one had encountered anyone who even emptied their trash. The Data was just there, like gravity to someone walking on a cliff.

But one thing was firmly established, one of Congress's last gasps before it turned Potemkin. In its third and last concrete response to one of HeadMan's edicts, Congress required the Minders to make formal notification – in person – of Elevation from the Null Set to Middling Severity, from MS to RoundUp, and from that to the Mirror. Get kicked up a Level, and the Minders had to tell you face-to-face the very next day, Christmas included. Middling Severity to RoundUp – from passive digital harvest to peeled eyeballs – was the crucial step to be avoided by the ninety-five percent of us below RoundUp.

The stark, single-sheet Elevation notice was hand-delivered in a pale blue envelope, the Minders employing their own squads – armed, silent, implacable. The operative phrase: Getting a Blue. Traveling in teams of three, the standard-issue goons didn't argue or explain. Everything about the Data was arbitrary and capricious. No transparency, no recourse. They just hammered it to your forehead with a rusty nail, leaving you to wonder which of your many sins theoretically ended life as you knew it. Theoretically.

Not that I knew anyone who'd gotten a Blue. My margin for error terribly thin, could I hope to keep it that way?

****

Amazing really, looking back over HeadFuck's increasingly repressive three years, that the Data's inner architecture had been exposed at all. But the zipper wasn't quite to its chin in the Data's earliest days, Congress still with a breath of life back then. Most of what we know slipped out at an aborted hearing convened by Rep. Webb Hendon (I-OH), the rogue chairman of the since defunct Subcommittee Overseeing Scrutiny. (Disgusted by HeadMan's rise from his party's ranks, Hendon had turned Independent but retained his chairmanship since no one else had the guts for the job.)

Doing nothing with the high-flown evasions that passed for answers, Congress gave up on anything but show hearings. What was the point, the executive so … unitary? What's more, an early HeadMan decree abolished congressional subpoenas; *invited* witnesses rarely appeared. Before they retired or were otherwise ushered off-stage – damn those unreliable little campaign jets – a few stubborn subcommittee chairmen would invite twenty or more officials, delving deep into the bureaucracy in the hope that a stout-hearted, mid-level toiler might appear to spill some beans.

A sore thumb who wielded his backwater subcommittee with aplomb, the wily Webb Hendon managed to insert his swollen digit in several deserving eyes before he died. The nine subcommittees that theoretically authorized and funded Homefront T initiatives held not a single hearing on the Data (or much of anything else) during those whirlwind days of HeadMan's first efflorescence. Hendon's the only hearing, he was also the only member of his subcommittee with the gumption to sit and hear the sole witness who showed out of the twenty-eight he invited.

And so the brave, doomed Data subcontractor spilled, making a big mess all over Hendon's hearing as the chairman intended. Testifying behind a screen, he emptied one can of beans. Then his strong, distorted voice indicated he was opening his second can just as an unseen but nonetheless imminent tornado interrupted the proceedings. Previously uncommon in Washington, tornadoes often forced the Sergeant at Arms, that newly engorged *manager* of democracy, to interrupt the rare hearing of substance. The weather so unsettled, any but ceremonial hearings soon faded away.

This a Friday, Hendon doggedly scheduled an immediate resumption for Monday. But fate deemed otherwise as he, his wife and his mystery witness died in a horrific fireball of a wreck that night following a late supper at an obscure spot way up in Northeast DC. Hendon was safeguarding his own witness for the weekend, for he had no staff he trusted beyond the one old lady who, having nothing else to live for, declared she didn't give a hoot about the threats that'd stampeded everyone else. Officially the subcommittee's librarian, the chairman couldn't even give Mrs. Chestnut a raise when she became his strong right hand.

Though Hendon had been avowedly sober for years, an empty

pint bottle of Everclear – pure rocket fuel – was found in his car. As if any driver wouldn't toss such an incriminating empty. It and a blood alcohol level *four* times the legal limit 'proved' he'd marked the day's partial triumph falling far too far off the wagon at dinner. The staunch librarian insisted at her one press conference that Hendon was sober dropping her off at her apartment before the short drive to his Maryland home. The foursome's only member to survive the night, Mrs. Chestnut vanished three days later. Said by HeadMan's tut-tutting henchmen to have fled for absolutely no reason, she was assumed to be as cold and stiff as the others.

She was roundly contradicted by one of the restaurant's waiters (soon elevated to assistant catering manager at a certain lofty think tank) who said he encountered a very jovial Hendon in the john who offered him a belt of some weird clear liquor that knocked him on his ass.

The accounts of the affair focusing on Hendon's alleged boozing, little was said of the hearing's witness beyond that he carried no ID, his facial markers had been destroyed beyond reading in the fiery crash and – as was increasingly common among security MoFos – his fingerprints had been chemically erased years before. His charred remains were buried in Ohio besides the crusading Congressman and his wife, their mourners serving for his.

And thus the Subcommittee Overseeing Scrutiny died also, neither Tweedledum nor Tweedledee willing to don Hendon's fatally independent mantle. Digging and scratching on some short-lived, pirate Dutch server, folks willing to brave the search were *sometimes* able to locate the testimony of Hendon's final witness, by far our best description of the workings of the Data. Should a (small) glass of Everclear ever accost me, I'll raise it high for the courageous subcontractor, old-lady librarian, a wife doomed by loyalty and the bull-headed overseer.

****

For most Americans, their Level and Tier were questions that loomed unanswered. In polite society, it was thought best to avoid Middling Severity Tiers One and Two. Rather than resting too, too perilously close to the Null Set, better to be an unobjectionable MS Three or Four, though some thought MS Three lacked ambition.

Both Nicki and I learned our Tiers when her chippy little ad agency, Fornix & Foyst, somehow won a huge Army 'minority' recruitment account. The home team faring so poorly, the prior agency had tripped badly over the hurdles to rustling up black and brown Boots. F&F's win pushed Nicki, who'd been churning it out to sell fake cheese and the like, into a T-tinged realm. And that was fairly astounding, her own boots on the ground at many an anti-war demonstration (before such Demos faded away).

Upon winning his first T account, F&F's owner, Ernesto Padwick, was informed of his employees and their spouses' status, and he was required to disseminate this information himself in a personal 'counseling' session. Damn embarrassing, said the office wags, Ernesto trying to keep his mail clerks straight.

Like all of our ilk, Nicki and I assumed we were in Middling Severity. She used to worry about my getting Boosted the odd times I published something with clout, then she stopped talking about it. It turned out our Tiers weren't close and, yes, that dangerous disparity helped show me the door. All the coupling since Adam and Eve, all the accommodation painfully forged between Man and Woman, and suddenly a whole new something to mesh. As the Chinese proverb does *not* have it: May you find a woman whose Tier fits. Nicki landed in the coveted Middling Severity Four and, like most at that relatively benign level of surveillance, could hope to stay there unless some harsh spotlight shone upon her. I perched uncomfortably high on MS Nine, only two thin Tiers below Roundup.

Had Nicki joined me up on MS Nine, Padwick told her she'd have been fired on the spot despite the fact that her bizarre verbal contrivances had helped lead a desperate Pentagon to Fornix & Foyst in the first place. As it was, cold inquiries were made about the health of her marriage.

Challenging the cops' train searches would probably Boost me to Middling Severity Ten. Insulting, really, that I wasn't already freaking in RoundUp. All my rabble-rousing – dripped word by word from a vein, as the old sportswriter had it – amounted to so much pissing up a rope I wasn't already in the 95th percentile of the nation's dissidents?

The Data Minders be damned, this citizen retained the right to lay siege and catapult a suppurating, dead cow over the wall. Forget strategizing with some earnest, civ-lib legal beagles (bless 'em) round a battered table littered with mis-matched coffee cups. Forget lining up behind a rumpled know-it-all in a checked sweater at the conclusion of some righteous panel for the question period's open mic. This galoot prowled alone, even if in that forest full of trees that fell with no noise.

You supposedly had to work it to hit RoundUp. RoundUp involved human monitoring and therefore cost HeadFuck money. I could hope my useless little one-man Demo wouldn't Boost me there. Not, post-Nick, that I gave much of a shit. And, you come right down to it, maybe that was why it fell to me.

Chapter Nine

Chilean Cassandra

I sat and scratched and finally hacked a path to a decision: let someone else deal my hand. Wednesday it was, and if there was nothing in the papers about Sarge and Statie throwing down, I'd count myself in the clear on that and time to head to Manhattan for my next bout of trouble.

The machine kicking into gear, I mused about stuffing a bunch of alley cats in a sack and riding the Huntington train in search of Boss Conductor. And … and … nothing about any fight on the LIRR. Saturday's hysteria was stillborn. What, the sergeant major and the trooper picked themselves up, agreed it had been a doozy of a dustup and went their separate ways into the night? Boss Conductor wrote a report capping a career full of artful fiction that made it all melt away. And all the passengers were too embarrassed as Americans – no, as Long Islanders – by this wrinkle in the fabric of their social comity to make a stink.

Perhaps the Army's overarching sway led the LIRR and even the State Police to hush it all up. Or maybe a cop and a soldier sparking a minor race riot on a train was so much dog-bites-man during our induced national nervous breakdown. Forget Statie. He was laid up in a hospital somewhere, his neck in a brace, an IV in his arm, a balloon on his willie and no notion of what landed him there. Forget living in fear. Let him fear my thundering response.

Alright, another of the quirky little participant-observer stories I'd chased of late. Someone had to cry halt to the damn searches – plus put their name on the resulting article given the new Reg banning anonymous content. They couldn't really enforce it on comment or chat, but just about all news sites, even the scoundrels who published me, required names they'd supposedly verified, certainly on an article as dicey as this. Why not me, all my milk gone sour.

Though my chest still ached, I needed something large enough to attract the cops' attention to prompt my high-minded hissy fit. What to carry in my new, bona fide East German Army canvas backpack? Hot and murky for the thirty-third day of Forever, I debated stuffing the pack with wadded-up newspaper so it would be light but not flaccid. (Ah, and weren't them the days!) But that might prove awkward should I get seized anywhere near a match. Books were the obvious choice, and not no Dick and Jane. Subtlety, after all, wasn't the key the MoFos sang in.

I got lost hunting down the right few manifestoes from boxes untouched since moving in. Why bother unpacking, not knowing how much longer my scrambling would generate the scratch for even the Hovel. Anyway, good old Tom Paine; *The Gulag Archipelago*; *1984* (duh!); Upton Sinclair's *It Can't Happen Here*; Roth's Lindberg as a Nazi; *Fahrenheit 451*; Madeleine L'Engle's marvelous fable about fighting group-think, *A Wrinkle in Time*; *Darkness at Noon* and *The Handmaid's Tale*; old-chestnut *Brave New World* and a couple of Philip K. Dick. And, to pound home the point from the flip side, *Mein Kampf*. I paused a moment before tossing in this last, but weighing it in combination with all the others, the hell with anyone who didn't get the point.

HeadMan banning whole-vid pacifiers expressly to keep folks from immortalizing the cops' antics, a simple open notebook would attract the attention of officers opposed to any record. And then play it by ear. Surely the seven shots to the head of that Brazilian electrician, courtesy of the London police way back when, had no bearing over here. Nor did that poor sick bastard exiting the plane in Florida they shot down donkey years ago, his wife yelling the whole time that he was off his meds and needed help. The NYPDs were *typically* professional enough to signal their intentions and offer everyone (pale) a way out. Gimpy ankle and a heavy pack in the heat, I wasn't making the Brazilian's fatal mistake of breaking into a run when he heard his train approach.

Baloney. His execution was merely an early warning shot sent round the world: you think it's a regular day in the life, but mess up in front of the wrong Protectors – lights out.

Just freaking approach them with both hands well away from your body, have the right puppy-dog ingratiation in a voice coarsened by jock jocularity, and bow before them with frequent use of the word, *Officer*. They weren't gonna shoot me at some mobbed Midtown location. Not with me getting all high and mighty on them, thrusting my wrists for the cuffs, playing to the gaggle of TV cameramen over my right shoulder, news-site dudes clamoring on the left.

****

I hacked my way to the train through a mile (how else could I afford the Hovel?) of the sweltering gray gauze we called air, on the verge of a major political statement. Heck, talk is cheap: about to launch an army of fellow refusniks. The resulting article couldn't focus too too much on the (my) swell ballsiness of it all before my clarion call for throngs to follow suit. And since I'd packed a couple of hefty PBJs for my big field trip to the City, I could blow the nine bucks in my pocket any way I liked.

I'd hit Times Square, 34th Street's Herald Square and then the belly of the beast, Penn Station, home to the LIRR, Amtrak, a slew of Jersey trains beyond any sane person's care or understanding, a bunch of subways and more searches than anywhere else. Take a public stand, avoid the cuffs or not as fate had it and make a hustling freelancer's penny telling the tale.

Proud of my chic, new backpack, one of my few recent luxury items, I risked a ticket propping it on the seat next to me, the floor sticky with goo. The crowd from the 7 train piled on at Queensboro Plaza, and a trim, well-dressed, older woman carrying a thick hardback planted herself in front of my pack. I came to and reluctantly plopped it in the goop (not goo). Well into her sixties, she sported thick, jet-black hair and chunky-chic glasses resting on an alarmingly long, elegant nose. Not pretty, per se, but you sure grabbed a second look. She wore an expensive old pale blue dress with bright, multicolored threads shot all through and stockings! – the only pair on six trains in the heat.

She settled herself, opened her book, but turned to me. "I'm glad the satchel is yours, and I wasn't forced to delay any number of trains contacting a policeman. There's one of the posters there: *You Can Be Embarrassed, or You Can Be Dead.* According to my companion, a man of some experience, yours is just the sort of bag – large and new in appearance – that is of particular concern."

She spoke with a cultured, old-world precision, her Spanish accent strong.

"No, it's mine. But that's interesting: new, like it was bought for something specific."

"You seem to have considered the matter well. Perhaps there's reason to call a policeman anyway? What would you do, I wonder, if you found yourself sitting in my seat next to such a pack accompanied by such a man? Judging by your looks, not that looks alone signify, you might be one of the Irish who've started up anew. Or perhaps one of the 'lone wolfs' the news readers like to talk about."

I thought street hexer me could orchestrate this little escapade, but I hadn't even made it out of Queens. Folks were awfully twitchy, and why not with the T Index given every ten minutes with the traffic and weather on the "all-tripe" stations. So helpful in deciding whether to grab your potassium iodide, the new numerical scale would shoot alarmingly from 89 up to 92 and then drop reassuringly to 87 two days later. A hundred indicating a current attack, the last time it fell below 85 was HeadMan's birthday. It hit 95 a month back, matching its high for the year. This followed the hijacking in Abu Dhabi of a sheik's jet carrying two prize stallions bound for Kentucky – like that had anything to do with riding the freaking subway. Yup, cower and marvel and thank our Wisers and Betters when the number magically declines, thank the gods when the volcano doesn't blow. But best throw another virgin on the fire just in case.

"Oh, come on, lady, you're making awfully free with some pretty inflammatory talk. I know they're discussing it, but they haven't outlawed packages yet. Besides, look, it's just books. Here – books." I flipped the flap. "I'm returning them to a friend so I can borrow some more."

"A generous friend, a regular Carnegie of books. Such friends, real or imaginary, are not to be sneezed at."

That her dismissal, she turned to her own book. "There is one thing, though. These really are my books. I just picked them out, these particular titles, Tom Paine and all, to make a statement."

"Of course they are your books. No person with any sense returns a dozen books at once, carrying a bag like that in heat such as today's. So, teach me: what 'statement' do you make transporting books in a closed satchel?"

"Well, I'm actually doing a little test, or more of a civil-liberties type exercise, finding where the cops are doing these subway searches they're suddenly so big on again and hoping they'll pick me. Then I'm gonna just say no and see what happens. See what the cops do. Because someone's gotta make – "

"Are you sure you have thought this through, or do you just not care? Maybe you think this is all a type of game – another American expecting flowers at his feet wherever he goes. Despite my years here, the sincerity of American ignorance never fails to impress. Do you not read your own newspapers or have any sense of HeadFuck's America?"

Head*Fuck*, OK. "What do you mean, 'thought this through?' The worst they can do is arrest me, right? And as for the news, isn't it mostly pretty darn sanitized? I get the real deal online some weird little places."

"Certainly on the most important avenue, television, one is hard-pressed to know this is a country sunk in many wars. But I am talking about developments here in Manhattan." The train brown-out slogged slowly through the tunnel under the East River, a long way between stops. "You say you do not fear arrest. If true, you have led an inconsequential life. But then that is the culture in your country: banality mixed with aggression."

"What?"

"Not a single policeman is happy conducting these searches, exposed behind their worthless tables. Why not just detonate there, a man in uniform always the richer target? Plus they have no defense against the youth with their silly loose clothing that hides everything. All this they know but do not say, and they are tense."

Given such systematized talk, was she a lawyer returning from court out in Queens, probably a defense attorney given her hep-cat dress? Or maybe a head shrinker with a partial crim-justice practice? "So are you prosecution or defense, cause I'm looking for a little insight about this new HateCrime. You see – "

"My position is not your concern, but you may assume I do not waste what time I have left. Your motivations seem sincere, however sliding off the tracks. So permit this: you benefit from being white and clean shaven, not brown with a mustache. With those glasses, your longish hair – why do you not grow up? – and a face relatively unlined for your age, you have something of the overripe graduate student about you. This may work in your favor."

"My hair isn't so long anymore. I just got it cut – well, cut it myself, it's so damn hot."

"Listen, please! Now, if you are going to make a speech at the police, which I do *not* recommend, think more of your body language than of what you say. Your political content will mean much to you, but little to them unless they think it might add to your charges with the new HateCrime, say. With that pack – do you not have a smaller one, an *older* one? – if you challenge them as you intend, they will be all eyes, not ears."

"Right. But not *challenging*. A principled refusal is all. I have to make a declaration so it means something. And the books I have, let me show you."

"I can imagine what books: *1984* et cetera, given Americans' tendency for the obvious. Personally, I would carry Zamyatin's *We*. Though it is good that Mr. Paine is again receiving some small portion of the attention he deserves. But I'm getting off here, a stop early, because I must say I am not entirely sure if you are simply foolish, or if this is all, what is the word, *artimana* – a ruse. Might it be that you feel compelled to make a confession of sorts – a boast, maybe – to one of your intended victims and are now just waiting until the train is more crowded in Manhattan?"

"Lady, you're talking crazy!"

"Crazy, or blunt, as my age permits. Given where I have come from and what I witnessed there – Chile, if that means anything to you – I banish uncertainty from my life as I am able. So I will indeed get off a stop early."

"Of course I know about Chile. Chile was the straw that broke the camel's back changing my life. You see, one afternoon, three different bankers – "

"I can imagine. Chilean bankers and their American masters have impacted many lives. Do you think you are the only person who has challenged an unjust regime? Who has taken a stand with far more than the carrying of books?"

She hid her face on her shoulder a moment, then turned back, her eyes glistening. "Nonetheless, I applaud you and hope you get to make your 'statement.' Perhaps you can write of this adventure if you are daring enough to attach your name. Outlawing first whole-vids and now the new Regs on anonymous commentary, HeadFuck's reach matches his grasp – so far. It takes a brave or foolish person, or perhaps just an uncaring one, to make a statement in such a country."

"You don't like us much, do you?"

"It is not my preference to be away from what family I have left. Some of my colleagues, people known still in my country, argue differently, but it is not for me to return. My heart would break to walk the streets of Santiago."

I stayed shut-up. She indicated a ten-year-old with his father. "Depending on your skill, on luck, on many things – who knows, you may fan a flame to help brighten that boy's way."

"A flame. Yeah, maybe."

"A flame to banish shadows – such as these 'Boostings.' Why, given the character of my and especially my companion's associates, do none of us know anyone who has received this Blue? We wonder what, if anything, the Data means."

"You'd think someone plugged in like you might know."

"Better to forget such shadows. More importantly, be aware of your body language, specifically your hands. Trying to get through their day like anyone else, the police are not as sure of themselves as they like to pretend."

The train slowing, I groped for what to say. Thanks, probably, but also that I knew what I was doing for Chrissake.

Her coda was worst of all: "Consider most your mother, if she lives. Think as a man much younger than you, more's the pity, should have thought of his mother. Carrying books – might that have saved my son, I wonder."

And with that she jumped up, darted around some big guy and out the door.

Like Emily, another woman slipped through buttery fingers. A dame with a past, that's for sure, if a bit of a know-it-all. She hadn't given me the chance to say I already knew about your hands. Nor had I gotten to tell her my own Chile story from my long stint as an informational handmaiden to Wall Street. To think what I'd get churning out oligarchic pap way back when – a buck a word and more in pre-Plunge dollars. Reward for producing such dry stuff, not to mention being on the wrong side of the barricades. After years of misgivings, plus a few good years sneaking *slightly* progressive views into a thoughtful monthly review, I found myself with a steady freelance gig writing on global stock markets.

Never mind that I knew nothing of such, I'd mastered the fairly easy lingo and had a smattering of world politics. Most importantly, I knew how to work the phone, top dogs with jeweled collars delighted to lead me by the hand in exchange for a quote. I coughed it up for years. But, as I'd have liked to tell Chilean Cassandra, came the afternoon that would've finally doomed me to a scraggily beard if I hadn't quit because I'd be unable to look myself in the mirror to shave. Three different global portfolio managers (not bankers, actually) echoed each other almost to the syllable: "That Pinochet," they blared into my phone admiringly, "perhaps he was a little rough around the edges. But, boy, did he whip that Chilean economy into shape."

If I had any spine at all, I would have hung up on the third one and gone off beating my breast in search of a blind person to help across the street. Not sure of my conversion, though, I finished the article, for I'd had many a moment over the years recoiling from what I'd heard and subsequently massaged into print. In fact, I gave this, what was indeed the last of my many enabling-the-Despoilers articles, a fine polish.

The Chilean patriot's words shimmering ominously before me, I shouldered my pack.

Chapter Ten

Moo!

And got out at the crossroads of the world to find rivers of people but no searches at any of the six entrances to the giant Times Square station. By my rough count, 163 entered in five minutes at one entrance west of Seventh Avenue. I figured that made the article's point well enough about sheer numbers overwhelming any search. I grooved a moment to the busker pounding away on the plastic buckets and tin pots that make such fine drums in the booming, hard-surfaced space, and only then saw the two cops standing way over to the side, one staring vacantly, one writing in his memo book. I walked over and planted myself fifteen yards away, turning to profile my bulging pack. But they looked right through me.

Strolling over to Grand Central Station further east on 42nd Street, I walked by a presumably huge hole in the ground where, amazingly, a post-Plunge behemoth was rising. Would have liked to play 'sidewalk superintendent' as little boys of all ages and sexes used to do in New York from time immemorial, helping supervise the initial stages of the city's skyscrapers through the holes cut in the plywood fence. But there was nary a chink in this one's armor. Another decades-old pleasure punted.

No NYPDs at either the Sixth or Fifth Avenue subway stations along 42nd Street, I hoped that Grand Central, with all those rich Westchester and Connecticut commuters, wouldn't be naked to the world, the suburban trains having their own Metropolitan Transportation Authority police force. And indeed it wasn't, one small part of the huge main hall quite safe, with three cops (one cradling a stubby automatic), two dogs and a sergeant standing around chewing the fat or lying chin on paws. My pack and I stood well within sight, planted near the famous circular information booth, watching for fifteen minutes as a sea of humanity broke around us. But, two cops with their backs to the crowd in the noisy station, none seemed particularly interested in their surroundings. A ways off, a pair of National Guard soldiers stood aloof, actually scanning the crowd.

My ankle and I limped down to the huge subway station at 34th and Sixth, Herald Square. No cops graced that entrance, so I tooled down an underground corridor and hit pay dirt a little after five o'clock. A couple of stairways descending from 32nd Street were roped off, and three NYPDs shuffled people into a cattle chute of the familiar blue, wooden police saw horses. Denied their usual quick jostle at the turnstile, a long, sweaty line of New York disappeared on up to the street at the sole open stair. Down at the business end of the line where I'd popped out of the corridor, the remarkably patient herd passed one or two at a time through the chute and then by a fourth cop, the Decider. Maybe one in five were sent over to place their bag on a table for the blind laying on of hands by two more cops, the rest were supposed to head for the turnstiles.

HeadMan and the vast swath of the populace he'd turned into security MoFos had things locked down so tight, it wasn't like there was any *crime*. So, all in all, a nifty little cop-full-employment scheme. Six cops at the same hundred-grand-plus their Coney Island brethren got, you include OT and 'fringes' to die for.

Though the Decider kept repeating loud and clear, "Unless I stop you, keep going," many commuters directed to continue their journey still bovined up to have their stuff examined. Knowing darn well they had no bomb, it somehow reassured to have some cop uselessly rifle their stuff for five seconds. Cops with X-ray fingers, for just patting the outside of the bag allowed the officer to magically divine its contents and declare them safe. A purifying act granting dispensation to the citizen who surrendered her or his rights.

An empty exercise all around, good for politicians covering ass and a sop for a guileless, gullible public quite deliberately frightened. Scared and thus compliant, unquestioning of endless war. *Take him – no her! – not me.*

As advertised and I soon verified, you could just turn and walk to any of this *same* station's other entrances, all of them unguarded. A mother hen subway clerk clucked around, but the token booth (Metrocard booth? nah) was unstaffed. So much for getting directions at this major tourist hub, or a map, or even selling a ride to some old geezer intimidated by the ticket machines.

A large man loitering with a big, bulging pack in a cramped, harried spot where no one lingers; a guy openly taking notes on the whole operation for crying out loud; then just standing there; then strolling around to observe it from all sides – I must've drunk my invisibility potion at lunch. Begging for attention, I planted myself within ten yards of the gauntlet's lead cop. But the threat declared to the trains, any accelerated rush of matter seemed immaterial this side of the turnstiles.

Humping it a lot harder than the MTA cops at Grand Central chatting with their backs to the crowd, none of these NYPDs looked any too thrilled. It wasn't what they'd signed up for, this overly tactile 'stickiness' with an ever-swarming public. No, not you, *you* – over to the table. And you, you, and *all* of you please keep moving. Too many sacks of meat incapable of following the simplest instructions. Oh, for sitting stuck in traffic in the cocoon of a patrol car, white-cop lite-rock on the FM – cops play the radio like anyone else marooned in traffic – Esposito in the passenger seat blathering on about sports, food, family or, the one constant, precinct politics.

The rush hour crush in full bloom, the trains' screech filling the narrow stairwell from below, the numb line stretched out of sight who knew how far. Was it simple lack of gumption keeping people from walking to a different entrance, or merely the commuter's comforting habit? *I always enter here and go stand by* that *pole on the platform to ride in the* third car. So much for the practiced New Yorker slipping past mothers with lagging children.

If I tried to make a statement here, would anyone notice in such a fractious scene, or even hear me in the shriek of rusty brakes from below? Nothing to see but the endless pas de deux of the Decider steering folks left or right, I wearied of waffling and left to find the other station entrances unguarded beyond a woman with a cup belting out "Midnight Train to Georgia."

So the far too curious dude with the big pack hanging close for no obvious reason was allowed to leave. Other stations, or maybe the mess of tourists queuing for the top of the Empire State Building, were a block away. What, some sort of anti-T triumph if they got exploded rather than the same number of people traveling underground?

****

I gimped the long block to Pennsylvania Station, the execrable rabbit warren tucked under a crappy officer tower and the round hatbox of Madison Square Garden. Loyal to the land of my birth, I pushed through the six-o'clock madhouse to peer down at the LIRR level to see two MTA cops funneling the very occasional passenger to a table on the side.

Going the long way around to another way down, I then lingered a few yards away from the cops for the third time that afternoon. People dashed or trudged through the chaotic swirl, others met and hugged by the little waiting area, one couple loudly admiring how big a friend's kids were. My pack and I galumphed around big as life, one of us taking notes, but earned not a nibble from cops focused solely on the relentless swarms off the escalators. Anyone of ill intent could approach them unmolested from the throng coming up behind. As Cassandra said, it would make any cop tense who allowed himself to think about it.

Then I saw that every time they sent some eager-beaver over to the table, one cop jotted something down. That meant they were being held to a standard of some kind, their efforts statistically evaluated. Despite the steady drum-beat about the *random* nature of the searches – everyone's equal when no one has any rights – I truly hoped these cops drowning in a rush-hour Niagara weren't denying the melanin-deprived our just props in the T Hall of Fame. (Though, following their attacks, many white men were described as merely deranged, including the anti-government Texan who crashed his plane into an IRS building.)

Still, reporters need to confirm the obvious. After, perforce, disappearing into the men's room (disassociating myself from that big-lug loiterer), I approached with a big chamber-of-commerce smile plastered on, all but wagging my tail.

"Jeeze, you guys are working hard today, huh?"

The cop affirmed that such was their lot. The sergeant edging closer, I got to the point.

"So, uhm, I'm kind of a curious guy, and I've always liked watching how police work. You know, this deal with these searches is really something."

Oops. However aw-shucks amorphous, that cut a bit close to the bone. His whole body stiffened as he glanced at Sarge but said nothing.

"I mean, with all you gotta do here, keeping track of all these hundreds of people walking by every second, it seems like they're dumping a whole extra chore on you guys." Nobody likes the boss, right?

"Sir – you're right. We are busy here. What do you want?"

"Well, I couldn't help but notice that every time you send someone over for a search, you make a little note. So I was just wondering if you were jotting down what type of person you picked. You know, their age or sex or whatever?"

"You're right again. We're keeping statistics on who we choose – on their approximate age, their race, their sex, class – like that. They give us our targets, and then they add up all the information from all the MTA cops doing this today to see how we're meeting our goals. That way we get a truly random search."

Class? Offering his professionally blank stare, he added, "Anything else?"

"No. Thank you, officer. That sums it up pretty good: a targeted, random search. I appreciate it, and I appreciate the work you do."

"During the Current Continuing Crisis, that's how we keep everyone safe. Now, you get home safe yourself, sir."

He stayed glued on me as I nodded and drifted off, our little exchange – Travis Bickle talking to the Secret Service agent about his gun – immortalized by any number of Penn Station cameras. So much for the PC shibboleth we all bowed before, the widespread contention that the searches were random. Random – like train tracks across the prairie.

On the big LIRR board listing departures, it read at the bottom: "IF YOU SEE SOMETHING, SAY SOMETHING. CALL MTA.PD." Now, a child counting on her fingers might figure that wasn't quite enough numbers. The nearest phone booth confirmed turning those five letters to numbers yielded the bum-number recording. Citizens! Remain vigilant, ready to report. Such misdirection is merely a test of your capacity to participate in your own defense.

Two National Guard soldiers were stationed by the stairs, one with an M-36, the other a sidearm, both vigilantly up against a wall at sort of right angles to each other, doing their best to watch each other's back. Their posture a far remove from the few willfully oblivious cops I'd seen, it meshed with the seriousness of the soldiers at Grand Central.

There were no searches at the Jersey Transit/Amtrak operation one level up, but the portentous Brit-chick train announcer with the Oxbridge upper-crust grated like hell. It was worse than all the TV and radio ads, including amazingly enough one for the Mets' farm team, the *Brooklyn* Cyclones, that featured her honeyed murmurings or those of her even more supercilious boyfriend. This same annoying creature informed us that a particular National Prerogatives of Reactionaries radio program was brought to you by the Smooth Over the Cracks in the Imperium Foundation. Puh-leaze.

Feeling craven about not jumping in with both feet at the subway search a block away, I made my way back to that LIRR escalator feeding people down to the MTA 'search.' Unsure how testicular my intent, I stepped off into muddy water. Giving my pack and me a hard stare, the cop I'd interviewed (whether he knew it or not) moved his hand quick to his gun. Leaving it there, he gave me the slightest of nods as I met his gaze invitingly. Ah, the dreaded experimenter effect.

Falling to entice at Penn, I headed back to Herald Square, thinking it would be less frantic there an hour past rush hour's worst, and I could nail my protest to the cathedral door with good, or at least audible, effect. But the cops had pulled up stakes and, my ankle barking to beat the band humping them damn books, so did I.

Chapter Eleven

The Wife Replies

I lay in a sweaty bed early Thursday trying to convince myself my fumbling the day before was for the best, that it enabled me to mine atmospherics. The few soldiers I saw were seemingly more on-point than the cops, for instance. Plus the scrappy New Yorkers at Herald Square submitted as meekly – no, eagerly – as did the generally snazzier Long Islanders a block away. Best, of course, was the decent little nugget that at least one police department, the MTA, organized its searches along demographic lines. For them, random was a lie.

The cops and I hopefully able to play our parts with a bit more collective oomph, feet hit floor determined to get to Herald Square and then Penn, if necessary, by nine o'clock. Shouting into a can on a string, perhaps, depending on any melodrama and my eventual publisher. But I couldn't think of a better route to some brief, mild satisfaction than to flee the Hovel and tell the men with guns I wasn't moving to the back of the bus, que sera what may. Write it on spec like usual and force some site to take it out of sheer marvelousness.

But first, I needed to write the Wife to declare my serious intent to someone. I hadn't e-mailed her in almost a week (five whole days, but who's counting), so I felt entitled to seize the excuse for contact, even if only via the screen she'd made clear she preferred. Work e-mail was about all she read … so. I doubted her bosses were snooping on a top-gun creative like Nicki, even with that huge new Army minority-recruitment account. No one in Fornix & Foyst would care that her estranged husband was showing a little spine with a puny, one-man civ-lib Demo.

At least I'd stopped fabricating absurd excuses to call on a Sunday morning, like the bleak embarrassment a scant *four* days after I got tossed when I called, entire minutes after nine, to oh so sweetly ask if she'd kept all three of our little can openers in the bitter flurry of my leaving. Wobbly from my obligatory post-breakup *Saturday* night, I'd been up for hours already that morning and by nine really needed that tuna fish omelet – about all I had on hand to throw on top of some eggs. No, I didn't have the head for wallowing through stacks of boxes on a potential wild goose chase. There'd been no labeling of cartons, Kitchen Stuff, etc. during my grab-it-and-gone. Just some: "No, no – that's mine, damnit. You never even heard of Savoy Brown before you freaking met me."

She hadn't yet filed for divorce and maybe never would if Fortune somehow tripped me and beat me to the floor. If I befriended Deep Throat, Jr., say, the two of us slamming into each other rounding some blind corner, wiping blood from our noses with his handkerchief as we got acquainted.

So:

Thurs. Mourning
Dear Nicki:
A little something going on that I thought I should tell someone about. Mostly just an excuse to talk with you – my quotidian temptation. And, yeah, I still remember you laughing when I used that word on our first date.

Hope the Big Town's treating you well, though not too damn well. I doubt you've found a fruit/veggie joint as cheap as out here. And I hope Charley at work isn't making you any crazier than usual – and that he doesn't freak if somehow this note to your work address sees the light of day during the, you know, Current P. Crisis. It's just I know you delete scores of home e-mail without a glance, and I want to ensure this note gets some play on the infinitesimal chance it proves necessary. It's not like either one of us is in RoundUp, thank God.

Anyhow, I've gotten awfully pissed about this lousy submit-to-a-search regime the City has resurrected. I encountered it in spades last weekend at the Coney Island music blowout we always went to. Looking to get some OT on stupid reefer busts, the cops were going nuts with targeted, not random, searches LEAVING the train. Worse than that money-grubbing was a disturbing incident the day before involving a trumped-up search on the LIRR of all places, me out to visit the Aged Ps.

They've sparked one of my little participatory/ observer deals to hold their damn feet IN the fire and get rich and famous all at the same time. Like Arthur Miller said, that we saw in Brooklyn – *that* night, remember when we got home? Anyway: "There's a universe of people outside that you're responsible to."

I'm surprised the hullabaloo on the LIRR didn't make the papers, it got so vicious and ugly. And, no, I'm not being my usual self-aggrandizing self. It all started when someone had good reason – an uncontrollable cat in a carrying case – to actually refuse a search and, shocko, shock, I got sucked in trying to help. Then this butthead psycho-cop poured a whole lot of gasoline on the fire, leaving me rather bruised and breathless. And, no, that's not a metaphor as I'll explain someday if your glamour-puss new life ever allows for an audience.

Which ain't to say, Baby, that I don't shoulder some of the fault myself for what happened to us. Problem is, as the weeks keep rolling on, our groove-thang fading quick and relentless, that's just brackish water under a rusty bridge.

As to the point for now: Gonna venture out today with my luxurious new East German backpack (and you say I'm in a rut) filled with some deliberately chosen books and hope to galoot around enough to spark a search and then draw myself up in high dudgeon for a principled refusal. Then I'll have a big boffo piece on it for the big bucks. A stunt, yeah, but drawing the line, damnit, with the sort of participatory/ observer stuff that's seemingly gone out of style.

So, a real martyr to the Fourth Amendment, maybe. Enough perhaps to rival the poor executed Brazilian electrician in London. No, I'm not gonna do anything stupid – I know how to mess with cops. Not that the Brazilian was carrying any political books, and I feel so damn obvious with *1984*, *It Can't Happen Here*, *A Wrinkle in Time* and *Mein Kampf*, etc. But they underscore the point I'm trying to make. (Remember your brother freaking when he saw me reading Mein Kampf, and I said, however evil, it was a 'necessary' document? I knew you were the one when you understood.)

Nicki, you should've seen it yesterday at 34th and Sixth: people were just delighted to trot up to have the cops trod all over the Constitution and *pretend* to paw through their stuff. One cop kept telling a majority of the people to just move on, but maybe a third of those folks – sheep who'd already been dismissed! – lined up anyway.

Yeah, just a metaphor, I imagine, about being a martyr to the Fourth Amendment – not that I give a flying fuck I miss you, Baby, oh so much. Anything happens, you'll know what to do.

Me

Lo and behold, Nick replied in the time it took to make a couple of PBJ club sandwiches, though it was still before eight in the morning. Must've been taking her damn promotion seriously. God knew Fornix & Foyst was paying her enough to churn out the suet, though it was a proper indication of where things stood that I hadn't a clue the precise number of $Ks. I forced respiration and opened it.

Hey:
I don't know what to make of your rambling note, though the emotional blackmail at the end is as clear as it is unwelcome. Just more of that rampant narcissism of yours from being an only child. Being a martyr is "just a metaphor,"

though you don't give a flying fuck – oh?? Well isn't that too, too clever and convoluted. As you never tired of telling me, even the day before we split, you're the real writer in the family, crafting your lofty shit.

Sounds to me like you need a job, but I'm tired being blue in the face on that one. So who are you writing this for, or is it another one of your 'adventures' you're going to end up publishing somewhere for fifty bucks? (See re job, ad nauseam.)

Still, be careful. There's probably better ways to become famous. Though I must say, both when the searches started and now since they're back, I'm pretty surprised no one has tried to challenge Walk-on-Water Ted about them. People talked big on that *Get On With It* site I used to lurk on that you used to laugh at for being so unctuous. But no one actually did anything I ever heard of. Millions of riders a day and not one stoned hippie chick, drunk model, coked-up Wall Streeter, righteous Hip-Hop Nationer, civil-liberties lesbian soccer mom or mush-mouthed Unitarian has irredeemably lost it in a sweat-bath of a station and just said no – plain old get the fuck out of my face, *No!* Sad to say, it just might fall on your beefy shoulders – *if* you can get anyone to pay attention. Though it'll be tough in this ONE instance, writing it up, focus on the story, not yourself.

Anyway, wasted too much time on all this – what, like nine years?

Actually, your dumb conundrums are more interesting than what I'm trying to nail down for this edgy new client. Maybe I should just quit this nonsense and sign on as some Mormon's fourth wife to keep his young slut-puppies in line.

I guess not all of those nine years were wasted. We had us some good times, especially those fool expeditions of ours all over creation. Don't know how many guys there are out there willing to take a subway and then a bus just to go walk along some shoreline and then a bus and subway home, maybe even getting wiggy with a five-dollar half-pint of Clan MacGregor on the way back. I'm too old for that swill now, but still. So, chum, you never know. The cat is way out ahead of me on this, but I do miss you.

Be careful. Is there any point in asking you to stop and think about this? You say you're not in RoundUp yet. But at Middling Severity 9, you're a hell of a lot closer than me. And remember about your hands with the coppers like we talked about once. You catch them standing around, tell them to go grab a broom. That's rhetoric or something, you big dope.
Nicki

I was spinning in my chair at this first positive indication of any sort. *Chum*! Of course my e-mail's talk of martyrdom was metaphorical. Something to catch her attention. Exit stage-left via cop? It wouldn't be remotely fair to the cop just trying to make his way uneventfully through his shift. Just my luck, he might skip the usual overkill, and I'd end up rolling around in a chair, a bag of piss by my feet.

Besides, *misses me*, she'd written right out loud!

Chapter Twelve

The Telltale Bulge

I re-read Nicki's e-mail a third time and floated to the subway almost at a run. Her biological clock winding down, had she decided she'd run out of time to cast about for the four guys needed to replace me? Would she stoop to dragging in our cat, Otis, if her little tease held no water? Uninflected e-mail – no notion of sarcasm or sincerity.

After yesterday's semi-formal ensemble, today's sartorial statement was an ancient, long-sleeved black tee shirt deluxe with thin blue and green vertical stripes. Dating long ago, I'd wear it dancing on a Friday, then wash it in the sink and dry it with a hair dryer to wow another quarry Saturday with its vintage quirk.

Floating, racing, I risked getting drenched hauling the darn books. Not carrying a hair dryer, I dialed it back and was soon hauling myself up, down and around the huge 34th Street station to, alas, find no cops. Off to Penn, the prior day's other seam of coal, before trudging up to Times Square and on to Columbus Circle if need be, hitting a number of subway stations along the way. Then home to phone a few of the usual civ-lib suspects for a quote or three underlining the swell chutzpah – I mean, necessity – of it all, write it up and hit send.

I headed west on 34th Street to see what might be left of the newsstand whose burning had so threatened the giant Macy's across the street. I found the rectangle of blackened sidewalk easily enough, but that was it. Well, they'd shipped steel ruined by malign neglect off to China before it was cool. Sold it as scrap right damn quick, never mind it was key evidence from a fairly major crime scene sixty or seventy blocks south.

My pack adding bulk to heft, I breasted the waves of commuters fanning out over the city, important types breaking on the prow of a heavily laden ship not given to unnecessary maneuvers on a bum ankle. Aghast at the impertinence of this slack vessel plowing doggedly forward, some of the sleek, overpowered cigarette boats barely veered clear. Why, it carved entire seconds from their day.

Crossing Seventh Avenue, I saw by a watch ad it was pushing 9:00 a.m. Almost Leslie time, the most informative few minutes of the day when the well-mannered pit bull graced hundreds of little radio and TV stations around the country with more real news in her introductory ten minutes of headlines than you'd get from hours of the mewling accommodationists on Narcissists' Permission Radio, never mind the tits-and-guts shouting elsewhere on the dial. Called *Redirection*, Leslie's assessment of another loathsome day, her measured jeremiad, brought to mind Brando's *Wild One*. Asked what he was rebelling against, he famously replied: "What've you got?"

I dug the Entertainment System, my little silver transistor radio, out of my pack. No inserting the latest, fantabulous McAllister to seal myself off from the world, 1950s technology was fine by me. (Though I did appreciate that more recent innovation, color television). I didn't walk along holding the radio cocked to an ear – too crypto-doof even for me – so there was the occasional odd stare at the curious bulge on my shoulder under a tee shirt. My yap closed, despite looking like a mouth-breather, the yakking wasn't coming from the fillings in my teeth. The last couple of blackouts, people crowded around this knucklehead to hear the news, no one snickering then.

So as not to drown out my pronouncement, I'd silence Leslie (fervently wished in many quarters) once she finished her ten-minute introductory take on the world. I certainly wasn't messing with cops carrying a bulky backpack *and* having some weird talking bulge tucked under my shirt. Weren't bulges one of the lies the bobbies initially hurled at the Brazilian? Anyhow, should luck lead to getting searched, my statement was short:

Officers, I hereby assert both my right not to be searched and to continue my journey. As you know, having sworn an oath to uphold the Constitution, the Fourth Amendment prohibits "unreasonable searches and seizures." The simple act of carrying a backpack by no means a reasonable cause for suspicion, I now require a statement from you that I am free to leave.

If they stood there scratching, I guess I'd take it from the top, repeating myself until sheer annoyance goaded them to respond – not a high hurdle. Focusing on the three key elements: 4th Amendment; no reasonable cause; and their acknowledgment I could go; I could fumble my way through it easy enough.

Leslie caressing me under my shirt with the day's news, I headed for the station's main entrance at 32nd Street. To the degree her professional persona ever cracked (usually just a 'hunh'muttered under her breath before her next question) she sounded quite exercised about a D.C. circuit court ruling permitting a U.S. "administrative annexation" of a vast swath of Venezuela for its own defense. The judges leaned on the IMF's "recent intra-oceanic decree protecting manifest-right resources" during the Current P. Crisis.

Crossing 33rd Street, basically a Penn Station/Madison Square Garden private loading dock there between Seventh and Eighth Avenues, I saw six cops on horseback hanging out mid-block. As opposed to the regiments of horse massed to intimidate the late-night crowds leaving hip-hop concerts, that merited a look so early in the morning. I walked up all but whistling I was such a happy-go-lucky fellow. The equally sanguine cops sat way up high bullshitting amongst themselves. Seeing them in their black leather boots and shiny helmets towering overhead on their choice NYPD horses, no wonder the Aztecs believed the Spanish horsemen were gods.

Cops on the clock doing their usual in a vastly over-policed town, no grist for my mill. There was an official entrance to Penn Station here between the office tower on Seventh and giant hatbox of the Garden on Eighth that I'd never previously encountered. It would allow me to scope out any search table and then stage a calm, full-frontal approach to prompt a safe encounter. Like Cassandra said, the cops knew too well they couldn't safeguard even themselves at their dumb table.

****

An escalator spat me out at Amtrak/Jersey Transit, so I wound down and around a staircase one more level to a narrow public corridor, signs pointing the way to the LIRR. I motored along at a good clip – otherwise you're left for the crows to peck in Midtown. Plus, having passed through this dump all my life, I was curious where this unknown corridor led. The wall on my right stretched unbroken; on the left a big opening lay just ahead, perhaps the main LIRR hangout where folks lingered to be shot from a cannon when their track was posted.

And Leslie started declaiming about the Disaffected Exonerated. The not nearly as amorphous as they liked to seem group of bike riders were suing the NYPD over undercover surveillance of the heinous crime of riding en masse through city streets. Such is the physics of a fluid mass – blow on a dandelion and try to corral the puffs – the last Friday of the month, their sheer wheeled numbers allowed hundreds and hundreds of them to thumb their noses at the NYPD. By simply saying 'No, we'd prefer not,' the group became a wildly disproportionate Walk-on-Water Ted obsession.

Month after month, expensive phalanxes of menacing uniforms lined the cyclists' presumed route, then scrambled to their vehicles to catch up when the procession took an unexpected turn. Undercovers with cameras peeking through a hole in their shirts, open whole-vidders capturing the biometrics of every face, helicopters thundering overhead to promote hysteria, mass arrests – playground-bully Ted achieved little beyond looking foolish.

Enjoying Leslie's account, I careened round the corner on my left and about knocked over the smaller of two MTA cops accompanied by a Guardsman as they came racing around from the other side. We collided but then were propelled back and apart like two magnets of the same pole, as much from the force of the lead cop and my involuntary "YAHs!" as from the jarring collision itself.

My chest still aching from a recent police encounter, he'd freaking clocked me with his nose in nearly the same spot, the lead cop maybe only 5'7" sense memory had it. I stood there panting, having stumbled back several yards into my corridor. Also propelled back around their side of the corner, they'd yet to reappear.

Granting three armed men the initiative, I froze, my hands

well away from my body and Leslie blaring away. Let her talk – I sure wasn't touching any piece of shiny silver metal I had secreted away until they reappeared.

Damn, oughta make 'em wear a bell, like cats in a bird-filled backyard. Double-damn, did I scare them or what? How freaking long was I supposed to stand there? Didn't these guys know this was *my* day, the intrepid citizen calling the tune with the forces of state control?

And then the three of them came around the corner, the short guy in the middle with – yup! – some blood bright on his upper lip, less so where he'd smeared it wiping off his chin. None looked any too happy.

Kee-riced! Just putting one foot in front of the other, I'd gone and bloodied a cop, broke his nose probably. And, like Jamie going after Cat Wrangler, he was gonna get payback one way or another. Humiliate a MoFo and you pay. We like to pretend otherwise, but we're still scratching and screaming and throwing rotten fruit at each other as we drag our knuckles across the forest floor.

The bloodied one was thirty-something, good looking with a shock of dark hair and wearing his uniform just so. The other cop was older, taller, bulkier and with the sort of '70s aviator glasses that did his face no favors. Crouching with his feet spread, the soldier kept his hands poised to snatch any passing West-Nile mosquitoes from the air.

Adrenaline shooting between us, no one but Leslie said a word. I'd stepped back into a pool of uncommonly good reception to hear that, amazingly, an NYPD honcho had agreed to grace her airwaves. She launched one of her usual, low-keyed, take-no-prisoners questions and said, "Deputy Commissioner Morris, your response please."

Morris replied in New Yawk cop-tawk about squashing groups with criminal intent. "And make no mistake about it," he warned. "I've seen the T in the eyes of these filthy young Subversives running roughshod on bicycles. The Disaffected Exonerated just don't get it that when the Commissioner *himself* says enough, you damn well better stop already."

A don't-mess terrier even – especially – with blood on his

face, the short cop erupted. "How's he got a NYPD white-shirt coming off a speaker? Who the fuck are you? Get your hands away from your body!"

Assuredly, they were.

The tall cop said, "Frankie, what the hell's he got in that backpack? And what's that on his shoulder? You see that boxy thing under his shirt there!"

Frankie answered, "Yeah, what the fuck is that under his shirt? And look at that cord going down the strap." Indeed, my swank, army-surplus pack featured a number of accoutrements and attachments, clips for water bottles and whatnot. Stepping back, Frankie shouted into his radio: "Homeless Disgorgement officers requesting a sergeant immediately! Corridor B-7!"

And the soldier said nothing, his eyes boring into me as all they retreated a couple of steps, their hands on holstered guns.

Then Frankie's nose started bleeding again, undoubtedly rendering him harder to control. I took a step forward. "Hey, man, I'm sorry about your nose. I didn't see you coming around that corner. I mean, it's not like you saw me either, right? Look, I got a paper towel with my lunch in my pack – it's clean."

I started to reach, but first to silence Leslie talking quite unhelpfully about a subpoena for records of police undercover activity. And Frankie said, "He's doing some kind of Demo with a tape about the cops or what? Who is this guy?"

They gave a gun to this man?

"Officers, no. This is a radio playing a regular station – well, damn unusual – but still right in the middle of the FM dial. Let me just get it so I can deal with you gentlemen properly."

I reached up across my body to my shoulder, my hand – shaking a little I noticed, and damn, I didn't like giving them that satisfaction – trying to push past the pack's strap and get under my shirt.

And one cop yelled hey! and the other yelled watch it! They all backed up another step, and Frankie stashed his radio back on his belt. Behind me came the determined clack-clack-clack of a pair of darting high heels, a sound that normally might turn my head.

I said, "No, man, come on. Let me just show you what the deal with this is – that it works."

And I pulled out my little shiny silver radio. Walking up one long, deserted residential Queens block and down the even more boring next, sneering at the people gathered companionably behind the lit windows, another tallboy of Ballantine surreptitiously in hand those horrible first weeks in the Hovel, the Entertainment System masked the break-up pain more than anything else I grabbed. Smiling at my dependence on such a simple thing, I saw the short cop draw his gun.

"Hey, maybe I should just shut it off. Or let me tune in something you guys'll like – the whole AM dial pretty much. You'll see."

Trying to position my hand to flick the tiny switch from FM to AM, I stretched it out to show them. And the bloodied, good looking cop with the crease in his pants and the shine on his shoes put one hand under the other and pointed that thing at my face. Our eyes locked, him looking all twisted and tragic and – Christ! sighting through one eye. It all too quick for me to get hysterical, I stood rooted as his face scrunched up like a five-year-old trying not to cry after his big sister walloped him. Then the gun exploded, the noise beyond measure in the metallic corridor.

Chapter Thirteen

An Iffy Diagnosis

The older cop screamed, "Frankie, what the hell are you doing? What the hell did you just do? Goddamnit, I told them you haven't been right since you got back." Frankie not answering, the other cop took out his own gun, aimed carefully at the floor behind me and fired.

Sounding like she was underwater, but all the louder for it, Leslie cut deep through the roaring in my ears. Before anything else, that pain had to stop. A tree hit by a car unable to hear myself, not knowing if I was whispering or screaming, I said, "What the fuck's your problem? Wait. Can you please just let me take care of this so I can deal with you."

And then this man standing fifteen feet away put his hand under his wrist again and again fired as the soldier leaped to knock the gun upwards. After a bit, I realized part of the throbbing in my head was a woman behind me screaming her fool head off, and who could blame her, shots flying all over. Then I felt the blood coming down the side of my face and swooned to the floor, top-cop Morris saying from my fist that he didn't have to answer that question, that he'd hang up if there was another like it.

It's true what they say: your life does pass before your eyes. I'd experienced it as a teenager lying near the bumper of a car that'd just screeched to a halt, your story in a fleeting whirl you never quite forget. Lying crumpled on my side, my pack of books half-humped on top of me, I looked up at the two guns dangling from two hands and was glad that no panorama-of-me flashed by. But my relief was tempered by the fear I might've wet myself when I felt blood on my face. I didn't dare move my hand down to check.

The blood dripping off my head to the floor, so much for any exalted martyrdom to the Fourth Amendment, so much for taking a stand. The master of disaster always thinking he could control any situation no matter how slippery. Amateur semiotician and first-rate fool, I kept telling them, just let me "*deal*" with you, a charged, murky phrase. My hand shaking, true, but I wasn't panicked beyond reason cause a couple of cops were pissed. Forget my clever mouth, maybe it was simply the radio, the classic transistor no longer safe in a micro-zap world. Radios, nip bottles and Siamese cats – all grease for the wheels – newly verboten.

What, after all the heartbreak, I picked the same morning Nicki shone the faintest ray of hope to fumble my way to the Exit? Just punch that button opening the elevator doors on an empty shaft and leave her with a lifetime of guilt? (A month, anyway.)

Shot in the head – not good. It's one thing to get rubbed out in some grand, Give Me Liberty or Give Me Death moment refusing a search. Me and the self-immolating Vietnamese Buddhist monks – right on, right on! Had mine been a principled, heralded checking-out rather than human fallibility writ large, years hence they might have named an elementary school for me in the Republic of Vermont. A fraught combo: a jumpy, dopey cop and a careless dope whose tongue flapped wrong. What the heck had his partner said about him not being right? Heaven knows how long-gone Moondog would've fared these days, the peaceful New York oddball who dressed like a Viking and carried a seven-foot spear. And to think I'd scoffed at that old-crone, Chilean know-it-all.

The soldier bolted towards me defenseless on the floor. Gonna finish the job with his big black boots? As he ran past, I turned and was confronted by baby-blue panties on a serious blonde sprawled on the floor, keening and clutching her stomach with both hands trying to staunch the blood seeping through her short, tight green dress. She was entitled to scream. Had the first shot hit her too, or the second bouncing off the floor that his partner had fired for cop-cover-up solidarity? Or was it the third, bouncing off the ceiling when the soldier hit his wrist – whatever the bloodied cop was called?

The soldier bent to the Blonde. Less than a minute since the third shot, maybe fifty people had come racing around that damn corner to jostle and cluck, a fox snuffling at their hen house door. Luckily, seeing two people bleeding on the floor and two cops with their guns out, the stampeders all shimmied to a halt, the newcomers craning their necks behind. I schlumped down further to rest my head on my arm on the floor. From this odd angle everyone led with their knees, their faces swimming awfully high up.

I tried to sit up, but couldn't shrug my way out of my rhinoceros of a pack. A couple of men, one a skinny yammerer in a sleeveless shirt, the other a bald guy with a gut in a pricey sports coat, started shouting questions and suppositions. Then a whole lot more of the crowd's who/what/why rattled round my head.

The older cop got out his radio and barked, "Dispatch, we got a 10-13, repeat, 10-13, officer needs assistance, in LIRR corridor B-7. Repeat, LIRR corridor B-7!"

Great. Now every cop within a square mile would rush up with his gun out, looking to protect his brother officers. Hey man, it wasn't the cops, but the civilians that needed assistance, our life's-blood dripping on a grimy floor.

The short cop – Frankie, *that* was his name – stood there mooning, his gun loose and disowned in his hand. Maybe he'd drop it and finish me off. He suddenly started kicking the wall's metal baseboard over and over, the booms in my head now worst by far, the cop squalling deep in his throat about how his wife was gonna kill him. That she was gonna be really pissed. That this'd probably be the last straw for the two of them, he got kicked off the force and lost their health insurance.

A jellyfish tossed up on a crowded beach, I lay in the middle of the floor with the crowd edging ever closer now that it looked like the shooting was over. I managed to haul myself to my elbow and then scooch back to lean the pack I couldn't unharness against the wall, some thick hardback, probably the damn Solzhenitsyn, assaulting my kidneys. The effort costing, my head lolled on my neck like a newborn's. The world twirled, then wavered – another thing that was never good. I got ahold of my hair on the side away from the blood and held my head upright. The corridor swam until it slowed and eventually righted itself. I found I could maintain.

Bending over the woman, the soldier pulled something out of that pouch they wear strapped to their leg and pressed it on her stomach before getting her to hold it there herself. Man, look at her! No matter what, she'd stolen my thunder on the searches, not that I got to make any. With a beautiful blonde gut-shot by one of our Heroes patrolling the perilous front lines at Penn Station, big-galoot me was damn sure getting cast as the villain of the piece once everyone started pointing fingers and covering butts. My ears roaring and my breath somehow rasping inside my skull, I tried to keep my head still.

The soldier rose from the Blonde, muttering and grabbing for his radio. He talked into it, then reached out and banged its base against the wall I was leaning against. Another bomb in my head, though not as bad as Frankie's boot on the baseboard. Striding back, he stepped over my legs and took Frankie's radio off his belt. The cop didn't seem to notice. Yelling with his arms outstretched, the other cop tried to stem the crowd. And the soldier, praise be, started hustling up medical assistance. Realizing I'd soon be passing through others' hands, I confirmed my drawers were dry.

A lady in a LIRR shirt elbowed her way through the crowd towards Frankie, demanding answers. That snapped him out of it and, ignoring her, he came over to me and bent quick for the radio. My hearing screwed, I'd spaced on it blaring there in my hand. Frankie refocusing my attention, I heard Leslie revisiting the Venezuela story, something about a proposed bombing campaign designed to spark a national uprising, though, improbably enough, by the people getting bombed *against* their own government.

If Frankie had bent for the radio nice and slow, I might not have reacted. But he darted too quickly, and I got a good grip on it. He started prying my fingers open, as I tried to command my hand. He picked up the whole limp noodle – to bite me? If he disappeared my radio, whatever I'd pointed at them could be said to have gone lost in the general confusion of the growing crowd, it then soon morphing to some kind of pistol. Poor procedure surely, but both cops had done their best.

"Hey, Frankie," I wheezed. "Leave me the fuck alone. Haven't you done enough for one day? It's a radio, like I told you. It's always gonna be a radio, and it's mine."

Saying nothing, he started digging his nails into the sides of my fingers. Lucky for me, intelligence from the far reaches of my empire wasn't transmitting all that well back to headquarters. But this little struggle obviously wasn't lasting long. I took a deep breath and remembered to generate volume from my diaphragm. "Help! Somebody help me! This cop shot me, and now he's trying to steal my radio so he can say it was a gun. Folks, this shit ain't right!"

My feedback loop rampaging since the first shot, I didn't know whether I was shouting or squeaking. But right on cue this big Asian dude with magenta hair and a slinky white girl dressed in a heat-wave smile and a sneeze, both looking about nineteen, pushed their way out of the crowd, the guy lugging an enormous, presumably licensed whole-vid. Not looking like officially approved media, he was probably one of the ever rarer film students grandfathered into one.

The girl bent down to see Frankie's badge and called out, "Marko, this guy said the cop's name is Frankie and his badge number is 5-9-4-7. Get both their faces – including their ears if you can get one or both – and then keep your shot nice and tight on the radio in the guy's hand. And get his head wound too, though it doesn't look too bad."

Some highly starched Despoiler started yelling at them to just let the cops do their job, but these kids, bless 'em, ignored the swelling pro-Protector chorus. Frankie said a whole lot of bad words jumbled all together, put one hand up by the lens and the other painfully on my knee to push himself up, and vanished through the crowd that parted for his uniform and his gun. Then six or seven soldiers came rushing up, two with big guns they used like halberds to push the crowd back. Finally a use for one of those damn things in a crowded train station.

The gutsy young girl was obviously a precocious med student who knew all about entirely superficial head wounds. Illustrating why HeadFuck had banned most of them, Marko's whole-vid became an instant press pass. He went over to film the woman who'd slumped to the floor, her head cradled by a female cop, the woman still pressing her hands into the dark, spreading red. And two paramedics came rushing up with enough equipment to invade Normandy, took a look at me and headed straight for the Blonde. Two more then barged through the crowd, and one put ammonia painfully under my nose – Christ! – cut my sleeve off and got some goop flowing into my arm.

The lifesavers didn't tarry. As the crowd grew and pressed against the soldiers and then a swarm of cops, they wheeled the girl past on a stretcher, the same lady cop running along besides her stretching a fluid bag awkwardly over her head, her other hand holding her gun against her hip. The crowd melted for them and then flowed back like wet sand at the water's edge where some kid has dug.

My two guys, the chunky one with the big stud in his ear stood up and stared down at me, while the skinny, hawk-nosed one tipped me forward and with some difficulty wrestled me out of my pack. He applied a heavy-duty band-aid of sorts, then wrapped some gauze around my head and taped it down on the good side. He asked if I had any kind of weird taste in my mouth, and when I said no, Skinny said, "You know what – relax, cause it just grazed you. Didn't even penetrate your skull. You're either lucky or the most hardheaded bastard I've ever seen."

"My Pop's been saying that since I was a kid."

Chunky detached a portable wheelchair from the back of his largest case. I told them I could get up myself, but they each got under an armpit and hoisted me into the chair. The walls going wavy again, I managed to pop the radio, hopefully unseen, under my ruined disco tee shirt.

A dough-faced cop in a white shirt showed up bellowing for everyone to move back, that he was the "Incident Commander." Maybe three guys retreated a step. He then yelled for someone named Frost, and Frankie's partner came up with a crisp salute. "Thought I told you to keep Reisner out of trouble," white shirt said. "Where the hell is he?"

"Captain, he's here. He must be gathering evidence."

"I see. You fired your gun too, Frost – that new, well, not Reg but … ?"

"Captain, I – "

"Right, Frost. Say nothing till the Response debriefing. I think Nenbach's running it today, thank God." Pointing down at me, "This the perp?"

"I guess so. I mean –"

"That's an affirmative regarding this Suspect. You have two daughters, don't you, Frost? I don't imagine you're going to try to swing college – not for both, post-Plunge – but still."

Rocking back and forth on the balls of his feet, almost strutting in place, the captain stared at his subordinate. Finally Frost saluted crisply and took two steps back, almost tripping over a weaselly guy crowding in with a rubber neck atop a stained tie that didn't go with his stained polo shirt. He'd already caught my eye by continually blowing little saliva bubbles.

The captain turned to Chunky and said, "This Perpetrator's, uh, *cut* is not life-threatening, correct? As the Incident Commander, I will rule on the timing of his release to medical authorities. If he cooperates, we can arrange a *free* visit to a city clinic soon enough. But right now he has several statements to sign."

Chunky smiled to himself, shrugged and half-turned away. The captain sputtered and almost reached out to grab the big EMT by the sleeve. Thinking better of it, he turned to his uniform and said, "Frost, you and –"

"Captain, not even close," Skinny intruded. "This man is our patient and forget that 'incident commander' garbage you guys have been trying to pull. EMS/FDNY doesn't recognize it – not from the MTA. As the senior EMS present, this man's health is my responsibility, and he's leaving for Bellevue immediately. He's at risk for swelling, intracranial hemorrhaging or maybe a stroke. I'd think you'd want him to get the quickest treatment possible. But either way – let's go!"

This last was directed at Chunky, as Skinny pushed him around to the back of my chair and picked up my knapsack and deposited it – umph! – in my lap, his hands soon full with his and most of Chunky's gear.

The captain darted in front of us, my toes up against his shins, his hand on his gun. He said, "Frost, write down this man's badge number."

Skinny turned to Frost and plucked his EMS badge away from his chest for easy reading.

The captain said, "All right big-shot band-aid man, you can take this Suspect to Bellevue for short-term medical clearance. After that, he's mine. And believe me, we're going to find out who's behind him, I don't care what it takes. I am not having Everidge's plans for so many of us loused up by a no-account Subversive. You got that, Frost? You play your cards right – that means starting *now* – and we can find a cush spot for you too. Though you should probably wait two more years till you get your twenty in."

"Captain, I'm going to ask you to get out of our way – now!"

"Sure. Sure thing, Mister MD. But just one more thing: whose pack is that you gave him? That's not yours?"

"That's his property," Skinny said.

"That means it's mine. This is a crime scene and that's evidence. Have you even bothered to check its incident significance? It looks awfully bulky to me, not exactly his laundry home to momma."

I gaped up at them, curious whether Skinny would defend my property rights. The captain bent to the pack. I put one hand on my shirt so the radio wouldn't fall out, and the other weakly gripped a strap as suddenly a bunch of bright dots flared up all around. "Hey, this is my stuff – my books – so keep your hands off and let me get to the hospital. Listen, I don't feel so good right now."

"So go to the hospital, Subversive. We'll be there waiting for you." And he knocked my listless hand away, but failed to scoop up my brand new pack with one hand. Getting a better grip, he handed it to Frost. Chunky wheeled me down the corridor to an escalator and spun me around none too gently to tip my chair and ride me up backwards. I peered down through my feet at a couple of hundred people milling around, the crowd densest over by where the Blonde had been. People started peeling off around the edges to start their day, a lot no doubt telling themselves to later micro-zap what that whole mess was about.

A cop outside helped hoist my chair up to bang painfully into the back of the ambulance. Chunky driving, Skinny got in the back, whipped out a blood pressure cuff, but then started listening to my heart. I asked what the matter was, and he told me to shut up and then banged on the wall and yelled at Chunky to go. One of the back doors opened, and an older guy with colorless, greased-back hair and a shabby, metallic green suit clambered aboard with surprising deftness.

Skinny bending over me with his back to the doors, I said, "Hey, is he coming with us?"

Skinny turned and, crouching low, advanced on the man. "You've gone too far. This is my bus – *mine*, inside and out. I don't care if you're deputy chief of the whole damn department, this is my ambulance and my patient. And you're getting out."

"Steady there, Sonny. Just making sure a crucial piece of evidence doesn't leave the crime scene. Now if you don't mind, I – "

And Skinny put his head down and charged forward and basically forced the cop back out. The cop grabbed a handle going down as his other hand scuffled under his armpit for the cops' usual helpmate as he disappeared. Skinny engaged a latch on the doors and banged *hard* on the wall – Christ! that went right through me – screaming to his driver, "Move! That's a direct order. This guy's pressure is dropping bad!"

Chunky made the siren scream, wheeled into a U-turn and full-tilt-boogied the wrong way up Seventh Avenue two long blocks to 34th Street judging from the hard right turn he wrestled us through. The guts of my brain wobbled horribly as we beat our way to Bellevue, still the best gunshot ER in the City.

The way everything felt loose and goosey upstairs and with all the dots flashing up and winking out, maybe that slinky girl who'd rescued me from Frankie wasn't such a great diagnostician after all.

PART THREE

Chapter Fourteen

The Crimson Colleen

After all the whiz-bang getting there, I fell off the ER's radar once Skinny and Chunky got me up on a Bellevue bed and left to go gab at someone in the middle of the room. With Skinny's help, I shuffled from my chair, each foot a slab of brittle concrete to be arduously lifted, swung slowly through a brief arc and then placed gently down lest it shatter. My ears remained full of gunfire seasoned with siren, two aural assaults I'd never encountered at such close range before, such had been my innocent shamble through life.

It felt like I'd just run a long way, and turning my head too quickly meant the contents took a moment to catch up to their container. I eventually managed to slow my shallow, quick breathing and fight off a patch of nausea, only to have a sandbag of exhaustion fall from on high. The ER a swirl of controlled chaos, the nurses' station in the middle featured a gathering of nations in a rainbow of scrubs writing, or peering at computers or murmuring urgently. The people crisscrossing before me moved with the sort of weary haste immune to a simple day off.

My bed near a corner, I noticed a great bustle of activity catty-corner across from me. The curtains closed, that stall's occupant was confirmed when a peppery little South Asian doc with dried blood flecked on his green pants came rushing up asking, "Is this the Penn Station shooting victim? Good – all right, her pressure's stabilized? Good. Let's get her upstairs, stat." They wheeled the Blonde out and away, amidst a swarm of people and two tall poles. I said my first real prayer in a long time for her, something beyond the incantation following an illegal U-turn of: Christ, don't let that be a cop.

What was my culpability for walking around with Leslie nestled under my shirt and a backpack full of admonitory books? For the pursuit of principle despite the warning from that prescient Chilean ghoul? For putting one foot in front of another in a corridor in Penn Station armed with a photo ID, nine dollars, a couple of sandwiches, a memorized statement and the sort of literature considered … unhelpful?

Frankie's face kept intruding as I lay back and drifted off, all tragic like he was the one getting shot. Had the bullet that got the Blonde ricocheted off my head, I wondered dimly – touched me last and so, like 'electricity' in a child's game of tag, was my responsibility?

I was immediately jarred awake by the grease-bag in the green suit who'd invaded the ambulance rifling through my jeans, grabbing them off the little metal table by my head. I snarled to leave my wallet alone and was about to muster as much noise as I could when a guy I hadn't noticed wearing a top-cop's white shirt told me from the foot of the bed to shut up, that they were MTA police. He was Captain Mumble and that was Detective Mangle.

"I don't care if he's Winnie the Pooh. Tell him to get his hands out of my pants and leave my wallet alone. That's your guys' favorite trick, isn't it? Lift someone's wallet, then they have no ID so you can force a match with some Fiend's biometrics and poof! – gone who knows where. Well, you're too late. Bellevue's already got my info."

He threw my pants on the floor and wrestled the metal table's one drawer open, as the white shirt clucked at me from the foot of the bed about proper police procedure accompanying a weapons discharge.

"Then go back to Penn Station where the shooter is. That's where your investigation is. You got nothing on me, cop. What – for walking through Penn Station with a backpack, some maniac shoots me? Get the hell out of here before I start making some real noise, Goddamnit! This is still a hospital, despite everything. Hey! Yo. Help!"

"Shut up, schmuck," said the detective. "Here's your wallet. It's so heavy, I can hardly lift it. You think with the nine bucks you got in it you're getting as good a lawyer as we're getting for my cop?"

He flung the wallet at my chest, then turned to the captain and said, "Let's go, it's not here. Leave this wannabe to this nurse I know. I'll tell her on the way out about the air bubble in his IV."

The captain said, "You sure it's not there? The one thing both of 'em said, the only thing they agreed on, was that it was silver. Frost said it was a radio, that he had some kinda pinko news on. And you know who, who never should've gotten his damn gun back, said – "

"Joe, how many times I got to tell you to zip it! Just cause this joker got shot doesn't mean his ears don't work. Let's get out of here before some jerk shows up with a press pass makes him think he shits lilacs."

They left before I thought to check my wallet for the license that was still there. A more thorough rousting would've found the radio wedged painfully between the hard plastic mattress and my lower back. I consoled myself musing about the supporters soon to mass behind my gurney rolling down Madison at the head of the Demo, strong lads competing to push it, everyone waving little transistors over their heads instead of the wallets used in protests long past. Maybe I'd milk my righteous celebrity in an ad – tastefully done of course and broadcast only in Japan: *Can't lose touch with the world? Paint it orange for your protection, but make it Whoever!*

A doctor came in as I was drifting off again, shined a light in my eyes and did some weird little hand-dance darting his fingers past my face. I half-yelped the first time he did it, but he told me to relax, that I was in a hospital, so everything was OK. They eventually moved me upstairs to meet my roommate, Luis, an older Puerto Rican gentleman who lay on top of his blanket in slacks and shoes along with his hospital gown.

Then a nurse dropped by, tossed me my own backless gown that turned you into a three-year-old, did temp and blood pressure and departed without a word. Some Asian kid who looked about nineteen but introduced himself with an embarrassed smile as Dr. Hwang, came in, unrolled the gauze from my head and spent a long time snipping the giant band-aid off in pieces to minimize the pain. Cutting off more hair than seemed necessary, he then scrubbed what he called a scalp abrasion none too gently, making things all wobbly again, and slapped on a truly giant band-aid. Again the little hand-dance and shining a light in my eyes which allowed him to conclude I'd had a concussion. He couldn't say how severe with these crude tests. But from talking to me, he thought it mild, and I'd probably be better in a couple of days.

Days? That ushered a whole new worry screaming on to my radar: who the hell was paying for this little sojourn? The MTA, right, which had landed me in Bellevue. And try telling that to the guy calling me down the road about some overdue thirteen grand.

A headache was inevitable, but I was to call a nurse quick if I got any sharp pains or numbness in my hands or feet, or if my vision deteriorated, Dr. Hwang told me. And, such are the joys of post-Plunge municipal medicine, he burrowed in his lab coat pocket for a couple of white pills complete with pocket-fuzz that I should take when the headache kicked in. Then he wished me luck, telling me I was going to need it, "politics-wise." Great.

Feeling quite breezy in a gown meant for a much smaller person – humiliation: hospitals' route to compliance – I despaired of hiding the radio in my bed. Scanning the room's few options, I realized that Luis watched me more closely than hospital etiquette normally allows, lying there on top of his ratty blanket. He said he'd gotten to the room with "pains in the stomach" shortly before me. Rather than ask what happened to my head, he rattled off a string of questions about where I'd gone to high school and college, what my father did for a living and did I belong to any political "groupings." I stared and grunted and ducked his questions. He then asked, "What's your favorite Internet pages, besides the porno, of course?"

Having to say something, I said I was mostly interested in baseball and tried to fend him off with sports talk, neither of us much interested in our rote assessments of the local nines. Then I told him, bright-eyed, curious bastard that he was, that I was feeling sleepy and so would pull the curtain closed round my bed. Back in bed, my head swimming from that tiny effort, I clutched the radio in my hand under the covers, determined to stay awake until I could hide it who knew where when my entirely too nosey roomie went to the john we shared by the door.

But it became apparent I was soon to drop off again despite digging my nails hard into my thigh. I tried to steer my dreams to some Nickilicious episode, or hell, maybe a cluster of them coiled hissing round my bed. Normally such achy nostalgia about the Wife was to be resisted, but I deserved some slack having just been shot. Besides, she'd said out loud, right in an e-mail, that she missed me.

I jerked awake knowing I sure didn't like the guy talking low in a Spanish accent out in the hall and tottered out of bed to explore the valance attaching the curtains to the wall. A lousy hiding place, but better than the rolling nightstand or wedged in any of the boxy, metal equipment all around my bed that I thankfully didn't seem to need. Any port in a storm, I stashed my exculpation up on the valance, up at least out of anyone's line of sight. Luis raising his voice in farewell, I slipped hustling back to bed, unleashing the sharpest pain yet right under my bandage. The rest of my head felt full of the stuffing you see leaking from the sodden stomach of a teddy bear washed up by a trash-strewn creek.

Damn, with the Entertainment System now officially hidden, I couldn't get any news. And the little plaque screwed onto the TV high up on the wall indicated the twelve-buck daily rental fee had to be paid by 11:00 a.m. Forget Bellevue's likely inflexibility regarding deadlines, as Detective Would-Be-Thief was happy to point out down in the ER, that was more cash than I carried.

I had to get ahold of someone, find out what the cops were saying about the shooting – saying about me – and whether reporters were buying it. And I had to get someone there to spirit the radio away. The Blonde checked out, God forbid, I hated to think how important it might become. So that meant my erstwhile in all but name wife. The two of us having endured a number of encounters with them over the years, Nicki plain did not like cops. Plus, our morning e-mail exchange meant this wouldn't come as a total shock. Probably, maybe, I still had a small pile of chips to cash in with her.

There was always Ralph, though we hadn't talked in weeks, not since that scrappy night he dropped by the Hovel. My only visitor so far, and boy was he impressed. Through thick and thin way back to college, Ralph had proved himself jake (enough) provided not much was required. Some fancy-pants twit got uppity at a party and needed a little verbal flaying, Ralph'd be right there to double-team his ass. But with something huge like this shooting, if some cop or reporter somehow found his way to leaning on Ralph, that might spark his tendency to drop the ball late in big games. Our king-of-the-hill routine meant he took nothing I did seriously:

Hey, Ralph, guess what. I discovered a cure for cancer this morning. Found it festering on a plate of pork chops I got bored with late one night about a month ago and shoved under my bed so I wouldn't step on it getting up in the night to empty out some beer.

Cancer? Cool. No, seriously man, that's good. So – what are we getting, pizza or Chinese?

Call the parents? Nah. Dad was getting frayed around the edges, and Mom had never been cut out for this kind of stuff. Best not to drag them into this disaster until I got a better handle on it. I had no siblings that Pop had ever owned up to, thank God, either here in New York or from one of his presumed, far-flung flings.

There were Rob and Owen, boulevardiers and friends, but steadfast circumspection didn't exactly spring to mind with that flighty pair. What about Millie, the local librarian Nick and I had hung with some – could I hope she might overlook working for the City in such a Minder-sensitive job?

Pretty slim pickings. Face it, with Nicki's far greater flair for friendship than sourpuss me could ever hope for, I'd been a tail to her kite for years. Better make it the Wife. I'd get to see her for the first time since getting booted, see how the big town was treating her – hopefully like heck. Maybe she'd put on weight, missing me so, though that'd be a first.

Then I remembered, with the possibility of spending hours in a station house lockup had I actually gotten to refuse a search, I'd left my micro-zap home for safekeeping. I sure wasn't asking

Curious Lou in the next bed for anything beyond a quick peek at his badge. There was always the nurse's station, assuming I could sweet-talk them in to letting me use their phone. Or maybe grab someone walking by in the hall, offer them a dollar. Reach Nick at work, tell her fate decreed a second lunch-hour that Thursday, and please hustle on over to Bellevue cause I needed her to hold on to something real important real tight.

****

Done with brooding, I sat up too quickly, and the room started to twirl, so I fell back. Damn, a slow-mo version of the spins (which I hadn't had since college) and not a drop to drink. As I tensed for another attempt, a celestial vision in a bright red V-neck sweater with a crucifix dangling just so loomed over me, a raven-tressed Grace Kelly the audience's first glimpse of her in *Rear Window* bending deliciously to a laid-up Jimmy Stewart.

"So you're the mad bomber all of Bellevue has been warned against? You look like more of a milk-lapper to me." Her smile coated the goofy insult with sugar, and her accent confirmed her a black Irish beauty, my nurse for the next however many radiant hours, fittingly enough named Maureen. "Walking with a backpack full of books were you? Well, that'll teach you. Now hold still while I make sure your heart is still pumping after the morning's glorious engagement."

The first nurse had naturally put the blood pressure cuff on my right arm on the easy-access, window side of the bed from which she, Dr. Hwang and Maureen had all approached. But this sweet physic saw fit for whatever obscure reasons of her own to bend close over me to attach the cuff on my far arm, the left. Surely that was inadvertent, the way she copped a not coy feel of my right arm with her perfect, red-clad martini-glassful. (There'd been inflation in aesthetics along with everything else since the French issued their famous dictate about the proper filling of a champagne glass.) Inadvertent, maybe, but pressed against me she deliciously remained.

Was it some sort of medical necessity, taking my pressure on the side closest to my now wildly beating heart? Or was I possibly encountering my first sympathizer, a gorgeous one not shy about manifesting support? Worrying about the cops and the jackals of the press, I hadn't stopped to think how the public at large – a phrase that did Maureen no justice – might react to the shootings.

"Milk-lapper? Like a kitten, huh?"

She smiled, but said nothing, leaning languorously and manipulating the old-fashioned cuff's little bulb. If I kept talking, would she have to start from scratch?

"So – 'glorious engagement.' What did they say happened? Did they tell you about Mutt and Jeff of the MTA?"

"There's talk of a few of the titles you were carrying, so I surmised you're a bloody fool. Actually, we don't know what to make of you despite what the cops are saying. Now quiet while I take this. Your pressure is much higher than it was an hour ago, and I'm daft if I can figure why."

This was the closest I'd been to a woman in far too many weeks, closer by far than dancing with Coney Island Emily who, despite her evident charm, was no dark-haired Grace Kelly. And that was bopping around vertically in a crowd, not lying nearly naked in a bed cordoned off from the world. Who could figure why the pressure in my arm should be so high with several liters of blood racing south. Well, she started it, so I decided not to fight it despite the thin hospital blanket.

It was all I could do to keep still as she leaned over and fiddled. Was that a wink as she finally stood up and said, "I'm afraid I'll have to try your other arm later."

And she popped an ancient thermometer in my mouth so quick I was saved from any dumb reply. She actually met my adoring gaze until I looked away, fighting the impulse to pull the covers up over my head like a three-year-old. Nurses – Irish nurses. Holy mackerel!

She took the thermometer out and went to the foot of the bed to write in my chart. Then she smiled again and said she'd be back soon for another try at my blood pressure. "Or, should I send Miss Tubbins in to do it properly? She's rather up in years, I'm afraid."

"You do it again, and I'm headed straight for the ICU. But,

Maureen, wait. I need a phone – no one knows I'm here."

"Just you wait, sonny boy. They will. One reporter has already snuck in up here, along with the couple who've made it upstairs to hound Ms. Fiore and the score and more downstairs."

"Ms. Fiore – is that the girl from Penn Station? How is she?"

"I was wondering if you'd be thinking to ask of her. You don't know her, a man like you? She's still in surgery, but there's a rumor it's going well. It's still true: if you have to get shot, even in the stomach – especially in the stomach – then make it near Bellevue. My girlfriend downstairs says the way the railroad cops are sweating and pacing, you must be innocent."

"I had books, and I was walking forward – that's it. Oh, and a ...." I almost mentioned my radio.

A pause, then, "And a what?"

"Nothing. Just books. Just putting one foot in front of the other in Penn Station."

"OK, books it was then. Let's leave it at that." And she jerked her head, her glorious hair jouncing to catch up, at Louie on the other side of the curtain. She looked at me hard, as I whispered, "I still need a phone. There's something...."

"Tell me you don't have a micro-zap, bright boy."

"I left it home." Then, whispering even more, "Deliberately. So what about sweet-talking my way to my one allotted phone call from the nurse's station?"

"You don't know, do you, boyo? You have no idea about the shite piling up around you, men in boots with calloused hands and stout shovels. And no, I'm not talking about the fool Minders everyone's shaking over, but no one knows why."

I assumed the cops'd play their usual mendacious games, probably unearthing certain past minor indiscretions. Nothing heavy, just the hardscrabble transaction costs of moving about the city of an evening manufacturing a certain hackneyed joie de vivre. Oh, and the standing up for free speech at Lincoln Center that Nicki and I had gotten tossed for. "Sure I know it's gonna hit the fan. That's why – "

"No, you don't have a clue about the shite-storm coming, what with cops roaming the halls."

"What kind of cops? MTA?"

She shushed me. "MTA is downstairs, pretending they're in charge. The main one is some old warhorse NYPD detective they sent cause he's friendly with the Commandant. That's what we call the nursing supervisor for this entire floor. A battle-ax, she's been here forever. She and the detective supposedly had the wee romance donkey years ago, though personally I think she's a virgin. Anyway, he's been up here before when the police blanket someone, this being the high-security ward that keeps the weirdoes and the death-freaks and especially the press out."

"What do you mean high-security? I'm on some kind of locked ward? They got no right – I didn't do anything."

"Calm down or your pressure will spike again, only this time don't blame me. Not locked, the doors open out. But they're locked coming in, and there's usually a Bellevue cop nearby. They have *two* of our cops on the door now, which I can't remember seeing before."

She went and sat on the window sill and stared at her feet. I was happy to watch no matter the storm on tap.

"You're in it deep, friend, though a fair bit depends on Fiore. She's young, thankfully, and some kind of athlete or dancer I hear tell. Supposed to have incredible abdominal muscles."

With cops lurking like she'd said, I had to smuggle that radio to safety. "Maureen, look. I still need to make that one call. It shouldn't be any big deal at the nurse's station for a minute."

"You look. That detective yanked her string, and the Commandant decreed: no phone calls for you. And no visitors – it's medically contraindicated. Which is pure shite. You respond to visitors quite well it seems."

She shot another devastating smile, this man-slayer who looked to be in her early thirties. A smart man knowing his limitations, I'd certainly never chased anyone remotely in her league, even back when I was her age.

"Anyway, gobshite, the bullet bounced, and you had the audacity to live. You're a walking rebuke who just might, you have that cussed air about you, make some noise."

"That's me, except I'm always borrowing someone else's soapbox."

"I'm wondering, carrying those books, might you have been planning on some marbles at their feet? That's rare enough these days, Americans such happy babies. So do you get why I'm soft on you a wee bit? My family back in Belfast, our politics tend towards the *preemptive*. You? You're locked in a box that's only going to shrink. Men close to me have languished in that box with nary a smile, so just think of me as the USO from the other side."

"You're talking about the New Troubles."

"If that's the stupid phrase you want to use. We don't since the high and mighty use it to obscure that sectarian violence returned only when the Celtic Tiger died. It's about jobs, lad. That's what we're killing each other over now, mostly. All the rest is just a gloss of old habits. Given the neighborhood we live, for my Da and my brothers, it's mostly self-defense – except for Donald, our redhead, when he's had a drop."

I decided to leap, no matter how cold the water. "Maureen, when's your next day off?"

"I said a *wee* bit soft, don't be going starkers." Then – and I started after all our whispering – she said, "As far as Bellevue Hospital is concerned, there are public pay phones at the far ends of each corridor. But you'll fall flat on your face you try to make it that distance under your own power. As your nurse, I'll speak to Dr. Hwang about ordering you a wheelchair."

And leaving me jonesing for another of those smiles, she walked out.

Weirder and weirder and still only mid-afternoon. Or so it felt, cause there were no clocks anywhere, I noticed, looking around. Man, even the lower right corner where the time would normally be displayed on the screen of the chest dilapidator was blocked by a dark stain etched into the glass. Nothing for it but wait and see if the doc would authorize a wheelchair, though I didn't see that giggly kid overruling anyone named the Commandant.

I lay back on an express to the land of Nod and thought I was already dreaming, such a bizarre voice accosted me. But it was Luis attempting a brogue. "Don't worry, boyo. I'll speak to Dr. Wang about getting you a wheelchair. I'm sure he'll be accommodating yourself." His bark of laughter sent him into a fit of coughing, a fit that lasted until I heard him strike a match and then smelled his cigarette. Guess Louie did as he pleased on the job.

Chapter Fifteen

Bedlam on First Avenue

I wriggled my way up from a deep dark pool towards the twilight at the room's window. Taking inventory, it felt like the Stuffing had fluffed some to press against my skull, and I wondered what it meant that I wasn't remotely hungry. I saw no wheelchair to go call Nicki, and it sure didn't feel like I was going for any long walks.

Nothing to do but lie back and ponder the cheeky enigma of my nurse. But worry over the Blonde – Ms. Something or Other Fiore – soon elbowed Maureen aside. Normally disdaining such competition, Maureen was thrown off-stride by a rare encounter with someone equally captivating though more of a juke-joint slap-and-tickle than her smoky jazz. Thankfully Ms. TK Fiore was a young … dancer was she? – God, my head – with presumably well-toned powers of recuperation. Imagining what the papers were going to make of such a glamorous, innocent victim, it dawned on me: I was an innocent victim too, Goddamnit.

Why would the MTA send two top guys to try to steal the radio if they didn't think they were to blame? I was peering through the wrong damn end of the telescope. Befogged, damaged to a degree unknown, flat on my back with my butt hanging out, time to stand up on my hind legs and rage to the heavens about some state control-type trying to kill me – and Carole – that was her name.

Or maybe Plan B: the civ-lib freak on a patriotic mission slugging it out with the cops in the ring of public opinion over the next few days – provided I wrangled access to a decent megaphone. Somebody with little to lose drawing a big fat line in the sand and sparking a groundswell of resistance. Wasn't that the point of this whole search-refusnik deal? Right on, right on. Time to call the National Lawyers Guild and the *Northwest*

Queens Disgrace to demand next week's cover to trumpet my intent.

I could already hear it: *What the devil did he mean, setting out to challenge the Protectors?* Far better, maybe, to maintain I was just listening to the Entertainment System and taking some books out to me sainted mum, soon to enrich her old age with a course of study of some of the more trenchant dystopian novels of the past century. What man born of woman could say otherwise?

Nick for one! it hit with a big, bright flash. Cause I'd sure spilled the beans in the morning's e-mail. Alright, time to reach her, both to keep my note under wraps and to come secure the radio.

His cigarette the unassailable proof Luis was a cop, let him jump up and try to stop me. This is America, damnit – hell, New York. Old-man shuffling round my curtain, any bluster would be a pretty thin reed, my head already pulsating like the forest inhaling and exhaling late at night if you lay in your sleeping bag and allowed its ineffable ebb and flow to wash over you. But, his mouth gaping, Luis was hard at it sawing wood.

Out in the hall, up came my man, a porter with a huge, multi-shelved food cart, a tall, skinny older beatnik dude pushing fifty with a gray soul patch, thinning black hair back in a ponytail and no chin whatsoever. And a micro-zap right on his belt.

I edged round his cart the long way so it sheltered me from the nurse's station thirty yards down the hall. "Hey buddy, what's doing? Got that primo food we've all been waiting for?"

"Man, you get two if you want 'em, as much money as the cafeteria's been making with all them reporters and cops downstairs cause of you. You're the dude got shot at Penn Station, right?"

"Yeah, the fuzz went wack on me, man. But thank God they aimed for my head instead of something important. So let me ask you, brother –"

"You can ask, don't mean I'll tell. But first let me ask you: since when we related?"

"Right – sorry. Anyway, I really gotta call my old lady. I'm not even sure she knows I'm here. The phone in my room ain't working, and I'd probably fall down I try to walk to them pay phones at the end of the corridor."

"You are looking a little green around the gills."

"So, whadiya say. Could I borrow your micro-zap a minute?"

"Call your girlfriend in Hong Kong if you want. Like I said, you got butter."

OK. Pushing seven I saw on a clock on the wall, Nicki wouldn't still be at work on a Thursday, not my newly unencumbered wife. Getting her voicemail, I asked Zeke if it was cool, and he waved his hand and bent to a lower shelf of his giant cart. I hung up and tried to summon up her new home number I'd been discouraged from using.

Suddenly, Luis called out from behind, "Henderson, you still on the clock? You still work for this department, or have you already quit to spend your life washing out that slut's panties?"

I peered around the cart to see some young Joe Friday with the requisite buzz cut, jug ears and blue, wash-and-wear summer suit standing slack-jawed at the nurse's station, bewitched by Maureen. Hands on her hips and her posture a marvel, she was smiling one of her smiles, tommyrot spilling from cherry lips, Henderson floating out by Jupiter's ninth moon. Having orbited there myself, I laughed for real for the first time since getting shot and said, "What's the matter, Louie? Your tummy hurts so bad you can't do anything but snoop and wear a smock?"

He swore as Zeke stood up holding a tray and yelled, "Henderson, you got five seconds to keep your fucking job!"

A startled Henderson looked up and started loping towards us. Trying to get a better grip on the infernally small thing (where's the status in being useless if your fingers are bigger than an eleven-year-old's?) I got Nicl's voicemail at work, which did me no good that evening.

Henderson arrived blowing smoke out his ears and startling Luis with his salute. An unruffled Maureen sauntered up behind; designed for it so well, maybe she just liked torturing men. Henderson said, "Sir, I need you to give me that micro-zap and return to your bed. You're a sick man."

"Why? I gotta do what you say cause you're wearing a suit from Woolworth's?" I would've felt better saying this if I wasn't barefoot with my drawers hanging out the back of my smock.

"Sir, I'm not going to tell you again. I need that device now. You're in enough trouble as it is. I mean – you're injured. For your own security, you need to remain in bed."

"I'm not *injured.*" Echoing something I'd heard some weeks back, "An injury's something you get playing basketball. I'm *wounded.* You got some kind of ID on you, Officer Henderson? Some indication of your command for when I sue your ass if you touch me? Some kind of, I don't know – writ preventing me making a phone call? You clowns shoot me, and *I'm* the one in trouble?"

And Zeke, who'd already neatly taken me down several pegs, came to stand by my side. "You're making mighty free with my phone. You on staff here, or can I just ignore you too? Cause I've been handing out slops and picking up the leavings here for seventeen years, and I've never seen you before."

Henderson turned plaintively to Luis. "Sir?"

An ally, no a Gibraltar, like Zeke at my side, I grinned over at Maureen, who just imperceptibly shook her head at me. I retreated a few steps. Luis yelled "Henderson!" as I dialed Nicki's micro-zap again. And Zeke – heck, what was his real name, my hero? – swung the enormous food cart at a perfect angle to block Henderson and throw Luis hard up against the wall. Henderson started to come around the other side, so Zeke swung his cart again, this time with a great clatter of trays and plates onto the floor, its long side pretty much sealing off the hall. Luis slumped against the wall, looking vacant and holding his left side with both hands. "I can hold 'em for about fifteen seconds!" Zeke yelled.

Voice-mail again. "Nicki, I'm stuck in – "

And a clever hand darted over my shoulder and snatched the micro-zap from behind.

"Hey – what the hell!" I yelled, forgetting my head and turning quick. The Stuffing doing leaps and bounds, I staggered and reached out blindly and pulled another tray onto the floor for luck.

When things stopped spinning, I saw a tall, busty broad in her sixties in a traditional nurse's uniform of starched white skirt and blouse and white stockings and shoes. Some stray wisps of steel poked out from under a nurse's cap that would have done a WWII home-front movie proud. I'd seen nothing remotely like this getup all day. She handed the phone to Zeke, saying, "Alfred, I believe this is yours. I suggest you store it in your locker while on duty as regulations require. Now please attend to this mess you've made while I inform dietary that we will need – I count eight trays on the floor – eight additional meals. At this time of night we will have to take what they can give us. So much for our patients' individual needs. I just hope, Alfred, that no patient's health is impacted as a result."

Zeke/Alfred had just assaulted two cops with a heavy, hard-edged metal cart. Luis was leaning against the wall holding on to himself, breathing heavily and trying to gauge the damage. Henderson was standing there bedecked with eponymous cling peaches, his gun out – of freaking course. Yet man of action Alfred cringed before this pillar of authority.

Ladling honey, Maureen drew close and said, "Officer Henderson, we don't need that here. Put your gun away, baby."

Two big Bellevue cops came rushing up from the door down the hall, but the boss nurse said, "Gentlemen, thank you for your assistance. But I believe I am going to ask you to wait on the other side of the door. We have matters entirely in hand here. Don't we, people?"

She looked at each of us in turn. I felt so infantilized I was torn between saying yes, ma'am and sticking out my tongue.

Ratcheted down, Alfred spoke barely above a whisper. "Commandant, I can explain. You see this patient here was shot this morning, and I couldn't see why he shouldn't be able to tell his family. I know – *absolutely* know – there's nothing worse than being stuck away inside somewhere, and your people don't know where you are."

"Alfred, seeing the obvious strain you are under, I'll overlook just this once the name you just uttered. Now there are patients to feed."

"Yes, ma'am."

He nodded mournfully and bent to a tray on the floor as I stumbled two steps to the wall, anchored my back to it and slid down, glad of my drawers. I heard the Commandant say, "Well that was not unexpected. Maureen, please get Richard and get this patient back to bed." And she turned to the cop. "Luis, your charade is over, so let me state categorically you know how I feel about guns on my ward. This man Henderson, who I am surprised was considered equal to this assignment, will leave Bellevue immediately, never to return. Is that clear? And I need to speak with you in my office. Little as it pleases me, I'm afraid Dr. Ralston must now be apprised of the course of treatment we have planned for this patient – under Dr. Hwang's signature, obviously. Now, we must – "

And I heard no more.

****

Someone was digging her fingernails hard into my forearm. Really hard. Then a hand went over my mouth, a hand attached to a crimson-clad arm that disappeared down over the edge of the bed. The hand released me, held up a shush! index finger, and I propped myself up to see the lustrous black hair crowning the rest of Maureen. Then she whispered shush! though I'd said nothing.

"Is it near morning? It feels like I've been sleeping forever."

"Not nearly long enough with that head. In fact I hated to wake you cause it's just past nine."

"At night?" Sending the Stuffing spinning, I foolishly jerked my head up to the window to confirm the darkness behind the light thrown by the hospital and the FDR Drive down below.

"Not too many oats in the barn on your best days, I suppose you did have a fifty-fifty chance of being right."

I scanned the patch of wall I could see and, as I stretched to look up past the unused machines to the wall behind me, she lay a hand on my arm. "Don't trouble yourself. No clock, and tomorrow you'll find Bellevue entirely uninterested in your twelve bucks for a television. The faster you're disoriented by a little isolation, the better they like it."

Tired of crouching, she settled cross-legged on the floor. "I must say they've got a heavier thumb on you than any I've seen.

Something involving the MTA brass *personally* somehow" She added that Luis – changed to a jacket and tie – that warhorse NYPD detective who was Luis's boss, the Commandant and her supposed boss, a Dr. Ralston, had all been closeted away arguing in the Commandant's office. Plus Carole was out of surgery and said to be doing well. Then, "I have a phone for you, that's why I woke you up, though it only accepts calls since you haven't officially rented it. Now let me leave before your Da calls. A little scattered, but still forceful, your father – the apple didn't fall far."

"They're starting to really piss me off. What is this with the phone calls? I'm calling Uzbekistan to report on my progress? I just want to let my wife – well, my about-to-be ex-wife – know where I am and that I need her help."

" 'About-to-be ex-wife.' That's nice. You know, I heard you altering your speech, you cute hoor you, talking to Alfred. Though God knows any kind of operational spontaneity is at a premium these days what with people spending half their lives being led by the nose by micro-zaps."

She ran her fingers through her hair – ah, do that again, please, nurse – and grinned up at me. "God knows it's going to get worse after Alfred's antics with his food cart. Word is the cops aren't going to charge him because otherwise it might – *might* – come out they're up here spying on patients. Still, that was a proper assault, cracking one of Luis's ribs. He refused medical attention here, but was wincing like nobody's business. I've never seen Alfred poke his head up out of the gopher hole like that before."

"People of all stripes are getting tired of getting pushed around."

"The bully-boys are mostly worried you're going to call a reporter. With Fiore out of danger, my girlfriend downstairs says the reporters are pacing around with nothing to do but get steamed there's so little on you. People are wondering what it is you were carrying in that big pack of yours. There's all kinds of crazy talk."

"It was books."

"OK. But what kind of books? Dangerous books? *Unhealthy* books? Taking them where and why so many, carrying them around in the heat, a big lug like you not exactly in the first bloom of youth?"

"You say the nicest things, nurse."

She waited for more, then finally, "Christ, I wish I could move back home! Just leave this Godforsaken country and its petty cruelties, every day a new thug with a gun on his hip.... So how is your mushy head? You didn't need that spot of excitement out in the hall."

"It's full of Stuffing."

"I'm not happy with how long it took you to respond to pain. Did you not feel me clawing your arm off?"

"It takes me a long time to wake up, that's all."

"Well, I'll see to it that Dr. Hwang orders you a CT scan first thing in the morning. Now let me go before your Da rings on that phone, and half the bully-boys in Manhattan come running. Tell him not to come in the morning, you'll be upstairs getting scanned."

She stood looking down at me a moment. I asked if she'd be working the next day, and she said she was on-duty until noon and then off for two days.

Then with a lilt that flirted with song, she said, "Don't worry, gobshite, I'll be charting your progress from afar. You're a funny one, and I may hear of you again. But, believe it or not, I do have other patients. So here's your nurse's instructions: talk to you poor Da, eat this marvelous Salisbury Mistake Alfred left you an extra large portion of, go pee – if you can't make it by yourself, call me on that buzzer there – and then to sleep with you. I'll check on you later."

And again she walked out without a look. Maybe having to do it too often, too permanently, she had issues with leave-taking.

****

How many years would have to pile on Maureen before I'd have a ghost of a prayer? A decade, assuming I didn't age a day? The alabaster skin framed by luminous hair, the cherry lips, big coal eyes, cheekbones marvelously mammary – wrap her up with a big red bow.

Saved by the bell. "This is your father," my father said, grave like I hadn't heard in years. "Schulman down the block called and said you were all over the news earlier. There's nothing on cable that makes any sense, and the crappy couple of radio stations aren't much help either. Are you all right?"

"I'm OK, Pop."

"The radio said the girl, the innocent bystander, was out of surgery and expected to make a full recovery. But all they said about you was you'd been shot in the head. And nobody would tell me anything at that stupid city hospital except you couldn't take any calls. They wouldn't even say what ward you were on."

"Yeah, well things are pretty weird here at Bellevue. It's like – "

"It's strange the way the radio made a point of saying there was no information on your condition. Usually they say critical or stable or something. Makes you wonder why they're leaving things so open-ended. Like anything might happen."

"Pop, I said I'm fine. It just grazed me, and I have a minor concussion and I'm kinda foggy, which will hopefully go away in a day or two.

"Nothing like what those poor soldiers get when something explodes near their head, huh?"

"Right. But things are creepy here. They had a cop in a hospital gown in the next bed, but now he's stopped even pretending he's not a cop. And they won't let me make any phone calls. They're actually physically stopping me."

"You need a lawyer, somebody who still practices law like from before. Not like everybody now afraid to defend a cow for kicking over a pail of milk. What about that kid you and Nicki used. He had some guts taking on the cops like that. Does he do defense or just civil?"

"Defense? Defense for what? I didn't do anything. Pop, I'm as much an innocent bystander as that Fiore woman. I was – "

"You don't know a broad like her, do you?"

"What? No. Listen! I was heading through Penn Station when this stupid-ass cop ran into me, I mean right into my chest with his face. I guess the cops are used to everyone getting the hell out of their way."

124

"So why didn't you get out of his way, you big stoop?"

"He came round a blind corner, and we collided. And he got all pissed off cause his nose got bloody, and so he ended up shooting me."

"The radio didn't say anything about any of that. No bloody nose or nothing. It did say the cops said you had some kind of silver device, some little square thing that hasn't been recovered. A micro-zap, or maybe some kind of gun or even a *detonator*. That's the word they used, can you believe it?"

"Pop, it was that little transistor radio of mine. You've seen it a million times."

"They said it got lost in the confusion after the 'weapons discharge' – another of their cute phrases, like the guns shot themselves. Plus you had an unusual number of books' – underground books or something."

"Yeah, books. So what."

"One of your stunts, right, more of this crap you write about for next to nothing? Look, you need a lawyer. I'll make some calls in the morning before your mother and I come in to see you. Parking's gonna cost me a fortune, but screw it."

"Pop, I'm shuffling around like an old man. I – "

"Look, don't say nothing to nobody. No cops, no foxy nurses – they do that with dames, you know – nobody. And don't sign anything."

"Pop, don't come till the afternoon. I'm having a CT scan in the morning – just a precaution."

"The afternoon, great. Just in time to hit rush hour coming home. So that girl who got shot, she's gonna live?"

"That's what I hear, thank God."

"The papers are gonna fall all over themselves over her, plus they're gonna back the cops. Hero this, Protector that bullshit cause they put their pants on without falling down in the morning. So listen to me – don't say nothing to nobody. We'll see you tomorrow afternoon. And, hey, I love you."

"Uh, me too."

Of all the shocks of an astounding day, that grabbed the biggest piece of cake by far. Even contemplating my father getting gushy made my head hurt in all the places it didn't already.

Damn! My mind so blowed, I forgot to tell him to call Nicki about doing nothing with that stupid e-mail until she heard from me. The Stuffing was messing me up cause, if that got out, I'm down twenty points starting the fourth quarter. Get her to bury the e-mail, then cling – in a 'shite-storm' – to the story that my new 'apartment' was so small, I was taking some books out to my folks' basement in Mineola. Yeah, the sort of books such a happy, commodious fellow certainly had no need of during the Current P. Crisis.

As Maureen promised, the phone wouldn't call out. So, time to march out there quarters in hand and *persevere*, damnit, until I found myself in front of a pay phone. I wasn't under arrest until somebody said so. Standing up, the walls still met at right angles. I yanked the cord out and put the phone on the night table by Luis's empty bed and shuffled out of my room to find they had indeed taken the gloves off.

An MTA cop in uniform ran up and basically got in front of me as I turned towards the doors at the end of the hall away from the nurses' station. The Commandant appeared and told him "to keep that patient in place, he's unwell." It wasn't hard, groggy me, barefoot and nearly naked against this buff, motivated kid. Then Luis showed, and the kid spread his arms wide. Though I didn't like turning my naked back to him, I tried a laughably slow spin move that sent the Stuffing whirling.

The Commandant came back, not that I'd seen her leave, dragging Dr. Hwang by the ear and saying that obviously I was experiencing post-traumatic delusions. Since they couldn't restrain me – I might do some real damage straining against the straps, or so she said – he needed to sedate me ASAP. He balked about sedating a concussed patient and then asked for Dr. Ralston's OK. But Ralston was off the ward, and there was no time to wait. I was in real danger as anyone could see.

I pushed against the kid, cursing and clutching my quarters tight in my little fist, all but expecting my mom to come and spit on a tissue to scour my five-year-old face clean as we headed up the walk to visit some smelly dowager aunts, having to sit still for way too long till they brought out the cake."I have a right to make a phone call – this is still America, no matter what you

MoFos say. I'm getting all your names and suing the piss out of all of you, personally and institutionally. And what the hell's your real name, anyway, Commandant?"

Though he hobbled himself with one hand on his gun, I kept pushing against the cop to no effect until two burly men in scrubs came up and held me against the wall and pinned my arms so Hwang could find a vein. I squirmed and twisted until the Commandant yelled at her gorillas to keep me still so the needle wouldn't break off in my arm, and the one's grip turned from a vise of iron to the jaws of death. Hwang hit it home, and I turned to rubber before the needle was out. As they none too gently marched me the few steps back to my room, I saw a blurry, crimson figure with her hand to her mouth shaking her head slowly back and forth, back and forth.

Chapter Sixteen

Lurch

Like surfacing that morning in my folks' garage – ah, the carefree days of Statie's assault and the riot on the train – I came to with little notion as to where or why. Again, it didn't feel like I'd been drinking, but I'd sure been doing something. Or, piecing it together, had something *done* to me, a doctor pouring sludge from a needle. Gingerly rising and turning, I saw that the curtain, his bed and Luis himself were all gone.

He'd been replaced by yet another large cop in uniform, this one sitting in a metal folding chair. He was an intense, misbegotten enormity, from his hooded brow, awkward nose and horse-teeth, to his cantaloupe shoulders and huge mitts, on down to the tug boats berthed in shoes way too fancy for his ill-fitting uniform. He called someone to report that I was awake.

Still needing to pee, I continued towards the john. He got up to block the open door to the hall. "No phones for you," he said. "They still have lots of needles right outside."

So I was indeed a prisoner, held incommunicado and without charge. All those ominous chickens had finally come home to roost. They'd been pecking and scratching ever closer since long before HeadMan, his status-quo predecessor most distressing of all.

"This is for your security," he continued. "It ever occur to you that a certain blonde's family, a bunch of them right downstairs, is looking to put some serious hurt on you."

"My protection – that's why you're gonna dope me again, I try to use the phone. Well screw you with an eggbeater." Hopefully Nicki had been out all night working a truck stop, with no time to forward the incriminating e-mail I sent her. Soon enough, the cop banged on the door to the john and yelled it was time I was done.

A Brave Sour World indeed. I took my time and flushed twice

to throw pursuers off my DNA since I couldn't recall them taking any blood yet. Though who knew what they'd done while I was knocked out; should probably check I still had both my kidneys. Him blocking the door like it was the portal to another dimension, I pretended to study the view out the window and caught sight of my little radio sticking out just a bit over the edge of the valance bracket.

"All right. Enough of that – get back in bed."

"Do I move my left foot first or my right foot?"

"What? No. Just get in bed. You'll be getting breakfast in a moment."

"All the narcotics I can stand, huh?"

"This is a city hospital. The city has agreed to work with us – with my employer – as to your level of care. Shut up and get in bed."

I lay down. His *employer*? They'd call it the department, sure, but no real cop would say that. I filed that away and tried to keep the conversation going. "Level of care, my ass, cause I haven't gotten any damn care at all. In fact, I'm leaving."

"You're not going anywhere until you're medically released."

"So now I'm supposed to believe you got two doctors to sign the papers overnight that I'm a danger to myself or others?"

Were they ever going to formally arrest me or, Lurch here barring the door, was all that moot? Did they even bother to arrest folks anymore, or just lay hands on you where and when they wanted? "I asked you a question, cop. On what basis are you keeping me here?"

I was just about screaming, my head paying the price, but maybe Maureen would hear me if she wasn't already tied up somewhere. Or was she one of them too, the strawberries and cream version of this guy?

A plump, black orderly bustled in with a tray for me and a glare for the cop. "Miss, can I ask you what time it is, please?"

"Why sure, Sugar. It's – "

"No talking to the Suspect!"

"Like I was saying, it's just after nine o'clock in the morning."

"Friday morning?"

"That's right. Now, I'm afraid this oatmeal has gotten cold

and lumpy, but the head nurse herself wouldn't let me bring it earlier. But there's juice and I got fresh coffee. Oh, and an apple I wouldn't feed my dog. For some reason the Commandant – you've had the pleasure? – wouldn't let me give you the pineapple that everybody likes."

"Miss – shut it!"

"But I'll make sure you get your lunch early. Your stomach's probably a little iffy right now anyway from that medicine they gave you for your seizure last night."

"Miss, that's enough! Or do I need to take your name?"

"My name's Aretha Franklin. What's yours, Bull Connor?" Turning back to me, she said, "Now, you need anything, you call me."

"Miss, wait! What seizure?"

"Your chart says you had a seizure, so they had to inject you with diazepam. And if you've had one seizure, that means you might suffer another and need another shot – you hear what I'm saying?"

The cop moved on her and barked, "Miss – out – now!"

She took her sweet time sashaying out, staring at a spot on the wall over his head – yeah, a clean, round spot where a clock once was. Gulping the coffee, I decided the Stuffing was a little more cohesive this morning. The truly ugly cop sat down, then stood right back up and made a big show of pulling a copy of the *New York Toast* out of his back pocket. He held it high to peruse its innards like a kid hiding behind a book to eat candy in study hall. As intended, I scanned its front and back pages.

The back-page, second-day story on the Yankees' marital dustup almost certainly would have been the front page except for the classic, Weegee-esque photo they'd found for page one. Since, aside from Carole at the beach in a yellow polka dot bikini stretching high to catch a frisbee, it would be hard to imagine a saucier photo.

Under the banner headline: *"Backpack Bungler, Beauty Shot; Startled Cops Forced to Fire"* vast real estate was devoted to an apparently candid shot of a very healthy Ms. Fiore in a low-cut, shimmery, midnight-blue spaghetti-strap number, leaning forward at a party or something and laughing fetchingly, all them pearly whites exposed, charm spilling all over the page. Below the photo it got worse the only way it could: "*Fireman's Fiancée Fighting for Life*". How long before phalanxes of uniformed smoke eaters lined First Avenue to waft their loud encouragement to Carole somewhere up above?

There it was, the whole story, no need to turn the page. The sex kitten (cat in her case), a wounded innocent hanging by a thread; the poor, frazzled cops, no doubt the victims of a sneak attack, who were passive-voice *forced* to unload; and the "Bungler" who laid them all low, no mention of his medical status. Man, I had to escape Bellevue and get my story out under my own damn byline, no matter how much any eventual lawyer shepherding my suit might squawk. This shit had to be answered and quick, cause once the Swift-Boat sailed, you had about a day-and-a-half till you sank.

"I gotta hand it to you, dickhead," Lurch said, "you raised the T Index to 94. That's the highest it's been since the Danube Six and that fire-hose fungus of theirs."

"You sure you're holding that high enough? I don't know if they can read it out the window over in Queens."

"Queens is that way, huh? Anyway, they got a little side article here quoting some big-shot prosecutors as to the right charges to ice you down good and long." He lowered the paper to – apparently – grin at me. "Let's see, the possibilities are: 'resisting proper authority,' and 'refusing a lawful order.' They'd work, but they don't give much time. There's always 'interfering with government administration,' but that's too weak for a double shooting. So is 'attempted disorderly conduct.' 'Resisting arrest' is out f or once, but 'attempted planting of a false bomb' ain't bad. That's actually, in some cases, more time than a real bomb. And here's one with some weight that sounds like I should have heard of it before – that you 'manifested a clear and present danger.'"

A clear and present danger – if that don't beat all.

Waiting me out, he finally said, "Actually most of them have decent time once they T-enhance them. It's getting tough to remember all the different kind of Fiends, but … an Anarchist, maybe? Or a Black Separatist – you wish. Homegrown Islamo?

Possible. Ah, the Lone Wolf – a sicko like you, my money's on that. Militia? I doubt you got the balls. Special Interest? I always forget – what is that, for fags? – so maybe. Or White Nationalist? Again, a balls issue."

"I guess alphabetically is easiest to remember."

"Right. Of course there's the whole other category of charges involved in your assault on Protector Reisner. First they have to enhance the Penn Station whole-vid, see what a skilled operator can cough up. Maybe we can loan them one of ours. Then, I *guess* they have to talk to that weasel, Reisner, before deciding on all the charges."

I liked this saying nothing, him spilling, cause what's *his* outfit if it's loaning the MTA a skilled fabricator? He shook the paper at me and said, "Cute chick, huh."

"Puppies are cute. I don't think cute is the first word that comes to mind with Ms. Fiore." Man, here I was male-bonding ogling my fellow vic with my jailer. "You know, her being a stone-fox doesn't do either one of us any good."

"Maybe … but how?" Way too slow, a poker face way beyond him.

"Oh, you know," I said, trailing off. Man, the pores on his face were enormous.

He eventually returned to his paper, this time holding it normally. "So what's the deal – you were carrying what the paper says were peanut butter and jelly sandwiches made with three slices of bread. It says, 'The purpose of this extensive supply of food remains unknown. It is unclear whether he expected some sort of siege.' "

Them clutching this straw, I laughed out loud. "Dude, look at the heft over here on this bed. I had errands to run. You have any idea how much it costs someone like me eating out running around Manhattan all day?"

Shit. Bad mistake: I wasn't running around the City. As I'd more or less decided, I was taking those books out to Long Island. But man, that's why they get you talking – just like on the idiot cop TV shows – get you trying to prove how clever you are.

On cue, he said, "And what about all those books? They don't list any titles in the paper so as not to give people ideas. But an

MTA buddy of mine says you had Hitler's book and also *1984*, which everyone knows is Red. And a book by a guy named Roth that's got a swastika on the cover. A Jew book – Roth, right? – with a Swastika? And something by some Russian guy, obviously another Red. You were humping a lot of weird, thick books around, the mercury up in the high nineties. So you into all that Nazi and Commie shit? That's what this is all about?"

Again I had to laugh at his disingenuous throwing bread on my pond to see what rose to the surface. "Man, if you're equating *Mein Kampf* and *1984*, then I don't know if I can properly discuss literature with you. Not to mention Solzhenitsyn's slice and dice on the USSR and Roth's anti-Nazi novel. American Nazis – you'd like 'em."

"You know, I've been looking to meet some American Nazis – off duty of course." Then, casual as popping the evening's eighth beer, "You know any?"

I smirked rather than strike at such a soggy morsel.

"You were also carrying *Catch-22*. That's against the Army, isn't it."

"Well, a satire."

"And what's this, porn? *The Handmaid's Tale*?"

"She's French, obviously."

"*A Wrinkle in Time* – that sounds suspicious right off."

"Way too many dimensions, dude. Plus, it's aimed at kids."

He stared right through me. "Targeting innocents. That's gotta add some major time. So what about this *Darkness at Noon* my guy said you had. What is that, Goth?"

"It's mostly updated vampire stuff. There's an eclipse, but it gets stuck, so the vampires can operate in the middle of the day. It's a whole new take on vampires you gotta check out."

"Maybe I will." Again the pause and, "So you know any – vampires, I mean?" And he started snorting through his honker, apparently how he laughed.

"Tell me, Lurch, someone have to teach you this nifty, hey-we-can-talk-here style of interrogation, all demotic and shit? 'A guy named Roth' – oh what a sly spider to the fly art thou."

"You lost me there, Einstein. But let me ask you this: it says here – "

"Tell you what. How 'bout I buy my own damn newspapers when I leave here in an hour or two and read them for myself."

"How about you just tell us what you were up to, Suspect, and I'll let you know when you can start thinking about leaving!"

"Screw you! And what's your name and your Goddamn command? Now that I look, you don't really have any signifiers on that uniform you're trying to fit into, do you?"

He had a big Glock or some such on his hip along with some cuffs and his micro-zap, but no name tag or bars on his collar indicating his outfit. His badge was kind of a blur, like the Oscar statuette's crotch. He and Statie, badgeless birds of a feather, unfettered, amok.

"Officer Krupke, Police Department, New York City."

"Fuck you, flatfoot. Or should I just call you spook?"

Some discombobulationist up from Fort Meade? Cause he was so proud of his *West Side Story* taunt, he flubbed the line. The formulation is, 'NYPD' or if you want to get fancy, 'Police Department, City of New York.' No one who's spent time within a hundred miles of the place would say what he'd said.

Where the heck was Maureen? Unless the Commandant had her transferred to the TB ward, the longer my sainted Mata Nightingale stayed away, the more she seemed the catch-more-flies-with-honey version of this brute. How come no one came to even take my temperature? Just sassy Aretha with that demoralizing pothole quick-fix in a bowl. I found the buzzer and pressed and pressed again, no idea if anyone heard, cared or was allowed to respond. Done trying to draw me out via the newspaper, Lurch flipped to the sports pages and settled more comfortably in his chair.

Came a knock at the door, someone no doubt coming to spray me with eau de wet dog. And Lurch asked *me* who it was. The ghost of William Kunstler, I told him, as he got up and admitted a muscular young guy in scrubs with a shaved head and Japanese(?) letters disappearing around the back of his neck who was pushing a wheelchair. The orderly said it was time for my CT scan, the one Dr. Hwang ordered back before I'd morphed entirely from patient to Suspect.

He studied the paperwork and finally said it was OK as long as he accompanied me upstairs. The orderly said he could fly to the moon for all he cared, his job was to wheel me upstairs. Neither sought any input from the slab of brisket they were fussing over. I consigned the radio to its fate and settled into the chair.

Lurch held us back with one hand as he peered out in the hall to see that no one was lurking, no Ed Murrow or hordes of Fiores with bags of feathers and buckets of tar. As we left, he nodded curtly at an older man in a fancy suit sprawled in a comfy leather desk chair across from my door, a big briefcase at his feet. He scrambled to his feet with a questioning look. Lurch ostensibly just a pot-scrubber in uniform, it was easy to see who was calling the shots the way the suit leaped up and, more tellingly, that Lurch alone approved my leaving to get scanned.

The dash of scarlet hunched over a computer down at the nurses' station was Maureen, who didn't look up. Were her hands tied or had she just cut me loose? Pusher-man scooted down the hall and then abruptly one-eightied so he could bang out the doors with his butt. The Stuffing got shaken *and* stirred, but my plea that he slow down went nowhere. The spook, or haint or general purpose scumbag playing dress-up in his vague uniform strode along unhurriedly in his seven-league loafers and, when it opened, ordered some frightened little Latina in scrubs out of the elevator.

Off the Restricted Ward and out in 'public,' it dawned that I could shout an appeal to anyone I met. How much of a commotion could I make and, more importantly, to whom? I'd need some big-balled doc or administrator to have any prayer at all of Lurch – armed and in uniform – not just blowing them off, my plea falling unheard to the faded linoleum as I was whisked away.

We got off on a lonely hall, and pusher-man barreled up to a door and wheeled around backwards again to bang through, Lurch right behind. But he stopped the spook in his tracks. "No, Man, you can't come in. There's way too many manifest gamma rays loose in this room for anyone to enter without first getting weeks of the antidote. I had to work in the kitchen for a month before they'd let me do the job I was hired for."

"Don't be stupid. I go where the Suspect goes."

"You married? I mean, like, actively? Planning on having any kids?"

Lurch not answering, it's the sort of question that gives anyone pause.

"OK then. I couldn't live with myself if I let you in here. You'd be lucky if the kid looked like a frog or something you could actually recognize rather than just a blob. You wait there in the hall while I take him inside."

What about me I wondered as, Lurch stymied, we banged inside. I planned on getting active again someday – if not exactly reproductively – like next week, damnit, with some ghoulish talent with a taste for cop-shot civ-libbers. The orderly turned me around to face the usual big metal donut with a bed threading the hole, then rushed to the back of the room, pushed through a door and disappeared without a word. An energetic young man.

Chapter Seventeen

Fleeing Lurch and All His Works

I sat for a minute waiting for the scan technician to appear. But where did that door lead, and how far could I get barefoot, in a smock and without a dime? Could I make it downstairs to find a reporter to smuggle me out for an exclusive limited to the tale of ferrying me home? Have her or him let me out three blocks from my door, promising not to follow? Cause what began as the small-beer tale of refusing a search had grown monstrously. Called "The True Tale of the Penn Station Shootings," it just might get my foot in some larger door and yield a couple of months' rent – not much over a grand.

More to the point, did I need Pop to show up to secure *me*, never mind the radio? Lurch had made it clear I was caught in their net, nothing remotely legal about it. So what came next, a ride in a small plane out over the Atlantic? The shootings splashed all over the news, how far could they take this here in the middle of New York? By locking me down, some might say they'd taken it pretty damn far already.

The door in back opened and in strolled Maureen cool as can be. She held a bag, hopefully a PBJ club sandwich, cause I suddenly realized I was famished. "Maureen, where the hell you been, leaving me alone with that brute?"

"Shush, eejit. They let none of us, not even Dr. Ralston – who surprised me, allowing himself to be kept from a patient – in to see you. They've got you locked down like I've never seen. And it was a ton of favors I used to get you up here and to have the CT technician disappear. So that cop, or whatever he is, bought Jimmy's story about how dangerous this room is?"

"Gamma rays. But why are they acting so crazy? They're just delaying my leaving, cause I feel a lot better already."

"A lot of people have made fools of themselves predicting how far they'll go.... Anyway, the papers are trashing you pretty good, with the police directing the coverage. That shite-storm I was telling you about is just beginning."

"I figure it's a fair fight."

"The last thing you need is to be fighting fair. They won't. How's your head, lad? That was a disgrace, a concussion patient getting injected with diazepam last night."

"I feel pretty good today, till Jimmy started playing ping-pong with my head, anyway. That MoFo jailing me in my room read to me from the *Toast*. Any papers any more on my side?"

"The *Toast* was predictable. But the *Daily Chirp* is questioning the shooting, which sounds iffy from the start.

"And the *Slimes*?"

"So it's sitting with our feet up, reading all day, is it? I'll draft a memo once I've read it. But the papers aren't your biggest worry. Some big-shot MTA cop was in the Commandant's office bellowing about your 'treatment.' He kept yelling that she didn't know how much was at stake. And that it should be easy, you already shot in the head.

"What kind of treatment?"

"Not to scare the bejesus out of you, but I moved heaven and earth to get you out of here *now* – not later, not even this afternoon. Cause they've got 'tests' planned for you that make getting shot in the head a walk in the park."

"What Goddamn tests?"

"Head injuries let them pick what they like, but they're all intrusive. And then things slip – instruments. And you're not the same afterwards, like those babies they give those horrible combination vaccines to, five diseases in one needle."

"Jesus, Maureen."

"They've had some bloke hidden away for the last six months up on the ninth floor somewhere, no one knows exactly where. And he didn't even stop one of their bullets or make it into the papers. Just came in from a holding cell spitting up blood and with an attitude like yours only worse – a genuine hard case. He pissed the wrong people off, got the 'tests,' and now he pretty much doesn't remember who he is."

"Who was this guy in the Commandant's office?"

"Some MTA white-shirt. He was yelling about how a lot of

people were hoping that ogre in your room this morning – who the cops all seem a little afraid of – could squeeze you. But tell me, boyo, you beat up an officer of the law?"

"Don't be ridiculous. I slay with words. He ran into me around a blind corner. Bloodied his nose on my chest and started this whole freaking misery. By the way, how's Carole?"

"She's fine, at least for a few years until gravity does a job on her. Just an accident it was then? So I'm risking ... *repercussions* for a civilian? And, no, I'm not talking about the Commandant, feck her very much. You're iffy, lad. Still, the *Toast* says you assaulted a cop. That probably covers things with the lads on my end – technically. Let's go with that. That and I like your guts tangoing with them not once but twice yesterday out in the hall like a drunken bear. So here I am on my white charger."

"That picture of Fiore the *Toast* got. She – "

"*Toast, Chirp* and the *Slimes* – above the fold – all three front pages."

"Jesus, a fireman's fiancée. You sure she's OK?"

"She's already sitting up in a chair."

"If only she'd rounded that corner first, she probably wouldn't have bloodied his nose."

"Smothered him, maybe."

Damn, she was fine, even giving her bitter little laugh. Five-foot-nine she looked, the perfect height, not that I'd ever stood next to her. A smooth throw through the gears from the moment she handed you the keys – and leagues beyond me (an intrepid carrier of books!) in the Troubles she'd seen, the hard-boys she'd known. What tempest had tossed her up at Bellevue, rather than ending up a craps dealer or weather girl or just some Despoiler's trophy vixen? She caught me looking and briefly flashed the sort of smile that'll curl your straight ones and straighten your curlies.

"Well this is a grand reunion, lad, but how about you throw your clothes on and get out of here. I was damn lucky to get them."

"No CT scan then?"

"You're fine. I can tell by the way you're talking. Nothing for it but stay quiet for another day or two. No excitement such as fleeing a hospital."

"I'm sorry, Maureen, but I can't go. There's something in my room I need to establish my innocence. You – "

"Your radio is gone. I was meaning to tell you, but as soon as Jimmy wheeled you out, that old spear-carrier outside your door went in and came out a minute later crowing and holding it in his hand. He ran to the Commandant's office and then came out with a grin that split his face like your ass. That's the only reason I was able to get your clothes. And it won't happen again, so get on with ya."

"I am royally screwed," I said, taking off my gown.

"Before it ends up on the bottom of the East River, that radio'll become a gun or worse – which they're already talking. You did have some pretty explosive books from what I've heard."

"That's right, *books*. Godfreakingdamnit! They shoot you, then they rob you, and then they frame you."

My poor ruined shirt already on, she handed me my jeans. The Stuffing kyboshing me on the second leg, my hand darted out to grab her shoulder. She steadied me, then bent down and – Jesus! – got close to reach around to pull up my pants. She rose and we were more or less dazzlingly eye to eye for the first time. I quit staring at the sun and reached for her again, this time for real. But she stopped me cold. "So what were you about, carrying all those books then?"

"What – oh, nothing. Just taking them out to my mother on Long Island."

And she laughed like maybe she hadn't in a while. "That's good, boyo. Maybe I'm finally teaching you to keep your big trap shut. Now your smelly shoes. Quick!"

She led me out the back door and down a short hallway to a flight of stairs. Walking in the hall was OK, but it got fuzzy negotiating the stairs, my feet too far down. She said she was afraid the six flights down were too much. So we'd go to Plan B.

The fuzzies reminded me. "What the hell is this the breakfast lady said – and put her on the same team as you and Alfred – that my chart indicated I'd had a seizure?"

"You'll probably be schizophrenic as well as epileptic before they're done. Never mind that the fake epilepsy diagnosis itself

– with all these new mental-health Regs forcing meds on you for the safety of the Realm – lets them inject you any time they want. 'Oh, our boy's looking cross-eyed, give him a shot!' That was another thing I was meaning to tell you."

"You were meaning to tell me a bunch of stuff, apparently."

She barred her teeth. "If you think this was fecking easy, arranging your escape from tests you don't recover from, then stealing your clothes, getting my girlfriend in cardiology – who I now owe feck-all, though she'll probably end up sweet on him, the ninny – to occupy the CT tech, then you can bloody well think again."

"Maureen, look – "

"And if it ever came out I lost a job on the Restricted Ward, which wasn't easy for a foreigner to get, for a mere civilian … well, paying my rent is the least of my worries."

"Maureen, I'm sorry. I owe you an awful lot. It's just this is all starting to fall into place way too easy. That bizarre, giant cop – did you see him? – buying Jimmy's gamma-ray nonsense, and you being able to get my clothes *just* as they find the radio."

"Well aren't you a piece of work, actually using your head for something besides catching lead."

"You come right down to it, I'm not doing them any real good hidden away in Bellevue. But if I 'escape,' the MoFos can see where I go and who I contact. See if my flailing about to keep my head above water leads them anywhere." I stopped and stared at the sun again, which smiled right back but said nothing. "You know, Maureen, I gotta thank you properly someday."

"Don't bother. I – "

Her voice suddenly breaking as she stood a step above me, her face went tragic.

"What?"

"I guess it all comes down to what they did to my brother – Michael, not Donald. A heroic man, a rock others once built on, he's not been capable of leaving our parents' house alone going on four years now. And if Donald was hard to control before that…."

"I'm sorry."

"So you'll understand why I don't get too concerned over

141

what fecking Data Tier I may or may not be in. Me and mine have been on the wrong end of too many men – very *tangible* men to worry about any of that."

She slipped her stern mask back on, led me out of the stairwell into a hall and then straight into a staff bathroom she unlocked. I willed the room to steady itself. "Maureen, I've never been held prisoner in a hospital before. So if I said some dumb things…."

"Don't worry, gobshite. It was worth it to see the look on her face when you demanded the Commandant's real name last night."

"So, you meant that about a one-way trip to the rubber room?"

"You end up worse than Michael. I've never seen them jump on anyone like they have you. It's like you challenge them in some fundamental way. Or maybe it's cause of all the front pages with the girl with the garbanzos and a headline about the mystery man with the metal head – who's about to get a whole lot more mysterious by disappearing."

"Damn. Carole couldn't be some big, goobery-ass dude or immigrant or something?"

"Are you sure you want to go home? I have somewhere safe you could hole up till you decide what you're doing. Talk to a lawyer, one of the real ones left who isn't in their pocket yet."

"Your place?" She just laughed. "Look, I did nothing wrong, so I'm going home, marching up my front steps and answering the phone when it rings."

"Maybe so. The old ways, taking to ground, don't work so well anymore, not with all their new tracking gizmos. OK, lad. Roll up your other sleeve to match the one that got cut off. Then turn left out the door here and you'll find an elevator straight down to the middle of the ER. Press G. It's the busiest spot in Bellevue, so hopefully you won't be noticed. Paste a smile on your face, do *not* meet anyone's gaze, and walk straight across to the far side and out that entrance by the ambulances. And then – you have money? – get in a cab and go."

"Maureen, I don't even know your last name."

"You're catching on." With another knee-wobbling smile, she added, "If you get dizzy going home, take this. A pinch of dexedrine – all the interns are on it. But try not to. Either way, sleep as much as you want, not that you'll have much choice.

And by tomorrow you should be better. If not – if your head is squirrelly in any big way come Sunday – go to a private doctor out in Queens, some Jew or Muslim who's open Sundays. But not a hospital, especially not a city – "

I leaned down to her. She kissed me back without hesitation, heaven on earth for days on end until I twisted my neck to get a better angle of attack and she pulled away.

"You have my number in my chart. Call me."

"So you're not such a goofus after all. But no calls. Let's try this: first Tuesday of every month, for a couple of months, anyway, I'll be having a bowl of soup in the coffee shop on the corner of Third and 34th at noon. The soup's good, and that's far enough away from the hospital. You got that, Writer-Man? Oh, did you think I'd not google you? Though I must be starkers to be even thinking of another writer. Now go – now!"

"Do I need to wipe any lipstick off?"

"Why? I don't wear any."

"You're kidding. First Tuesday, Third and 34th, noon."

"You can remove that bandage Monday. Till then, try to stay quiet. And no boozing, you – for a couple of days anyway."

And with that she reached around me. I puckered up for another kiss as she leaned in, opened the door just enough and pushed me out.

I melted into the ER's frantic swirl, a United Nations of scrubs, white coats and patients' families, a worrisome couple of cops sprinkled about. The giant band-aid on my head clamored and throbbed as I pasted on the sales clerk's vapid half-smile, stared off over everyone's head and shuffled forward, my invisibility ring slipped on for the bored hospital cop by the door.

Then I was free, outdoors if not off the Bellevue campus, out in a tangle of ambulances, a couple of EMTs leaning on them smoking, one reading a paper festooned with Carole in all her cheesecake glory. If I ran into my ambulance crew from the day before, Chunky wouldn't care, but would Skinny just assume I'd been discharged?

I strolled out the old, ornate front gate, misjudged the distance to my feet and staggered, the ground rising up at me. Waves pooling gently around my ankles, I waded across First Avenue and raised my arm for the cab I couldn't afford.

PART FOUR

Chapter Eighteen

The Morning After Nick's Big Night

But of course I could, I had nine bucks.

No lipstick! Was I really to believe such a professional man-slayer was set to purring all on her lonesome by the sight of me in a pale blue gown? If not a rock like her brother, might Maureen someday come to think of me as particularly cohesive landfill?

Who was I kidding? Awfully convenient, her being able to grab my clothes like that. And what about all those *pertinent* questions, like about my books and how Frankie had bloodied his nose? Formerly hot grease when they toss in the fries, Lurch had been stymied awfully easily by gamma rays, as Maureen wasted time with tales of ice-pick lobotomies. Holed up in Bellevue I wasn't exactly helping them figure out what I was about, so why not arrange my daring, slow-mo escape – right past the hospital cops in the ER?

Regardless, there was no doubt I'd been held prisoner, denied even a phone call, doped when I'd tried to make one, and warned that more needles plus tests to permanently scramble my eggs were in the offing. All a strong case for leaping in a taxi and gone, my first cab without Nicki in years. But first to make sure the wife sat on my idiot e-mail – Minders Turn Elsewhere! Just pray she hadn't already sent it to some obscure haven of discontent to then blossom far and wide, cause I really needed to think about whether I was disclosing my mission at Penn Station.

I stumbled on the curb and paid the bleary price between the ears. OK, barely out from under Bellevue's roof, so much for holding off on the intern's-little-helper Maureen slipped me. A bitter pill, indeed. At the phone booth that hopefully shielded me from prying eyes in the hospital across the street, the Wife started hyperventilating from hello.

"Nicki, wait, let me ask you. That – "

"I didn't know what to think. I mean, last night I get this message, you sounding all breathless, that you're "stuck" somewhere, and then you never called back. So, I figured, I don't know, you were stuck in heartbreak hotel – some of your usual nonsense."

"Believe me I would've called back if I could. Wait till I tell you. But first – "

"Then this morning I hear you've been shot! So I called Bellevue, and they were a total joke. One guy mumbled in an incomprehensible accent he totally put on cause I heard him ask someone about you, and his English was fine. Somebody else hung up on me, and then this lady said the computer had no patient by your name."

I'd shunned the ballooning implications of no one coming to even take my temperature when I woke up. Were they really thinking of turning all my verbs to the past tense, simple as that? It happened to perceived irritants – writers who knew of the wrong politician's drug history, say. But it was usually in roadside motel bathtubs out in Indiana or somewhere, the lonely truth-seeker just happening to succumb to a final bout of depression despite being right on the verge of a big score. Hell, concussions cause blood clots often enough, and once they start traveling round your body…. I could only hope my wife would fight to keep my perfect body safe from autopsy.

"Nicki! Did you send out that e-mail?"

"Yes, of course. But don't worry, I edited it like you told me to. I took out all that self-serving crap of yours."

So much for any decision on what exactly to say about Penn. "Christ, who'd you send it to?"

"Wait, forget the e-mail. You have to hear what happened to me coming to work. First, how are you? Are you OK?"

"I'm fine. A little woozy. And I literally had to flee Bellevue. So who did you freaking send it to?"

"You know, I told you all your wise-guy snarking around at my advertising parties was going to come back to haunt us, but I thought it'd be me at work. So, Mister Big Stuff in all the papers, do you remember the CheeseSpray party?"

"CheeseSpray – Nicki, what the hell are you talking about? *Who* did you send it to?"

"Well, someone remembered you from the CheeseSpray launch party. Melanie Artenunotte of *The New York Slimes* remembered you waving that tray around. And some *Slimes* police reporter knew our last name from me getting some award – he started out as a clerk on the business desk – and he asked Melanie if I was connected to you. And she told him yeah, that's who you were. It had been bugging her since news of the shooting broke yesterday."

"She told who?"

"This police-beat twerp, Eric Benson. He ambushed me outside my office before eight this morning. I didn't even know what planet I was on at that hour."

"You spoke to him? What the hell did you say?"

"I don't know, not much. I thought he was joking at first about you getting shot, and he thought it was weird I heard it from him. Kept remarking on it like it's some kind of duty to remain glued to the horrible news the world churns out every hour."

"Well, we are theoretically married."

"Yeah, anyway. So I told Benson about your theory that participant/observer journalism is one of the last best avenues open to a freelancer."

"*Nicki*. What else? Wait. First, Goddamnit, who did you send the e-mail to? And why did you send it without checking with me first? How long we been married, you don't know better than that?"

"Screw you! I have your stupid e-mail hidden right here in my drawer, and – wait – here. You ended it with, 'Anything happens, you'll know what to do.' Well, something sure as fuck did happen, so I followed your orders."

"That was in case I got killed, which wasn't going to happen."

"Sounds like to me you came awfully close."

"I hadn't done anything yet. That's important: I was just minding my own business, *walking* through Penn Station. Which is true. But with that e-mail out, now I'll get painted as some kind of freak challenging the fuzz –a T-symp or maybe even a Fiend myself! Plus Carole getting shot is gonna be all my fault too."

"*Carole* – you know a girl like that?"

"I'm supposed to call her Ms. Fiore cause we've never been formally introduced?"

"You better hope you don't get Boosted *two* Tiers for this, not one. Which I do not want to talk about at work. And what's all this about a detonator?"

"See what I'm saying? It was my idiot radio – you know, the Entertainment System – which they stole from my hospital room. I haven't had a chance to tell you they had a Goddamn cop in my room the whole time, first acting like a patient, then one in uniform, if he even was a cop. And when I tried to bull my way out of my room last night to call you, they shot me up with dope and I was out for hours. And now I just – well, I just kinda escaped."

"They made you a prisoner, and then they drugged you?"

"Yup. And they put in my records that I have epilepsy. I'll have horns and a tail next."

"What a minute: you had to *flee* Bellevue? This is New York for Christ's sake, not Washington with that storm-trooper cop they got running things down there."

"Flee, as in down the back stairs and out. So, Nicki, who did you send it to?"

"I couldn't think after that *Slimes* guy got me so twisted. He was practically skipping down the sidewalk he was so thrilled with interviewing – well, your wife, I called myself. He said you were the huge black hole at the center of the story, and he had an exclusive with me."

"Who, Nicki!"

"*Naked Opposition*. You know, you seemed to like them, the couple of articles they published of yours."

"You sent it to Stanley?"

"I didn't know anyone's name. I just sent it to their general mailbox. But you'll be proud of me, I put a really good subject heading on it."

"I'm sure."

" 'Civil Liberties Crusader Sets Out to Take a Stand.' "

"Jesus. Maybe I can sweet-talk him, or threaten him somehow, not to run it. You sent it from work and told him to run it?"

"Not my official work e-mail. People all over the office have already been giving me the hairy eyeball, and God only knows about Charley, who's been closeted away upstairs all morning."

"You sure you sent it to his main mailbox?"

"Their staff page wouldn't load. I think Fornix and Foyst's system blocks *unhelpful* sites. "

"I'll call you later. Don't do anything until you hear from me, OK? But wait, you got 'twisted' with the *Slimes* – what the hell does that mean?"

"Nothing. I mean, he came up and catches me right at our door when I'm just trying to make it to my desk to suck down a Dr. Pepper. He said he'd found pictures of me from awards dinners, probably that horrible, goofy shot of me laughing with my mouth open. And I'd had nothing to eat. All – "

"What do you mean, Dr. Pepper and nothing to eat? You out all night or what?"

" All I knew was that blonde bombshell was on all the front pages cause, for once, everybody on the train had a newspaper – *everyone*, it was amazing. But I was reading my book and figured I'd catch it when I got to work."

"You didn't answer me."

"You want to hear or what. So this puppy in a brown *velvet* jacket – something weird in this heat – jumps me by F&F's door and asks if I know you. And – I don't know, it was something about the ritzy jacket and he was cute and all. So just goofing around, I said, 'Why, does he owe you money?' And he fucking wrote that down, can you believe it. I mean that's a joke, that's a line, everyone knows that. But he kept pushing that there was some money angle, like you set out to get shot so you could sue the City."

"With my metal head."

"So I just blurted out that well, of course there was a money angle. That you're a writer, that's what you do."

"Nicki, for Pete's sake!"

"Listen or I'm hanging up. I mean I didn't even know you'd

been shot. Plus no one knew anything about your condition. Even the *Slimes* had been trying to pry it out of Bellevue all night, he said. So of course I was bothered by that."

"Perturbed, verily."

"But I did *not* say anything about protesting the searches or anything. I figured you'd want to tell the world that in your own words, in that e-mail. So then he went back to the money angle. At that, I just said I was late for work and had to go."

"Money angle. Maybe I should just go find another shaky cop with a gun. This guy was real young?"

"Yeah. Why?"

"He's gonna make it as sensational as possible to make his bones on my ass. What else?"

"I don't know."

"What else did you freaking tell him, Nicki? Come on, I gotta go reach Stanley before it gets ruined even worse."

"I didn't *ruin* anything. I'm not made for all this, some twerp bushwhacking me first thing in the morning about somebody I know getting shot. I'm just an advertising hack, remember?"

"I said before *it* gets ruined – I didn't say *you* ruined it. Now, come on. Stop getting hysterical and tell me what else you told the Goddamn *New York Slimes*."

"I don't know. Just that you were probably looking for another big score like when you caused those hearings and testified before Congress."

"You sure you told him about Congress?"

"Yup. And I said you were kind of a nut – you know, in a good way – about the Constitution, though then I remembered about your e-mail and just left that hanging. That you'd been kind of floundering lately, having trouble getting published, but that now, after getting shot, maybe you had a big story. Something to get you back on your feet."

"You told him that? Do you ever listen to yourself, how that sounds with that Blonde having to get her guts stitched up?" The Wife – at her absolute best in an early-morning twerp crisis.

"Look, no one told me to get up early and have a big breakfast cause some reporter was gonna leap out of the bushes at me cause my chump-change husband is in all the papers for all the wrong reasons. I mean, it was kind of a big night last night if you really must know, and I might even have still been a little drunk to tell you the truth, nothing in my stomach to soak up the alcohol."

"Spare me the freaking details. So: 'somebody you know,' huh?"

"What?"

"That's how you referred to me before. Pretty much says it all, doesn't it?"

"Go reach Stanley. Tell him I made a mistake, and he'll just have to understand, that's all."

"Sure. He'll be delighted to punt the biggest story he's ever gonna see – dropped out of the clouds into his lap."

"Appeal to his better nature. You're sure your head's OK?"

"Yeah, I think so. See you later, alright?"

"I guess."

The silence dragging, hard to say who hung up first.

****

Time to appeal to some scrambling web-dude's better nature and tell him to forego a sketchy and premature disclosure regarding that little Penn Station imbroglio. The Stuffing fluttering, I stood in the street waving for a cab, nothing but trouble beckoning back, the sun emanating from wherever it had gone. Bleating horns the only sign of life from the stalled traffic three long blocks from the copy/net shop, I got out to beat the meter turning over again. My feet in better focus thanks to Maureen's pill, I motivated a block, feebly swinging my arms to grab some momentum, then stopped to call Pop. Amidst his concern over more Bellevue weirdness when he called, Pop was glad I'd felt well enough to get discharged. He wanted to drive in with Mom, but I said I was probably sleeping most of the day. We agreed they'd visit on Sunday, high time they found out why home was called the Hovel.

So Nick had had a "big night." Hotdiggity, raise the curtain on a standing-room-only engorgement. Hard to say which was worse, that she'd felt the need to tell me, or felt that she could. Hell with it – all of it, including her lousy sacral dimples. I woofed down a corn muffin from one of the carts the City amazingly hadn't shut down in favor of stores that sell worse for twice. Munching, I wondered the number of morning-after Dr. Peppers it was going to take to get over the Wife.

Chapter Nineteen

Stanley the Obdurate

Pushing up my one long sleeve, I trooped into the copy joint feeling odd among people whose hopes and concerns probably didn't involve the cops, the Constitution or even their own plummeting reputations. *Naked Opposition* was happily commentating on some same-old same-old. Since Nicki sent my e-mail with such a marvelously vacuous subject line, it was probably still worming its way to the top of Stanley's pile. Come on, "Crusader Draws a Line" from such a highly paid wordsmith? That'll leap from eyeball to mouse-click. Why not the ever fanciful, "Minder-Savvy Tier Reduction."

Stanley had published some of my unadulterated musings (he had space to fill with my recycled thumb-suckers, me the urge to be heard), a tasty morsel or two, plus one, very hasty stick-to-the-ribs dinner to prevent getting scooped. Yet I'd never spoken to one-man-band Stan to gauge his age or anything else. I didn't even know what state he lived in, though some of his own rants hinted at rust-belt. Whoever he was, he ran a good site – a bit raw, sure, though fundamentally legitimate, a good daily clearinghouse of raked muck, dug truth and alternative buzz.

At least Stanley never had me sign the damn release that pervaded freelance work, the one that stated that if the subject of any story so much as says boo, never mind how airtight the article, the publication washes its hands of the writer, with all the blame and exorbitant cost of settling or defending falling on that poor schmuck's head. Small journals and national heavyweights alike employed this delightful little codicil to wrap themselves safely around the trunk of the tree as they cut off the limb where they'd happily sat next to you on publication.

Stanley, instead, trusted to his wits. He published for the love of it, sheer cussedness and – with maybe forty thousand readers a day – a little money. It took guts to poke the big dogs in the ribs whenever someone handed him a long enough stick or he dug one out of the weeds himself.

Debating contacting him at all, I turned to see an abandoned *New York Slimes*, still the key shaper of opinion even on a tabloid-special story like mine. Lo and behold, the trifecta Maureen mentioned, the *Slimes* also fronting a photo that was really starting to grate, Carole big and brassy above the fold. The décolleté picture, seemingly the only one ever taken of her, leaped out even more surrounded by all that gray. It was like the drawing of a pretty, long-haired girl playing the sousaphone leaping off a dictionary's sober page. Re-cork your tongue, brother, and join in offering a lonely city's concupiscence for her recovery.

The *Slimes'* coy headline was perhaps worst of all: "Man Carrying Books, Woman Shot at Penn Station". Fair enough and, depending on the story's speculation as to my intent, perhaps even favorable that they immediately saw the books' significance. But then the headline continued: "Mayor Declares, 'Wider T Link Not Yet Apparent'". Great. Not that no terror link existed, nor no reason to think me part of some wider plot. But that no link was visible – yet. Thank God they slowed that guy down shooting him.

The headlines cued the demonization drums, exculpatory cops conducting, the mayor facilitating, a crescendo coming, newsstand guys furiously making change, all bathed in Carole's overripe glory. I couldn't wait to read the *Daily Chirp*.

God, I wanted to scream. Why didn't I have a damn job? Then maybe I'd still have a wife I didn't have to e-mail, but could just whisper my plans to. Kind of a big night, she'd had the gall to say, showing up residually boozed at work. What, some Wall Street schmuck who's gotta start despoiling at dawn, so he couldn't take her to breakfast like any normal jerk screwing some guy's wife, however estranged? She woke up in her own bed the morning after the night before, no way she was leaving her apartment without breakfast in her belly to soak up the booze. I'd taught her that at least, while also demonstrating its corollary: excessive amounts of food don't really compensate for lack of sober sleep.

****

Having his personal e-mail, I quickly reached Stan the Man to find him stewing over Nicki's note. I asked for his micro-zap, figuring dulcet tones in his ear a better chance to browbeat him into not running a missive that inadequately explained my motivation at Penn – Christ, was it really just twenty-five hours before? Two mangy, self-righteous mutts fighting over scraps, I owed him one, but not this.

Stanley wrote back:

"Revealing my phone would violate a security paradigm of long standing, especially with the lens now focused on you, friend. Still, congratulations on the wide coverage your action – not that it's described as such, yet – has received. *WashPost, USA* Maybe. There was even a decent AP account in my local fish-wrapper.

"But tell me, friend, how do I know you're not some governmento trying to finally uncover my location asking for my micro-zap?"

I told him the Minders didn't move in real time on Middling Severity Tiers like mine, so how could anyone but me know Nicki had sent him my e-mail?

"This shouldn't come as any great surprise, but innumerable spooks monitor my traffic. But, assuming for a moment that you are you, let's hear some more about "Nicki," because frankly your relationship appears to be under something of a strain."

Gonna grab a little color and kick the happy couple's can down the road, Stan? I told him to leave my wife out of it and realized my disadvantage not knowing how much of my mawkish crap she'd included in what she'd sent him. Back on my heels, I threw a decent counter-punch that he couldn't have it both ways, pretending it wasn't me and also pumping for info.

He cleverly resolved our little security dilemma so we could then proceed to our real argument by asking me to name a fact-checker we both happened to know. I easily remembered his oddball first name: Wrenfield. Stanley wobbled a bit over why didn't I remember his last name, but even he realized that was silly.

My identity proved, he congratulated me again. So we got sidetracked admiring our deep appreciation of the shit raining down on us all, as well as the tattered umbrellas our kind offered to a discerning, thumb-sucking few.

"Stanley! Enough claptrap. You can't run that *private* e-mail of mine. I'm screwed if that's how it comes out I intended to challenge the cops. It'll color everything and give them room try to blame me for getting shot in the head."

"What's wrong with a laudatory challenge to the cops when they mutilate the Constitution right under our noses, and no one says a word? 'Nicki' — if she's not actually a mechanism to fuel your own disingenuous disclosure — did you a favor, friend. Round up the band, the bloggers, dykes on bikes, whoever you can get and march down Fifth Avenue. A lot more people will support your action than you might think."

"Stanley, it wasn't an 'action.' As of now, far as anyone knows, I was walking through Penn Station. The demonization already bad enough, the cops dredging up who knows what wretched excess from my checkered past, I'd just as soon keep it that way for a day or two until I'm able to tell my tale properly. But I need that time to stop being woozy from getting shot in the head. That was a private e-mail to my wife, and you have no freaking right to it."

I could hear him laughing through the copy shop screen, not least because I'd probably just nailed Nick's identity for him by calling her my wife a second time.

"Friend, an e-mail sent to a general delivery address at a public news site that gets more than 42,312 uniques a day is not exactly private. You certainly don't own it. I doubt that even I own it. Sent unbidden to *Naked Opposition* for the benefit of its readers, if anyone owns it, they do."

"Spare me. I'm not including in an e-mail – cause of you know who – half the stuff that's happened to me over the past 24 hours, and I'm not even home yet. This is off-the-record, damnit, you are NOT allowed to use this. But I was physically prevented from calling my wife to tell her not to send my note out."

"As to your coy little reference to the Minders: step on a crack, break your father's back. That is, embrace them and whatever they might do, or at least turn agnostic. It's the only stance that allows one to soldier on without whiplash from looking over your shoulder. I have to figure there are already so many alphabet-soup agencies on my case, it's only a matter of time."

"*What's* only a matter of time?"

"No one knows – that's what makes HeadFuck's America so interesting."

"I'll sue. I'm serious, Stanley."

"By all means go right ahead. I could use the diversion, could use the several trips to New York you'll eventually pay for. You know deep down you don't have a prayer, and I just hope, fellow traveler that you are, that it won't get too, too expensive for you. Either way, I'll enjoy the pro se exercise and write regular updates that'll just drive eyeballs to *N. O.* Hopefully you'll get your own site (finally) to counterattack, and all in all, the Beast will get fat and happy."

I told him my head was full of mush, that just typing this nonsense was leaving me exhausted, and I was going home.

He said fine, but since he was indeed posting my e-mail to Nick – his obligation to his readers demanded no less – he needed to get a couple of things straight.

"Let's square this away, and I'll let you go get some rest. I've had four concussions myself over the years, so I know what they're like. The last two freed something up in my writing, broke in the gears a bit better somehow.

Anyway, you wrote of 'confronting the cops.' That's great, folks should stand shoulder to shoulder on that. But what exactly did you mean?"

"Stanley, that's self-evident."

"OK. You also wrote that you 'hope to galoot around enough to spark a search' etc. I don't know that word as a verb, but I guess you were planning on approaching the cops in, according to my dictionary, a *foolish* manner?"

"I was goofing around with my wife. You never heard the phrase, *big galoot*?"

"So you were using a word ungrammatically because it was

not for publication."

"Nail the jello to the wall, dude. Could you be any more anal?"

"Anal, if you insist. But for your own protection as well as mine, enough lies soon to be printed about you as it is, brother. I recall you burrowing pretty deep yourself when it's your byline."

"And another thing: what's with the ugliest, skimpiest type I've ever seen? Talk about passive-aggressive."

"Saves on archival costs. Until it's printed – and imagine a top-notch site like *N. O.*'s volume of correspondence – I don't consider it saved. But here's one I don't get considering your normal realm: 'Then I'll have a big boffo piece on it for the big bucks.' "

Damn, I'd been hoping Nick'd had the sense to delete that. Like her "big score" admission to the *Slimes*, it was the money quote in all the ways that counted.

"That's sarcasm, you dunce." My knees wobbly, I swung wildly, praying for the bell and back to my stool in the corner. For all I knew he was dating Maureen's sister or living with Carole Fiore's mom, so this next bit was truly pathetic.

"Sarcasm, like you use with someone who knows your sensibility, someone you trust. You got someone in your life you trust? Don't answer that, I don't give a shit. But if you 'shoulder-to-shoulder' print that about a boffo piece, you better hope your head swivels enough to watch your back for a long, long time."

"Anytime, anywhere."

"Rock-'em, sock-'em, Travis. Last question, and I'm out of here."

Hah! Got a gun on a doohickey gonna slide down your arm, Stanley, to go with that mohawk? Like any good reporter, his questions got trickier as he went along, though I would've saved that "boffo" bit for last. Quoting my e-mail, he wrote:

" 'So, a real martyr to the Fourth Amendment, maybe, enough perhaps to rival the poor executed Brazilian electrician in London.' How did you get the fuzz to even draw their guns, let alone shoot you? You never impressed me as the reckless type, debating every tiny edit like you do.

"And finally – says you, not me – how did you know your head is like Wonder Woman's bracelets?"

" 'Fuzz?' Stan, you nostalgic bastard. Hell, I was carrying a backpack, and I was going to refuse to submit to a search. So anything was possible. And no, I'm not depressed. Life's peachy. How's by you? You getting enough of whatever rows your boat, I shudder to think?"

"So the shooting was all just an unfortunate set of circumstances?"

"Read the damn papers, which I haven't even had the chance to do yet, then flip whatever they say sideways and let your conscience be your guide. My head is swimming, and I'm in a freaking copy shop spending money by the minute on this with you, and I got a long way still to go – and that's not in a taxi – to make it home. Anything else?"

"That's it, except this that might cheer you up. You wrote of maybe being a martyr to the Fourth Amendment. Well, my publishing your note might end up making you a martyr of a different sort, a punching bag, maybe, for the Movement as a whole. Cause the MoFos are gonna make an example of you, brother. Challenging the cops on these SOP searches is not that huge in and of itself – entirely worthwhile, entirely necessary, certainly, but not exactly striking at the heart of the Imperium. Still, if refuse-and-resist ever catches on about something like the searches, it well might lead to bigger things. And trust that I'm going to do my utmost to boost – sorry, highlight – *N. O.'s* revelation about your political intent as much as I can. Sorry if that means you fall pretty far. But the greater good demands that I focus on the oak and not the acorn.

"A good plan of attack on your part, absolutely. Though any hint of praise only inflates your worst tendencies which are easy enough to spot just below the surface of your writing. Otherwise, why all this retro, self-aggrandizing participant-observer material, constantly conflating yourself with the story?

"Whatever Demo you were planning has blown up in your face and you are now a symbol, like it or not. Also, fate couldn't have handed you a worse fellow victim than Fiore. It's almost laughable. If you alone had gotten shot, revealing your intent might have left you smelling like a rose to the noses that still discern flowers from fertilizer.

"Maybe you haven't previously faced a crisis big enough to uncover whatever hidden resources you may have. Well, this is your crisis. If you own a parachute, grab it. Any skeletons in your closet, haul them out into the light yourself, cause a lot of snoops and spooks have you in their crosshairs. Any kiddie porn — how you rectify that, I'm not exactly sure, though I think I can put you in touch with someone — any back taxes, any gun with one of those nasty, multi-burst trigger activators down under your old shoes in the bottom of a real closet (though again, guns don't go with being an effete, strictly rhetorical bomb-thrower), excise them yourself before that skeleton starts dancing on Page Six.

"And as for effete, relax. While we've been enjoying our little chat here, I've tracked down a picture of your wife, which I will not use. (Her name, yes — my responsibilities to *N. O.*'s readers demand that. But let someone else dunk her pretty face in your lumpy porridge.) Which raises the interesting question of why you have to e-mail her at all to discuss your plans. When I want to talk to my wife, I just roll over. But, to quote the man of the hour: 'Don't answer that, I don't give a shit.' Good luck — and try to remember who your friends are."

Stanley scoring points in a flurry with both hands, including rubbing my nose in my obvious estrangement from Nicki. But hell – *N. O.*'s "revelation" my ass. Ah, the Left. Gotta love us mutts so willing to tear each other to shreds. Writers mine their experience. It's what we do, all well and proper in nonfiction like my pending "Penn Tale" as long as it's indicated as such. (I find novels rather tedious when the writer leans too heavily on the autobiographical, conflating the authorial self with the narrator in various too clever ways. If you can't make shit up, why bother?)

"You finished, Dr. Freud? First off, a true ally would let me tell my story in my own way. A twenty dollar bill falls out of someone's pocket walking in front of you, you yell – plain and simple. As to the participant-observer stuff, it's what you're limited to when you contact editors and tell 'em your last piece was in *Naked Opposition*, but they get first crack on this new one, and not a soul gets back to you.

"Also, given that I got shot in the head yesterday and don't really need to be a punching bag for anyone right now, exactly what 'Movement' you talking about? It's got a name, got leaders, a set of principles or any agenda aside from getting you more attention than you deserve? So screw you and the galoot you rode in on.

"That's right – watch out, baby, black power's gonna get your momma. Cause you know damn well what you're doing here is wrong, Stanley, a smart, solidarity-forever, man-the-barricades type like you. A guy who put his body on the line trying to take a stand, someone who's now getting denounced on every front page in town, should have the right to control the raw material of his own story. Control his own damn text – a private note to his wife.

"Just cause you got ahold of something by mistake doesn't mean you have the unalloyed right to publish it. So, should we ever talk again, which I assure you will be too Goddamn soon, spare me your namby-pamby, Kumbaya load, cause you're nothing but a snake like all the rest, handing the Swift-Boaters all the fuel they need. I hope your scrawny ass looks lousy in the wispy, scraggily beard I assume is all you can grow, since you're not gonna be able to look yourself in the mirror to shave for a long time. That I leave you as my curse."

Bruised and abused, damn right it made me feel better to nail Stanley as the rheumy piece of cheese he was. Though, unfortunately, he was as sharp and forceful as *N. O.* would lead one to fear. He'd quickly realized, for instance, that I hadn't seen Nicki's e-mail. At bottom, I had little but a personal appeal, just as she'd suggested. *I* was the self-involved know-it-all? Screw him, his galoot and the horse they were spooning on when they rode in.

160

I waited a bit, but there was no reply. Could my outburst have cowed him into submission? I'd find out soon enough assuming I didn't keel over on the way home or get snatched off the street. Adrenaline fading as I cut the juice to the machine (always, with a public computer), my feet felt further away than ever.

Chapter Twenty

The Hovel's Sheltering Arms

Sticking close to the sidewalk's slow lane abutting the stores, I shambled the couple of blocks to the Queens train, an old hobbler with a four-tipped cane at one point rushing past. I brooded over what Lurch had read from the *Toast* and also the dreadful *Slimes* headline. Wasn't anyone questioning the shootings?

I got the papers as I hit the subway stairs. Man, my depth perception stank, and I clung to the rail. The post-rush hour brown-out already in force, the train plodded under the river taking folks from around the world home to Queens. So I had plenty of time to peruse the first rough draft of *my* story, damnit.

The *Slimes* evinced its usual predilection for official pronouncements, starting with the mayor tarring me in that headline. And it quoted the cops high up in the story regarding the " 'silver device' " I was said to be " 'brandishing.' " The MTA police spokesman said it was unfortunately lost in the post-shooting melee as " 'bystanders first panicked, then pressed forward.' " But the cop added, " 'Whether it was a micro-zap; an old, illegal whole-vid cell phone; an outmoded radio of a rare type no longer in common usage; or a gun or even a detonator is yet to be determined.' "

His stilted reference to what it actually was, a radio, reminded me of when they catch a plagiarist and run both texts. The copy, being a lie, always sounds all-thumbs next to the unself-conscious original. Still, it would take a rare reporter to conclude the spokesman doth perhaps protest too much about this silver embodiment of mutability .

The *Slimes* then quoted the MTA dude on my " 'antique satchel of East German military design crammed with an inordinate number of printed books.' " The police regarded the specific titles " 'a matter of the highest security since several agencies are subjecting the books to retroflex analysis to determine their underlying significance.' " What, gonna read 'em?

The article said the police had to delay questioning the "Suspect" – bingo, you bastards, that the *Slimes'* own term, not quoting anyone – since doctors forbade it due to my "grave medical status." That nicely redolent phrase prepared a grieving world for my potential exit stage left.

The MTA mouthpiece – country mouse to the NYPD's city mouse – stirred things ever frothier with talk of "an atypical configuration of an unusual amount of semi-perishable food. We're studying whether the subject was self-supplied for a siege of some sort."

Self-supplied. Not catered? Get a MoFo before a cluster of microphones and any fool thing he said, into the paper it went. I weighed – well, in England it'd be a lot of stones – and I had two solid sandwiches. On a normal day moping around the Hovel, let alone out upright schlepping an "inordinate" library around, they wouldn't last past three in the afternoon.

Carole, I was happy to read, was expected to make a full recovery after getting her no doubt gorgeous intestines stitched up. From Ridgewood, Queens, the twenty-four-year-old was heading to her job at some big real estate outfit when shot. She was also studying nights at Queens College – that is, when this walking wet dream with the heart of gold wasn't spreading cheer at local hospitals and nursing homes with the rest of her amateur modern dance troop. Carole's slightly older fiancé, the fireman, was no slouch in the looks department himself, with a nifty forty-five dollar haircut and de rigueur, rakish mustache. Thank goodness no pictures of me had surfaced, at least there in the *Slimes*.

The paper spilled some ink interviewing Homeland Control Deputy Chief Undersecretary Diego Smith and Prof. Wallace Jones, the Alexander Mitchell Palmer Professor of Civil Control at MIT, about the pressures on cops making split-second decisions. Said, Smith, " 'After Manila, we all recognize the importance of targeted kill-shots. At the end of the day, public safety often dictates that the risk the Suspect presents – his guilt, in effect – is established post-neutralization by sophisticated Homeland Control techniques, including our new, post-facto neuro-forensics.' " For his part, Jones hoped " 'the Suspect might recover sufficiently to shed light on his motivations, however obscure.' " Shed like a white cat on a black bedspread, Jones.

The *Daily Chirp*, bless 'em, had a coy headline framing Carole (who I was definitely getting a little sick of, like your third piece of wedding cake): "Cops Shoot Penn Pair". Then, below the bodalicious beauty: "Woman, Man Fight for Life at Bellevue". Inside they had the same MTA garbage about a gun or detonator. But the *Chirp* also harped on whether the police should even draw their guns in Penn Station during rush hour, particularly the machine pistols they increasingly favored. It wondered, "Of the 300,000 who pass through Penn Station daily, how many will now cast a justly fearful eye on the Protectors charged with safeguarding them?"

Walk-on-Water Ted instructed *Chirp* readers in no uncertain terms that the random searches, " 'will get the job done and are here to stay on my say-so.' " He added, " 'Though I don't trouble him with policy specifics, I'm sure I have the mayor's full backing.' "

A third *Chirp* story was headlined: "Penn Protector Called 'Shaky'; Officer Questioned During Sands". It identified the shooter as one Frankie Reisner, a Guardsman and "heroic, four-times Boots". Both he and his partner, Phil Frost, were family men and seasoned MTA officers. However, "The circumstances of Protector Reisner's last deployment Stateside remain cloudy," said the *Chirp* in probably the only real reporting – as opposed to taking dictation – I read that morning. "He has been formally interviewed as a 'person of material interest' regarding an incident with numerous fatalities outside Salakmahest, according to one Army source."

What's more, the MTA had temporarily placed Reisner on desk assignment. This followed " 'a possible T incident with a gun placed to a Suspect's head, the Protector's weapon not forced to discharge,' according to a senior MTA leader unauthorized to speak since, he said, 'the matter is before one of those damn vestigial courts.' " This official regretted Reisner's transfer to Penn Station from the 125th Street Station where the incident occurred. " 'He was doing a fine job applying Sands techniques to one of our own outlying areas.' " Frankie escaped desk-duty and got his gun back about a months before nose met chest.

My man! Head over heels in some Fomenting Democracy mess, shaky and shell-shocked and carrying it home to rile the folks uptown. Didn't one of those MTA cops rifling my stuff in Bellevue's ER say something about he should never have gotten his gun back?

The Guardsman accompanying the two cops was named Marlede, his last name omitted for security reasons. (That got out, next thing you know some sharp-eyed Fiend kidnaps his daughter's Shih Tzu.) He took a buyout a few years back from his plume of a job as a union electrician, hocked himself to the hilt and bought a failing car mechanic's shop in East New York that was thriving until it went bust during his third Boots.

So. The war-vet cop (however compromised), the avuncular, family-man cop, and the pillar-of-his-community, war-vet soldier on the one hand. The heart-of-gold fox on the other. And little old me on a wizened third.

As to the *Toast*, Lurch had hit most of the highlights up in my hospital room, though he'd overlooked Carole's boss saying, "They need to find out about that jerk who forced the cops' hands and then throw the book at him. It's no accident that *both* officers – both experienced men and one a Fomenting Hero – felt the need to fire."

Indeed. The *Toast* accompanied this with a photo of Carole playing after-work softball. A pitcher, of course, she'd just released the ball and was standing straight, her left arm in a graceful follow-through. A tasty rainbow sherbet in pink sneakers and tall purple socks, even her knees appealed, and how rare is that? But no one would care about knees topped by such a long pour of creamy vanilla thigh, then lemony short-shorts and a tight cherry tee, *Real Bricks*, the name of her company, stretched to the breaking point in chocolate sprinkles. A marvelously intense look was topped by all that platinum whipped cream piled high.

The games co-ed, she undoubtedly got numerous strike-three-lookings.

None of the papers knew what to make of me, and none had connected the dots to my published journalism. My instinct not to identify myself at Bellevue with my formal name, which doubles as my byline, proved sound. The *Chirp* painted me as a victim – sorta – though several leagues removed from Carole, while naturally the *Toast* had me sipping jihad-tea. And, using the term, "Suspect," the *Slimes* was perhaps worst in its sly, authoritative way. But depending on what Stanley spilled, I still might get to dance on stage in some measure to my own music – once I got it written.

Subways were not eponymous where I lived. Enjoying the AC, I gazed out at what TV and radio chock-a-block with Spewer ads insisted on calling 'haze.' Western Queen's low, foreground jumble did nothing to obscure the apartment towers a short leap over the East River. Yet the tall glass sheaths, curved or jagged, bronze, green or blue – meant to shimmer and dazzle and pronounce about their occupants – were barely visible through the lung-searing smear.

****

The Stuffing giving notice that I soon needed to get horizontal, what right did I have to assume refuge behind the polite fiction of my own locked door? Not that I felt showered in serenity at the Hovel. It'd be a long time coming before I wiped from memory the balls-in-a-vice panic attacks I feared still.

Startling and unexpected and the first of my long, sketchy life, the attacks reared up as I lay down my second night there. (The first, the night Nicki kicked me out, I'd been way too fractured for anything as *integral* as a panic attack.) I'd reluctantly turn the light off a bit later each night only to be gripped by the certainty that I'd stop breathing, maybe in ten minutes or maybe along towards morning, but a done deal that night if I let myself fall asleep. I felt no panic sitting in a chair mourning Nick, my eyes drifting aimlessly over a book. But upright in a chair was no way to spend the night. I'd go take another piss and several calming gulps of water (that dumb cycle) and reluctantly return to bed. Getting ahold of myself, after that I'd perhaps marshal the belief that respiration might continue.

Breath somehow ongoing, I'd then confront the sensation

that something amorphous but malevolent, some smothering ill vapor, was collecting itself up in a corner to soon fling itself down from the dark recesses of the tiny bedroom. No, I couldn't see it, but that didn't mean something bad wasn't coalescing up by the ancient mansion's peeling ceiling far above. Leaving the light on soon lost its power to vanquish the vapors. Fearing something was up there when I could clearly see otherwise – fear of my marbles rolling loose – was perhaps worst of all.

Knowing that a dissolving marriage birthed the night terrors, but unwilling to blame something beyond my control, I finally, laughably, attributed the Blue Meanies lurking amidst the cobwebs to the oddity of the once luxe old pile's ten-foot ceilings. Tall, wide and still shabbily handsome, built for some minor shipping magnate in the 1850s, it had been carved into a dog's-breakfast of apartments – cells, really, most of them. Such cramped little cribs hard to find, even in Bumfuckville, at least it was down by the river. Even there, most of its large, shabby peers had been replaced by a brick box with walls that vibrated when struck, the few windows the size of microwaves. (The builders pocketed another dollar deciding residents didn't need light or air.) My home had escaped demolition cause, aside from its dicey, ass-end location, the quirky Greek landlord, almost as old as the house itself, refused to sell.

From his enormous, gloomy apartment behind the columned front porch, Mr. Staphilopoulous terrorized the all-male gathering of misfits who lived in the rabbit hutches above. Such was his fierce mien, peering out from under bushy white eyebrows that clashed with his improbable, pomegranaty hair, he even spooked some of the younger project kids passing by.

What's more, Stap was rich, his fortune resting on the one thing they weren't making more of: a stupendous back yard. Deeper than it was wide (and it was plenty wide), it was aswarm with junk. Near the house, a listing, vine-encrusted aboveground pool was missing a few side panels. Further back, a couple of Detroit's finest dinosaurs rusted away, including an ancient, luridly purple Plymouth Road Runner, more's the pity. As to the vast stretch of brambles leading up to an uncertain, high wooden fence, human foot had not touched earth for some time.

Nicki lowering the boom right when the former tenant was carried out feet first, I was lucky enough to score a prized pad high up and in back, far from the Greek's prying ears. So our only real tussle was when my friend Ralph dropped by and committed the crime of leaving his bike by the porch while pondering which of the fifteen indifferently working bells rigged up by the front door of this ostensibly private home was mine.

I got back in Mr. Staphilopoulous's good graces explaining to him on his porch one fiendishly hot night, the murk pressing down on every crease and cranny, what a presidential vest-pocket veto had been. He'd heard the phrase on TV from a HeadMan partisan, one of the dozens who dominated the airwaves once it became clear whose bread was buttered, how, and by whom. The shill had argued it meant nothing that Congress had allowed itself to be stripped of its subpoena power. Nobody would miss that anymore than they'd miss the vest-pocket veto. And Stap had been driving himself crazy trying to make it parse literally in his decent English cause he couldn't remember any president in his many decades in America wearing a vest.

In time, more porch chat revealed his other chief occupations: massaging his almost worthless, post-Plunge shares of ACME Cement and the like; torturing his corrupt city councilman (a yuppie who'd had the nerve to unseat Stap's thieving countryman) with a string of handwritten letters laboriously translated to English with the aid of a tattered Greek-English dictionary; and bemoaning the fortunes of his favorite footballers, AEK Athens.

The entire first floor Stap's faded domain, there were grim single rooms on most of the second and the entire third floors, many with no window, and all sharing the floor's one kitchen and bath. The Albanians, Chinese, Guatemalans and Mexicans et. al. found them a steal at $450, usually two (three?) to a room. The Albanians, far as I could tell, were hard-smoking burn-outs who manned the local produce stores; the Chinese, younger, hard-smoking strivers; and the Latinos – by far the majority – were nonsmoking grunts of all work who blossomed briefly each week from around seven Saturday night through the duration of volleyball Sunday.

Some little whippet of a white guy who favored short-sleeved checked shirts with white pants and went running every morning at six, had lived on the second floor for years in a real apartment. Marvin even had sole access to a criminally unused terrace on the big porch roof. A computer mumbo-jumboist for Chase or Capture or some such Plunger, Marvin saw no need to buddy up to yet another of the losers passing through, especially since Nick tossing me had goosed my usual cleverer-than-thou snarl. Our sole conversation, Marvin mentioned that Saturday night was the house's one night to howl, Stap purposely out. But it wasn't too bad, he prissily assured me, because "the laborers" wanted to be up early for Sunday's catch-and-toss volleyball games in the local school yard.

And at that, Marvin slipped through his door. Him staring past me, I'd scaled back my grunt of hello to a nod. No longer riding on Nicki's social coattails – bye-bye giant shrimp and oddly sour Heineken – I needed to exercise my flabby talent for friendship.

The Hovel: the two-room (real bath and kitchen, of sorts, included) locus of my struggle to inflate my lungs despite the Blue Meanies. After some increasingly rough nights, I quit my bedroom and made a nest for myself on the floor in the kitchen/den/rec room under my one window. No air stirred as I stared at the backyard's towering tree and wondered which was older, it or Stap. After a few nights, a sore back and the long-term soul-sickness that replaced the immediate, Mickey-Mouse fear of crib death sent me back to bed in my glorified closet.

Oh woe was fucking me. They say the most stressful things in life are divorce (mine in the offing), the death of a spouse or a major illness. No argument here.

But, assuming no one crashed through the door – this was still New York, not Tulsa or San Diego – the Stuffing would compel a night or two of sleep. I was heading home to my two-room, six-bills-a-month, fourth-floor lair that I was going to learn to love real soon. Just click my ruby slippers three times and say it loud.

****

Riding the bus home with the project ladies clutching their shopping bags, I fretted over finding Mr. Staphilopoulos on the porch, waving a copy of the *Chirp* under my nose, my stuff heaped on the front lawn, my landlord yelling about needing no troublemakers. Like most in HeadFuck's politically demobilized land, we hadn't veered to politics (beyond vest pockets). Given his general rules-and-regulations mentality, one could guess. Aside from ancient cars – his own a well preserved barge of a Crown Vic, dark green with seats of the finest burnt-sienna plastics – he seemed to find himself at an unenthralled remove from most things American. That presumably included such quaint anachronisms as political dissent.

Trundling up the block from Bellevue, the porch was empty, Mr. Staphilopoulos perhaps inside brewing another espresso. Far as I could tell, the bitter little cups were his sole sustenance aside from cigarettes, the odd, rich snack – fried eggplant, anchovies, and pearl onions smeared on crackers or pesto spooned straight from the jar – and a genteel sufficiency of Metaxa. The Stuffing was doing back flips by the time I hauled myself four flights up.

I fired up the machine, glad to see that Stanley was still linking to the same garden-variety scandals as before. Could my tirade have possibly hit home? Ideally, I'd have gotten my side of the story out before he, that twerp Benson at the *Slimes*, the cops or some haircut on TV heaved another bag of slop my way. But, those four flights up the final blow, the floor was going all wavy on me when I stood up. Brushing my teeth for the first time in a day-and-a-half all I had in me, a cogent and impassioned account wasn't spilling from the Stuffing just then. Whatever I wrote getting boatloads of scrutiny, it couldn't be no Dick and Jane.

I decided against a chair by the door. Aside from hardly slowing 'em down at all, I feared surrendering to that level of paranoia in my very own Hovel. Plus, how would they get in if the Stuffing went south, and I had to crawl to the phone to call a *real* ambulance (assuming I could)?

I unplugged my phone and turned off the micro-zap. Setting the alarm for late afternoon to get up and make a stab at "Penn Tale," I tottered off feeling like I'd dragged a heavy stone by a strap round my forehead. The room stale and sarcophogal, a concussion still trumped the walls closing in. And so out I fell. I had no memory of squelching the alarm, but did recall getting up at some point for a feed and staring at some idiot cop show for fifteen minutes.

Actually, like most, it was far too clever and instructive, teaching that suspects should never demand a lawyer before sparring with the cops. As I knew well, such behavior-modeling embedded in a TV show's story line is by far the most powerful form of mass inculcation. Hence the struggle every few years over actors smoking in movies and why, leaping into their cars, even the worst desperado and most desperate pursuer fasten their seat belts before burning rubber. Start blabbing folks, you're smarter than the cops.

I sat there watching the MoFo's easy triumph that Friday evening, dumbly spooning pineapple-laden cottage cheese and wondering how such an oddity arrived in my fridge. After this quarter-hour cultural and gustatory triumph, sleep reclaimed me.

Chapter Twenty-One

Two Below the Waterline

The vertical coffin's door somehow shut and my pillow drenched, I leapt from my bed too quickly, staggered and clutched at the door. Downing a small pond after an interminable three minutes clearing the lead from Stap's 1850's pipes offered some relief. And not even a lousy breakfast of cereal doused in evaporated milk from the cupboard wiped off the relative shine of waking up Lurch-less, lord of all I surveyed in two hot, little rooms.

Dulling that shine figured to belong to a certain lefty wanker and the *New York Slimes*. I spooned away over an article that swam to the top of the kitchen-table pile. It detailed the treatment accorded a certain showpiece Fiend, my brief interlude at Bellevue a day at the beach by comparison. For I'd suffered no long-term sensory deprivation. My windows weren't cloaked, guards hadn't covered my eyes with dark goggles and worn dark visors themselves to prevent ocular intercourse. There were no sound-proof headphones clamped on my ears. Having escaped their 'tests,' I hadn't been rendered "docile as a piece of furniture."

The Stuffing trimmed by caffeine, I logged on, just another Saturday of big-foot abuse. Perhaps getting shot had shown Carole the error of her shallow ways devoting her free time to making orphans and old folks' blood race. Her perfect belly already irrevocably scarred (several interns fighting over who got to keep the cat-gut once her stitches were removed), maybe she'd decided to donate a kidney to some mortally ill smoke-eater who rode the truck with her fiancé.

If so, Stanley hadn't caught up, *Naked Opposition* ballyhooing its "EXCLUSIVE: Wounded Activist-Journalist's Goal to Challenge Illegal Police Searches. Alerted Spouse His Intent to 'Spark a Search ... for a Principled Refusal.' Deemed Arrest

'Likely.' Amid Police Smear, Left Endorses his Planned Action."

Staking his claim to me as a "stalwart *N.O.* contributor," he led with a properly skeptical description of the shootings and riffed on the unconstitutionality of suspicionless searches. He then echoed the widely held belief that – like all the new T-apocalyptic TV shows – they're nothing but security theater designed to flog fear and cow the populace into accepting all manner of abuse.

Then Stan the Man anointed me as the standard bearer of some rag-tag movement – dream on, Stanley – and he called for "legions of self-reliant, constitutionally aware citizens to follow this activist's lead."

Carole Exhibit A (Exhibit A forevermore), he decried the danger to bystanders in a crowded train station when cops unholster their guns. No, no, no – 'bystanders' as evidenced by *both* of us, Stanley. He said it was a danger I recognized. As I stated in an e-mail exchange with *Naked Opposition* – my "only interview to date since the unwarranted attack by the police – *'I was carrying a backpack, and I was going to refuse to submit to a search. So anything was possible.'* Indeed, this citizen-activist was willing to put his body on the line to take a stand." Great. My pen gone dry, I chose to tell my tale not to, oh, the *Daily Chirp*, or *Redirection*'s Leslie, but to *N.O.*

He questioned the MTA's characterization of the conveniently missing silver device as a possible detonator or gun and ran my denial of carrying any weapon. Regarding the shooting itself, he then quoted something that had seemed clever typing to a (former) colleague, but darn peculiar in a story helping to shape me for the world: " '*Read the damn papers ... then flip whatever they say sideways and let your conscience be your guide.*' " Shit.

He noted my claim to be suffering a concussion and said I seemed, "even through the beclouding, pixeled scrim" – writing with all ten fingers, Stanley! – "to be under considerable stress given the contrast with our previously harmonious relations." So now I was unhinged to boot.

He ran my germinating complaint that, "*I've gotten awfully pissed about this lousy submit-to-a-search regime the City has resurrected*" followed by my disgust observing the searches in action: " 'People were just delighted to trot up to have the cops trod all over the Constitution and pretend to paw through their stuff. The cop told a majority of the people to just move on, but maybe a third of those folks – sheep who'd already been dismissed! – lined up anyway.' "

Unhinged, but oddly superior as well.

He let me articulate my plan, " '[H]ope to galoot around enough to spark a search and then draw myself up in high dudgeon for a principled refusal.' " But then he channeled his inner schoolmarm: "His granting himself license to employ a noun as a verb is in keeping with – alone among the close to nine million and more victims of these police-state tactics – his decision to stick it to the Man." Thanks, I supposed.

As I'd feared, he quoted the impecunious freelancer's optimism expressed to his flown-the-coop wife about big-BIG bucks, maybe even four hundred of them should fortune fall all over herself: " 'I'll have a big boffo piece on it for the big bucks. A stunt, yeah, but drawing a line, damnit, with the sort of participatory/observer stuff that's seemingly gone out of style.' " He compared "a hungry writer conflating himself with the story to walking the railroad tracks searching for lumps of coal tossed from the train."

Shooting himself in the foot, he alerted everyone to the fact that after a couple of decent scores on domestic policy scandals, I'd fallen on hard times, reduced to "publishing several articles for free on this site, such is the antipathy of the day for the true rabble-rouser."

He quoted my denial of sending him the e-mail anonymously myself to surreptitiously disclose my intent to the world. "And that well may be true," he said, running some of the Internet circle-jerk proving that the cut-and-paste of my note to Nick came to him from an anonymous Fornix & Foyst account.

Whether sanitized by Nicki or him I couldn't say, but at least there was none of my icky, oh-Baby, personal stuff, nor any of that sappiness about Fourth Amendment martyrdom. Several e-mails and calls to Nick's voice-mail at work were not returned, he said, and a Queens number under her name was recently disconnected. "That may explain the curious tenor of an intra-spousal e-mail." Getting all ham-handed, Stan? He added that I'd apparently sent it to alert Nicki to my plans since – and here he repeated the money quote – I "admitted," said Stanley, that, yes, anything was possible.

Screw you with an eggbeater, Solidarity Boy. It was a *statement*, not an admission, which you're flogging to ram home the nonexistent shreds of my culpability. Willing to bear the risk myself, I was also, according to him, willing to consciously endanger everyone around me. You got a lawyer picked out for Carole to sue me with yet?

He ended by twisting a guilt-by-association shiv, quoting out of left field (way over by the foul pole), one "Comrade Timmy Refneski, Chief Dogmatist, Bakunin's Rebellion, the Republic of Bushwick." Couldn't reach the Center for Constitutional Rights or the National Lawyers Guild, Stan? Though decrying that I'd written for the bourgeois press – yeah, all those glossy-paper, celebrity-adoption stories I spew out for four bucks a word – Comrade Refneski applauded my intent at Penn Station. But he also offered this. " 'The police astound me by shooting two so-called Caucasians. Those two pigs are in obvious need of re-indoctrination.' "

Stan, the master of the smiling screw, tarring me with both Bakunin's brush and this nincompoop's inflammatory claptrap. Cheap and obvious, calling a cop a pig does nothing to advance your cause. Did Timmy even exist, I wondered, or had Stanley conjured him up to add rust to the knife? Timmy got a grand total of twenty-nine googles, I detoured to see, my grandma thirty-years gone probably getting half that. Stanley must have been repaying a debt of some sort plugging *Timmy* – a proper trust-fund revolutionary name. Besides, didn't it take all of Brooklyn to constitute a republic?

Stanley ended with another shovelful of purported liability from some twisted sister at an outfit called Citizens' Obligations. An awesome twenty-three googles for her whole organization, obligated citizen Hannah Soledad seemed like she'd be a blast sharing an adult beverage at an appropriately licensed, smoke-free tavern once our IDs were scanned at the door and we presented affidavits regarding the evening's duly arbitrated intended intimacies. Cause she thought my plan " 'potentially worthwhile, but I would advise against unwarranted soloing. Anyone seeking to properly discharge Citizens' Obligations must inform the police in advance and obtain Commissioner Ted's arrest permit so as to coordinate a legitimate, peaceful arrest with properly accredited media coverage. Deviating from procedure invites at least a tazing, as this sad case indicates, a young womyn fighting for her life.' "

Arrest permit – darn. Must have missed Walk-on-Water Ted's memo on asking permission to get popped. I'd failed to "coordinate" with the cops, so by her lights, of course I'd gotten shot, Carole too. As to accredited media – licensed? – that excluded you, Stanley, you bastard. Quoting these two morons completed a nifty hatchet job, the blood on his shoes hard to see. Go ahead, lap it up all you scribblers building on this garbage, all you cops loading your biggest buckets of slime. Semper Solidarity, Stan – your feet all comfy up on the desk wherever it is you foul the air.

****

The Stuffing throbbing, I swore steadily though without much flair. My last real meal Thursday, two days before, man, I needed to hit the local Chinese. There was one every block or three, the supposedly bulletproof plastic barrier optional. But first to see with how heavy a fist young Benson banged his keys. Eric *Keith* Benson, I saw, three names crowning the ambitious typing of the site's second offering. Tops was the confirmed downing by an RPG of an ancient B-52 accompanied by a link (the *Slimes* declined to run it itself) to a Pan-T agency photo of a delirious crowd hammering the huge jet with their shoes.

At least they'd used F&F's PR photo, Nicki looking fine, a woman any dope like me would be thrilled to have identified as his wife under the cigarette-while-pumping-gas headline: "Penn Shooting Figure's Wife Wonders if Money Woes Sparked Attack". Damn, Frankie was broke along with everything else?

There was also that dreaded little tag (if you're the article's focus): *News Analysis*, which meant they gave the writer free rein. It was the only way to justify the front-page treatment, cause Benson had little to hang his hat on but Nicki's nonsense. After sugar-coating the shooting in a quick intro, he went anecdotal, talking of meeting her as she arrived at work. "Asked by means of identification if she was related to the Penn Station shooting figure, his wife immediately replied, 'Why, does he owe you money?' "

It came out of her mouth, so Benson could legitimately write it down and then print it – devil take the hindmost. Almost gleeful, he added that though Nicki "would not confirm how onerous his debts, she did acknowledge that her husband had hit a professional dry spell. She said, 'He has been kind of floundering lately, having trouble getting published. But now, after getting shot, maybe he has a big story, something to use to get back on his feet.' Asked to clarify, she said, 'Well of course there's a money angle. He's a writer. That's what he does for a living if you can call it that.' "

All that a fine start on Wen Ho-ing me, time to screw Nick by making sure the Feds made the connection to their latest Boots campaign: "A newly minted vice-president and star copywriter at hot ad agency Fornix & Foyst (which recently landed a $167-million U.S. Army minority recruitment account – the first of three to be launched this year), she seemed oddly unaware her husband had been shot less than twenty-four hours before. When informed of what still might prove a fatal accident at Penn Station, she declared, 'No, you've got it wrong. Some absurdly stacked blonde is on all the front pages, not my husband.' Finally convinced that he was indeed the attack's Suspect, she protested, 'But nothing was supposed to happen! It was all just a test!' "

Suspect – my *Slimes* title. Carry a decibel reader around with you, Benson, to justify those exclamation points?

Mining more Nick ore, Benson wrote, "She seemed to search her mind for a possible explanation of why his antique East German military satchel was crammed with an inordinate number of printed books: 'Well, he's put on a little weight, and it's very likely he was just getting some exercise carrying them around somewhere, getting out of his little apartment which isn't wired for air conditioning. If he thought it was worth six dollars for the train to Manhattan and back, he might've ended up in Penn Station just to walk around in its AC.'

"Adding confusion to the Suspect's murky and apparently financially strained circumstances – who can tolerate *un*conditioned air these days? –his spouse refused to clarify their living arrangements or why she referred to it as 'his' apartment."

So, a fat, cheap grifter. I hoped like hell she was still drunk off her ass, cause the Wife didn't even let me roll up my pants leg before shooting me in the knee.

Benson rolled on. "The Suspect's condition is listed as 'grave,' with sources indicating it is likely to deteriorate during a delicate course of treatment. It remains unclear how he managed to ensure the bullet did not prove immediately fatal. One theory was advanced by Dr. Wally R. Littlesmith of Lexis/Nexis-Nassau Community University Medical Site. 'I've heard from contacts in our T Community of a new, top-secret, plasticine *super*-Kevlar, if you will, that can be appliquéd to the body. Of course removing it later from the head – required within forty-eight hours lest it painfully shrink whatever anatomical structure it encases – necessitates shaving the scalp. But, at the end of the day, that would seem of little consequence to someone pursuing the extortion scheme the *Slimes* has detailed so thoroughly in its questions.' "

Set up the pins and knock 'em down, E. Keith. The police-beat cub added helpfully, "The MTA police still hope to locate the missing 'silver device' the Suspect pointed at Protectors to prompt the shooting, an item the police have identified variously as either a detonator, a gun or perhaps some other implement." The caveats grew ever fainter, including the possibility – initially endorsed by the police – that it might be a radio.

Combine the *Slimes* with *N.O.*, and I emerged as someone who'd set out to challenge our Heroes' T Paradigm, designed to keep us all safe. Plus I'd gotten a classy – no, iconic – American broad shot, a fireman's very own. And all for the worst of money-grubbing reasons and nary a word of contradiction from this quarter.

The Stuffing both soggy and oddly light, I plowed through my crappy mail, only an enterprising 187 strangers tracking down my e-mail address. It was actually far less, I saw, since maybe a third of the notes repeated the same awkward slogans, such as "Patriots Obey Protectors" and "Expose the Satchel!" and – my favorite – "Unbuckle, Unzip, De-Latch!" So it was probably the same male dork or two (women have lives) armed with a bunch of sending addresses. Another guy complimented me but wanted a call – at a New York number – to explain what it was all about so he could replicate it down in Philly. Whatever you say, MoFo.

The vitriol was leavened by inquiries about my health from some reporters and drug policy activists I knew, everybody asking way too many questions. A few folks even applauded my intent.

****

Shite, indeed, Maureen. Assuming Carole recovered, and I managed with a compelling (and true) account to deflect the tide of blame rising past my waist, maybe it did come down to taking one for the team. Rather than the usual fusillade on some late-night corner in a black or brown neighborhood – the circumstances obscure, the investigation contrived, the truth foggy, the outcome fudged, the penalty minimal (a month off without pay for killing a blameless kid on a Brooklyn project rooftop because the cop was so scared he'd had his gun out on routine patrol, his brain on hair-trigger) – let the world see that the quick-draw artists were spreading to the realm of the white and coiffed.

It was time for some four-dollar protein, starch and grease, hopefully in that order, and back upstairs to make a stab at "Penn Tale." I lifted a twenty from next month's rent, Stap's annoying insistence on cash proving useful. I still had a death-grip on the banister heading down the four flights, but my feet didn't flounder quite like the day before.

179

Chapter Twenty-Two

But Mr. DeMille, My Boots Are Muddy, My Spurs Rusty

Sugar-monkey! Down on the porch I heard Mr. Staphilopoulous yelling in far less-accented English than usual, "Hey, News-Man, get that truck from blocking my driveway. Move it before something happens to your windows. We got no news here!"

I'd obviously joined Officer Henderson in floating out by Jupiter's ninth moon, cause it hadn't dawned I'd be prey way out in Bumfuckville. Why, it was a full two days after the shootings, and I'd traveled under an entire river! My phone wasn't listed, and no one but Nicki and my parents knew where I lived. Them and Ralph, damn him if he coughed it up.

I looked down at my work boots, baggy, saggy, *old* cut-off jeans and faded, shrunken Hot Tuna tee shirt I'd put on to cheer myself up. The only band shirt I'd ever bought, amazing it made it home with me with what they started passing around up in that theater's balcony, Tuna marvelously electric, none of that Jorma's gotten old picking-and-plucking crap. Long before Nick, Sally was her totally wrong, white-bread name, my brief fellow-flinger. Not going much of anywhere for either of us – but, boy, where was she now, *twenty-four-year-old* Sally for even an afternoon? Her fetchingly unshaven pits swam to mind, two flaxen snatches migrated north.

If it was a truck, that meant TV and, Mr. DeMille, I was decidedly not ready for my close-up. But, having consumed an entire muffin and some cottage cheese in the prior 48-hours, my skimpy breakfast hadn't cut it. The floor going wavy on me, attempting four flights back up and then four down was out. Screw it, I wasn't making it to wardrobe. Like Benson, only worse, the haircut in that truck would just edit his sidewalk Gotcha! to emphasize any slip-ups. No, the next communiqué lobbed from my foxhole was passing through my own fingers.

Nor was I ready to confront my landlord, the Greek presumably furious I'd brought the locusts down on his gritty little patch of paradise. I crept out the long back hall, Stap still yelling out front, got past the pool missing a panel front and back, through the overgrown ramble of a backyard and out a hole in Stap's fence into the neighbor's backyard. The Stuffing's airiness deteriorating to dizziness that Saturday morning, I rested a moment in the neighbor's driveway, hands on knees, then scooted down the sidewalk with barely a glance at the fish-kicking-a-field-goal TV truck on my dreary block. That resurrected Nicki's theory about making out in a dark bar: if you pretend you can't see them, then of course they can't see you.

I did, however, foolishly catch sight of myself in the window of a "Comidas-Soul" joint that failed despite its valiant effort to appeal to most everyone in the projects. Skip the faded tee shirt struggling to meet its responsibilities and the disgrace of my shorts. I'd totally forgotten the giant band-aid pasted on my lank, unwashed, thinning, too-long, self-cut former Breck-Boy glory. Jesus, I looked like Cat Wrangler with her skewed lipstick and sister's sock taped to her hand, except I should hope to look half that good.

I hit the bodega for a rare, unhung Dr. Pepper and a two-pack of Lady Linda chocolate cupcakes – the ratio of frosting to cake to ook-filling exactly right – to carry me through the afternoon. Plus some baked beans and bright pink, Dominican hot dogs for dinner, and the *Chirp* and the *Toast* I almost forgot, sweating provisions.

Under the headline "Beauty's Miraculous Recovery" the *Toast* had Carole leaping off the page in a pink leotard performing at some hospital awhile back. The line below: "City's Prayers Answered". True enough, I for one having joined the chorus. The *Chirp* had the same shot – had to love it when the tabs got burned like that – only smaller because below Carole was a shot of her chiseled-jawed fiancé over the headline "Fire Fiancé Demands Answers". I could hope it was answers from the MTA – right after I ran off to join the circus as the bearded lady.

I'd find out after I ordered from the closer, lousier Chinese that served only white rice, rather than the brown-rice joint a block further. Cause I was awfully unsteady on my pins, hopefully at least partly from sheer starvation.

I ordered goop to go and sat watching molecules dance in the murk outside, telling myself it was just a trick of the sun refracted through the smeared window. Only there was no sunlight. The general hope was someone would catch it someday in a bottle to show little children. The place deserted that early, the fierce old Boss-Man soon grunted at me, and the effort of just getting to the counter for my Three Kings Displeasures convinced me I was wolfing down at least one to forestall keeling over the second flight up. But man, I did not want any reporter finding me there. Aside from being mentally, physically and sartorially not equal to it, I was Goddamn not in the mood. Hell, no paycheck-guy was pushing on Boss-Man's masking-taped cracked glass door. Nothing but the spiffier joint up the street for the likes of them.

I coughed loudly to mask the noise of opening my Dr. P. and hid it on the seat next to me. Opening the *Toast*, I basked in a study of Carole, yes, at the beach, not with the frisbee of my fantasy, but emerging from the surf, her over-matched bikini ajar, hubby-to-be with the photo credit, a scandal in two-dimensions. Only the *Toast*'s push to canonize her kept it from the front page.

Already feeling steadier for the metallic-tinged pork, I was glad to read she was up and at 'em on her Bellevue ward. The *Chirp* had some sketchy stuff on me supposedly "absconding" from the hospital. But Carole kept grabbing my eye – an action shot of her running the bases – until the subhead, "Suspect to Face Assault Charges?" got me by the throat.

But the Chirp was just musing aloud. According to one MTA honcho, they were " 'waiting on interviewing the regrettably absent Protector Reisner before deciding what charges the Suspect will face.' " There it was again, capitalized even in quotation, traveled from the columns of the *Slimes*, to a *Chirp* subhead, to a cop's mouth with never a clear indication of what I was suspected of doing. I flipped the page to – wow! – see the headline, "Soldier Held Fire, Why Not MTA?" Add that to its prior revelation about Frankie's involvement in the Salakmahest cluster-fuck, and the *Chirp* was cooking with gas.

Racing through the article, which initially focused on bystanders' peril, I was interrupted by a young guy lugging a surprisingly compact TV camera festooned with NYONLY logos, a stout chain linking it to his belt. He went to the counter and spoke to Boss-Man in Chinese. His background tough to pin down, whether he'd learned it at home or during a junior year abroad I couldn't say. Way too thin, with greased, spiky black hair doing a just-so leap off his forehead, he was dressed like *West Side Story*'s Bernardo on his way to the dance in a dark purple shirt, some kind of severely cut black jacket, and pointy-toed Beatle boots Pop would've called them.

Neither shot nor starved, he had no call to sit down at the other greasy table and said in English to make it to go. Bolting then and there would only trumpet the hounds, so I was glad when he looked right through the Bumfuckville goober bent over his kibble and took to sighing and sticking his pacifier. It pained me to think my type of dense, baroque reporting down the drain, people getting their infotainment from those things in eight-word bursts. Feeling slightly more human with each bite, I gulped a surreptitious hit of soda and, articles on my mess off-limits, read about the Yankees' latest blow-up. One of the owner's horses had about kicked down his stall trying to get at another horse. Nothing to do but wait this guy out cause I wasn't burning my backyard entrée with him watching.

My nose buried and mouth working, the restaurant was suddenly flooded with light. The camera on his shoulder boring through me, NYONLY studied his pacifier and then walked up, saying, "You're him, aren't you, the Penn Station Sus – I mean the Penn Station shooting victim? Right? This officially licensed camera is rolling, by the way."

Done nothing wrong, I had nothing to hide and said, "Yeah, I'm the guy those cops shot. But I'm eating right now as you can see, my first real meal in days. If you give me your card, I'll be glad to schedule an interview at our mutual convenience. But I'm afraid now is not a good time for me."

And I turned and clutched at the can on the seat and took a long swig, spilling some down my chin. Blind to the napkins at hand, I reached awkwardly to rub my chin on my too short sleeve, a contortion that sent the Stuffing into a back-flip. Damn, the last time I was on TV I wore the same blue suit I got married in, and they sent a long black car. This time, some guy was trapping me all dishabille in a formica booth. Adjusting his lens, he spoke excitedly into the top of his camera of "a chance encounter with the man the entire city has been wondering about since he absconded from Bellevue Hospital."

"Just curious: where'd you get my picture?"

He peered over his shoulder at the door, then shrugged and turned off the light. "Let me turn the video off. Not that I *have* to answer that, but I've got a source in the Commissioner's office who sent me your address and a photo from a Penn Station surveillance camera. They're spreading it around cause there's an ABC truck parked outside your place – no way you own that big pile, right? – and I heard FOX was here until he ducked out to get shots of a dry-cleaner explosion up in the Bronx since you're so close to the Giuliani Bridge."

I chewed the Displeasure I'd crammed while he spoke, crazy-nervous and trying to rehab the Stuffing on the fly, and tried to remember if I'd ever heard of a dry cleaner exploding.

"Now look," he continued – and just why did every schmuck I encountered lately feel free to immediately start barking orders? – "I'm going to turn the video back on in a minute, and I can film you saying nothing and gorging yourself on a lot of nasty food for this hour of the morning. Or I can shoot you running away on up to your front door, which" – he bent down to see that the half of me under the table was no more prepossessing than the visible half – "you probably don't want. Or we can do a short interview here, though I would suggest you try to fix your hair a little. No, not the bandage – that gets the sympathy vote, right?"

"So on your exalted say-so, I got no right to tell my own story how and when I want? That is, in print and whenever I'm damn well ready?"

"Your story's getting told, like it or not. You lost control of it about two minutes after you made that cop shoot you. So how about telling the world what you were really doing in Penn Station. Like somebody said, control what already happened, and you control what's going to happen."

"You mean that somebody named Orwell: 'Control the past, you get to control the future. And, rule the present, you own the past' – something like that."

"Whatever. Do you have any idea what the cops are saying about you? Doesn't matter whether it's true or not cause all they have to do is get some little outlet to repeat it, and then it's fair game ten minutes later for us professionals, a story this big."

"Maybe the cops should be worrying about what I'll say about them. Ever think of that?"

"Tell you what, and I say this as a friend. You got any deep dark secrets in the backwaters of your life that might float to the surface, get 'em out now yourself. Put on a jacket and tie – you own a jacket, right? – and come on down to the studio. Cause I guarantee there's about eleven cops digging in your dirt right now."

"I didn't know we *were* friends. That's mighty generous of you considering I don't even know your name. And exactly how do I know you're legit and not some cop trying to get me to spill? No, I'm sorry, waving some card around your neck proves exactly nothing. Maybe if I wrote down all those ID numbers."

"No way am I handing over my license to carry a video camera to someone like you. Not after the profound background check I went through to get it."

"You mean handing it to a reporter who figures he doesn't need the government's permission? What, I'm gonna rub my DNA on your *license*, get us all twisted?"

"Like you're a great advertisement for being an outsider."

"Ya know, I'm not feeling quite well enough for playing the dozens. My head feels like it's made of tapioca – something about getting shot probably. But let me ask you: *I* made that cop shoot me?"

"Dozens of what?"

"Never mind that. You think I *made* that cop shoot me?"

Jesus, I needed to shut up. My dry, faint sarcasm had gotten me into trouble more than once, usually in swilleries at two in the morning. So I was damn glad he'd turned his camera off.

"Why would a trained police officer – a Protector who's marched through hot Sands defending the Homeland – shoot you if you didn't have a gun or a detonator, right? Let's start with that. Which one was it?"

"You drink your Kool-Aid in a sippy-cup?"

"What do you mean?"

"It's an historical reference. Anyway, it ever occur to you that we're competitors in telling *my* story?"

"What, you think you're a *journalist*? Living around here and looking like that? Not for money."

Nicki been bending his ear? "Now get this: I didn't go to all that trouble lugging that backpack around in this heat to not try to make a chunk of change off it. I mean, you got to pay the rent somehow, right?"

"How much were you hoping to make?"

"A couple of hundred bucks for writing about it. It's called participatory journalism, popular back when you were playing with mud pies."

Man, I'd better be careful when this guy turned his camera back on, cause none of this sounded on-target. I could *physically* feel it up there somehow, my head not firing on all cylinders. I sure didn't need to be talking about money before discussing my primary concern – that's right, damnit – the searches' assault on civil liberties.

"No, I mean how much were you counting on for getting shot in the head?"

"You ever use your brains for anything but keeping your ears apart? For instance, how did I manage to arrange it that that cop would only graze me? Tell me that, bright boy. Not that it wouldn't be nice to have the MTA pay my rent for a while."

He stared back, and then Boss-Man interrupted to say his shrimp roll was ready. Guess I'd have a TV gig too if all I had for lunch was a damn shrimp roll. He threw two bills on the counter and said, "These witticisms are too priceless to waste. I'm going to turn on the camera, and you decide your next move."

The bright light caught me delicately finger-combing my hair, the suddenly enormous camera searching for zits from three feet away.

His cool, disaffected drone perked right up. "Tell New York: *You're ... the ... Only... One!*" He then gave a lying little intro about an interview with the man of the moment at a local restaurant I'd chosen. Great, cause that meant I chose to dress like that too. Before I could protest, he launched right in. "So it wasn't just about the money was it? You maintain you had some other purpose involving the police?"

What the hell, this guy had found *Naked Opposition* so quick? "I'm not quite sure I know what you mean?"

"Is it that you don't know, or is prevarication how you make it through the day?"

Oh spare me, vocabulary-boy. With his Protector-coddling sound bites. no way he'd let me challenge the whole search paradigm. But if he'd read Stanley's article and caught me fudging about my plans, that'd brand me a liar for good. I fell back until the ropes caught me at the edge of the canvas, the crowd roaring for blood. "*Prevarication*? You know, I'm just a simple lad who's washed up here in Queens."

"Washed up – no kidding."

I tried to beat him to the punch. "That wasn't correct what you said before about me 'absconding' from the hospital. I haven't hid myself away anywhere. I went home because I wasn't happy with the level of care I was receiving at Bellevue. The morning I left – Jesus, yesterday it was – no one even came to as much as take my temperature. So, free, white and over twenty-one – I mean, over twenty-one of any color, of course – I don't need anyone's permission to check out of a lousy hospital."

"OK, let's talk about that. You got yourself discharged?"

"Look, Bellevue's a funny place. A lot of weird stuff happened up in Bellevue that *I'll* write about myself in my own good time."

"So you got discharged? Got your bill and left?"

Obviously they were putting it out that I skipped on the bill. Well, I'd sound a fool just blurting out wild accusations for this guy to carve up about cops in the next bed, and Lurch in his fake uniform, and docs with knock-out needles. I needed to make a cogent accusation all laid out carefully in print. No good was coming from this line of talk. Besides, usually contenting myself with two Displeasures at most, this meal he was ruining had cost real money. All I wanted was to eat and loose myself in the sports section for a few minutes before returning home to try, somehow, to pull my chestnuts from the fire – that and maybe a visit from the Wife. Was that asking for the moon?

"Look, unlike revenge, this gourmet offering is not a meal best served cold. It's my first real meal in – "

"Is that some kind of threat?"

"No, that's Shakespeare – an English playwright."

"Very clever. So what's your response to the engendered discharge wounding innocent bystander Carole Fiore in the midst of your planned encounter with the police?"

"I feel terrible about Carole, obviously, and I'm thrilled to read that she's recovering. You're right, she is an innocent bystander. Like me, someone just putting one foot in front of the other."

"Really? That's what you were doing in Penn Station?"

"I was just going from Point A to Point B as far as those cops who shot Ms. Fiore and myself knew."

"But that's not the whole truth, is it?"

"You tell me. Why, cause I had a backpack?"

"What about your anti-anti-Fiend intentions? Because a peculiar website called, *Naked* – "

"Right, of course. *Naked Opposition.* I was about to steer you there myself for background if you were interested. I e-mailed the editor there yesterday a bit about my plans. You might find it useful."

"You mean useful to know that you had set out to obstruct T Containment?"

"Nothing I can do to stop you putting that traction on it if you like. But I would urge people to go read *Naked Opposition* themselves."

"Protectors have deemed these quotes legitimate. One minute."

And he adroitly scrunched up his shoulder to pin the camera to his chin, his hands free to scroll. He tut-tutted to himself a moment, then said, "According to material posted this morning by a blog called *Naked Opposition*, you stated – I guess the word 'I' is missing in a pathetic attempt to avoid blame – 'Hope to galoot around enough to spark a search and then draw myself up in high dungeon for a principled refusal.' I'm not sure I get all that. Galoot – what's that? And a dungeon. What, you were going to refuse somehow from your jail cell?"

"Words, you know. They're neat – especially in a private communication with your spouse. More to the point, what the hell are the cops doing 'legitimizing' my private e-mail? Another thing: That wasn't 'material,' that was an article published by a respected news site. Got almost a half-million hits already this morning." Maybe. Stanley my first conduit to the world on this, might as well buck him up.

He sticked his box some more, then, "Here's the money quote: 'I was carrying a backpack, and' – wait a minute, *here*: 'I was going to refuse to submit to a search. So anything was possible.' "

"Well, That's right. Someone had to do it. People going about their daily lives cannot be stopped and searched for no reason. Period. Aside from the fact that it doesn't work, given that you can *usually* turn and walk away, it's against everything this country used to stand for. And maybe it's time we took it back."

"Took it back from who?"

"Oh, please. It's no different than the cops on trains with dogs and submachine guns, the helicopters everywhere, or the police racing through town in caravans of fifty – all it does is frighten people so they'll agree to whatever the government wants. And we've all seen where that's gotten us."

"Where's that?"

"You know any Boots?"

"Not personally. That's not my scene. Anyway, you wrote, 'Anything can happen.' So you were willing for civilians to get shot as well?"

"Civilians *as well*? Does this look like a uniform to you? Hot Tuna? Hey, stay electric, Jorma!"

"Hot what? Never mind. So, you *were* willing?"

"Look, you can play gotcha all you want, but if you don't mind – and even if you do – I'm gonna go home and finish my goop, cause it doesn't seem you're going to leave me alone. Viewers at home, I'll be writing about my ordeal as soon as the Stuffing permits. That's, uh, my little pet name for what happened to my head. So, uhm – hi, Mom. All that baloney. And to Ms. Fiore, Godspeed on your recovery."

I stood up, realized I couldn't manage an open soda along with cupcakes, newspapers and the rest of my food, and so drained the Dr. P. Over at the counter I asked for a plastic bag to dump it all in and suffered a Boss-Man lecture on not bringing soda into "my store when I got orange soda like that." Not wanting to be rude to a man who regularly made me food, I turned too late to see NYONLY filming my leavings. I stood behind him a moment wondering what was so fascinating, then saw he'd flipped my *Chirp* from the sports to the front page for a shot of Carole and her fiancé amidst my cold, greasy mass of picked-over food. I tapped him on the shoulder to move, waited, then – though I knew he'd use it to ill effect – brushed rudely past to the table as he intended.

Damn my head for not allowing me to flee when Boss-Man handed breakfast over, cause that had been one stone-bad encounter. I banged out the door, hitched up my shorts and trudged off, compounding any number of gaffes by looking (guiltily) over my shoulder to see him standing in the doorway filming away. A wonder I didn't flip him off.

I certainly wasn't disclosing my back-fence route, so I headed straight for the ABC truck by Stap's front gate, finding it blessedly locked and empty. First stroke of luck since meeting Maureen – who seemed of a more innocent time, when all I confronted was murderous cops, not online 'Movement' mavens and pretty-boy TV reporters. Thank God his camera was turned off for most of that embarrassment. I couldn't remember if he'd turned it on in time for a decent quip about the playwright, not that he'd ever use it.

Chapter Twenty-Three

Nickilicious No More

My luck continued to hold as Mr. Staphilopoulos came charging up the hall from out back, his shirt particularly faded for the occasion and his pomegranate hair awry. I braced myself, but he was grinning. "I see you not thief anymore – you use the front door."

"I'm sorry, Stap. I needed something to eat before I could talk to anyone."

"You a tough guy to figure, mister, dressing like a bum, staying up there all day doing whatever you do. Then going out at night with that little radio of yours playing stupid baseball, but going where, still dressed like that? Now it turns out – I have friends with Internet – you some kind of writer. Somebody who tells the government to get lost!"

"Look, Stap, I can explain, or try to anyway. It's all about protecting basic rights. This bit with the subways – "

"I don't know about subways if that's what you mixed in now. I don't ride them, don't care about them. But I asked and my friend, the Turk, found stuff you wrote from years ago – OK stuff."

(He'd told me the story: he'd had a fling with the Turk's sister back when dinosaurs roamed and, though properly affronted, the Turk initiated their cats-and-dogs-sleeping-together friendship by bowing to the sacred compact among husbands and helping to conceal it from Stap's wife, long since fled on numerous grounds.)

"Oh, that."

"You don't think I understand all that, a man who had to leave Greece, go up mountain in middle of the night with clothes on my back, no goodbyes to nobody?"

"You mean with the colonels?"

"An American knows about them? So, Mr. Bird-Brains, no

more dress like this, you got the TVs after you, OK? And don't worry. When you getting beauty sleep last night, I sent them away?"

"Sent who away?"

"Two men in suits, said they were from the railroad. Shit-hole cops. I told them come back with papers from a judge. Told them I pay a lot of damn taxes on this house. More than anyone around here with that backyard no good to nobody till I'm dead. They should look that up before they bother me. Me or my, my *housemates* – that's the word."

"You sent them away? What'd they want?"

"They wanted you, 'to talk' – ha! And a woman, dressed nice, *looks* nice – she made me laugh, laughed right in her face when she said she was your wife. Said she was worried about you. No cop, I don't think. Probably newsie, always being a sneak. She wanted your bell on the door, said you weren't answering your micro-thing. She was funny. Like a man like you living here got a wife like her. I said sure, *that's* his bell. I pointed, you know, to all those bells there, and I went inside."

"Stap!"

"She stood ringing those broken bells and then she just yelling your name, yelling loud as hell. A lot of noise out of a skinny girl – not *too* skinny. I stand behind the door, can't believe it, think maybe she climb up, go knock on a window upstairs."

"Jesus, Stap. She – "

"Wait. Then some coloreds, three or four hanging out down on the corner, come up cause she's yelling. And they all want to be a big help, but she ignores them. It was almost ten o'clock, and I thought for a minute they were gonna come in my gate, and believe me, I be out there quick with my knife, asking no questions. Not because of newsie-girl, and not because they colored. But this is *my* house, and they better know that. But she's smart. She sits right down in my chair on the porch and crosses her legs like a cool cookie waiting for a man to come down. And then she left, soon as they go."

"That *was* my wife. Technically we're still married."

"Sure, Big Stuff, whatever you say. You not like my other guys upstairs, right? So listen, no fights over a girl – wife, sure – you got that? OK, I send her up. But I don't think she come here again. She don't like it down here by the river, no yellow taxis every twenty feet."

"Damn. Shit, Stap!"

"That's right. Women: damn shit."

"Maybe it's just as well. I was in a fog last night with my head, and that's not like I want to see her cause I got maybe one or two more chances with her. Hell, I'm still in a fog. And thanks about those cops. They said they were MTA?"

"MTA, what's that? They flash a badge two seconds. American cops I don't care about except they sit on my balls. But these damn TVs, their trucks in everybody's spot, the whole block a mess. There were two last night, so Georgos had to park around the corner and walk back alone, old as he is. How long they chase you?"

"Only until I get my story out – write it myself and then they'll lose interest. I'm not so good today, but I'm gonna try to start."

"You got shot, mister. Messing with that blonde I saw her picture on TV – how you do it, a guy like you? That pretty woman you call your wife and now this blonde, a young man's dream? I give you a beer for your secret, a big bottle like you buy. Walking through train stations with what – a pack? I know you not running away leaving all your stuff upstairs."

"What stuff?"

"Your junk. All those boxes of paper up there."

"What the hell, Stap!"

"I looked in your rooms yesterday. I want to know if you have bombs like they making little talk about on TV – what's the word – not *jokes*."

"I don't know – hints."

"Hints, right. But a man who got nothing don't leave what little he got. Going over mountain late at night not your way. Me? I had a lot in Greece, but that's a separate story."

"Mr. Staphilopoulos, you're right. But let me get out of here before that TV guy parked there shows up again. Meanwhile, if my wife comes back – who knows? – do me a favor and send her up, OK? And Mr. Staphilopoulos, I appreciate all your help, all your guard-dogging. Cause we got colonels over here too."

"You got money? You need ten dollars?"

"Stap, I'm good. Ask me next week."

****

Wow, keeper of the keep, Staphilopoulos, refugee and politically astute new friend. Upstairs I saw that *N.O.* was bouncing like a red rubber ball, number three on the day's ranking behind only a particularly well-lit beheading whole-vid, and the global-exclusive from Jacquine's steady limo driver that she's really a he, the itchy-pants driver claiming to know. Christ, number three! Not bad, Stanley, for a piece that, for all its nonsense, did discuss the politics of challenging the searches. So maybe something might come of that *if* the civ-lib aspect didn't get swift-boated overboard.

I forced myself to the mirror to contemplate the snug Hot Tuna tee, decades old and an indeterminate color. Man, NYONLY's video would probably bounce too, the already infamous wastrel scarfing grease in a shabby Chinese, talking trash before beating an ignominious retreat. I turned and caught the horror-show band-aid I kept forgetting, and then Frankie loomed up in his cold-blooded, two-handed shooting stance. And I cracked. But only for a second, damnit! A sob, a choke and a single, long, loud "Aaarrrgghhhghhgh!" was all I gave them. Let the many buzzards circling low fight over that. That's right. Panic attacks, sure, but I'd shed not one tear over Nick. None of that *Tears get in my ears/Lying down crying over you* garbage.

Collapsing in the big wing-chair wedged between fridge and window, my refuge since college, my thoughts dragged against my will to our first date when I'd thrown my sole, time-tested seduction strategy out the window. (Kiss her till both your jaws ache on the first date, but touch nothing covered by a bikini. Not foolproof, of course, but the gentlemanly lack of a clothed grope blossomed over the intervening days and typically rendered the lucky lass horizontal come your second date.) Rather, a few kisses in, I'd startled myself – certainly not Nickilicious – by reaching out for her succulent right breast on the street by her apartment. My left hand the one wired to the pleasure center,

194

therefore her right breast. Sitting there, I couldn't conjure how to re-spark a flame that for most of the last nine years she'd help fan right along.

Pushing noon, I was entitled to call. She'd journeyed to Bumfuckville the night before, so she'd just have to come again, come sit an hour in my kitchen looking askance. That and hugging me twice, damnit – coming and going. And then I could think of facing the future, would be forced to by how she turned to offer a cheek where once she'd melted at the end of a tentative left hand.

No answer at home. Dialing her micro-zap, I realized she'd have some reaction to Stanley and Benson's beat-downs, so best to have my print-outs at hand when she started yelling. Low and intense and angrier probably than the night she smashed the Christmas tree ornaments, she poured molten ice in my ear. "Did you see what they did, your idiot friend Stanley, and of course that prick at the *Slimes*? What – Charley? Forget Charley. Padwick himself is going to shit a cow that Fornix & Foyst got dragged into your nonsense. That twerp at the *Slimes* knew exactly what he was doing mentioning my promotion and that new Army money in the same sentence. Everybody knew I was going to be the lead writer on that. A $167-million-dollar ad buy! Do you have any idea how much F&F creams off the top of that and how much would drip down even to me?"

"Nicki, he had to put in where you work cause that's where he encountered you. And that bit about Army recruitment is just boilerplate on Fornix & Foyst cause it's a big new account. Anyway, where are you?"

"And that damn Stanley putting in all that Internet stuff to prove you contacted me at work about your plans in advance. It's like I'm an accessory before the fact."

"Accessory to what? Come on, you know I wasn't doing anything illegal. Besides, I thought you approved."

"I'll be lucky if they wait till Monday to fire me. And I got a big nut to make now every month in the City."

"They're not going to fire you. Tell them you don't even live with me anymore."

"That'll be the least of it. But look, I came all the way out there to your ridiculous … *home* to see you last night, and your bizarre landlord was no help at all."

"He's OK. He thought you were a reporter, couldn't believe I have so enchanting a wife, however temporarily. Besides, he told two MTA DTs to scram if they didn't have a warrant, so I can't complain. So, uh, Nick, what happens when I call you back at home?"

"Why don't you fucking grow up. I don't even know if I'm getting escorted from F&F with just my picture of Otis in my hand in about forty-eight hours. They're sure not gonna let me work on what's a hell of a challenge convincing black and brown kids to step up. I already had a tagline working: *Army. Because we ALL bleed red.*"

"Do you ever listen to yourself? Huh, Nicki? Sending kids to a Sands isn't exactly CheeseSpray…. Nicki?" Ah, going all silent – my all-time favorite Nick tactic. "So how is Otis?"

"He's fine, though he doesn't like it that the windows in my new place don't open."

"Smart cat doesn't want to live in a sealed tomb."

Our cat, torn from my bosom, the clever black and white tuxedo job who Nick appropriated as a matter of course.

"Look, Nicki, I know we're down the tubes, but I'd still like to see you today. Some nurse told me that depression kicks in with a head injury, and it's just – things are tough right now."

"I can make it tomorrow, but not tonight."

"What about this afternoon?"

"It's just not a good time today."

"Busy, huh?"

"Look, tomorrow I'll be able to tell you all about the great theatrical sensation. Someone scalped tickets for like five-hundred each – and he was lucky to get them – for *Abu Ghraib, the Musical*. You know, the one that Jacquine dropped out of over artistic differences about her nude scene."

Someone.

I let it alone cause what was the point. Besides, like everyone else, I was distracted by Jacquine. Some thought the musical's subject a bit outré. But, so many years later, the argument that sufficient time had passed to allow for a light-hearted reconsideration carried the day. Especially after the producers circulated opening-night pictures of HeadMan's brittle, waxen girlfriend cackling away in the eighth row, most folks surprised she could move her face enough to laugh.

Its first-half-closer, featuring hundreds of little lights winking out in the backdrop, represented the fate of Boots and even others (it was said). Then the second act opened with an aircraft carrier steaming on stage, hurrahs turning to horror as it catapulted little souvenir planes out into the audience. The Sands brought to Broadway, the tickets with the same waivers in infinitesimal print that baseball tickets had about foul balls.

Two female guards did a competitive striptease in front of the chorus of prisoners, and a mousey female guard's first-half flirtation with a tough-guy mercenary blossomed into a precarious, love-conquers-all romance in the second half. But the noose tightening, the brute turned state's evidence against her, and she tragically chose not to head home to her family in disgrace. The mercenary's bathos-laden, self-lacerating lament was all over the radio for about three weeks until it was pulled one day – often in mid-song – never to return. All in all a boffo show with hen's-teeth tickets despite its dependence on drum machines.

"I hope one of those little planes gets him. So, you told the *Slimes*, now I'm supposedly fat as well as a scam artist too cheap to cough up train fare."

"I told you that creep shocked the shit out of me telling me you were the other shooting victim. I was back on my heels the entire time. I know you're just big boned even if your head alone weighs thirty-seven pounds. But even you must know you have bigger problems than your stupid vanity, cause they're saying you had a detonator or a gun."

"And you believe that shit?"

"Of course not. I know that's not your scene."

"Screw that and screw the *Slimes*. What you don't realize is that *Naked Opposition* is the more important story. Wait – listen! That's cause it gives some idea, in my words and Stanley's, of the civ-lib stuff I was doing."

"It ever occur to you that that kind of twisted thinking is why your career never took off – even when you had that big score – thinking that some blog is more important than a front-page story in the *New York* fucking *Slimes*!"

"Look, I'm gonna get the truth out on Penn Station, but I'm kinda foggy and can't really write right now."

"How about you skip the writing and call a lawyer. Your father probably still knows somebody cause I don't know if you want to use ours. Jesus, what's his name, it's been so long since we even heard from him."

"Steve. Yeah, well, he's working contingency, so we'll hear from him when we hear from him. Did you punt all the personal stuff from my e-mail you forwarded, or did Stanley delete it out of the goodness of his heart?"

"I deleted it. That Stanley is a joke. Miss Universe gets shot, you get shot, and he's worried about you using goofy verbs in an e-mail."

"I am so screwed. Look at that freaking headline in the *Slimes*: 'Wife Wonders if Money Woes Sparked Attack....' " I could hear her shushing someone, her new Mr. Right-All-The-Time. "I could catch Moby Dick in my hat next week, and that headline is all people would remember. I gotta go. Gotta go 'flounder' my way through another 'professional dry spell.' Or so I hear tell."

"I'll call you tomorrow to let you know what time I can come over."

"Yeah, well, hopefully he'll kick you out of bed by noon."

"Bye."

And she hung up, like I was the one messing up. Hell, maybe I was and for a long time too, the past week just icing. A thousand freaking dollars to go to a show, the Wife had a hot thang going with some moneybags and couldn't be bothered to hide it. I could just hope MoneyBags hadn't discovered that special little live-wire spot on her lower back yet.

****

Work my best refuge, the stakes weren't high, just clearing my name. Man, the going was slow, searching for words and fumbling details. Surprised I didn't have to look at the keyboard.

After a rough hour, my head pitching forward towards the machine, I was hitting the hay or the hay was hitting me. I printed out a couple of pages of scrambled notes – Stan the Man right again: until it's on paper, it ain't saved, not really – and called it a start.

Slipping off, something that had rankled since my first exchange with Stanley propelled itself to the surface, its subcutaneous tickle finally breaking through. Both he and that NYONLY slickster – God, had he really turned off his camera like he said? – had warned me in no uncertain terms to boot any skeletons from my closet. And, yup, I did have bones to kick to the curb, bones so new, bits of flesh had yet to fall. I wrote *Indiana* on my palm and fell instantly asleep.

The phone jangled after what felt like a long time, Pop sans preliminaries. "You did it for money? Why didn't you come to me if you needed a couple of hundred dollars?"

"Sure, Pop, I did it for the money – a lot more than a couple of hundred dollars. The only problem is I won't see it for like two years. Pop, that's ridiculous. How in the world could I know that cop would only graze me?"

"So you're being sarcastic. I get it. Your being so clever, boy, is gonna turn around someday and bite you in the ass."

Some might say at Penn Station it sorta already had. We didn't talk long. Too dazed to work, a snooze topped off my main nap till hunger drove me to those Dominican pups, a fine, tasteless platform for mustard and ketchup.

I tried committing further halting words, but damn tough to concentrate with that ink on my palm. Heck, any claim to being a regular Joe had flown out the window through the barrel of a gun two days before. So go ahead and empty my closet before someone else did, not that the two bastards with their own bones – twins to mine – would be so inclined. Short and sweet and don't even try to get paid for such a confession. Just hope the damage would be outweighed in a day or two by the sheer news heft of "Embarking on an Exemplary Refusal." Or simply, "A Sad Farce." Either of those "Penn Tale" titles would set mice to clicking.

I started musing happily on where to publish … "Shot by a Nose." *Blackboard*? Nah, they'd chop it off at the knees with the ripe nonsense that no one read more than five-hundred words online. *Defiant Obeisance* or *Big Buckets of Hail*? Hell, aim big: *Morning Dyspepsia* and be done with it.

In the meantime, I still had a boringly sober, soberly etc. Saturday evening to get through, both baseball teams having played day games. I plodded uphill through the spelling of 'cat,' not quite able to summon the name of that other one with paws and a tail who chases cats. The walls closing in (not far to go), I ventured out to the hall around ten, it feeling oddly like the locked, 3:00 a.m. study-room in a college library. This a Saturday, the one night Stap granted license to howl, yet there was no 'salsa' (it was all salsa to me) throbbing up from the third floor. Heading to the stairs, I heard no feet pounding from room to room, no calls in Spanish or faint phisst! of a pop-top. Two guys down there were *whispering* for some bizarre reason.

Gazing mournfully out the hall window to the towers lost in murk across the nearby East River, I gave Otis a wave in case he was futilely trying to sniff some 'air.' Beyond, despite vast expenditures of candlepower, the Times Square behemoths merely hinted their presence, the Despoilers paying big for something barely seen. Finding little solace gazing west, I went to the opposite window to sneer at another damn TV truck – late to the party, boys – and look out over the low rooftops to the planes stacked up over Cheney Int'l.

Soon curled defensively on my side, I peered up at the vertical coffin's ceiling far above. Hell, we'd had a good run and such larks as I'd probably not see again. Turning forty had hit Nicki like a ton of bricks, but then her career took flight, what with her string of quirky successes de scandale. And clients with nothing to lose (fifth or sixth in their category) soon beat down the door at a fusty old Fornix & Foyst gone unexpectedly edgy. Rejuvenated man-about-town, Ernesto Padwick, had gladly bid adieu to the old fogey who'd quit in disgust, especially since the latter's main client, a blue-blood private bank, had been recently gobbled up by a South Korean manufacturer of steel buildings.

With her every outrage and subsequent raise, Nicki seemed to regard ours as some sort of morganatic marriage. I kept walking that plank pointed Left till eventually the Big Town stole her away. No, we weren't destined to grow old together.

Static with the police and the press not nearly as dire as love gone sour, I laughed at the post-Penn coven of MoFo demi-ghouls gathering high up in the corners trying to amass sufficient weight to descend upon me. I turned the light out and rolled on my back to summon visions of succor (not daring to aim for true happiness) that began with a bowl of coffee-shop soup *and* preceded the crushing, (Neil) LaButian revelation of Maureen's true intent.

Chapter Twenty-Four

The Frying Pan Flips

The Stuffing felt darn good come Sunday morning, and I lay there pondering a downgrade to Breadcrumbs. Approaching an age when you don't wake regretting having had five too few, my satisfaction at such *Saturday*-night virtue, plus feeling somewhat like myself, was tempered by the day's foreboding confession regarding Indiana.

Heeding Stap's advice, I threw on some slacks (absurd in the heat) and a real shirt, and caught sight of myself on the way out. Oddly enough – not that the poor bastard made it that far – it was Orwell who noted you wake up at fifty with the face you deserve. But then, water unavailable, he'd shave with wine during the Spanish Civil War. The dawn of fifty no longer dozens of years off, I wasn't exactly hollow-cheeked, but the past days of irregular eating and no beering lent a nicely gaunt(ish) look.

So a relatively cheery lad was I heading out for the *Toast* and *Daily Chirp* and an egg sandwich, never mind the Wonder Bread the bodega couldn't transcend. Still before eight on a Sunday, hopefully it was too early for any newsies downstairs, or perhaps they'd even lost interest, NYONLY having beaten them to the punch. Assuming he wasn't sitting on it, I'd check out Mr. Fabulous's story online after breakfast.

Sweating some by the time I galumphed down the stairs that stayed largely in place beneath my feet, I passed a couple of Latino dudes sweating their way up. They met my grunt of a greeting with angry stares. Word had obviously gotten out that I was responsible for the cop cars cruising outside, the Fuji blimp no doubt overhead to immortalize all our features for the new Domesday Book. (Back before people grew so politically demobilized and demoralized, Fuji let the NYPD use its blimp to observe and presumably record demonstrators down in the streets below.) After resolving some of the niggling little issues haunting my life, I needed to organize the boycott Fuji so richly deserved.

I tossed a goofy grin at the plain-clothes with a crew cut lounging in the dark Ford out front, a cluster of electronics under the dash. Turd-Touch spooking the Latinos (hence the hush on the floors below me the night before), had I also halted commerce by the projects a block away? How soon before everyone, including Stap's buddies objecting to the TV trucks usurping their parking spots, united to pressure the Greek to throw my disruptive ass out? Rather than nodding appreciatively at my geek duds, the cop just eye-fucked me, then reached for his radio. Which raised the question of why the Red Squad bothered with an unmarked car. Less theoretically, how did I know he even was a state security MoFo rather than a private goon – and which was worse, assuming there was any real difference?

At the bodega, my buddy the counterman interrupted my gasping dash through the *Toast*. "My friend, we give big thanks to you for all the TV people here with Manhattan money. Cops too. Many cigarettes and coffee and even food we sell because you a big star."

"Big freaking star – right here on the front page, my whole life in the toilet."

"We see that this morning and big surprise. But any story in newspapers is good. Tell me, more TV people today – what do you think? I need know how much bacon to cook."

"Who knows. Maybe there'll be a funeral instead, and all my friends will come – big eaters and drinkers all three of 'em."

"No, no – no funeral, I *personally* will see to that. A young man like you, many women ahead, now you a star. You know already – that's why you dressed up today."

"OK, you personally guarantee no funeral. That I'll take. Thank you in advance." He made me a damn nice sandwich.

I stumbled home staring at the *Toast*'s front page surveillance camera photo of Ms. Hubba-Hubba striding down that Penn Station corridor "seconds before the engendered shot" said the caption. You could almost feel the oomph of her parade in that dress. But even Carole paled before the headline picking my bones clean.

PENN SUSPECT A HITLER FAN
MONEY-SCHEME WITH AD-BIG WIFE AT ARMY AGENCY
CRIMINAL PAST, BIZARRE LINCOLN CENTER ARREST

Something was as rotten as could be. Forget the photos gracing the page 4/page 5 spread: my ancient, chock-full-of-nerd high school yearbook photo, and the (sexy) drunken-slattern shot of Nicki laughing uproariously that she was afraid would surface. Cause five cherry-picking, *Toast* scoundrels, led by one Nathan E. Tredwell, had culled details of my e-mails, incoming and outgoing both, along with my phone call the day before to Pop.

BARMY BACKPACKER COURTED DANGER
By Nathan E. Tredwell

According to a host of officials who must remain nameless so as to escape censure for prejudicing the potential jury pool, the Backpack Bungler who caused a defensive police shooting on a jammed Penn Station concourse Thursday, staged it as a "stunt" to, he admitted, make the "big bucks." What's more, he showed a shocking indifference to innocent-bystander casualties; has both Nazi and communist East German Army linkages; plotted the attack with his wife, an executive at an advertising agency crucial to American military readiness; and is freighted with a tawdry legal history suggesting a vendetta against Mass Transit Protectors. The *Toast* has also learned he refers to his fellow New Yorkers as 'sheep' for following proper, lawful orders from the front-line Heroes who daily keep us safe.

Conferring by phone with an unknown colleague and potential paymaster who he referred to as 'Pop,' the Penn Station shooting Suspect was heard to say on Saturday, two days after the near-massacre, "Sure, Pop, I did it for the money – a lot more than a couple of hundred dollars. The only problem is I won't see it for like two years."

T officials are still working to uncover the projected use for any money obtained in what appears to be, as one put it, "A deliberate, find a broken sidewalk, trip-and-sue scheme." And several issues remain to be clarified. For instance, noted one senior police commander, "How did he know to be lurking in that Penn Station corridor just as the officers and their National Guard escort rounded the corner?"

Another source feared the worst: that any eventual court award might have been slated for a neo-Nazi effort since, shockingly, the Suspect carried a copy of Adolf Hitler's hate-book, *Mein Kampf*. In a communiqué prior to the incident with a woman apparently his wife, the Suspect referred to Hitler's officially condemned hate-screed as "a necessary document."

A subsequent source wondered at the training that enabled the Suspect to dodge his head so precisely to ensure a non-fatal grazing after eliciting Thursday's weapons discharge. "That's treading a fine line, and that sort of expertise doesn't come cheap and it doesn't come easy," this close-arms combat veteran said. He added ominously, "I doubt it's even American in origin."

In a statement somehow captured by a marginal cable outlet, the Suspect thundered, "Not that it wouldn't be nice to have the MTA pay my rent for a while. Just get this: I didn't go to all that trouble lugging that backpack around in this heat to not try to make a chunk of change off it. I mean, you got to pay the rent somehow, right?"

This was his admission of a direct, mercenary plan to challenge the lawful *random* search paradigm so beloved by the public. As subway rider Denis Naufrasen of Tidal Basin, Brooklyn put it, "When no one has any rights, we're all equal. I just thank God for Commissioner Ted and hope to be voting for him for higher office soon."

TAWDRY AND ALARMING CRIMINAL HISTORY

The *Toast* has also learned of the Suspect's criminal record, a history both alarming and tawdry that he himself recognizes as a liability. In an e-mail to his confederate, one Stanley Netherhall, whose obscure blog has published a number of his musings, the Knapsack Knucklehead expressed concern about "the cops dredging up who knows what wretched excess from my checkered past."

Wretched and excessive indeed. He was arrested and charged with trespassing and disorderly conduct at a free, outdoor Arlo Guthrie concert at Lincoln Center. It took five New York police officers to subdue him and his confederate/spouse after a dozen-member Lincoln Center security detail shrank at the prospect. A senior NYPD source noted that though the Suspect was declared "an imminent threat to public order of unknown severity," the police were able to contain the dangerous duo and defer action until the concert's end so as not to disrupt the folkie-heaven event.

In fact, such was the Protectors' skill, there was no need to resort to the commonplace orange plastic netting which has so improved New Yorkers' quality of life. "He was speaking out of turn, so he paid the price. We made sure of that," said the senior Front-Line Responder. "He had beef with Lincoln Center – their guards were really ticked off. They told us what to do, and we went to work."

****

Whoever was stuffing my life down Tredwell's maw also fed him my couple of standard-issue open container violations on city subways, plus the "pending offense involving foul language directed at the person of an official MTA Public Facilitator. These malfactions on the trains may indicate the source of some sort of personal vendetta against transport securers."

Tredwell, et. al. then slammed into Nicki at top speed, discussing her work for the Army's minority enlistment campaign. "Given the manifest need for patriotic replacements to plug holes in the T Campaign's defensive projections, the Pentagon is anxious for new initiatives to drive enlistment. The previous nonwhite campaign – *Shoot Someone Over There Cause You Can't Kill The Bastards Here* – was initially praised for its off-beat charm, yet it was discontinued when only 117 African-Descents offered themselves last year."

Then there was this, which speaks for itself:

"The Normative Forensic Diagnostician on the case, whose name is being withheld since he lives with his mother, is still researching the import of the Backpack Bungler's statement, "My head feels like it's made of tapioca." The Endowed NFD theorized, "Is he so delusional that he believes his head is constructed of a pudding? Or is he signaling co-conspirators about liquid explosives hidden in a lavatory – as the vulgate would have it, the 'head?' "

The Diagnostician did admit to total bafflement trying to decode this instruction from what he termed a driven antiestablishmentarian: "Spare me your namby-pamby, Kumbaya load." The reference may be to "some sort of new threat we've not yet seen," the NFD warned. He added, "I can only hope the authorities follow HeadMan's leadership in remaining *Bold, Extolled, Impregnable!*"

Finally, in a homoerotic passage that days later still drips with psycho-sexual significance, the Suspect threw down a hirsute gauntlet to a co-conspirator with whom he would seem to have a complex and cantankerous relationship. When Netherhall directed him to clear anything incriminating from his "closet" and declared him "effete," he shot back, "I hope your scrawny ass looks lousy in [its] wispy, scraggily beard...."

Admitting his inability to fully interpret this statement for an advertiser-supported newspaper, the NFD did note the seemingly bifurcated appeal of underdeveloped yet nonetheless hair-covered buttocks. "I'd be the first to acknowledge their appeal," he said. "Still, it's an acquired taste not for the uninitiated. It may well be tied in somehow with his taped statement characterizing his own mother as 'baloney.' Such strained relations with the primary initial imprint-object are definitely T-normative."

I was eventually linked to Communism, Satanism, child pornography, anarchists, illegal weapons, East Germany, pyromania, and North Korea. Everything but the sinking of the *Maine*.

Not bad, not bad at all I concluded, daintisly smearing a morsel of egg from my lips with the back of my hand. A single phone call and a few woefully unguarded e-mails – sent a day or two before, in more innocent times when I foolishly dared think of them as off-limits to the press – were all that the *Toast* needed to chop-suey my life. Voila, America, your latest violent, delusional psychopath.

All that, yet Tredwell couldn't find room for a word on my civ-lib concerns. Nothing of my statement to Nicki that it was high time someone took a stand. And certainly no mention of Stanley's musings that resisting the searches just might spark something bigger. Nor was there anything of my mutterings to Stanley about being physically restrained in Bellevue. A neat bit of stove-piping indeed.

I pictured poor Nicki sitting across from a permanently tanned but nonetheless apoplectic Ernesto come Monday morning. No ad agency got the fifteen percent commission on media buys that was standard when dinosaurs roamed. For the sake of argument, halve that and say that F&F got 7.5% – an assumption – of the $167-million campaign. That rounded off to $12.5 million, right, Ernesto? If I somehow ever spoke to the Wife again, I'd just have to say she was far better off growing radishes or whatever it was she found for herself. Hell, I sent the damn e-mail to her job to make sure she got it – I didn't mean anything malicious.

Nor did it sound remotely good about NYONLY. Time to see the damn thing, which I'd certainly been in no mood for while my useless Saturday unspooled. I sprang to the machine – that is, turned slightly in my chair – and, what the hell: "Access Denied." How could I not freaking get a cable channel's home page? I beat my head against a couple of digital doors and finally pried one a crack to see that *my* machine was specifically denied. It referenced the Net gobbledygook address of the box on my kitchen table. I threw it across the room.

****

No I didn't. Man, the *Toast* was gonna suck all the air out of the room, leaving none for some actually positive *Daily Chirp* articles. One was an exclusive with the slinky girl from Penn Station and her boyfriend, the big Asian dude with the Mohawk. They said I'd been holding a simple transistor radio which they whole-vid minutes after I'd gotten shot. But that was minutes before the cops confiscated their legal, college-sanctioned whole-vid. His name was Marko (as I maybe recalled her saying), and she was Bethany, both of them film students at Brooklyn College. They'd contacted the *Chirp* to demand the return of their camera and everything it contained. Marko had stored a semester's worth of work in two courses in it and Bethany one – courses that neither could afford to flunk.

The cops let them have it, citing their prior disorderly conduct arrests for 'unauthorized documentation' of that infamous vegan-rights Demo that turned ugly when the lamb that protestors symbolically released spooked a police horse. The intrepid pair had whole-vid a cop Tazing the lamb. Plus, like me, they had their own frictional costs of riding the trains. Marko had the standard, late-night open container ticket besmirching his record, while Bethany had been caught smoking a cigarette on one of the elevated platforms out in Brooklyn.

For pity's sake, hide the children and the old folks.

The next page featured Carole in her high school cheerleading outfit, pompoms aflutter, next to the welcome news that, such was the outpouring of restorative love from the entire city, she was feeling well enough to probably be released on Tuesday. The TV chat-fests were already making competing offers for her first interview – a bout of penetrating political analysis surely on tap.

The *Chirp* also reported that, "MTA Protector Franklin Reisner has yet to return to his Staten Island home and has been reluctantly reported as missing by his wife, Vivian. He has also failed to report to duty or even to consult with police union officials about the engendered shooting."

But most devastating was the article on my vanishing from Bellevue. Apart from pinning it entirely on a desire to skip out on the bill, "The Backpack Bungler apparently miscalculated on this as on so much else since Bellevue had already verified that his address in Queens is…." Then big as life – heads-up every disaffected looney in town – came my Bumfuckville address. Screw them and their paper-thin pretext for printing my address. So much for the Hovel as haven.

The up-and-at-'em, Sunday morning voicemail was from our lawyer, Steve. *Ours*? Though I could no longer refer to the toaster Nicki kept as ours, nor would I be schlepping *our* laundry anytime soon, perhaps I could gloss over such technicalities regarding legal-beagle Steve. Nick and I remained co-plaintiffs in an endless suit against the NYPD and Lincoln Center. Steve, our hungry young attorney, had been prodding the contingency-fee case slowly forward, trying to prompt the federal judge to rule on motions profound (ours) and absurd (theirs).

He'd returned late Saturday from hang gliding off some cliff, and his message was torn between anger at our small-bore suit getting overwhelmed by the shooting and barely contained glee about the far bigger suit Penn represented. He said he didn't think he could invest any more time or resources on Lincoln Center if he wasn't also hired for Penn. Though, conversely, he also didn't think he could take on the enormity of the shooting if I was charged with anything beyond the standard, no-account disorderly conduct. Anything beyond that, well, trouble just seemed to find me, and he'd reluctantly have to conclude I needed other representation. And since he was entitled to recoup a fraction of his uncompensated time and effort, he'd be happy to provide copies of his Lincoln Center file for a reasonable fee.

In other words, if the cops couldn't pin anything on me in regard to Penn, and my suit thus had decent prospects (dependent, of course, on getting an old-school judge), Steve would back me to the hilt. Otherwise, he'd sell me our case files and, welp, have a nice life.

My best hope for that dim prospect was to offer "Penn Tale" to history near the start of the week's news cycle. For Maureen's sake, I'd have to fudge my escape from Bellevue. Finagle it, somehow, or maybe just include that part out – an interesting technical challenge. Speaking of *technical* challenges, Jesus, was I really pursuing Maureen beyond speaking loud enough for the wire she'd wear?

I actually got to stringing a few words together on "Penn Tale" when, of course, the phone rang. Some politician, no doubt, offering big bucks to say I once dated his opponent.

PART FIVE

Chapter Twenty-Five

Corporate Spook

But it was Ralph, falling all over himself that I'd been brought so low. "Nice shorts you got."

"And why do you care?"

"You haven't seen it, haven't seen yourself on NYONLY yet, have you? I forgot. You're the only person in New York who doesn't have cable even though you get nothing but ghosts on your TV."

"I tried to get NYONLY online, but it's blocked on my machine – my *specific* machine. You believe that?"

"They got you by the nuts, dude."

"Maybe – maybe not. But what about my shorts?"

"You mean the world's oldest, baggiest, somebody-shat-in-them-and-died, blue-jeans shorts you got on. Throw in them boots you wear even in the middle of August, and some tee shirt that's way too small and so old I couldn't begin to tell you what color it is. And that's with my new Osmosis-Screen I been telling you about."

"So I was dressed like a bum going out for ten minutes – shoot me, for Chrissakes. The guy ambushed me. But what did that jerk say about me getting shot? And – why, yes, thank you – my head is feeling better."

"Wait. So the best part is when he ends it saying something like your path forward remains uncertain given all the trouble you're in. And there's this long, zooming-in shot as you shuffle off down this crappy block of you in those shorts. First all of you, then just focusing right in on this, this – *remnant* – that you're wearing that you really should burn except the EPA would come after you."

"I promise to call you for sartorial advice before leaving the house from here on out."

"Suit yourself, wiseass. But what were you eating, man? It looks like, I don't know, pig vomit or something. All greasy and dull at the same time, and you couldn't identify any of the ingredients when he pulled in real tight. That was the other thing he kept the camera on. Oh, and that bandage on your head. He loved that too."

"So he screwed me every way he could just to show the world how clever and superior he is. I should've stolen his damn change off the counter."

"Don't steal anything, man. You need to be clean as a whistle, buddy-boy. And wash your hair, for fuck's sake. You've been on TV before, you should know better than that."

"Look, Ralph, for the last time: I was starving and I stupidly went out without bothering to think. It'd been less than forty-eight hours since I got shot – in the head! – and I snuck out the back hoping they'd miss me. But this turkey showed up to get a damn egg roll. That's all he freaking ate for lunch was one egg roll!"

"Well, you are well and truly fucked. And they're saying there's gonna be some kind of videotape of you casing Penn Station released later today. Apparently shots of you carrying that backpack in the heat."

That weird pain started up again on the side *away* from the abrasion.

"So what were you doing in Penn Station," Ralph continued. "Looking for the right cop to shoot you and almost miss?"

"That's it, exactly, Ralph. How come I never recognized before how gosh-darn clever you are."

"Yeah, and I'm sure it's a good time to piss off your friends. But you know, it was weird."

"Weird how?"

"Weird that his camera was busted or something. Cause he kept jumping to himself back in the studio with this smirk on his puss listening to you just talk, no picture. Then he'd jump to shots of you in that Chinese, the audio and video both on. He kept flip-flopping like his camera was fritzing in and out."

"What a minute, what was I saying during just audio?"

"I don't know, your usual wise-ass."

"*Ralph!*"

"Alright, let me think. The thing that leaps out – and you should've seen his little grin with this – was when you admitted making that cop shoot you."

"What the hell are you talking about?"

"He had you saying, 'I made that cop shoot me.' Though it sounded like you were asking a question. Not that that's not getting lost in the sauce."

Christ, he said his damn camera was off. He'd made a whole big production about turning– shit! – turning the *video* back on. Lying scum. Goddamn sarcasm. Never, ever resort to sarcasm, the world wasn't made for it anymore.

"That was sarcasm, Ralph, answering his stupid questions. Jesus, I am fucked. What else?"

"He said you refused to answer whether the device you carried was a gun or a detonator. I almost choked on my sandwich, that a punk like you had a bomb or even a gun. It's like – "

"It was that stupid transistor radio I carry around that you and everyone else find so amusing. Go on."

"Well you'd better get a big, big picture of that radio up in Times Square like tomorrow. Another thing – I remember this perfectly cause it just nails your ass so bad – he had you saying something about wouldn't it be nice to have the MTA pay your rent for a while. And then you used one of your phrases, something about making 'a chunk of change' carrying that backpack around in the heat."

"You really think I'm dumb enough to say that? I was talking about getting paid for an article – a lousy couple of hundred bucks – and he just sliced it up any way he wanted. Well, the hell with them, cause it doesn't make any sense. The big hole in this whole smear campaign is how did I make that cop shoot me, but just nick me in the head? Tell me that, Goddamnit!"

"Dude – my ear! You still think logic has anything to do with this? They brand you a 'dirty bomber,' and that's it. The war hero and the deserter, remember? Only in your case, you got a gorgeous blonde with tits from here to Hoboken – and real by the looks of 'em – shot in the gut, a *fireman's* own personal playpen. Then there's the cops – sorry, our 'Protectors.' And a Boot. On the other side of the equation we got you looking homeless *and* talking about doing it for money. Whatever it was you were doing, challenging these useless searches that nobody cares about except they make you late. Yeah, I read that lefty blog of yours, *Naked Opprobrium* – whatever. The King of fucking Bushwick rushing to your side."

"Like the cops can tell anything patting the outside of your bag for half-a-second."

"People just want to get out of there and get on with their day. Nobody's getting X-rayed or felt-up. Hell, nobody even cares that companies nakedly buy elections, so why should they care about their *stuff*? Just keep your weed in your pocket in tin foil and don't go near any of their damn dogs. You think anyone's gonna care that Mr. NYFabulous sliced up your words? Go ahead, prove it. And then get a real big megaphone."

"I am so screwed."

"The fork just fell *outta* your ass, you are so done. But yo, you ever go pay a sympathy visit to that Fiore action, make sure you bring me along. I can be your cousin or something, cause she can butter my toast any side she wants."

"Sure, Ralph. You're first on my list. But I don't think I'll be seeing Carole anytime soon. I gotta go."

"Alright. Make sure you watch the news tonight. That cop video might even be on your TV."

"Right. Thanks. Bye."

My anchor in the storm whose wisdom beckoned. But he was right about one thing. Hunkered down in the Hovel or not, I was at that moment servicing vast swaths of a fearful and/or bemused public, the MoFos on top.

****

Not knowing the store with a megaphone sale, I couldn't think what to do about NYONLY just then. But it was pretty damn clear that if the cops were spoon-feeding the Tredwells of the world incidents like Lincoln Center – and no mention that the charges had been dismissed – then I'd really better shove a certain skeleton into the light myself. Both Stanley and NYONLY had urged that, and neither carried a light load between the ears. Wasn't the cover-up worse than the crime? Depended, probably, on whether the crime stayed blanketed.

So, time to bellow and bluff like my betters, with the slight difference that I'd aim for the truth. My linen then clean, anyone who dared make a stink was a sore loser – get over it and move on! Destroy the village in order to save it. A full recount violates voters' rights. These Boots are made for Fomenting, don't worry about why. Time to look forward, not back. Anyone paying the least attention knew the drill.

Back at the beginning of June, still joined in connubial bliss – well, tethered under one roof – I was $287 short on my half of the rent. And, astoundingly, a corporate espionage assignment fell out of the sky, some unidentified big schmoes having need of a newshound with a certain flexibility. No excuse, of course, but who was to say a chunk of cash might not help preserve what, all in all, had been a pretty slipericious marriage? The dumb thing was, when a Mr. Bettinger of Bettinger, Smoot and Associates called out of the blue, I hadn't a clue what to charge, so I asked for a chump-change fifteen-hundred, when I certainly could have doubled that. All I was risking was my byline – my name – a bit faded, sure, but still capable of a spit-shine if I somehow encountered the right big-time story. As the Man for All Seasons observes, "Why … it profits a man nothing to give his soul for the whole world ... But for Wales!" That's right, for a measly fifteen-hundred clams.

So, confess, really? Muddy the waters more, though I already couldn't see my feet?

Nicki pretty levelheaded despite her recent flibbertigibbet ways, I would've loved to run it by her. Pop? Part of our problem was he didn't take my work seriously cause of the paltry pay, so the journalistic ethics involved would mean little. He'd just start muttering about a lawyer – which I plain did not want to think about. Who I really wanted to talk to, both our heads on the flip-side of the pillow recently under her ass to improve the angle of attack, was Maureen, savvy devil that she was.

216

If I confessed, it had to be public, and it had to be quick before somebody beat me to it. Not that anyone who knew of this little peccadillo wanted it exposed. Would *The Symington Referendum* even take such a stark announcement? Or what about Bill Syriac's blog on the press, basically a well read bulletin board? He always seemed to have a whiff of the father confessor about him.

That was if I didn't just let this mangy dog sleep, hopefully to choke on a piece of gristle fallen from an abscessed tooth. Or not. Cause two days after Bettinger called, I found myself flying out to Lester, Indiana to attend Heavy-Duty Manufacturing's dog-and-pony introducing its next generation death-crate.

Yup, working for "the competition," as Bettinger said more than once, I was to go learn what I could of HDM's new Hillbilly Grinder – ground-up Boots' near-universal term for the tippy vehicle – as it was introduced to the press and Pentagon brass. The decade-long, billion-dollar military contract didn't include the billions more that, oh, *challenged* American males might someday fork over for an eventual civilian model. Drivers looking to tumescefy their lives could drape themselves in watered-down élan borrowed from younger, poorer and more virile American fighting men and women.

After instructing Bettinger that requiring an e-mailed report was a deal-breaker, he finally agreed I could report in with a pre-paid card from an Indiana payphone. Let them work out their own security at their end.

America at war, not to put too fine a point on it, I was spying for the Germans, cause the only "competition" was Chrysler's Jeep. The Germans had been trying to unload Chrysler for years, but were still looking for that greater fool. The Pentagon had narrowed it down to two vehicles, a new generation HDM on steroids and a new Jeep on human growth hormone. So the German-owned Jeep was HDM's competition to replace the old Grinder that had proved so unstable and breakdown-prone in the Sands. (I'd read of far too many combat related rollovers – heck, fatal rollovers just driving scared along a riverbank.)

But, Christ, didn't Bettinger even google some of my man-the-barricades articles of recent years that should have disqualified me from working for a defense contractor? I certainly bothered to learn of his tainted background. Maybe he did and figured I was broke enough to be desperate. Maybe he was right.

I figured to get in, learn what I could of the prototype new light tactical vehicle, get out, and then go scrub with lye soap and a wire brush. So I dropped everything, a light load for a longish time, no publisher clamoring for my proposed book, *A Pernicious, Underreported (Except by Me) and Insidious Slice of the Drug War and Why It Demands Attention* – a working title only.

More's the pity since, just being lucky out in Indiana, I encountered an HDM machinist (or he encountered me), a disgruntled vet who'd dodged round several Sands in the tippy, existing Grinder. And he dropped a scoop on me that would've had my byline bouncing. But I couldn't publish it without shooting myself in the foot exposing my false-flag operation, though my client, "the competition," would've obviously been thrilled by any HDM bad news. If I confessed, however, I could then let loose a scoop that might save some lives. I sat and sweated, my head hurting in ways I couldn't blame Frankie.

I finally decided to at least write the damn thing. Get that done and then decide if Syriac should hang my skeleton in his window come Monday morning. One thing was sure: with another video salvo coming, the cops weren't letting any grass grow under their trotters.

Sweated and sat and was about to start stringing words when the damn phone rang again, probably someone caught drowning puppies wanting me to testify as a character witness.

But it was Pop, informing me, "You're right, those searches are dumb. And maybe sometimes it's a dummy who doesn't care anymore is what this country needs. OK? But the real reason I called is, why'd you have to e-mail Nicki at her job talking about this stuff with the cops and the searches? You think maybe that e-mail was a deliberate … you know, a little 'fuck-you' as, your marriage over, you headed out the door? Checked out one way or the other?"

"Pop, what the hell are you talking about? No. I sent it to both her job and her own e-mail to make sure she got it cause I didn't know what was going to happen with the cops. And e-mail – especially Nicki's at home – gets deleted without a glance."

"So this deal in Penn Station was so uncertain and so dangerous, but you still didn't care what happened messing with men who got more guns than sense."

"Pop, what're you trying to say?"

"I don't know. Back in my day, you break a cop's nose, they would've just taken you down the alley and gotten their message across in about a minute-and-a-half. Nowadays, especially in a place like Penn Station with cameras everywhere, they can't do that. So everything gets escalated. All the wars we're in, nobody cares about them shooting some big lug who pissed them off. Except for you being white, it happens all the time."

"I guess I scared them, holding that radio out at them and carrying a pack."

"And why were you doing something so shit-for-brains? No kids or nothing, you're way old enough to do what you want with your life. That's always the big question under every other question, isn't it? Still, a girl dumps you, I say, walk away with your head high. Make her wonder if she made a mistake. Don't do this petty shit, screwing her over at her job with an e-mail. That's too easy, just hitting a send-button."

"Pop, you got it all wrong. Jesus, you're starting to sound like one of these damn reporters. Before this happened, before getting shot, Nick and I were *estranged* – that's all. We had some hope, maybe. I mean, she wrote me back that morning before I left for Penn Station and said she missed me."

"Yeah, 'missed you.' But she didn't say anything about wanting to see you, did she? OK, mister, none of my business. But the next dame, leave the damn e-mails alone. Though all these big shots making big money never seem to learn that, do they."

Ours was not a warm goodbye. Shit – e-mailing Nick at both addresses was basically like swimming at a lake with no lifeguard: you employ the buddy system. With all her cutsey-poo crap about lesbian soccer moms in reply, she'd certainly said nothing about not writing her at work. Still, Pop was right about one thing: yeah, she'd said she missed me, but there was nothing about any getting together to ease her pain.

Chapter Twenty-Six

That'll Knock 'Em Back on their Heels

Pop throwing punches wildly with both hands, but not scoring, damnit. Aside from the odd, arch comment at an F&F party, I'd never messed with Nicki's job. Hell, I'd helped her tweak her copy, trash dropped on consumers who, it turned out, enjoyed marketers rubbing their noses in it.

I went to my window, but it didn't help, my breath shallower still, and I suddenly, no kidding, needed to get out of there. Head up by the train maybe – sure, treat myself to my first five-buck coffee drink that the chrome-table set so favored. See if the Backpack Bungler's new status might sway any of the perky, dead-eyed lovelies up there, a haughty Greek, or snickering South American, maybe, arch Asian or askance Muslim. Shoot the moon.

About to step off the porch, I heard, then saw an NBC truck lumber round the corner looking for a driveway to block. Damn – just a minute quicker! Cause, in my Geek long pants or not, still reeling from Pop's flurry and lacking the head for an *encounter* just then, I fled back up.

I'd missed a call, probably Bellevue saying since I'd never been officially discharged, I owed for all the meals, including extra desserts, that Zeke – Alfred, rather, my hero – insisted on delivering to my room. But it was Nicki saying she wanted to see me before hitting work on Monday, and why didn't we have dinner at our favorite (i.e., less snooty) local Greek. Her treat. We could get some of that grilled calamari we both liked. Gotta be able to make a formal declaration at work, huh, Nick? Cause that sure sounded like applying our no-breakups-on-the-phone vow that we'd pledged on our two-month anniversary – about the time, we both well knew, when inflamed affairs like ours tended to peter out.

Like condemned-man Barnadine in *Measure for Measure* who

declares, "I swear I will not die today," and then, oddly enough, stomps unmolested back to his cell, I was in no mood for the axe. Plus, I had to write Syriac and deal with his potential caveats, make a further stab at "Penn Tale" and cope – or at least watch – the cops' impending video.

Not to mention working up the nerve to remove that dead-mouse bandage and wash the grease from my attractively thinning locks cause I had prior, pressing business to conduct out in the world on Monday at a court of sorts. Monday the deadline and not wanting any legal irregularities pending(!), I was set to handle it Friday except I'd woken up in a hospital bed with a goon barring the door. So no, I was a mite too busy to dissolve my marriage that evening.

Shrinking from calling her micro-zap to interrupt her second (third?) frolic of the day with MoneyBags, I called Nick's home machine and proposed she come by Monday night. Might as well get her crossed off my dance card to focus on the many other names. Waiting for her machine, I envisioned MoneyBags' paunch and little rat eyes scrunched by bloated cheeks, a light dusting of dandruff gracing the shoulders of his expensive sports coat.

Enough marriage shit. If I'd indeed dabbled my toe in Stygian waters by messing with the cops, I needed to so roil them no one could cross. I sprang to my métier, the keyboard, to cleanse the stain from my escutcheon, confound my foes and maybe even pluck the bowstrings of Nicki's successor, aquiver at the overburdened suppleness of my prose. Its hearty verbal chunkiness would lay the groundwork for me unmitigated. She'd be a mere six years younger than the Wife – no, eight. Nothing extreme, right around Maureen's age.

I fell to typing my Syriac statement.

Actually, still not convinced I'd ever send it, I switched immediately to a pad and pen. Even with my machine always offline when offline, the MoFos' new, *retroactive* keystroke monitoring programs were awfully slick.

Dear Bill:
You may have noticed I've been in the news lately, which came as a shock to me too. I've certainly lost

control of my own narrative, but as I discussed with the editor of *Naked Opposition*, I thought it past time that someone stood up to the *non*-random, suspicionless search program here in New York City that, in total violation of the Fourth Amendment, subjects anyone dicey enough to resort to public transportation to immediate search.

The way the searches have been incorrectly portrayed, passengers are supposedly able to refuse and hoof it to another station though it may be a half-mile away. Never mind that you might be old, or late or traveling with little kids – or all three in a downpour. I'll have more to say on all this when I publish my account of getting shot in Penn Station as I set out to execute a principled refusal to this illegal policy. While I didn't shy from the risk of a civil-liberties protest arrest, I had every reason to expect that would be the worst of it.

Far more luminous individuals, though on issues of similar import, have been arrested for similar non-violent protest. It's a legitimate and worthwhile action, one that I believe should be both endorsed and emulated in these perilous times. Yet I've heard of no one just standing up and saying 'Get-out-of-my-face No!' in a city of almost nine million. As the poet has it, "The best lack all convictions, while the worst are full of passionate intensity."

I did indeed intend to write about it – and to expect my normal pittance for my words. For what good the tree that falls on deaf ears, what purpose in making my statement of refusal before twenty commuters left to wonder what that was all about? It's the sort of old-fashioned, shoe-leather, participant/observer work that most reporters with weekly paychecks feel beneath them these days. They'd rather flog a mouse and call that an investigation. So I ended up taking one for the team as a result – my team. Because it's past time to choose sides. You're either on the bus or off the damn bus.

And speaking of those on the wrong side, on whose 'authority' were my private e-mails and a transcript of an obviously private phone call to my father obtained? And then who gave them to the *New York Toast* as manna for the absurd fictions it published this Sunday morning? In the midst of all this stove-piping from illegally obtained material, the *Toast* failed to mention that these private communications discussed my intent to protest the searches.

But to the impetus for this letter and the reason I hope you can post it forthwith. I'm proud of my intent Thursday in Penn Station and sorry that a simple pedestrian accident rounding a blind corner ended up forestalling it – for now. Let me extend heartfelt best wishes to Ms. Carole Fiore, whom the MTA police also shot that morning, and express my delight that she is apparently well on her way to a full recovery. (As to my head, time will tell.)

I write today driven by a bona fide skeleton in my closet, something well beyond the normal frictional 'transaction costs' of the hardscrabble passage through life (not to mention the city's subways) of someone who – on occasion – finds dry, unmediated, *dry* existence a tad dreary. These costs represent the human condition rather than a true skeleton, people throughout history having maintained their right to cognitive autonomy despite the advent of the eight-dollar glass of beer.

But there is something I regret, and let me attempt to mitigate its impact by disclosing it here myself.

I dissembled on behalf of Chrysler, my target the soon to be retired Hillbilly Grinder's current manufacturer, Heavy-Duty Manufacturing. As you may know, Jeep and HDM's Grinder are locked in a stiff competition for the contract to produce the next generation, light-tactical vehicle for the Sands. I did so at the behest of a Mr. Bettinger of Bettinger, Smoot and Associates.

Though I might maintain that I intended to write about it, nevertheless I am owed a very small sum of money for traveling under the flag of journalism to Lester, Indiana back in early June to learn what I could of the new vehicle being show-horsed that day to the press and then to report back. And yes, it was a fraught experience, both that day and since. That I've yet to be paid is of no consequence to anyone but my landlord.

Funny thing is, I learned something out in Indiana of fairly enormous consequence to our troops when the new vehicle *hits* the road. So now that this stinking cat (skeleton of a cat – no mixed metaphors here) is out of the bag, I'll tell that tale too and maybe even save some lives in the process. HDM's new death-crate, the new Grinder, is far from general production, so there's no harm in my having tarried a couple of months. That my (near-deathbed) conversion took getting shot in the head and then smeared by every paper in town – well, we are brought into this world far from perfect and try to progress from there.

Somewhat cryptic, I know. But I managed to make the key point about my misdeed, and I hope, numerous curs nipping at my ankles, you can publish this statement come Monday morning. Thanks a bunch.

Sincerely, etc.

Having been blasted as a Fiend, I couldn't resist a few rhetorical blandishments in this first *self*-penned salvo from my bunker. So, type it up and hit send? A cover-up is worse than the crime only when it fails; you don't hear of the ones that stay blanketed. Easy to write, easier to send – but repent at leisure. Man, who could I ask or, rather, get to tell me what to do? Maybe get Mr. Staphilopoulos to convene his chorus of Greek buddies (and one Turk) down on the porch to shift the entrails. Yeah, confessing to something few knew of and none wanted exposed. *That'll* send the MoFos packing!

Still mid-afternoon, I decided to sit on it and, suddenly weary, succumbed to the call of my chair.

****

"Nice shorts," said the voice on the phone that woke me. "So now we gotta be on the lookout for the naked, fat homeless guy you stole 'em from?"

Ralph doing a bad Brooklyn tough-guy, and why was he obsessed with my nether regions anyway?

"Very funny, bright boy."

"We figured you were the genius. In fact, that's why we're leaving you loose, doing our job so good for us every time you open your mouth or leave that little rat-hole of yours. But we we're still thinking about inviting you down here for a little chat. Informal-like."

"Look, pal, like Sam Spade said, 'If you want to see me, pinch me or subpoena me, and I'll come in with my lawyer.' And aren't you supposed to identify yourself at the start of the call, maybe be a little professional?"

"I was getting to that. Everyone's in such a hurry these days. You going on *60 Minutes* tonight and gotta make sure to get that filthy bandage changed? We figured – "

I slammed the phone down. It rang again. "Hey, *bright boy* – BEI. You ever stop to think, maybe, that T has got this country screwed down pretty tight?"

"Ya never know, MoFo, the right stone in the right pond, what kind of effect it might have. But unless I hear who I'm talking to, I gotta go wash out my ears."

"What – you're gonna, oooh, *hang-up* on me again? The wetbacks in that house of yours – maybe three of them legal? – making you feel at home, an ass-wipe white boy like you? We'll be shaking that rat-trap pretty good. You might want to spread the word about the happiness you bring wherever you go."

"I'm counting to five, cop. One, two – "

"Sure, sure thing , punk. There's a desk here I gotta go put my feet up on. My name is DeBrunt –one word, capital D, capital B. Detective, MTA. So tell me, you're just some schmuck they recruited to probe the politics of the searches, right? I mean, you gotta be somebody's pawn, arranging that interview with NYONLY looking like something my ex-wife's cat threw up. That supposed to add to your street cred with the maggots already lining up behind you?"

"All over the country, DeBrunt."

"Not for long, what we got in store for them."

Them – who's them? Cause that was just a dumb line about all over the country.

He went on."I got two suggestions, punk. First, make the most of the temporary little slice of freedom you got. Probably with a ho since your wife is so ... *occupied*. And second, I'd watch the local news tonight if I were you. Any channel. We were wondering if we got your good side – with the cameras, not Frankie. We got much better shooters than that asshole. Very patient guys, all sizes, all ages, all colors. All hanging around Northwest Queens keeping the public – that's the public at large – safe."

And then the baanhhh of a dead line. Jesus, good old fashioned, bare-knuckles intimidation, the best sign in days. Cause if the MTA thought they had me nailed, they'd feel no need to alert me to their damn video. They were the ones running scared over a bum shooting.

Chapter Twenty-Seven

Artless Fabrication

Alright, what the heck time did the local news come on anyway, before *Belly Up to the Beast Within* or after? The paper said six o'clock on Sundays – in a little while. Of course there was a Nicki voice-mail. Sounding again way too sweet, she said dinner Monday worked cause, "It's been quite a full weekend to tell you the truth, and I'm bushed."

Spare me the details, darling. Going down to the hall window to shoot malevolence Manhattan's way – rise, oceans, rise! – I heard some laughter from the floor below and scooted down to see two of the friendlier guys. I asked about any 'autos de periodicos en la calle' – newspaper cars in the street. One snarled as they pushed into their room, "You bad. You bring la Migra. They already get two men with children need food back home. You go to Hell."

Turd-Touch! turning everything brown and smelly. Time soon enough for the tube, any channel, 'DeBrunt' said. That meant Channel 10, pretty much the only station that came in at all clear since the prior citywide television antenna was malignly neglected to dust.

(Damn peculiar that nowhere in New York's hundreds of square miles or on one of the dozens of tall buildings, not a single spot was deemed suitable to build a new antenna for the biggest TV market in the country. That the miserable reception forced most everyone to pay big for cable month after month was no doubt entirely coincidental. So, along with the drinking water they'd made great inroads on, they managed to privatize television as well, never mind the publicly owned airwaves. Privatized the schools too. Amazing how bad a beating you can inflict, the alley dark enough, cause nobody wrote a word about the missing antenna. Ralph was right, basketball courts got a mite crowded on my TV, everyone shadowed by his ghost, twenty players running around.)

The cop's video was XYZ's lead story. "Metropolitan Transportation Authority police have this afternoon released dramatic, never before seen video of the so-called Penn Station Shooter." Wow, they were focusing on Frankie? Who woulda thunk it, and why was DeBrunt wetting his pants over them showing Frankie shooting me? Clutching and grabbing, I knew it wasn't so.

They had maybe forty-five seconds total, the telling bit a nifty mis-spliced fifteen seconds that turned reality inside out. The MoFos having traveled often and far down the mendacity trail, blatant misrepresentation came easy, certainly when dealing with a nobody like me. Well, they misunderestimated me, cause I have truth on my side, with goodness and beauty right behind.

As reported by one Cloud McNamara, the video started off with a clear view of me talking to the Penn Station cop who'd been jotting down demographics on Wednesday. There I was in all my earnest glory, looking, yes Chilean Cassandra, a little like an aging grad student in my button-down shirt with the sleeves rolled up. They'd helpfully circled my bulging pack, not that you could miss it, and the news puppy allowed as how the cops were "unsure what threat it might have contained since the Suspect was, unfortunately, not apprehended on this the day prior to the shooting."

Big-time threats in that pack, Pup – little black marks on paper. There was a break in the tape and then a view of me walking past that same cop a second time when I tried to spark a search but the cop didn't bite. "Having probed the Protectors' defensive perimeter, nineteen minutes later the Suspect returned. But he thankfully loses his nerve, or perhaps there was a technical glitch, and he moved on without incident."

Glitch, yeah, the ray beam from the orbiting Mother Ship deflected by a low-flying blimp's biometric cameras.

He continued. "Stated MTA Deputy Commissioner Walton Everidge, 'If an attack or mandated discharge had occurred in this much more crowded waiting area rather than in the next day's more isolated corridor, I shudder at the consequences.' "

And I quiver, Everidge, at the thought of a particularly

228

righteous meteor crashing through the roof onto your lying head. News-Pup got more breathless still. "Now here's the tape from the actual day of the shooting that imperiled commuters and sent hundreds fleeing. Be advised that due to a suspicious technical glitch potentially similar to the previous day's, uh … malfunction, the video is of poor quality."

That gobbledygook apparently meant I was too incompetent to blow myself and a multitude to high heaven on Wednesday, but somehow possessed the magical power to incapacitate hidden surveillance cameras on Thursday.

"As the tape starts, police advise viewers to observe – there! – the Shooter comes into view."

Which technically speaking was true. The image of much poorer quality, you could see just a touch of blue uniform, Frankie's knee maybe. But I dominated the screen, jerking oddly into view like stage furniture whose guide-wire has suddenly gone haywire. Was it that bald-faced and direct, the phrase 'the Shooter comes into view' justified by Frankie's knee but obviously referring to me, the unarmed, bleeding man rushed off in an ambulance? As with issues more momentous than ruining some mope's life, just repeat the lie and….

"The tape resumes here, and police instruct Homelanders and others to note the flat silver object in the Suspect's hand – right there! Police sources have theorized about it, given the bulky nature of the Suspect's backpack. But the exact nature of the threat remains to be determined."

There was a brief, grainy, slow-mo shot from the rear of me pointing some kind of … *something*. Though it was again helpfully circled in white, it could be a lump of plutonium, or the Holy Grail, or a used condom dried all stiff or, sure, some kind of very rectangular weapon. Whatever floated your boat.

"Unfortunately, in the melee that followed the tragic engendered-discharge Thursday morning, the weapon itself was secreted away, presumably by an as yet unidentified co-assailant. Protectors are asking Homelanders or others with information to report to their local precinct with a change of clothing."

Co-assailant – a nifty step up from co-conspirator.

"Fearing for their lives, MTA Protectors felt it necessary to 'mechanically accelerate' the Suspect's East German Army rucksack rather than risk it exploding." Then, of course, came video of a nice, medium-sized boom and ball of fire down at Floyd Bennett Field, an NYPD helicopter framed nicely about twenty yards away. Knowing exactly how big the charge, having placed it themselves, they felt no need to move a multi-million-dollar aircraft. Of course, Lurch knew all the titles I'd carried, so they'd opened the pack no problem.

Gnawing on my bones was about all that was left.

He continued, "Senior MTA officials have ruled out releasing the footage of the actual discharge due to the sensitivities of the Protectors victimized by the incident. However, they were able to provide two other pieces of evidentiary video that shed light on the dastardly attack."

Out of sequence, since they'd already shown me brandishing the Entertainment System, they then showed Frost ministering to Frankie around the corner, the soldier standing in front of the two cops in a defensive crouch. The video no longer cloudy, blood flowed crimson down Frankie's face.

Betty, let me hear! Always with the questions. The guy had a gun – or something – and the cops had their guns. They haven't gotten to that part yet. Maybe they don't know themselves. You know, the 'fog of war.' Now, look at that, my fish-sticks got cold watching this. Be a doll and nuke 'em for me."

Violence the main course, they offered some cheesecake for dessert.

"MTA specialists, aided by state and federal agencies, have carefully reviewed literally tens of thousands of feet of videotape over the two days in question from Penn Station's 184 video cameras, searching for the soon to be captured co-assailants. And, I'm happy to say, they unearthed a last piece of tape that speaks for itself: never before seen, candid shots of someone who at this point certainly needs no introduction. Ladies and Gentlemen, by generous permission of the MTA PD, permit Cloud McNamara to proudly present Ms. Carole Fiore!"

And a well-hinged and very determined Carole came sashaying down the corridor prior to the shooting in that tight, alarmingly green dress, this tape's color hormonally saturated. Shoulda seen it coming, the *Toast*'s front page a still from a sequence where a human overrode Penn's camera. Too bad since on a face that gorgeous, her haughty *stare if you must, but out of my way* expression was even more riveting than the usual foci, however spectacular. They ran it twice, the second time with just a tasteful touch of slow-mo of Carole hurrying (I remembered the determined clack of heels) down that corridor.

"Betty! Get in here and look at this cupcake – a three-layer cake more like it. I hope for that lucky-stiff fireman's sake none of the good parts got hit."

Cloud wrapped up with security-camera shots of ambulances and cop cars tying up traffic on Seventh Avenue. But, despite capturing Carole for the ages, they had nothing of me walking that same corridor seconds before, nor of the two dumb bunnies' collision. Just me leaping into the frame as "the Shooter" and then pointing that silver thing.

They showed the whole package that Sunday evening on every channel in New York. But, I would learn, the "Silver Weapon" video was deemed too "sensitive" to ever broadcast again. It got what they wanted out there, it's job was done. It's not self-censorship, man! Some sights – a rolled, burning Fomenting Grinder, for instance – are too fraught to inflict on a fragile public. The hens might stop laying. Never mind that Boots were shown daily on TV in every country but their own doing horrible and having horrible done.

Sorry that I'd waited all afternoon to write Syriac and his audience of scribblers (plus whatever bounce I got), I typed my letter off that legal pad, inserting this right before my confession:

"And just now the TV news aired an obviously manipulated and out of sequence set of surveillance videos that seek to place me in the worst possible light as I walked through Penn Station carrying a back-pack full of books (*quel horror*) hoping to spark a search so I could just say no. Just say, in effect – to cite an ostensibly spontaneous, but similarly planned action – that I wasn't moving to the back of the bus.

Of course, having blown up my backpack – which

they owe me for – amazingly enough, there's now explosive residue on it. It ain't rocket science. At Bellevue, a 'cop' wearing no insignia knew all the titles I carried, mentioning them one by one. So they didn't have to explode my pack, they'd already opened it.

The narration I heard on my local XYZ station referred to me as the "Shooter," though I was unarmed and rushed to the hospital bleeding from a bullet to the head. Let me state categorically: I had no gun and no detonator. The citizen's responsibility to keep an ear on events is more crucial than ever in today's political climate. To that end, I was carrying a silver transistor radio that was audibly playing. The man who shot me remarked on the content of the news, and its presence was attested to by two independent eyewitnesses in Sunday's New York Daily Chirp.

As your readership will appreciate, Bill, writers – i.e., typists – often go to great lengths to free sore hands from static loads, however small. So the radio rested under my shirt on my shoulder where I could hear it.

The MTA was able to supply an irrelevant tape of Carole Fiore, Thursday's other cop-shot, walking down the same corridor I'd traversed seconds before. (As mentioned, I certainly do wish Ms. Fiore a speedy and complete recovery.) But they somehow had no footage of me in that corridor from that same camera since that would harm their fabricated and, let me reiterate, out of sequence video-narrative that tars me as the 'Shooter.' Nor did they show the blameless collision round a blind corner that I had with the short cop who shot me, inadvertently bloodying his nose.

Finally, most crucially, the MTA withheld the tape of the "bullets' actual discharge." (Apparently they leaped out of the cops' guns of their own accord.) According to XYZ's Cloud McNamara, this was supposedly "due to the sensitivities of the Protectors victimized by the incident." Not because it would show a panicked cop – who only recently had his gun returned – shooting me for no reason. The MTA is obviously floundering. Otherwise why release such a botched job destined to turn and bite?"

Sure, this would steal some thunder from "Penn Tale," but this video had to be refuted and quick. Focused on what I'd just written rather than my confession, I pretended to think about it, cried havoc and hit send.

I cobbled together another scrumptious meal from a can of curried kidney beans and a block of ice-encrusted peas over some couscous I unearthed. Forcing this down, I re-read Tredwell's chop-job. Though I was mired in a heap of vilification and abuse – hell, drowning in lies, plus childishness like NYONLY focusing on my shorts – it was clear that the *Toast* had crossed a line. Though one of the smaller besmirchments lobbed my way, once the paper dragged in my and Nicki's brutalization at Lincoln Center, it obviously needed to indicate the charges against me were dismissed as silly.

For there was an innocent third party to consider, our lawyer, Steve. God knew how much time, effort, expense filing all those briefs, and on and on this hungry young attorney just starting his solo practice had invested in our lawsuit against Lincoln Center and the City. Tredwell wrote rubbish about the "dangerous duo" of me and my "confederate/spouse" successfully staring down a large Lincoln Center security force (though we had). So "Penn Tale" would have to tout the charges' dismissal as well as our lawsuit. That way any jury eventually hearing our punitive damages case would know I was an innocent man slandered and smeared. Steve's mountain of uncompensated, contingency-fee toil and time demanded no less.

And all because a huge, rich institution snapped their fingers for five NYPD forelock-tuggers, enough to handle two troublemakers at an old-fogey folk concert they *thought*. And yet the cops showed, but there we remained, burrowed amidst the tight rows of spectators, counting on Lincoln Center's abhorrence of a mid-concert scene. Out on the street, the Wife and I wouldn't have had the means or the nerve to resist. But by the simple act during an ongoing concert of keeping our butts glued to a metal chair in a cramped row several seats in from the aisle, we told them to go to hell and made it stick. Told that NYPD sergeant who requested I come to the aisle for a "conversation" that I could hear him fine from where I was. It was obvious that, once in the aisle, they'd smoothly, *quietly* give me the bum's rush to the back of a patrol car. That was plain unheard of, Bartlebying the cops with a simple: actually, I'd prefer not to. And so, at concert's end, we got slammed and bloodied as hard as they felt they could get away with in front of that crowd.

A happier time, Nicki and I still tight. Lordy – the two of us holding hands and pretending to ignore fifteen angry men (including the ten Lincoln Center guards) stuck to their flypaper twenty yards away. And, oh, the glorious few seconds of telling that guard who'd informed me I was permitted solely to clap exactly what he could do with himself. A simple, clear, concise get-out-of-my-face no! Like AIDS activists said way back when, "Where's the outrage?" I wore that knee scar proudly.

Any discussion of our lawsuit was the functional equivalent of citing my name. And that I'd been loath to do, it certainly not in my nature to beat my breast in the front row of the temple. Shying from undue disclosure, I'd seen no particular reason to make this whole civ-lib quest I'd embarked on unnecessarily personal. No cause for fulsome detail about myself, my life, my family, my circumstances. Do that and soon enough you're talking about food, drink or sex, for crying out loud. My particulars unimportant, this was a simple Everyman's tale. The story of a somewhat political New Yorker – his veins clotted with peanut butter, his countenance just then unmediated by Ballantine, his struggle against undue semen buildup proceeding unaided – who sought in his own self-effacing way to push back against the forces of quotidian repression, the Hammer raining down on short and tall alike.

So … my name is Daniel Forbes and the musty, old, ancient, should've been a slam-dunk suit against Lincoln Center and the City was mired in U.S. District Court in the Southern District of New York. Perhaps it'd be best to footnote the details.

[FOOTNOTE ONE] The damn thing growing mold on some judge's desk, it was akin to knowing you're the potential heir to a very modest sum come the demise of a hale and hearty thirty-year-old with no predisposition to illness: you don't rush to spend the money.

One footnote typically bequeaths another. And, in fact, the cops' unprovoked attack on us that night was so shocking and brutal – them flying through the air full-length to tackle me, audience members then encircling us chanting "Shame!" and "The Whole World is Watching" – that, unbeknownst to us, a bystander in Arlo's sophisticated audience filed a Civilian Complaint Review Board case on our behalf. [FOOTNOTE TWO] We learned of it months later when a hobbled, but nonetheless dogged CCRB investigator contacted us out of the blue. She gave quite the look when I placed my own little tape recorder on the desk next to hers for her interview.

****

One heck of a Sunday: lies in the paper, confessing to the world, my marriage kaput, Pop's nasty accusation, a cop calling with threats, and an artless but nonetheless powerful video that dropped me off Stap's tall roof. Hell, I no longer batted an eye at cops anchored downstairs monitoring my comings and goings. Not that I had anywhere to go. Shoot, deal with it tomorrow, all of it and all of them, happy at least that my head seemed better, and the week – one heck of a *week* – was finally over long as no one came crashing through my door before the clock struck twelve.

1. United States District Court, Southern District of New York. 1:05-cv-07331-NRB.
2. Civilian Complaint Review Board: CCRB Case Number 200408189.

Chapter Twenty-Eight

Syriac Swollen, Stap Primed

Kee-riced! I woke with a jolt from a combustible mix: the Sunday *Toast*'s mention, stolen from my e-mail to Nicki, of an incident with a cat and a cop on the LIRR that left me "bruised and breathless"; the cheap malice of the *Daily Chirp* printing my address; and the MTA fairy-tale video featuring my pretty mug. Mix, season and bake for twenty-two minutes at 612 mega-Hertz and Statie would have no problem wrapping his warped brain around two plus two equaled me. In fact, any of the "USA, USA!"-chanting louts in that LIRR car could tie me to a prior attack on a Protector.

The large stone dropping from the ceiling that Monday pinned me until a foot spasmed free of the sweaty sheet, almost toppling the cartons stacked up against the wall. They contained files for articles that had made their mark, some of them. My other foot could almost touch the closet harboring the ill-fitting suits from my biz-writer days. Should the LIRR riot surface, I'd cope with my usual knife-thrust alacrity. Meanwhile, toss it to the top of the teetering pile.

My appearance, motives, work, finances and marriage all scattered on a Times Square sidewalk, getting shot was still strangely liberating. Lightning never striking twice, it wasn't like they could shoot me again. Can't touch me, got that DeBrunt? Plus, Penn Station five days prior and the cops with the weekend to think about it, if I didn't get arrested as Monday played itself out, time to back-burner the legal threats the papers pondered so lovingly.

First, I needed to confirm that Syriac had played his part in my exceedingly odd rope-a-dope rehabilitation. Then I'd hightail it off to Brooklyn so they couldn't arrest me on a weeks-old, new HateCrime ticket whose witching hour was nigh. Then back to the Hovel to finally polish off "Penn Tale" and send it to maybe three sites – and screw 'em if they couldn't cope with a simultaneous submission from the man of the hour. (Much to Nicki's disgust, I never held editors up for money. Unseemly, somehow, disseminating Truth; whoever responded first snared the prize.) Then noodle around for reaction to my confession, followed by a beer or three to hornswoggle things properly for Divorce-Dinner with the Wife.

That bit of bother dispensed with, Nick riding off into the fantabulous Manhattan sunset, perhaps some trolling round the haute-chrome environs by the train. But first to see that my mea culpa was loosed upon the world, no doubt adding to my peculiar allure.

Syriac's note leaped out of my mail's queue of garbage and abuse. He said the Net nuts-and-bolts ferrying my letter the night before were identical to that accompanying my prior mail, and that this satisfied his vetting. He'd posted it early to garner the maximum exposure. And thanks for thinking of him – for free – despite my new notoriety. Right. Combined with sheer bumpkinism, eschewing pay for a confession was the sort of squeamishness that helped explain landing in the Hovel at my ripe, lonely age.

The way of it these days: the writer calling up a screen to see what the world saw as it sees it. No e-mailed confirmation from Bill or – heavens! – phone call, no massaging of the text or consideration of any liability. OK, Bill, fine. I wrote it, and sent it and, yeah, take responsibility for the weightiest prose I'd ever committed, heavier by far, really, than painting the White House dung-brown. Swamped, his site took its own sweet time loading. At least he ran my letter unmolested below his backhanded intro:

PENN STATION SHOOTING *VICTIM'S* STATEMENT

The economic and other pressures on journalists, particularly freelancers, are exemplified by the case of an independent reporter who once carved a decent niche for himself exposing government foolery. Or perhaps these pressures apply very singularly to the long strange trip of Daniel Forbes, a publish-anywhere scuffler. He'd once commanded front pages nationwide with his detailed and devastating series in *Salon* revealing that the White House Drug Czar instituted a convoluted scheme that ended up paying the TV networks millions to let his functionaries oversee the scripts of some of the biggest sitcoms and dramas of the day. [FOOTNOTE ONE] His revelation of the government's secretly inserted, anti-marijuana propaganda caused an uproar and led, if I recall, to four congressional hearings and even, as he'll tell you at the drop of a bong, to his testimony before House and Senate subcommittees.

His right to publish was attacked by the White House, but the work held up. He exposed the bought scripts as ludicrous, with such examples as: find a joint in an otherwise exemplary daughter's room and exile her – that night! – to live with a relative hundreds of miles away. Or refuse an accident victim life-saving surgery until he reveals the name of his pusher-man.

A follow-up piece indicated that several newspapers and magazines, including *U.S. News & World Report*, *Seventeen* and *Parade*, also participated in the indirect cash-for-content scheme. [FOOTNOTE TWO] Then came the less surprising news that the Channel One 'news' programming beamed to a captive audience of millions in the nation's schools was also bought and paid for by the government. [FOOTNOTE THREE]

But then, perhaps inevitably given Forbes's milieu and the general tenor of his associates (his work has appeared in *High Times* and *Rolling Stone*, and he even addressed a NORML conference), things seemed to roll off the rails. His byline appeared less regularly and in obscure outlets given the heft of the scoops involved.

For instance, he obtained an on-the-record accusation that John Ashcroft would allow Protectors to appropriate money intended for school kids. [FOOTNOTE FOUR] Were it not for its obscure placement, that should have at least delayed Ashcroft's confirmation as Attorney General pending further investigation. He pointed out some early, cabalistic conflicts of interest by one Judy Miller,

238

a now somewhat tarnished member of the Fraternity. [FOOTNOTE FIVE] His pork-fried titillation that Jayson Blair traded sexual favors for drugs with men, not women, probably deserved its obscurity given the far-fetched notion that any woman might pay Blair in any currency for the privilege. [FOOTNOTE SIX] And Forbes's exposure of a popular plagiarist rocked the blogosphere, however briefly, but really….[FOOTNOTE SEVEN]

His account of a vicious raid on medical marijuana patients, did indeed pluck the heartstrings, the gendarmes demanding a woman rise from her sick bed, her wheelchair not within reach. [FOOTNOTE EIGHT] But he crossed the line from journalist to participant (never a good idea for even the unaffiliated) by helping to lead a small section of an antiwar march, as he himself detailed here. [FOOTNOTE NINE]

A model of popular textual analysis regarding whether the Russians were working against U.S. military interests by spying for Bad Guys and disseminating intelligence over the Internet, argued for wide dissemination and discussion. [FOOTNOTE TEN] Yet it sank virtually unnoticed. One might argue, Boots at stake, that it rivaled in importance the violated sanctity of the television sitcom, but apparently not.

Forbes was even reduced to writing a long, well-studied manifesto on political malfeasance perpetrated by the Governor of Ohio – talk about fish in a barrel! – that surprisingly found no takers among respectable media outlets. [FOOTNOTE ELEVEN]

Another effort that argued for more notice but for its obscure placement was a rigorous study of numerous high, middling and low government officials using the powers of office to swing upcoming elections. [FOOTNOTE TWELVE] It dovetailed neatly with his disclosure that the White House bribing the TV networks was nothing but a scheme to steer voters against the statewide medical marijuana initiatives they overwhelmingly approve every time they're offered the choice. [FOOTNOTE THIRTEEN]

Under the guise of helping kids, the government subverted elections. Some found this troubling.

And then, his byline flitting hither and inconsequentially yon, his name exploded (so to speak) on Thursday in very peculiar circumstances. He maintains he was seeking to resurrect the shady old practice of participant/observer journalism. Due to its disastrous outcome, his Penn Station prank has achieved wide notice. But he apparently preceded sans assignment, doing it on 'spec' as it were. And no wonder, for no professional editor would approve of setting out to challenge a practice that stands between us and perdition: state control of our movements. Worse, he aimed to publicize his stunt with an eye towards emulation! 'Spec' as in *spectacularly* brain-locked!

Armed with a bulky backpack, he sought to balk at the random (but fully clothed) searches that keep all New Yorkers fearful, especially, one hopes, those seeking to embrace Perdition. He states that he was carrying, oddly secured on his person so as to free hands pained by too much keyboard use, a small … transistor radio is probably the term. This contention – however harmful to an economy dependent on churning through generations of gadgets – was corroborated by eyewitnesses professionally quoted in yesterday's *New York Daily Chirp*.

This much is known: Forbes was shot in the head. That has not impacted his capacity to generate the workmanlike prose he claims as his that I have generously provided room for below. Looking back on his oeuvre to prepare the present contextualizing (for which this correspondent receives no direct extra remuneration – click on any of the donation buttons scattered throughout this site), it's apparent that he never quite mastered the oratorical rotundity, the necessary rodomontade of the Professed Journalist. He never quite rose from the *reporter's* ranks.

As to what might be termed his statement of 'guilt' below – such an archaic concept applied post-Plunge to the media! – I remain agnostic. Who can but limp soberly along on even a major-league staff job's remuneration? As long as it's done delicately, there's room for a certain, oh, *stretchiness* of standards. That is, as long as there are no overt attempts to profit from directly moving stock prices, say, which even today retain a whiff of the improper. Or certainly nothing as dire as a respected, national newspaper withholding a potentially election-swinging scoop on improper government spying on Citizens/others until long after the president running for re-election had stolen safely home. But, to merely provide competitive information to a private client, a respected global defense contractor – well, to coin a phrase, *no blood, no biggie*.

As the Continental Op might tell him: "Y*ou talked too much, son. You were too damn anxious to make your life an open book for me. That's a way you amateur criminals have. You've always got to overdo the frank and open business.*" Still, as I bring this analysis to a close before turning my expensive bandwith over to Forbes's statement – A WORLD EXCLUSIVE! – permit a personal observation.

Some shred of standards remains, my role to encourage same. To wit, I do not approve of the absurd designation of Forbes as the "Shooter," as has crept recently into some professionally generated accounts of the affair. The duly sworn Protectors had guns, Forbes carried a radio according to a leading tabloid. Not to bow too, *too* unfashionably before logic, but to nod perhaps anachronistically in its direction: who the shooters and who the shootee would seem apparent. Nor can I sanction an obviously manipulated videotape that the Metropolitan Transportation Authority released last night. Meaning still has its place, and frameworks need to be observed. Ridding us of T requires no less.

Finally, friends, please note that I'm a whisker away from nailing down Big Pharma sponsorship of my next, soon to sell-out Practitioner Conference: *Stretchy Standards,* featuring a keynote address by yours truly on "Situational Elasticity." Given the sold-out success of its predecessor, *Bed Your Embed*, check this space daily to avoid disappointment.

As always, *arrivederci!*

Well, at least the exalted one ran my statement unmolested, googled me decently and actually skimmed some of the articles that popped up. And since I hadn't manipulated any stocks, I was aces in his book.

Stanley also weighed in in his normal, inimitable fashion:

Comrade:

Though it's certainly open to debate why I should grant you that encomium. Not after you royally screwed me on Saturday with your failure to follow through on our agreement regarding a picture of you holding up a tabloid shot of Ms. Fiore. Soon as I can track down contact info for her (pretty closely held, let me tell you), I'll be offering her a regular column in *Naked Opposition*. Unpaid, of course, but I like to think she could benefit as much from the high-toned exposure as our readers – notice I said *our* – would appreciate her youthful bent.

By the by, you don't know how to reach Carole, do you? Too soon to have heard from one of her lawyers, I imagine.

As to _NO,_ I'm thinking of dropping the periods in the logo, closing it up and adding an underscore. Build on the updraft in traffic as it were. Though why solicit your opinion on graphics or anything else? Nothing but silence from your quarter – and after I gave you such a Boost running our interview. You should know that Bakunin's Rebellion's Comrade Refneski might well have proved an ally. He could've provided, not security I wouldn't think, but a 'shadow' or two to help document the further outrage headed your way. But your failure to contact him after he went to bat for you in my story Saturday has cost you his support. A simple courtesy note would have preserved your access to his ability to stage a countervailing video to the cartoon the MTA released last night. I'm sure you've seen his devastating efforts regarding the Gnome of Greenpoint, the little fellow born with no arms from the decades-old oil spill in the water there. Yes, *that* Refneski.

Admittedly, I do applaud your little disclosure on Syriac today. By all means bring the global armaments elite to a screeching halt (or at least slight braking) with any monkey wrench in the works you can grab. Get all the monkeys clawing and biting, and if it takes trashing a once perfectly good byline to do so, I at least am among the few who appreciate that you're looking at the bigger picture.

Have you considered a pen name? Keep your first name, thus: Daniel Hill. I've always thought Hill would be a good moniker. Short, sweet and you never have to spell it. Of course, it might be tough to establish a new byline at your age. In fact, I was a little surprised at the cops' video of you. Frankly, you write younger.

Stanley

****

I was none too thrilled with the prospect of prying off my gnarly grey bandage. What if little bits of Stuffing came with it? But last Thursday five sticky days past, this boy was taking a shower, no ifs or buts. I couldn't then leave it there, a sodden, congealing mass. Besides, didn't the wound demand a look-see? Prolong the agony by removing it slowly and carefully, or peel it off with a roar to mask the pain? A little worried what might accompany it if I yanked, I chose the former.

And it didn't look too bad. Inside the little crop circle of hair that Dr. Hwang had harvested lay the inconsequential mark, longer than wide and about the size of a small wooly worm, of a gun fired from fifteen feet. Damn lucky, even if the upshot was a job grading manure under an assumed name.

Eating the seed corn stashed away for Stap's rent, I grabbed fifty to (hopefully not) pay the HateCrime ticket and forty cause who knew what might befall before night fell; shat-showered-shaved; ran a damp paper towel over my slightly dressier black boots; pocketed a paperback and a slim reporter's notebook; made the requisite sandwich; headed on out. One flight down, I copped to a band-aid. The scab intact during my ablutions, that didn't call for exposing it to the world. Man, nothing but some large, ugly, orangey band-aids *perhaps* less alarming than the scab. Leaving, Nick had thrown them in the plastic bag that constituted my medicine chest. I also grabbed Bettinger's 'assignment memo' off the table in case some 'professed' scribbler demanded proof I'd spooked.

Spiffed in a pair of black chinos and a *laundered* blue shirt over a sweat-barrier black tee, it would've been nice to find a newsie downstairs to denounce the MTA's fairy-tale video. Or maybe they'd want to discuss my confession if it had already bounced. Syriac gone so Hollywood, I didn't know whether to take comfort from him pooh-poohing any thought of wrongdoing, or see his license as confirming my transgression.

Usually open in the heat, Mr. Staphilopoulos's door was closed as I crept by. Usually you'd see him across a dark expanse of living room seated on a wooden folding chair reading the local Greek newspaper under a window. At first I'd wave, thinking it ruder not to, but he'd just stare, enforcing the invisible privacy-curtain that hung at his open door. A closed door meant hope Stap was out, cause I wanted to let things at least marginally calm down – yeah, hold my freaking breath – before we spoke again, and he could toss the troublemaker on out. But he was out on his porch in nothing but an ancient pair of khakis and an even older pair of sandals, a surprisingly good chest for a guy pushing eighty, with most of the curly hairs still black.

"Ah, Mr. Staphilopoulos, taking the air this lovely morning."

A slow grin spread over a face that had seen too much sun. "You take it, Mr. Excitement Man. I don't like this air. An animal coming from a deep hole don't like this air. You make it better with a snap of your fingers."

"That's me: control the weather when I'm not making the world spin."

"You did *something*, wise guy, I not do my thirty-six years here with all my yellings. Your friends parked here babysitting you mean the project boys don't bring their dogs to shit on my sidewalk no more. That's good."

He pointed to the MTA cruiser I'd been trying to ignore, its cherry top gyrating red and blue, the bored guy behind the wheel fond of toys.

"Stap, I'm sorry. But look at that idiot with his lights just in case the whole block can't see him. I don't – "

"Hey, this best excitement here since the lady across the street got sick in her head and kept running around with her dress off.

And that was way back with the President who dyed his hair."

A couple of third-floor men slunk out and pushed past, one of them jostling me roughly though there was plenty of room on the huge porch.

"Hey, what's the matter with you guys – don't you know we got a big fish living here now?"

One kept walking, but the other made a big deal of turning on the walk and staring first at Mr. Staphilopoulos, then me, shaking his head all the while and then spitting showily on the step below where I stood.

"Hey, mister!" Stap yelled, loud but still amazingly sanguine. "You want to spit on him, I don't care. You're all big boys, do what you want. But out the other side of my gate. No fighting upstairs and no spitting on my house, the house you living in – however long that is. You got that, amigo?"

"OK. You the boss in this house. But tell him no more Migra. They in this street every day, and already two men gone. Some stay upstairs, scared. So they lose their jobs. All cause of this big pendejo."

"Look, pal," I told him. "It's not my fault if the cops are going nuts. That's what they do in this country. Your country too. But look at that car. It says 'Metropolitan Transportation Authority.' That means it's railroad cops. Got it: *el train*. They don't care about you. All they care about is me."

Looking up at us and shading his eyes with both hands for some reason, the sun oppressive but unseen as usual, he spat again, only this time off on Stap's rocks and weeds. "It's your problem, you fix it. Before somebody fix it for you. OK, *pal*?"

They left. So the South American Syndicate was after me too. Pile on the heap with the rest, boys.

Stap started laughing low. "Mr. Popularity – you got big talent make people happy."

"I'm glad you find it funny."

"I like funny at my age. I don't get much funny. I told you before, I like a guy mess with cops. Nobody does that since HeadFuck came in. Long as things not get too crazy, you OK here."

"Thanks, Stap. It's good to know I have a home."

"So what you all dressed nice for? You going to a lawyer? You want good Greek lawyer, very expensive, all the judges in Queens in his pocket?"

"I think I got a lawyer. I'll let you know."

I stuck out my mitt and we shook and, holy mackerel, he palmed me a ten-spot. Not a lot of rope thrown my way, who was I to insult the man whose roof sheltered me?

The MTA was tossing money around too, cause along with the standard-issue big glowerer behind the wheel, a female cop sat in the passenger seat, exhaling cigarette smoke out the window like it was her last act upright. And the sheer dingbatism of their flat-footed stalking rose up my throat and out.

"Hey, officers, thanks so much for the extra security. The whole block appreciates it. Since there's even less for you busy guys – pardon, Ma'am: guy and gal – to do once I leave, how about a ride to the subway in this heat so I don't get my nice clean shirt all sweaty. Maybe I'll start babbling, and you can crack the case."

I was babbling already, the request for a ride impulsive, silly and almost genuine once I realized how beastly it was out on the naked sidewalk, nary a tree the mile to the train's AC. Besides, what the heck was the point of their syrupy intimidation? The woman, too jaded to be really cute, took another drag, and the glowerer just shook the day's Kangaroo Krap at me and disappeared behind it. Guess it was a bum assignment, sitting there to no purpose, few folks drifting by to break the monotony.

But still an affront every time I opened the door. "Come on, how 'bout a ride? You guys are public servants, and you got a member of the public here looking for a little servicing. Whadiya say, Sunshine?"

The object of this last blasted the siren so sudden and so loud, I yelped and staggered back. I sure didn't like giving them that satisfaction though, unlike when Statie's club connected, these two couldn't hear my cry. Christ, it was a *lot* louder than a normal siren – a twin, almost, to the aural weapon the cops used in their fake ambulance to break up that anti-war Demo years and years back that Syriac mentioned. I fell further back, holding my ears and crouching down as if that would make it hurt less. Holding

246

his ears too, Mr. Staphilopoulos charged down the steps, his eyebrow tufts primed for battle. The sonic assault lasted a long moment; then we stood there twitching, its aftershock concrete.

Finally able to open the gate, Stap laughed. "More Mr. Popularity, huh?" He hitched up his beltless pants and then yelled far louder than was necessary, maybe from the clamor in his head.

"Hey you cocksuckers! I pay taxes here, you got that? I know people – people you don't want to know you. I'm talking Mister Bigs for the City. So be nice, you want to sit all day in front of my house in *my* spot. Or maybe time for you to go get coffee. Charge it to Staphilopoulos. Charge it anywhere, they all know me. S-T-A-P-H-I-L-O-P-O-U-L-O-S. You got that? Write it down! And then you go fart on my balls."

The dude stared, then – already way too hot for it – disappeared behind his paper again, while the siren-queen curled her lip. Stap said something unpleasant in Greek, hitched his pants back up, turned and marched up his porch steps and in.

Cocksuckers – wow – not to mention that farting bit I'd never heard before. In all my tangles with authority, I'd never had the guts for such endearments. So Stap thought his old-school connections still counted for something. Maybe.

Left alone, I half expected the cops to spring out after me, but there was just the barricade of newspaper and the flashing lights. Across the street, one of Stap's Merry Men stood on his porch shaking his head and wagging his outstretched finger at me. But I wasn't worried about my landlord. If he was pissed at me, he would've said something right then. He always did. Besides, yelling at those cops was the most fun he'd had in weeks.

1. Daniel Forbes, "Prime-Time Propaganda" and "Propaganda for Dollars" *Salon.com.* http://www.salon.com/news/feature/2000/01/13/drugs/index.html and http://www.salon.com/news/feature/2000/01/14/payola/index.html.

2. Daniel Forbes, "The Drug War Gravy Train" *Salon.com.* http://www.salon.com/news/feature/2000/03/31/magazines/index.html

3. Daniel Forbes, "Reading, Writing and Propaganda" *Salon. com.* http://www.salon.com/news/feature/2001/08/08/channel/index.html

4. Daniel Forbes, "Missouri Cops Said Ashcroft Agreed to 'Look the Other Way' on Forfeiture Law": The Progressive Review. http://prorev.com/bush4.htm

5. Daniel Forbes, "Judy Miller's Partisan Baggage" *The Huffington Post.* http://www.huffingtonpost.com/daniel-forbes/judy-millers-partisan-bag_b_5064.html

6. Daniel Forbes, "Blair Talks Turkey" *DrugWar.com.* http://www.mapinc.org/drugnews/v04/n000/a108.html

7. Daniel Forbes, "Noted War Blogger Cops to Copying" *Wired.com.* http://www.wired.com/politics/law/news/2003/04/58346?currentPage=all

8. Daniel Forbes, "Bound by a Patient in a Chair, the Feds Call Local Cops for Help" *DrugWar.com.* http://www.mapinc.org/drugnews/v02/n1684/a03.html

9. Daniel Forbes, "New York Used City Vehicles, Extreme Noise as Weapons Against Peaceful Protesters" *The Progressive Review.* http://nyc.indymedia.org/media/text/high-speed.txt

10. Daniel Forbes, "Did Russians Use Blog to Aid Iraq?" *The Progressive Review.* http://www.informationclearinghouse.info/article2951.htm

11. Daniel Forbes, "The Governor's Sub-rosa Plot to Subvert and Election in Ohio" The Institute for Policy Studies. http://www.fornits.com/anonanon/Forbes/ohio/ohio.pdf

12. Daniel Forbes, "White House And DEA Work to Defeat Michigan Drug Initiative" *DrugWar.com.* http://www.mapinc.org/drugnews/v02/n1636/a06.html?1163.

13. Daniel Forbes, "Fighting 'Cheech & Chong' Medicine" *Salon.com.* http://www.salon.com/news/feature/2000/07/27/ondcp/index.html

Chapter Twenty-Nine

HateCrime

Some drivers collect speeding tickets like lint in a fat man's belly button. Riding the Iron Horse, I accumulated my own frictional transportation costs, including this new HateCrime hogwash I had to beat or pay by that Monday's close of business. Otherwise there was nothing to stop them from issuing a warrant and showing up at my door that evening and off to the land of stale baloney sandwiches and its attendant thrills. So, no, I wasn't fleeing a bigger, more intractable problem (like a defaming police video) by heading to Brooklyn on something I could actually wrap my hands around.

It hadn't been my proudest moment, chiding a deliberately balky civil servant, back when Nick and I were still tethered but on the verge of Splat. An anti-incarceration, harm-reduction maven who ran a quality drug-policy boutique was looking for a director of research. There was a chance he'd be glad to get a stickler. It paid more than twice what I was scratching out freelance and, though I shrank from the thought until too late, my marriage was at stake. Emasculating, really, to quit reporting and be a flower girl carrying this guy's train, but I'd worry about that after I got the damn job.

Running late for the interview, I saw the nose of the train appear far down the elevated tracks and motivated the last block to the station. Though I'd emptied my MetroCard the day before, if no one had the gall to be on line ahead of me, I could thrust six soggy singles at the clerk, grab a MetroCard and levitate to the platform, the doors closing on my butt. No time to limp-noodle those bills into a machine.

I hauled up the stairs to the mezzanine, the train's rumble ever closer, and – yes! – no one on line. I thrust the bills in the slot, held up two fingers and half-danced a little importuning jig like a kid afraid he can't hold it any longer. My jitterbugging yielding nothing, it came time to venture a little encouragement.

"Come on, buddy. Train's coming! There's the money."

Doing some bookkeeping, the man behind the glass ignored me. He shouldered a tough, relentless job for not much money and less respect, serving rushed schmoes from all over the world while keeping his totals straight. I invested a third of the time to the train's arrival in silent propitiation. No avail. So, almost wagging my tail to get the clerk to spend a second on a customer, "Come on, pal! There's six bucks. All I need is a two-trip."

By rule, three token clerks later separately told me, they're required to stop their bookkeeping for a customer, and usually the clerks do everything they can to help you make the train. This guy finished with a pile of money and jotted down the total, his cue to dispense with me. Never looking up, he reached for a fresh stack of bills. The stairs down from the platform full of whoosh, I glanced at the turnstiles to make sure they weren't jammed with people, noticed a cop on the other side and turned back for a last-chance plea to this willful obstructionist.

Picking up that fresh stack of bills his Rubicon, I met him midstream. "For Christ's sake, you're doing this deliberately. Can I just get my damn MetroCard? The train's coming!"

Immune to insult as well as plea, the sneering clerk all-thumbs inched his way through my very simple transaction. They can seem to comply, fumbling just enough to scotch any hope. I finally grabbed the MetroCard and dashed, still with a glimmer of a ghost of a chance.

But not with my path blocked by an authoritarian in blue.

"Get over there, sir. Stand over there now!" The cop ordered me to one side.

"For what – the train's pulling in!"

We argued over where we would stand for the ensuing argument. The third time he told me to move, he puffed up and started reaching for his cuffs. The train starting up, I groaned and moved ten feet, staring at a young, with-it, skinny transit cop sporting a fine Frankie Valli duck's-ass and ink on his forearm of a face crowned by thorns.

I reached for pen and paper and peered for his name and badge number. He recited them proudly, did Officer Brian Malone, and then demanded, "Is that courteous, raising your voice like that?"

"I was talking in a perfectly normal tone," I barked.

"But was that courteous, talking to the clerk that way?"

"Look, being rude isn't against the law. I don't need to listen to this."

"So you admit you were rude?"

"What the hell is this all about, your ticket quota?" Kiss any hope of that job good-bye, I missed a second train. I took a step forward, he held his ground, pointed his leather ticket book at me and ordered me to stay where I was.

"That's precisely what we're talking about: profanity. And you're just digging a deeper hole for yourself with more."

In the years since my and Nicki's pounding at Lincoln Center, I'd actually moderated my diction some when circumstances demanded *and* pride permitted. "What profanity? What the heck are you talking about?"

"Sir, the booth surveillance system has recorded you taking our Lord's name in vain, and – "

"What're you talking about – whose Lord?"

Was I gonna have to call my prospective boss and tell him I was delayed wrangling over free speech? It wouldn't exactly improve my odds with that rather dour soul to hear I couldn't make it into Manhattan without tripping over the cops.

Perhaps not wanting to answer a theological question that had proved somewhat dicey down the centuries, he said, "Sir, it's everyone's responsibility to remain aware of changes in the Regs governing Homelanders/others' behavior. Hate leads to T. Are you not aware of the latest HateCrime Regs?"

"Cop, I got somewhere to be. What the heck are you talking about?"

"Jesus Christ" – the good little First-Communion boy bowed his head – "is revered by Christians and respected by all other religions. More Americans define themselves as Christians than Israelis do as religious Jews. Therefore, assuming that clerk is a believer, he shouldn't have his beliefs spat on while serving the public. Under Public Law 19-033, written by the Commissioner himself and signed by the Mayor last month, any offense to an on-duty City employee's beliefs is a Class Three offense punishable by a fine of up to $300. Since – "

"Three hundred dollars – you're out of your cotton-picking mind! What the hell – "

"Sir, I'm warning you. I will not tolerate any more such talk in the performance of my duties. As I was about to say, I follow His path as best I can and practice forgiveness. Since you were ignorant of the new law, I will fine you only fifty dollars. Now hand over your identification."

"You're the one fining me? Since there's no judge involved, maybe I should just pay you directly."

"If that's a bribe, this can turn real serious real quick."

"Bite me, pal. Though that's probably a bribe for you as well."

"I'm going to ignore that, and follow His path as best I'm able. But you should know the fine is the last part of the ticket I fill out. Now give me your ID or I'm calling for back-up. Which is it?"

I coughed up my papers and as he bent to write, said, "I'll fight it, I'll drag you to court."

"Fine. Do it on my day off so I get the overtime."

He then asked for my Social Security number. I told him he had my ID, he didn't need that. He primly pointed to a space on the ticket for it, telling me there was a line for it that had to be filled. I refused and managed, astoundingly, to make it stick. Then it was my work address and phone number, just so they could mess with your livelihood then – and with your SS number – for the rest of your life if they wanted. I told him I was self-employed and refused to say how.

Up on the platform, lucky not to have missed a second train, I swore satisfyingly for real, though none too loudly, and read that in Officer Malone's opinion I'd committed a 1050.7(r) offense. As his short narrative explained, I'd been "observed by PO being loud and boisterous and using religious hate speech." Boisterous – a classy, infinitely elastic word.

Being late for the interview and how that spoke to my "maturity" hadn't helped, my policy maven subsequently sniffed in a turn-down phone call that came one day before Bettinger surprised me with his clandestine little offer. Failure to get the job a straw dropped on an arthritic camel, Nicki pulled the plug right after my day-trip to Indiana. So trashing my byline – my name – to try to save my marriage was moot. Should've left for that interview five minutes earlier, should've had a valid MetroCard. Shoulda done a lot of things.

Chapter Thirty

Know-It-All Al

Amidst the weeks of intermittent fuming, a sporadic search unearthed a spoonful of mention of the City expanding HateCrime. But the text of the new law remained elusive. Was it so ridiculously broad that the phrase "For Christ's sake" qualified? I'd planned on uncovering its Swiss-cheese legal basis on Friday, maybe even venturing to the local cop-shop to see, however improbably, if they'd let me read the law there – assuming they had a copy. Tied up Friday, here it was Monday morning with my one o'clock court appearance fast upon me.

Time to read the damn thing and measure the rent I'd so boisterously torn in social comity. I managed to make it to the Transit Adjudication Bureau, housed in a once stately temple of commerce in downtown Brooklyn, without offending anyone. But there was no law to read – they said – just a ten-page pamphlet, the official Rules of Conduct, pried from the unwilling receptionist's grasp. Chock-full of prohibitions and circumlocutions, the brochure gave the cops innumerable excuses to fatten the City's coffers. Just sitting on the stairs waiting interminably on a train – a late-night practice for generations willing to sully their pants – could cost two-hundred bucks.

It was a cautious little instrument in some respects, taking five dense paragraphs to define who could use a guide dog and how. But it also reached for the stars. Section 1050.7(i) read: No one shall "Conduct himself or herself in any manner which may cause or tend to cause annoyance, alarm or inconvenience to a reasonable person...." That tie with that shirt, sir, truly alarming. Seventy-five bucks! Moving your lips while reading, Ma'am: fifty. If someone's boom box blared away in an otherwise empty subway car, would he be liable for a hundred-dollar tendency? But the brochure stopped at .7(i); progressing all the way to my (r) meant they'd really used the old noodle.

I set off for the Transit Authority's headquarters a few blocks away, twelve stories of glossy light and dark stone, to find a copy of the law. The guy in reception scanned his clipboard and determined that customer service was up on the third floor. He then confided about the law library on twelve, though he wasn't sure they'd let me up there. But I was required to *leave* my driver's license to go up, an awfully good deterrent to anyone reluctant to be permanently recorded as seeking redress.

No indication of where customers were served, two guys soon appeared, one with an unlit butt already in hand, and said Surface Transportation occupied the whole third floor. They pawed the ticket, but knew of no customer service or public affairs department at TA headquarters that could offer a copy of the law. They hadn't heard of the new HateCrime and, career civil servants, wouldn't opine on the ticket's validity. But they encouraged my quest for information and started musing about this one guy, Al, over in Bronx buses who knew just about everything. They led me around a corner to a bunch of cubicles and a youngish Al, who I'd assumed was some graybeard. Four or five people gathered round, glad of the novelty of someone attempting to run the City to ground.

Al said customer service used to be on the third floor, but it had been disbanded, not that anyone bothered to tell the lobby receptionist. Crappy little stores offered a customer-service window, but this sage knew of none for us millions of riders and suggested the law library upstairs. I assured them I'd never seen any of them and said I hoped to make it up to the Bronx for a bus ride real soon.

As I stared at the numbers over the elevators, someone stage-whispered my name. Al said, "I thought that was you, Forbes, but I didn't want to say anything in front of the others. There's something you should know, and let me tell you quick."

"I'm all ears."

"My girlfriend works upstairs for one of the MTA big Kahunas. And she says they've been working overtime to smear you."

"That's just the papers carrying the cops' water like usual. And TV – who cares? Here today, gone tomorrow."

"Really? Cause that NYONLY clip of you wearing those

254

disgusting shorts is bouncing all over. What the hell were you thinking?"

His shirt crisp and his hair slick, he sported the sort of rimless glasses that add twenty points IQ. "A smart guy like you, Al, getting caught up in sartorial gaffes too?"

"I've no time to argue the obvious. Look, some people in this building are behind you, however subterraneously. There's some weird stuff going on, if you catch my drift…."

"Well sure. I mean, no."

"Ever hear of an MTA police deputy commissioner named Walton Everidge?"

"Yeah. On TV."

"All over TV last night commenting on that ridiculously fake video they worked up on you. You know, 'the shooter' without a gun who gets a head wound."

"I am really glad to hear you say that about that video. I was hoping it was obvious to anyone who saw it. Can you nail that down for me?"

"Not without risking my job even more. You got 'em panicked, man. A guy getting shot just walking through Penn Station with a backpack – even someone like you – threatens their whole scheme."

"People'll start thinking they might be next."

"Right. So they demonize the shit out of the guy, not least with video of him with some kind of, quote, 'weapon.' I doubt you were pointing anything dangerous at two cops and a soldier."

"That's me, Mister Milquetoast. It was a little radio, just like *The Daily Chirp* quoted those two kids saying."

"You mean a transistor radio? They still sell them?"

Jesus. "Al – what scheme?"

"Alright. Listen and get this good. Everidge – "

The elevator I'd called popped open with a ring, and we both froze and stared obliviously up at the numbers. Empty.

"Everidge is slated for a big-ticket job with something called ASPIC."

"The outfit run by that nut-job who keeps marrying twenty-year-olds to save them? Got their hands in every security-MoFo pie there is. Drug-testing and bounty hunting, right? Plus mercenaries and private space-flight. And they got this facial recognition scanner that IDs you from the other side of a football stadium."

"I pegged you for a prairie dog too – up on your haunches, scanning the horizon. They pack that scanner in a drone's nose to pick out the right guy – you know, the Fiend with a *mustache* in the crowd at the market – and bingo! Like zapping bugs with one of those purple lights and too bad about any of the other bugs flitting around."

"Like John Doe says, 'The world's been shaved by a drunken barber.' "

He grimaced, put off by me trying to be clever too. "Look, you have no idea the risk I'm taking talking to you with what's going on upstairs."

"I appreciate it. I gotta tell you – "

"Alright! Now ASPIC, which is definitely one of the ultimate Beltway bandits, has the ball rolling for a huge new five-year contract to privatize the MTA's – quote, unquote – 'random' searches, which are totally useless, by the way. And Everidge is their soon-to-retire tool on the inside. They've got a sweetheart, no-bid deal pending – some MTA board member's wife is supposedly getting a big cut as a 'consultant' – to have ASPIC jack up the whole program to like $159-million a year. Then multiply that by five for the five years. Which is insane since right now the MTA is doing our little sham display for something like $9-million."

"Jesus, Al. Wait, that's like – "

"Just short of 800 million bucks."

"No wonder they were gonna scramble my brains. So what's the wife's name?"

"I don't know. Sorry. But even lining a lot of pockets, they'll still have to turbo-charge the whole program for that kind of money. So they'll be searching huge numbers of people and doing facial and/or iris scans on the spot of anyone who says boo."

"Using one of those hand-held *Gotcha!* machines, huh?"

"Forbes, HeadFuck et. al., is constantly looking to get folks in the system *and* get 'em comfortable having their biometrics read. It's not like a fingerprint, right, doesn't leave a stain, doesn't even physically touch you. Only it's worse, with cameras everywhere zooming in to pick you out of a crowd, the cops with those towers with like five biometric cameras in them all over the place."

"They had a tower at the St. Patrick's Day parade for Chrissake. Filming everyone marching *and* the crowd. Oh, and at a Mets game, too," I said.

"The NYPD has a saying: 'If you can see the Chrysler Building, we can see you.' Dominance and control – plus pure ego. And it's not just the cops, man. The New York Public Library, the one with the lions where nothing ever leaves the building, they're – "

"I used to use that all the time."

"I had to walk out," Al said. "About two months ago because they wanted a digital photo and your birth date – the month and the year only, like that slick little subterfuge matters when they have your name, address and face. Just for looking at a book right there in the building or using the Net. I told them to get lost. It's all about getting as many people as possible, in this case, the 'problematical' sort of person who uses sophisticated libraries, into their giant mug-shot file."

"What, the cops back-alley search their files?"

"Forbes, you think way too small. That's good. That's what it takes to walk around with a backpack to challenge this T-crap from the ground up. You're not naive, exactly, but you are willing to look foolish. Or maybe you just don't care. Like Aldous Huxley said, 'What fun it would be, he thought, if one didn't have to think about happiness!' "

"Happiness ain't been much on my radar lately, Al."

"So you end up leaving the house looking homeless the day after you're on every front page in town. Great. But either way, you're still a threat, so they're coming down on you like a ton of bricks."

"I'm glad they have such nifty reasons cause this nurse and I were trying to figure out why so many bricks."

"What might happen if you make the right Demo in front of someone with a whole-vid – legal or not – and it bounces?"

I nodded, though my damn *written* account would still be key far as I was freaking concerned.

He continued, "So go ahead, start with these idiot searches and take it from there. I've seen guys in suits *skipping* over to the cops' table. But it's all of it: libraries, ASPIC on the trains, getting DNA from anyone arrested for anything – that's *arrested*, not convicted – the radio chips people have been getting implanted in droves, so you can access your medical records in an emergency – yeah, right."

"Shit, I got my picture taken at the door to go have a beer, some idiot place my wife dragged me to. Plus now Easy-Pass combined with Automatic Plate Recognition systems, and – "

"Tell me this: back when they first started pushing user fees to drive into Manhattan, how come none of the articles ever mentioned that it would require cameras tracking all those cars. I researched it, did some radio archives, too. And not one story in a hundred mentioned that crucial little fact which might've really creeped people out. The fucking 'press.' "

"Now, now, Al."

"Say they have your markers, and someday a robot camera encounters you out in the world somewhere doing something bad, like maybe writing something down. Thirty seconds later you get spit out as that guy arrested years ago protesting cruelty to the horses at Aqueduct – or close enough to that guy – and down they swoop."

"Writing in public does seem to freak people out."

"Just be glad this is a government building. We don't like to spy on ourselves so much, but a private building, there'd be a hidden camera catching all this. And then I'm guilty of conspiracy just being seen with you."

"Freaking conspiracy of what?"

"*Conspire*, from the Latin for breathing the same air." With a rueful grimace, he really looked at me for the first time. "Let me finish about ASPIC, brother, before someone comes. ASPIC has all these bonuses built into their prospective contract to grab illegal aliens, deadbeat dads, registered sex offenders too far from home. Plus all these stealthy new offenses to get you into the database like your HateCrime nonsense."

"Christ."

"Stop saying that, Forbes. Who knows how many Red Calfers are running around here now."

"Just exactly whose Lord did I offend with that clerk is what I want to know."

"Anybody's Lord, man – whatever it takes to get you and the rest of us *processed*. What's more, the ASPIC contract authorizes some real black-boot stuff, their guys tootling around with submachine guns and full powers of arrest and initial detention in this huge warehouse they got cheap at the Brooklyn Navy Yard where they run your name and face through the mill till something pops. And cause they're private, no names and no badges – so no badge number. They kick your ass, go ahead and prove it."

He shut up and stared up at elevator numbers as two women yakking away walked past behind us. "Those two wouldn't see us if we fell out of a window at their feet. You know, people are all over the map on you since you got shot, some on the left trashing your 'ill-considered' action, some libertarians jumping to your defense. Either way, the Barmy Bibliophile Bomber – a Nazi, right? – helps scare everyone into accepting the searches that ASPIC and a bunch of newly retired train cops are gonna get rich on real soon. You're a bona fide, American-talking, white dude up to who knows what, so obviously no one's safe. Just search everyone. And calling it a Commie backpack was a nice touch. Army surplus?"

I nodded.

"Do yourself a favor, Forbes. Stay squeaky-clean as long as this lasts. No open-container bullshit, pay any back taxes."

Still before lunch, thank God he hadn't run across my Syriac confession yet. I smiled, wondering his reaction when he stumbled across it.

"Laugh if you want. And a haircut wouldn't hurt either. You cut it yourself? You know, it's not a done deal my girlfriend will pick you to unload her ASPIC poop."

"You don't mess around do you, Al? I know a certain Chilean ghoul I should introduce you to. It's not like everyone's got a cush government job to throw away twenty bucks on a haircut."

"Look, I'm on your side. Why else am I risking this idiot job standing here, a job I really need cause of something I wouldn't wish on anyone. You represent something bigger than yourself right now, so act like it."

"You know about the running of the bulls in Spain, right – well *I'm* the one chasing the damn bulls. People keep trying to draft me into some kinda 'Movement,' but they never can tell me much about it. I got nobody. I don't need anybody. It's Me against Them and screw every – "

"Rebel without a clue, huh? You ever stop and think of what grew from a female cop slapping the wrong Tunisian?"

"I'm not setting myself on fire, Al – way too painful a way to go. Besides, I'm a print dinosaur, so screw the little talking pictures."

"Fine. Look like you fell off a Mott the Hoople tour bus – fell and bounced hard. Just try not to be a four-flusher, that's all."

"A what?"

"Go take care of the stupid ticket. Maybe you'll get a decent judge over at TAB. They still exist, believe it or not. Cause your chances of looking at the new law with the Gorgon running the law library are slim and none, and slim just fell in the river with rocks in his pocket. I couldn't find the law's text anywhere online. And, believe me, I looked."

"Yeah, pretty damn weird. I spent less than an hour looking for it, but still…."

"Well I spent over two, and with a Masters in public administration, I like to think I know what I'm doing."

"So, Al, a young dude like you with a masters degree, fire in the belly, on the right side of the barricades – talking of *Gorgons* for crying out loud – I mean, what the hell you doing?"

"Bronx bus routes? Simple. My ex-wife and I have a five-year-old daughter with brain damage. Fucking says it in four-point type right in the combination vaccine's product literature: *may cause brain damage*. Not that we read that till much, much later. Fools that we were, we trusted our pediatrician. And, no, it's not the mercury anymore. That's a straw man."

"Holy shit. I've heard of that. That's terrible! I'm sorry."

"Don't apologize to me. It's her life they fucked, the only one she's ever gonna get. Anyway, I got Plunged and needed a job.

Believe me, even these days, there's still no health benefits like city benefits. With my daughter, end of story. Besides, having pretty much conquered the Bronx, I'm hoping they let me go play with that kick-ass little train down on Staten Island next."

"I'm sorry about your daughter. I don't know what to say."

"I start talking about it, I won't stop. That's one reason we got divorced. Look, my girlfriend's name is Elaine Livingston. Not 'stone.' She's even angrier about ASPIC maybe getting this contract, cause her heart is pure. Women, you know. She was bitching over what Everidge and his buddy, her boss, did to you with their absurd video last night. They didn't even try to hide what they were doing making it in this little den they have upstairs. She was already planning on contacting some reporter about ASPIC, once she found one with guts. They exist. But then you got shot, and she said it'd be poetic justice to pick you despite all your baggage. And here you are. Kismet."

"That's me, all the luck in the world."

"All you really need for a story is a copy of the ASPIC contract, and" – his whisper fell even further – "I know she's already got that. Now she's trying to get ahold of her boss or Everidge's employment contract too, and you're good to go. The girl's got balls. But either way, *if* she agrees you haven't been too compromised by your recent travails, you'll have enough initially with just the pending contract. Call her tomorrow, Tuesday, and we'll see."

"I call her *here*?"

"Are you nuts? No, at night. Call her – " and a man in a sharp suit strode down from the far corridor, one arm pumping, the other holding the papers he studied. Without a glance, he marched up and hit DOWN. I'd punched UP when he appeared, Al scurrying down the hall. Great, Al – just start dialing numbers at random till I reach Elaine? Sure. Maybe I'd reach Coney Island Emily along the way. But DOWN came home a winner under my heavy whip, and I turned to Al with a palms-up plea.

"Brooklyn," came his whisper. "She's in the book, there's only two Elaine Living*ston*s. Tuesday evening – and from a phone booth if they haven't shut them down by tomorrow."

261

Chapter Thirty-One

The Major Knows *What*?

The bell rang for UP. Maureen said she'd never seen so heavy a hammer, but an ASPIC dollar sign fronting almost $800-million explained a lot. If – *if* – Lurch was an ASPIC thug, that's why the cops, mere public servants, were afraid of him. The LIRR an MTA railroad, the pending ASPIC deal also helped explain why news of the LIRR riot was suppressed. Cat Wrangler objecting to a search had sparked that whole conflagration. Showing what might ensue – or worse, that it was even conceivable to refuse – no, no, no, nix that news.

Yup, on the very day my idiot confession shredded my hard-won credibility, a source swimming among the big fish of the MTA had potentially offered a whale of a document. Hell, just say Indiana was to make some money (not that I'd seen any). That floated any boat these days. No – to write about the experience. Having since confessed, brazen it out like everyone else. "Senator, I'm not here to discuss the past." And, "There's no point in prosecuting past offenses."

Three suits and a white-shirt cop crowded on the elevator on eight, and I faded into the back wall. My shooting would provide the wham-bang anecdotal beginning to an article on big-bucks corruption and the private thugs soon to be toting submachine guns on the trains. And my incarceration at Bellevue would be "Penn Tale's" perfect fulcrum. So a three-headed monster of a scoop and worth some money, especially if Elaine cooperated.

Getting out at the lawyers' plush lair on twelve, my incipient tantrum went nowhere. What chance would someone not professionally accustomed to flailing away against officialdom, or without English as his or her native tongue, or someone with a nine-to-five have had? Most people would have sworn loudly, maybe even boisterously, and mailed a check. And so our rights eroded as the MoFos gorged on bitterness, fines and arrests. I sat and ate my sandwich, enjoying a sports section someone had tossed. The Yankees were one-and-nine over their last ten, and the *Slimes* primly hinted at revelations to come involving a blimp pilot and a ball girl.

****

Upstairs at the TAB for my one o'clock hearing, I was taken aback to see the little sign hidden way over in a corner: Civil Court of the City of New York. Maybe the ticket referred to the Transit Adjudication Bureau so people took it less seriously, not realizing (Social Security number and all) the potential real consequences down the road when trying for a job, a loan or an apartment. Some sixty blue plastic chairs filled the room, and a sign commanded: "Please Remove Your Hat." Two dozen people were scattered around, three of us white, the rest brown or black, the median age two decades less than mine.

None looking gleeful and a few quite glum, folks eventually began emerging from the hearing rooms in back where they'd been ushered by one of the three administrative law judges. So did I prefer Hate adjudicated by the pale, orthodox Jewish man – probably not, given my offense – a black woman in richly tight pants, or, as it turned out, Administrative Law Judge Judith Feingold, a tall, hawkish dame with her own brittle appeal dressed in a loose purple sweater and straight red skirt?

"Well, Judge," I intoned, barely room to cross my legs sitting in her 'court,' "I hope you'll agree that today's case has nothing to do with what happened to me last week. And I also hope we can discuss this cockamamie new religious HateCrime law which I'd never heard of and which sounds like a gross violation of the separation of church and state. You see, Judge – "

"Tell me one thing. It's obvious you think you're clever. But that doesn't mean you're a Nazi like the papers say, right?"

"I was carrying a bunch of books, books that deal with over-arching state control. They've chosen to emphasize only one. But Judge, they're pawing through our bags any time, any place, anyhow. And now this new law I'm here on today is about controlling how we think. I mean, how did that cop know when

263

I told the token clerk: "For Christ's sake, give me a MetroCard," that I didn't mean it literally? That I wasn't late on my way to proselytize or something."

"The narrative is bare-bones, but then the police are told to write as little as possible since at least nine in ten New Yorkers just mail in a check. The less written, the less people have to dispute. Are you sure that's all you said?"

I nodded.

"As much as I might like to dismiss this ticket by highlighting your challenge to the underlying law, I can't. Wait! Luckily for me, Officer Malone has written it so poorly, I'm taking almost no risk in just dismissing it."

"It's a feather in your cap, Judge, that even with all my baggage, you're deciding the matter correctly."

"Way down at this level, there's still some judges – well, out of sight, out of mind. On the federal bench…." She held her smile a beat too long, wrote a moment, then picked up the top piece of paper on the tall pile near her elbow and bid me gone.

The ticket garbage on a technicality, Judge Feingold had written: "The NOV [Notice of Violation] does not state a prima facie case since it alleges only that RESP[ondent] was observed by PO being loud, boisterous and 'hateful.' It describes but does not identify the city employee allegedly impacted. Therefore, on its face, it does not allege sufficient facts to state a violation."

It sounded like the cop hadn't mastered a basic tenet of the new law: identifying the offended city employee, someone aside from himself. So I wouldn't get to channel Clarence Darrow on up to the Supreme Court. Having saved the price of dozens of slices and tallboys, I smiled my way down in the elevator. A tonic to meet an honest arbiter, someone looking to slap down this new law from her very low perch – if both she and some eventual misdemeanant had the guts.

****

The coming evening with the Wife my last, I'd get my first good meal in days, maybe even a few laughs with Nicki over old times. Anything had to be better than this death by a thousand cuts. Hell, just get it over with, perhaps even storm out. What, and skip dessert?

Mooning over a broken heart, the sudden, sickening realization slammed home with such force I was lucky the elevator cable didn't snap. I should've hit the STOP button and dangled in space awhile to get my bearings. Jousting with the MTA, I'd been fleeing buried doubts about my Syriac confession all day. No, not about its necessity. But, enjoying my cleverness addressing Bill and the world, I hadn't forced a halt to examine my basic premise. Beyond dumb – cause it was 'only' a letter to Syriac – to not exercise the due diligence an article demanded.

In other words, 'Who else could it be?' wasn't nearly enough of a justification for such a stark accusation against Chrysler. Not close.

I staggered out of the TAB building and collapsed on the same bench where I'd read the sports section, back when still anticipating my next triumphant whirl on the merry-go-round. That's right Al and Elaine, the boffo investigative reporter is at your door, hand over that ASPIC contract. You can count on me – never mind I may have botched some basic shit right, like who'd hired me to spook.

That cookie, Bettinger, had intimated his ass all over the lot, mentioning the Hillbilly Grinder's "competition" at least three times. Right, but he'd never specifically named our client. Damn, I never would've been so cavalier with such an accusation in a real article; that, or some editor (certainly Stan the stickler) would've sheep-dogged me to prove it. My stomach lurched, and for a moment I thought I might foul the sidewalk right there, a fitting commentary on my recent accomplishments. But who the freak else could it be cause DoD had already limited the competition to the Grinder and Jeep.

The online function on my antediluvian micro-zap went on the fritz back before Nicki and I did. And, concentrating on fluff like storing some rent away, I hadn't replaced it. Recalling a cyber-café two blocks from the TAB, I raced there ignoring an ankle at that stubborn stage where, the easy healing done, the rest was going to take a while.

Syriac had helpfully linked to Heavy-Duty Manufacturing's

denunciation of me and demand for an explanation. As its statement put it, "If these disturbing allegations from this peculiar individual in New York have any basis in fact, the Germans needs to address them quickly. Such tactics, if true, only underscore the Terminator's [HDM's name for the Grinder] overall battlefield superiority in a wide range of theaters from the Sands to any remaining Snow. Only a full disclosure of their relationship can allow the Dept. of Defense to properly award a contract that's crucial to America's Heroes Fomenting Democracy on so many fronts worldwide."

This did little but turn up the heat. Mid-afternoon and no word yet from Chrysler, I entertained the hope that my rash unbosoming might hold up. Who else could it have been? Syriac's comments page didn't shy from those decrying "journalists debasing themselves by dissembling." Still, about half sided with him in exonerating me.

Most of my personal e-mail I deleted unopened based on the malevolent subject headings. One tricked me, though, with what appeared to be a threatening reference to Nicki. But opening, "As soon as able get Money from Wife," revealed the same bilge I'd been punting for days:

Forbes, Mike Tyson was right, the only thing to do with toilet waste like you is to "eat your children." That's assuming you found some hoe to rut with. If you got no kids, me and Arthur will make other arrangements. You don't know Arthur, but that's okay. He does what I tell him – mostly. Sometimes he gets a little excited & then things get messy. But that's okay to because by then we're always way deep in the woods. Way, way back cause Arthur is real strong at dragging things. We don't never worry about cleaning up the mess. After me and Arthur get done – and that can take all kinds of time – the bigger animals take care of the big parts, the weasels take care of the smaller stuff & then the bugs clean up the rest real good. Leastwise, that is how it works so far.

So, you piece of twat, before you can mess with any more MEN putting their balls on the line keeping us safe from T-scum like you, me and Arthur will be making the trip up to Queens real soon. Right, as soon as we can make Arthur's wife turn over her

266

disability check for a couple of bus tickets.

And this is signed, so even on the computer you know it's for real – Me & Arthur.

Another note I foolishly opened praised the *Daily Chirp* for printing my address as "a public service." It got down to business quickly, something about extension cords that I didn't bother to finish.

Then the subject heading from a gobbledygook Hotmail address jabbed me in the throat: "I've got the real deal on Chrysler. Call me."

Nothing but two phone numbers with 703 area codes (DC's Virginia suburbs), one with a 1:00 pm time, the other for 3:00 pm. Plus the warning that "This e-mail account is already terminated" and the command to "Call securely." I'd long since missed the one-o'clock window and would have to hustle to make the three o'clock. I jotted down both numbers, reached under to unplug the computer and ran, the café dude screaming at me in Urdu or some such.

A half-full phone card in my wallet, I started racing to the corner when I realized it was already compromised by old calls to the listed number Nick and I once shared. I turned for the bodega the other way and it all magically fell into place three minutes before three, the name of my unattainable third-grade crush my new PIN.

"Hello."

First surprise: she was a she.

"It's me, Miss. I certainly appreciate your contacting me. Plus this is an anonymous call on my end."

"Good. Not that we're talking long. My name is Lois – not that you can refer to me in any way in print, not by gender or anything else. This is all on a not-for-attribution basis. Agreed?"

Second surprise: she sounded black, though with more than a touch of the South in her speech, it was hard to say.

"You have my guarantee … Lois. You're pretty experienced dealing with the press if you say not-for-attribution, rather than the useless 'off-the-record' that's been twisted and abused into meaning exactly nothing."

"Actually, no. This is my first time, and I'm not happy about it.

But I had to contact you rather than let my thief of a boss enrich himself while my brothers and sisters under arms are getting blown to pieces all over the world."

"You're in the military?"

"Major, United States Army – a fact that is most certainly off-limits. But to get down to it: Yes, you were hired to spy on the new Grinder, which, rumor has it, may be as much of a death-crate as the old one. I encountered your letter to that Syriac site today, but Chrysler was not – repeat, not – the client. I know who did hire you, and I can give you the e-mail to prove it."

Shit-fuck.

"I wish you would. Cause, assuming you're right – and I do – I really messed up. And I don't need that in my life right now. It would really help if I could rectify that ASAP."

"I have the documents. How you're able to use them is up to you. But you did mess up, which is surprising. Because it was the quality of your work that got you hired to check out the Grinder in the first place."

"It was?"

"Two points: I have what you need to make the case on where your assignment emanated from. Whether you contact that individual for his bullshit denial is up to you. Either way, you should understand that things are going to get hot for you up in New York because of your Syriac posting. That means as of now, today. I have no idea how far he might take it, but he can be a snake when cornered."

"So I got to add someone else to the list of crazy bastards out to do me harm. Sure, make it an even half-dozen – what's the difference?"

"Listen to me. This is some serious shit you've got yourself involved in, with barrels of money at stake. Your best bet safeguarding yourself is to publicize this man's involvement – like tomorrow. Go stay somewhere else tonight, cause I would think twice about going home."

"You're serious, huh?"

"In an operational context like this, I am tied down tight at all times. Something you might want to copy. Now look, I'm only saying this once, and then I'm terminating this call. Tomorrow,

Tuesday, I will be in the northwest quadrant of Farragut Square, a park in downtown Washington just north of the White House so it's easy to find. Northwest – like the only part of DC that matters to most people, that's how to remember the quadrant. I'll recognize you, but have a copy of *The Washington Times* on the bench next to you. I'll be there at both 0800 hours and at 1730. For your sake I hope you make it there by morning. You know north from south, right? And dress decently because you'll need to move around DC inconspicuously. Leave those nasty shorts at home."

"Wait. This is an awful lot to take in at once. What – "

"Farragut Square, tomorrow at eight. Like the man said, the journey of a thousand miles begins with a single step."

"You really think I'm in some kind of danger."

"About eighty percent probability. I can give this story to somebody else if you want. But, having screwed up on Chrysler, you need it more, and there's something to be said for that. And – well, there's something else that I'll explain when I see you."

"Well, OK. I guess – "

Baannhhhhnh, the line went dead.

Chapter Thirty-Two

Short Leg Goes Pfhifft!

So Chrysler wasn't the client said a voice on the phone.

****

Deep down, I'd always known I'd end up swelling my prostate inching a cab around midtown. Maybe just track down Statie or Frankie or 'DeBrunt' to finish the job the first two botched. Or finance Me & Arthur's trip with the rent money I wouldn't need and spare Arthur's long-suffering wife. Meet them in Van Cortland Park up at the top of the Bronx, the densest forest in the city, to save pack-mule Arthur some wear and tear.

Or take my rope-a-dope stab at redemption on Syriac a step further by exposing what sounded like a big-shot Army officer who, for obscure reasons of his own, had hired Bettinger, who'd then hired me. A story on that, plus "Penn/Bellevue/ASPIC," would make a nice one-two punch cause apparently I'd just agreed to drop everything and race off to DC. Soon to flit from one Green Room to another, willowy junior producers vying for my time on-camera and off, getting shot was just the tailwind I needed to leave Nick in the dust.

Absurd to jump like that cause a voice beckoned, someone on the phone speaking of a mistake, and a threat (only "eighty percent" probability") and its antidote – containment, anyway – which she just happened to possess. She built a nice, scary straw man, herself with a lighter at hand. A trap? Everyone knew where I lived since Sunday's *Daily Chirp*, so they could damn well trouble themselves to do it on my turf. Too unsporting, surely, to lure me to DC just for their *convenience*.

Right, time for Divorce Dinner – Nicki having hopefully done something horrible like chopping off her hair or getting coals-to-Newcastle fake ones – and then up way too early to catch the train to paint my way out of my dunce's corner.

The walls tottering on all sides, it was the absolute worst time for a galloping assumption leading to the worst mistake by far of my career. Self-publishing even a grocery list on the Net, you gotta, gotta, gotta self-edit. And then sit on it and then cogitate some more. And, for God's sake, don't drone on too long. Forget a second source, I had no affirmative statements of any kind. Bettinger's nod and a wink, misdirection from someone I didn't know from beans, was it. Me who'd always made that extra call, always been willing to further annoy a source.

Did I need to take Lois's warning seriously and head to Chinatown and one of those cheapo buses, a sketchy driver with two fingers on the wheel? Followed by a night in some flea-bag if I could even find one in ever-glossier, money-swollen DC, the local industry going great-guns. Go ahead, Major, lengthen the list, but please, whoever claimed the prize, do your damn job right. Don't leave me pissing in a bag, a nip bottle or three secreted away in my wheelchair, trying to rouse images of the Crimson Nurse – what the heck was her name? – hers the last breast felt while still a man even if only with my arm.

****

Rounding my corner, nary a news truck or even cop car in sight. Had fortune propelled me off the radar, my shoals plumbed so thoroughly by so many liars and cheats? Marvin, the self-righteous computer geek with the fantastic, criminally unused second-floor balcony, stood by the front gate talking with some bald doofus in a sack of a green suit. Getting a better look at the garish, orange tie askew, the glasses with masking tape at the hinge and the mole sprouting hairs on his chubby cheek, he looked too ill-stitched to be some shyster lawyer or even a cop.

A reporter, obviously. He'd prove easy enough to blow off, though I couldn't stop him getting some nasty quotes from Marvin. I had half a mind to stride up snarling incantations and drawing symbols in the air – give his readers their money's worth. Neither scrawny Marvin nor the bulky stranger moved out of my way by the gate. I waited a moment, then brushed past with downcast eyes so as not to crack the door to conversation. The guy had an odd twist to his foot and was wearing the built-up shoe of someone with a shorter leg.

Marvin said, "Right, that's him. See what kind of jerk he is like I was telling you."

Great. That didn't augur a pleasant chat, so using the front door risked rubbing Mr. Staphilopoulos's nose in the fact that Trouble leaving that morning was Annoyance coming home. I veered off across the grit and weeds that passed for his lawn and headed around back.

And the stranger asked, "You're sure, absolutely one-hundred-percent sure, that's Daniel Forbes?"

Marvin said, "Do I look like a man to make reckless statements? He's the newbie who thinks he's a big wheel around here. But he'll get taken down a peg or two before too long."

Some might say, Marv, that I'd recently been knocked down a fair number of pegs. I motivated around the side of the house, confident that with that foot the reporter wasn't catching up to fire any questions anywhere near me. A few steps on, I turned to see he was moving fast himself and with some kind of long-barreled pistol out, held low against his body but clearly visible when his arm swung out to compensate for his leg.

Christ, Statie! My address got published, and it took him all of one day to get this sweaty joker on me, only he didn't look like he was joking. I grabbed at the back the house with both hands wheeling through the turn as one of the little windows in Stap's tumble-down garage shattered, scattering several of the rats-with-wings who lived there. Man, not joking at all and a silencer to boot. The back door fortified by a rusty lock, the one key good front and back, I couldn't risk fumbling with it. I started praying for real.

What – where?

I dashed through the broken front panel and into the wreck of a pool, almost slipping into the swamp low in the middle.

And, kicking his leg oddly, he ran past the open panel, stopping to pound on the locked back door. Thank goodness it was locked so he couldn't get in to accost Stap and the lads. Shit, go on in, pal. Roam up one hall and down the next and look under each and every one of all those beds on the second and third floors. Let me flee to my new life washing cars in some broke-down western Massachusetts mill town.

He stopped pounding and took to kicking with that built-up shoe, bellowing in a husky wheeze, "Forbes, an atheist like you isn't disrupting our plans. You hear me? Not for us deserving few. So get down here and open this door now!"

I peeked over the edge of the pool and saw him with his ear up against the door, one hand clawing at it softly, the other holding the gun straight down against his leg.

"Forbes – let the Devil take you! This one is guaranteed to have no white hairs in its tail. We're not letting a non-Believer like you screw up our plans. You get down here now – and with that semen!"

What?

The hole in Stap's fence, the one I'd used Saturday morning sneaking out to the Chinese! I turned and again almost skidded into the swamp before edging around to the pool's missing panel in back. Out again, I had the momentary, fool impulse to jump in the purple Road Runner mired in the mud and try to fire it up for the first time in years. The keys dangling from the ignition winked at me as I dashed past bending low.

Pressing his ear against the door, the gun dangling, he was almost moaning it sounded like. He reached up and pounded on it softly. I scurried across the *long* patch of weeds and made it behind the one big tree to look again. He was looking up at the sky muttering – or praying.

Praying myself that the bloodhound stayed fixated on the door where he thought the trail led, I scrunched through the fence. With any luck, I'd get across the neighbor's yard and then up her driveway to head for the hills. His muttering grew louder till he declared, "And Amen!" His big dome visible over the fence, a light bulb appeared just above, and he turned to Stap's pool with an odd, strangled cry and stormed in. Good, fall in the swamp while Lois appeared overhead in her Army chopper, Maureen at the door lowering a rope ladder and ready to hand me a Ballantine.

I scooted across most of the neighbor's yard before cracking that twig. Should've known to wear my moccasins leaving the house that morning. Short Leg popped his head up over the wall of the pool and our eyes locked over the fence. His slow, slobbery grin led to a triumphant "Ha!" as he moved to the wall of the pool to steady his hand. "Pfhifft!" He grinned again and waved me closer, a cat toying with its prey.

I lept to the neighbor's back door as another "Pfhifft!" splintered the side of her house. Hey Up There, any deal you want, long as the back door was open to race blindly through *and* I could make the front door work without a key. Through a kitchen window I spotted the clunky, compensatory shoe scrabbling at the top of the five-foot fence, a fleshy athlete not to be denied.

I reeled down the dark back hall, bellowing. "Hey, whoever lives here – it's me, a guy from Mr. Staphilopoulos's house next door. I'm just passing through real quick. Don't worry about me!"

I shot a look into the dining room – empty. "Yo, wait, that's not fair! There's a guy with a gun! Dressed in a green suit. I think he's after only me, but if you're here somewhere, get behind a locked door and call the cops! Though he might be an off-duty cop himself, I don't know. Bye!"

Best I could do. I took way too much time fumbling with the front door's two locks till flinging it open. I screeched to a halt on the porch, but he wasn't lurking in the threadbare little bushes that dotted the front yard.

Down the steps and … where? To the projects? Not that they'd daunt this kook, but the buildings' zigzag footprint offered slightly better prospects than the grid of treeless, baked streets the other way. Maybe get through the projects' maze to find a loitering gypsy cab on the other side and then where, exactly, was I headed? To the local cop-shop?

Well sure, mister. We'll take a report. What color suit you say this gunman's wearing? Look, don't get excited. We'll send a car down there as soon as one frees up. Stop yelling, I said. So why don't you catch a bus, go to the movies or something. Or maybe you should avoid public transportation, huh, wise guy?

Crashing through the neighbor's front gate, I got such a pain in my chest I had to stop. But the count of five found me running for the projects. I kept waiting for the final "Pfhifft!" but made it to the corner. I looked back to see him coming out of the yard of the house the far side of Stap's clutching some kid's scooter. He saw me, beckoned again with goofy insinuation and then bent over to pump that scooter.

Hell, I'd gotten more than two score in – which was a lot more than way too many twenty-year-old Boots cut down mid-Fomentation.

OK, make him shoot me in front of a bunch of people. I dashed the half-block to my local bodega to burst through the door gasping for air. Everyone startled, including the two cops in uniform who must've strayed in for a soda or cigarettes, people on the clock eating better than that.

"Officers! There's a man with a gun. He's after me. In a green suit. He's already fired like three shots and he's not trying to hide it. Though he's got a silencer. A green suit, kinda bald, glasses and one of those built-up shoes when your leg is short."

One cop got on his radio and the other drew his gun and took a defensive position behind the Lady Lindas' display, peering over it out the window.

"Green suit? How tall? What's he after you for," one yelled.

The other yelled, "You're that crazy fuck that lives around here, right, the one in those shorts that's messing with MTA cops?"

"I don't know what he wants – not too short, chunky. But I gotta go, cause he's not fooling. He stole a kid's scooter, and he'll be here in a second, so – "

"Mister!" It was my buddy, the counterman who'd prophesized fame-driven fortune with women. "Come on!"

The one cop yelled, "Hey, wait!" and turned and pointed his gun at me. And the other one stopped barking into his radio and yelled, "Rick, here he fucking comes, gun in his *right* hand!"

The counter guy grabbed my wrist and jerked me through a slippery kitchen and out back where he bent to boost me over the tall fence into someone's back yard. Not knowing I could still do such a thing, I scratched and scrambled up and over and – Christ! – down far below, though my good foot took most of it. He yelled "Run!" and I turned to thank him. But he'd already grabbed a mop and was racing back into his store.

PART SIX

Chapter Thirty-Three

Heading South

I heard no shots as I ran up the driveway. And with all the sirens that rent the air as I ran, then jogged, then strolled, whistling, through Bumfuckville's little riverside park, and then zigzagged to the subway station two stops down the line, there was no way to distinguish the sound of any ambulances.

Waiting on a train heading to Penn Station, a picture loomed up of the assassin beckoning with his gun, wearing the demented grin of a father finally getting his toddler off to bed, mom out unexpectedly late. The gunman obviously not caring about getting caught, was I such damaged goods he had license to all but sit and have tea with Marvin, my tool of a housemate?

And I suddenly crouched down behind a trash bin on that distant subway platform. My viscera squashed, I soon couldn't catch my breath and finally reared up, scaring the heck out of some girl mooning away on the other side of the bin. The slight thing gave such a yelp, just the two of us down there at the end of the platform, she almost darted off for help until I managed to convince her it was some type of exercise for a bum knee.

Man, that queered things, someone wearing orange to my Bambi. That long stretch under the river to Manhattan, I forced my breath to slow and tried to divine who lusted so to see me cold, they stole some poor kid's scooter. Speaking of which, why was I heading straight for Penn Station – DeBrunt *and* Statie's lair – Short Leg certainly unhinged enough to be one of Statie's running buddies? Nope, I needed to take the back-alley PATH train and catch the DC train in Newark. The Hovel inhospitable, head to Washington to see about Lois's 'evidence.'

I eased up Ninth Street between Fifth and Sixth towards the

276

sleepiest of the several PATH stations. And, yikes, look at the soldiers – and not least because there were no cops in sight. Ten soldiers all on their lonesome searching bags at this rinky-dink PATH station, American cities the defeated South circa 1868.

Having seen enough soldiers scattered all over Manhattan in recent years, I should have taken this group in stride. Already shaky, I crossed the street and lurked by a panel truck to watch a military squad shunt folks into their little circle to be searched. *Not* NYPD-devil-may-care, two soldiers stood close, their eyes fixed on people's hands; two others flanked the entrance, their heads rotating, the tips of their rifles nosing curiously forward.

I stuck a foot out to test the waters in the street between us, got halfway and froze. A honking car materialized, and I leapt back to the far curb by the truck, my head throbbing again, this time the side by the wooly worm. I needed to breathe, stroll through the soldiers and get to Newark to fall out on the train to DC. Get out of Dodge before those two cops in the bodega put out an APB on me as a Concerted Witness or something – assuming they still could. Short Leg a doughy, older white dude in a suit, could I hope that improved everyone's odds of maintaining the number of holes they came with at birth?

Man, it was a *bunch* of soldiers out on their own recognizance, not just one or two palling around with the cops like usual, the latter at least offering a fig leaf of local civilian authority. The pistol on the hip of the sergeant running things was somehow more puissant than any three cops' exact same gun. None of the Jerseyites heading home said a word, neither the few picked for the plucking, nor the majority shuffling along staring at the ground like me at Coney Island. Happy couples chatting side by side were stricken silent and alone. *Do it to her. No, him.* One guy stage-whispered, "I hope this doesn't turn into another Penn Station, when that guy went nuts attacking that Protector."

I went nuts? I donned a far-off stare over a slack mouth, hunched down in on myself and, thus disguised, made it through the soldiers. Downstairs, shaky hands kept jamming four wet-noodle singles into a machine that spat them back. I tried to stiffen my bills cause, no, I wasn't using my credit card. Some chippie in a hurry behind me basically grabbed my inadequate

277

funds and swiped me through on her card. I didn't bother about the forty cents change.

In Newark, the cops were busy with a woman whose skin didn't quite stretch over her face and her drunk companion wearing many socks but no shoes. She kept screaming, "I got a check coming Wednesday. Talk to me then." Newark with enough homegrown issues, I caught the DC train no problem.

****

Safe, perhaps, for a couple of hours, I grabbed a seat on the left to groove on some fine decaying infrastructure as we rattled and thumped our way south. It was somehow too effete for a country of spewers to maintain a decent national railroad. The moon cloaked like the sun, Mother Ocean would offer her inky embrace south of Philly, dark water racing up to threaten the train.

Drooling there at Stap's back door, what had Short Leg bellowed – something about me not screwing up their plans? And that everyone had a purpose, and I wasn't defeating theirs, the *deserving few*. That sure sounded like a few top MTA cops about to hook up with ASPIC money. Al pegged himself as so damn smart, yet there he stood mouthing off in an MTA hallway – yeah, after I'd left my license down in the lobby.

And what about that other nonsense Short-Leg yelled, something about believers and no hairs in the tail? And I had to get down there with *semen*? Though not exactly my type, as little as I'd been getting lately (i.e., none), the fat bastard didn't have to come after me with a gun. A lot to think about on a parched throat, not to mention I was suddenly starving. To the snack car for a beer and some pretzels, those ten-dollar sandwiches out of my league.

Swaying to the rhythm of the rails with my two-buck-extra bottle of National Bohemian (a splurge since I hadn't seen one in years), a voice rang out "Yo, Forbes!" and I almost dumped it on the slinky woman I was admiring. It was a kid and, man, look at him, with his blonde tints, lime-green polo shirt with the collar turned up just so and Nantucket-Red pants looking extra-fetishy on someone so young so far from ACK-land.

I kept going, but he said, "Yo, I thought I recognized you from the news last night with that ridiculous band-aid on your head. You're the one getting Boosted sticking your nose in the cops' T-control."

Jesus, saying that right out loud about a Boosting! A lady got up at that and pushed past me to another car."Getting out of town, man? I don't blame you bro, with pictures of you in those shorts flying all over making you look like a Null."

"I have some business down in, ah … away. Why would I need to leave town?"

"You tell me, messing with New York's Finest, even if only the train cops. But dude, where's your entourage? You're like famous, all the stuff they've been saying about Mr. Metal Head. My girlfriend – we're in this special pre-Capitol Hill program down at Georgetown – said people were talking about you and this anti-search crap of yours at a party last night. And that's unheard of. Nobody at Georgetown talks about current stuff, not in pre-Hill. All political talk can do is ruin your chances."

I drank in the idiot flip-flops – Jeeze, his ankles were enormous – the buttery leather shoulder bag and matching suitcase scattered over three seats, the copy of *Maxximus* open to a comparison of picking up a woman to picking up a bowling ball, the absurd pants, the muscles, and the tints, not to mention a laptop frozen on an improbable female writhing on a stone altar. Movie or game I couldn't tell, not that there was much difference anymore.

A laptop! Cause with Lois and Short Leg running over my day and then backing their vehicles up for another go, I hadn't a clue as to Chrysler's response to my confession. Not with my busted, on-line-less micro-zap. So, "Politics have grown a bit problematical, haven't they. But, tell you what, friend. There's a piece of news I gotta check out, so if I could maybe look at your machine a minute, I'd appreciate it."

"You still communicate with smoke signals? *I'll* tell you what: fifteen minutes online for that beer. That little dictator behind the counter got all high and mighty on me when I gave him my step-brother's ID that says I'm only like thirty-two. I guess that boy's got an attitude problem, cause it works all over Georgetown."

I handed over the seven-buck Natty Bo as he complained he thought it was an Amstel, but he'd take it and half-tossed me his open computer. Laughing hard mid-swallow at my fumbling – I'd never had occasion to catch an open laptop on a moving train before – some beer foamed from his nose. He quickly wiped it with his collar (so that's why they wear them like that) and said, "Dude, that puppy's stone-ground military spec, its hard-drive resting in fossilized amber. You couldn't dent it if you dropped it from a plane." And with that he buried his nose in *Maxximus*, the skin book that dry-hump didn't show real skin.

Using his already open browser, I hit Syriac's link to the befuddlement emanating from the German's North American headquarters in New Jersey. Here's the relevant part, which made some thin sense a second time through:

We state categorically that no corporate officer here or abroad authorized, participated in or was even fully aware of the attempt to breach the security of our partners in the Greater Global Fomenting Campaign. Corporate staff in New Jersey met with surprise the 'blogged' claims made today by an individual so marginalized – a person recently exposed as opposed to Protectors' measures that aim for keeping us all safe – as to be almost unworthy of comment.

However, stated Marilyn Foster, a native-born, Externalities Presider, "The product launch for the 'Hillbilly Grinder' (as this second-rate platform is popularly called by Heroes of the Sands) was in fact a public meeting. Some twenty-three authorized journalists filed reports, and there were a 47 percent increase in the normal daily vehicular traffic through just the *front* gate of its Lester, Indiana plant.

Officials at Chrysler, a company embraced for now within our corporate family, stated from Auburn Hills, Michigan that they had no knowledge of any passive harvesting of competitive information.

The head of Chrysler's Washington Disbursement Office, Walter Pantly, was unavailable for comment. His deputy, who declined to give his or her name, stated that the office was studying the matter but could not comment at this time. However, sources within the W.D.O. office declared a "rogue operation that interfaced with the Disbursement Office" to be of interest. It was conducted by a senior leader of what is said to be a separate "organization." Said one source, "Sure the lever was in place – that didn't cost us anything. But no one in this shop has seen the need to pull it as of yet. Frankly, the unfortunately eponymous Grinder's overall stability is so poor, even that minimal extra expense seemed unwarranted."

We wish to ensure our 34,000 employees worldwide that we are studying the import of a remark we hasten to note emerged from the W.D.O office anonymously.

Finally, to return to the scurrilous individual who lodged today's unproven allegation – a man, it should be noted, whose intemperate actions engendered the tragedy of what affiliated, *official* press reports have termed the "forced" shooting of an innocent bystander – an examination of his so-called 'career' casts a long shadow on any statement he might make. Not only has his 'work' been rewarded by a drug-legalization organization backed by shady foreign-born billionaire, G. Soros. But he's also shown a tendency to baselessly attack powerful and respected institutions in the past. In fact, the White House itself once found itself compelled to try to censor him for bias. [FOOTNOTE ONE] That the White House effort failed doesn't lessen its significance.

A respected specialty publication, one arguably familiar with his milieu, made reference to a statement from an advocate for innocent young Homelanders regarding his "great affection" for "wacky weed" as a catalyst to his work. [FOOTNOTE TWO] No doubt that helped fuel the verbiage that appeared under his byline in such respected [sic] organs as *High Times*.

In fact, we could mine this rich vein for some time: for instance, he has acknowledged helping to organize the actual takeover of a public street as part of an anti-Fomenting Demo. [FOOTNOTE THREE] Accredited journalists representing official organs please contact this office for heaping *scoop*fuls of dirt.

In short, nothing stated by this person – who, for reasons rooted in a deep pathology, opts for extreme shabbiness when being interviewed by a New York cable outlet – should be granted any weight.

Finally, as a matter of personal privilege, the members of our New Jersey-based corporate office solemnly affirm and avow that we knew nothing of any of this."

Surely "extreme shabbiness" was harsh; wouldn't mere *remarkable sloppiness* have served? Thus the German's peculiar card, not that it bothered to cite *The Boston Globe* [FOOTNOTE FOUR] defending me against the White House, or me blowing the Partnership for a Drug-Free America out of the water in *Alternet*. [FOOTNOTE FIVE]

Syriac also linked to Heavy-DutyManufacturing having a conniption fit about this statement's oddities, concluding with: "Their man Pantly has been locked in a closet for the eight hours since their spy issued his statement this morning? Their telephone doesn't reach all the way to wherever he's pulled the covers up over his head? Since the Germans admit 'the lever was in place,' it seems they should pull it to produce Pantly to explain that 'rogue operation.' That or withdraw their inferior, foreign-owned vehicle as morally unworthy of transporting America's Fomenters heroically doing God's own work subduing Global T."

It ended by treading awfully light on me since I carried big buckets of HDM water.

I resisted the impulse to toss the pup's laptop back, thanked him, gave him my back and switched cars. Had Chrysler hired me or not? Should I be encouraged by its waffling non-denial/denial? What did that mean, the lever was in place: *The Moon is round, lads, but sail on the ebb tide*. They're "studying the matter"? Wallowing in it chest-deep more like it. Sure, the White House had accused me of bias – cause they couldn't dispute any of my facts. And forget the Partnership for a Drug-Free America saying I was on "wacky weed" (how *precious*, how positively fey) when I nailed them for like the 11th time, in that particular instance for plotting to interfere with state elections in Ohio that Syriac cited.

Needing to say something before the sun set, the Germans promulgated crap – including smearing the sugar daddy who'd given me one quite small, but welcome lollipop – crap so mutable as to be twisted any way they liked depending on how things unfolded. Twist slowly, slowly schmucks, cause there was a certain gorgeous Army major giving me the goods to nail somebody, whether Chrysler directly or as collateral damage, my assignation in Farragut Square would tell.

Baseless character attacks, fine. But some nebbish whizzing shots my way didn't sit right, not with entire continents full of women I'd yet to leer at. Master of a crowded editorial calendar and commander of the low-three-figure fee, let Lois help me nail it down, then publish quick as a first step towards resuscitating my byline and raising my profile too high to shoot.

1. Robert Housman and Daniel Forbes, "White House Blasts Salon" *Salon.com.*
http://www.salon.com/news/feature/2000/04/20/housman/index1.html#story_full_842f9804a9db0e4a2a011afba97e3735

2.Richard Linnett, "Adages," *Advertising Age.* http://adage.com/adages/post?article_id=51978

3. Daniel Forbes, "New York Used City Vehicles, Extreme Noise As Weapons Against Peaceful Protesters" *The Progressive Review.* http://nyc.indymedia.org/media/text/high-speed.txt

4. Mark Jurkowitz, "Online Journalist Tangles with Feds Over Antidrug Ad Policy" *The Boston Globe.* http://www.mapinc.org/alert/0161.html

5. Daniel Forbes, "Open Letter: Daniel Forbes Responds to Richard Linnett," *ALTERNET* http://www.alternet.org/module/printversion/13365

Chapter Thirty-Four

Indiana Wants Me

Man, I didn't need to pay extra for that Natty Bo just to give it away. I glared at the morose face glaring back from the dark window and searched for openings in the Germans' weasel words.

My false-flag trip to Lester, Indiana a couple of months back wasn't supposed to be so damn complicated. Bettinger had hired me for a pittance ($1500, or six or seven of my typical articles' worth) to travel under the flag of journalism to check out the proposed new Hillbilly Grinder. Get in to Heavy-Duty Manufacturing's dog-and-pony introducing its new light tactical vehicle, get out and report by phone to a Mr. X. Cash Bettinger's check at a check-cashing joint rather than fouling my bank account with something so fetid and put it in the rearview mirror. Then go scrub myself all over, the money salvaging my marriage for another month or two. Maybe.

Flat-backing a mattress for money, I'd treated myself to a Zounder! A final desperate grab for a lifeline, it was the last new Lincoln ever made. Clunky for a two-door and cobbled together from mismatched parts from Ford Europe, they sat untouched on dealers' back lots for years before being dumped on bottom-feeding outfits like the Rent-a-Heap at the airport. While the exclamation point seemed to help on hills, I was just as glad to have no time to master the 53-channel TV embedded in the steering wheel.

Bettinger had insisted on faxing me my marching orders rather than taking a second to summarize them by phone. And he was mighty ticked-off when I said I'd report in by phone or not at all, cause no way I was e-mailing anyone. Awfully dunderheaded of him to commit the assignment to writing on his letterhead, but maybe he was too busy marshalling private Boots hither and yon. For instance, it didn't take much digging to unearth his firm's role helping to quash that big immigrant uprising at the meatpackers outside Sioux City.

Five years back, HDM had sold the Army a brand new Grinder, the Terminator, its name a nod towards maybe someday reintroducing a version to the civilian market. But it proved so fatally unstable, so tippy, that a mere five years later – lightening speed by military standards – the Army had cancelled the contract. Here in the new contract's final round, after prototypes from such Fomentingly plump death merchants as Lockheed and Grumman had fallen by the wayside, it came down to Jeep's Repulser and HDM's not quite new enough Terminator.

Bettinger's fax ordered me to snoop on the Germans' presumed behalf in three areas: hidden foreign content (for obvious reasons, since they still owned Jeep despite all their efforts to unload Chrysler); secondly, had the prior model's woefully inadequate engine, transmission and suspension been improved; and, third, was its armor still so mismatched to the underlying vehicle that the damn thing rolled unless driven – at war, often on roads that barely deserved the name – like it was tootling around Mayberry for a quart of milk.

Amusing myself that morning pressing buttons on the Zounder! dash to no discernable effect, I wondered if I'd even get past the front gate. HDM's in-house PR, a Mr. Faxil, was decidedly vague when deigning to take the fifth call from one Preston Lestwick, who I said was doing a story with important T-logistics implications for *Untoward Vitiation*. And yes, Mr. Faxil, it was on spec, just a further indication of the story's significance that I was risking my own time and money. *Untoward Vitiation*'s editor, a far glossier rat who I'd met once or twice, us both scrambling for cheese, would've busted a gut to hear I was in Indiana on a nuts-and-bolts defense procurement piece for his scandal sheet.

Out in Indiana, Preston had some business cards identifying me as *Untoward Vitiation*'s Senior Econometrician; a *very* occasional contributor, I'd failed to crack the masthead. I was costumed econometrically in a tight, mostly green plaid jacket, yellow shirt and brown slacks unearthed from deep in my closet.

Then it hit, what if I ran into my old running buddy, David

Kiley, a big-time auto reporter down from Michigan? I'd pre-submission edited his two best-sellers (in some circles), fun books both, one a history of Volkswagen, [FOOTNOTE ONE] the other of BMW. [FOOTNOTE TWO.] He'd have been shocked to find me there, my biz-writing days long past. Might've gotten awkward trying to finagle an explanation the savvy Kiley would buy, especially since I'd skip lunch with him to report in to Mr. X . Hell, even if he figured it wasn't kosher, he wouldn't squeal to HDM.

I forgot Kiley – writing major stories on Detroit's fall and uncertain resurrection, why the hell would he trek to Indiana – and went to smile my way inside a defense plant with nothing but a homemade business card. Sweaty palms gripped the Zounder!'s wheel pulling up to the HDM gate. It featured a guard tower and enough fencing and razor wire to safeguard the $2,700-an-ounce gold in Ft. Knox – what was left of it.

The two guards wore the standard-issue stompers and goggle-like black shades, plus silver and black baseball caps. No name or insignia adorned grey uniforms that seemed to shimmer somehow as they moved. One slung a machine pistol over his shoulder and approached my window with a clipboard. The other went to the passenger side with the same gun cradled in the crook of his elbow, a mirror on a pole in his other hand.

The first had Preston's name on a long list – one hurdle cleared! – and, icily polite, told me to pop the trunk and hood. Blinding lights switched on at ground-level as the other guard busied himself with his mirror under the car. I found the little latch for the hood, but for the life of me couldn't find the trunk latch. Cars backing up behind, I importuned with a look. Frost forming on my glasses as he spoke, he advised that the morning's presentation would wait until everyone was "situated." Almost pushing him with the door, I eventually got out to stand blinking in the fierce light to bend for a better look under the dash. But no. He finally reached in and found it in a nonce, a damn *button* up under the dash, not a latch like the hood's.

There was a moment's panic signing in on whether Lestwick had an 'e' on the end. But I was ushered into a cavernous presentation area, the working part of the factory curtained off with floor-to-ceiling industrial curtains. Among the couple of hundred people milling around were a bunch in dark suits and maybe twenty in dress-blue uniforms. Engineering types in khakis and short-sleeved dress shirts trailed the officers. Numerous workers in jeans clustered back by the refreshment tables laden with soda, chips, cookies and untouched fruit, competent looking men with serious arms, some with serious bellies. The very few women wore skirts to the knee, not a pants suit among them, their blouses featuring a frill or bow to conceal the bustline.

Up front, there were rows of chairs before two long, draped tables with name cards and more chairs behind. The guest of honor graced the gap between the tables so as to appear in any shot of the speaker at the low podium. Painted in camouflage, the Terminator wasn't much bigger than the current Grinder, just a lot angrier. It's windows opaque for some reason, I was glad to see one parked in back with its doors open for the assembled press to sit inside and play soldier.

I skirted one of the scrums around the competing local-TV beauty queens (no concealing frills or bows) and looked around for someone with a tongue loose from too much soda, an engineering type maybe – they always like talking about their work. Ah-ha, *there* was my guy. His double chin ill-shaved, his enormous red and white checked shirt stolen from a scarecrow, his darting eyes pleaded for relief from standing there alone. Yup, that was a pocket slide rule nestled among the pens. Math. That meant he knew … something. OK, my standard ice-breaker from the good old days.

"So, whadiya think of all this wretched excess?"

Wrong move. He wasn't some lissome lovely at a crowded party I was trying to maneuver out to the fire escape for a private chat. Hell, the two of us would probably tear any fire escape from its moorings. He looked at me uncertainly, swiped at an oily nose with a meaty paw, but said nothing.

"I mean all these cookies and stuff. TV-girls – generals, for crying out loud! Some of those guys gotta be generals, right?"

"I only had seven cookies. We got an e-mail about minding our manners. Decorum they called it, with the reporters here. So I

287

asked Mr. Kearney, and he said there was no *numerical* limit as long as we were polite and didn't stuff our pockets."

"Well, I had ten myself, but they can't touch me. I'm a guest."

"The peanut butter ones don't look it, but they're really the best."

"Plain old chocolate chip for me, my man." Jee-zus – next! But all I saw was a sea of backs; talking to the cookie monster hadn't raised my meager stock. Besides, he had that slide rule….

"Just looking at it, it's obvious that your Terminator is going to wipe the floor with the Repulser."

"You've *seen* the Repulser?"

"No. How? I mean, isn't Jeep – hah, that's a laugh. Aren't the Germans showcasing it next month?" He nodded. "I guess I was thinking of Raytheon's new APC." No point harboring my scant lingo.

"*Raytheon* is doing a new armored personnel carrier?"

"Yup. Very hush-hush on the QT. Shouldn't even have mentioned it, so if you could forget you heard it, that'd be great. They don't want to tip, uhm … Mack Trucks to their plans."

"*Mack Trucks*?!?"

I shushed him with a finger to my mouth as he fished a cookie out from among the pens and chewed in obvious befuddlement at the shocking competitive info I'd so casually let slip. Why the freak couldn't Mack make an APC, they put their minds to it – or Studebaker for that matter.

"So, that Terminator, that's a beautiful hunk of metal."

"Metal's the key component," he declared. "But I don't know about all that dark green in the camo. I sent a couple of section chiefs an e-mail on it and got a rather rude reply about sticking to my area. One even grabbed me in the cafeteria and said just cause I have a Ph.D. doesn't mean I know everything."

Wound up, he waved a hand around clutching a cookie from who knew where. Plucked it from my ear perhaps, though I was the one dressed like a vaudevillian. He complained sensibly enough about the green not working well in the Sands.

I cocked an eyebrow at him. "Maybe it's not meant for the Sands."

"Is *Norway* our next pre-emption? It's not like there's many

Christmas trees in any of the Sands, right?" Giggling at his own joke, he choked loudly on the cookie, and several heads turned our way. Damn!

"So what is your area of expertise, Doctor?"

"The most important of all, the bottom hull."

"Of course."

"The half of the bomb that makes a big hole in the ground we don't care about. It's the half of the bomb that goes up, where the soldiers are riding, that counts. And if stupid HR, not an advanced degree in the whole bunch of 'em, would just leave me alone, I might be able to save soldiers' lives!"

More heads turned at his outburst. "It's always the visionaries," I comforted him, "who suffer with marbles at their feet." Come on doll-face, let something slip before they drop a net on you.

"And that stupid Indian transmission. The bean counters, who don't come close to understanding my work, are insisting on it. Something about a whorled gear. All I know is it bumps out and totally messes up my hull coating. Transmissions are mechanical – you can bend them if you have to. You can't *bend* metallurgy. Besides, who cares how much it costs the Indians to reconfigure. Let them charge us an extra $270 per vehicle."

Of course the Plunge had hit the casinos hard. But since when did Indians make transmissions? I tried to ask, but he had a full head of steam.

"IED transverse penetration causes even more fatalities than the rollovers. And aren't rollovers one of the main reasons the Army cancelled us after only five years, hoping we could fix it this time? Well, *that*'s not my area, thank goodness."

Catching sight of a tall, fit man in a blazer striding our way, "Yeah, rollovers. What's the deal – "

But steam was leaking from his nose by then. "If they'd only listen about my reversed-ion, tungsten hull coating. I've achieved a 27 percent improvement in blast dispersal in the third quadrant of the hull alone. An extra $4,000 per Terminator is *not* that much. The Army's got to see that. When you compare it to the medical costs of somebody with no legs for the ten-year care-allotment they get under the new Enlistment Regs. I don't – "

"Wilson! Introduce me to our new friend here."

The man in the blazer was smiling so hard, he made *my* teeth hurt. I looked from the part in his hair you could set your clock by, to the crease in his slacks sharp enough to be illegal on airplanes, on down to the idiot tassels on his shiny oxbloods. So much for getting any more out of Wilson, and a damn shame, cause his sugar-high or something had really kicked in.

"Can't, Mr. Kearney. He never said his name." For a big man, Wilson sure shrank in on himself pretty small.

Preston shook hands with Wilson damply and Kearney wincingly.

"So, Wilson, what have you been telling our friend Preston here with such gusto?"

"My usual, Mr. Kearney. Reversed-ion tungsten. You know that's all I talk about to anyone who'll listen. That or Purdue girls tennis."

Picturing Wilson slavering from the front row over the young lovelies on the court, I hastened to assure Kearney we hadn't gotten to the tennis yet.

"Of course, Wilson. But I thought we agreed, you and I, after that unfortunate incident with that Marine colonel, that your tungsten wasn't quite ready for public discussion." He turned to me with his fierce smile. "Don't want to push it out of the nest before it's ready to fly."

"I know, Mr. Kearney. But still, the more people who know about it, that's more who can bring pressure on the Army. You get those ions hot enough, and once they start reversing – "

"Wilson! Zip it, now! Talk of ions with a guest is way out of bounds."

"That's OK, Mr. Kearney. Look at him. He won't understand any of it."

"Wilson, remember the e-mail from Mr. Samuelson himself on decorum with our guests. Now, have you – have you had any cookies yet? What? Good. Try the peanut butter, I hear they're best."

"Oh, I have, Mr. Kearney."

"Well go have some more. No – bye-bye, Wilson. I'd like to have a little chat with Preston here."

Kearney watched his broad back a moment, then turned to me a second before pasting on his smile.

1. David Kiley, *Getting the Bugs Out: The Rise, Fall, and Comeback of Volkswagen in America* Hoboken, NJ: Wiley, 2002.

2. David Kiley, *Driven: Inside BMW, the Most Admired Car Company in the World.* Hoboken, NJ: Wiley, 2004.

Chapter Thirty-Five

Windows You Can't See Out

"He's a brilliant metallurgist, you know," Kearney informed me. "Set the entire department at Purdue on its head getting his Ph.D. there. Some kerfuffle involving that tungsten of his. We're lucky to have him, of course. But Wilson's not quite ready for public consumption, not after we cut his meds cause he kept lying down on his lab bench. Not ready for – I assume you're press."

I admitted as much as various muckety-mucks started to drift over towards the two tables with the placards. Not wanting to fry Wilson's considerable bacon any more by linking him to my crucial question on rollovers, I temporized with something he'd said that made no sense. "So, Native Americans are making transmissions now? That's a nice, heavy-duty business. That's down in … Oklahoma somewhere?" They had Indians there, right?

"The Germans did what? Really – you've heard that? Son of a gun, going all affirmative action on us."

What? I almost fished for a cookie in my own pocket. "No, for you guys."

"Boy, that's news to me. I wasn't aware that Native Americans did that kind of manufacturing."

He beckoned with his eyes to someone over my shoulder.

"Neither was I. I guess there's a lot of crony-capitalism floating around these days, you get the right representation in DC." I gave him a complicit smile.

"Well, Native Americans can bid on that piece of business like anyone else. Bring it on."

The silence went from awkward to tortured pretty quick, both of us waiting the other out. I cracked first, trying to worm my way to any foreign content. "So, you guys dropped a Volvo engine in there?"

"Volvo? You've got some funny ideas, friend. No. We're sticking with the tried and true, a good, hard-working, fuel-sipping General Motors V8."

Of course your ideas get funny, plucking them from air.

"A V8 works OK, a vehicle that heavy, long as you keep it under 50 miles an hour, huh?"

He grimaced and smiled and again importuned someone over my shoulder. "It's worked fine for years. With the right down-road security projection, there's no need for our Heroes to exceed 50 m.p.h."

Un-huh. Bettinger was interested in whether they'd beefed up the power plant. "You ever think about going with a Caterpillar engine or a Detroit Diesel or something with some oomph that truckers use?"

"If you had any notion of this category, you'd know that the Krauts own Cat and that Detroit Diesel is also foreign owned. Post-Plunge, our heavy manufacturing isn't what it was, or haven't you heard. But we're glad to have a – well, that's right, a 100-percent American vehicle."

"All home-grown?"

"Like I said, various GM V8s have been working just fine for us for decades now."

"Quite an advantage that, fighting for a defense contract. Wouldn't want our Heroes riding around in foreign metal. So, 100-percent American, huh?"

"Ah, Colonel, there you are. Have you met our new friend, Preston Lestwick – a *special* friend, Colonel. I wanted to make sure you two met."

I turned and was confronted by a ball of wire that rendered the exceedingly crisp Kearney a rag doll by comparison. His hatchet of a jaw aimed way too close at my Adam's apple, he grabbed my elbow to pull me even closer as he abused my hand.

"Ah, the military perspective we've been lacking, Colonel...."

"Kubark," he growled. "I saw you talking to that brilliant Mr. Wilson a moment ago. Just generalities, I trust."

"Wilson and I plumbed deep platitudes, Colonel Kubark. And under Mr. Kearney's tutelage, I've forgotten them already."

"I'm surprised Wilson was allowed to attend this event,

Kearney," he said, staring dead at me. "So, Lestwick. What exactly are you looking for a military perspective on?"

"Now that you mention it, those windows on the Terminator there. Not to put too fine a point on it – but can troops see out of them? See where they're going?"

"Damn glad you asked that, cause that *has* come up for discussion. But we've got seven cameras mounted strategically round the Terminator's exterior. Catch you picking your nose a mile away, Lestwick. Upload your picture to Florida, and with their real-time, biometric enhancements, we'll *know* it's you in just over ninety seconds. They're heat sensitive and provide night vision and motion detection. Given those capabilities, we went for the full blast protection over mere unaided human vision. The naked eye is for the last war, not the next Fomenting Democracy on tap, right Kearney?"

"Whatever our Heroes need on the full-spectrum battlefield," Kearney offered.

"That must cost a pretty penny, seven cameras."

The colonel snarled, "You going to be the one, Lestwick, to knock on some brand new widow's door, her about to drop another kid, to tell her *her* Hero has gone to his Reward because the Army decided to save a measly $37K a vehicle?"

"No, sir, not me. But if you can't see out, why not just metal it over entirely?"

"PR, you come right down to it, for the populations we're Fomenting – plus our ever expanding Homeland duties."

Looking alarmed, Kearney said, "Don't you think it best, Colonel, that we focus overseas, what with American Heroes conducting three Democracy Fomentations and one Pre-emption."

The colonel coughed, but remained focused on four very shiny shoes, plus mine. "Ah, currently, that's *two* Fomentations, one Pre-emption. One, the hoped for surge petered out, and it's been downgraded to a Holding Action."

Wow! They'd bowed to the obvious, and thrown in the towel on one of the wars? But which one? I wasn't even sure which were Fomentations and which a Pre-emption. Us so chummy, I almost asked Kubark, but before I could get it out, he said,

"So, Lestwick – *Preston Lestwick*. I thought I was familiar with all the reporters – sorry, journalists – on the wheeled-vehicle procurement beat. But that's a name I haven't heard."

"Well, my magazine thought it would be interesting to approach such a crucial topic from an, uh, econometric point of view."

"And what magazine did you say you're doing this for?"

A particularly interested Kearney took a step forward.

"And how, for instance, that meshes with defense contractors' typical distribution of work among key congressional districts. Building, of course, on the pioneering work of Styron and … Cheever regarding the defense budget's failure to intersect with the country's overlaying macros and never a discussion of why or how. I think our Terminator here represents a very specific iteration with its innovative camera configuration that obsoletes unaided optics."

That left them understandably gasping for more, but always leave your audience hungry. Finally, Kubark said, "And you're working for who exactly?"

"Oh – ah, *Untoward Vitiation*." A gossip rag, one with pretentions, but still.

"*Untoward …*"

"*Vitiation*. It's a technical journal, well that and with a bit of celebrity gloss to carry the freight, of course. Its influence far exceeds its modest circulation."

"New to me. I'll be very interested to check that out." He again thrust his chin at my neck.

Kubark was getting more steamed and Kearney more pained with every breath I took. People drifting towards the rows of seats, I flung caution aside. "Does it still roll?" They stared, four lips pressed tight. "I mean, of course it rolls. It's not like it's tracked."

"What the devil are you talking about," demanded the colonel. But I couldn't bring myself to utter the offending phrase, *roll over*. "I mean, does it still tip?"

Kearney stared me down. "You mean *over*?"

"Yeah, like on its side, down the bank and into a river, Heroes laden down with equipment gasping their life's breath away?"

Formerly unflappable, Kearney exploded. "That trial at

Aberdeen was biased. Everyone knows that. A tree stump would've rolled, the way she was driving it. Besides, that is highly classified info – *toxic* in the wrong hands. *Directly* toxic to the hands holding it. You following me, bud?"

Licking his chops and trying to remember where he'd left his knife and fork, Kubark said, "Kearney, I'm just glad it was you, a patriotic private Citizen, and not this spear-tip of the United States Army instructing this ... person on what is what."

Aberdeen. What, the proving ground where apparently a woman had rolled a Grinder? And wouldn't Mr. X like to know. So, "Well: Aberdeen. I don't have to tell you how big a place that is, with all kinds of people wandering around. Why, I heard – "

"Alright. Listen up maggot, and you listen good." A beet-red Kubark was all up in my face talking low. "That test-range perimeter was as tight as a drum. I'm security for this entire program, and when I say it was locked down, that means it was clean enough to cook a grilled-cheese sandwich on its ass. So if anything got out, it came from inside. Which means it's only a matter of time before I'm breathing down that traitor's neck. You tell your source that!"

I would, soon as I met him. "Why, Colonel, I'm sure I don't know what you mean." I batted mint-julep lashes at him. "I see the union rep is free. Let me grab him while I can. Labor's view can be quite telling, econometrically speaking. G'day, gentlemen."

Jim Kowalski, president of Local 3 of the United Electrical, Farm, Service Workers Amalgamated – a rump, military offshoot of an eviscerated United Auto Workers – scurried off to one of the TV-girls just as I was getting him all warm and squishy for the kill on rollovers. Then someone tapped the microphone for us to take our seats, and I barely had time before the shilling started to grab not nearly enough cookies to keep the demons at bay. (The chocolate chip beat the peanut butter by a nose.) I plopped down in back, my notebook propped on my knee like a good pup, a hard wedge of a man in uniform who I'd seen huddled with Kubark glaring from across the aisle.

I'd come all this way on assignment, damnit, a professional who didn't like to disappoint. And while I could offer Mr. X.

a few frayed strings to tug, I had nothing conclusive. Man, I should've caught the five a.m. plane Nicki had pushed and gotten in some more schmooze time. Cause I got nothing from Congressman Howdy Doody and General Hosanna but happy talk about "the 100 percent all-American Terminator" – a "USA-united vehicle from right here in the heart of the Homeland." At that, the workers clustered in back got the TV cameras turned their way with some less than spontaneous chants of USA! USA! Never mind that the Repulser was made a couple of hundred miles away.

Luckily, the HDM boss invited guests to get a closer look at the two Grinders on display, so we weren't hustled right out. That a fancy gent with white hair was chatting up a terrified looking Wilson (ah, Turd-Touch strikes again) when I trolled by was moot since Kubark's bullet-headed subordinate trailed me closely. I joined the crowd of workers, engineering types and military men milling round the Grinder in back. But any time I ventured a hello, my new shadow was breathing down my neck. So all I got were versions of "Rah, team, here in the heart of the Homeland."

Once that became all too plain, I figured to at least sit in the monstrosity like everyone else was doing. I could offer Mr. X the pivotal intel that the cabin had nine screens, five gauges and seven dials. Oh, and a steering wheel – probably. I stood in line, but gosh if they didn't shut it down right when I was next. Too bad, cause it looked chock-full in there, enough doo-dads to fly a jet. Despite my protest, they made it quite clear – what with all the Fomenting, not to mention Pre-empting – they had to get back to work. Yes, at that exact moment. And thunk went the doors. The two young reporters behind me made not a peep, one reassuring the other they could make do with the handouts.

And that was that. Welp, time to fake it with Mr. X. Time to see if the campaign to restore pay phones to enable the post-Plunge fifth of the populace w/ithout a phone or micro-zap to call an ambulance had gained any traction in a place like Lester.

Rinsing my hands in the men's room – what the hell! – someone jostled me from behind. This subway rider instinctively clutched his wallet as a hand slipped something into my jacket's side pocket. Shrugging him off with an oath, I turned to see a well put together worker with a finger to his lips."A good one," he whispered and strode out, laughing to himself.

The deft precision of the hand-drawn map, coupled with his confident air, convinced me to follow his directions out to the fields a few miles from town. That and the promised "SCANDAL" – just the one word in block letters below the map. I could hope it was both about the Grinder and passed the smell test. If so, Mr. X would be glad of the delay.

Chapter Thirty-Six

The Man Who Didn't Give Two Shits

Two months back, standing on a baking back-country road fifteen minutes from the HDM plant, I tried not to gulp the blessedly cold beer mystery man slapped in my mitt when I went to shake. Still looking like he was laughing to himself, he'd been leaning on his small old beater of a pick-up at the crossroads in the fields when I pulled up.

"I figured, instead of a voice out of the dash leading you by the nose, you were old enough to know how to read a map." He was a little younger and just a little shorter, with jackhammer forearms, a drinker's loose, skinny face, and an assertive, tired voice, not too deep despite his size.

"I got that left turn by the water tower that was easier to see on your map than in the sky – they're taller where I come from – so I was OK. But, Jesus, a Genny Cream Ale, man. How'd you find them out here in bum-fuck Indiana?"

"Indiana's not so bad a place if you got to be from somewhere."

"No, of course not. I mean – "

"You're from where, New York? Guy I met in We're-Fuckedistan from there talked like you. A real zero, but I guess somebody's got to be from there too. Genny Cream, they're all I drink – when I'm drinking beer. A local guy has got some kind of pipeline to 'em for like $4.89 a six. They're weak, and that's good, as many as I been drinking since I got back. Developed a taste for 'em way back, when I was active-duty at Fort Drum. Just a baby then, I guess I liked piss-water beer."

"Still in at your age, you Guard or Reserve?"

"Guard. You never served your country, did you?"

I shook my head and introduced myself, unthinkingly using my real name. Christ – so much for the day's stage name. He crushed a hand still smarting from Kubark and said, "Everett."

"It's your dime Everett, cause I got fish to fry."

"I guess I'm supposed to trust you on the fly. Fine. My life insurance is paid up for the rest of the year. And my HDM job – forget my job. Except for losing that, I don't see this coming back on my wife and daughter. And they'll cope, she's got a big family. Nothing worse can happen to me than already has – not with what I've seen and done. Ain't no point sitting in the back of a Grinder with both your hands hid behind a ceramic vest and your gun at your feet – over in a Sands or here."

Not liking talk of life insurance and that the worst has already happened, I said, "Sounds like you got it sewed up tight."

He gave that the grunt it deserved. "OK, let's do it. I was enjoying the legs on that TV girl all the bosses were elbowing each other to talk to, her camera off or on. The brunette, not the blonde. And there you were standing behind her – who're you supposed to be, Jimmy Olsen in that get-up?"

"I'm just glad I haven't ripped a seam in this dumb jacket."

"Weirdest thing is, ever since I got my blast concussion, my balance is shot, my memory's not so great, and I get 'fogged-in,' I call it. Oh, and my wife and little girl love the mood-swings. But my hearing's been like 20-20. Better."

"I'm sorry about your head injury. Jesus, your brain getting messed with, I can't imagine. I mean, it's never happened to me, thank God. We all certainly appreciate your – "

"Can that shit. So I'm staring at the TV girl, hoping she'll drop that little gold pen she's waving around. And I hear you getting under that colonel's skin about the new Grinder. About the Indian transmission that's supposed to be this big secret till we get the contract. Even though it's not half-bad – better than the Allison spider trap we're using now, anyway."

"Indians, right. Why are Indians making something like transmissions? I mean who even knew they could do such a thing?"

"What are you talking about, all those billions of people over there. But wait – no, wait. So that shit-hole dictator, Kearney – who likes abusing anyone who can't talk back, especially that fat guy who ain't all there you were talking to – and that colonel had a cow when you started asking about how the Grinder is still way too top-heavy. Which is why I brought you out here. Cause anybody making a colonel unhappy – "

"Look – *you* wait." I was finally able to interrupt. "This is a conversation, not a lecture, or I'm leaving. If you won't let me ask questions, I can't do my job. OK?" Never mind that it was a whole other job than what he thought. He stared a bit too long, and I almost took a step back he was so intense. Finally he nodded.

"What kind of Indians are making your transmissions? From where?"

"From over next to We're-Fuckedistan. You know, the people put chutney on their curry. What, you thought they set up a tranny plant out in South Dakota somewhere?"

"So that's why Kearney freaked when I asked about that. Come to think of it, he never did answer my question about it being one-hundred percent American. The more foreign content you got, the less you can wave the American flag about the Germans owning Jeep."

"No shit, Shirley. But that whole 'home-grown' argument is shot, or it should be, with how many foreign *aspirants* they call 'em we got in the regular Army. Anyway, I start wondering about you asking about the transmission and especially about the Grinder still being tippy. Most of those reporters back there look mighty comfortable at the trough, but you look like maybe you gotta elbow your way in from around back."

And, finishing the bottom half of his beer in a single, smooth swallow, he squinted at me for an answer. Out there in farm country, there was even some sun this city boy hadn't seen in a long time. "Everett, I figure coming the wrong way to the trough is what this trip is all about."

"Good, cause I need a reporter, and they don't run in my circles."

He started ripping the label off his empty bottle. "My wife taught me this trick. Peel the label all the way off before getting another beer. Probably doesn't make any difference in the total come the end of the night, but it slows you down a little. We still love each other, I'm pretty sure." He caught my eye yet again. "Shit, ain't no doubt in my case."

I laughed to myself thinking about having to vouch for Nicki's happiness just then.

"Barbara's her name. She says this whole thing is because I'm mad the Guard is charging me 599 dollars for losing my helmet. Shit like that happens when you roll over in the middle of an ambush. So I grabbed Willie's helmet. He didn't need it anymore with his chest gone like that. So that's what I wore cause we didn't exactly police the motherfucking area getting out of there. Who knew the Guard was going to check serial numbers on the helmet they got back."

"I'm sorry about Willie."

"So's Willie. All the guns and ammo we give to 'friendlies,' you think it stays with them? The Hajis we're supposedly training, half the time they're too afraid, or indifferent, or doped up one way or the other to even leave their compounds."

"Nobody stays bought right anymore, huh."

"Not like in this country. Out West, Montana and Wyoming, they want to go fight Canada for all the water they're sitting on up there. Fine – long as you're straight that that's what we're doing. Hell, in the Sands a lot of these crazy Red Calfers talk about fighting for Jesus. It was half the officers – no, *leaders*, yeah, right – bite me! That's right, a new motherhumping crusade. Go for it, but do it proud."

"I wonder what excuse we'll come up with for Canada."

"They speak *French*, man. Anyway, I'm freezing my ass off up on top of this mountain drinking water out of a bottle. They're sniping us, we're shooting back – nothing but a piss-hole for miles around, it don't mean shit. Turns out they bottle the water in Colorado and ship it clear round the other side of the world in these little plastic bottles."

"What do they say: strategy's for amateurs, logistics for professionals. We might as well bore a hole through the earth and drop it down."

"Costs a million bucks a year to keep a Boots in your average Sands. They got hash, sure, some of them. But not much booze, and almost no hookers, but plenty of Big Macs and ice cream. Kids who didn't have money in their pocket for that crap at home go to war and get fat."

"Welp, war sucks, so I hear. But what can I do you for, Everett?"

"You're not as bad a wiseass. But you're still like that other damn New Yorker. Alright, the whole-vid I'm gonna give you might even make it on *Up Yours Truly* or *Breakfast Raunch*."

"Right. Cause you got some whole-vid that neither you nor anyone you know is willing to put their name on under the new Regs – but it's perfect for me. Whadiya got, HeadFuck and the Pope getting it on, one in a dress, the other in a chicken suit?"

"I only have one way to protect my brothers under arms from out here in 'bum-fuck Indiana.' And that's to see that HDM, which I've been working for for seventeen years, doesn't win the new Grinder contract."

"How you gonna do that?"

"I'm not. You are, with the whole-vid I'll be *mailing* you – like from the Post Office – starring the Secretary of Defense. Remember awhile back when she got banged up and had to cancel her appearances for a couple of days. Then she showed up with a big band-aid on her chin and joked to some reporters that she cut herself shaving. Only reason you would've heard about it was some yapper on TV worked up a spoof showing her shaving. So they nailed him for HateCrime cause of all the talk about her being dyke."

I admitted to some vague familiarity.

"It wasn't shaving, not that band-aid, anyway. Nope, she rolled our prototype going barely 35 miles an hour. I mean, she could hardly see over the steering wheel. HeadFuck's just trying a little misdirection with a woman, like they used to do with those black cabinet members they liked to shine a light on. Anyway, the SecDef ended up jerking the wheel – a little, not a lot – to avoid embarrassing herself driving over an orange cone on the course – "

"At Aberdeen!" Showing that you already knew stuff was one of the best ways to cultivate a source. But then I remembered I was only playing reporter that day.

"You knew about Aberdeen, or did you hear it today? Cause it ain't exactly the world's best kept secret around here."

"And you have proof of this?" Even play-acting, I still got that tingly feeling.

"Course I got it. You think I'd risk getting fired going AWOL from work the way jobs are around here just to chat? I'm sorry about your name going on top, but something like this, you gotta follow the Regs to get it pubished. At least you'll get a hell of a scoop out of it. Here's the deal: a little birdie gave you the whole-vid, and I'm the cut-out. Then you forget my name."

Shit, might embarrassing the Secretary of Defense, PC figurehead that she was, earn an Elevation to RoundUp? Not that I was actually doing the story. "It all falls on my shoulders, huh – *Minders Turn Elsewhere*!"

Everett would remain good looking till the Genny took its toll in a few years, but he got real ugly real quick. "Screw the Data. This is the real world we're talking about here, men's lives at stake. Besides, I don't think the fucker even exists. You know anyone the Minders have messed with?"

"There's one guy, but that was mostly back taxes."

"It ain't happening to the boys I'm drinking with after work – or anybody any of us knows. Let the Minders worm their way deep, deep down, have a party for all I care. Clause *I* don't feel 'em."

"I still need some sense of where you got the whole-vid. I mean, all the Regs on video cameras now, how'd a guy like – "

"You mean how'd a nobody-autoworker get ahold of a whole-vid of the SecDef herfuckingself proving the new Grinder's gonna chew people up as bad as the old one? And she wasn't some scared, lead-foot kid in-theater. She was driving slow and basically just yanked the wheel a little."

"Yeah – a guy like you or any other source, you come right down to it. I haven't made a career-threatening mistake yet – not up to today, anyway. But you're only as good as your last story, especially a freelancer like me."

What the heck was I talking about? I was just stringing Everett along fishing for details to phone in to Mr. X. No way I was putting out such an embarrassing whole-vid to draw all kinds of attention to my little corporate-spook trip.

Ignoring my question about its source, he said, "Which reminds me, we gotta talk about where you're going to send it. Cause our whole-vid is funny as shit if you don't think about what it means. First you see the SecDef hiking her skirt up to her butt so she can haul herself *way* up into the Grinder. Legs that should not see the full light of day. Then she's driving for a minute, which they can edit out."

"I don't know if you want to edit it any, so they can't accuse you of anything."

"Maybe, maybe not, given people's attention spans these days. I'll have to talk to the guy who took it. Anyway, then she does this little jog to her left – nothing big, not at all. But over she tips, sliding on the driver's side. She was going so slow, she didn't flip. And all hell breaks loose. Three emergency vehicles come roaring up, and a fire suppression team sprays this aqueous-film foam all over it. And they're running around putting a chain on it to pull it back over. But then a dozen guys just go push it over, and she's flopping around inside cause she's taken her seatbelt off. That's when she cut her chin; you get to see the blood dripping pretty good when they finally haul her out. So it'll bounce pretty high."

"Who wears a skirt to Aberdeen?"

"Gotcha. As to how we got the whole-vid – come on! The Grinder comes from here. Don't you think we had some folks babysitting it, going to Aberdeen and back?"

His bottle stripped, the label peels at his feet marked our rendezvous. He whirled and tossed it far.

"Great. So now some kid's gonna get broken glass in his corn flakes after the combine gets ahold of that."

"I doubt it, seeing as how that's sorghum."

Rasping his hollow laugh, he turned abruptly for his truck. What, I'd screwed the pooch ragging him about littering? He rummaged around under the front seat for two more Gennys and sneered mightily when I declined a second. "Can't drive on two, a big guy like you?"

"No. It's just that as a writer, I got to keep my wits about me."

"Unlike the dumb-ass who spends his day messing with machines that'll take your arm as quick as look at you?"

"Were you always this pissed off?"

He took a step towards me, stopped and stared, a little shudder passing through him. "You always such an arrogant prick? But Barbara'd tell you no about being always pissed off, that she married a cuddly ol' puppy dog. She wouldn't have married the guy who came back, not from that last tour."

"It was worse?"

"My first two Sands were SOP death-and-destruction. But we took so many casualties that last one, the officers lost control, and things got ugly up on that mountain. Some things you can't really imagine how they'll hit you till you see them for yourself. Like the fountain of blood when a man's head gets cut from his body. That was after we found three of ours from the neck down."

"Jesus, Everett."

"Never heard about that, did you? Theirs or ours. Anyway, all I did was watch, but I could've left. Just about every night now, I wish like fuck I had."

No way I interrupted the silence that dropped on him. Finally he looked up and said, "Somebody's gotta try to protect the boys HeadFuck's gonna send out Fomenting 'Democracy' in that thing. Since I don't give two shits anymore, it might as well be me. Like I said, the worst has already happened to me."

"Been there and out the other side, huh?"

"The main thing is I've seen too many dumb-as-dirt rollovers kill too many good people. Hundreds of needless fatalities, you count up all the Sands. It's so fucking bad, the Army built these shake-and-bake things they call HEAT – Humvee Egress Assistance Trainers – and trucked 'em all over to teach you how to 'survive' a rollover."

"They built some kind of carnival ride so you knew what it was like to roll?"

"Right. Except not 'was' – *is*. They threw 2,600 pounds of armor on the one they been making since 2010, and it's a fat broad in a miniskirt. When it's not flipping like a coin, heavy as it is, the transmission or suspension fail. Or the motherfucker sinks to the axels in any kind of mud. And the payload is so skimpy, you get blown up twice making two trips instead of one."

"Or you can't carry the gear you need to kick in doors that night."

"What I want to know is why is it always some shit-for-brains kid driving? The sergeants are always messing with laptops back to Florida so they can tell you from six-thousand miles away who's living in some house down the road. Split the blame so you don't have to feel so bad when some farmer gets killed."

He peeled his label a minute, then said, "Listen hard to what I'm asking you to do with my whole-vid, man. Has your life reached the point that you don't give enough of a shit? You fed up enough with what's going on – from HeadFuck on down to the bully with a badge down on your corner – that you're willing to try to make a difference?"

He stumbled so hard he almost fell, and I made the mistake of stepping forward with my arm out, asking if he was OK.

He slapped my hand away hard. "I am *not* drunk, damnit! That's my first two of the day, right there in front of you. And me not even done with the second one." He rectified that. "This morning I had *none*, not with all the bosses sniffing around that stupid ceremony. That's the damn blast-concussion I told you about messing up my balance. I'll probably fall face first into a machine press and that'll be that."

"I'm sorry about your ... injury."

But he wasn't listening to me. Then, finally, "An *injury*'s something you get playing ball. Mine is a damn war wound, a simple little IED that didn't leave a scratch. But the blast-wave hits you at 1600-feet a second. Then all the air that got moved out rushes back in at pretty much the same speed and clobbers you again. And your brain gets so shook – first one way, then the other – it ain't the same for a long time, if ever. I know I'm not close to getting it back."

"I'm real sorry to hear that, man."

"Tens of thousands of us with this blast-wave, and the Army doesn't do shit. It says, oh, it's just a concussion like you get in football. No treatment or compensation, and sure as hell no Purple Heart cause your skull stays intact."

"I thought they decided to give Purple Hearts for that."

"Nope, HeadFuck rescinded it. Didn't hear about that either, did you? They try to pin it on stress or depression and slap you on the ass out the door with a happy-pill. And all *that* does is turn you into a limp-dick tub of lard so you really got something to be depressed about. My deal ain't from me freaking out cause I killed some people who were trying to kill me. IT'S BECAUSE MY DAMN BRAIN GOT PUT IN A BLENDER! Got it?"

Jesus, he was scary. He looked off over my shoulder awhile, then grabbed my arm. "The main thing is stopping this new Grinder. It's one thing to get shot up in a fire-fight. That was another big difference in We're-Fuckedistan, them going toe-to-toe. Or even to buy it from a bomb in a goat. Spam in a Can ain't much, but it's something. But to get killed cause your own stupid vehicle can't take a curve over 40 miles-an-hour, that's just sad."

"Alright already. Send me the Goddamn whole-vid. I'll see what I can do."

"Both of us'll be interested in seeing what you can do. Look at it as your contribution as a civilian – a big one. I know the Regs on putting your name on top are messed up, I'm the first to say that."

Un-huh. But I gave him my bricks-and-mortar post-office box. Sure, that was a Data-screwed thing to do. But standing there in the stupid *sorghum*, it wasn't like I could start up a pirate Dutch anonymizing address, one of those supposedly stealth jobbies that usually last about three weeks before it got shut down.

We had drifted over by his truck, and he leaned in and took a picture off the visor. "Let's get this shit done, and you come on back sometime after the damn Germans get their Grinder contract. Maybe a year after it all blows over – assuming we're *both* still sniffing the air – and contact with you is a little less … sticky. Long as you drive. No flying coming to see me. See a little bit of the country before they stop you crossing state lines."

"You mean me, or everybody?"

"You tell me. Anyway, I'll let you meet Barbara and my daughter. We already know, what Barbara went through having her, she's our only kid."

He handed me the photo, and I gave a sincere whistle. Yellow-haired wife and daughter, sunburnt and pretty both, solid looking inside and out. Barbara wouldn't stand out amidst the foot-bound wraiths hobbling round Manhattan, and she looked all the better for it.

"Ain't Barbara a honey after all our years together? You notice I don't say my daughter's name. You gotta earn that, so we'll see. After sixteen months of me falling off that stinking mountain, she was scared of me at first when I got home. That broke my heart more than anything. She went from a toddler to a little girl, and I missed every second of it. And you don't get it back."

"That's horrible, man. I give soldiers props like everyone else, but I never stopped to actually try to … comprehend what that means."

"You know anybody been in combat the last couple of years? Huh, Mr. New York Writer Man? A good friend, not just somebody from down the block."

"To tell you the truth, no."

"It's the hicks like me and the foreigners, plus our home-grown Spanish, and a few black folk thrown on top to pepper the stew. No writers doing important work they got to stay sober for."

"Bottom line, Everett, there's no draft. So most of the country just skates by. All these wars, where's the Demos? We used to do 'em, hundreds of thousands of people freezing their asses off. Are people just scared of getting Boosted or what? Any Demo now, it's over getting abortion rights restored, or college kids worrying about their janitors' pay. But nothing about what soldiers are doing in the Sands or the MoFos are doing home here."

"Gotta keep your head down so you can buy the new micro-zap next year. Me, I'm trying to keep grunts from getting killed in a new Grinder just as tippy as the old one. So, you in or you out?"

"You're asking a lot, dude."

"OK. So we won't shake on it – for now. In the meantime, I got to get back to work. Look, the wife makes a mean beef stew. We'll drink some Gennys. They're a fuck-lot better than Hose-'Em anyway. "

"Hose-Em?"

"Hoosier. They dropped the regular beer, and all they're selling now is Hoosier-Dried-Ice, Hoosier-Clam Juice, Hoosier-Meth – whatever they call that one. Wash your dog in it maybe, but don't let it pass your lips."

We parted such friends, I fired up the Zounder! – roar chipmunks, roar – wondering what his little girl's name was and not where I'd toss the package soon to hit my post-office box.

****

Mr. X was pissed I called so late. He said he'd heard the presentation had ended by 11:30, so why was it pushing one o'clock? Then he surprised me saying he didn't like being away from his desk so long. I hadn't thought of him with a regular-type job. But I mollified him with news of the Indian transmission (he shared the general incredulity about Native Americans until I got him to shut up and listen) and especially the VIP rollover. He got so excited about that, I finally told him it was the "SecDef herfuckingself," and he just about swooned. I figured, what the hell, maybe Everett's scoop would see the light through this unlikely channel.

Mr. X was intrigued to hear of the Christmas-tree camo, but he already knew about the substitution of cameras for windows. I decided at the last minute not to mention Wilson's tungsten, which sounded like it might actually help protect Boots someday. No problem, cause the tranny and the SecDef sure stewed his prunes. Hanging up, I realized there was a sibilant little 'S' in his speech when he got excited telling me what excellent work I'd done, and that he'd tell Bettinger to cut a check that afternoon. Not that that freaking happened.

Chapter Thirty-Seven

Nick Spills Beans

Musing on Indiana, sheer nervous exhaustion eventually overcame me as we clackity-soothing-clacked down to DC. No rest for the wicked, my jangling micro-zap pulled me awake and away from Everett's groaning board. Forks in hand, Barbara, he and their handsome daughter – introduced as Betty – had all been laughing nastily, the child harsh beyond her years, at my tale of leaping long ago over a rat in a subway tunnel. Not growing up pressing their nose to a subway's greasy window during trips to town from Mineola, they didn't grasp the tracks' dark allure, punctuated by mysterious lights of many colors, cryptic signs and the occasional post-Plunge ghost station. They'd never sat astride a local, flogging hopelessly as an express cantered up, toyed with us a moment and then galloped by. The other train's adults flickered into view, first one then another framed perfectly for a moment as my local gave her all, and then quickly past, all of them oddly unmoved by the desperate race. I tried to explain to my phantasmagorical hosts that embarking decades later for the next station's half-moon of light was a drunken, manly scaling of the only Everest at hand late of an evening.

Unable to remember the last call with good news, I was tempted to ignore my micro-zap and seek sleep and a different dream, perhaps discovering if Maureen had had her appendix out. But it was an old friend calling, Nicki on familiar ground – angry rather than her recent patronizing over-solicitousness.

"Damnit, Danny. I'm paying a fortune in rent so I could quit riding to Queens on that train. Where the hell are you, and why aren't you answering your home phone? It ever occur to you our meeting tonight might be a little, oh, important – to me if not to you?"

My dulcet-toned wife, a little tipsy by the sound of it and a lot furious. "I'm on the train. Something happened, and I had – "

"The train? So you're late, and I should just meet you up by the subway? You get a kick out of me sweating my way all the way down here giving a hundred-and-fifty creeps *another* opportunity to comment on each and every part of me? Just cause I wore that yellow dress you always liked so much – you know the one – for our little whatever the hell it is, *ceremony*, tonight. That and having to flaunt it at work today after how you've fucked me over. That dress is probably the only reason Ernesto the slime overruled basically the entire rest of the agency who wanted to fire me on the spot."

Ah, the clingy yellow number, normally reserved for rats-chasing-cheese parties, not plucking Bumfuckville's strings. That she came so sculpted to highlight my loss thrilled me no end. "Listen, I'm on the train, a real train, headed – well, never mind where I'm headed. I'm sorry about your job. I really am. But I got a hot tip on fixing a bum steer. Did – "

"You're still funny, you know. I hope you don't lose that, all the shit going on with you. It's your most appealing quality."

"Advice on ensuring your successor is worthy of a dress that – *bright*, Nicki? … Right, you're just being all friendly. Sorry. Well that's sorta the role you're supposed to play, isn't it? … Cheery, right, to get us both over this little rough patch."

Finally, "Are you going to be a total asshole about this?"

"So *you're* getting all quiet and hurt now. I'm allowed to be an asshole if that's how I want to play it…. Anyway, this is doing nothing but amusing the dudes listening in. So did you happen to catch Syriac today?"

"Syriac? What are you talking about, with the world falling down on your head?"

"Something happened, something bad. So I'm headed to DC to fix what I can." Shit, I should not have said that right out loud.

"Something bad – something new bad? Or the same old bad as of five days ago when you threw your life in the toilet and pulled me in after you?

"Something new. And it's not good."

"And I'm supposed to care that Syriac, the great and powerful, added his two cents about you, like that's going to change anything? Will you please get real and maybe worry about what the cops are saying about you on *television*, for Chrissakes?"

"That is not something I'm worried about, the man with no gun and a bloody head who's called the shooter. No, it's something I wrote on Syriac, not vice versa. Anyway, look, I'm on to a couple of big scores – and no, that does *not* mean money – out of all this. So maybe it all happened for a reason, long as Carole gets better."

"She's better. She's going on *Breakfast Raunch* or whatever that new macro-transmission is for something like $40-grand on Wednesday. She'll probably be wrapped in cellophane. But wait a Goddamn minute. What do you mean all this happened for a reason? I'm probably getting fired from a hot agency's vice-presidency, when less than two years ago I was a glorified secretary living with you on rice and beans."

"Nicki, look, it – "

"But it's all OK cause you're getting some lousy little civ-lib articles out of it? The Minders are the only ones reading them, the crap places you publish. Times have changed, Danny, since HeadMan clawed his way in. I mean, F&F found out you're flirting with RoundUp as it is."

"Not on the phone!"

"Sorry. You know, I was doing pretty good, captain of my own keyboard, until you dropped this stink bomb on me."

"I'm sorry. Sorry about Fornix & Foyst. But I had to tell someone what was going on before I set out last Thursday to challenge the searches. Just in case. Jesus, I don't know who's more suspicious, you or Pop."

"Your father's a smart cookie. He'd be elbowing Fiore aside on *Breakfast Raunch* so fast her tits would spin. Car alarms would be going off for three blocks."

"How freaking drunk are you? Cause this is the most honest conversation we've had in a long time."

"Not nearly drunk enough. So what? I wasn't looking forward to this evening, long-time coming or not. Plus I had to mollify someone pretty pissed off I was seeing you at all."

"Ah-ha! So the yellow dress's true target is revealed."

"He's gotten awfully … proprietary awfully quickly. It must go with money. *Noblesse spoiled rotten* or something. He got

313

ugly, yelling I should call you and do it by phone. I think he's worried about one for the road, but I told him you've got too much self-respect for that."

"Don't be so sure in that do-me dress."

"I wish the hell he was here now so I could get out of here. He offered to drive me, but he'd probably get car-jacked down here in his ridiculous heap of metal. Though I do like the baby kangaroo-hide seats. You know, 'outrage' as a prestige branding device that was so big right before the Plunge. But him driving ran the risk of you two meeting – "

"Kick his ass for him."

"Probably. I haven't had two boys scrapping in the dirt over me since high school, though it'd never do for him to see where you live. I still wish he was here now to drive us home."

'*Us.*' '*Home.*' "Why, where are you now?"

"On your damn porch where I spend half my life these days."

"Jesus, are you? Look, Nicki – seriously, if you run in to some fat doofus in a green suit with one leg shorter than the other, keep going. Fast. He's bad news, real bad news. Don't talk to him, for real. And for God's sake don't tell him we're – that we know each other. He's dangerous."

"I haven't seen anyone like that. And who the hell wears a green suit? I'm sitting here in one of these nasty chairs waiting for these two jerks on the sidewalk to get bored staring at me so I can get out of here. I called the two car services whose numbers I remembered, and they both said there was too much craziness on your block right now."

"Why, what's going on? Aren't there any cops sitting around scratching their ass?"

"Nope. Just some remarkably unfriendly Spanish guys in and out. Oh, and your landlord, Mr. Stapapoopous. We had quite the conversation. A very 'subtle' visual undressing, part of his old-world charm, I guess."

"Nicki, you're hot, OK? All of Bumfuckville is in a tizzy, big-time reefer dealers throwing commerce to the winds to melt on the sidewalk. I got it. I sorta discovered that when we met, remember. Jesus – what's gotten in to you?"

"Maybe I just decided to live a little after hibernating so long.

So, hey, you're coming in really clear. Did you get a new micro-zap so you can finally get back online? Or is it still that same old dinosaur with no Internet and the fuzzy GPS that leaves you floating out in space?"

"The old one."

"OK. So no accurate GPS on you, right. Anyway, Stapapoopous – "

"Just call him Stap like everyone else but me does."

"Oh, only *you* can master it, you who grabs success by the throat and feasts on it. Of course. Mr. Poopous and I got to talking after I demanded he take me up to your 'apartment' let's generously call it. You didn't answer either phone, and I really did, you know, want to see you. I mean, I haven't even seen you since you got shot."

"Your concern knows no bounds."

"I didn't know if you were up there worshipping an open stove or what. So I got Poopous – who really is kind of sweet, bringing me an espresso and almost getting me to try one of his nasty little Greek cigarettes – to take me up there. So now you're fleeing all your problems running to DC to do one of your week-and-a-half jobs for three-hundred bucks?"

"Yeah. No. Just go read Syriac." Jesus, I shouldn't have freaking said that either. "Let's just say I had to leave in a hurry. So, look – walk the other way, you see that guy in the green suit."

"OK, no green suit. But, Danny, you gotta get some plants up there or a Farah Fawcett poster or something. Living like that, no wonder you're running around messing with the cops, getting yourself shot."

"Nick – for the last freaking time: I was walking through Penn Station minding my business when they shot me. That's important, OK, for your next sterling encounter with the jackals of the press."

"So that was all just your idea, right – all that with the searches? Nobody else involved ... *feeding* you the concept?"

"What? You know I work alone. What the hell's gotten into you?"

"And our bed. It looks absurd, that big bed crammed into that

315

little room. You can't even put your feet on the other side, all those stupid boxes you have up there. For what? No one's suing you over a story from five years ago."

"*Our* bed? The narrow little bed of nails I ordered is still getting sharpened."

"So ... what're you working on going to DC?"

"Nothing."

"Come on, Danny, you know I've always supported your work."

"You should remember one of the keys to our former happiness: you're a terrible liar."

"Yeah – screw you. Cause of you, I'm off the Army's African-descents recruitment – "

"Nicki!"

"That's what the government calls them. Our big plum, *my* big plum. Plain off it. Not even any behind-the-scenes tweaking the copy."

"I'm sorry. No, I am. What do you want me to say? I never thought I'd get shot refusing a search. Not really."

"Life sucks. But what the hell happened here tonight? Stapapoopous assumed it was 'Mr. Popularity.' Cop cars were screaming up to the bodega from every direction, he doesn't know why."

Where's Stap now?"

"Inside using the john. That's why I'm calling now."

"Did he say anything about any cop getting – *injured*, or a bodega guy?"

"No. For Christ's sake, Danny! You get mixed up in any more shit, just tie a rock around your neck and jump off the roof here into the river."

"Look, get Mr. Staphilopoulos to give you a ride. He's probably happy to do it."

"Only too happy. So, come on, you won't tell your wife what you're working on in Washington?"

"Nope."

"Well, where're you staying? That old dump we stayed in when you where down there messing with Congress, the Harrisburg?"

"Yeah, probably. Ah, Nicki" – and damn me if I didn't almost lose it – "those were the days, huh? Remember, pre-Data and all, you leaving that Senate office building ahead of me and walking on the other side of the street so you wouldn't get tarred with my brush. What happened to us?"

"That was fun, bringing the Drug Czar to heel. But cut it out. It's been a long, horrible day, and I still have to get back to Manhattan somehow."

"Jesus, Nicki, hearing your voice, even so pissed off and asking all these weird questions like I don't know what – it's tough. I've never had the greatest talent for friendship. I left that up to you for both of us, and it worked OK for a long time. Now…."

"Look on the bright side, dude. You're getting out of town, your luck's due for a change. Can't get any worse, right? And the Harrisburg's not so bad. Just bring your own towel and don't get naked between its sheets."

"Will you stop Goddamn mentioning it. It's not like I need to broadcast where I'm staying, some maniac taking shots at me."

"So that was you out here tonight. There's a shock. Some guy was shooting at you – what does he look like? I mean, I'm curious. Plus I gotta make sure I don't run in to him. Height, hair color, anything special, any – what do they call it – distinguishing characteristics?"

"What the hell kind of kool-aid is in that drink of yours? You haven't even asked me if I'm OK."

"Somebody shooting at my husband, a girl gets curious. But you're OK, right?

"Pretty shook, but OK."

"So can we stop being quite so self-important about this dumb call. Like with all the T out there – supposedly – all the *chatter* anyway, the Minders are wasting an actual live human listening in on you in real time to hear where you're staying in a couple of hours."

"Draw 'em a map, why don't you. Christ!"

"Hey, you there listening! Send a chopper quick to airlift me out of Bumfuckville. Yoo-hoo!"

"You saw the Goddamn *New York Toast* yesterday, with details of my calls and e-mail. Or were you too busy yesterday."

"I was busy, thank-you. I saw it very early this morning, or heard it, Ernesto reading most of it to me. I couldn't follow it all, he was so mad. His accent gets worse when he's angry. I do remember that like every third sentence was about me."

"I should sue that bastard, Tredwell, and the *Toast*. It's outrageous – "

"Just what you need, Steve racking up endless hours on another lawsuit neither one of you'll ever see a dime from. So read *Sy-ri-ac*, huh? That's easy enough to spell, right? That's what you're going down to DC for?"

"Nick, what the fuck's this all about, worrying about my micro-zap's messed up GPS and everything? You know how to spell Syriac's name. You're the one who freaking turned me on to him in the first place, *Nicki*!"

"So enjoy the Harrisburg. I mean it's right downtown, right? I – "

I hung up. So they flipped her, must've scared the hell out of her. Or maybe somebody leaned on Ernesto about his big Army account and told him to let her keep her precious job if she pumped me for info. Damn, that was dumb, mentioning the Harrisburg out loud. And, God, the way her voice went all cotton-candy: *Aren't you going to tell Wifey-poo why you're going to DC?* Surprised I didn't, cause angry, tipsy and dancing me round the floor to who knew whose tune, Nicki still had me rapt tight by frayed bonds that, Lord knows, should've ripped a long ways back.

****

Forget her *and* MoneyBags' damn kangaroo hides too – the porker, since she figured lover-not-fighter me could kick his butt. With her incessant parroting of its name, did I dare still stay at the Harrisburg? Had I been elevated to RoundUp and its real-time spookery rather than my Middling Severity's passive harvesting? That is, did I need a different hotel? Along with its busted Net access, my old war-horse of a micro-zap had only fudgy GPS, as Turncoat Wife had delighted in pointing out. Hell, stay there and just lose any tail going to meet Lois the next morning.

Lois thus protected, un-huh, did I have it in me to worry what might befall little old me? Screw it – Harrisburg here I came, come what may. Yet another in a string of long, lousy days, sniffing out another place to sleep was beyond me. If they wanted to mess with me, they knew the Hovel's address, and they hadn't yet. Nope, nothing beyond hogging the Greek chorus's parking spots, intercepting calls and e-mail, fake videos, la Migra rounding up my housemates, lies and threats, incarceration at Bellevue, a lame shooter….

I stared out the window to see an inlet racing towards me, a canoe perched on a dock, a new life washing dishes in some shore town a paddle away. Stop the train! Shave my head and sprout a beard. Was it possible to still disappear in America, start anew in a room over a shop – assuming I could beat out the hungry locals for a subsistence job? Where was the town without cameras grabbing eyeballs on every corner?

Chapter Thirty-Eight

No Blonde in a Red Dress

Unless Lois proved unexpectedly and marvelously hospitable, this trip to Washington would be far from my best. Probably the most fun was sitting next to a senator (back when that meant something) on the little toy subway that shuttles around Capitol Hill. Rushing off to vote and back, Sen. Byron Dorgan (D-ND) asked me to run it by him one more time, so I earnestly explained his devilishly complicated hearing to him. The matter was deliberately tangled, the Drug Czar seeking to obscure the $22-million he shunted to the TV networks for White House approved, viciously anti-marijuana storylines in the most popular sitcoms and dramas of the day. Good of him to mention my original articles, Syriac also cited the one proving the propaganda's raison d'être. The whole thing arose in response to the passage of the first medical marijuana initiative in California; it was social marketing geared to turn other states' voters against reefer as medicine.

Dorgan and I got off the train together, me yammering, him nodding, and strode to the elevator to the floor of the Senate. I was still talking as the door closed in my face. His anger grew in the twenty minutes it took him to return to the hearing room, and he was a far more aggressive questioner. Nobody cared about all the fancy charts and graphs that Ogilvy & Mather had tricked up around the room, the same ad agency later discovered to have tried to steal millions of taxpayer dollars through blatantly fraudulent overbilling.

A friend who caught it by chance on C-Span told me later they enjoyed the way I calmly interrupted my disquisition at the witness table to sip some water. Even better, if not as giddy as my ride with Dorgan, was hearing that Sen. Ben Nighthorse Campbell, the subcommittee's chair, said I'd done the country a real service. Some months on, a staffer and then Campbell himself called me, trying to steer me to the story of a guy named Abramoff who was ripping off a bunch of Native Americans. The story was complicated, and Campbell hadn't been able to interest any of the local big-foot reporters, so he thought I might be dogged enough to give it a go. But casinos? lobbying? Indians? How the hell was I gaining traction on any of that from up in New York, and I passed. Feast on success, indeed, Nicki.

Later it was the House's turn for a hearing, and I'll never forget getting a little choked-up raising my hand and swearing to tell the truth before Rep. John Mica, an unreconstructed drug warrior who didn't particularly thrill to my testimony. Small beer nowadays, of course, people basically laughing at Congress when they pay attention at all. But it wasn't then, back before the Plunge, and HeadFuck and the Disruption and the Data and all the lousy wars. Back when I caught lightening in a bottle.

The World Series is still a valid statistical benchmark they can't muck up with nonsense about this or that record in 'post-season play.' And there's quite a list of luminaries tied for second after Reggie Jackson for most home runs in a World Series. Jackson, the straw that stirs the drink, had five. Then, with four each, come such titans as Babe Ruth, Lou Gehrig, Duke Snider, Barry Bonds* and – that's right – Gene Tenace of the Oakland A's, the '72 Series MVP. He began the year as a young back-up catcher and hit only five dingers during a regular season that saw him bat .225. He went on to an entirely respectable major league career, but nothing like the bottled lightening of that week in 1972. Pausing to collect myself with that gulp of water and smiling for the C-Span camera, I liked to think I channeled Mr. Tenace OK.

****

Tints and all, Nantucket Red was easy to spot moving off in the crowd up ahead. I hung back as this strapping youth carrying a small suitcase and a shoulder bag sought out an incredulous Red Cap. I couldn't spot a tail in the crowd or on the Metro and headed for the Harrisburg Nicki was so fond of mentioning. I'd lumber out from under the net they'd toss the next morning – sure thing. In other words, I hoped Lois had weighed the consequences of summoning the likes of me.

Or maybe I wasn't making it till morning. As I approached the H-burg's front desk – just another Joe off the street – the pale pudding of a clerk barked, "Mr. Forbes, so good to welcome you to the Harrisburg this evening."

Exhausted, I plain lacked the oomph to turn on my heel. My (post-Plunge) fifty-six-dollar room was as I remembered from Nicki and my two stays. There was the rod that opened the vent for the air conditioning, whatever temperature management decreed. Threadbare towels – check; lumpy plaster walls – check; no shampoo; old-fashioned walk-in closet with a dime-store mirror hanging on a nail; the riot of miscellaneous hangers, yours for the stealing; the parchmenty window shade that recoiled with a snap; the dark, heavy furniture made of real wood; the sagging bed with the nubby, pale pink bedspread; the apathetic TV: check, check, check and check.

I wrestled the bureau up against the door – laughing somewhere, were you Maureen? – and took out the micro-zap the Wife had turned Judas. Old and therefore built to last, I repeatedly slammed the bureau drawer home on it to no effect. My eyes suddenly fuzzy – damn you, Nicki! – I went bat-shit, swearing loudly from way down deep as I abused something even more defenseless. Finally smashing it on the tub, I emerged victorious from the Battle of the Phone, pieces resting on a carpet mottled with stains.

Man, I was hungry. A cabbie lolling by the entrance had said I'd be lucky to get some over-priced gristle at the one joint open within blocks. Yup, downtown a little after eleven in what was laughably still called the capital of the free world, God forbid there should be a deli open to get a cheap egg salad hero.

Still breathing a little ragged, I sat and waited for the thump on the door that never came. Screw 'em. Statie got slammed, Frankie bounced, the papers smeared as much egg on themselves as me, the MTA's obviously fabricated video fell flat (says me), Short Leg's only casualty was Stap's garage window (I could hope),Carole was healing and Turncoat Wife was a smoldering cinder, the pain cooling. Sure, I'd nicked myself screwing up over Chrysler. But the only one who'd scored a real hit – so far – was that damn NYONLY chippie, a sartorial hit. The rest of you motherhunchies, get behind that electronic fence with the Garden City guard dog. That's right, *Can't Touch Me!*

Stomach grumbling, I fell asleep watching flickering Angels (I half expected to wake up to a test pattern on the H-burg TV) taking a lead on the White Sox on a walk, a balk, a squibbler and then a monstrous three-run homer by an emergency call-up second baseman in his fifteenth major league at-bat at age thirty-one.

****

Abroad in the glossy, shuttered downtown at six and no coffee for love nor rue. Why hadn't folks from any number of far-off lands gotten rich fixing that, and why did the locals tolerate it? Only the closest of friends ever wondered aloud how their government had gone so wrong. But last night's proffered plate of gristle and the morning's forced fast made it clear: folks with any sense or standards stayed far, far away.

I set out to meet an undoubtedly beautiful Army major armed with the documents to shift my chestnuts to a different fire. That, or slink back to the Hovel leaving my Chrysler boo-boo unrectified. No big black spewer with tinted windows following me at five m.p.h., I cast searching looks at the cab and truck drivers, the porters hosing down the sidewalks, the odd office worker getting an early start, the many! homeless just starting to stir from the ledges they'd found for the night. No one looked back but the guy I handed some change. "May the Tail be red," he intoned. Right – fresh from a spanking.

Jeeze, it was already hot. Waiting on a light, a staring crew-cut man spooked me onto a bus at the last second. Fifteen minutes north into steadier deterioration and then the subway back, no blonde in a red dress dogged my heels far as I could tell. Can't Touch Me! Strolling with one eye in the back of my head towards Farragut Square after seven o'clock, I finally encountered some food, its over-priced drabness (powdered eggs?) mitigated by its skimpiness. That some grinning lout greeted me with wild enthusiasm at the door and pointed me to the counter five feet ahead did nothing to redeem it.

The eagle-eyed oaf darted, sorta, into a Metro station, lingered, then out a different way. And finally I noticed the American flags everywhere. Leaving the Harrisburg an hour before, I'd been too wigged about spooks behind the wheel of every cab to notice them draped over office building doorways and taped to the inside of windows up above, as bunting in store windows, as street furniture on poles at corners, and plastered as ads on the sides of buses, a credit line thanking a chief Despoiler.

Such my normally circumscribed haunts, it *was* good to be walking round a far-off town, however thin an excuse for a city. Not allowed to over-awe the Washington Monument, the office buildings marched down K Street in lockstep height of a dozen or so stories, and this New Yorker enjoyed the expanse of visible murk overhead. Slices of bread in a stale loaf, the buildings echoed the government marble and limestone, a beige façade following khaki and preceding tan, the rare glass or metal skin a marvel.

Man, that *was* a gun on the hip of the private guard outside that private office building, then another guard packing a half-block on. The Disruption, after all, had started a few miles away in that first food riot in Chevy Chase. Alright, focus on my meeting with Lois. Keep my eye on the prize – and my hands clearly visible.

Farragut proved a pleasing spot of green surrounded by a bevy of red, white and blue. Pushing 7:40, I decided to sit and stew rather than running around aping sweaty 'tradecraft.' To check on my progress on any number of fronts – heck, Carole's too; when did Nick say she was going on *Breakfast Raunch*? – I bought a *New York Toast* from one of the many boxes on the corner. But I didn't open it, content to sit gazing about in the southeast corner of the park, catty-corner to my assigned quadrant. The northwest, right, was where Lois wanted me, where the white people hang, she more or less said. And how likely that a white person would say that? Could I hope her boss was a general and not 'just' a colonel? Along with the color of my whistle-blower's finely sculpted skin, I'd learn his rank soon enough.

The traffic was mild and unhurried – until sirens announced one of the regular mini-caravans of spewers, their lights dancing as they ushered some muckety-muck to his desk. At one point, three seven-ton camo trucks lumbered to a stop as a bus stalled up ahead. Momentarily mired in traffic, maybe ten soldiers leaped out in vests and helmets and all kinds of unfathomable gear, pointing their M-36s every which way. They scrambled back up only as the trucks were moving. No one but me as much as blinked.

Tuna-on-white (extra celery and mayo), a mess of people headed early to their desks to paper over cracks in the Imperium or siphon money from its maintenance. Most wore two or three plastic ID badges around their neck. The men, many of them former captains of their homeroom intramural volleyball team, sported short sleeve shirts, baggy slacks and, for some reason, garish ties infantilized with old-school VW Bugs or little hula girls in grass skirts or the like. Perhaps it was their subconscious comment on their day.

The women tended towards the amorphously appealing in that they were young, healthy and clean-scrubbed and wore clothes that offered a few palpable hints. Echoing the buildings' palette, their knee-length dresses with complicated, concealing bust-lines were typically worn by New York women thirty years to the bad. They looked like former powers in the French club or debate team, and a vast number were pregnant I soon noticed.

My mind drifted to the Wife's betrayal nattering on endlessly about 'You sure you're staying at the *Harrisburg*?' When would I stop calling her the Wife? Her lobbing the MoFos' questions at me in her icky new, overly insinuating manner – forget her boyfriend, that settled it. I wrestled off the inscribed band of gold – copious spit lubricating it painfully over the knuckle – and parked it with the pocket lint under the one key I carried.

La-de-fucking-la…. Down the tubes, and the day beckoned.

****

I strolled half a football field to my assigned sector, passing an entrenched encampment (that *was* a bookcase full of books) of eight or nine homeless folks right in the middle of this small park surrounded by deluxe office buildings. They were of a piece with the multi-hued homeless all over the place, visible but unseen and apparently unmolested. Unlike the strident defense of any horizontal surface in Manhattan, the DC ledges and cubbies they slept on were unspiked. Gripped by money and policy and failed conquest and clamping down – and money – the local Despoilers and Deciders' sole contact with the street (unlike in Manhattan, were they *might* conceivably walk a few blocks from office to restaurant) was three ushered steps from back seat to guarded front door.

I felt slick picking a bench commanding a view of anyone approaching from basically anywhere in the park. Three minutes past eight a passerby said, but no sign of her. Major Lois was so damn military-precise, she'd punted our meeting as I was coming up the walk?

Her contralto from behind made me jump.

PART SEVEN

Chapter Thirty-Nine

A Fan Led this Lamb to Slaughter

"Forbes, I told you to display a *Washington Times*, not that out-of-town garbage. This won't work if you can't manage basic operational coherence regarding a very simple order."

Was I supposed to jump up and salute? I turned in my seat and gaped at her, not because she was indeed black, but because whatever I'd expected, Lois wasn't it. Her broad, appealing face under short, spiky processed hair was set off well by oblong, almost-green glasses that any gay graphic artist would be proud to wear. Tall – really tall – she was perhaps just starting to benefit from slightly slacking off years of intense physical conditioning. She came around, sat down and, yeah, another damn soldier made this typist wince when we shook.

"You can close your mouth Forbes, or did you not pick up on me preparing you for the shock of a black female officer. Speak up – you're supposed to be good with words."

"I, uh, no – nothing."

"Relax. Since getting moved from Intel to Procurement, professional glad-handers who make a lot more than you get all flustered meeting me." She gave a little laugh. "A shame really, you messed up on Jeep, cause I don't know if the new HDM Grinder is any better than the one chewing our boys up now."

"You hear what happened at Aberdeen?"

"Aberdeen? You hear all kinds of rumors, but suppose you tell me."

Yeah, tell the security MoFo – not *unfathomably* gorgeous, but certainly a foxy, formidable woman sent to put me at ease. "How about you show me yours first?"

"Watch your tongue, Forbes. I am not in the mood, taking who knows what risk meeting you here. Not that I care all that much anymore. I'm never making lieutenant colonel, not with the 'pious' fakers running this man's Army like it was a high school clique. I have three short years left to put in, so let them come after me. Still, I don't imagine you have any idea if you were followed here. If … *people* know you're in Washington."

"I wasted some time coming here taking a bus north and doubling back by subway. Getting off the bus by myself up where it was pretty empty, I didn't see anyone. As to knowing I'm in DC, yeah, they know. My idiot wife – sorry, ex-wife – for some reason took great delight in repeatedly mentioning during a call the name of the hotel I stayed at last night, the Harrisburg."

"The Harrisburg! God, they haven't torn that down yet? We had a suite there, maybe a third of my senior prom. All we could afford. Six weeks later I was doing push-ups at Fort Jackson."

I told her about the clerk knowing my name when I walked in off the street.

"He probably freelances for this out of control T-Squad run by a thug named Cummings. He treats DC like his personal playground, and if half of what you hear of Cummings' back room is true, it's no wonder most of the *cops* are afraid of him."

"Scared cops. That worked out well for me in Penn Station."

"Maybe it did – for the rest of us, if not you. This ill-advised conversation with your wife was before you arrived in DC?"

"*Ex*-wife, Major. But yeah, well before."

"Easy as pie then, especially since I'm sure this maniac Cummings is at least lip-service Red Calf, what with a job like his. But enough chit-chat. Penn Station means, unlike most people, you're peeking your head up out of the foxhole to see what's going on."

"Isn't that how heads get shot off?"

"You're going to die anyway, mister, or didn't you get that memo? A man like you, no kids, right? Act like it's already happened, and then maybe you can try to make a difference."

What the hell did that mean, *a man like me*? "I thought I was pulling on my end of the rope OK. It's not like it's crowded, that end of the rope."

"It's not, I'll give you that. OK, the guy you're down here to

328

get, General Parnell Whitaker – "

"Your boss is a general? That's great, that means our story will bounce higher."

She slowly let out a lot of air. "Nothing *ours* about it, like I told you. He's big in this Red Calf nonsense that's flourishing up and down every corridor of the Pentagon. Anyway, I got ahold of a couple of e-mails from Whitaker to some corporate crook up in New York, a guy named – "

"Bettinger!"

"Forbes, I know you know Bettinger. The whole world knows that now. Don't interrupt and maybe I'll tell you why I feel guilty in regard to you and Bettinger. Anyway, yesterday morning Whitaker was bellowing into the phone like usual, like he's six beers into watching football, something about a website called Syriac. Imagine my surprise when I went there, and it turned out to be you."

"Why surprised? Cause it involves a nobody like me?"

"Negatory. Because it involves a *somebody* like you. Yesterday, Whitaker stormed out like a headless chicken, and I took the risk to root around this private laptop he doesn't even lock in his desk. That's how self-involved and reckless he is."

"Hubris seems characteristic of our leadership."

"He's my 'leader' in name only. And please tell me, why did the Army drop 'officer,' a perfectly good term it'd been using for hundreds of years, right when this grunt got her commission? Anyway – and thank God it was a private computer, not a superior officer's Army machine – I found the e-mail where he introduced you to Bettinger."

"*Whitaker* introduced me? You've got that?"

She patted her camo shirt pocket with a smile. "But here's the screwy part: I was the one who introduced Whitaker to you."

"Get the hell out of here – I mean, how?"

"It was his doing, really. It was a couple of weeks after I got involuntarily transferred to Procurement, which is as slimy as you might imagine. After my last Sands, I got a dream job where I was able to use my masters in international relations from Hopkins – "

"Where you no doubt drank buckets of Fomenting kool-aid."

329

"Not necessarily, though there were big *tubs* of it sloshing around. Look, an Army career wasn't exactly in my original plan until I blew my knee out in a scrimmage against Elizabeth Seton – those proper young ladies doing us a favor even showing up on the same court as Anacostia High School – before I got to play a single game my senior year. And that was going to be my year. I already had three scholarships on the table from mid-majors, but I had to get greedy because a Missouri assistant coach got friendly after a playoff game junior year I had 34. All that went bye-bye when that Seton pig pushed me under the basket."

"Guard or forward?"

"Shooting guard. Just give me the ball! Anyway, we had no money – none, not with four kids, Mom sick, and my father working for the District. Coming from Anacostia wasn't the wrong side of the tracks, it's the wrong side of an entire river. After that Seton gorilla blind-sided my ACL to smithereens, I didn't like where my life was headed. So time for push-ups."

"The military the only option at hand, huh?"

"The Army put me through undergraduate in dribs and drabs, and then full-time through Hopkins. Now with HeadFuck and way too many Sands, some of us have to stay in to try to keep the Army from going entirely off the rails."

Head*Fuck* from this officer in uniform. Well, she was meeting the likes of me to turn over purloined documents – if I passed whatever test she was giving. "That's a heavy load for your, uh, slender shoulders."

"Uh-huh. Anyway, that dream job was crunching intel and *not* in one of those shops where they dial up the report they want as political cover. But I got shunted to Procurement for asking too many questions, which makes Intel seem honest by comparison."

"Follow the money, some famous screenwriter said."

"It was getting all Bohica this Spring, when we were massing troops in our little puppet, Kyrgyzstan, so we could menace Kazakhstan."

"And where's Bohica?"

"Nowhere. That's Army for: Bend Over, Here It Comes Again. They had a big natural gas discovery two years ago in

Kazakhstan, and the Russians were freaking out cause it looked like we were going to invite ourselves in."

"That would be Sands number what since HeadMan burrowed his way to the top, cause I'm never quite sure, to tell you the truth."

"DoD pays a lot of retired generals to go on TV and fan that confusion. But it came to our attention that a certain Russian blog, supposedly private, but well connected and full of retired officers, was doing a lot of high-level description but, more to the point, sophisticated prediction about our troop deployments in Kyrgyzstan ready to go over the border. It was probably mostly just Russian satellite imaging, but someone was dumping high-quality intel into this blog, *Asian Sovereignty Alert*."

"Just like they were doing way back during one of those first Sands, the one in Iraq."

"Iraq II. And I came across your old article as historical research on the real-time intel they were giving on U.S. tactics and strategy *during* the Iraq II invasion. My lieutenant colonel and I started making a stink about the Russians doing the same thing this Spring, only pre-invasion of Kazakhstan. And your story was part of the proof."

"Imagine that."

"Open source textual analysis – half the time that's all you need. So my boss and I made some waves – not the first time for that, either – and it rubbed a big bull two-star the wrong way."

"Honor among thieves, or professional courtesy or something with the Russians?"

"Right, because my colonel got shipped out to Fort Hood, overseas his next stop, soon as they figure out who needs Fomenting next. I was 'offered' that too, but I'd just got back, so, technically, they couldn't order me. Working for Whitaker was my only other option, even if I know nothing about Procurement you can't learn in a PX. But I'd just bought a house, my first – I'm still in the middle of renovations – so here I am."

She kicked at the gravel at our feet, inadvertently sending a stone at the ankles of two pregnant women walking by. One turned to glare, and the other hissed "Army" and grabbed her friend's elbow.

"And so, Major, mad at me for obscure reasons of your own, you sicced Whitaker on me?"

Man, she could flash some choppers.

"No. Shortly after getting to Procurement, I had your article up on the screen still just kind of wondering if there was anything I could do. And Whitaker came up behind me and put this soft hand on my shoulder and bent way too close and asked what I was reading. I scrubbed for a week to get the stain of his hand off a uniform I am still proud to wear."

"You wear it well. No – Major. I mean, it obviously means a lot to you."

"Uh-huh. I told him if he ever touched me again I'd file charges so fast his desk would spin. That I hadn't slept overseas with a knife in my hand for a total of 66 months, and counting – fifteen months twice, fourteen months, twelve and ten – to put up with any part of that Stateside."

"So those stories we hear are true?"

"The mortars, the IEDs, the women in black working their way close to explode – forget all that. The worst was sleeping with that knife. Some girls wore diapers so they wouldn't have to get up in the night to pee. Hot as it was, I'd risk dehydration every night having nothing to drink after 1800-hours."

"That's terrible."

"Affirmative. Anyway, Whitaker started pretending he'd just been bending close to see what I was reading because it didn't look like anything to do with seven-ton axels. Five combat tours and my Hopkins degree, if the Army wants to waste all that…. Three years, and I'm gone. Whitakersaid he couldn't figure why a 'lovely Negress –' "

"He called you that?"

"Not to my face, but blabbing into the phone the day after I got there. Anyway, he couldn't filter through his little pea-brain why I'd be interested in something from IraqII when we've already had IraqIII. And he ordered me to e-mail him your Russian article that was on my screen. I tried to laugh him off. That it was just obvious nonsense that someone had sent around as a laugh."

"Now, now, Major."

"But he gave me a direct order. That was months ago. Then

yesterday, I heard him wetting himself over your Syriac post. Your writing is a little fancy there, don't you think?"

"It had been a long weekend."

"Maybe that chow you were eating in that Chinese 'restaurant' went to your head." She laughed. "Your little stunt was tactically poor, marching round train stations with a giant backpack looking to tell cops to stick it. But from a psy-ops standpoint not so bad."

"Shout it from the rooftops, right?"

"You never know where a Demo might lead. I was in mufti the other week on the Metro, and one of those bastards comes up with his damn dog wanting to stick his nose in my lap. Said the dog had 'alerted' on me. I didn't see the dog do anything but react to his handler trying to get his mind around a black female reading a book. Here in the *Homeland*, it's just part of militarizing the civilian population."

"I wouldn't mind sitting here talking all morning … Lois. But don't you have to report for duty or something?"

"I took a couple of personal hours. Alright, this isn't easy cause I'm not used to apologizing to civilians." She stopped and worked the gravel with her boot. "But I am truly sorry for the trouble that's found you because I sent shit-magnet Whitaker your article."

"Hey, no one put a gun to my head and made me go out to Indiana." I looked up to see two more very young, very pregnant women walk by, both in the same dowdy, frilly clothes the other expectant duo wore.

She saw me looking. "Isn't New York overrun with post-adolescents dressed all Sunday-go-to-meeting and churning out Christian warriors?"

"Future cannon fodder, huh. But speaking of guns, what kind of insanity is your boss capable of? Cause I'm afraid you were right saying I was in danger last night." And I told her about Short Leg.

"That's Whitaker's bag-man for his petty little Red Calf schemes. I didn't know he did wet work too. I hope you hurt him."

"No, just melted away – more my style. What's his name"

"That I don't know. He apparently doesn't believe in e-mail."

"The e-mail you had access to."

"Don't get me started on the drivel I had to wade through between Whitkaer and his girlfriend. As to you, there's three: I have him introducing you to that crook, Bettinger. Plus one he sent Bettinger on the foreign content and rollovers he wanted you to focus on at the HDM plant. And finally, a summary of your phoned-in report that he sent to Pantly, the Germans' lobbyist, talking about the Indian transmission and hinting at some catastrophe during the Grinder's test at Aberdeen. He was tooting his horn about the job his 'operative' did. It sounds like you did OK for someone who doesn't come from this world. Your hair was shorter then, I guess."

And again giving that little grin I was really starting to like, she reached up and gave my dangling split ends a flick with her finger.

"Don't run into too many men in your world with hair long enough to play with, do you?"

"Forbes – not that it's any of your business – my men, their hair is short and crinkly."

"Ooh-Kay. But wait a minute. How in blazes did you hack his account?"

"His wife's frou-frou dog's name is his password, a name written on the back of a photo on his desk. He was braying over the phone about it in that voice of his to his girlfriend. She's a 'lobbyist' – like my mattress lobbies me to sleep. But what happened at Aberdeen?"

In deep enough, I spilled. "Just the SecDef herfreakingself rolled a Grinder at low speed trying not to hit an orange cone."

"So that's what happened to her 'shaving.' Going slow, you're sure? The whole point of cancelling the contract and rushing production of the new one was to fix the damn rollovers that have been costing us hundreds of troops a year."

"Yup – slow. Awarding the contract is funneled through Whitaker?"

"He's the first hurdle, and he hasn't farmed out any of the initial decision making far as I can tell. So how do you know about the SecDef?"

"I have – I mean, I've *seen* a whole-vid of it. Somebody

showed it to me."

"Somebody not up in Queens. Who had it out in Indiana?"

"Lois, Lois: a gentleman never tells. Besides, wouldn't it make more sense that somebody at Aberdeen had it."

After it arrived in my post office box, I'd hidden Everett's whole-vid under the kitchen sink, and, yeah, that'll stymie 'em for entire minutes. His blistering harangues to get the damn thing out regularly hit my stealth Dutch e-mail address. I read them on a supposedly Minder-proof, illegal machine behind a curtain in a Bumfuckville Laundromat, but never gave Everett the false hope of a reply.

Jesus, she was slick with her sneaky little smiles setting me up to finger Everett. Who the hell had mentioned Aberdeen first, her or me and was foxy 'Major Lois Abernathy' (her last name on her shirt) a DoD MoFo playing me for what little I was worth? Had the Army caught on to me from Everett's end, or was it just pulling on the loose string of my ridiculous Syriac posting?

As if on cue – either to help or to knock me further back on my heels – Lois handed me the latest HDM statement that she'd printed out at home that morning. Its salient guts:

In accordance with the Protect-the-Protectors prohibition on unlicensed visual recordings, U.S. Army T Regs prohibit filming of its personnel, either by standard methods or overtly. However, once T-Irregularities are ruled present – such as a visitor to a Heavy-Duty Manufacturing General Readiness facility refusing to fully yield his vehicle – Army Regs encourage all imaging short of capturing troops' biometrics.

HDM believes it has Whole-Vid™ the German spy entering its facility. The company's security enhancers have bio-densed our Whole-Vid™ in conjunction with the tape issued by New York Protectors regarding this individual who calls himself Daniel Forbes.

The amateurish nature of the New York imaging, however, rules out full Bio-Meshing™. Homeland

Control Secure-Transport authorities are currently confirming this individual's rental of the vehicle seen <u>here</u> entering our South outer perimeter."

A bemused Lois described the whole-vid the statement linked to. "You know, they don't actually need lights that bright. In fact, their dark glasses cut them by sixty percent. It's just done to disorient the target. Which by the look of you standing there chewing spit, they could've done with a flashlight."

She gave me her most devastating smile yet as I hauled out Bettinger's assignment memo, its logo up top particularly catching her eye. It was an overwrought, mystical hodge-podge with an elaborately spoked wheel, a cross, tongues of fire, six or seven candlesticks, a unicorn springing free from a slathering pack of dogs and an insipid looking baby cow.

"Bettinger doesn't have any of this stuff on his bare-bones web site," she said. "I guess it's just for insiders like you who've earned paper-based communication. But it's got some of the same elements as the graffiti that Army bible-thumpers have been spraying on walls all over the world. The candlesticks for instance, and this calf here – she's red, by the way."

"That's like the third time you've mentioned a red calf."

"What rock you been living under, man, you don't know what it takes for the Messiah to deign to appear in this lousy old world? First off, they have to rebuild a temple on Jerusalem's Temple Mount – where the Romans destroyed a prior temple. But the guy with an excavator can't start digging the foundation until he's been purified with a dab of the ashes of an *all-red* cow. And though they've been trying for years and years, always a couple of white hairs sprout out somewhere before the cow reaches age three as required. Meanwhile, people who *pretend* to believe this mumbo-jumbo are taking over all over DC."

"No real believers?"

"Some of them, sure. Mostly it's just a fancy way of one hand washing the other. But enough background Intel, cause we need to get out of this park. First, take this ticket to the big Defense-Theft Association party tonight up at the top of the Hart Senate office building. Whitaker will be there, so you can pound home how your fates are linked, how anything happens to you, he's busted. Plus, here's his direct line, though I wouldn't be too eager to call him any more than you have to." She wrote and ripped a page from this little notebook. "Basically, do a reporter's bare necessities, and get your story published linking him to you as best you can. That's the only way Short Leg, or more likely someone worse, doesn't hound you for the rest of your very short life."

"I suppose. But being boat-loads more famous and powerful than me didn't stop G. Gordon Liddy from offering to off Jack Anderson."

"Whoever they are. You have a better idea for staying left of the Boom? Gonna go to the cops? Move to Fiji? Live under my bed?"

"Now you're talking."

"You wouldn't like all the noise. Look, go to the party and tell Whitaker you have him nailed. You have his e-mails, end of story. Suggest strongly that you got them at the other end."

"I guess I'll spot him from that weird 'S' in his voice when he talks. You really think he'll be there?"

"Ah-ha. You did report in by phone. I was saving asking you about his little lisp. There's pictures of him on the Net. Plus he's not hard to pick out; he'll be one of the few in dress blues who look, I don't know, kind of *doughy*."

"This one hell of a shindig tonight?"

"Not for you. Have one drink, two tops – that's an order, Forbes! You occupy the high ground, or so both you and Parnell should come away thinking. You can enjoy yourself without getting drunk like the rest of them, right? There's lots of females nodding and smiling and ... you'll see. They don't let the pregnant ones go. These booze-fests get pretty out of hand, and pregnant women would remind all the self-righteous drunks of their wife and kids."

"In a Senate office building?"

"Especially in Hart for some reason, crowded with the sort of field-rejects I've spent my whole career avoiding. I don't suppose you brought a suit and tie, or even a sports coat?"

"Lois, I jumped over a fence fleeing an imbecile with a gun.

I didn't pack for the trip. Am I going to be able to fit in at all?"

"No. But without a jacket, you'll look like a chicken scratching itself. I've got a fancy one haunting my closet, actually two, and a couple of ties. Left there by some civilian who got a little too stuck on himself – and his 'prerogatives.' The sleeves will probably be a little long, but…. Get to my place by 1700-hours. We'll have a fashion show. Plus you'll benefit from a little hosing down by then."

She wrote and ripped and handed me an address in Southeast. "That's Anacostia. First metro stop on the other side of the river. Paint the right look on your face – you can do that, New York? – and it'll be early enough nobody should mess with you."

I stared at the paper till she laughed. "You look like a recruit I just ordered to get a can of striped paint."

"I was just thinking you remind me of a friend of mine." Well, Everett, his fingers reaching for my neck, but still. "He wondered if maybe I didn't give enough of a shit to tell the truth, come what may. You – you've given up on making colonel, which limits their leverage."

"Un-actualized self-sacrifice. Otherwise it's somebody else telling their story, not you telling yours. That's *un*-actualized, Forbes."

"The only way to get our country back is if enough people – civilian and military – don't worry who's telling the story long as it gets told."

She stood up, working her mouth but not saying anything, and looked down at me with a funny look. "It's not like either one of us has any kids, right, Forbes? But, look, you've got real work to do, and I've got some axels Humpty Dumpty pushed off the wall."

"Humpty Dumpty should kick butt for once, all the King's Horses and all the King's Men lying in a pile instead."

"Maybe someday he will."

"Maybe." She turned and started striding. I hissed, "Wait! The e-mails." Still upset over what we'd said, she sat back down, slipped some folded papers to the bench by my leg, said "1700-hours," rose and cut fast through the civilians.

Chapter Forty

A Great Capital Worthy of its People

She could whip my potatoes anytime. *Lois.* Have to ask how she got such a white-bread name when we met for our date later. Sure it was a date: we were meeting in the evening at an assigned time and place. Her place. Never mind it was just to borrow a jacket I needn't worry about fitting aside from its too-long sleeves. Exactly how humongous was her ex, someone overly concerned about his *prerogatives*, someone with so many jackets he could afford to mark his territory abandoning not one, but two?

Whitaker's automatic office signature leaped off the page with all its gobbledygook about his particular Procurement unit and internal Pentagon address. Was it maybe just the plain dumb belief you can't get caught?

But his e-mail introducing me to Bettinger was, face it, probably all too accurate. For while Whitaker praised me as a dogged reporter – "a plugger" – who could probably handle the dissembling required out in Indiana, he also declared me "small-fry enough to be desperate enough to do it." His second note to Bettinger relaying what to emphasize in Indiana was straightforward enough. Last came his boast to the Germans' lobbyist, Pantly: "What one of my most trusted operatives unearthed at Aberdeen makes me tingle. As we'll discuss in person, he represents the sort of *flexible* insider I've nurtured over my twenty-five year career that might prove invaluable to your shop." Not that I'd know you to spit at, Parnell.

It'd be basically a short, wire-servicey job nailing his ass. Yup, the truth – wrinkle-free and stain-resistant. I flipped the *NY Toast* open to find a puff piece on Carole hyping her appearance on *Breakfast Raunch* on the morrow, Wednesday. I threw it down in disgust and vowed it was the last paper I read till I left DC. That's right, boycott their asses. Giving it to a passing homeless guy, he said, "Thanks. I'll enjoy catching up on the Yankees hitting bottom. But there's no real news in this. I get that mostly online. You should try it." I allowed as how I might.

A bus belched by, a single ad on its side amidst the flags: "T is the threat. Complacency is the accomplice. Silence makes YOU guilty too! Be aware and speak up. Doubt is no one's friend." Darn tooting. Doubt and I were motherhumping estranged. Time to find a computer at some informal, local outfit that took cash. Failing that, I vowed not to worry about Whitaker's henchmen – Can't Touch Me! – instantly alerting on my credit card at some brand-name joint. How deep did his tentacles reach?

Three Washington go-get-'em types strolled up, the two nodding at the tall one with his hair parted in the middle and particularly fierce aviator glasses. "Look, it's a T disbursement allocation – nothing more. If we invoke Article 49, it doesn't absolutely *have* to get printed in the *Congressional Record*. Not that that matters anymore."

They actually responded to my Hail-and-Deliver, the shortest one with the biggest briefcase pleased as punch to spout the locations of three Unfettered Desks within a five-block radius. But no, he didn't know of any café or mom-and-pop place that might, as I incautiously put it, "be casual about those Regs that some folks get all caught up in renting out computers."

"This is the nation's capital," he said with a start when he realized what I'd asked. He took a step back, put his briefcase down and planted his feet squarely, as if I might rush the three of them. "We go for the tried and true national brands here. An unsanctioned machine – that's barking up the wrong tree, fella." The tall one swore and took to polishing his glasses on a tie featuring greenbacks falling out of helicopters. I counted eight credentials around three necks before beating my retreat.

A dude on a skateboard said, nope, he'd never encountered an "informal net café" and pointed me to a nearby Deskless. Neither did a long-haired lass in one of those old-school peasant blouses that offer so much opaque intrigue, nor a Rasta man know of such a place. The latter said, "Maybe you find one, Mon, you look hard somewhere like Forestville or District Heights over in Maryland. But you need some luck there too, Mon, looking like you do."

Alright, a comprehensive enough sample to decide that a big chain was the only option at hand. Eight bucks for twenty minutes on Deskless's machine (I didn't bother doing the math on what that came to an hour), credit card only at a monitored machine at a timorous, national copy shop.

I willy-nilly punted the day's queue of e-mail abuse, opening only Stanley's whining demand for material for *NO* and a fond note of appreciation for my "efforts at the front lines of Patriotism" from Millie the librarian. Well, well, Millie – yikes, no thanks! Oh, and a Dutch-server note from an anonymous Al looking forward to the evening's meeting that I had to tell him was getting punted, no way to safely reply from that credit-card powered machine. But great news that he and Elaine had apparently decided to give me the ASPIC documents.

Revealing none of my hole cards, I sent off a pointedly vague query to three editors who'd previously ushered my typing to a panting public. Yes, I'd perpetrated a large boo-boo. But I'd since come into possession of the *physical* evidence to nail the party who'd hired me to spy on HDM. I just needed to contact this person for a response, along with one or two ancillary scoundrels, and we were good to go. My thousand-word *J'accuse – the Retread*, plus the aforementioned evidence, could soon hit their desk – by fax – for publication the next day.

All three replied with some version of: Gee, ain't that interesting, and we'd love to talk about Penn Station as well as subsequent, attendant mysteries, including this little snag with the Grinder. As to an article under your byline on your peccadilloes out in Indiana, sorry, but the water a bit murky at present, perhaps we should wait to see how (if) it clears. In the meantime, they all wondered if I might sit for an interview ASAP with one of their top political reporters; they promised a fair hearing, including on my quaint Fourth Amendment absolutism.

Nah. I wasn't tossing my crumbs upon the water of someone who gets paid just for showing up.

It was like trying to get that story Syriac mentioned, the one on Ashcroft, published quick before the Senate J-Committee approved him as AG. The drug reformer who'd tipped me breathing fire, I cast a wide net over many reluctant editors; the guy at *Ozarks Magazine*, a non-crusading lifestyle magazine from Ashcroft's home state, was particularly surprised to hear from me.

So I dropped down a notch to someplace I'd graced before. *Off the Warpath* got play – some – with the right piece, plus they'd actually relish the chance to display a general's dirty undies. Probably pay an entire $200 for a scoop from the man its betters would interview but not publish.

Off the Warpath's Joe Francessa chortled yes to the tune of $250! provided I could swear the e-mails were legit and I secured some kind of response from Whitaker. Anything, no matter how hostile or tangled his non-denial denial. Sure, Joe, the e-mails were legit. Some dame I knew nothing of beyond generous hints of how she filled out too eponymous a camo uniform handed them over this morning. Joe was also amused to hear our next contact was by fax; supplying the number, he said he'd have to check his machine's paper hadn't turned to dust.

Got a publisher's imprimatur, so time for some reporting to save my scalp. Time to mess with an Army general, plus Bettinger, the big-time, light-weight spook, and a lobbyist named Pantly. All from a pay phone in a strange town, armed with a phone card and buckets of self-inflicted mud, and no way for them to call me back cause I wasn't giving out my location to someone who'd already dispatched a mad gunman.

Leery of confronting Whitaker, I temporized by unplugging the Deskless computer and cranking out the story's bare bones on a different one. Procrastination by writing – a switch. No e-mailing myself story drafts for everyone and his brother to read, I bought a micro-zip to store it. Sure, they might track down the credit-card powered computer and unearth my work. But, assuming I wasn't already in RoundUp, quick publication would render that moot.

I then had to worry about losing the stamp-sized micro-zip fumbling for change in my pocket. When were manufacturers going to realize that miniaturization-chic had long exceeded its diminishing returns? I put the gizmo in my wallet and decided not to count my cash. Hell, it was *Whitaker's* heart I clutched beating weakly in my palm. Searching for a payphone, I saw a truckload of soldiers roll by, accompanied by three Grinders, two with big guns mounted up top. I clenched from the bottom up, but, again, saw no one else give them a glance.

****

"Whitaker speaking."

"General, Daniel Forbes here. Tell me, sir, how is it possible that an e-mail from you refers to me as 'small fry' and 'desperate,' but that a subsequent e-mail – mere days later to a different recipient – applauds me as one of your 'most trusted operatives?' Frankly, the cognitive dissonance of melding these two wildly disparate characterizations leaves me reeling. Now, if I may – "

"What? That's ridiculous, Forbes." Ah, there was my boy's little whistle on his 'S's. "I'm sure I did call you small fry and desperate. That e-mail proved an excellent judge of character, I'd say. As for the other I'd have to check my records."

"Thanks, Parnell. That's damn jake of you to confirm sending that e-mail," I said, scribbling furiously.

"Wait a minute."

I did.

"Can the damn fancy talk and tell me how someone like you has this secure Pentagon number."

"Doesn't Bettinger call it regularly. Remember, I've worked for him. It's not like you two are seeing eye to eye at the moment." Nothing like spreading a little chaff.

"Bettinger! I doubt it. But rest certain I'll ask him if he ever answers his damn phone."

"Yeah, well, he's running scared too – trying to. He was foolish enough to send me a fax on his letterhead with your instructions for my trip to Indiana. And you, Parnell, are knee-deep in rapidly drying cement since I'm in possession of three very trenchant e-mails, from you, re me. All, astoundingly enough, featuring your automatic office signature, all emanating from Pentagon room number 3D877. Seems like I've got all the evidence I need, so let's talk motive. Was it all about getting the big-bucks job with the Germans to keep your slick little mistress all comfy in baubles and beads?"

"*Baubles*? I'm a very busy man, Forbes. Do you have any idea how many Fomenting Campaigns we're involved in right now – four or five when you add the imminent to the on-going. We'll have to speak again in an hour. What number do I reach you at? Perhaps we can work something out, something advantageous to us both."

"Sure, Parnell. Always happy to talk – advantageously. But make it an hour-and-a-half. *I'll* call you. And no Short Leg, got that?"

"Who? Oh, him. I believe he's being detained up in New York. Some little unpleasantness that won't keep him long."

"*Unpleasant* – my ass! The two of us are joined at the hip, so your threatening me is over. Not with the letters I've mailed to three editors to be opened should anything happen to me."

"Believe it or not, Forbes, I actually am busy. So, 11:30. I'll see if I can clear five minutes to deal with you properly. Anything else?"

"Nope."

I told Pantly's secretary I had an e-mail addressed to him from an Army general offering inside connections developed over a long career that "might prove invaluable." Dripping venom, she said he was "in conference for the balance of the day."

And I promised Bettinger's voice-mail I'd e-mail a couple of questions for an imminent story he'd find of interest. I could hope for his denial if he was foolish enough to lie, then blow it out of the water with his memo to me and the two e-mails Whitaker sent him.

Having tooled around within a stone's throw of Farragut Square way too long by then, it was past time to decamp. Ah, a rare teenager in this corporate/homeless enclave. Should've grabbed one from the get-go looking for my net café, cause this kid was happy to help.

"Yo, Shorts-Man! You clean up nice, except for that thing on your head." Jesus – but I asked my question. "Dude, you in luck. I went high and low a couple of weeks back looking for an advanced-copy bootleg of the new Pol Pot's Revenge. You've played it, right? Mad-shit! I went to this one weird place

344

people talk about, down Near East – down by that shell of the new baseball stadium that got Plunged and this old Army fort that's falling apart. The joint had everything, dude: old-school phone cards, computers you can't trace, race-neutral condoms, shit, maybe even a micro-zap that takes whole-vids, Minders Turn Elsewhere."

Called Connexions, it was on the corner of First and N Streets SE.

Chapter Forty-One

Making Connexions

Dodgy, down-market Southeast did not entice, not with its garages and cab companies, spewing power plant, shuttered businesses and, of course, the shells of a couple of partially built, pre-Plunge condos.

Connexions proved a long, low, listing affair that might've started life as a machine shop. The bright sign over the battered wooden door featured a riotously laughing black man in a top hat framed by a red, black and green rainbow. Its one sprawling room was littered with floor lamps resting on worn oriental rugs. A long maroon couch anchored one wall, and beat-up armchairs were scattered about. Three computers sat on tables by the wall opposite the couch. A teenager sat before a big screen noisy with slaughter.

A small Subcontinent guy well used by life raised his gaze reluctantly from his book resting on a dusty glass case displaying novelty beer mugs and old board games. Another case held stacks of magazines, a presumably fake gorilla's head, and an assortment of shrink-wrapped sneakers. Behind him hung a splayed snakeskin tacked to a framed piece of red velvet.

He held up his book. "A history of your civil war. Your fields ran red not so long ago, and yet America, that *exceptional* nation, instructs us all. Good morning. You may call me Zafar."

The machines were five bucks an hour, cash only, not the Deskless's $24. (I'd worked out the math on the train.) A great price and no credit-card trail – break free of the chains, buy local, Minders Go Hump Yourselves! Plus he said he had a working fax machine.

His address on his faxed letterhead, I e-mailed Bettinger some straightforward questions about him and Whitaker and their e-mails, plus one self-indulgence: "Why did you insist on faxing me your advisory on my HDM trip, a document that features your logo and letterhead? Did conscience prick, and you wanted to get caught? Or are you just sloppy?"

I hit send and walked through the draft I'd just written, clarifying and curlicuing, adding some atmospherics about the fatuous speeches out in Indiana. Oops! Gotta know when to stop stringing words together, cause it was time to go drape a noose round Whitaker's neck and tie the other end round my waist like Lois had said.

****

Zafar directed me to a pay phone around the corner "in front of the candy store that sells few candies." Past an empty lot's banner-crop of broken bricks, smashed bottles, crushed cans, old tires and a dishwasher with its door open and dishes still inside, I found Jaimo's Candy and Notions. The two big windows still shuttered, the smeared glass door allowed for a few hard-worn men and women in and out. They were of all ages, but one body type: skinny. That I was, for once, overdressed was the least of it. Using the phone meant standing with my back to all that traffic, but so be it. The phone was plastered with fliers offering "Real Down-Home Meals from 3 to ten, Friday, Sat & the Lords' Day, $4.95 complete, corn bread too." Only Tuesday, or I might've stuck around.

"Whitaker speaking."

"So General, I guess we never had our discussion about those e-mails I have, two to Bettinger and one to Pantley, all three involving my trip to Indiana on your behalf."

"Wait a minute, Forbes. I am *not* hanging up on you." His phone disengaged in an odd way without hanging up. Fine, let him record the call, that'd keep me on my toes.

"Got your recorder going ," I said when he came back. "Well, I got mine, too. It's called a pen."

"Forbes, in a world with T raining down right and left, do you have any idea the level on which the upper echelons of the United States Army operate? Levels far, far beyond someone like you. For instance, why would Bettinger have faxed you instructions if not for your small role in a very sophisticated, on-going check on vendor security. We had reason to pick you."

"And what – what was that reason," I sputtered, hoping I could read my rushed scrawl.

"A varied body of work combined with obviously flexible standards."

"Right. Tell it to the Marines."

"The Marines! What the hell do they have to do with this? They are strictly back-seat, mister, this allocation cycle. You got that?"

"That's a – never mind. So now you're telling me, out of all the Army's vast security MoFo apparatus, there wasn't a single soul you could grab to whistle past the HDM gate? Not one? Far better to trust this 'sophisticated' operation to someone you didn't know from Adam and didn't know how he'd perform."

"We – it was thought best if the HDM people googled you, they'd come up with some published writing."

"Except I didn't give them my real name, you dolt. And if I had, they'd come up with just the sort of hobble-the-empire writing guaranteed to put a defense contractor at ease. Stuff like my article on hundreds of millions of dollars of government ads paving the way for war. [FOOTNOTE ONE] HDM'd love that.

"Forbes, I – "

"So you presented me to Bettinger, who sicced me on HDM. Which raises the question of why this *sophisticated*, United States Army operation involved Bettinger in the first place. You like mustard on your Swiss cheese, General? Cause everything you say is full of holes."

"Not everyone eats lunch this time of morning, Chinese-slop boy. But, Bettinger, now he's a …."

We plowed through some silence. Then, "A what? Hard to say, isn't it. But let's talk about you, General, and those three e-mails you sent. You should know they're going to appear in print immediately, me and you holding hands, draped in infamy. One single hair on my head gets mussed, and the … the authorities are coming knocking on your door."

"*Authorities*? What authorities is that marching in the front door of the Pentagon? Who's cutting that order, maggot?"

My turn to let my mind race and my tongue rest

"Right. But those e-mails, they're obviously part of that same sting operation."

"Is that the same sting, Parnell, where you had to report in to the Germans fifteen minutes after HDM was done to fuel their PR response?"

He ignored that – my rock, along with his e-mails and Bettinger's idiot assignment memo. "The proper form of address is General Whitaker, Forbes."

"And my proper form is *Mister* Forbes. Or do you try to avoid words with 'S' in them? You know you're going to sound awfully funny on the tape I've got of you soiling your fatigues when I told you about the Grinder's Indian transmission and the SecDef rolling the damn thing on its side." Two could lie as well as one.

"Release that tape and – Christ help me – see how long you last."

"Just remember those letters to three, nationally prominent editor buddies of mine nailing you if anything happens to me." Not that I knew any editors I could trust except, oddly enough, maybe Stan the Man.

"A *letter*. If you were serious, you'd have rented time in an authorized whole-vid parlor."

"Screw that – I'm a print dinosaur, a wordsmith."

"Mailed from Washington, I bet."

"You got the manpower to intercept mail throughout the entire District? Sure you do. That's why you sent a clown like Short Leg up to New York."

"He was itching to go for his own reasons as much as I sent him."

"Right on, General, cause you just admitted to being in league with a failed assassin."

"No such thing and you know it. Forbes, I – "

"You nothing, Parnell! Now – "

Feeling them, I turned to the three guys glaring at me. One said, "Yo, that's my motherfucking phone, unless you be wanting four more band-aids on your head."

Scrawny, but three of them and entirely their turf … fuck it, come what might. Fuck Nicki too, harping on the Harrisburg. "Looks like a public pay phone to me, gentlemen," I said and gave them my back.

"Alright, General, let's wrap this up. There wasn't a single soldier you could spare for a day-trip to Indiana, so you plucked me out of the blue to, unbeknownst to me, do my part for the Fomenting by testing HDM's security. Bettinger was involved because, well, he needed the money let's say, and you dated his sister back in college. And you needed a phoned report immediately following their dog-and-pony because, well, that's the type of take-charge dude you are. Right. You stick to that steaming pile of nonsense, I'll write the truth, staple it to your e-mails, and we'll see who the public lines up behind. Not that it matters, because *my* health and *your* freedom are linked – at the hip! No slipping and hitting my head in the shower. Got that, Parnell?"

"You're delusional, Forbes. I don't even know if Bettinger has a sister, let alone dated her in college. I can prove that because, working hard to put myself through school in *addition* to ROTC, I didn't have time for dates in college. Now get this and get it good: the people I am piously aligned with have resources beyond – "

"Yo! Your phone call be finished one way or the other." I turned to see a fourth guy, shorter and scarier than the others, and making meaningful gestures with his hand in his pants pocket. I nodded my compliance.

"Look for the story tomorrow, Parnell. Bye."

"Tomorrow, you say? I – "

I hung up, realizing too late how dangerous it was to let him know he had the rest of the day to play with, and shouldered my way past the four of them. Damnit, I still had to check in with Pantly. That done, I could fax the fool thing to *Off the Warpath* cause I doubted I was hearing from Bettinger.

A bit peaked from a very iffy confrontation with an Army general, surely the local entrepreneurs wouldn't object to me buying some M&Ms. Making Connexions seem like Bergdorfs, Jaimo's Candy and Notions was little but a card table with an empty chair behind it lost in an expanse of curling, grey linoleum. Drugs of however many sorts moved through a slot in the wall. A man looked up at me, grabbed something and was gone. Another swore and rushed out empty-handed. But there was a pack of M&Ms among the dozen candy bars and four warm sodas arrayed on the card table. Why couldn't I get what I wanted – a Goddamn bag of M&Ms – in the normal course of things? Just once, this one time in my life. I picked up the candy as a scraggily guy came a few steps into the store, saw me and fled. I came to my senses, put it down and fled likewise to find the street deserted. Alright, six straight days in the wringer meant the local pillars of commerce Can't Freaking Touch Me! either.

I used the their office phone to hear his reptilian secretary say, "Mr. Pantly is unavailable until next week. You can try to schedule an appointment for mid-week – provided you appear in person with *micro-embedded* credentials from an approved publication."

I told her I'd take that as a no-comment.

****

Too bad the kid who'd been slaughtering space-cats who look like Hitler was gone, cause he might have shielded my screen from the big lunk ensconced at one of Connexions' machines. The way he was two-finger pounding the piece-of-fluff keyboard (pounding his default mode by the look of him), I hoped Zafar had a replacement lying around. Though in jeans and tee shirt, from the crew cut up top to the boots down below and all the chiseled slabs of beef in between, everything about him hollered Hoo-Ah! Damn, Whitaker was lightning-quick tracking me at that phone booth cause bingo! – a Boot on the ground. Of course that explained his odd little machination at the start of our call, not recording it as I'd foolishly thought. Rather than worrying about getting quoted correctly, Parnell was gonna ensure our little chat and especially his e-mails never saw print at all.

I sat down to a grin from a tanned open face not particularly marred by an undulating nose. I nodded hello and – fuck it – micro-zapped my story up on my screen to insert Whitaker's lies.

"Nothing like a nice clean, no-tell-motel kind of computer to keep up with your buddies," he said.

351

"Unlike the ones where they get your DNA first."

"Riki-tik, friend. Technically, my 'treatment' – there's a joke – requires disengaging from the field of battle. Let JSOC prove it was me using the Dutch e-mail down here in the jungle. Cause this boy is gonna find out if his squad's got any casualties. And nothing but the crotch-rot Swanson was born with."

"Glad to hear about the no casualties. We certainly appreciate your service."

"*We*? Oh, you mean all them people going shopping. How about you send my wife a case of peanut butter instead. We got two boys gonna be bigger than me sometime next month the way they're going through a case of it every other week."

"So you don't care if they catch you e-mailing?"

"Do I look like I give a shit, my college-boy captain e-mailing frat bunnies all over the East Coast, sending 'em *pictures* of himself standing with his shirt off in front of our fire base, for fuck's sake. He's using a Dutch pirate like everyone else, cause no one's supposed to be e-mailing till the Army acknowledges the country we're in."

"Your captain's not worried about the pictures going viral if he's good looking?"

"We're hanging it way out over the line on a daily basis, people's heads – enemies and friendlies – like pumpkins sitting on a fence at 700 meters. So a pissant order from some numb-nuts in Florida who gets to change his socks every morning ain't gonna stop you from checking up on your wife or girlfriend – or both." He grinned again.

"You got both, I'd bet."

"Me? Boy, we be nothing but ghosts where I been, hush-hush up the ass. So any vows this side of the ocean don't carry no weight. But we kill enough of 'em, then buy off the rest, get somebody running things who's got his mind right, we won't even need an official Sands." This tumbled out in a syrupy, good-old-boy rush.

"That'd be good, cause we got how many Sands going right now?"

"Three official, two probably never gonna be official, where we're using proxies and mercenaries – only difference being their color and their pay. And I don't know how many hush-hush jobs to prop things up like the one I was in for 140 days and would still be there except for the wrong damn NATO field-reject."

"Yeah, what happened?"

"Army says I got the yips from pulling the trigger too much. Like a little shooting is gonna ruin my sleep. Ain't nothing but politics – international relations – them saying I need to calm my ass down. That NATO scum-sucker I walked away from after he pulled his weapon on me – he's *calm*, you got that shit right. They're saying how I could've killed him. Like if I wanted him dead he wouldn't be stiff right now."

Him getting excited, I said, "Hey, my name's, uhm, Nick."

He smirked. "OK, uhm-Nick. How about you call me Mac. So what boogalooed your ass down to the shady side?"

"Trying to get some … stuff out, down here off the beaten track where nobody'd bother me."

"I hear that."

"And you don't worry about the Minders messing with you cause of this e-mail?"

He met my gaze. "The hidden tip of the spear, man! Snake-eaters don't waste their time worrying about the shit the rest of the world worries about."

Jesus H., no wonder. Cause the whites of his eyes encircled his irises 360-degrees. Like the circle of the sun all the way around during a lunar eclipse. Looking permanently fierce and alarmed since birth and, voila, a stone-killer sent to Connexions to attend to a little spot of bother on the side.

Damn, I had to tip Whitaker to my location, had to do my job right calling him though I'd probably never write for even a supermarket shopper again. He must swing big weight to have a whole posse sprinkled around the city so spear-tip here could show so quick. Hopefully he wouldn't mess with Zafar too, listening avidly as he pretended to read.

"Lucky you, dude," I said and turned back to my screen. Make him blindside me. My scrawled notes held up, and I plugged in Whitaker's crap. Good that it was wire-servicey, cause waiting for Mac – pounding away there at arm's length – to make his move didn't exactly facilitate my usual chaste webs of prose.

I hit print before it dawned I had no idea if Zafar had a printer, but heard an old ink-jet chugging away over by his display cases. I thought about grabbing it and gone, but, Deskless faxless, where else to find a fax before Mac rendered me room temperature? Zafar made it moot, saying, "I see you have printed – ah, only two pages single-spaced. They're on the house. Now for a fax, which no one has asked for in many a moon."

I smoothed out the e-mails and Bettinger's memo on the display case and gave him *Warpath*'s fax number.

"Doing business here in NearEast DC, I am able to shrug off most official burdens – Minders Turn Elsewhere!" Zafar said with a smile. "It took but a short time after purchasing Connexions from Mr. Howard's widow to appreciate the local advantages. But, since this fax machine *is* registered, may I glance at your material?"

I hesitated, but hell, I wanted it disseminated. Zafar recoiled after studying Whitaker's e-mails with their bold heading: For Official Use by Authorized U.S. Army Personnel Only and his auto-signature at the bottom with his Pentagon address. "You are into it deep, faxing private U.S. Army e-mails from a *general*!"

"Could you please shush!" I said, indicating Mac with my finger pointing into my chest.

"Him? He is no worry. This is his fourth time here – nothing to do with you. We see much worse than him in my country."

I turned to see Mac lounging back in his chair, his hands laced behind his head. He stood up. Bigger than me where it counted, younger, someone who turned heads to jelly! He ambled up and said, "Most business this guy's had in weeks, at least the times I've been here." He turned to perusing the dusty cases as Zafir said he'd fax my stuff. I handed over a ten and sat back down to scroll through the day's abuse to confirm that Bettinger remained his usual silent self.

A tall, skinny, almost albino-looking dude dressed in fatigues burst through the door. His small eyes set in a pale, squinty face, there was nothing washed-out about his intent. I logged off before he was on me, but couldn't pull the plug. No talk, no shilly-shallying, he grabbed my wrist and sore shoulder and hissed, "Get up! Playtime's over. You're coming with me!"

I made myself heavy in the chair and flailed away as Mac rushed up. Two of them, Christ, I guessed I was leaving. I looked to Zafar, and he held the faxes up and signaled OK. Why in the world had Mac let them sail through?

Jabbing my weirdo attacker sideways in the knee as he dragged me up got a grunt but no more. No matter, cause he never saw Mac grown huge, his face a snarl. Mac hit him in the neck, and down he went neat and clean, Mac catching his head before it hit. He groaned and started to rise, but Mac did something to his throat. He slumped down and stayed there.

"Jesus, did you kill him?"

"Fuck no. For what? Cause you owe him thirty dollars for bending over his wife? You've never come close to killing anyone, so trust me: you better have a reason – or an officer to hang it on. Let's go."

"Where? What? I mean, where?"

"Out of here. Or do you want to be here when he wakes up? He's not gonna be any too happy, and you weren't exactly kicking ass before he got mad."

"I don't know. I don't – "

He grabbed me by the arm, and I stood up and shook him off. "I'm tired of you people putting hands on me, damnit!"

He shrugged. "No skin off my balls. Shit – you see this rear-echelon motherfucker's tattoo?" He pointed to a red cow on his forearm. "Probably some numb-nuts Academy-boy. They're big-time Red Calfers. You coming or what?"

More Red Calf shit. So, leave with my ostensible savior? Would Mac really have caught the guy's head like that if they weren't on the same team? No point striking out on my own on foot, cause I wasn't shaking Mac if he wanted to follow.

He reached under the table and yanked out the cords to his and my machines, rose, pulled some bills out of his jeans, and in two strides was at Zafar's counter.

"Sorry about unplugging the machines, friend. I hope this takes care of that – and Sleeping Beauty." He threw the money down and picked up my papers. "He'll be out for about ten minutes. I wouldn't dump him nearby. But that's up to you if you know the right place and you got a back door and a vehicle to bring up quick. Your best bet is call 911 and say he fainted. Don't worry, *you're* not the issue. You coming or what, tough guy?" He tossed me my work and was out the door.

1. Daniel Forbes, "$226 Million in Govt Ads Helped Pave the Way for War" *Antiwar.com.* http://www.antiwar.com/forbes/?articleid=2679

Chapter Forty-Two

Home on the Home Front

Mac grinned over at me from behind the wheel of a tall, full-throated pick-up with a workmanlike gleam inside and out. I made the compass and the radar detector, but the four or five extra gizmos mounted here and there eluded me. Having just been saved by another damn soldier, I didn't feel like small talk about his toys, certainly not the lunch-pail-sized motor with gauges and ports and a thick wire snaking up into the dash where the center console should've been. He was wearing the "CAT Machine" baseball cap he'd grabbed to shield his face from light-pole cameras; I was reduced to a grimy brown one from under the seat smeared with the name of some unpronounceable cattle drug.

He peeled away from Connexions for a few blocks, more intent on his mirrors than the windshield. Finally encountering a red light at an intersection too busy to run, he pounded the steering wheel hard and give a whoop. "First action in weeks if you don't count disciplining my broke-dick sons."

He punched a button, and some twangy, pained country singer started up loud about the small-town verities of "*You can bite me, anyone who ain't like me.*"

"I'm glad you enjoyed it," I yelled. "No – I mean, thanks a million, man."

"No problemo." He sang along to the chorus a minute, "*My kids are growing bedrock roots/How 'bout yourn?*" Then, "Anyone sending out a general's e-mail, I got their back. That is some deep shit. So you a blackmailer or just a reporter?"

"A reporter. Doing a mickey-mouse story on – "

"Shut it! If it affects me or mine, I'll hear about it. Otherwise, who cares. Either way, I got deniability."

"Okay. So where we going?"

"We're getting the hell off the streets until Twinkie back there wakes up enough to go back wherever he came from. Personally, I'm not too worried. If he had back-up, they would've jumped in. Plus he's not calling any kind of cop, I don't think. As to you – well…."

"So where we going?"

"My house."

"You *live* around here?"

"Sure, my crib. Do a little relaxing."

Great. What, this guy wanted his pound of flesh for saving my bacon? We drove past a giant, half-completed shell, which Mac took great pleasure in pointing out as the Washington Nationals' attempt at a new stadium before that all went to hash, and they stayed in that empty old barn on the other side of town, RFK Memorial. It had been delayed by defective concrete, a big scandal when a ramp failed during construction, killing three illegals and exposing a bribed inspector. That delayed it a good year-and-a-half, and the Plunge did the rest.

We crossed over into Southwest, which featured run-down residential blocks sprinkled among various shed-like little businesses whose best days were long gone. Down on First and R, down by where you fall off the edge of the world into the Anacostia River, he steamed to a stop across from a surprisingly ramshackle little ranch house whose shabbiness didn't match his or his pick-up's crisp air. He strode hunched over through the wreck of a yard and waved his hand behind him to lock a truck which didn't beep back.

We kicked through the dust by the side of the house, but kept going rather than turning towards a back door reached by a couple of stacked cinderblocks. He warned of dog shit in the baked swamp of naked dirt. On cue, a large mutt stirred himself from the hole he'd dug under the yard's one tree and came up snapping and growling till Mac raised the back of his hand and snarled. As the dog turned, I did the same. We passed through some bare bushes into a neat backyard with grass and flowers and then through a spiffy little house's bright red back door.

We kicked through the dust by the side of the house, but he kept going rather than turning towards a back door reached by a couple of stacked cinderblocks. We passed through some bare bushes into a neat backyard with grass and flowers and then he was unlocking a bright red door.

Inside the sunny yellow kitchen I was surprised by the formal, framed photos of Malcolm and Martin; in the living room were tolerable paintings of Martin and JFK amidst the chintz. A big, flat-screen TV was over in a corner, its giant packing box in the corner opposite. I drank in the red-roses couch encased in plastic, the blinding yellow carpet, the dried flowers overflowing a vase on the table, the Beatrix Potter bunnies here, the coffee-table antiques books there and looked at Mac and his muscles and laughed and said, "I'm sorry. But all this crap isn't exactly what I expected."

"It's not my house, shit-bag. Look here." Deep red curtains blanketing both of the living room windows, he pulled one slightly ajar. Across the street, a long expanse of weathered brick wall stretched out of sight in both directions. A little to our left, the two halves of a hurricane-fence gate were so askew even I could have crawled underneath. Beyond lay an expanse of tall scrubby weeds. I said, "What's that, an old TB hospital they've closed down?"

He moved the curtain more to look himself and gave a chuckle. "You'd never know it from here, but that's Fort McNair, home to the Capital Region Homeland Defense Battalion. Twenty-three-hundred grunts sitting on their asses waiting to lock down any rebellion. The Army should move most of them up to Baltimore, the shit they got going down there, packs of dogs gone feral roaming the streets. But HeadFuck wants them here. Wonder what he knows he ain't saying. Anyway, the best way to stay out of sight is right under the Army's nose."

"What're you, AWOL?"

He was on me quick, grabbing a fistful of my good shirt. "Do I look like the sort of pussy to go AWOL, the men I'm supposed to be getting home safe getting shot at four times a week? That the kind of staff sergeant I look like to you, you sonofabitch?" If he ripped some buttons off, how the hell could I present myself at Hart that evening to confront Whitaker?

"No, of course not. It's just I…."

"Just you what?"

359

Doing nothing for my nerves, he did a quick frisk, released me and stared.

"I don't know, man. I guess you don't follow the news."

"Any news I need, I get when they cut my orders."

He went over to the couch and started fiddling with something in a drawer in the coffee table. "You a drop-kick dog, dude? One of them dogs going through life getting punted into one wall after another?"

Was I? A damn interesting question for another time, I shook my head.

"Un-huh. Somebody who likes to hitchhike with a piano? Look, I got a spade in my squad in-country – where I'd fucking be right now if the Army had any balls. This is his momma's house. For fifteen-hundred bucks for the time I got to report to Walter Reed three days a week, she figured she could go live with her sister."

"What's happening at Walter Reed?"

"You know what PTSD is, that the shit-for-brains newspapers are always yelling about whenever somebody punches a door or has a DWI. You know what it stands for?"

I nodded.

"Wrong! It stands for Pussies and Titty-Sucking Douchebags. The whole damn deal was cause of this idiot college-boy lieutenant, not mine, but this asshole from The Citadel walking out of his way to tell me about needing to shave if you can fucking believe it. One of our own got killed the day before, and I got his shirt up over his head and his hands behind his back before he could spit."

"But you didn't hurt him?"

"Only a little. If he was a Red Calfer, I'd be sitting in a cell right now. So there's that, plus wiping the floor with that NATO dickhead who took his gun out at the wrong party. So now I'm sitting around singing Campfire-Girl songs to calm my ass down so I only shoot Fiends. Which tomorrow we'll be 'mentoring' after we buy off the long-beard running their tribe."

"All part of the cost of war, huh?"

"Look, America's not at war. America's at the mall, feeling for the money that used to be in our pockets. That's what, almost

340-million that don't count. They're just for getting their asses kicked or to fuck a soldier on a Saturday night, depending."

"And pay the tab."

"Whatever. Then you got your roll-around-in-the-mud regular grunt – good and bad both, even all the foreigners. Finally, there's the little slice of men that do what I do, the snake-eating tip of the motherfucking spear. The Army knows we gotta get regular maintenance. Used to be they'd send us to Greece or Spain or someplace to raise some hell. But now, that's too *dangerous*, American personnel on everybody's shit-list with HeadFuck making friends all over the world. Instead of sitting with German broads going topless on a beach in Spain, I'm at Walter Reed talking about my *feelings* cause the Army says it's got too much invested in experienced Special Ops to flush us down the toilet."

"Meanwhile, regular Army, or National Guard anyway, can't see a shrink till their eyes are spinning in their head."

"Yo – you're not here to be talking about eyeballs."

Him even angrier than when he grabbed my shirt, I nodded and said, "So you came to the hood to chill."

"Nothing wrong with a little freelancing to keep the reflexes sharp. I had to get that one asshole's mind right, the one down the block wanted to know why I'd kicked Boo-Right's Momma out. Like he gave a shit about Momma, been scaring her white for years. Boo-Right used to be just like him till I had him in my squad for six weeks, and he was riki-tik A-OK – especially the time he basically saved all twelve of us when they were shaving our monkey good in We're-Fuckedistan. We put him up for a Bronze Star, until that butt-fuck colonel blocked it, saying the first Bronze Star in a Sands that big was going to a Red-Calfer."

"So all the Sands we got going, the Army's taking all comers?"

"Look – most our guys are riki-tik to the max. The Plunge upped quality. But every recruiter's still got a bottle of urine-flush to wipe away the recruit's pot. Or they got some kind of legal trouble. Or they're White Power, in it for the weapons training. The skinheads are OK, you get their attention. But they get all secret and embarrassed you catch 'em in a group talking their shit, 'Blood and Earth' and all this Homeland crap."

"How do they get on with all the foreigners who've signed up?"

"They don't. But that's another joke. A while back I was helping babysit some regular Army in a nasty part of We're-Fuckedistan – like we're really gonna Foment a country that big. And I needed a translator to re-give the order I was giving to a kid with an American flag on his arm. You fucking believe it? The company was half foreign, one hell of a mix with all the hillbillies like me. They kick ass, some of 'em, once you got 'em pointed in the right direction, but damn."

"And they're the ones that are always on-point."

"Damn right. You gotta be lucky, and you got to be good to end up with USA stamped on your ass. Unless it's posthumous, which just means paying off the grunt's kids growing up eating tacos somewhere. Give 'em that, shit yeah, growing up with no daddy. It's only money. Thank God my two, the thirteen-year-old anyway, are mostly growed. So the motherhunchie likes to think."

"So where's your family – your wife and kids – live?"

"Away. Out in the country three hours from here. We're pretending the gas three times a week to Walter Reed and back was too much. But fuck it, I left. Had to or I was gonna kill the big one – my *firstborn*, little, uh, Mac, Jr., let's call him."

"Thirteen's a tough age, I mean, I would imagine."

"How I know your sorry ass ain't reproduced itself? Anyway, he's into death metal. Fine by me, he'll fit right in the regular Army till he gets he's head blowed off at twenty. Hopefully he'll have his momma signed up on the insurance – ain't no way I'm making it till then with HeadFuck – and not some twenty-year-old gash telling him her third baby is his. Problem is, I been away so much, he's got hair down to his ass now, and his mother says that's his *prerogative*. You believe that shit? Like you give it a fancy name, that means it's OK."

"Language covers up a lot of sins."

"Let the kid go queer with that hair. Like I give a shit. Right before I left – what set the fuse – he shows up one Saturday morning with a candy-ass bracelet on, and that is where I drew the motherfucking line. He tried telling me I should like it, it was

362

a warrior thing."

"What'd you do?"

"Whadiya think – I took it off him. He was a strong little motherhunchie, stronger than I woulda thought – so that's something. Plus we were out in the backyard, so the only thing got broke was her damn rose bushes."

"Get with the program, Mac. They got so many rubber bracelets now, you can have a rainbow up and down your arm."

"Not my kid." He laughed. "Hell, we were both picking thorns out for hours. Plus the beer bottle he broke and came after me with – give him credit for that – his mother bitching that I shouldn't even be having a beer in the morning cause we had the other one's damn soccer game to go to. Like I worry what the foreigners think, the kid's coach probably the cousin of somebody I shot last month."

"No, no, man. Somebody you were *mentoring* ."

"Even though I had to pay Boo-Right's Momma this extra cash, she said I needed to get away, do some thinking about what's *important* to me."

Mac looking ready to snap something in half, I futilely tried to switch gears. "So what is important to you?"

"It sure ain't the motherfucking extra life insurance she was on my ass to get, saying the Army death benefit isn't enough to feed them two ingrates on. I needed her to co-sign a pipsqueak twelve-grand loan to buy a new truck. That one around the corner is eight-years old even if it doesn't look it cause I'm never home long enough to put any miles on it. Making the most money ever, so how'd I end up driving the oldest truck in my life? And I tried to tell her buying a new one was as good as life insurance, she could just sell it when my time came."

"Come on, Mac. You're indestructible, you know that. You're gonna end up sitting in a rocking chair with your knees hurting, trying to remember where you put your teeth."

"Fine. Just as long as there's some gash detailed there who's lost her teeth too."

I grinned all friendly-like, not that he noticed. He'd rescued me, so I was his sounding board. Nobody from the neighborhood was dropping by to yuk it up with the big, intense white soldier, so he was getting his money's worth with me.

"That damn one-year term policy she wants me to get from that shyster she met *on line at the store* – right – the premium totals forty-seven percent of the death benefit once they hear you're special ops. And she already told him that, said she was bragging on me. Hell, I can go down to a Tunica, Mississippi casino and do better than that, cause the money's gone when the year's up."

"What do you play?"

"Poker. Nothing but. That piece-of-shit insurance is about as fubared as them Navy cocksuckers figuring out if an engine or something is broken by throwing it overboard. If it floats, it ain't broke. Tell me a truck ain't a better investment than a policy only pays fifty-three percent of what you put in.... I said tell me a new truck don't make more sense than that, damnit. What the hell you grinning at?"

"What you said – about the Navy. Sorry, it took me a minute to get it. Look, don't worry about the insurance. You got a rich uncle you don't know about waiting in the wings."

"Not in my family of dirt-farmers. She thinks with me being away so much, she's calling her own tune now. But I showed her ass. Took the cash I was gonna buy the truck with – had it all picked out, color and everything, and would've locked that money away sitting on rubber in the driveway. But, no, she wouldn't co-sign that itty-bitty loan. So, fuck her, that cash ended up here with me, what's left of it, anyway."

"Whadiya mean, 'what's left.' How much money can you spend on booze and broads how quick?"

"Don't forget my present to Boo-Right's Momma." He pointed to the new TV, frozen on a picture of a girl undraped in seaweed. "No way I was up here for weeks watching her little toaster oven. Not that there's anything on to give a shit about. Fake laughing, fake explosions, fake tits – it all goes blank after five minutes after what these eyes have seen. Baseball once in a while. I like how the pitching coach has to get up and go talk to his pitcher, not the other way round."

"Who you root for?"

"Been gone so much, I kinda lost touch. The Indians, probably, before they moved down to where'd they go – Knoxville? – after the Disruption. I gotta pee."

I fought the sheer nervous impulse to walk around the room and look at Momma's tchotchkes. He came back and started messing again with something in the drawer in the coffee table. Eventually he looked up and said, "Till our day comes, motherhunchie, we do got to amuse ourselves. And I found something here, right on Boo-Right's Momma's block, helps power-up all that *important* thinking my wife's so worried about."

Pulling it out of the drawer, he said, "If you and Twinkie back there are setting me up cause I got sloppy e-mailing too many times from Connexions, then *you*, motherhunchie, are the most squirrel-nuts JSOC investigator there's ever been. Or you're just damn good with this little doofus act of yours. Either way, you don't have a weapon on you, so we'll just have to see what happens.

Chapter Forty-Three

Mac Tries Crack to Relax

And Mac brought out a little glass pipe along with a plastic lighter and lit up and sat back, holding in smoke with a rictus grin. He exhaled, not that much came out, reached into the drawer for another few pebbles for his bowl and made them disappear. Crack. That'll calm him down.

"Unless you personally been under fire, I am taking no motherfucking looks from the likes of you."

"Hey, knock yourself out."

"We got about six-hundred Special Ops wrapping up that gas pipeline dust-up I was in. The one they say ain't worth shipping me back for. Unless it gets blown up into an official Sands and time for the regular Army to go roll around in the mud. Either way, Army says I'm headed to West Timor in a couple of months." He fired up again.

"East Timor. I didn't know we were there."

"Pay attention, damnit. I said *West* Timor. And we won't be there either, not least anybody owns up to. We gotta … *take out* – that's the word the brass-hats with big balls like to use on TV – forty-two 'Fiends,' let's call 'em. Do that and get out, I get to sit on my ass and drink for one solid year. Twelve whole months, they can't fucking touch me!"

"Sweet. A year on the beach."

"That's if I make it back to my wife's loving arms – the ones getting a workout while I'm gone. A job like West Timor, you got a one-in-five chance of getting dusted. That means a candy-ass like you don't get to say shit about how I relax."

The pistol he took out of the drawer and laid on the coffee table was big and thick and had the usual dull gleam."Don't mind Henrietta there. She helps me relax too. You want some of this?"

I could feel my mouth hanging open as I stared at the gun. An armed, unhinged killer, on the pipe – I was so freaking glad he rescued me. "Uh, no. Not my scene, man."

"All this is is plain old cocaine. Not all that strong, but they sure boil it down. Don't make no difference if you're smoking it. That's just white-boy thumb-up-your-ass, you think you're better if you're snorting it and get your nose chewed up. Your lungs will grow back – they're a wet organ. Your nose ain't gonna fix itself."

I sat there staring at him, him and Henrietta. "So I asked you a question, Squirrel-Nuts," he said on the exhale.

"I'm sorry, Mac. What's the question?"

"Hey, don't go squirrelly on me, Squirrel-Nuts, just cause a cold-blooded killer in the Secret Army of Northern Virginia is enjoying a little cocaine. I've killed 56 assigned targets. Extremists, Insurgents, Fiends – fucking *Bad Guys* – whatever they're calling them this week. Check the T-box, squeeze the trigger soft, and bingo, Miller Time. We call it the Propaganda of the Dead. Works real well keeping the locals in line."

"You don't have to put any heads on a pike?"

"It's civilized, man. They don't know till it's over. And that's not counting who knows how many I've done standing on a ridge in the moonlight spraying on full automatic. You watch your step, and Henrietta and I don't need no more till I get back on an airplane."

"That's damn white of you, man." That's right, time to emphasize our shared heritage.

"All them airstrikes I called in ain't on my head – no way. You drop the bomb, they're yours, flyboy. And I've never killed a kid in my life, he ain't shot at me first. I don't care what they say about that one maggot, him supposed to be fifteen and had a beard Abraham Lincoln would die for. Shit, I'd have had more confirmed kills except for that whole stretch when they went nuts with the damn drones the pussy-shit CIA is so crazy for. That shit's important, cause now you get promoted based on your number of kills. They used to fudge it – never came right out and said it. But now with HeadFuck turning us loose, they got a formula."

"Promoted based on the number of kills – doesn't that creep you out?"

"They're *Bad Guys*, man! It's just my damn job, and if they had the same promotion ladder going all along, I'd be a master sergeant right about now. That's what you get for sixty confirmed kills, and believe me, I'd've found me four more. Be rolling in dough and not taking shit from anybody under a captain. That's another reason to hate the drones, even if they ain't stealing one of my squad's good honest kills."

He stopped for another bowl. How much damn rock did he have in that drawer, and how twisted was he gonna get?

"All this T is bullshit, anyway," he said on the exhale. "Americans – you know, 'Homelanders' – are more likely to die in the bathtub. Hell, especially you. Anyway, work was slow for a few years till they loaded the drones up with so much shit – cameras and geospatials and electronically scanned array radar and satellite uploads – that now they're worth more than a hunter-killer team. The CIA got a lot more careful with their expensive toys, so we were back in business."

"Raining death from the skies doesn't cut it anymore?"

"Doesn't matter how many bombs you drop, Numb Nuts – ever hear of a little skirmish called Vietnam – the Air Force ain't never won a war, and it never will. So let us do our thing, kill or get killed, and leave us the fuck alone."

He had another hit and held it, polecat-white circumnavigating his eyes.

"So, Mac, why am I more likely to die in my bathtub?"

"You don't think faxing some general's e-mail out don't lead to getting dizzy in the shower? And don't answer that, Squirrel-Nuts. I don't want to think about you naked."

His silence didn't last long. "World War II, they say less than one in four soldiers *under fire* shot back. Now think about what I do. That means the Army made me who I am. I didn't steal people's kittens and torch 'em as a kid. I didn't even go hunting – too boring, nobody shooting back. So now I'm supposed to quit and go sell Chinese cars, that Caddy knock-off they got for like nineteen grand?"

"Hey, your Campfire-Girl treatment is gonna make you good as new. Good for another fifty-six anyway."

"I'm good for 'em now, motherhunchie."

"You got a beer, man?"

"You should get yourself some of that seroquel the Army gives out like candy – you crush it and snort it. All I got is some bourbon in the kitchen. Give you a hit for every hit you take off this shit here."

I shook my head as he fired up again, Henrietta plopped in his lap. "So, uhm, you know what time it is?" I looked around for a clock. "Cause I got somewhere I gotta be, and I'm not quite sure how to get there from down the ass-end of wherever we are."

He'd been exhaling up towards the ceiling all that time, but this time gave me a nasty face-full of cat-pee/burning-solvent smoke. "Wherever it is, you got plenty of time cause I'll drive you. Right now your job is to sit there and shut the fuck up and be clever. And, just to prove I ain't a hard-ass, you can have some bourbon if you want."

"Nah. I still got some reporting to do later – face to face. The guy'll smell it on me."

"So, that's against the law, having a drink? You worried the cunt-sucking *Minders* might find out? Speaking of which, I ain't even told you about my wife. That's all she wants now. Don't get me wrong, I don't mind munching a little carpet once in a while – fair's fair, change of pace. All that shit. But that's *all* she wants. Said I was too rough fucking her. She used to like it rough, but what, her boyfriend's a lapper, so now that's all she wants?"

He stood up, sat back down, turned and put his feet up on the couch.

"And when I wasn't too rough, she said them pills they had me on at Walter Reed till I tossed 'em, were messing me up – *me*, who's fucked his way all up and down the Irrawaddy and back again."

There was no way I was encouraging this alarming heightening of our intimacy, him prone and fiddling with a pistol. "Hey, uh, maybe a hit of bourbon would be a good idea."

"Fuck the bourbon, Reporter-Man. You don't deserve it. Not the way people like you have fucked everything up. The damn Army lost its way when we stopped feeding ourselves. Living in dorm rooms half the time, for Christ's sake, going out on shifts like we're punching a clock, some third-country national smiling at you, loading your plate, pushing cake on you so you can't move, spitting in your food in the kitchen. That's what happens when you 'occupy' a country – try to fucking *build* it – instead of beating it down and moving on."

"Can't move on till we got the pipelines laid in the right direction."

"Sit and crack two-thousand eggs in an hour, like I did way back when, you figure stuff out. Maybe that's why they got the Filipinos in the kitchen now, to make sure nobody has any time to think. That and privatizing everything that ain't nailed down, people sitting home on their fat asses making big money. Half the dudes you run into in your typical Sands ain't military, the geek Americans the worst."

"How's that?"

"Fucking think they know what they're doing cause they sat in a cubicle somewhere mapping *tendencies* versus *actualities* or some shit. The Army's so hard up for specialized Boots, they slap six weeks of training on them and call 'em interrogators. I could do better. Hell, I have done better, the only thing I got up my sleeve is a couple of Marlboros that – don't you be giving me no look – I give 'em to *smoke*. Your average raghead goes bat-shit for a Marlboro. Not that sympathy is my big play."

"I don't know, man. I can see the milk of human kindness flowing through your veins."

"Ain't no doubt a bullet can solve you a lot of problems. The court's weren't taking them, and even when they do, they say shit in open court ain't right. Plus jailing 'em for life costs too much. But sometimes you gotta grab somebody cause you think you can get some intel. And these dim-bulb contractors, when they're not shooting at shadows, they got no sense of how to fake friendship with a raghead. Unless they're ex-special forces. Then I won't even talk to the motherhunchies, selling out their unit for buckets of cash."

"Never tempted?"

"If you're killing somebody, but you're not under oath to wear that flag on your shoulder, then you're just a fucking killer – no more, no less."

"Serious shit, huh?"

"You think? Shit, they call it 'simulated drowning,' but there's nothing simulated about it. It's *interrupted* drowning. The bastard is drowning. Freaks you the fuck out. Freaked me out a little, just standing in a corner watching. That's the price we pay for crawling out of the sea: can't stand to have water in our lungs no more."

"Mac! You believe in evolution."

"One of the few, buddy boy. Don't get me started on the cult they got running the Army now, especially since HeadFuck barged in, not that it started with him."

He ejected Henrietta's clip and took another from his pocket to ram into her butt. I couldn't sit there anymore – waiting. With all the people after me, to have it fall to some cracked killer offing me from sheer ennui though he didn't know my real name. I got up.

"That front door is nailed shut. And no way you're making it out the back door. So walk around, have a party. Just be clever. *Clever* – not too clever. Anyway, Snake-Eaters like me should be hunting and killing, that's it. Charlie-Mike, son: continue mission. Kinetic operations. Shift all this nation-building shit – '*clear, hold and build*,' my ass – to the hold-your-hand-crossing-the-street regular Army. 'Hearts and minds.' Shit, tits and ass as close as I'm getting to that. We pay 'em to turn in their weapons, and they give you some piece of crud Thomas Jefferson shot his first moose with."

"They gotta make room for the new ones we ship in by the truckload."

"Plus the Army wants us to get blowed up making sure somebody's finger ain't painted purple twice? Like it matters who they 'vote' for. You're not on Uncle Sam's payroll yet, just torch a couple of Grinders, you will be. *If* you can get to them before they roll over. But don't get me started on the motherfucking Grinders killing soldiers."

"So that's true about the Grinders rolling?"

He stared his fierce weird stare, then had another hit, but at least exhaled towards the ceiling that time. "You didn't hear: *Don't get me started*? But I'll tell you a natural fact. I will get my own damn leg blowed off – below the knee, no biggie. I know just how to do it. Spend my days sitting on the porch before I let them send me back to the crybaby regular Army like that psychologist – a civilian couldn't find his ass in the dark with both hands – was threatening me with my last Campfire-Girls up at Walter Reed"

"Look, Mac, I still gotta go." Whatever time it was, I *had* to leave. My brains were starting to twitch.

"Fine, go! Cause you're being very un-riki-tik. You want Henrietta's little sister to deal with Twinkie or whoever your general deploys next? She's small enough you could probably handle her without blowing your foot off. Please tell me you know how to handle a nice clean little Beretta."

"Thanks, pal. But no guns. I've known for a long-time I ever get my hands on one, I'd hurt myself one way or the other."

"Another surprise. Alright, let's go. That crack-ho down the block's been sniffing around long enough. This shit" – he held up the pipe – "your first time, it's like sex at seventeen times ten. After that one first hit, you're hoping maybe the next bowl or the one after that equals it."

"You know you're never gonna find it. You've been on it what, a week?" He nodded. "That's long enough to know. What happened, some guy down the block gave you a taste or two for free, just to be friendly?"

He stared. "You know, it wasn't so Goddamned easy coming off the Army speed this time back. Maybe cause we we're so far in-country they gave us more than usual. Plus I got pulled out of theater so quick. Usually we *try* to taper off before going home. I figured this shit'd ease me off it."

"Medicinal crack – cool."

He threw his feet on the floor, Henrietta who'd been resting in his lap shifted to his hand. "Screw you, Squirrel-Nuts. I've spent less than three-grand on this shit. That means I have got myself locked down. And if I go through the six-grand I got left, well, fuck her too. Less for her to get when she files for divorce. That's money she coulda had sitting in my driveway."

"That's a lot of money, man."

"And you are definitely tip-fucking-top of my list for handing

372

out advice. Alright – I need me some rubbers, cause I am definitely wrapping my pile driver before I let that skank neighbor of mine touch it with any part of her that gets wet. Or maybe not. That'd give Mrs. Mother-of-my-Brats – second one don't look nothing like the first – something to bitch about. Her telling me she ain't so damn Christian she signed up for living with a mean drunk. Have to see how she likes me on cocaine."

"You know it's only a matter of time till you flunk a drug test and you end up with a dishonorable discharge."

"You think I give a rat's-fuck about bad paper? It ever occur to you maybe I don't want to get dead? That maybe there's a bunch more women I need to get naked with. Ever think maybe I used up my quota of luck, the last little crumb of it sliding down the side of a mountain chasing a Toyota? I got thirteen years in. What's the Goddamn odds rolling the dice for another seven with HeadFuck deploying the judge/jury/executioner Secret Army of Northern Virginia like he was tossing empties out his truck window? Huh, motherhunchie?"

A noise outside, he rushed the window and raised that big pistol. I made out the sharp ping of an over-inflated basketball hitting the sidewalk. It faded down the block, and he turned to me, still pointing the gun.

"Late one night, all of us tanked, this major let slip that all Snake-Eaters combined have done something like 58,000 'executive actions' worldwide."

"Executive – that means it comes from the dudes wearing suits."

"You got that shit. All I know, you pull the trigger enough times, it all kind of blends in together and you put it over in one little corner of your brain. It's the other shit you remember. The ho with the butter lips after you been on top of a mountain for months. How cold it got that one January. The cake Martinez's mom shipped us or the day Swanson butchered and cooked a whole cow we acquisitioned."

"Don't need any steak sauce, meat that fresh."

"Just a little salt. Now do I need to repeat my question?" Henrietta nosed inquiringly forward.

"Uh, no."

"No, what?"

"No, I never thought about the odds."

"*My* odds over seven long years of seeing the world killing for HeadFuck and whoever's running him. Him with only three years in, you know he's taking another five – if his health holds up, cause he wasn't looking any too healthy the last time I say him on TV."

"He has been looking pretty weird lately."

"So, standing there looking like you couldn't make it through a regular Army Search-and-Avoid mission sitting in a field all day, you don't have to consider them odds, do you Squirrel-Nuts? Not that you really give a shit about yourself, right? I saw the way you went all pussy with Twinkie, a big dude like you. I see you're not wearing a ring – you ain't got nobody. Me, I got two boys to raise. The younger one ain't past all hope. So I do not need to be hearing shit about bad paper from somebody never worn the flag on his shoulder in his life. You got that?"

"Sure, Mac. You're the king of you."

"Riki-tic, boy. Now I am getting me some rubbers, some cocaine and the skankiest ho I can find."

Henrietta pointed the way.

Chapter Forty-Four

Across a Slow River

I offered to drive "since you've had a couple of bowls. You know, no offense."

"That'll be the fucking day I can't operate my vehicle cause of a little cocaine. Besides, I got plans, motherhunchie, so we're just going to the local Metro stop so you can hop a train back to the World without getting your candy-ass handed to you."

Telling him I was actually headed across the river to Anacostia knocked him back on his heels for the first and only time of our little sojourn. He allowed as how he'd drive me there since he could maybe score some cheaper crack there. He waved away my carping about the idiocy of two big white guys trolling Anacostia in a loud, look-at-me truck and punched in the twangy singer, this time wailing about *Folks coast to coast letting those in the know protect our libertieeees!*"

We drove past tidy, two-story brick homes painted in various pastel shades, a colorful counterpoint to tired looking Ft. McNair. Sailing through another red light, a cab on my side had to screech to a halt, and I lost it. "Look, man, I'm going to a lot of trouble pursuing Truth and shit so I can maybe have a better life expectancy than your average Ramone. Now what happens when I ask to get out at the corner there by that bus garage?"

Fishing out the little Beretta from his waistband and nestling it in his crotch, he blew off a third red light. OK, we were skipping that particular corner.

"Running red lights go with a gun in your lap, Mac?"

"You think I'm worried about some punk DC cop? Bring it on!" He fondled the smart little pistol, but did stop at the next light. Trying to keep it light, I asked if he was curious about my errand across the river.

"Look, Broke-Dick, do I care what you're doing? You're at least double age twenty-one, so go chase tar-bush all you want.

We can compare notes later." He made the singer even louder, something about *"Our queers round here think the closet's fine by them."*

The hot shank of a hot day, the truck door burned my dangling arm as I scanned the cross-streets for patrol cars and barked to make him heed a stop sign. And then we were on the Frederick Douglass Bridge, the Anacostia sluggish, dirty and low in its banks there in late summer. And thank God for a little speed and breeze.

Sliding by a tangle of freeways, we passed a threadbare park, and within a couple of blocks we'd accomplished the journey from Momma's scrappy, spare-parts neighborhood – but on the right side of the river – to a wide-porched, broke-down southern town, many of the houses leaning, their yards overrun. Trees cooled some side streets, and the faded awnings over the occasional window helped too. Then there were the blocks of grim two-story brick bunkers, a bunch with plywood windows.

Sullen, curious people stared at the white men in the loud truck, one overdressed, the one with the crew cut chewing his teeth. If cops, they were sure flaunting. If not, then who, what and why? We cruised the main drag past a big Baptist church, empty lots behind wire-topped fences, check cashing joints, abandoned storefronts and at least two take-outs promising an improbable cornucopia of Subs, Chinese, barbecue, fried chicken and – the topper – *fresh* fish. The We Buy Houses signs fastened to trees and poles were torn and faded.

Mac eased to a stop in a bus stop, rousing a clump of teens across the street all arrayed in some program's blue tee shirts. He shot me the genuine grin – not crack-grimace – pretty much missing since our introduction back at Connexions.

"Sorry, Broke-Dick, about not having any beer. Me a snake-eater on leave – very un-riki-tik. Word of that got out, shit'd be bouncing off my back awhile. So, look – don't let 'em catch you down here with nobody else around. You sure you don't want to borrow Henrietta's little sister? A good Boy Scout like you never got your prints captured, right? Not too many people my line of work still got their prints. Anyway, this Beretta's clean like my conscience – you got that? Clean, so you can get somebody's mind right and just drop her as you slowly walk away. Not that you stand any chance of blending in down here before his homie shoots you in the back, but at least you'll have left your mark."

I shook my head about the gun.

"Your funeral. But tell you what. I was boring my balls off bouncing off the walls there in Momma's living room. At least you didn't go all wuss on me, so we're free and clear."

"Well thanks, Mac. That's a good deal cause, you come right down to it, I guess you saved my life. Probably. So, uh, you know, thanks."

"My name's not Mac."

"I know. Mine ain't Nick."

"No shit. Now make tracks before this gets too disgusting."

****

A couple of the staring teens sidling my way, I motivated a block, and in that heat they weren't all that interested. A block on, I came upon Best Booze, a thriving establishment with heavily fortified windows. The only other white guy I saw was exiting a red Mustang convertible with the Virginia vanity plate: SEBOOZE. Southeast Booze? Staring back, he ambled inside, a pretty damn curious sight himself in his shades and pompadour, checked shirt, red shorts, knee-high basketball socks and old white leather Converse.

Lois's directions from the Metro to her house on Mount View Place were easy enough to extrapolate. I turned on a relatively leafy block and then another and soon found myself before a small-ish two-story home with a neat lawn and porch. The first floor was newly painted a cheery yellow, the second story remained a faded pea-green.

And hello, Lois! coming up the walk behind me in gym shorts, sneakers and a snug Army tee, returning from circling the track at her old high school it turned out. As opposed to the morning's camo, in this get-up curves outdueled muscles – and she had a lot of muscles. She shook my hand and said, "You're early, Forbes. So I won't apologize for my informality. I was so depressed when I got transferred to Procurement, I did nothing for weeks but sit around and eat chocolate. No exercise at all. But I'll get it back."

"Improving on perfection?"

"One for your team. But come inside. We've given Old Lady Gaston enough gossip for a week. Hi, Mrs. Gaston. You drinking enough water in this heat?"

She smiled up at me, and I saw she'd shed the goofy glasses, and that her eyes were almost yellow. Fumbling in after her, a *long* stretch of bare leg led me up the steps and into the kitchen. Rooms brightly refurbished here and various shades of grime there, the kitchen had a gleaming new sink, but the fridge would've felt at home in the Hovel. Following my glance, she said, "That's piece-meal redecorating on an Army salary. I only moved in a few months ago."

"Actually, I was looking at the map. I don't get it." Taped to the refrigerator door was a map of DC with a bunch of big white spaces scattered around. In one towards the bottom, an arrow pointed to a drawing of a house labeled *Home Sweet Home*.

"There lie monsters – Negroes. They don't put Anacostia on the tourist maps. I got this one at Union Station at an official, DC booth. Heavens, boy, what if some nice couple from Rhode Island brought their children cross that river?"

"They might benefit from a little education."

Post-graduate. Still, this is *my* Home Sweet Home, a bona fide detached house cause I've lived in enough pre-fab barracks to last a lifetime. Girlfriends were telling me why did I want some fix-it-upper in the hood instead of one of those attached townhouses in the Buppie ghetto down by the Maryland border. They're just barracks someone put a skirt on, drive in, drive out and nod hello. Live there for years and know three people's names."

"Come on, Whitaker does something dumb, don't you want to be able to come home and punch a hole through your bathroom door? I mean look at that door there – you couldn't get through it with an axe."

"Basically, after all the years overseas, it was time to come home. My mother still lives eight blocks away. My two brothers are OK. Never been arrested either one, amazing for males around here. They got out, one of 'em up to Alaska, you believe that? And my baby sister's still running the streets eight blocks up the other way. She just turned twenty-two, so the jury is still out, maybe. Anyway, it looking like I'm not getting any young minds of my own to mold, maybe I can show the kids around here how to do push-ups right."

"Come on, a young woman like you."

She snorted. "So, your day: report. You didn't hurt anyone with one of your fancy words?"

I almost blurted out about the albino, but then I'd have to explain my escape: *'Oh, I've learned a thing or two in my time around the block, Lois. It's incumbent on any man with any scrap of self-respect in this mean ol' world.'* No. Mac would end up introduced into the equation, who I'd merely allowed to drive me within blocks of her home. Instead, "I pissed Whitaker off, that's for sure. But that was safely from a pay phone. Otherwise, mostly pretty busy sweating the story."

"You don't sound entirely sure."

"It's not easy doing a story in a day." I started looking around her kitchen, and she eventually let it pass.

"Well, it's good you're early, even if you are catching me a little sweaty. Given the complexity of the mission – making you presentable – it's not like we have all kinds of extra time. You saw the two jackets hanging there in the dining room; I say the blue one, not that reddish one. No man over the age of twelve should wear red, not even one with skin as dark as his."

I tried to elbow the hard-charger with long arms off-stage with the Whitaker article. She frowned down at the print-out, allowing me to map her contours unimpeded. If that wasn't reward enough, she flashed a big smile. "Pretty good for reporting and writing this in a day, Forbes. Till I was halfway through Maryland, formal writing came slow. You combine a DC public-school education with years of writing Army-speak.... "

She advised me to slam Whitaker's assertion that his three e-mails were part of a private check on vendor security; as a principle in the procurement process, no way he could've initiated such an operation on his own. And why in the world pick me rather than someone with a security background? Plus,

I needed to wed him more strongly to any future trauma visited upon me. Needed to basically make him responsible for my safety, she said.

"I was hoping he'd assign you that mission, Lois."

"I pick my own assignments in my own kitchen."

She tossed the article aside and came towards me, reaching her hand out high – the better to reach for a kiss? Yeah, writing was supposed to save me, but I hadn't really contemplated this outcome. Man, I could use a glass of water first. "Ah, Lois, I – "

"Wait, before I get to that band-aid of yours, who'd you send this to?"

"Yeah, uhm – not the biggest outfit in the world, but well respected."

"Where, Forbes!"

"Uh – *Off the Warpath.*"

"Where? Oh Lord, I can imagine. But the article's tight, that's what counts. Or at least it should, not where it originates. I'll get a couple of friends to start it bouncing round the Building, and hopefully your publisher won't matter since you have those e-mail. You included them?"

"Faxed them out with the story."

"*Facsimile* – my man. OK, it'll bounce out the Pentagon door to some political site and then we'll see."

"I just need to get in front of a computer – hell with it, I'll use e-mail – to punch up those couple of points you want emphasized. Plus whatever I get from Parnell tonight. So, uh, Lois, where were we?"

"Ain't you something, going all Barry White on me. I was about to address that nasty band-aid of yours. Get over by the sink where the light's good and sit down. You were shot on Thursday, right? Writing like that, you're obviously over any concussion and, unless something bad's happening under the band-aid, the outside of your head should be OK too. You don't whimper too much, you might even get your hair washed. It needs … something."

"Fertilizer. The Harrisburg gives you nothing but deodorant soap, which this former Breck Boy did not use on my hair. You're a lifesaver, Lois."

380

"Right. Then there were the times I wasn't. The ones you lose, especially when you're in command, all them boys watching and waiting for the black female to screw up, are the ones that keep you up nights. Doing civil affairs, supposedly non-combat and still: should I have gone down that street, or might I have lost *two* going down the alley over there?"

I had nothing but a grunt for that. So smooth I barely noticed her removing the band-aid, she then took my head in strong hands to tilt it to the light and said, "It's crusting over nicely. Nothing to do but keep it clean and dry and hope the hair grows back. Now take the blue shirt off, which, no, Aunt Jemima is not going to iron for you. But keep your tee shirt on. We don't need things getting too crazy like long ago back when I was a corporeal in Korea."

She said back before her promotion to sergeant she used to cut hair for money because she was basically sending her whole paycheck home after her father had his stroke. Men she'd run the clippers over their fuzz the week before lining up so they could talk to a woman for five minutes. Fun times, the peace-time Army. Joining up, she never conceived she'd pull a career or make it to major, nor that that little slice at the start would be the only peace-time stretch. She went to work with the little dish sprayer hose, me in a chair and leaning back over the gleaming kitchen sink.

"You've gotten a good whacking lately, haven't you, Forbes – incoming from all sides. So maybe a little treat isn't out of line. Talk is the odds are good tonight."

She refused to elaborate, asking instead whether the SecDef whole-vid was clear or blurry and could I get ahold of it again. I fed her thin trash about a chance encounter I didn't know if I could replicate. (Yeah, somebody on line at the store had turned and said, 'Yo, you gotta check this out.') Eyes closed while she worked the lather, I ignored the harrumphs that nonsense elicited.

Leaning back with my neck bared by the big knife in the drainer, I certainly trusted the woman plying warm, soothing water over my weary head. But I still wasn't giving up that whole-vid till I loosed it on the world on, yeah, *Morning Dyspepsia*. That'd be the ticket to the top of its home page, if they – and I – had the stomach for it. Not that it wasn't a moot point just then, the damn thing thankfully stashed hundreds of miles away.

We waited each other out, till she harrumphed again and said, "Well something's got to be done, cause those people at Hart tonight, the big death-dealers, are riding high. Everyone is so damn triumphalist in this town – and based on what, aside from the fact that it's 'unpatriotic' to question the military about anything. We'll get it right the next Sands, the generals say. But nobody ever says why there always, *always* has to be a next one."

"What about West Timor?"

"West Timor! How the hell do you know about that? Who're you working for, mister?"

"Me? No one. I mean, just myself. *Scraping by*, that's my motto."

"Maybe not. Your protest-the-searches, one-man Demo might actually have sparked something. I know all my neighbors are furious about the dogs slobbering on them on the Metro."

"It's been creeping up on us on little cat feet in steps big and small since long before HeadFuck."

"This old political scientist at Princeton, a guy named Sheldon Wolin, called it sleight-of-hand, smiley-face, fascism-lite."

"Not so damn smiley – or slight."

"*Inverted Totalitarianism*. Wolin figured it was rooted in that original seizure of power down in Florida. They got away with that without a murmur of protest, no street Demos like in the Ukraine or Teheran or even London last year. Nothing. *Just get over it, that's so last week* we were told. Florida showed them what they could get away with. Wolin put it this way: 'Accepting something as true is not the same as agreeing that it is.' "

"Sounds like half the people I know."

"It's the majority in the military, but we don't talk about it. Charlie Mike: complete the mission. After Florida and then them looking the other way to let the Towers come down, time for Grinders to start flipping in the sand."

That – the great Taboo – just wasn't said in HeadFuck's America. Incredulous, I asked, "You mean that about the

Towers?"

"Shush! Those two Supremes who recused themselves to let HeadMan in – right all the way to the grave, Forbes. All people care about now is how their family and a few friends are doing. Three houses down they won't even wave at the old lady on the porch cause she's not part of their world. So they sure don't care if there's soldiers with automatic weapons down on the corner."

She mused about wanting to give me a trim except my head presented the two fields virgin to her scissors of long and thinning hair. Rinsing off the conditioner her nail caught the wooly worm Frankie had given me.

Jolted, hurt, I jerked violently, dislodging the sprayer from her hand, wetting her down and propelling my face into her chest. She'd been leaning close to reach around and get the hair down my neck. Splayed in the chair – holy mackerel – had Lois actually added a little wiggle disentangling herself?

"Mother Hubbard! Sorry about your head, Forbes. I hope that wasn't too terrible." She batted her eyes – God, the unearthly yellow – and added, "That takes me back, cause you could teach those GIs in Korea a thing or two."

Speechless, I offered the towel covering my shoulders. She started patting herself down, but seeing me watching, tossed it in my face and told me to dry off while she went in search of a brush cause a comb might catch in a way I couldn't afford.

****

I figured she'd change what'd become a marvelously clingy shirt, but she just returned with a brush and pointed me to the mirror over the table. My glasses back on, I took my time brushing, staring. Unperturbed, Lois leaned against the sink. *Jugs* was the word that came to mind, jugs that wouldn't spill.

Re-plowing the same shallow furrows, I finally put the brush down, and she led me in to the jackets, ablutions over, the fashion show to begin. But first I had to laugh at her dining room. That and the living room were totally refurbished, all creamy off-white walls and dark wood and floors buffed within an inch of their lives. And, yes, she'd done it all herself, learning as she went. But the living room had a lot of empty floor around the couch and chair and a chock-full bookcase that also harbored an inadequate little TV. The dining room was worse, just six stately chairs arrayed around a missing table.

My snicker launched a giggle, and then she was laughing too. "I guess I got used to how odd this must look. Count your blessings you won't see the rooms upstairs with the wallpaper with the brown roses. No one but my mother's been over here since I got the chairs. She's just thrilled I bought in Anacostia, though she worries about the place being empty when I deploy God knows where sometime next year. Keeps telling me now that I have a house, time to fix the empty part. Just go down to the bank like I did with the house and apply for a man who maybe won't get himself killed being a hero."

A choke caught her, and I stayed shut up. "I normally eat in the kitchen. But I sat in here the other night with a plate in my lap and my wine glass on the floor, imagining someone at the other end and a couple of kids on either side. And if a little tipsy role-playing is as nuts as I get after slinging Intel through five combat tours, I'll count myself lucky."

"Wouldn't you need four kids to fill up the chairs?"

"Two tops, mister. Like I need to be churning out kids at my age. Anyway, I've decided you're not getting this ridiculous red jacket. I didn't go to town on your head like that to turn you into a fire truck."

Fine by me cause the blue one was gorgeous, some kind of weightless worsted or silk or both for all I knew, an almost imperceptible pattern of dark and darker little blue checks. As to the ties, even Lois's ex-dude wasn't immune to the unmanly silliness. Both expensive shimmery silk, one featured a cartoonish giraffe crammed into a little car driving with his neck and head popping out of the moon roof. A bit martial for my tastes, but still nifty, the other featured several realistic World War I biplanes scattered in dogfights over a blue-sky background, darting in and out of clouds, one spiraling down in flames. It would go over well with the evening's death merchants.

The jacket fit fine, except for the aforementioned sleeves which were a whisker shy of having to be rolled up. It was by far the richest piece of fabric that had ever graced my frame. "I appreciate the loan," I said.

"I don't care if I ever see it again. I've asked him to get his stuff three times, the last time saying I was going to throw them out. And he had the gall to say he'd get them when he was good and ready and they better be here."

"So what's a fella got to do to get a drink around here? It's been awhile."

"Nothing. You're showing up sober. This is important tonight between you and Parnell."

On that ominous note she went to change her wet shirt to drive me to the train. Lois introduced the wizened neighbor on the other side to her friend from work, then pointed me to an old dark blue Chevy Impala. She said she wanted an American car with some size so as not to get pushed around playing the bare-knuckles dodgeball common to DC's highways. "A Spec4 about to deploy had nowhere to park her and didn't mind some cash for a last party heading out right when We're-Fuckedistan was heating up that first time. Thirty-six hundred bucks later – for under 60,000 miles cause he was never home to drive it – she was all mine. And I hope like hell he spent it all, cause it was his last party."

"I'm sorry."

"So's he."

"No, Lois, I mean it. It never really registered with me before – before I got, I don't know, mixed up with soldiers. But – "

"Yeah, well, can that shit. He doesn't need anyone's empty words, and neither do I."

Taken aback by her vehemence, "So, what's the car's name – you know, like a boat? It needs a name to make it yours."

"Have to make it some old-fashioned, oddball name like what my parents gave me. 'Trying to get your feet pointed in the right direction,' was all they'd say the couple of times I asked. My brothers too – Claude and Henry. He used to say he was surprised it wasn't Herman. I get it now, but boy did I hate it coming up. I ever get a dog, have to name him Otto."

Stopped at a red light, two young bloods in a flash car with gleaming wheels stared from five feet away, everyone's windows down. Making a gun of his fingers, the driver coolly shot me point-blank in the head as his passenger yelled over the 'music,'

"That's right, bitch! Take that boy back over the river 'fore the same fucking thing happens to you!" They peeled out laughing their nasty little heads off.

She said, "Just the way the big boys like it: all of us in our own little pots on different burners boiling away to nothing."

That nastiness killing conversation, we pulled too soon into the Metro's little drop-off area. She turned to me and said, "Be careful of flabby old Parnell. He's not as pitiful as he seems."

"He warned me about his 'resources' when I spoke to him today."

"Just tell him he's guilty, like your article says. Shit, I left it on my kitchen table. Have to rip it in little pieces and flush it down."

"The standard reaction to my work."

"You write your own material? Anyway, forget hinting to Parnell about your source for the e-mails like we discussed this morning. Just *tell* him you got them at the other end, from Bettinger, and it's time for him to ride off into the sunset with his dumb-bunny wife or dumber girlfriend if either one'll still have him now that his days as an Army big shot are over. You can tell him he's looking at charges of fraudulent concealment, obstructing contract proceedings – that's half the town – and defrauding the United States of his honest services and the right to have its business conducted without improper influence. Tell him all that and put it in your article too. You need me to repeat them?" I did and she did. "And then tell him he's going to be too busy defending himself to mess with little old you."

"So, Lois, I gotta thank you. This has really cheered me up – the realest fun time I've had with a person in a while."

"You mean with a girl. But hey, you're fun too, Forbes – deep down."

"Whatever that might mean. So, uhm …."

She leaned towards me, and at the last second I closed my eyes for her kiss. They opened with alarm as I felt her fumbling around down by my lap. She freed me from the seat belt, opened the door, pushed me out and drove off with a smile and a wave, not a word about our next where or when. I didn't even know if she liked coffee-shop soup.

Chapter Forty-Five

A Feather in Their Caps

Crestfallen, I rode the long Metro escalator past competing Grinder ads and then a big splashy one for the new Chinese 'Cadillac' with the headline "A strong want is a justifiable need." I clutched at the sense memory of Lois lifting slowly off my face with, damn right, a hint of a wiggle. Otherwise, why hadn't she changed a very wet shirt?

At the first stop back in 'DC proper,' two cops and a particularly unfortunate German Shepherd came aboard. Enormous in the head and chest, the dog's back sloped horribly to the breed's characteristically inadequate hindquarters. A weasel on ice, he slunk forward, his long purple tongue lolling and dripping. Pants tucked into black boots and hands crammed into those horrible tight gloves, the dog handler was short and pretty with a ponytail begging for a tug; her large, red-faced partner glared at everyone all at once and cradled a complicated, not terribly large gun.

My heart thumping from carrying an Army general's purloined e-mail, I tried to ratchet things down to deflect the dog. I stopped myself reaching for my book the better to bury my nose. Dogs can sense fear, was it as simple as that? The trio advanced towards the middle of the car, the dog calling the shots. The handler flicked his leash to get his attention and nodded towards a slight, dark-skinned kid about twenty sporting an afro, spiked leather bracelets on both wrists and a tee shirt adorned with a garish cartoon of a man with a similar afro pointing a gun. *Yeah – he'll do. Take him!*

Ignoring the dog, the kid eye-fucked the cops. But the boss kept plodding forward, his hind legs slipping on the slick floor. The dog looking the other way, I stared into the middle distance as the woman passed and couldn't help but see those man-tailored uniform pants did her no favors. Bored, the dog stopped, sat, then plopped, nose on paws. Nails clattering for purchase, he rose to a prod from a boot, turned and caught me sneering. At least I hadn't bloodied his nose. His lip lifting in a snarl, my gaze drifted ever so slowly off over his shoulder to alight on the male cop's gun. Hopefully that wouldn't alert on me.

A large, older black woman across the aisle foolishly eyed the dog to beat the band. He stared balefully back as she started plucking at her face and breathing fast and shallow. That's right, lady, stare at him wide-eyed. Mean dogs conducting a lottery love that. What's all that junk in that big bag by your feet anyway – huh, lady? *Take her!* The white boy over here in the slick jacket and stupid tie is riding proper: nothing that doesn't fit in my pocket, including a few radioactive documents.

Intrigued by her attention, the dog hunkered down and edged closer. Whimpering, the woman jerked her bag off the floor away from him. Growl met whimper as the dog pocketed his tongue and lunged. She screamed and thrust her bag to ward him off, the short cop bracing both feet and yanking his chain barely in the nick of time. Straining furiously, the dog dragged the cop off balance as her partner grabbed the leash and jerked. Down the car, a woman shouted, "No, no! – don't!" His front paws dancing in air, the dog growled and snapped and slavered two feet from the quivering, wheezing woman. Sobbing behind her inadequate bag, she kept gulping out variants of "Do what you want, do whatever you want! But Mother of God! get that animal away from me. Please, Jesus, make him stop!"

Mission accomplished, the two white cops together managed to drag the dog towards the door, and the man spoke into the radio on his shoulder. "Search and Suppression Team 23. Official canine alert, center-mass full lunge, bag present, 18:42, approaching Waterfront Station." There was a staticy question off his shoulder, and he said, "That's a negative, Central. No back-up requested."

More garbled talk from Central, then, "Look, Joe. This ain't nothing. Maybe got to get a car cleaner here, this dame's so scared. But the damn dog did his thing – right, unmistakable. Like to take her head off. And the car's camera caught it on tape, so Reynolds here, right?" – his partner nodded – "and me are not willing to just whistle down the car. We'll take her off at Waterfront, pace out fifty steps, Reynolds'll keep everyone behind that, and I'll clear her stupid bag – which these people have got to get the message through their thick skulls to stop carrying." More static from Central. "Affirmative, Central. Her bag will be cleared under a 13-37. Worst thing'll happen, Joe, is I find her dirty undies." Static. "10-4."

He turned to the woman desperately trying to catch her breath. "OK, Lady. You play ball, and I can fix it so I don't need any more guidance from our canine sensor. Alright? We get off at this stop, I look in your bag a second, and we run your ID through a couple of databases. Nothing there, right, an old dame like you? No outstanding warrants for skipping community service? You got your papers, right?"

Moaning yes, yes, just keep the dog away – though she was going to be late for her job cleaning offices – just please, Jesus, keep that dog under control, the woman stood up, shielding her most vulnerable parts with the bag.

"OK, Lady, let's – "

"Yo, cop!" The kid with the afro started laughing and pointing at the dog handler. "You wearing some kind of quilted diaper, or your ass cheeks be made out of cottage cheese?"

She whirled, yanking the dog, who'd again been nose on paws. He crouched, rumbling low in his throat, eager to confront a young male like himself.

"What the fuck did you just say?"

"I forget," the kid said. "But this shit ain't right. That lady don't have a damn bomb and you both know it. Yo, your partner said it right on his radio. You got your thumb on us so heavy, you don't even care what you say right in front of us no more."

"You always such a wise-guy? Huh, kid?" The big cop barged up.

"*Kid*? Yo, I'm twenty-two years old. I'm grown, so that's the way you need to be talking to me."

The man looked to his partner, who was busy looking over her shoulder trying to catch her reflection in a door window. "Alright, *mister*, let's go! Off at the next stop. Won't take me long to find a warrant on you – something – if you even got papers on you. What's that in your right pocket?"

"None of your business. I ain't gave you no just-cause by insulting your female. And I'm damn sure not consenting to a search."

"Cross *our* turnstiles, Mr. Constitution, and you've consented. You'll see, once I get you off this train."

"Yo, People! This shit ain't right, searching this old lady cause she's afraid of dogs." The train started slowing. "Niggas be pissed, and we need to be representing on this shit. Like that white dude up in New York said, that freak in them shorts. Word, the bullshit's been rolling downhill too long. We need – "

The doors opened and the male cop hustled a really decent kid – sacrificing himself to rescue the lady, cause she did not look at all well – out the door, dog and handler following. The woman across from me sweating freely despite the AC and struggling to catch her breath, I smiled and said, "You're gonna be OK."

And HeadFuck and a Fiend clinked glasses somewhere, the whole fearsome, expensive exercise a feather in their caps.

****

Goosing my nerve for the coming confrontation, I switched trains and was soon up on the street amidst the spiffed Capitol Hill types flitting past tourists consuming chunks of space. On some secret signal, they'd halt five-abreast to stare up at that dome full of hot air. Dogs and their human handlers lounged everywhere, soldiers too, only half content with mere pistols. A couple of Grinders with machine guns up top nosed out of a loading bay.

I waved my ticket at the white mustachioed guard leading the platoon at Hart's front door. The old gent said, "Sir, this is a public building. Folks don't need tickets to enter, so if you have business inside, you're welcome till closing time."

Hart was one of those waste-space buildings with an enormous interior courtyard and floor after floor of office windows peering down on a *safe* Calder sculpture plopped down to consume some of that empty space. Steeling myself, I circled the bright, content-less pile of metal, giving the many cameras a shot of my so far unidentified best side. Was I really hitting that elevator over there and on up? Lois termed her boss a fumbler, but she hated him. Of all the various scoundrels after me, Parnell was the one who'd clawed his way to the top of the heap to send not one, but two weirdoes after me.

Christ, look at her and oh my goodness, *her*. I saw that on the Hill, single ID cards had migrated south to women's waistbands, and there was a decided absence of concealing bows or flowing Amish dresses. Nothing but tight silk shirts and tighter skirts for the tall, slender, buxom women with drop-dead – you, not them – exquisite faces and casually complicated hair. Their legs went from here all the way down there, ending in those pointy witch shoes that had largely disappeared in New York during the *let's-walk* pragmatism of the Plunge. Men, who came in various sizes, shapes and ages and wore boxy summer suits, did almost all the hiring on the Hill. So res ipsa loquitur: the thing speaks for itself.

Hell, aside from my wedding day, my high-water mark was etched on the wall of one of Hart's larger, more ornate hearing rooms – so screw Parnell. Riding up to room SH902 on the ninth floor, I worried about getting in, but there was nothing to it. No one wanted to know, let alone record anything. The no-nonsense silver fox at the reception table passed my ticket through some whiz-banger which whirred, then lit up. When it beeped, she tossed it into the Memory Hole under her table and waved me in. The three gorillas at the door behind her wore dark, somehow indistinct uniforms with no names or insignia, and one carried the same slick machine pistol as half the cops outside. My indifferent nod acknowledged their facilitation of the evening.

It was a vast, vulgar room with marble walls framing floor to ceiling windows on three sides, a dark ceiling with sparkly lights unneeded at that hour, and a fruit-salad carpet. The giant spaceship of a dome menaced the longer wall of windows. An angel, the hem of whose little black dress just about met the hair shimmering down to her waist, straddled a harp on a spotlit, revolving platform off to the side.

Not that anyone could hear a harp over the din, the booze having already flowed for some time. Those party goers not braying held a drink to their lips. They looked like the people

I'd seen by the Calder, only raucous and more so. The women outshone the beauties downstairs, their qualifications for rising nine floors above Senate drudgery on ample display. The men had sharper haircuts and of the half not in uniform, many wore those clownish white collars and cuffs with blue, striped or even pink shirts.

Talking as they chewed, several hundred of America's best and brightest and their barely wrapped candy jostled for space. Bosoms heaved and liquor spilled from carelessly held glasses – there was more. Only slightly less devastating than the guests, waitresses in short, flouncy little nothings struggled with their trays as they dipped around large men rooted in the wide stance needed to chew and slurp and bray. Some bellower cut through the noise, "Hank, you dirt-bag! Never thought I'd see you Stateside, leaving you sliding off that mountain. Get over here and hear about the pile of H-27 funding Ray's talking about."

Back-lit by the blazing dome through the window behind him, an indistinct guard stared my way. I turned to hear a suit pause as he lectured the general he was tugging on a leash. "Look, Garret, all these micro-robotics and neuron sprays and turning their grassland to desert is fine, far as that goes. But I learned at Mr. Parker's knee longer ago than I care to admit, that the real money is always, always in the hardware for a major land war. Whether we fight it or not doesn't really matter. By that time, we're way past my slot in the appropriations cycle. Now I want your shop to generate a report by the middle of next month on three-turret – Nelson, you dog! I heard you got back. Is that why there's so many females here tonight? Jesus, you can't swing a dead cat without hitting one in the tits. Hurt the cat by the look of 'em. You know General Garret, right?" He gave a tug, and they strolled on.

Jumpy there in the lion's den, I turned too quickly when someone tapped me on the shoulder.

Chapter Forty-Six

Hijinks on High

And I nearly bowled over a tall, young lovely apparently given to speak. Apparently with me. As she apologized for me almost spilling her frightful purple drink, I saw she was merely pretty – Jesus, very pretty – with long dark hair and glasses and a brown, sleeveless dress that actually left something to the imagination. A girl, really, a home-spun beauty compared to the barely wrapped pneumatics.

"Hi. My name's Delores. What's your first name? This is only the second time my boss has let me come to one of these parties. She says I need 'schooling.' But this is such a big one – the Appropriators' Ball we call it – it's all hands on deck. At least I've learned enough to know that no one has a last name." This tumbled out in a breathless rush.

I told her my name.

"That's a nice name – *strong*. God, my feet are killing me. My boss, April, runs my firm's House Liaison, and she insisted I wear these heels that Mr. Lawson told her to get for me."

Almost invited, I leaned back to take in her shoes and – it still a party dress, not a shroud – my-my, *Delores*. "Those don't look so bad. But then, look at mine," said the doof wearing glorified black work boots.

"Of course this is the first job I've ever had where I didn't wear sneakers. A colonel in my father's battalion who's friends with Mr. Lawson – they were in I don't know how many Sands together – got it for me after Dad was killed in Were-Fu – you know."

"I'm so sorry. That's terrible. We certainly appreciate his service and mourn your loss."

"No, please. Anyway, it's all so unreal. Everyone wants me to be all broken up. And I *was* for the first couple of weeks. But it wasn't like my brother and I ever saw him except a couple of weeks a year – if he was even home. My mom divorced him when I was fourteen, he was so crazy and violent every time he got back from a Sands."

"HeadMan asks a lot of our men in uniform *and* their families."

She looked up at me and then remembered to smile. Golly. Do that again, please.

"We're not supposed to talk about ourselves, but ask the men about themselves. April gave me this pill to relax, but all it's doing is making me go on and on about myself. Maybe I shouldn't have asked the bartender to make this drink so weak cause I guess I'm still nervous."

"What in the world is that noxious potion you have there?"

"I haven't a clue. The girl on line ahead of me – I couldn't stop staring, she was such a knockout. I asked who she worked for, trying to network in case I mess up at this party like last time and maybe get fired. And she laughed and said she works for herself cause no one else lets her work only three hours a day. I was still thinking about that and in a panic just told the bartender to give me what she was having, only half the liquor. But here I am still talking about myself. Wasn't that great in the House today that they passed, I think it was, thirteen supplementals to the Defense Appropriations bill. All on a voice-vote. That really shows that the country is behind our Heroes, right?"

"Passed by acclimation, huh. How much do they all add up to?"

"I don't think anyone knows. But enough about politics. April said to ask about your work first and then steer it more personal if the Quarry seems comfortable with that."

"Quarry?"

"Oops. Maybe my drink is strong enough."

"Delores, look, this Quarry is comfortable talking about whatever you're comfortable talking about."

"Thanks. So you must be some top-gun scientist or something, am I right?"

"Something, yeah." Trying not to laugh, I had to turn away. Sammy Cahn had it that what is dancing but making love set to music. But he probably hadn't pictured the amorous water buffalo enveloping a short young maiden and hunched considerably to ensure optimum contact. This to a harp no one could hear. I turned from the sight as one would from a bad wreck to see far across the room a group of Marines helping two girls up on a table.

"That's OK. You had a ticket to get in and you're a man. That makes you a genuine Quarry. My first party, the Appropriators' Ball last year, I was so scared. I'd never done anything like this before – you know, with someone I haven't been dating for like *months*. I still haven't. And people can sense fear, just like the dogs on the Metro. So I had barely a nibble. It's not like I'm *hideous* looking, right. The party ending last year, I was practically throwing myself at some big House chief of staff. And April was furious I didn't know he was gay. She says I'm supposed to follow the political gossip sites on my own time, but come on! I don't do much news – I get more from books."

"I can assure you I like girls."

"You promise? I know I'm not the sexiest thing here. I mean, look at *her*. But I'm nice, and maybe you might like that. It's just I'm afraid of most of these guys. They are serving the Homeland, I know. But *implements* – that's what I hear, down in this suite of like nine rooms they have on the sixth floor," she said in a whisper. "But you don't seem too stressed, like you have to get rough, right? My dad hit me enough to last a lifetime. So that aspect of – did I say something wrong? You won't tell on me, will you?"

Aspect! Jesus, I had to call Al and Elaine to tell them to hold on to those ASPIC documents for me. And quick. Al didn't seem like the type to be kept waiting. I should've freaking called from Anacostia earlier, where I'd seen some phone booths. But I was too all-a-'tizzy from my close encounter with Lois to think of that. "No, of course not. Tell on you for what?"

"Is it my glasses? I'm sorry. I can take them off. I know I shouldn't wear them, and April wasn't happy, let me tell you. It's just I have this tiny little infection from my contacts – goodness no, it's not contagious – and I wanted to be able to see to duck if they start throwing glasses like last year."

"Don't be silly. You're gorgeous. Scrumptious as a matter of fact."

"You're sweet."

"Delores, seriously, you're positively scrumptious. But I just remembered there's something I absolutely must do."

"Please don't get me in trouble, promise? I really need this job. It pays pretty good – I mean it should, considering. I'm paying for like half my brother's tuition, and he's only going into his junior year. I promised my Mom he wouldn't have to drop out of college like I did when Dad died."

"Look, Delores, you're wonderful. Besides, I wouldn't know who to tell even if I had any complaints. Which I don't. Believe me, there's nothing I'd rather do than get to know you a little better." Were those really her marching orders – pray, God – as simple and direct as that? "But before I can throw myself at your feet, I have to make a call, and then track down a general for a brief, private conversation."

"Avoiding formalities of any kind is exactly what tonight is all about for the defenders of our freedoms," she recited blankly. She drained some purple drink, made a face and rushed on. "Promise you'll say hello to April when we leave, maybe even put in a good word for me? She said I couldn't afford to mess up like last year. Plus she was awfully annoyed at how I was dressed – that brown is too restrained, a 'hands-off' color."

"Restrained like salmon swimming upstream. I'll be delighted to sing your praises to April if I'm not struck dumb by your beauty by then. So look, if I can find my general, I should be able to wrap this up in half-an-hour. And I'm sure if April knew who I am – I'm actually kind of famous in a weird way – she'd be very pleased with you."

Absolutely the sort of dude April and Mr. Lawson wanted to curry favor with. Was I really leaving her swimming in that pool of drunken sharks? Leaving dewy, seemingly done-deal Delores for something as speculative as Al and Elaine's APSIC documents to beef up "Penn Tale"? Cause my botched Syriac confession and cancelling the evening's rendezvous hadn't exactly poured honey on my prospects. I glanced back to see some big thug in uniform descend upon her to hopefully scare her all the more into my nonthreatening arms.

Exiting the room to a glare from a guard – just ignore them like everyone else – the silver-fox at the door assured me she'd remember me. Asked why, she said she was particularly taken with my shoes, the likes of which she had never seen in Hart. Well goody-goody for us both.

At least there were a couple of pay phones off in a corner beyond the elevators, dusty relics of another day. Assuming they worked, surely the Senate wouldn't let its own phones be bugged. Al and Elaine were less than thrilled with Syriac and with my missing our meeting that evening. They'd have to see about things when I got back, which they hoped was soon cause something new had surfaced, a specific something.

One of them on an extension, they started wrangling whether I was worthy, with Al pointing to the value of my fame. Infamy more like it, Elaine said. He countered that it wasn't like they had another reporter they could trust on tap. She reminded him who was taking all the risk, and Al yelled back about the danger of Monday's initial overture. Declaring the call dangerously out of control, Elaine hung up. I tried to mollify Al, but he said Elaine was crying, and he had to go.

The man with the Turd Touch working his magic on their groove-thang, another generous scoop of uncertainty plopped down on my overflowing bowl.

OK, Delores! After – I'd almost forgotten – I slapped Whitaker down hard. If I could find him.

****

Things had ratcheted up a notch in the enormous room. For one thing, there were six or seven women dancing on tables, not two. They were still clothed – technically – though I couldn't swear for the pair in back who'd attracted the largest, loudest crowd. Some lout yelled at the harpist, "Hey, girl, how about you put that silly thing away ain't nobody can hear and do some *dancing* on that platform you been hogging up there. Or step aside for some gals who will."

No one had anyone gotten any less drunk in my absence. Slithering through the crowd. I tarried a moment to eavesdrop on an Air Force officer talking to someone in pinstripes. The airman said, "If General Allen and his team pick the one I'm crossing my fingers for, the next Sands will be one beaucoup effort, I'll tell you what. About time to let the Air Force loose."

The suit replied, "Throw a dart at the map, though I still think we have to keep our focus on Greater Mesopotamia. Sure, natural gas – I recognize its importance, *BEI*. But we still gotta dance with the girl that brung us."

Ah, there was my Delores pinned against a window, looking like she wished the lit-up spaceship hovering outside would beam her aboard, away from the big lug of a soldier waving his drink around as he talked at her. I had no idea how much right of refusal Delores could exercise long as she left with someone, anyone – me. Even if within the evening's rules of engagement, would she have the gumption to slip away? High time for my little tete-a-tete with Whitaker and then go elbow the brute aside.

Cause damn, she looked fine, *especially* in just a normal sexy dress, standing where I could drink her in, all of her, in one long gulp. The back of one wrist at the end of a long, perfectly toned bare arm fluttered to her mouth as she pretended to laugh at some sledge-hammer witticism. An arm like that spoke volumes. All right darling, you've laughed enough, and no, no, do not toss the dark luster atop your head like that.

Feeling my stare, she dodged from behind the crew-cut slab to give me a teeny smile and the briefest of nods to meet her *over there*. The trained assessor of the field of battle turned quick to catch me holding up my finger in a 'one-minute' gesture and ground me into the ridiculous carpet with a glare. I beat a strategic retreat to line up for Lois's second and last sanctioned beer.

Watching a soldier, sailor and marine with their uniform jackets off in a furious push-ups contest – they'd drawn a loud profane crowd – it took a moment to realize I was being addressed by the two suits ahead of me. "So whose interests you representing here tonight, cowboy?" the older one asked. He reached out to knead away absentmindedly on my sore shoulder. "Those new green jakes with the bacteria that eat the poop, the ones the Poles are trying to sell us, saying we owe them for their 'contribution.' Whadiya figure, Fenton," he asked the younger suit with the shining shaved head, "all the Sands combined, the Poles lost only a little north of eight-hundred personnel last year? Something pissant like that."

"Careful with the merchandise, pal. You squeeze that melon there too much, you're gonna have to buy it." I ducked awkwardly out from under fingers that grew more painful as he gained purchase.

"Some picayune number like that, Mr. Kratos, *BEI*. Maybe not even," said Fenton. Then cracking himself up, "Wait, no. Just look at him. Our guy here has a new *solar-powered* armored personnel carrier."

How drunk was Fenton, cause that little joke didn't justify half his hilarity.

"Gentlemen, I'll tell you cause I like you. But very hush-hush."

"Hey, don't drop any violations on us, Cowboy. Not during the Current Permanent Crisis," said Kratos. "It's just we've never seen you, or anyone like you, at the Appropriators' Ball. No offense – got that, mister?"

Gee, his squint was reassuring. "I certainly appreciate your interest in my affairs. But let me pose a query if I might. Just what is it – "

"Pose a what?" barked Fenton.

"An interrogatory, Fenton," I said gently. "What is it exactly that marks me as … *different*, not that I accept your premise in that regard. Is it the jejune tie? I assume that's the right plane getting shot down."

Kratos grabbed it with hors d'oeuvre-greased fingers for a look. "No, the tie is the one thing that works. Very festive. Look at Fenton's there, not that I'd ever insult someone's beliefs – no profit in it."

Fenton flapped his at me, then snatched it back. "Don't touch! This one's special."And indeed it was, with the cutest red cow prancing before some old stone city, a blazing light piercing through the clouds above.

"It's interesting what marks you, friend" said Kratos, warming to his topic. "Takes me back to my old days doing field intel. It's not the jacket – perfectly fine for Pimlico. Nor even those shoes – perfectly fine for raking leaves. And the less said about your hair the better. Like all good assessments, mine confirms initial impressions while penetrating to the heart of things. Cause you don't really like people, do you, you self-satisfied prick. These days, Washington is a friendly town – if you've got the right friends."

"Bold, Extolled, Impregnable," Fenton piped up.

Ignoring him, Kratos continued. "What it is beyond your outfit and the wise-ass manner, I'm not sure. But it's as plain as day. '*Jejune*.' How come a smart guy like you can't see that's not the sort of word to use in a room like this?"

I stood there dumbfounded as some syrupy, disco-strings version of a Sinatra ballad boomed from hidden speakers, the harpist finally bludgeoned into silence. Had I ever heard this, among the many indictments of my character over the years, that I didn't *like* people? Was that why all my friends were Nicki's? "Well, I certainly appreciate you gentlemen working to help me reform my character."

And Fenton got chesty all of a sudden, as drunks will. "All right, fella, enough wise-ass. How about you just tell us how you came by such an exclusive ticket."

"Well, gentlemen, strictly entre nous, it all started with my gig as a consultant on Paraguayan deep-sea fishing rights. Complex stuff, the amount of pink dye you're able competitively to put in a catfish to call it salmon and what-not.... What's that, Fenton? Why yes, of course Paraguay is landlocked, now that you mention it. That's what made it such a devilishly tricky assignment. As to tonight, a marquee American firm – which you'll understand I can't name in such a highly charged competitive environment – is seeking to monetize the technology involved. With obvious DoD support, of course. Men, I believe the good barkeep awaits our order."

Chapter Forty-Seven

Whitaker at Hart

And though Kratos looked like he'd swallowed something that wriggled on the way down and Fenton turned a sputtering red, I grabbed my beer and sought the cover of the scrum before the dancers. The biggest crowd was drawn by the newest venue, the harpist's revolving platform usurped by the most ... professional dancers so far.

The woman exposing a generous portion of a generous derriere by bending over to wave to the crowd from between her legs apparently felt competitively driven to such by the two girls creatively sharing a big leather divan. The absolute knockout shimmying away over on the left merely held her own.

Elbowing my way forward, I heard it, the slow, slight drawl and sibilant 'S' first implanted during my phoned-in report months back. Not talking to anyone in particular, my man Parnell was one of many encouraging the dancers to ever greater depths. Drifting past to look for a name on his uniform, I saw the slightly darker oblong where it had been removed. A glance around the room confirmed what I should have already noticed: not a name in sight. *Doughy*, Lois had said, though not by my necessarily more forgiving standards. About five feet ten, with thin hair greased back, his head – his skull, not his face – was somehow fleshy, as were his pink fingers. He had the usual fruit salad pinned to his dress uniform, though less than most, and I tried to imagine what it must be like to have your deeds and character displayed on your chest.

Discarding the notion of cracking my bottle over his head (wouldn't do to waste my second and last beer) I sidled back around and said, "Nice party, huh Parnell."

Sparing not a glance, he gushed, "Better than last year's even! But hold on a minute, and let's see if she gets the one with the superstructure into that chair. Goddamn, they'd give those two skinny ones there a run for their money!"

If *they* were skinny, what did that render some of my past stabs at happiness? Alright, time to lay down some law about not killing me, not with Short Leg, Twinkie or his own damn self. "I know your wife doesn't mind you choreographing things here, Parnell. Everyone in D ring knows that. But your girlfriend still might."

He turned, crunching ice furiously as a grin took hold. "And your wife, Forbes, it's taking half a Fusion Center to keep track of all the men she's thrown herself at recently, including a tall, young black. Though she seems to have settled on some rich old Jew for a while. You must have had some money when you got married, just short of ten years ago was it? Cause what other reason would a broad like her have to get hitched with someone like you."

So MoneyBags was old. I almost did a little jig.

"What the devil are you smiling at? Do you have any idea how easy it would be to snap my fingers and have your butt whipped."

"You just gave me a piece of good news, Parnell, but don't worry about it."

"So how the hell did you sneak in here? People all over town scheme all year to score a ticket to this gang-bang."

The crowd yelped as the other two girls took to a divan as the Captain and Tennille's "Muskrat Love" purred from the speakers. Delores's brute barged up and saluted, the first of those I'd seen that night. "May I be of assistance, sir? Nothing would give me greater pleasure, sir, BEI!"

"BEI. But thank you, Major, no. I think we have things well in hand here, don't we, uh, Dan? Quite a party, don't you think, Major? Enjoy yourself." Whitaker raised his glass vaguely in response to his parting salute, and the major did a nice cha-cha-cha about-face and melted off.

"You know … Dan" – God, it pained him, this sudden chumminess – "you did outstanding work out in Indiana. Her rollover. And that intel on the Indian transmission was top-notch. Imagine the effort involved in HDM keeping that from me. I would've thought that might have borne fruit by now, and you'd be due for some sort of bonus – a signing bonus I guess you'd call it."

"Yeah, what kind of fruit is that?"

"Low-hanging fruit, nothing exotic. Certainly not by the standards of this room tonight."

Man, he wasn't that tubby. And he didn't look nervous at all. Needing to pop something in my mouth, I swiped blindly at a passing tray, snaring a stuffed mushroom.

"That's a fungus – no damn benefit in eating that. During wilderness training, they teach you not to waste time on them. Stick to meat, friend, that's what your body needs. There's some outstanding beef circulating here, I can get them to bring you a plate of it with a knife and fork if you like. Leave those little skewers alone where you can't get a big enough chunk in your mouth for a proper taste."

"I'm good. Now whadiya say we stop all this pussyfooting around and get down to business."

"What's the matter, you don't like watching women express their true debased nature? Fine, stare at the floor if you want, but I find it invigorating to occasionally test my self-resolve…." I made to go, so, "Have it your way if you insist. OK, that illegally recorded tape you made out in Indiana, what's its price? As we both know, everything has its price, including you."

Tape – what freaking tape? Oh, right, that tape. "Not for sale, Parnell." Though of course it was. "Unless you want to buy one of the six or seven copies I got floating around various places – for your own archival purposes."

"I look at a someone like you crawling along on stumps, and I don't think you're making and distributing seven copies of anything, let alone something so inconsequential."

"You mean something that's going a long way towards keeping me alive?"

"Please, such melodrama. Alright, this is fair, more than fair: a thousand for each of the copies, seven grand total. Add that to whatever you got from that crook, Bettinger – I'm figuring ten grand – and a pipsqueak like you is making out OK."

I had to laugh, laugh dead in his face at that. I looked up with a big grin to see Delores drifting by thinking it was for her. She gave a lovely little smile in reply and again cocked her eyes to *over there*. I turned and asked Whitaker, "Ten grand – how the hell you figure that?"

"I paid Bettinger $25,000, so I figured the person who took most of the risk got a third of that and more."

He stopped for a gulp from his glass. Jesus – this was why I'd come. All on the record unless one of us said otherwise, I had to stifle the urge to get out my notebook.

"Look at it this way," he said, "Oh, hi, Charlie – talk to you in a minute. Who's this? Oh, just an old soldier gone bad. You know a hustling 'consultant' like the rest of you shysters."

Paraguayan fishing rights, Jack! "Soldiers gone bad – takes one to know one, Parnell. To answer your question, Bettinger promised fifteen-hundred, I haven't seen it, and I wouldn't take a dime now that I've re-embraced truth, justice and the good, old, *old* American way."

"*These* are the good old days, friend. Look around this room, you see anything here not to like? What about her – hello, darling," he said to some broad trolling past in a suggestion of a dress. "But, fifteen-hundred! You're as bad a sucker as I was, just on the flip side. I paid way too much, you charged way too little. I figured big-time corporate operators like Bettinger, that's what they got. I got a damn high overhead these days, and he wiped my checking account clean."

"I bleed for you, Parnell. You know about the tape I got on you. Now, about your e-mails, you should also know – "

"Your crap is coming out tomorrow, you say? " He downed his short drink and then grabbed a half-drunk one that looked similar off a busboy's passing tray. Staring at the two busy couples revolving before us, he shrugged, knocked back his scavenged drink, tossed both empty glasses to the carpeted floor under a little table and took a staggering step towards me. "After twenty-four years in, it's time to get out and make some money. Get myself situated for the next ten years."

"So why not a revolving-door job like everyone else here? Why'd you have to screw around with me and ruin both our lives?"

He held his hand up and rubbed his first two fingers against his thumb. "I needed an in to maximize my return, something fancy to bring to the table." I committed that to memory as he added, "As the great Rushdoony said, 'All law is a form of warfare.' Well, I'm at war against the ridiculous conflict of interest Regs."

Riding the self-pity train straight downhill, that last drink hadn't done him any good. "Knives are getting sharpened all over town," he whispered. "The jackals that slunk away when the HeadMan first stomped through the water hole are slinking back. It's almost as bad in his circle, I hear, as it is in the Pentagon. You don't get much protection from being even a top Calfer anymore. Not when that's half the senior ranks Building-wide, or a Dominionist, or a Reconstructionist or Re-establishmentarian or whatever someone chooses to call himself."

His mouth smeared on his face, Parnell drew even closer to share the whiskey fumes. "You know I had to fake a hell of a bout of stomach flu to miss HDM's launch. Made myself throw up all over my desk the day before, and my absence still raised a lot of eyebrows. But I figured with you already out there, I couldn't risk a security vid of us in the same room. Besides, you got people talking – seem to have a talent for that – and found out more than I could've officially."

This the man who'd sent two weirdo killers after me, I laughed at his shaky attempt to suck up. "Been a reporter a long time, dude."

"Look, mister – the job you signed up for is done. So just stand down."

"I don't know, Parnell. I kinda promised the guy who gave me the whole-vid of the SecDef tipping the stupid thing that I'd use it – out of concern for our Heroes and all."

Poleaxed, his mouth worked before the sound came out, "You have a *whole-vid* of her tipping over?"

Oops. Jesus, wise up. I stared, the correct response eluding me.

"Forbes, what are you worried about little old me for? Save some lives, man! It's not like a one-star procurement manager can stop a project with momentum like this one, everybody yelling about the damn rollover Grinder we have deployed now. Hell, neither one of those platforms, Jeep or the Grinder, is all that fucking stable. Not that the HeadMan cares, he's focused on

405

consolidating the domestic scene."

"What'd he say, his last time on TV when he looked so weird, 'Let the commanders on the ground decide.' "

"You know the old saying: War's too important to be left to the civilians. Plus I've heard he thinks casualties – a lot of them foreigners, thank God – work to inflame Homelanders. Make you more bloodthirsty."

"You're kidding."

He looked at me slyly. "Why do you think the whole-vid of that barracks bombing got 'leaked' last month, the one with the footage of that fox second lieutenant all bloodied?"

I looked up to see Delores's brute talking earnestly to the two guards who'd been eyeing me, and damn if here they didn't come. I turned to my new *friend* Parnell, who looked like he was assessing the need to puke. The taller guard said, "Good evening, General. This guest with you, sir?"

To his credit, the bastard lost his fuzziness round the edges riki-tik. "No, not *with* me, men. Certainly not, are you, Dan? Not yet anyway. But I do want to talk to him a moment more."

"You OK, General," the shorter one asked. "Want to sit down a minute, let me get you a ginger ale?"

He stood up straighter, his eyes darting. Christ, was an Army general actually afraid of these private MoFos? "Fine, boys. Never better. Appreciate you looking out for things tonight. You know, men, I hear there's a surplus of females here this evening. I know you're on duty till midnight. Still, a little tip to keep in your back pocket." And again the same casual wave with which he'd dismissed Delores's brute.

"Speaking of security," Whitaker continued, charged by the fog-clearing interruption, "there's a certain captain I know, pretty weird looking, you come right down to it and not exactly a big hit with the ladies. The kind of guy who spends Christmas at the movies, and he's not Jewish. Probably why he's so good with extracurricular work."

"All your henchmen are weird somehow, ain't they, Parnell?"

"It's *General Whitaker*, fuck-face. Anyway, he was really looking forward to tonight's guaranteed dick-wetting now that the Ball Committee has finally stopped nickel-and-diming us.

So he was *primed* until he had an unfortunate encounter down in a little shop in Southeast, of all places. He said he was way too humiliated to come tonight, waking up on the floor with a DC EMT shinning a light in his eye."

"Is he really an albino?"

"It's a matter of degree." Deepening his voice, he sneered, " 'Hey, thanks, General, for admitting to sending him after me.' Like I care. Besides, go ahead and prove it, Mr. Zero. So the question is, what the hell happened to my captain? He can't figure what you did to him, how you caught him unawares when you were basically putty in his hands. He'd really like to know what the hell you did – you know, for his education's sake."

"What *I* did? Sure – *right*, what I did. Whadiya think, I go down these mean streets naked to the world, depending solely on the kindness of strangers? OK, it's a simple little … North Korean move whose main virtue is it's so hard to see coming. If he can't track it down with those two clues, he doesn't deserve it."

"North Koreans – they're known for leaving no marks."

"Unlike, speaking of your crackerjack henchmen, Short Leg spewing shots all over Queens. Huh, Parnell?"

"Do you have any idea how much Red-Calf influence I had to spend to get that idiot out of jail? Having to make all kinds of promises to a top NYPD Calfer to get an unlicensed gun charge reduced to disorderly conduct."

"I'm supposed to feel bad, he flubbed *that* particular assignment?" Damn, too loud, cause even in the midst of an ever more raucous circle-jerk, several heads turned our way, including those two guards. I split my face with a friendly grin for the general, who grinned back when I nodded at the menacing guards.

"Rising in a meritocracy like the Calfers is too tricky for someone so reckless, as you saw up in Queens. A lot of people like to pretend it's sin that's preventing the Second Coming. You know, gay sex and abortion – not the lack of a pure Red Heifer."

"So you think cow ashes will do the trick for a sinner like you? Out, out damn spot! Looking around this room, I figure it's gonna take more than a cow to clean up this bunch. And I'm not talking about the women."

"What's your mother's maiden name?"

"Why, you want to mess with my bank account? Gonna send somebody to Queens in an iron lung to shut it down? I don't think there's enough there to cover the trip."

"If I was interested in your dwarfish finances, I'd already have access. If you're Hebrew, my explanation goes one way, if you're a regular religion, another. I'll cut it down the middle, like Solomon. We have to get a Red Calf with no white hairs. Totally pure red. Wash your hands in its ashes and then you're purified to enter Temple Mount in the Holy Land so you can build a new temple for the Hebrew Messiah. You and I – judging by your features – call Him Jesus. He'll be coming again soon, so we can start thinking about Glory Days. Us and the Jews who convert."

"So that's why Short Leg was screaming at me to get the semen. You told him I had some from the right bull."

"He was told you were going to sell it to infidels to pour down the sink. Why should he care about a murder rap? He believes if you don't give your all for the Red Heifer you might get a stroke like that Israeli prime minister way back who was stricken for giving Jewish land away."

"And that's why he stole a kid's scooter – for semen."

"We know our reward isn't in this world. You think I care about money serving my country all these years? Our Faith is a force-multiplier.. That's what American Exceptionalism is all about, serving the Lord. We're doing His will, all these Sands. Fomenting Democracy is just the icing on the cake."

"You leave me breathless, General. So you sent me to Indiana cause you don't care about money."

"These wars endure until He ends them. There's other stuff, OK, worthwhile stuff. Saving their women, combating evil, securing resources – natural gas, mostly, our current Sands. All under the heading of Fomenting. I almost forgot: fighting T, of course."

"You think all that still applies, the shining City on the Hill raining salvation down with the bombs? Don't all these defeats mean something?

"Haven't lost one yet, maggot. Did you see any foreign tanks rolling around on your way here tonight? Throw in the pansy Air Force, and we've still got the best, most efficient killing machine on the planet – fuck the Chinese very much. We're supposed to ask Christian Homelanders to pay all that hard-earned money, and then just stockpile the hardware? Not use it for a higher purpose? I don't think so."

"So it all comes down to kill a Haji for Christ."

"Listen up and you listen good. The time of our stealth infiltration of government is over. When I look around this room, I see the people born to lead this country. Homelanders and others will follow as they're able to perceive the reality we create. Look at the caliber of men here tonight, and then tell me a nonbeliever like you is on the right side of history."

A roar erupted as some soldiers hauled down a sailor trying to join the fun on the revolving stage, which, I noticed, featured the first unabashed bare tit of the evening. "My bank account, sure. But what exactly qualifies you to comment on my faith, Whitaker?"

"Don't make me laugh, someone like you. Most people want to submit, to follow a leader. But not you – wearing a sports coat to a high-toned affair in a Senate office building.

"Alright, Parnell. This little colloquy is all well and good, but I got fish to fry."

"Listen to how you talk – so full of yourself." He stumbled closer again. "Well get this, sausage-jockey. You're giving up those e-mails and that tape – all of them. And then you're going to go somewhere. Disappear. Go slop pigs out in *Indiana* if you like. And this whole nightmare will never have happened."

"Don't you think Bettinger gave me those e-mails for a reason? Just be glad I got them from New York, and not out of your shop. Not that it matters, cause you're the one disappearing, pal, and for a good long while. You're facing" – what the hell had Lois said? – "federal charges of concealment, and, uh, fraudulent contract and, right, defrauding the Army of having its business conducted without improper influence."

"*Improper influence*? What stupid, *old* history book did you get that out of? Look around you here tonight, shit-hole, at who's got their hands on the tiller."

"In the till, you mean. You sure you got the juice to avoid a traditionalist judge, assuming there are any hanging on down here?"

"Third time's the charm, Forbes."

"Third time for what?"

"Twice you've slipped past my men. OK, you want a job done right, you gotta…. Easy as pie, with you already branded as some kinda kook Fiend for messing with Protectors up in New York. Hell, I'll just plant it here in *Cap Dispatch* – the editor's a Calfer – that you were done in by others in your cell to keep you from exposing your plot."

"Only problem with that is my only co-conspirators are those three independent editors I clued in, tying my safety to you with a big red bow."

"Nobody gives a fig about you now, so why is anyone going to care once you're toast?"

"Or how about I just jump up with the girls there and make a little speech about our joint endeavors?"

He started turning away at that, and I grabbed him by the arm and pulled him close. "You don't got the sense God gave geese. I go down, you're getting locked up for the next twenty years cause my story – *our* story, Parnell – is getting published in a few hours, and there's not a damn thing you can do about it. What, you gonna shut down the Net between now and then?"

"You never know, I get some Calfers pulling together."

"And, yes, my publisher already has the e-mails you were stupid enough to send, plus the assignment memo that idiot Bettinger faxed me."

"What makes you think any of that matters a lick towards keeping you safe rather than both of us going out in a blaze of glory?"

"Bottom line, Parnell? Cause you're a coward. A flabby, desiccated rear-echelon motherfucker. Otherwise you wouldn't have been a desk-jockey all these Sands."

"How about I staple your ass to your mouth. That way, the goons where you're ending up can fuck you twice without having to get all sweaty about it. You'd like that, wouldn't you."

Delores trotted up as I fumbled for the right response. She stood baling with her back foot, but still trying to help, bless her. She said hi to me, then lobbed Parnell that bit about knowing to ask his first name only and wondered if he was enjoying "a very spirited party."

"Beat it, Missy. And leave my damn first name out of this. This pantywaist is toxic, you got that? Off-limits. There's plenty of All-American Heroes here tonight for you to satisfy your obligation. With the extra females present, if you don't score one, I got a captain off-site can punch your ticket for you."

Arms out, he advanced on her to bodily shoo her away and then lunged. Yuck. Like Lois said, he was doughy, I found, my hands on his chest as I jumped between them. He was easy to fend off, for his target was another glass on a passing tray. And Delores, wow! Her glasses were off and hooked into her high neckline when I turned to her, her hands kung-fu cocked.

"Stop that. You'll just get in trouble," I hissed. Arms that delicious, I could only hope I remembered how with a woman that young. "Now, I'm almost done, and we can get out of here. We'll go yak at your boss a minute and then vamos!" She nodded, finally put her hands down and gave me one of her smiles.

"A piece of advice – if you're capable of it." Ich, Parnell leaning in confidentially was worst of all. "Little Missy here is certainly fertile, young as she is. I already know you don't have any kids, so given what's happening here in the Homeland – Europe is already lost – as a white man, you absolutely must breed in whatever short time you have left. Just drop your load, she can always give it up for adoption."

"What the hell are you talking about?"

"It's the white man's burden, even a maggot like you. It's a shame that old Quiverfull movement didn't take off like it should've back then. I mean it's back in spades now, especially with the HeadMan's new incentives to couples who were married in an approved church and qualify under the Race Regs' new Nascent Minority clause."

"You take an awful lot for granted, don't you Parnell, talking like this right in front of her, a young lady I've just met."

Both of them stared incredulously as a bunch of guards rushed off to smother a sudden brawl in the corner. I told Delores, "Just go over there a minute, OK, please. I'm just about done."

"That's right, fork-in-your-ass done. What's the matter, Missy, somebody in uniform too much man for you? You know, shit-hole, that's why this little piece of skirt is into you."

Old man Kratos and his bald brass knuckles came charging up, Fenton basically shoving Delores aside. He said, "See, Mr. Kratos. See how he's bothering one of our Heroes in uniform. I've been trying to tell the Committee all along these anonymous tickets are a bad idea. We try, but with over seven-hundred tickets, it's too easy for one or two to go wrong. There was that *journalist* last year we had to take care of, and now this, this…."

Apparently he couldn't think of a term low enough for me. An annoyed Kratos said, "Speaking pretty much *as* the Committee, I'm tired of hearing this shit, Fenton. Anonymous tickets are the only way business gets done. Everything OK here, General?"

"Hard to say, Gentlemen. Maybe, Mr. Kratos, it's time for this boy's rear end to be scraping sidewalk."

"I thought that the moment I laid eyes on him. But first I'd like to know what the hell he's doing here."

"Right. Where'd you get the ticket, mister," Fenton barked, all up in my face.

"Your momma left it on my night table as a tip. Said I wasn't charging enough."

"Alright, I've heard enough," said Kratos. He deftly deposited his sputtering muscle behind him.

"Just one thing," Whitaker said as four guards materialized from nowhere. "What was that this morning about me dating Bettinger's sister? Have I forgotten something? Do you know what she looks like now or where she lives? It's his *younger* sister, right?"

"How 'bout you take what's offered here tonight, Parnell, and then start worrying about your criminal defense. You're going to be a busy boy with that."

Kratos said, "You want him searched, General, before he leaves?"

"It might be interesting to see what kind of … documents he's got on him – but, now that I think of it, probably not. It is, after all, a night for fun, Gentlemen, and I wouldn't want to put you out. "

"No documents tonight, huh, General," said Kratos.

"I told you, Parnell, they've already been delivered."

"So what's that make you, King Turd on Shit Mountain?"

"I was thinking it made me more like a phoenix rising from the ashes – you know, one of those mythical creatures, like the so-called female orgasm."

"What are you talking about?"

I looked over at old-man Kratos, who stood there sourly letting a general hold the whip, and gave him a big wink. "I should've known you've never encountered one, Parnell."

"Get him out! Out now! Out before I teach him some fucking manners!" The dancers stopped to stare he yelled so loud, even the nearly naked one.

The guards started bellying me towards the door, Kratos following. I looked back to see Whitaker striding towards the bar and Delores standing with the back of her wrist covering her mouth, shaking her head slowly back and forth, back and forth. I gave her a shrug and mouthed "No" at her so she wouldn't follow. Bypassing the line, Whitaker ordered a drink and turned and gave me the finger.

I stopped abruptly, a guard running into me. "At the hip, Whitaker!" Then really loud. "Remember, you and me, *General Parnell Whitaker and Daniel Forbes*, joined at the hip!" Along with the *Warpath* article, bellowing it out like that to that particular crowd would forge the bond. I gave that sweet girl a last smile – damn, I couldn't freaking win! – as the guards started pushing for real, and the room surged towards us with a roar.

Whitaker yelled, "I won't be the horse to your Lady Godiva, Forbes. You hear me, Goddamnit!"

I did, no problem. A beehive tipped over in the corner would have created less of a commotion. Fenton twitching and clenching, Kratos turned to the Silver Fox sitting serenely behind her desk outside and said, "No way to identify this man's ticket, is there, Miss Smythe?"

"No, sir. According to procedure, I'm afraid not."

"Very good, Miss Smythe. That's exactly the answer I was hoping for. Norda, I believe only two of you are needed to escort him out. See him to the sidewalk – that's it. Got it?"

"BEI, Mr. Kratos," the tall one said.

"Fenton, attach yourself to General Whitaker. *Discretely*, Fenton. It's probably time to get him a girl – one of ours, Cynthia'd be best – and a car and driver."

Fenton barked, "*Bold, Extolled, Impregnable.*"

"BEI," Kratos sighed. Then, "You two men, come with me. There's a certain young lady in there I want to talk to. Though she's one of April's, so I doubt she knows this piece of trash somebody tossed into our midst. She was probably just looking for an easy time of it tonight."

Kratos turned and jabbed me hard in the chest. "I encounter you again – which, believe me, can be at the drop of a hat – you'll find out I never let someone off so lightly twice. Your kind, your time is done!"

Sparks came off the short guy in the elevator, but the tall one, Norda, reminded him of its cameras. Then he told me, "Don't bother waiting for chicken-bones upstairs. No guest'll touch her, tainted like she is. Kratos'll probably give her to our guy, Lembowski. He likes bringing a piece of fluff to heel."

Whitaker was right about one thing. I'd worked my Turd-Touch magic on Delores, turning her evening – if not days and weeks hence, depending on how brutal Lembowski proved – brown and smelly. She was also probably in need of a new job. And then I was on the sidewalk being told to get myself gone before Mr. Kratos changed his mind.

414

PART EIGHT

Chapter Forty-Eight

Floundering Across that River

Either one of them able to take me apart, I stifled the smirk and turned on my heel. Damn, Delores had given me the sweetest little c'est-la-vie smile on my way out the door. I ruefully pictured my nervous, chatty charmer turning starkers from her fridge to offer me a beer, then doing that thing with the back of her wrist covering her shy smile, her long, pale legs welded demurely, her tousled hair playing peek-a-boo with her not terribly large, perfect breasts, our first bout accomplished, Delores purring for more.

No wet-shirt tease or vagaries over soup weeks hence. Man, she probably had the silkiest damn fur, girls like her just did. A working dog and his glaring minion passed going the other way, and my foot nearly spasmed out to trip one or the other. After all, how much longer would my soggy bag of luck hold?

I suddenly needed to pee like a bastard. Maybe a nice outdoor piss was a stone for two birds, cause I had no idea where I was laying my head in a couple of hours. Wet down those bushes there over by all that white marble. Sure, the Library of Congress the sign said, a fitting comment on my 'career.' Couldn't ride the subway all night cause it mickey-mouse shut down. Still before nine, there was always a late Chinatown bus back to the Hovel – yeah, to end up back at my too well known address before the morrow's *Off the Warpath* story inoculated me from harm (uh-huh).

I took a left onto a leafy street cause – maybe it was stress of bellowing at Whitaker– but I was emptying my bladder one way or another. And there, a block on, down some steps, the name in green neon above the door, was The Bite Boite. Cripes. It proved all dark wood and cozy tables with little lamps with red shades. The man greeting me from behind a podium blanched when I informed him I was meeting the, uh, Hendon party (a nod to the late, lamented Congressman) and motored past, the men's room thankfully off to the side. Searching futilely for a Hendon on his clipboard, he called to me as I reached the door. Jesus, I won't use any soap, OK.

His sputtering growing louder, I locked the door behind me. Ah, sweet relief interrupted by banging on the door. "Come on, get the hell out! You're not allowed." Someone with a deeper voice and heavier fist than the greeter.

I took my own sweet time. Unlocking the door and pushing a cautious inch, it was wrenched out of my hand so violently I almost tumbled out into the arms of a man with a slab of gut dressed in a blue tuxedo shirt, no tie. Arrayed behind were three Latino workers in those checked kitchen pants and filthy white shirts, two of them grinning broadly, the third slapping the boxy business end of a meat tenderizer into his palm. Thirty or so diners staring, for the second time in ten minutes I was the object of a crowd's hostile curiosity, this group at least looking less likely to rip me limb from limb. The man said he was the owner, and he was sick and tired of riff-raff off the streets abusing his hospitality. "But you have. So now I want to know what you're going to do to fix it."

Riff-raff? And me dressed the best I'd been in I didn't know when. "Whadiya mean, am I going to go back in there and *reabsorb* it? By the looks of 'em, most of your customers don't flush. But I'm afraid I did, so that means you're piss out of luck. And if you want me to flip you a dollar for the privilege, you can go suck eggs."

"I'll have you arrested for trespassing and libel against my customers. No, for T Crime. That's right, I – "

"Yeah, what T is that – for telling you to suck eggs? How do you know the eggs won't enjoy it?"

I brushed past, one of the grinning kitchen workers giving a little bow to usher me out. I mean, which Goddamn pound of flesh did he want? The man grabbed at my sore shoulder, but I ducked away and turned to see him beckoning for meat-tenderizer dude. This for a piss – enough was, yeah, too freaking much.

I grabbed a knife from an empty table's place setting, really not much more than an elongated butter knife, and brandished it wildly. Then Zorro yelled, "OK, Fat Stuff, you really want blood all over your nice carpet here – yours, mine, maybe both? Tell you what. I'll mail you a dollar for the water and the *one* paper towel I used, hold your damn breath. Now I'm walking out the door here, so come on if you want to."

I felt for the door behind me and got it open. A diner yelled, "Watch it! That's that Fiend from New York, the one in the shorts. He's all dressed up as a disguise!" Great, and me waving a knife around. I tossed it on the carpet and showed them my back. Cause I really did not care. Ruining a general's life and then breaching his lair to rub his nose in it, I was supposed to blanche at some lard-ass restaurateur acting tough?

The Battle of the Bathroom. Hell, wasn't that why Mailer's literary ex-con killed that poor young waiter, Richard Adan? OK, no pee inside me to earn a place for the night, so where?

****

It took one short block to admit Lois had been my fallback all along. Come on, not changing her wet shirt after our intimacies by the sink? The contacts to show off her cat eyes, *plus* those shorts – I hadn't been that darn early. What was her saying no one but mom had been to her house for months but the anguished plea of the lonely and bereft?

Hell, she was flirting with me from the jump, flicking my hair like that in Farragut Square. Sure, Delores would've been stupendous. But she was obviously snatched from my sweaty paw to propel me to the arms of someone closer to my age and outlook.

The cab driving by made my decision for me, though I had to club the driver to understand I wanted him to pull up to the side entrance of Union Station and sit with the meter running while I scanned the street behind. A variant on Deep Throat instructing Woodward to cab it to a hotel, then duck in, out a different entrance and quick into another cab on his way to their meeting.

English seemingly his fourth language, the second cabbie at the station's main entrance was even more obtuse when I asked him to drive me to the nearest Metro station, insisting there was one right there. Well, if I didn't want that one, what line was I looking for? What did I mean it didn't matter, just please get the hell out of there? My yelling finally motivated him to the Chinatown Green Line stop straight to Anacostia. Security theater for an audience of one – if Lois even opened her door – the cabs were an expensive way to hit her porch in good conscience.

I lingered on the Anacostia platform a moment but spied no one white getting out with me, so figured no tail. Up on the street a cop drove by and then pulled a U, came back and stopped the one time some teenagers seemed moved to amuse themselves with me. So I made it to Best Booze's wire-meshed door unmolested in search of their absolutely most eponymous nine-buck red.

The hollowed-out old clerk in his plastic isolation booth just pointed vaguely to "the wine area." When I pressed him for a recommendation based on my exacting criteria of price and color, he said, "Do I look like I'm getting paid enough to care about some over-dressed jerk coming down here looking to get laid on the cheap cause she's black?" I didn't bother with the unassailable defense that my budget applied to white girls too. Nor did I inquire of the booth's second white guy, a glum young dude in a protective vest, blue pants with a yellow stripe down the leg and a pistol on his hip. Hoping Lois had some beer on hand for me, I got the only red under ten dollars with a fake cork, not a screw-top. From Portugal, how bad could it be.

I braved deserted residential blocks rather than the main drag with too many people out escaping the furnace inside. Zigging and zagging – the more trees, the safer the block, I decided – I pondered my uncertain reception, then woke up enough to stow the tie in a pocket and shed the jacket. Not that holding it over my shoulder would blend me in. Some old lady hollered down from a porch did I want to come in and call a cab, and two kids from another porch cursed and told me where to go and what to do with myself getting there.

Damn, only a small light downstairs, an upstairs room blazing away at Lois's. Subject to an early reveille all these years, had she retired for the night, though not much past nine? No way round it but mount her porch and ring her bell. Pushing her gate open, a particularly bright motion-sensitive light kicked on. Up on her porch, I could hear Lois pounding down the stairs, so I lunged for the bell before she could find me lurking unannounced.

She flung the door open and stood coiled, a big bat held effortlessly in one hand, a club of a flashlight in the other. She was magnificent! Pointing to the flashlight, I tried to laugh. "How far do you chase me in the dark after I run from the bat?"

She stared at me balefully, waved the bat at my chest and finally put it down. "You don't have anywhere else to go, do you?"

"I got plenty of places. People clamoring for my company. What I don't have is your zip code – you know, to mail this stupid jacket back."

She came out past me holding the bat high again, peered around, turned and shoved me roughly inside. Her hand felt good on my back. Lois shut the door and, *right on*, locked it. She was wearing a faded University of Maryland tee shirt, the Terrapin looking mighty smug, gym shorts and nothing else far as I could tell. "Stop staring, boy. Or ain't you never seen a woman ready for bed before. I thought I made it clear I'd seen the last of that jacket. What time is it? You think Anacostia's so dark and scary I won't dare send you packing? Or am I supposed to take pity on you cause you're some kind of druggie, civ-lib freak like I've been reading tonight?"

"Lois, I'm sorry. It's just a little after nine. I, uh – look, I brought a bottle of wine." Taking it out of the bag to show her, she caught sight of the label.

"Thanks. I can use that the next time I cook spaghetti – in the pot!"

She stared. All I had was a palms-up shrug. Finally she laughed and said, "Trust you, Forbes, to leave the Appropriators' Ball alone."

"So you know about the women's 'obligation' as Whitaker put it. He got real ugly real loud to snatch a young damsel from my grasp. She'd seized on me as the most undemanding option at hand – little did she know."

"An excess number of females, probably, she wanted to lock down a sure thing."

"Thanks, I think."

419

"So did they start throwing stuff? Any Marines get their asses kicked?"

"All it needed was some lions and Christians. And better music. You wouldn't believe the 1980s-dreck they were playing."

"Most of those rear-echelon turkeys are pretty played-out, so that's all they can handle. You didn't get drunk, that's something. So skuzzy old Parnell sent Missy packing, and you figured you'd turn to Old Reliable sitting at home reading?" And she reached up and flicked my split ends for the second time that day.

"We both made enough of a commotion – him first – that half the nation's T-Industrial Complex will have no trouble linking our two names. Not after I bellowed them out both loud, saying we were linked at the hip."

"You did that? Well, it's not like there was any decorum to maintain."

"They were already throwing me out. And don't worry, the lady at the door told head security there was no way to identify my ticket."

"And the e-mail?"

"I stressed that it came from New York. Parnell seemed to accept that. Though most of the time he was just buffaloing his way straight ahead."

"Speaking of which, you're already inside, so no point standing here in the hall." She led me into the living room and plopped down right in the center of the smallish couch. I took the chair. A coffee table still in the offing, she reached for the half-empty bottle of wine on the floor by her feet, poured herself a healthy glass and raised a grinning, mock salute.

"Since you've offered, thanks, Lois. Wine's not my thing – "

"Obviously."

But I'll take a beer if you've got one."

"Let's see if you've earned it. So did you get anything for our article? I re-read it before flushing, and it's good, but a little skimpy."

"So now it's *our* article. You putting your name up top too?" She laughed. Watching her sitting there *breathing* at me, wearing the challenging, quizzical look that seemed hers for the evening, it was all a blur except for Delores's lovely smile and Whitaker's hissy-fit. "For one thing, I can add the super-dooper atmospherics of dancing on tables and four women getting progressively less dressed and more entwined."

"Dancing on tables – in a Senate office building! That's sweet. Saw it with your own eyes, so in it goes. Too bad it doesn't specifically serve Parnell's head on a platter."

Jesus, of course! "The main thing is he admitted to paying Bettinger $25,000 to hire me. Wiped his checking account clean, he said. So there's a record of it. Plus he told me it was time he quit the Army and made some money."

"That last goes without saying, but he told you about a twenty-five grand check? What is it, people don't feel threatened by you, so they just start spilling their guts?"

"I've been a reporter a long time, girl, supposedly having learned a little technique in that stretch. But the truth is, he was flailing pretty wildly. Maybe he thinks I won't be around long enough to tattle on him, so...."

"Nobody followed you here, right? You're sure of that?"

I proudly recounted my taxi-machinations and that only black folks coming home tired from work got off the train with me.

"Look at Maxwell Smart! I don't think Parnell has it in him to get a brother working for him, his mind isn't wired that way. But damn! Twenty-five grand for a day's work. And how much did you get, half?"

"Me? Nothing. I was supposed to get the grand total of fifteen-hundred, but I haven't seen a dime, and I'm certainly not taking any now – not that that's gonna happen. He also said that neither of the new Grinders, HDM's or Jeep's, is 'all that fucking stable.' I suppose I can quote him. He knows I'm writing an article, and neither one of us said anything about on- or off-the-record. I didn't have a notebook out, but, hell, *on* is the default assumption."

"He sends some guy to New York to kill you, and you're worried about that?"

"That's not the half of it. Today, well...."

"Today, what? What the hell happened today."

Man, she got fierce quick. "Nothing. *Tonight*, just all kinds of, you know, vague threats, stuff about no one caring about me once I'm 'toast.' And he should do the job right himself and get it over with."

Lois not buying, not at all, I plowed on. "That's about it for the party. I overheard a lot of stray talk about various weapons systems. Not that I saw any cash changing hands over in a corner."

"We're the ones writing the checks."

"And along with every woman there being at least strongly encouraged to go home with someone, just before getting tossed, I saw my first unabashed bare tit up on this little revolving stage. God only knows what happened after I left."

"First of the evening or first of your life?"

"Hardy har-har. I feel bad about that poor girl getting tarred by my brush for picking me out. After tossing me, the security MoFo was headed back in to interrogate her, plus she's probably out of a job. She said she screwed up the only other party she'd been allowed to work chasing some House big shot she was supposed to know was gay."

"Too bad about your little whore, but this town chews 'em up and spits out the bones. Sounds like she'd be about right for the Navy. But what about you, Forbes? You heading out west to pick apples? Gonna live outside the Bar Code?"

"Nah. I got a story coming out tomorrow that's gonna bounce wide and far and make me a big-time two-hundred-and-fifty bucks."

"Two-fifty. Jesus, you need to enlist. You're worse off than the grunts with kids who qualify for food stamps. But you done good, getting Parnell to spill about that check."

"Yup. Confronted him right in the fundament of the T-Industrial Complex."

"You like confronting people. Gonna tell 'em where to stick it when they try to search you, everybody else staring at their shoes. So what are you, a nihilist, a transit recidivist, some weird, lone-wolf loner, or a Fiend like they're saying in the papers up in New York? This isn't the first time you've messed with the cops is it?"

"I guess I didn't get enough hugs as a kid."

"Maybe not, cause I came across an article in a New York legal paper about you suing the cops and Lincoln Center. You couldn't go to a *folk* concert without raising a ruckus, and then they didn't tell you to shut up politely enough."

"Refuse and resist. Me and the Ex are suing their asses, and when I adopt some foster kid, my share of the money will be just in time to help *his* kid go to college – enough for books for a whole semester."

She yawned and stretched, her hands high and her feet out straight – as if I wasn't staring every chance I got. She gave me a look and said, "Things are getting ripe in this country, HeadFuck on top long enough to wise people up. You can feel little eddies of it starting to move."

"Tonight, it was some dog and his cops scaring the bejesus out of a woman on the train."

"Let me guess: a black woman, an older black woman?"

"Old enough. Five minutes after we parted, me verklempt – "

"Talk English, show-off!"

"*My mind troubled.* Troubled, OK, from wondering if I was ever going to see you again.... Anyway, I thought this lady just trying to get to work cleaning up other people's trash was gonna keel over right there, she was so scared. The cop even told Dispatch it was nothing, but the dog had 'alerted,' so that was that."

Lois shuddered, quite a performance. "I can't stand 'em, the dogs always trying to sniff you. You don't see them 'alerting' on men."

"Someone's got to strike a spark somehow, get something going to build up people's morale. Get enough sparks until, eventually, the whole thing goes poof."

"It'll be a nasty fire," Lois said.

"People are fighting their own MoFos the world over, so what makes us immune? It's not like some fraud *election* is freaking gonna do the trick, deep as this crew has their claws in."

Another hit of wine and Lois sighed. "Elections didn't mean diddly when we voted against those early Sands. It's going to be tough on the stone the flint hits to make that spark of yours. Ever think of that, bright boy, setting out to tell the cops to kiss off about the searches?"

"Like Sancho Panza said, 'Whether the stone hits the pitcher, or the pitcher hits the stone, it's going to be bad for the pitcher.'"

"Whoever he is – like you're the only one who reads books."

She gave a devastating smile as I watched her slow journey across to the one bookcase to fumble around behind the shelved volumes. I'd never seen such *round* muscles. What, a joint to goose my nerves even worse, maybe some gooey Afghani hash home in a duffel?

Chapter Forty-Nine

Not Tonight, Maybe Never

She turned and handed me a book.

"This is what I was telling you about: *Managed Democracy and Inverted Totalitarianism*. You may want my oven mitts."

I pretended to study it a moment, but didn't open it.

"I heard about Wolin from some freak at Hopkins – well, freak by the standards there," she said. "And the funny thing was, the library had his book listed, but the librarians could never produce it no matter how many times I requested it."

"Funny things, libraries these days. At the famous Lion Library up in New York – ."

"Wait! So I forgot about it till I ran into it in a musty little bookstore way out in Maryland. Against his principles to throw out a book, the owner said he was glad to see it gone. After I read it, I was glad I paid cash, and there was no record of me ever getting my hands on it at Hopkins."

"Hot-stuff, huh? Though I doubt that some dusty old political science tome, I don't care how perspicacious, is nearly as transgressive as some of the books I was toting around Penn Station."

"But those were novels. If they're any good, of course they're more true than even the best analysis. Footnotes just get in the way, you come right down to it."

"And just how the hell, Missy, did you know they were all novels?"

She started, smiled, and when I didn't smile back, narrowed her face alarmingly. "I don't know what you're trying to insinuate, but whatever it is, I don't like it. After I've let you into my house twice – once, uninvited – with you being all vague about who knows who tailing you all over DC. I just assumed they were novels, based on the type of person you are."

We looked at each other unhappily. Finally she said, "It's just I like talking about books. Tell me one you like that you carried."

"I don't know. I guess one I *like* is called *A Wrinkle in Time*. A really profound book if you give it a chance."

"OK. My Wolin for your *Wrinkle*. I don't get the chance to talk about anything but Army procedure manuals that much anymore since my fool got himself killed. You probably grew up with your parents reading to you all the time. Momma was too exhausted mostly, being sickly with four kids, and I don't think Daddy was much of a reader. He could, don't get me wrong. It just wasn't his thing."

"That's me, a real Wind-in-the-Willows childhood. Well, thanks for the suggestion on the Wolin. I'll have to check it out – later."

I gave her my best Cary Grant as she went back to the couch, sitting encouragingly to the side, not the middle. But she was stuck."You know all the shit we've been doing to the rest of the world for years, right? Now HeadMan and his gang are doing it to us."

'Blowback grown big."

"Think about it, Forbes. Counting the Cold War and all the hot ones small and big, we've been at war one way or another for a lifetime now. That does something to a country – to its people."

"Maybe all that stuff carries within it the seeds of its own destruction. At least we're smart enough to never pick on anyone who has an air force or a navy."

"It's not so easy, fighting an idea."

She reached for something in the corner of the couch and pulled out a fancy, gold-colored cigarette case and removed a substantial, brown-paper number. Apparently weighing her decision, she stared down at it, then lit up. "You don't need to be giving me any looks for a *clove* cigarette. The basketball player isn't allowed or something? You know I haven't picked up a ball since that thug destroyed my knee. Sure I could have sat out a year and limped through a career at Drexel or someplace and maybe had some fun."

"More fun than cutting hair in Korea?"

"But it wouldn't have been the same. Drexel ain't Missouri, and neither my first step nor my elevation was ever going to be what I had. Three different doctors told me that."

During the long pause, I sought the right, baby-I-understand look for when she finally came back. Despite my best efforts, she inexplicably didn't pat the couch next to her in invitation.

"Going to kiss some village elder's ass my last Sands, we got two men killed out of the blue in a village that was supposed to be totally pacified. Bought and paid for. A bunch of new wells, a new school, the lot. But it had been all shot up that morning, six civilians killed, including two kids. Now this was our sector. *Hearts and minds* – shit, we weren't supposed to off a dog without my colonel knowing about it. Turns out the Secret Army of Northern Virginia – "

"Special Ops."

"Look at you. Anyway, JSOC had been pursuing one of their private little vendettas without bothering to tell us that maybe people might be a little pissed off at Am ericans, you head south into that next valley there."

"Special Forces living large?"

"If you call that living. They get awfully twisted awfully quick, doing what they do. A law unto themselves, I try to keep me and my guys the hell away from them. In-theater, a Special Ops sergeant is just as likely to stare right past me as obey an order from a black female major."

"Speaking of chain of command, you couldn't have reported Whitaker internally, gone through channels."

"Five or six years ago, maybe. But now – a black, *female* subordinate accusing a Calfer general? They'd file some pro forma paperwork, toss it and try to force me out before I got my twenty in as a lesson to anyone else even thinking about it."

She looked around the room a minute, then whispered, "I just wish Marcel was here to talk to about all this."

"You mean Jacket-Man with the long arms?"

"That jerk? Give me a break, Forbes. No. Marcel's dead, the damn fool. He had to get all heroic saving three of his men. They're still alive – though I don't know if one would call it living – and now Marcel's momma's got a bronze star framed on her wall. Whoopee."

What the hell was I supposed to say?

"We met in officer candidate school. It wasn't rocket science, us getting together stuck at Fort Benning with all them Calfers, even back then. He got killed us bringing Turkmenistan to heel after they kicked us out that first time. That boy was finally ready to get down on one knee to get both our mommas off his neck. But look."

She waggled her naked left ring finger at me.

"Funny thing is, even sitting like a lump over there, you remind me a little bit of Marcel, your Charlie-Mike vibe, you know, Continue – "

"Mission!"

"Charlie-Mike got him killed. Nobody expected him to cross that road, the fire they were laying down." She drank. "I should've known better than to love him. That he'd get himself killed. Cause Marcel was the one who taught me what we were talking about this morning: give up the ghost and take it from there. Did you notice how freaked out I was in Farragut right before I left, with you basically repeating his philosophy of you can't worry about yourself? I'd hate to see you get killed too."

"Sitting here with you, Lois, I'd have to agree."

"Any hope of it saving you, you better pray our story bounces, cause *Off the Warpath* ain't gonna cut it on its own."

"Like a red rubber ball. Bare tit in a Senate office building – should put that up top. That's still slightly surprising."

"You like mentioning that, don't you? I guess you haven't been around the military much, cause – HeadFuck setting a tone killing so many civilians in the Disruption – things have slipped, man. I mean, look at those mercenaries doing vodka shots out of each others' butt cracks years ago. Speaking of which, let me get you that beer. You probably earned it just showing up tonight to get in Parnell's face."

She got all girlish with a little ballerina twirl out of the room on long, sculpted legs and returned with a big green oil can of Fosters ale, not the tasteless blue beer. Rather than hand it over, she leaned against the door jamb scratching her back like a bear on a tree and smiling prettily at the gaping statue who'd sprouted in her living room. Just a little like a very delectable, formidable, *round* bear. Seemed like I was gonna have to stand up to get that ale. Neither one of us moved after I took it, all of Lois entirely within reach.

I told myself to remember this the next time I aped indifference to my fate, Short Leg spraying shots or an albino clutching at me. The delicious anticipation, the first step on a wire without a net – man, I was rusty, years and years with none but Nicki. I gulped. Nice, Fosters not normally in my price range.

I just brushed her lips with mine. Then I did it again. She took her glasses off but kept her eyes wide open, or at least did until the kiss deepened and I closed mine. Holding the idiot oil can in one hand, I pulled her close and started to melt into all of that. She slipped me some tongue, then pulled suddenly away. What, I didn't taste good?

I gave her my best Cary Grant imitating a scolded puppy.

She nodded across the room. Marcel's ghost had materialized? Cause I didn't see anything "Could we be any more on stage here in my home with that window wide open and all the lights on?"

"If they don't have switches, we could cut the cords."

"I've got a better idea." She brushed past me close. God, it was all I could do to not cup one as she went by, but everything about Lois shrieked she was not the woman for a cheap feel. Following her to the foot of the stairs, I reached, but she laughed and dashed up. I stayed to watch. At the top she turned and slowly peeled off her shirt. I whooped and took the stairs two at a time until I tripped. By the time I caught up to her in her bedroom, only the elegant little art deco bed-side lamp was on. Going to her, I couldn't help but notice that one of my *Salon* articles was on a laptop on a narrow table by the blessedly curtained window.

We kissed by her bureau. Prolonging the delicious anticipation, I confined my explorations to her back. Then, almost swooning from what Lois was doing to my neck, and my old friend the Stuffing acting up a little, I laughed inside thinking of Mac and our unstated competition that evening. I said almost aloud, *Man, if Mac could see me now*.

Lois stopped fumbling with my shirt buttons and said, "Who's Mac?"

"Uh, nobody. Just some white guy I know who's expressed a

certain fondness for black women."

She stopped and held me at arm's length, allowing me to finally reach out for really the most amazing pair I'd ever encountered. And no matter the shank of experience in a man's life, long or short, that's saying a lot. She slapped my hand away, and no, not kidding. Alright already. Us about to get slippery, maybe it was time to stop lying to Lois. I dragged my eyes north. "He's just this soldier – well, this Special Ops killer, you come right down to it, who saved my ass this afternoon. Don't know quite why he did, except he likes spitting in their eye. Plus he's bored."

"Likes spitting in whose eye," she demanded, stepping even further back and catastrophically crossing her arms. "And don't lie to me, mister. You know how many men have tried to lie their way into my bed? I'd have liked to think you were different. I left the Building at lunch to confirm that your wife's moved to Manhattan, so at least you weren't lying about her. Now spill it. You've been lying all along about what happened to you this afternoon, haven't you?"

My hard-on was just about gone. "Alright. After phoning Whitaker – remember, this *general* threatening me, siccing Short Leg on me, hiring me to spy, the whole nine – so if I've been a little scattered…. Anyway, I'm in this little joint down in Southeast working on our story. A little place off the beaten track that lets you pay cash for a machine. And – "

"Connexions. You found that your first morning here, huh? Does it still have that sign with the fool in a top hat?" I nodded. "And?"

"There was this good-ol'-boy soldier already there when I got back from the pay phone around the corner. Lois, look, I didn't mention either about getting threatened at the phone by the drug boys. I can't keep track anymore. Anyway, this beefalator sergeant was there e-mailing his unit somewhere they're not supposed to be. Like Gary Cooper on steroids, a real killer if half of what he said was true. Turns out he was ordered home for treatment for the yips. So I do my thing and fax the story and the e-mails to *Warpath*. I'm just about to check my e-mail and skedaddle when in strolls this albino dude."

"Motherfucker, Forbes! You've come to my house twice now

and, idiot that I am, I've let you in. Goddamn standing there grinning on my porch. Albino – you sure?"

"No, I made it up. Of course I'm sure. I mean, not totally, but tending that way. He doesn't say much of anything, but just goes after me and tries to drag me out."

"And you, having learned a thing or two over the years, incapacitated him no problem."

"Actually, Mac did that. Did something to his neck and made him pass out."

"Unarmed combat 101: compress the carotid artery. So you thanked this Special Ops – great! – for taking care of skeazy Captain Bybee, who is one of Parnell's junior Calfers and a very nasty piece of work, and slunk out of Connexions and led them all to my front door? Probably brought Cummings along for the ride too."

"Jesus, no. Mac and I piled into his vehicle and off to this house he's renting right outside this decrepit old fort down there. We – "

"Fort McNair."

"Right. He relaxed by smoking crack and fondling his gun and messing with my head. Finally he drove me to MLK Avenue up about eight blocks from here, and then he peeled out. No one followed me from there. I promise"

"Says you."

"How? He didn't call anyone. Besides, he didn't hear about Anacostia till the last minute." (Though, Jesus, he did use the john, I admitted to myself.)

"You ever hear of GPS on his vehicle?"

"Lois, you're getting crazy."

"I've seen what these people can do. I don't know about you, but I still have a future I'm interested in pursuing once I kiss the fucking Army goodbye." She forgot herself and started waving her arms for a wonderful few seconds.

"Look, the guy running Connexions said that Mac had been there like four times before already. So he had nothing to do with me. If it walks like a duck, sometimes it's just a damn duck. Now come on…."

"What else?"

"What else nothing. Now let's be nice."

"Look, I won't throw you to the Anacostia wolves, not at this hour. You escaping Bybee , it'd be too damn stupid to catch it from someone who only cared if you got fifteen bucks in your pocket."

That didn't sound encouraging. And indeed, her shirt on the floor in the hall, she turned to her bureau and, bending down marvelously, got out another damn tee shirt for a final stupendous display putting it on before the curtain rang down. So close! So freaking close. And to think that moments before I'd considered simply catching her braless in that Terrapin number a bona fide erotic achievement. Damn the Stuffing and damn saying what I thought I was merely thinking. I sank down on her bed behind me and half-laughed so I wouldn't cry.

"Get off my bed and come with me."

At least I thought to grab the oil can off the nightstand. Undoubtedly not making it back to her room, I looked around on my way out. Pretty, the most fully realized of her rehab efforts, the walls a pale yellow, the ceiling cream, the floor gleaming, a classy mirror adorning another bureau on the far wall and various framed photos and weird narrative abstracts, paintings that were *constructed* in a way I didn't have time to take in. Considering all the horrible places she'd slept since her knee got ripped, it made sense this was her home's first truly finished room.

Yeah, they were her paintings, mostly, she said, showing me down the hall to a room with the brown rose wallpaper half stripped off, a big section of floor removed in one corner and a torturous army cot. She came back with a nice pillow, but a rough green blanket and went over and unlocked the window and threw it open.

"Too bad cause you're a nice guy, mostly. You should've been straight with me. Though if you were, I might not have let you in even this afternoon. So you played your cards best you could. Too bad you didn't keep your fool mouth shut back there, cause I'm damn good. Fifteen years since my last white guy, I was looking forward to a change of pace after someone too slick for his own good."

"You *do* say the nicest things."

"I did get a kick out of you sitting anchored in that chair downstairs like a fish out of water. And then up here how you were looking at me. But I'm sorry. Lying to me about operational security, which you did like three times, is not something I can tolerate at this stage of the game. The bathroom's down the hall. I'll leave you a new toothbrush. I'll also leave you with a question: do I still sleep with a knife under my pillow?"

She stood there a moment looking at me, punched me lightly on the arm, said "Too bad" again and left.

Lying there listening to the sirens loud or far away and afraid the damn cot would collapse under me, I vowed not to freak out come morning wondering where the hell I was, sleeping on such a contraption.

Chapter Fifty

Or Maybe Someday

I woke remembering the fiasco of the night before all too well. Dewy, signed-sealed-delivered Delores and a nearly naked vision beckoning me to her bed. And nothing but a little sweet kissing. Had Nick hexed me cause she'd settled for some rich old bastard? Forget the Wholeness of the Oneness – yeah, like I was getting laid any time this century. Lois was still an ally, maybe, but I'd sure shred a budding friendship.

Or maybe not. Exiting the bathroom after some basic sign-of-the-cross ablutions, I smelled bacon cooking. Even better was the lilt of a woman singing some maddeningly familiar little ditty. Had her anger evaporated, or did Lois just like to whistle while she worked?

"The bacon alarm clock worked, huh? Did you sleep OK on that horrible cot?"

"Like a statue – afraid to move in case it collapsed on me."

She gave a little grin and turned back to the stove in her sunny kitchen, looking oh so different in her camos and boots than the sight of her at the top of the stairs burned on my retinas. Speaking of which, she wasn't wearing any goofy glasses.

"First time ever cooking bacon in this kitchen. I was surprised I had it buried in the freezer from my old apartment. Jacket-Man always fled as quick as he could. He wasn't making any money sitting around talking after he got his. Marcel, of course, never got to see this place."

Maybe last night's mess was for the best, cause she was obviously still deeply grieving. She broke the silence. "I felt a little guilty about that cot, a big guy like you. I almost came and got you – just to *sleep*. You're still in the penalty box. Though, judging by the way you looked when I put a shirt back on, I don't know how much sleep you would have gotten."

"Oh come on, what's the big deal?"

"Uh-huh. Been lonely since your wife split?" I finally nodded. "And it's not like things were all warm and cushy before she left."

"Now the single girl is offering me her insights on marriage." She turned abruptly. "Hey, Lois, I'm sorry. I didn't need to say that. You were indeed a sight for sore eyes, who am I kidding? … So, feels like another sulfurous day on the planet Mercury kicking into gear." Almost nine o'clock I saw. "You're going in late, or does the Army keep bankers' hours now?"

"The day after the Appropriators' Ball, things'll be a little slack any office having anything to do with procurement."

She motioned me to the table and plopped down bacon, eggs, toast, juice and coffee.

"I hope you like your eggs sunny-side down. Done properly, that's considered a great luxury in the Army."

"I like 'em whatever way you fry 'em. My local bodega, you get it on Wonder Bread." Had she possibly forgiven me?

She murmured at that and fell silent. Not getting quite enough to eat as a kid, maybe, the six of them carried solely by Dad's municipal paycheck, did she stick strictly to business at the table? Stirring milk into my coffee – what the heck, the spoon's handle was a young girl dressed in an old-timey party dress. I looked up to see Lois displaying what looked like her sister.

"I was waiting for you to notice them. The Dionne Quintuplets. They only come out for special occasions – and, yeah, the first frying of bacon qualifies. Daddy got them as a boy from his Momma, who got them from hers. Man, did we fight over them, us four kids. Made eating the same store-brand sugar-flakes year in and year out tolerable – sorta."

"They're cute. But you better count the spoons before I leave, Lois."

"Why, there's only two, Yvonne and Annette, and they're right here."

"Sure. But what about all the silver a desperado like me might steal? You know, the guy who got himself shot in the head for money."

"The silver what? I don't have any jewelry, if that's what you're talking about. Never having a place to call my own till now – not really – I never wanted to worry about it, and then it just seemed, I don't know, not me."

Before blundering into an insult explaining the cliché about counting the spoons, this scion of one of Mineola's finest cramped split-levels said, "So you still have the other three?"

"Nope, we all took one, Momma too, when Daddy died. Only reason I have two is my running-wild sister admitted it was only a matter of time before someone stole it from her to use as a cooker. Not that she's ever messed with smack – far as I know."

I busied myself with my plate.

"See," she said, holding up the spoon again. "A pole up her butt. That's half the Building, the self-righteous bastards, especially when the lemmings start saluting and marching off the cliff. But they're nervous. HeadMan's not as easy to control as most commanders-in-chief, not as predictable. So they lash out – all of them, from the private spooks getting rich in those office parks in Virginia, to all the men with guns in more uniforms than you can keep track of, on down to dogs on the subway scaring old ladies."

I waved a piece of bacon at her and tried a new tack. "No crypto-doof glasses this morning?"

"Whatever shit this day is going to bring, it's no time for self-effacement. Besides, maybe I don't feel the need to fend anyone off this morning."

"Oh really?"

"This is nice. But not all of us are freelance and fancy free. And don't you have a cake coming out of the oven you're supposed to put some icing on this morning? You can't go back to Connexions, that's for sure, but I think I have that solved."

We found ourselves grinning at each other. I reminded myself that, hell, I was older than my lovely major and more worldly in small, inconsequential, Sancho-Panza ways. It still around six in the morning *Warpath* time and the cot upstairs belonging to the night before, I was in no hurry to break the spell of sharing a breakfast table.

But she mopped up some egg with her toast, got up, went to the dining room and back with the two jackets. Holding up the fancy-schmantzy one, she demanded, "You sure you don't want the blue?"

436

"I'll be getting a Blue soon enough."

"And for that I'm sorry, OK? Whoever you might be, Minders, Go … Jump in the River! But I'm still throwing it out for real this morning, no fooling if you don't take it. The ridiculous red one too. And no, I am not even a little worried if he decides to show up to claim them after leaving them here for months."

I mounted a vague protest about not tossing something so nice. Not that I wasn't hoping for a huge fight between them.

She switched gears. "Don't think for a minute I'm not still mad at you for lying to me about maybe bringing a psycho like Bybee right to my door. Since I still have to report for duty today, I'm going to assume you didn't. But I had a little trouble sleeping myself, thinking about things. You don't have a whole lot of support do you? None of these freaky websites you publish on even know what you look like, right?"

"Not unless they've seen me in those shorts."

"Crazy like a fox, those shorts: you're the guy next door everyone can feel sorry for cause no self-respecting Fiend would wear them."

"You say the nicest things."

"Look, I've faced some shit in my day – serious hit-the-fan. But I've done so as part of the most lethal organization the planet has ever seen. Never mind that half the time the shit has had United States Army stamped all over it. You, on the other hand, operate under a kind of pressure I don't know much about cause it's all on your lonesome."

"It's easier being responsible to no one."

"Maybe. But somebody's got to attach their name to our article, or it's not allowed to be published. That's why your source hasn't succeeded in getting that SecDef whole-vid out yet. You've put your name on top of some heavy material."

"We'll, Lois, that's damn … nice of you." Jesus, I almost said *white* of you.

"Uh-huh." Her stare cut right through. "Maybe you should shut up so you don't mess up a good thing, which last night would indicate you have a talent for. But, seeing as how you're hanging on by your fingernails all alone in a hurricane, I've decided to cut you some slack. Provided – and try to keep it in your pea brain that you're talking to an experienced intel analyst who's been lied to by hard, cruel men, warlords and sheiks, all over Pipelineistan – *provided* you never, ever tell me as much as one tiny little fib again."

"I promise. I mean, I swear." I held up my right hand and stupidly said, "Last time I held my hand up like this was before Congress."

"Yeah, yeah. I read all about it."

Brother. "You know, you're wrong about one thing though. I'm not all alone. Like when I was in Bellevue after getting shot, there was this nurse – I mean, a whole bunch of people trying to help." Jesus, concentrate. "An orderly, all kinds of people. And my landlord has shocked the mess out of me watching my back. A little spark, maybe, is all it takes to maybe get something moving. You're Exhibit A, of course."

"No, no, no. I am Exhibit Not-in-the-Alphabet, boy. Now let's saddle up riki-tik before this gets sloppy."

I joined her at the sink with my dishes. "You want me to do these dishes while you, I don't know, water the horses or something?" She turned to me with a quizzical smile way too close, and I was damn lucky not to break it clattering the plate into the sink. "I mean, you cooked, I'll wash."

"Well look at you. But we do not have time for nonsense like – "

There was nothing tentative about our first kiss of a new day. She finally broke. "Good – nice. Now I am going to work and so are you. You remember what you wanted to add into our article, right, that $25,000 check more important than all four of the tits you saw last night."

"See, now that's the trouble with this fool country, placing mammon above mammaries."

****

Leaving, Lois was real glad Old Lady Gaston hadn't made it early to her porch. Passing the boarded-up library and driving deeper into Anacostia, she apologized for deserting me far from the train. I dismissed that and fell to brooding. Solid and, shit-yeah, gonna bounce, our Parnell story was still freighted with a big *say-what*? Man, I had to get "Penn Tale" out into the world, both to push search-refusal and to mitigate some of the weirdness clinging to me so tight.

"Alright, the librarian you need – you still with us, or are you thinking again? Before we get to her, you remember the two points you need to hammer home that we discussed yesterday afternoon?"

"Sure," I said. "Link the bastard preemptively to anything bad happening to yours truly. And … shit – sorry."

"No way Parnell could have run an independent check on vendor security, certainly not using his private e-mail. That kind of freelancing just doesn't happen in the Army. And double-no-way plucking you from deep, deep on the bench."

"Except I nailed the assignment better than nine out of ten GI Joes."

"Maybe so, hot stuff." She eased to the curb, pointed and said the library was two blocks up on the left. Then, "OK, the girl you need to latch on to is Shandre. My age, she's the only one of my teammates who hasn't moved to the Maryland suburbs if not a whole lot further. Including a couple to the next world. I called her this morning, and she's on the look-out. Not that there's going to be a whole lot of other big white guys walking in there. But just in case, tell her that 'Gimme' sent you."

"Gimme being you, cause that's what the boys said when they saw you?"

"No. At first I was mortified getting that name. Down two in a playoff game at our gym, time about to expire, my point guard was just standing there dribbling, frozen. So I yelled loud enough to hear in the locker room, 'Gimme the damn ball!' So many people started calling me Gimme, I decided to embrace it."

"And?"

"And what?"

"What the hell happened in the game?"

"Please. Let's just say I made sure both feet were behind the three-point line."

"You're sure you want to involve Shandre? What if they pull the string from the other end, from *Warpath* back to an Anacostia library?"

"You don't think we've thought of that? For instance, Shandre isn't demanding ID before letting you use a machine. Even though they've been requiring that since *four* days after HeadFuck got in. It was like they had it waiting in the wings to implement, because I'd hate to think cracking down on the DC public libraries was tops on his to-do list."

"They've had it in the libraries up in New York for years – way before HeadMan."

"We're slow here. That, or the District just doesn't have any money, which can be a blessing these days. Anyway, Shandre'll log you on with this Memory-Hole password she's got. And let 'em prove it. What, you couldn't have found your way to an Anacostia library your own pale self? Lots of people cross that river for all kinds of shady reasons. Some of them don't even bother buying cooking wine first."

Gosh, she had a pretty smile.

"Reading up on you last night before you spooked the crap out of me ringing my bell, I saw – "

"You were that surprised to find me on your porch?"

"Yes I was. A lot of women who've served are real particular about their personal space, so on any given night that could've gotten ugly. For whatever reason, last night wasn't one of them. Anyway, I got your address from the *Daily Chirp*. Right by the river in Queens – a happening condo with a swimming pool on the roof no doubt."

"Uh, not really. It's – "

"I saw online. Some big old house a block from the projects. I can take it from there."

"It's nice enough. For the short term. For a guy who'd just got thrown out of his home. And moved quick. And didn't care he was so tore up. It's a little like Anacostia, though not so leafy and without a drop of Southern charm. It's not like I'm going to be there forever – not with my ship coming in, its smokestacks visible on the horizon."

"You make it sound so appealing. But here's the deal. We both know where we live, so face to face is our next contact. And that does *not* include tonight or any other time this trip of yours to DC, got it? No phone and certainly no e-mail, phony Dutch address or not. We both lay low for awhile – not that that's an option for you. No contact for two months. Then who knows, I might be willing to give Manhattan another chance, now that I got someone to show me around."

I nodded. Man, I was starting push-ups *tomorrow*. That'd give Stap something to chew over, another scintillating woman crossing his porch in search of my bell, her race the least of it. (Far as I knew, his delight in his fellow creatures lashed everyone equally.) /

"Good – so that's settled," she said, like she was talking about inspecting a barracks. "OK, *Off the Warpath* goes live about 1200 hours our time?"

"Pretty much. I'm glad I don't have much to write."

"Right. You mission-ready?"

"Absotively, Major."

"Uh-huh. The song says, *You got nothing, you got nothing to lose*. Well, we are definitely starting at the bottom of a long steep climb. Taking down a corrupt Calfer general is a good day's work. Maybe having to look over their shoulders a little will slow them down some. Get to near the top of that climb and maybe heads will roll. Whether we're there to see it…."

We sat a moment, looking, then each of us looking away in turn. She took my hand, placed it on her breast and leaned in to it. I was too agape to make too, too much of it through the heavy camo, tee shirt and bra. Hey, even all muffled, that pleasing weight felt wonderful. But parked on a busy street and Lois looking solemn, it was at least as much of a bond as something sexual. She dropped her hand and, after a good squeeze, so did I.

"So you're not so broke up over last night. I'll be laughing for a while, the look on your face when you collapsed on my bed after realizing Santa got stuck in the chimney. Nice to have someone not take you for granted. Now de-digitate yourself, man. And two things: write real. Ain't no time for windbags."

I waited till finally she said, "I'm almost reluctant to say this, all the shit raining down on your head. But if you're willing – and that's a real *if* – get that SecDef rollover whole-vid out soon as you can. You do decide yes, don't procrastinate. Tomorrow is promised to no man – or woman."

The depth of her gaze, a kiss would've been anticlimactic. "I'll never wash this hand again," I said, getting out. She smiled and waved and peeled into a U-turn. I stared, joking to myself that she was so stung by tears, she'd side-swipe a parked car. A block on, she stopped – what, to beckon me to race to her side and away from all this (and her pension) to shared bliss over a live-poultry store, Lois to clean the cages, me to bite off heads? She got out to hang the jackets on a church's iron fence and back in and gone without a look.

Chapter Fifty-One

Teammates

A fine red brick building with a sloped green shingle roof, the library was deserted at that early hour except for an old man and two young boys pounding computers. Shandre came out from behind the reference desk as I approached and asked if she could help. Too tall to be the somnolent point guard and more matronly than Lois, she stood smiling until I woke up and said, "Uh, Gimme said I might drop by to see you this morning."

"I thought as much, but you can't be too careful these days. How long do you anticipate using my machine?"

"Well under an hour."

"That's a good answer. Go to that magazine rack there and look at one a moment. Then go to that "Staff-Only" door over there." She nodded in the other direction. *Popular Mechanics* – it'd been how many decades? The door opened as I reached for it, and I entered a small, immaculate bathroom. I leaned against the door to the throne, she against the sink, maybe a foot between us. Man, a smile at our forced intimacy wouldn't hurt, but one look and I decided not to hold my breath.

"I understand you're inserting a last-minute update." I nodded. "Gimme said your evening had proved fruitful."

It had? "What?"

"Your *reporting* last night. Is it worth the immediate, real-world risk to both of us, my job the least of it, to add it to your story from here?"

"Absolutely. What I got takes it from good to over-the-moon."

"Right. She said she wouldn't bring you here unless she thought it worth the risk. You're using an anonymized address, and your editor is expecting it? Good, cause I think once you send it, you should do your full turnaround and be gone from here within ten minutes. Is your editor the sort of person to appreciate that and not swamp you with endless, niggling TKs?"

"I think so."

"Most important question: when you sent her – "

"Uhm, him."

"OK, sent him the bulk of the article yesterday, did you use this same anonymized address?"

Man, my name required on top of the story, I hadn't much worried this. I *wanted* notoriety to fend off Whitaker. Besides, I'd been writing on computers I'd never see again – a luxury denied Shandre. I told her I'd first e-mailed Joe from a different address and had faxed the article to him.

"If you e-mailed him even once, that fax was like taking a shower so you don't get knocked up. Now was it from an address they – the Minders the least of it – have any reason to associate with you?"

Duh, just one with my name on it. "Yeah, I'm afraid so."

She sighed and sunk further on the sink. "And this general of hers is a Calfer. OK, not for anyone but Gimme. And also because one of those damn dogs got fresh with me last month on the train – understand?"

"You mean my stillborn anti-search campaign up in New York?"

"Even a stillborn Demo can strike a chord, all the play that yours is starting to get. For both our safety, ten minutes tops from sending it, to closing the story and then pulling the plug on that computer. And then I never saw you. How could I help it you snuck in when I was helping some old man find West Indian cricket scores – Minders Turn Elsewhere!"

I got lost pondering how much Turd-Touch had screwed Zafar with all my machinations at Connexions. Shandre staring, I woke up to mumble, "Minders Turn Elsewhere!"

"Use the computer in the corner opposite the magazines. It's the only one in a study carrel. And look – I read your Syriac confession – save your flowery touches for your Christmas card."

"Jesus, everyone's a critic." Neither one of us was smiling. "Hey, I'd just gotten shot in the head and – well, all kinds of crap was raining down. I felt entitled."

"Gimme and I both sticking our necks way out on this, your

entitlement just ended. Give me a nod when you're ready to send, and I'll start my shut-it-down clock at ten minutes. Then I'll come tell you how you're to exit the building. You're not physically limited?"

I realized she was waiting on a real answer. "Well, Shandre, how exactly do you mean, *limited*?" I gave her only my middling Cary Grant, full-bore saved for women on their couch of an evening.

"Uh-huh." She unlocked the door, stopped and said, "If – *if*. You better treat her right, you hear me. Or I'll make it painful for you." As she left, she whispered, "And Forbes, good luck!"

And wouldn't I like to know what girlish infatuations Lois shared to have Shandre order me to treat her right. The computer already up and humming, damn weird not to be able to check my e-mail to see if *Warpath* Joe had any problems with the stuff from the day before. Anyway:

Dear Joe:

Personal Safety – no kidding – requires publication this morning. Unable to check my standard e-mail for any prior queries. After I send this, I can monitor this address for exactly eight minutes for any questions regarding yesterday's or today's material. Anything else, resolve it best you can or excise with a minimal incision. But, yes, IMPERATIVE to publish today.

Today's additions are air-tight – all direct quotes to me or my direction observation. The one tiny caveat (it's only 99.44% certain) is characterized as such.

Joe, relying on this article to save my skin is a thin reed, I know. Come what may – la-di-dah – it's all I got. Regardless, it'll strike a spark. Don't stint on the headline. And thus the long, steep climb starts. Good luck to us both.

(Byline is)Daniel.

Shoot, I was so Delores-bereft getting thrown out of Hart, and then focused on not getting mugged making it to Lois's, and then not mugged *by* Lois, and then making nice, I never jotted notes on Whitaker's statements. I had his reason for sending me to Indiana nailed: "I needed an in to maximize my return, something fancy to bring to the table." Fine, sure, and it went right up top. Would have been nice to have three or four more statements between quote marks.

But all I really needed 'verbatim' was the bit about the $25K check to Bettinger cleaning out his account and his threats about no one caring I was toast after he finally sliced the bread himself. Plus this gem I just remembered: "I'm at war against the ridiculous conflict of interest Regs." Still, it was my first time ever crafting words out of someone else's mouth. If I made his *but* a *however*, and he was wearing a wire, that little 'lie' is all they'd harp on to torpedo the whole piece. Go ahead, make my day, dude, you got the guts.

I beefed up the two points Lois reminded me to emphasize and added a splash of the evening's debauch. Having next to nothing to drink, I could've written awhile, but didn't, restricting myself to some color on the fights, the drunkenness, the cozying up between suit and uniform, even a sneer about the horrible music. The hundreds of circulating women got their due, but the four pros entwined on the revolving stage were the stars. Oh, and bare tit on my way out (and ain't that too telling a phrase). I read it twice, found it actually somewhat restrained, and gave crack-the-whip Shandre the high sign to start her ten minutes.

What was she coming over for, cause I sure wasn't letting her edit it. Pulling up a chair, she barked, "Move over, please, so I can show you how this program works."

"What are you talking about? I know how –"

"Shush! Are you always so hard-headed, cause I need a reason to come over here. Well go ahead and send so I can start the clock."

"I don't know." And I didn't. "I'm not too crazy about accessing my Dutch account with you watching. Or doesn't that matter with you and Lois maneuvering me so nicely to this keystroke-recording machine?"

"I don't know any *Lois*. But ain't you a piece of something. Or have you forgotten that you showed up at someone's house unbidden last night and she let you in?"

"I guess you got me there. Look, I don't care. I trust you – go ahead and look." She made a big show of turning away. "Should I keep it open awaiting my guy's reply, or go back on in a few minutes?"

"Who am I to say. You're the security expert."

"Oh for Pete's sake, Shandre, do you know how many time's my life's been threatened this week?"

"Still time for one more, though I guess you have had it rough. When you're done, go back to the staff bathroom and – "

"You're crazy if you think I can fit out that little window."

"*And* keep on going down that same hall to the "Emergency Only" exit. The alarm hasn't worked since I got here, and I'd hate to admit how many years ago that was. Out that door, go straight to the ladder I just put there over the back fence. Just climb down the other side best you can. Do not break an ankle, cause once you get up from this chair, we've never met. You got that?"

"Sure thing, Mata Hari."

"I'm supposed to fawn all over you cause you mention an historical figure? Assuming you succeed in getting all of you over that fence, head on through the trees, down the hill, out that house's driveway and do not get caught. Somebody messes with you, flash your wallet at 'em real quick, act official – act *white* – say something about an 'ongoing investigation,' and don't stop until they get you on the ground. Which it's your job to see does not happen. You can do that, New York?"

"Sure thing."

"You know what, the homeowner comes after you, just tell 'em you work for this psycho DC cop named Cummings and watch them run. Then turn left out of the driveway, keep walking, though not too fast, and catch the first bus you see going that way. Any bus runs into MLK. You have four singles on you? Please tell me you know to always, always carry singles."

"Uhm, probably not."

"You have two, don't you? Cause all I have on me is two myself."

I nodded as she held up some singles, folded. "I can't take – "

"Boy, wake up! You can't take a few dollars from a black

woman? Whether you give a damn about yourself or not, we're talking about my safety here. And I need you off the street, not fumbling around big as shit in a store round the corner from my library making change. I got three kids to raise – and that's by myself!" She jammed the money in my shirt pocket and continued. "If the bus turns right at MLK, stay on, it's going over the bridge to the District. It turns left, stay on too, it's going to the Metro. Got it? Hit send and you have ten minutes." And she clamped her hand hard on my wrist. I let her, and looked up. "Remember what I told you before, Forbes."

"I will – I mean, what?"

Her squeeze intensified. "She's the best person I know."

"Sure. Me too, I guess. I mean, we've just met."

"Uh-huh." She let go, wished me luck again and left. *All of me* over the fence. Watching all of her motivate back to her desk, she was a fine one to talk. I hit send and waited for the screen to go kerflooey cause of my Dutch sending address. A long four minutes later, Joe's minimal queries appeared.

From the big chunk of it the day before, he wanted only a rock-solid assurance that I had reported to Whitaker by phone from Indiana following the HDM presentation. Doing so violated Joe's sense of how a legit investigation would work and therefore helped indict the general. Plus, from that morning's installment, had Whitaker really said that about being at war with the conflict of interest Regs? And had I really seen bare tit in a Senate office building, cause he wanted to pump that big. I offered to describe them. He passed "unless they were in some way remarkable."

He offered congrats on a boffo piece, said it'd be up in half-an-hour once he ran it by his partner and would bounce big given the "oddities that abound with you right now." And he told me to get the hell gone from wherever I was. Plus he wanted more stories, especially my tale of getting shot. And shouldn't I clear up the disturbing rumors about my stay at Bellevue, rumors traceable to a certain competitor of his. Joe said he could do three-hundred bucks for either article, five hundred for both. Yeah, big bucks, liked I'd bragged to Nicki several eons before.

Rumors. Thanks, Stanley, you bitter little man.

OK, half-an-hour before even more infamy rendered me safe

and cozy. The first hurdle on the journey home was an eight-foot hurricane fence out back, the kind with lattice strips you can't see through. Sure, Shandre's ladder would get me up, but it might actually hinder the transfer from windward to leeward. I stashed it by the dumpster and decided I'd be too visible from the street at either corner to take advantage of the fence's right angle. Hell, good for the soul, climbing a tall fence *unaided* every decade or so.

Right. Scale the Goddamn fence for the sake of two Anacostia women definitely cooking with gas. Plus, the unfinished business of how did Lois's right breast feel compared to her left. Maybe I'd get to testify, with full immunity, against Whitaker in some court down the road. And get "Penn" out, past time to own my story or kiss it goodbye. Punch MoneyBags in the nose, sue the MTA for a new pack *and* my books and get that damn SecDef whole-vid out too – probably, maybe. A bunch of stuff. So scram before Whitaker's latest henchman, the Man with One Arm, dropped from a tree.

Bumfuckville's bodega counterman was far, far away. Nothing for it but crab my way up, hope my sole wasn't pierced and vault over and down. Almost up, I thought to go get the ladder and peer over for a soft landing spot rather than the discarded Chevy truck engine I might be heading for. Robbed of momentum, I got my cuff hung up and kept going, thinking it'd pull free. It didn't, the cloth ripping only after turning me half-upside down to crash in a heap on soft earth further down than it looked. Competing in the Unaided-by-Bodega-Dude Division, the Republic of Bushwick's was the sole judge who scored it above a 2.6.

But no blood, and the tear in my pants wasn't too glaring if you didn't look. A quick inventory showed I still had the three e-mails, my book, wallet, keys, pen and notebook – enough to assault a whole den of Calfers. A scamper through the back yard and down the driveway, and a quick bus took me to the Metro rather than the bridge. A cop car came screaming up behind, shrank me in my seat and kept going. I was glad of the folks off and on and on and off on busy MLK, glad that the Whitaker story was out of my hands, and gladder still to sit and try to think of nothing but Lois grinning at the top of her stairs. But one happy puzzle kept intruding: what to make of Shandre's surprise. Sandwiched between her two singles were a couple of twenties. Lucky I didn't feed them blindly into the bus lock-box gizmo, cause there was a big sign saying "NO CHANGE FOR ANY REASON!"

We'd just have to see about that, MoFos – me and my women.

Chapter Fifty-Two

Reckless Everett's Stink Bomb

Lois soon to descend on the Hovel and no time like the present for a little exercise, I marched up and down the platform swinging my arms. Go ahead and snicker, friend, I got plans. Sure, I embodied the necessary chutzpah – she liked me. Plus I was different, uh-huh, than Lois's usual young, athletic, black soldier. Damn, this stab at exercise indicated I gave a shit. Dangerous that.

Along with getting sweaty in the Metro's more cavernous heat, I had to check that Joe's partner hadn't kiboshed the story, plus answer the note from 'Pop' that Bybee interrupted leaping on me in Connexions. So head back to the District (as us Anacostians said, like Brooklynites heading in to 'New York'), get the digital lay of the land, then sit in a museum café relaxing like the dude without a care that I indubitably was, stare at the tourists, and complete – finally – "Penn Tale." Then maybe a stroll to generate a thirst and a couple of beers.

It became apparent that my time to deliver was soon. I rode a few stops and got out at Chinatown, but those crabbed little restaurants weren't conducive. Walking on, I found myself staring up at the Hay-Adams hotel as matters became more precipitate. A venerable old pile, there was no sign in the rococo lobby. I pasted on a purposeful smile and scooted up a staircase to a promenade. Bingo.

Mission accomplished, I encountered another of the many reasons this is a great country. Every time I shifted – gotta shift for access, no way round it – the toilet's maniacal laser eye concluded I was done rather than pursuing the necessary paperwork, and it flushed, spraying me with a great whoosh of unclean water. If this was progress, I wanted none of it. (Used to be you could flush a urinal with your elbow all neat and clean – until someone who'd never used one installed those little push-buttons right on top. Haven't touched one yet.) I ruminated a moment to lull the laser eye asleep, then leapt off before it got me. DC in a nutshell.

Out in search of a writing pad and somewhere with free AC but not *too* much distraction – my God, was that willowy brunette up ahead Delores? Cruising up alongside to see, I felt rather than saw some schmuck pass, stop and turn.

"Forbes, is that you? Stop!"

I closed the last step, turned gracelessly and confirmed nope, not Delores. The startled young beauty whisked away.

"Yo, stop! That's you, I know it is."

Ah, new excitement rearing its loud, ugly head, his bellicosity demanded to be answered in kind. I turned to see some young guy in a khaki summer suit charging up wearing, yup, the same dumb heifer tie as my buddy, Fenton the night before, though his added an amorphous, dark presence opposing the light coming from the cloud. He pulled out his pacifier as he came, stopped, thumbed it, looked from it to me, me to it, and said, "Are you harassing that fertile young woman? I'm surprised you're still out on the streets bothering right-minded Homelanders."

"I was just inviting her to watch while I sent you packing. Old-hat, sure, but she might find it amusing."

"Not half as funny as you getting tossed from the Appropriators' Ball last night, BEI. You should have stuck around, cause kicking you out, you screaming like a girl, was just what that party needed. Even better was when they dragged out this piece of baggage who looked like a kindergarten teacher. She kept yelling that she didn't know you, that you two were just talking. She put up such a fight against like four of our gorillas, people were rooting for her. They were going to taze her right there on the floor after they threw her down. Would've been fun to watch her twitch, but some damn admiral had to intervene."

Turd-Touch in spades. He caught my distraught look. "Bad news about her, huh – like maybe you did know her and infiltrated the party together?"

"Nah. She was just disappointed not to stick around to see you service those Marines. Three at once I saw on the whole-vid making the rounds this morning. That must take years of priming the pump. You're a talented dude, dude – your momma must be so proud."

I leaned against one of the countless flagpoles, crossed my arms and grinned as this guy – young, athletic, and enough of a dick to have scored a ticket to Hart – took an angry step towards me. Might as well get rolling around on a DC sidewalk over with, this trip to HeadFuck's seat seemingly headed there all along.

"I'm surprised you have the nerve to mention whole-vids. As a key persuader for Crutchem and Baggit's DC office, I'm on a very restricted list-serve belonging to the Tethered Manufacturers' Alliance. And I was wondering why this morning they were bothering to *again* push that over-exposed vid of you eating refuse up in New York wearing those shorts. Any normal person would've had the sense to crawl under a rock after that. But you – "

"A rock: to consort with your family."

"You're so clever, I'll bust a gut, BEI. Not like I needed to see that whole-vid again. We watched it about six times at this party I was at the day it came out. Thirty people laughing their asses off at this one pathetic loser."

"Glad to have been the occasion for merriment."

"You don't know how merry things are going to get. The manufacturers, the lobbyists, my shop – the Army itself – we're all gunning for you. What makes you think you can smear a Red-Calf Plenipotentiary like General Whitaker during the Current Permanent Crisis? Not to mention how pissed off ASPIC is that your nonsense about refusing the random T searches is starting to spread. Do you know how much money is at stake in privatizing the searches – here, New York, Boston, who knows where."

"Spread how?"

"How about you tell me." I stared blankly till he almost whispered, "Another, even more confidential, T list-serve that I only have irregular access to – so far – said there were nineteen different search-refusals on transit systems around the Homeland yesterday. In Oakland, it was like a big, organized group. And chatter indicates there'll be more today. Like you and your T-symp friends didn't know that."

453

Always so eager to show off access to inside poop. "Nineteen, huh?"

"It's only a matter of time before we fully penetrate your network. A lot of folks on that super-secret T-list were wondering how you got that Blonde bitch to accompany you down that corridor in Penn Station. Cause she was damn sympathetic to you on her macro-transmission this morning – blamed the Protectors. A talented girl like her, what a waste."

Carole, really? "What did she say?"

"Like you, or someone a lot smarter, didn't write her script for her. She didn't even show any goodies, the way she was dressed."

"Alright, dude, I got smelts to fry."

I turned, and he grabbed me by the shoulder and twirled me half around as we grappled. I surprised him by suddenly spinning the way he wanted and slamming him hard in the chest with both hands and off me. After a week of abuse, enough was too much. That felt good! Should try it more often. I upped to him and he fell back, both of us breathing hard. His cow tie askew, I'd finally touched one and remained unsmote.

"Why are you messing with a general, you T-symp! Libeling a senior officer is T right there – "

"What T is that – for telling you all to go suck eggs? How do you know the eggs won't enjoy it?" I was starting to enjoy that line.

"Calfers are off-limits in this town, everybody knows that. I just read your *Off the Warpath* little nothing. People are laughing so hard, it's bouncing all over even though – you self-indulgent horse's ass – it's like fourteen-hundred words! No one's going to believe it'd take more than twenty-five dollars to hire scum like you, not twenty-five-thousand."

Cool, it got published. "That money wasn't for me." Jesus, had Joe screwed up that bad, saying all that money was supposedly for me? If he wrote that I was supposedly spying for real money, just pry open the nearest manhole cover and drop me down.

"You know, along with that whole-vid of you in those shorts, Tethered Manufacturers also linked to a site I'd never heard of, *Deceit Nest*, that had your 1040 from last year. They had that, plus some off-the-shelf, enhanced porn everyone's already seen, plus some crap rehashing an old steroid scandal."

"So, a site you bastards created solely to embarrass me."

"Real embarrassing, cause Whitaker's check is more than you made all last year. And you're taking on people who make twenty and thirty times as much. *Bold, Extolled, Impregnable.* Don't you get it?"

"Your tethered jerks did me a big favor getting that out. That I make so little just enhances my prestige – credibility, I mean. That I pursue truth for its own sake. Folks will applaud me for what I do."

He crossed his arms and shook his head. "They're shredding the ticker-tape right now. Don't move, while I get a Protector here to see about those e-mails you fabricated. I – "

I swore, turned and booked, managing to head north like I'd been. I looked back to see him gesticulating wildly, his pacifier to his ear. The damn article was supposed to protect me from Whitaker, and maybe it would. But what about all his friends: institutional, institutionalized, otherwise? Time to get the hell away from people who might recognize me, though where exactly was that?

A block on, clown-boy not following – nothing like a salutary little two-handed chest slam – two Grinders full of soldiers came screaming round the corner, headed towards me, and kept going. Pacifier still to this ear, he jumped out to flag them down and just barely jumped back as they roared past.

Man, I had to get off the streets till my *Warpath* screed worked its magic. It'd be good to get in front of a screen to ensure Joe hadn't royally screwed up about Whitaker's check to Bettinger. I cut east and ended up zigging and sagging north through a quiet little homeowners' neighborhood as NW eased into NE. A tolerable 96-degrees according to a passing car radio, I considered a walking beer, not quite sure where I was walking beyond – *away*. Right, pop a beer and round a corner into the arms of a black cop pissed at someone thinking white skin would let him skate in a black neighborhood.

I plodded, sweated, thought about Lois keeping her eyes open kissing, had a Debbie to confirm her inferiority to Linda based on cake-to-goop ratios, sweated and plodded, got cursed to "get the hell back to your own country" by some boys young enough to not really worry about (probably), and finally came across Connexions' glossier big brother, one ThinkTanked by name.

The kid behind the counter forbade cash. Independent and out-of-the-way, maybe this joint wasn't as spook-friendly as Deskless and its ilk. Or maybe I was done turning tail, a *story* saving me. Like I told Lois, I wasn't ready to kick a family of squirrels out of their hollow tree to go live off the Bar Code.

****

And there it was making a nifty splash on a traffic-slowed *Warpath*. Preceded by "Exclusive" in red, Joe's nice fat headline pulled no punches: "General Admits to $25,000-Corporate Espionage to 'Maximize my Return'; Declares, 'I'm at war against the ridiculous conflict of interest Regs'; Threatens Reporter at Bare-Tit Capitol Hill Debauch" Then, in just slightly smaller type: "Female Party Favors?"

I raced through it, and of course Joe hadn't screwed up about the money. His sole edit, an improvement, involved my one slight surmise. He changed my "The stunning young women, each more of a knockout than the next, attended under 'obligation' to service any man present" to the slightly softer "The stunning [etc.] were encouraged to be generous with their affections." Whitaker's e-mails and Bettinger's assignment memo all surfaced bold and brassy at a click. So off to the races, you and me, Parnell.

Joe wrote me that it was bouncing higher than anything on *Warpath* in years. *Morning Dyspepsia* had even resorted to a rare midday update, and several outfits wanted to interview me. Joe told them, truthfully enough he figured, that I was secreted away for my own safety but he hoped I surfaced soon.

There was also a note from Stan the Man, weighing in with "deep disappointment over your betrayal of this site and the Movement both, publishing today on that parvenu's little rag." There was also the usual torrent of threats, abuse, come-ons legal and otherwise, and appeals to fold my "case" into this or that.

And two notes from Pop, Wednesday's stronger than the prior one. What with my "cell" (as he still called it) not answering – did I need help with the bill? – and my home answering machine full, he and Mom were so concerned, he'd endured rush-hour traffic in to the Hovel Tuesday night when I hadn't answered his first note. He'd encountered Stap, who knew I wasn't upstairs. And Pop concluded:

"Your landlord, whatever the hell his name is, is decent enough. He said there were a couple of people sniffing around after you, but no one showed any warrants, so no dice. He finally got convinced I was your father. He said I was too old to be anything else, though I'm in better shape than him with his funny little foreign cancer sticks that he almost got me to try just curious how it tasted. Like I need to start that shit again. The funny thing was, once he got who I was, his English got a lot better. Made me laugh cause the old guys used to pull that shit in Brooklyn all the time, but I forgot living in piss-assed Mineola.

Hey, I know things were rough during that phone call Sunday, but answer your damn e-mail. If you'd answered yesterday's, it would had saved me a trip to town which I really don't need, all those assholes driving like they got to get somewhere to save the world.

Schulman down the block called again this morning, asking if we got macro-transmissions, like we're worrying about that crap at our age. He's a little too caught up in your troubles, you ask me. Anyway, turns out the girl who got shot with you was on something called Breakfast Raunch. And Schulman, when I finally got him to stop bitching about her not wearing a see-through shirt or something trying to pretend he's some old goat, said she blamed the cops

about you two getting shot. The TV guy tried to say, well sweetie, your memory aint good, the trauma and all. But she wasn't having none of it. A girl like that turns out to have a head on her shoulders too. Go figure.

Look, I know you're in the shit, but just write four letters – I'm OK. Your landlord said I should come back, he'll take me to his little Greek social club to play cards. Even just looking for new money on the table, nice to get an invite. Spell his name for me so I can get it. Write back and don't be a jerk cause I got enough to worry about right now. Love, Pop."

Again with the *love*, the dude going soft in his dotage. I replied that I was down in DC, and he should check out a site called *Off the Warpath* to learn why. Said I wasn't proud of myself, but – whoopee! – at least the whys and wherefores of my disgrace appeared under my own name. I cut and pasted *Warpath*, said click on its links for the dirt it was grounded in, and spelled Staphilopoulos for him. Them two a team – look out!

Then up scrolled the disaster of the day, a whole new barrel of trouble. Lester Genny was Everett's handle for public consumption, "You Lying Sack of Shit" the subject heading on his note.

All those weeks of bitching at me, Everett had never violated my idiot e-mail account with my idiot name in it. But included at the bottom of dozens of articles, it wasn't hard to find. And here he was violating that radio-silence on this of all days, standing on a chair waving a red flag and pointing a gun at both our heads. He'd obviously decided to forfeit my claim to continued respiration, a claim I'd so far staked by declining to smear mud all over the SecDef's flabby legs. His hands darted out the screen at my throat:

Sack:
Bottom line up top, you boasted in your ridiculous letter to that Syriac site that you were going to tell

what you learned at the HDM plant and "maybe even save some lives in the process." So when the fuck is the whole-vid I sent you of the SecDef rolling the new HDM Grinder at Aberdeen coming out? That's a hell of a lot more important than some general trying to line his pockets. Like that doesn't happen every day in Procurement.

All you do is ignore your Dutch address, so using this one is maybe the spark that all my ass-kissing through Holland ain't been. Let the bright light shine on me, Whitaker, the Army, HDM, you, everybody.

No, we didn't officially shake on it, but I thought we had a deal. There's probably five sites, including *Off the Warpath* and that weird little uptight *Naked Opposition*, that'd be glad to run that whole-vid if only I could find someone to meet the Regs by putting their name on top. And believe me I've been looking. No one gets back to me.

That was supposed to be where you came in – pushing a LIFE-SAVING whole-vid out the door since you can't get in any deeper shit than you're in starting up this business about the searches. That's right, you got nothing more to lose.

Big news out of Indianapolis this morning, a bunch of black kids who take a public bus to high school sat on the bus and refused to get off after a cop's dog alerted on one of them. Said they were targeted, not random right from the start with the cop stopping the bus like that. They started rocking the bus from the inside after the cops took the adults off and said they were all arrested. One kid they interviewed mentioned your blow-hard Syriac letter. Though he wasn't too crazy about you comparing yourself to Rosa Parks.

Look, if the cops blew up your pack to say it had explosives – nice Catch-22, huh – plus they're manipulating video to try to turn you into the shooter, and they already locked you up in Bellevue (that's what people are saying) why the hell are you worried about putting out a whole-vid? You're way too deep in the crapper to be worrying about exposing the SecDef rolling a Grinder.

A Demo that catches fire is like T. The bomb doesn't have to go off for it to work. Even failed T works when it makes people nutty. And now your little aborted Penn Station action is rousing people up. Like the Wobblies say, "Direct action gets the goods!"

But I don't give a shit about the civ-lib stuff. That's for civilians. I'm trying to save some grunts. Cause if the Army awards the Grinder contract to HDM, that's it, they aint going back. Just get the paperwork ready on 300-plus non-combat deaths a year.

Do the right thing, dude, or I feel a road-trip coming on – thank you *New York Daily Chirp* for your fancy address down by the river. You never know when I might catch the sniffles and need a day off. So just get it the hell out before me or some HDM criminal bangs on your door. Cause then it's too late. Do it, man, and earn yourself a bowl of mean beef stew.

Genny

The man liked that piss-water beer. *The whole-vid I ... sent ... you of the SecDef....* He had screwed me up, down and blue. Hell, Everett had been a blast-concussed loose cannon since way before grabbing me off the factory floor. He was right, however, that a whole-vid taking down a multi-billion dollar program to save hundreds of lives outweighed hill-of-beans Whitaker by a lot of beans. My name so black, my prospects so bleak, they couldn't get any blacker or bleaker? Nothing for it but shine a light on the SecDef rollover?

So I added the SecDef's merry band of MoFos to the posse after me, turned the simmering HDM thugs up to a boil, and didn't e-mail Everett back. Damn him and his whole-vid, which

I'd had no reason to grab as I left the Hovel two mornings back. At least a bunch of folks had had the guts to actually refuse a search – as I absolutely must do my next opportunity.

Warpath Joe would alert me meanwhile if anything devastating materialized, like an artful whole-vid of me with those shorts round my ankles skewering a red heifer. Too wigged to just get up and walk out, I decided to check out the search-refusals that were apparently rising like water in a cracked basement. Nineteen the day before! And suddenly this weird screen sorta *shimmered* into view on top of my mail. Never seen anything quite like it wavering there so oddly.

Dan –
Get out now! Pull the plug, walk out the door and keep going. NOW!
A Friend Inside.

The plug out of reach, I flicked the power off and on and split, just managing to duck behind a cluster of flags across the street as an enormous, candy-apple red, civilian-model Grinder with dark windows roared up and parked where it pleased. It was one of those idiot pick-ups with a covered bed too small to carry anything but a few cases of cat food. Still ugly as sin, but natty in the threads he favored when not impersonating a cop, Lurch from Bellevue marched into ThinkTanked. I picked north and ran like I hadn't in a long, long time.

Chapter Fifty-Three

Ridden Hard, Put Up Wet

I sat in the back of a Mickey-King, the only sit-down joint for many a block, nursing fries and making a stab at "Penn" cause – Lurch hot on my tail – obviously I needed more firepower than *Warpath* on Whitaker. Mostly I bobbed and weaved, Lurch's unfortunate mug swimming before me. That contempt was his strong suit up at Bellevue had pegged him from DC. But who the hell did he work for in that ill-fitting cop costume and then jacket and tie?

Unwilling to sit and wait for the net to drop, I walked hither then back yon along blocks of comfy homes mingling with desolation. Bates Street was spiffy, as was First and O. There was a nice uncluttered feel about things as you'd turn a corner and find an enormous athletic field attached to a school. Suddenly light-headed in the heat (or such was my excuse), I fell into a little cinderblock joint called The Liar's Alibi figuring it'd welcome me with open arms. But after ignoring me for several minutes, the bartender in gold lame pants and a fiery wig finally came up and demanded proof of age from the likes of me. Circularly beset, I plain didn't need nonsense just to sit and gulp a beer. Badly overestimating me, a customer yelled as I left, "That's right – goodbye! Your kind been Plunged, boy. This neighborhood ain't for sale no more."

Despite Washington's lack of hospitality, I was in no hurry to return to the Hovel, my dangerously known address. (Thanks again, *Daily Chirp*.) Best to let *Warpath* fester overnight, rendering me all snuggly-safe as dawn broke. So, a room for the night for cash; use a credit card, and I'd still be on my second beer when the MoFos barreled in. And then they'd just steal the rest of the six-pack. I doubled a few blocks back to a no-tell motel to hear the guy refuse my fifty-three bucks in cash, even when I offered to bring him the room phone so I couldn't stiff him on phone charges.

"What makes you think my customers need a phone, man? Ain't nobody staying here looking to be bothered by the shit they came here to get away from."

He sent me packing to a place eight blocks down, six blocks over. And why didn't I have a credit card, the little foreign man there wanted to know, before his English deserted him when I waved the required fifty-nine dollars under his nose.

At a loss, my dogs barking, I blindly caught a bus heading downtown. A woman across the aisle was reading one of those ubiquitous, free papers, slight trash that the *Post* foisted on an indifferent city. I admired the photo on the back of the Oklahoma City Roughneck young phenom, Callaghan-Perez, sliding into second, spikes high. The headline said, "Payback Tonight?" and there I was with my plan for the evening. If tickets were available – ha!

Out in the world but safe, sequestered among dozens of Nationals' fans – the Roughnecks, sure. They'd stomped all over the Mets three, four weeks back. And after the Nats lost, well, I'd stroll out on the arm of one of the many lonely, morally casual women known to frequent night baseball games.

I hopped off for the train out to the Stadium-Armory stop.

And then sat on it wondering how Lois had made out amidst the swarm of Calfers where she worked and when, if ever, I might find out. Fleeing that, I took to scratching out more of "Penn." And some easily excited dweeb started and said, "Hey, what are you doing? What are you writing? Who are you to be writing stuff down in this car? None of us did anything. I've been in this car since before you got on, and nobody's done a blessed thing. Besides, with that shirt, you have a job, so how come there's no ID round your neck?"

I curled my lip, decided against giving him the bird as he kept sputtering, and set to telling of the green-suited greaseball who'd invaded my ambulance outside Penn Station. I didn't think that particular violation had been committed to the pages hopefully still on my kitchen table awaiting my return.

We pulled into a stop and Dweeby jumped up, declared "the

whole incident preserved by the car's cameras" and announced that he was going for help. Good – lawyers, guns and money, make it snappy, pal. I grinned around at my fellow passengers to elicit confirmation of his evident illness, but everyone just stared at their feet except the woman who shook her head and busied herself with her personal pacifier. The train pulled out not quite fast enough.

Thirty-six bucks to get in – $27 for the cheapest ticket, $5 for "handling," though I was standing at the Nats' window paying cash, and $4 for "T-enhancement." No searches, oddly enough, but plenty of cameras. Curious, I joshed with the ticket-taker about the lack of a search, and he said they'd dispensed with them late last season to save money. "Long as you don't try to smuggle in any sandwiches, you're OK. Why, you got some kind of problem? I can arrange for a supervisor to search you real quick if that makes you feel safer."

Me safer? I was about to point out that particular idiocy, but I'd just dropped a lot of money and, besides, had nowhere else to go. Half the folks scattered in the upper deck behind home were dressed in Nationals bright red, including some dame pushing seventy in uniform pants, stirrups, the works. Neat to be off the streets, amidst the few, the loud, the committed, no MoFo coming up on me unawares.

Moving from Cincinnati after things deteriorated there, the Roughnecks were in the National League's new Southern division, the Central having been disbanded once the Disruption hit Cincinnati hard and a new owner hightailed the Pirates off to Las Vegas. Despite their Gatorade-green uniforms, they were fun to watch scooting all over the field, the Nats actually pulling their catcher mid-inning after three Roughnecks stole second with embarrassing ease.

Good to galumph my feet over the empty seat in front, slump way back and groove on a game in an old football stadium making no effort to be anything else, everything distended and far away and out of scale. Even the distance between home and second seemed off somehow. I finally broke down and hailed one of the black vendors who far outnumbered the black fans there in that black city. Peanuts, the cheapest offering, a mere eight bucks. Cracking your way to the puny reward took enough time to pretend you got your money's worth.

Around the fifth inning, the dicey little question I'd been trying to smother raised itself irreducibly: where was I getting horizontal? Sure I'd been catnip to women since getting shot – long as I didn't think about actually getting laid. But the only women remotely approachable in the entire upper deck were the two youngish moms over there yoked with three preadolescent horrors begging for more soda. They could fight over me, the loser saddled with all three kids.

In other words, time to call this editor I knew, Richard – whatever his last name was – from a joint I'd published some, *The Monthly Mordancy*. Call to see about a vacancy on his couch, if his micro-zap miraculously hadn't changed, *and* I still had it scrawled on a piece of paper in my wallet from back when people wanted to hang with me. The stadium so old as to feature an actual working pay phone, yup, there was his number, and there was Richard, recognizing my voice at hello. And how in tarnation was that possible, I asked him.

"I guess because we were talking about you at a story meeting today, which had us watching that absolute classic NYONLY vid. We were wondering if we should interview you about how that no-search seed of yours is starting to sprout, plus all the … curiosities in your life lately. With the proper editorial controls, of course."

"Control under my own byline is what I like best."

"I don't think that would be possible right now."

"Yeah, fine. Already been offered that."

"I can imagine. Your *Warpath* story, it'll be interesting to see how it unfolds once they try to walk it back. But it got quite the bounce with those e-mails your general was dumb enough to write. Who knows, maybe things are starting – *starting* – to get a little interesting, not that that's going anywhere. As for you, you better hope your piece stays tight."

"Tight like the rope I got around Whitaker's neck. But anyway, Richard, I was wondering … a little favor. Any chance your couch has a vacancy sign on it for tonight? Just the one night, I promise. But I think I should stay in DC for another day to wrap

465

things up and, well, things have gotten complicated."

"*Complicated* – try radioactive in your case. Tonight, right, the day you took down a big-shot Army Calfer? That's a 'little favor' I'd tell my own mother to stick it."

"It's just, you told me once if I ever needed a favor, not to hesitate to call."

"That was a long time ago, my man. Way, way before the HeadMan. Forget the cliff you're driving your own self off, things *have* gotten complicated, you know. Uhm, BEI. The answer – hello, everyone – is categorically no-way-Jose. I gotta go. Don't call here again."

Seemed there was no end to people invoking BEI, fervent or desperate people. I sat down within hailing distance of the two moms – hey, one might be single, all the kids belonging to the other – not that either responded with anything but a grunt and then silence to my friendly, insightful observations about the game, one of their girls sticking her tongue out at me. A good game, anyway, a Nat having clubbed a three-run home-run – that I missed, of course – giving Washington a one-run lead.

But the Roughnecks' sheer speed and guile tightening the Nat infielders' collars, they manufactured two runs in the top of the ninth as we all knew they would, and the dejected home-nine's last licks were a quiet one-two-three at ten-fifteen, too late for the 10:30 last Chinatown bus home. I followed the half of the crowd heading for the Metro rather than the parking lots intending what, exactly? That I'd stumble upon some drug policy buddy, reefer's tendency towards contemplation suiting baseball? That someone of any sex was gonna swoon at the very sight of me? Sure thing, it had happened 24-hours before with poor Delores, who was probably wishing she'd thrown herself at some battle-scarred Marine. Everyone disappeared down the steps of the station as I walked away from the lights of the city.

I passed a spooky old hospital there in the dark by the edge of the Anacostia River, then scuttled by an even spookier giant new jail – one old, one new, do the math. Some doggerel was spray-painted on the jail's far outer wall:

Marching to future Depths,

The Powers seek None of More.

Emboweled lower down,

Leap from the Stump whole.

Little HeadFucks peel our eyes,

Mad to remember, we pray to forget.

Marching, shouting, scurrying, shooting –

Avaunt, Horatio – the Tanks!

That's right, baby, avaunt! The two institutions were succeeded by a well appointed neighborhood of single-family homes. And what had apparently been my fallback position all along elbowed its oddly liberating way to the fore. It had been gaining momentum since the two sleaze-bag motels declared my cash unclean.

Radioactive, unfit for human company, it was time to go to ground, time to sleep under the stars like a proper revolutionary. Good for the soul and no one the wiser, what was I afraid of? That I'd find it all too easy? That the Farragut Square lending library wouldn't soon welcome me, though I had a book to contribute? That I'd regret, as DC's version of Fall came on round about Christmas, not taking that jacket from the last woman I'd ever kiss. That I'd soon be buttonholing tourists to fling a hand at the Capitol dome and draw them as close as uncertain hygiene permitted. "See that – I testified there, not once, but twice, back when it mattered. I used to be a contender, but right now, buddy, I could use a bite."

Hell, I'd been spending like a drunken sailor, a king's ransom for the ball game and my crunchy dinner. Save some money and burrow away somewhere resting on soft lichen (DC lousy with it), and dismiss the MoFos for the night. Not under that bridge looming there, I wasn't a troll. But, yeah, down by the river.

Lordy, yup, a cemetery behind an easy enough thick brick

wall. Congressional Cemetery it said – well, Congress needed one. Old trees graced the paths meandering through the modest headstones and disappearing down a gentle slope towards the river. A cemetery, was that good luck or bad? Teenage couples were always fooling around in them – yeah, right before the haint got them. Awfully inviting, the main thing was to get in without being seen. All the houses across sleepy 17th Street were dark except for one or two rooms with a blue flicker.

The six-foot wall sloped down to well under four-feet by the corner of 17th and H and so up and over easy as pie. Nice change of pace to hop over something and land gently on my feet. I hunched over and scrambled further in, tripping only once on a broken headstone, then veered closer to the street lamp shining in the land of the living.

Man, was I really doing this? Sure, welcomed by folks who meant me no harm, and where else could I be sure of that? OK, behind that tree looked pretty soft. I went over to seek benediction from the nearest resident, one Fielding Ablegar, 1818 – 1879. Shit, sixty-one long years sounded damn good, the wolf huffing and puffing at my house of straw. Lucky, probably, with the Civil War age-wise, had Fielding found his allotted time sufficient? His faded epitaph unreadable in the dark, I'd get it come morning. A pastrami hero and a forty would've settled nice, a propitious sip poured on Fielding's grave. Throw in the Entertainment System for company, and I'd have been in clover – or lichen.

I curled around a root, my standard recent posture so alone in a bed so big. Everett, you reckless bastard – though maybe he was right. His e-mail the cherry on top of the free-floating bad at my knees and rising, maybe it did fall to me to get that SecDef whole-vid out. Save a couple of hundred lives year after year and, more importantly, charge a nice fat fee for the few paragraphs I'd write on Grinder non-combat casualties to accompany my top-five, Keystone Kops whole-vid. Except the only sites with the guts to run it had no money. Sexual indiscretions about the only ones that saw the light of day, if I had something meaningless like the SecDef (yuck!) rutting with one of HeadMan's chief gangsters – sky's the limit.

Speaking of nastiness, was I so far south I had to worry about snakes and whatnot? Fire ants, poison lichen? Needing someone to examine all my parts for ticks was the emergency that'd send me to Lois's door on the morrow.

I woke up cold still a long way from morning. Cold and feeling awfully exposed, not that I was moving to a darker precinct among the shades. I rolled over, away from the street light I'd been hugging. And what was that way over there? Forgetting to hunch over, I got up and – yo, momma! – a green tarp covering the loose dirt next to a grave dug for the morning's festivities. Fleeing the open grave, I dragged it back to my spot by Fielding, he and I pretty jake by then.

Half the tarp ground cover, half a blanket, I snuggled in and hugged the earth, invisible to the living, the dead hospitable.

PART NINE

Chapter Fifty-Four

Two Guys, Lonely but Not Alone

The birds finally drove me awake. Cool, cause it promised to be a thrilling day, though I hated to think how. I was outdoors, the root gouging my back said, but where and wrapped in what? Working up the nerve to look, a sudden hot breath on my face forced my lids open.

Its muzzle way too close to mine, I couldn't tell how big the dog was, not that it mattered, his teeth within striking distance of so many important parts. Growling and snapping, it had me pinned down pretty good, my hands caught under my green-tarp blanket for, of course, I'd spent the night in the Congressional Cemetery. A man's voice trilled out, "Sydney – that's OK. It's just a bum dirtying our cemetery. Come on boy, let's go."

But Sydney was enjoying himself, and from the next "Come on, boy" I could tell his owner had turned away. Trying to bring my hands up under the tarp elicited a couple of even closer snaps. Scared of something creeping up in the night, I'd slept with my glasses on. So I'd be able to admire the disfigurement of my nose and mouth if he didn't just go for my throat.

"Hey, mister!" I managed to call before the dog silenced me with way too close a feint. OK. I smashed him in the nose through the tarp, pushed him away and scrambled up as he yelped. A wire-haired Jack Russell well capable of biting the mess out of a prone victim.

His owner came rushing up. "What did you do to my Sydney?"

"Kept him from going for my throat. You enjoyed that didn't you, pal. You thought – "

"Never mind any of that. If he's marred right before the Greater Richmond All-Dog Invitational, you will pay, believe me.

470

Members pay $200 a year for the exclusive right to use this field as a dog park. You have no dog, not that you'd even be allowed on the waiting list, someone vicious like that to a defenseless animal! You apparently didn't read the signs prohibiting admittance after dark – cause you slept here overnight, don't deny it. This cemetery is on the National Registration of History Sites, so that makes you a T-Felon!"

"Why should this morning be any different? As to 'defenseless,' he was going for my face unprovoked. You got no – "

"Naughton told me to never leave our house without my micro-zap, but here I have. Or you'd be running from the Protectors soon enough. Sydney, we're leaving!"

"And the horse you rode in on, pal. Jesus H. Christ!"

As if knowing that Fielding was *my* protector, the nasty little thing darted close to lift his leg on his headstone before I could stop him and then scampered off. I bent and stretched, trying to iron the kinks out of my back.

"I've never heard what the 'H' stands for. You wouldn't happen to know, would you?"

I turned to see a big, laughing old guy with shades (not that there was any sun), brush-cut white hair and some faded tattoos on meaty, tanned forearms. "H stands for, 'How the hell do I banish the ass*holery* haunting my life?' I'm sorry – I'm sure you're jake. It's just that twerp was getting his rocks off letting his dog mess with me, and I've had my full of that kinda stuff the last week or so. Plus I really don't like this rotten town of yours."

"A visitor, huh? Well, of course, sleeping rough like this. Stupid me. Sorry, I don't get to talk to too many folks, people who talk back, I mean. My name's Lou." And he stepped forward to shake as I told him mine.

"I like dogs, don't get me wrong," he said. "But, man, they do not belong in cemeteries. Not one with hundreds of Civil War veterans. These Yuppie idiots with their fancy little dogs, they toss balls, frisbees even, and the dogs trample all over the graves. This is consecrated ground, but the cemetery lets them pay to turn it into a dog run. And don't get me started on the dogs lifting their legs on headstones – or worse."

"Speaking of which, me and Fielding Ablegar there got a little simpatico during the night. I was curious about his epitaph, which I couldn't read in the dark. Kind of an impromptu sojourn last night, I didn't bring my flashlight."

I started over towards the stone but, standing behind me, he recited: "Search the World Over, but Find thy True Beacon upon Offering your Surrender."

Surrender.

"Man, you're really into this cemetery – cause how many headstones have you memorized?"

"None. My eyesight isn't 20-10 anymore, but it's still good enough to read that. I'd have memorized Matthew Brady's inscription if he had one. His grave is over there. You know who he is, right? Ever since I came by and found dog shit on him, I've been dropping by most mornings to stand watch and send the dogs over to J. Edgar Hoover."

I studied Fielding's inscription a moment and thought about the turn life had taken till he said, "Pardon me saying, but I don't see any provisions. No skin off my nose, but if you want an egg sandwich, our house is that green one there you can just about see the attic window of."

"See, Lou, I said you were jake."

I returned the tarp to the waiting grave. Walking to his house, Lou – apparently hungry for talk – said he'd spent his life as a petroleum engineer in oil fields all over the world, happy with the work, not the people. He'd made decent money and raised his family, but knew something was missing. So he came to DC to teach high school math. He stuck it out for two years, but it was awfully tough at his age. I said I could imagine, trying to pound math home, given kids' attention spans these days. No, the classes were fine, he said, sparsely attended, but the kids who showed really wanted it. It was all the rest that he couldn't hack, the homeroom, plus the cafeteria and hallway duty. It was a young man's game.

Then, life was such, it got beyond him to think of moving. Besides, he liked his sleepy neighborhood, though he was sorry the Nationals hadn't left. Hitting his front walk, I asked if he was all alone in the big house, and he said might as well be, that his wife wasn't much company anymore. I said, well, that happens in a marriage, but he said it wasn't like that.

We walked down the side of a tidy, green house with a beaming yellow door and neat hedges and lawn. A wooden table and chairs anchored one side of the back yard, a screened-in enclosure with a couple of chaise lounges the other. A natural-cut big black poodle roused herself from under the table to greet us. I laughed, and he said he told me he liked dogs, just not pissing on war vet's graves. He told Lucy to keep me company and said he'd be back in a moment.

Through the kitchen screen door I heard him talking low. He came back a moment later with soap, washcloth, shampoo, a towel, disposable razor and a brush. He said he'd had his sense of smell pretty well burned away in an oilfield accident, but he imagined I was a little gamey, sleeping out like that. "You can take a whore's bath on the driveway there with the hose if you want. Whatever your day brings, it'll probably go down a little easier if your hair isn't dirty." He then dispensed the tonsorial advice everyone felt entitled to give me. "You should go with the brush-cut like me, a lot less maintenance." He left to get some eggs going, and I decided to take him up on his offer, stripping to the waist, the key thing not to get my lower half too wet. Shaving was easy in the side mirror of his green Saab convertible.

Man, people took one look at me and felt compelled to offer ablutions. The blue dress shirt I'd put on for the Transit Adjudication Bureau on Monday was finally incapacitated by sleeping out. As for the sweat-hiding black tee, it stank. No more, no less. So when Lou came out with a tray and a black polo shirt over his arm, I accepted this even more generous offer. He tried to get me to take my two shirts with me, but – traveling light, not galumphing around with two dirty shirts in a bag – I insisted on a trade.

"Eat these before they get cold, and if you feel like it, tell me a bit of what brought you here. I've encountered a couple of people sleeping in Congressional Cemetery before, but never one who cared about an epitaph, and certainly not one I invited to my … backyard. I hope you understand." And he nodded over his shoulder towards the house.

We sat at the table, Lou with coffee, me the same, plus, wow, what tasted like fresh squeezed OJ, which I hadn't had in forever, three bulls-eye eggs nestled in their hollowed out toast of thick black bread, plus the toast squares and a quarter-cantaloupe. Maybe it was all too easy a way to get me blabbing, but so what? I'd already hung a bunch of tawdry laundry on the *Warpath* line.

My mouth full, he said, "So, your 'sojourn.' All kinds of people have been making alternate living arrangements since the Plunge, but you're not a hobo. Not unless you hid your kit away somewhere. And no one who's really homeless lets his kit get too far."

"I sometimes wish I was homeless, everything that's been raining down on my head." Hell, some guy all set in life tossing everything to teach in the inner city at his age, I decided to trust him. I told him I was a baseball fan, had gone to the game and just ended up in the cemetery, and had actually had a pretty good night's sleep once I got that tarp working. I'd been unwilling to use my credit card for a hotel and had pretty much gone to ground, I told him.

"I wouldn't imagine you're too intimidated by that ridiculous Minders' fairy tale – like any system with that *supposed* amount of data is scalable, or even readable. Whatever the Minders are, if anything, they can't be half as bad as the psychopath running the DC cops' Terror squad. But can I also hope you're chipping away at the façade known as HeadFuck? '*Bold, Extolled, Impregnable*' – jawohl!"

"Only in the most indirect sense. But I did manage to publish a story I was down here researching. On a little site that's actually quite good called *Off the Warpath*."

"So this is you, huh, Mr. Forbes. That orgy in that Senate office building was probably a lot worse than you wrote it, right?"

"Slime oozing all over the carpet."

"You sleeping under that tarp, I thought it might be you. With that article, I figured you'd be in Washington and, well, you lead a fairly nonchalant life. I mean – "

"I do?"

"Devil-may-care, let's say. The *Symington Referendum* made

474

a big deal out of you taking down that general, and collected all kinds of odd-ball stuff connected to you. So now you're in the vanguard against these security-theater searches?"

"You tell me. I've been out of touch the last day or so trying to stay in one piece."

"The DC 'searchers' specialize in dogs going after blacks – young, old, male, female – long as you're black. Works fine to keep them scared and beaten down."

"I saw it in action. Thought the lady was gonna expire right there."

"Your letter to that Syriac guy is bouncing all over. Though it does seem an odd statement – disjointed if what you're trying to do is spark protest about the searches. How's your head, by the way?"

"I know. Lou, I gotta get home and generate something coherent. You know, explain where I'm at and how I got there. My head's better, thanks, but it's been tough."

"You never know about things sometimes, about the effect a simple gesture like refusing a search might have. People have to be ready for it, of course. But look what happened when Lutherans started invoking the Sermon on the Mount in a Leipzig church. It took years, but you get some folks praying in church, and you turn around and it's seventy-thousand marching, and then the Wall came down."

"As simple as that?"

"It's like a run on the bank, the difference being it's the top guys who've lost confidence, not the depositors."

"My thieving-scum general talked last night of infighting at the top. We'll have to see. Meanwhile, Lou, I gotta go."

"HeadFuck's gotten so weird – ineffectual like – anybody new might be worse. So you have to eat and run, huh?"

"I wish it was five o'clock. Cause I didn't celebrate my article like any writer should, not at RFK Stadium's prices last night. After five, you and me'd be having a few and solving the world's problems – until the wrong helicopter flew overhead."

"I've been looking for a reason to break open that six of Natty Bo growing stale in my fridge."

"Don't tempt me, cause it doesn't end good for people when

Turd-Touch starts working his magic. The eggs were delicious. Plus the bath – and, oh, the shirt!"

"Sure thing. But earn your breakfast first."

"Name it."

"Elizabeth would love it if you went to the screen door there and said hello. We don't get many visitors. Just a simple hello, the less said the better. And no matter what, keep the door between you or you'll scare her half to death."

"It'd be my pleasure. She's probably the first person I've met in a long time who won't immediately think of me in a certain pair of shorts."

"I decided not to mention them. Elizabeth rolled my clay into something out of nothing and gave me forty-six of the best years anyone could give – and now three of the worst."

"My mom says old age isn't for the faint of heart."

"Not unless you're lucky. So if I'm friendly to a guy in a cemetery, you'll understand. You're not supposed to say this, but I get so bored and lonely. I tried getting Lucy to talk politics, but it didn't take, the old flea-bag."

She was waiting for us by the door, tall and slim in a white sleeveless gown, her long grey hair a bit jarring through the screen. I was glad she was lovely her whole life before her face took on that cast. I said, "Good morning, Elizabeth. I'm so glad to meet you. Lou has been telling me how happy you've made each other all these years." She nodded gravely, smiled, then frowned, but didn't speak. Lou took me gently by the arm.

"Thanks, that was perfect. But anything more will just make her nervous wondering why she doesn't remember you."

Down on the driveway, I gave Lucy a good rub and, I couldn't help it, Lou a hug – a real one by two lonely men, not one of those scared-of-your-shadow excuses. I was halfway down the drive when he called me back to press thirty dollars on me. "Take it, damn it! Consider it a contribution to your civil-rights campaign. Take it, I said! Look, money's not an issue for me – I got out before the Plunge. Besides, what do I have to spend it on? I wish it was more, but I never have a reason to carry cash." I took the twenty, balanced the ten on Lucy's head, and said thanks, my socks were sticking to my feet, and I'd let him buy me some new ones if I encountered a store in DC that sold such exotic fare.

"It *is* a pathetic excuse for a city," he said. "I go over that bridge there, do all my shopping in Maryland." I turned at the end of his drive for a wave and saw him crouched, whispering to Lucy. "Forbes! I'll be following your progress. You don't have any kids, any *young* kids, do you?" I shook my head. "Good." Nothing to say to that, I waved again. He cuffed Lucy to get her going and headed out of sight towards the screen door that framed his day.

Chapter Fifty-Five

Whacked out of Wack

I headed for the train to a computer to see if Everett had upped his threats, happy to be clean and rid of two shirts past their sell-date. An old dude my size bestowing a slick black shirt good for the sweating on tap – figure the odds. Lurch falling out of the sky well off the beaten track at ThinkTanked, no point in not presenting myself all big and bold at the nearest Deskless. That's right: Can't Touch Me! The *sixth* Washingtonian I importuned once off the train actually stopped and pointed me to a Deskless.

Joe was in a happy lather over *Warpath*'s site being attacked like never before. Before he lost interest, he traced several of the attacks to "one of those loony end-times churches in Colorado." He'd been forced dark for about ten minutes, but otherwise his server's defenses held. Not that it mattered anymore, dozens of sites running with the story. His traffic was up eleven-hundred percent. He added:

WELCOME UNAUTHORIZED READERS OF THIS EDITORIAL CONFAB. HOPE I'M NOT GOING TOO QUICK FOR YOU.

SO, DAN, YOU'VE OBVIOUSLY SHED ALL SELF-REGARD. ME, I DON'T CARE MUCH EITHER AFTER MY LATEST CT SCAN. I'VE GOT SIX MONTHS TO GO — IT'S *ALL* MEDICINAL, SON — AND OUR WHITAKER STORY IS JUST THE START OF ME CHECKING OUT WITH A BANG! OF THE THINGS I'VE GOT SIMMERING, SEVERAL MIGHT BE RIGHT FOR YOU, YOUR BYLINE ALREADY SO FRAUGHT. WE'LL CONFER AS PER USUAL.

No surprise, but HDM was blowing steam out of both ears, Joe said. He linked to its statement and also to the Germans' tangled effort regarding my disclosure of Whitaker's e-mail to its man, Pantly. Buried in a bunch of expensively crafted words strung together, up, down and around – most of them swallowing their own tail – came a faint glimmer of them, yes, talking to Whitaker about potentially, down the road, perhaps "accessing his knowledge base so as to fortify our efforts to protect the Homeland's Heroes."

There you go, pop the cork, Joe! – in what little time you got left. Jesus, is *that* the only way to grasp at truth these days, as simple as that?

Joe ended, "So, MANY THANKS FOR WHITAKER'S HEAD ON A STAKE. A CHECK FOR $250 WAS MAILED LAST NIGHT TO YOUR ADDRESS A LA THE *DAILY CHIRP*. MORE OF THOSE BIG BUCKS WHERE THAT CAME FROM, SO REMEMBER: THINK *WARPATH* FIRST!"

Along with far more than the usual amount of trash in my queue, someone with the intriguing handle of "Lester's Honey" offered: "From his wife – a warning here."

Hello:

I feel I know you, I've heard your name so much around my house, said in hope the first week and then more and more angry. Of course yesterday, he liked to blow the roof off he was so mad you published that story on the Grinder and the General but did nothing about you know what. I tried to tell him people do what they can, and maybe you're not the right man for it, but you know how he is.

See, he's been fixed on you off and on for months now, so it just seems natural to think you two know each other. Though I guess you don't. All he says about picking you out that day is something about a hunch.

I don't know if you have any kids or not. Probably not, you even <u>thinking</u> of putting that out under your own name. But I am writing you with a heads up. I saw the e-mail he sent you yesterday and I know how reckless that is for everyone involved. I saw it after it was sent – too late. We don't hide stuff from each other, but he's a man, he goes his own way.

Anyway, he was out all night last night, ordinarily no big deal. No one's stopping him or his friends from drinking and driving the back roads. Unlike most, at least he drives slower. He parks and sleeps it off somewhere, then wets his head down, brushes his teeth and gets to work by the seven o'clock start. He refuses to carry the micro-zap I got him, but he always stops to call me driving in.

Except today he didn't. And then a friend called me that he didn't make it in to work. And we had a deal about his job. No more no-doctor's-note absences after he had a string of them when he got back from his last Sands and instead of putting him on leave like they should've, him with his head all messed up from that blast concussion, fucking HDM put him on probation.

He's so tore up about how bad the new Grinder still rolls, I really don't know what he might do to you. God knows he tried to find another reporter with the guts to put his name on it to get it out under the new Regs. He contacted five or six, but they're all too scared. I don't blame them, and I don't blame you, even if you did make him some kind of promise.

I love my husband and his little girl needs a father. It was rough when he got back, trying to be a daddy again. But they worked it out, and they're each other's whole lives now just about. That means he's not looking to check out. If he shows up in Queens, don't hurt him, but don't let him hurt you either. He's not doing his girl any good being in prison till she's grown. I can't believe that newspaper told everyone your address. Maybe if you could just go stay somewhere for a couple of days till I can track him down and shake some sense into him.

I know this is tough on everybody. Good luck to us all.
His Wife

I freaked, but only for a minute cause I was tired of it, way tired of running. Move Everett to the top of the heap, goody-goody. Sick of DC and bone-tired of scuttling under the fridge every time someone turned on the light in the kitchen, I was sleeping in my own lonely bed that night. Hell, I was still Everett's best bet for getting the whole-vid out. So no way he'd just blast me to kingdom come without first trying to force me into doing it.

Ah, a posy from Turncoat Wife. At least there at Deskless, I didn't care if it deliberately harbored some super-dooper Trojan worm. She skipped any salutation.

Look, here's my damn address, which I can't believe I'm giving you. But your shitty micro-zap is out – trouble with the bill or, about as old as me, did it finally die? It's the third tower east of Third Avenue on 73rd Street, Apt. 47-J. (Across the street, the buildings only reach about thirty stories.) Building security has scanned a photo of you I hadn't thrown out for some dumb reason, so you're pre-screened enough that they'll call me. Great – another link to you. But otherwise they won't initiate any contact.

I caught Carole on *Breakfast Raunch* yesterday morning. MoneyBags with the wandering eye insisted, not surprising after the splash her photo leaving Bellevue made, miles of thigh disappearing into a red leather miniskirt and a midriff-baring top highlighting her big shooting scar. But yesterday, she was disappointingly demure in a white dress. Short and unavoidably tight enough, but up to her neck for some reason. The 'interviewer,' who at first kept adjusting his package like he had a hard-on just sitting next to her, finally complained that he didn't know if the "Network" – there's a laugh – got its money's worth.

Turned out he was talking about content. You used to talk about those Chaminade guys you encountered growing up in Mineola, how on-the-ball they seemed. So maybe it's her Catholic high school, cause she was pretty articulate, her sentences actually more than six words long.

The interviewer's main problem was she blamed the cops for both of you getting shot. They cut her off with a video of her va-va-va-vooming down that corridor the first time she said it was obvious you were holding a radio because she could plainly hear it. Then she saw it in your hand and wondered what kind of a goof actually still used a transistor.

They tried to get at her off-camera when they showed that vid, but she didn't budge. Cause here's the really cool part.

481

She said – and it's bouncing all over, that's why I can quote her directly – "I don't care what you're trying to get me to say or how you threaten me. I'm the only other civilian who was there, and Daniel Forbes was just talking to the cops and showing them all he had was a radio. It was playing loud, some weird news show. Then I saw that short one, Officer Reisner, with his gun out, and I started rushing up thinking I could stop it. Cops like talking to me. But then Reisner fired, and I stopped, for which I blame myself. Finally I got moving again, but then I was shot, and so here we are. And I'd like to thank the hard-working folks at Bellevue and – "

They broke suddenly for commercial, and no more Carole, though when they were hyping the spot for days they said she was the whole half-hour. Amazing thing was, I liked her. And you wouldn't believe how she's getting trashed today, something truly horrendous about a joint in a park as a teenager.

So a deal's still a deal – Sunday night is your damn deadline, Danny. If you want to talk, now you know where I live. Cause I am not trekking out there to stand on your porch any more. I think the guys from the projects have started selling tickets. Besides, I'll probably be too busy looking for work.

Nicki.

Well, well, Nicki, 73rd Street – further south than I would've thought *and* with a 47th-floor monthly nut. More to the point, Carole proved a mensch and got kicked off the air as a result. Just like what happened to me on CNN [FOOTNOTE ONE] for stark truth-telling. Despite everything that had been painted on her generous tabula rasa, all I knew was she volunteered to cheer orphans and old folks, was getting married for love not money, and hid none of her light under a bushel. And here she was standing up to the Protectors at least as much as I was, and with a hell of a lot more to lose: *Mel, Mel, commere! Look at this dame – she's got star quality! Who's her agent, we can plug her right in.*

Joe was wrong, I did retain a scrap of "self-regard," Cause I suddenly thought of Lurch, unplugged the machine and ran three blocks. Alright, no need to rush home to the Hovel, time to play tourist. My private, sergeant and lovely major had shown me the soldier's rough road, a stretch untraveled by a nation on cruise control speeding off a cliff. So I decided to pay my respects at the new Sands Memorial. Plus, yeah, I was curious, it causing such a ruckus when HeadMan personally unveiled it back when he still did such things.

****

At first there wasn't much to the Sands Memorial but a modest pavilion with razzle-dazzle displays on T in all its useful multitude. But kids from all over the country quickly wearied of pressing buttons to cause explosions. Fed out of the building into a shallow bowl at the far end of the Homeland Mall, polished marble arrows in the grass directed our attention.

One view featured a starkly realistic hologram, a movie projected on air, of the Towers, standing immense, then hit, burning, hit again and falling miraculously within their footprint, all in under a minute. Initial viewers might gasp, but the kids grew distracted as, after a brief pause, the buildings reappeared to endlessly stand and fall. A blank check as the years elapsed – summoning, tempting, invoking, justifying.

The other set of arrows directed viewers to a giant, shimmering Cross, sparkly and majestic. Not nearly as tall as the Towers, it was shot with color, a fireworks display without gunpowder's smoke or smell. An eager, buoyant Cross. A plaque on a low, unobtrusive stand was the only marker in the inviting little meadow. Acknowledging the controversy attending the memorial's opening, it read, "The Cross is darkened on five special days to respect our Heroes' diversity and honor our Homeland's ideals." And, to much wailing and gnashing, the Cross was indeed extinguished those five days, the Towers doing double duty.

Feeling queasy, I turned to go and only then saw it. I avoided a dog-cop and asked one of the many other officers sprinkling the grounds. He said the giant sign was about a week old and then beckoned for another cop to take my picture. *That* very brackish water under a rusty bridge, I struck a leering pose and then turned to look.

Across the Potomac in Virginia was a colossal billboard of HeadFuck himself wearing a vaguely martial tunic, pointing at us resolutely, his big bald head gleaming. One word flashed red, then the next: *Bold, Extolled, Impregnable*, a bromide that was getting harder and harder to laugh off. He occupied much of the space between the Towers and the Cross.

Pushing three o'clock, my slick new shirt gone damp, it was a hundred-and-one degrees I heard someone say. The day before almost balmy by comparison, it never ceased to amaze the difference a few degrees made. I was glad of the water fountain, but baffled by its instructions: "Push Button. Wait for Water." Only in DC. What I really needed was some AC, but I wasn't going back in the pavilion to hear more explosions. The Sands Memorial the last straw far as me and DC were concerned, I slogged east towards Greyhound, questing for two slices and a soda – six bucks. I gave the White House a wide berth, vowing to see the famous new gun emplacements on the lawn some other time.

Cops, soldiers, dweebs with IDs, sneering ex-presidents of the French club with legs down to there, pairs of shy, fecund women in their updated Mennonite dress – they all started to waver in the heat. I resorted to my own damn slogan: *Boundless, Exemplary, Unflagging*! but kept stumbling and finally quit my quest in favor of a ten-buck "personal pan pizza," total intake of cardboard less than two regular slices.

Get me to the bus on time! Restored mostly by the clip joint's AC and gulp after gulp of water in its bathroom, I pressed on. Barbara – "His Wife" as she loyally called herself – had written around nine that morning telling me not to go home. More than six hours later, surely Everett had shown, chagrined about being too hung over to face an arm-chewing drill press, still boiling mad at me, but safely confined to Indiana. Turd-Touch certainly never darkening Connexions' door again, I decided to check at the Cyber-Bound a block back – Can't Freaking Touch Me!

Nothing from Barbara or Everett, but someone had sent a Milwaukee IndyMedia story about the search-refusals spreading.

It focused on a concerted little Demo four woman had done at the bus station there with suitcases stuffed with brassieres. Man, I had to get "Penn Tale" out to add my bit to – shit-yeah, call it a Movement.

As I was closing my queue, up popped the day's second from Lester's Honey.

I write because I scared the piss out of you earlier today. Which was for your own safety. Now I'm the one scared. Everett's HDM buddy and I decided to go look for him around noon. Ev's been afraid in the Sands, he knows there's no good reason to make someone fearful. So it wasn't like him to not contact me on his ten-thirty break.

His buddy and me split up to look. I found his truck, off the road, but not in a place where Ev would have sleeped it off last night. It wasn't even really hidden, cause it had taken out a wide path of late corn. And that's not something Everett would do, no matter how drunk he got, wasting money and work like that.

But here's the thing that's really scary. Inside the truck was about fifteen empties of Hoosier Meth. The man loves his Genny Cream, right. But as much as he does, he hates Hoosier Meth more.

What I'm trying to say, no way he would 1. drive through that corn or 2. drink one, let alone fifteen of them H-Meths. Somebody has snatched him and is trying to set it up to look like he took off somewhere. Moved to Nevada to work in a silver mine or something.

HDM loses that Grinder contract, that place is gonna be a ghost-town. This whole county would shut down. How many goons does a billion-dollar contract buy? And my fool husband is threatening that. No, I'm not worried who's reading this now. They already have him, so let them know that I know. Let him go free, and we'll just slink away I promise. Or I'm making the loudest noise I can starting with this letter.

I sent our girl away before I went out to look. And not to anyplace obvious. Nobody can find her. Let them come after me. I hope they do, because I will show those motherfuckers. Let them think cause I'm a woman I can't. Trying to make it seem like Ev is the guy to go off and kill himself somewhere. Like he'd do that after surviving three long Fomentings, one Sands was almost two years. Night after night with a bulls-eye on his back going door-to-door. Watching his best friend get fried up in a stupid rollover. Bullshit.

Part of me wants to just grab my girl and run. But that's a small part. He loved our girl to death. As hard as we worked having her, Ev freezing his sperm before deployments, and all that other business, he wasn't checking out while she was still Daddy's little girl. They're going to paint him like all the other vets killing themselves cause they got the shakes and can't sleep, depressed and all that. Maybe when his daughter turned 14 and started running wild, but not now.

So, they got him and they killed him. Be with a man for twenty-three years, something like that happens – you <u>know</u>! You don't have to be told.

And you helped kill him, sitting on that thing. So what are you going to do about it now, mister bigshot New York writer? A writer like that old band of his made music to vacuum by! Getting it out now doesn't mean shit to me. What I want to know is are you coming out here to help bring some justice to my man? Justice to protect me and my child, to clear his name and get the bastards who did it. Well, are you?

His Wife.

Everett was playing in leagues bigger than he knew, and he'd screwed both of us from the moment he slipped that map in my jacket pocket. Sorry, Barbara, but Turd-Touch was clean on this one.

But of course I wasn't. Everett brought the big smelly bucket, but I provided the ladle.

I stormed blindly out. Jesus, get a pint of whiskey, get on the damn bus and sit and stew and be safe for however many marvelous hours it took. Hopefully Homeland Control would be up to its usual idiocy and prolong the ride. Buy food, a thriller – something dark for the times – and a pad to write on. They sold all that stuff up near a big-city bus station, even in DC, right?

And just sit, night falling not quick enough, glad of the baby screaming his fool head off and the couple fighting viciously in some foreign tongue – racket trumping thought.

Screw Everett, the smug, macho – I almost bowled over a former math club president, turned to apologize and couldn't help but admire.

And some skell, raggedy and nappy and nasty and dirty, loomed up from nowhere and slashed the meat of my palm between my thumb and forefinger.

It took a moment to register as the girl screamed and ran and the blood began to flow. And in a charming, drawing-room accent the skell said, "Take this if you would, please. It has everything you need. Clean the wound with the swab – it'll sting a bit, I'm afraid – then apply the bandage. And don't worry, both contain military-spec coagulant and self-cauterizing agents. Besides, I only penetrated the stratum granulosum, maybe the stratum licidum at most. Just apply them both without delay, and you're right as rain. Off you go."

Floored by this performance, I half expected him to slap me on the butt and back onto the pitch. Instead, his rubber-gloved hand – the pristine gloves a far remove from everything else about him – thrust a neat little packet into my good hand. He dropped a gleaming scalpel on the sidewalk and leaped into the back seat of a spewer that drew up with its back passenger door open. It tore out as the people gaping at me turned and fled. And no, I couldn't make out the half-covered license plate.

Marked and in pain, worrying I'd offend – heck, the *Vic* fearful of MoFo attention – I ran around the corner and behind a big planter sprouting three flags. Jesus, a thin trail of blood followed, but the flow was already slowing. Maybe that guy did know how to inflict a flesh wound. Of course he knew, a professional in disguise like that, talking of stratums – even if made up on the spot, they sounded good – plus two well paid comrades in a very expensive vehicle, one to drive, one to open the door in back. A garden-variety DC cop wouldn't have laid a glove on them.

I fumbled my gift open to find an antiseptic wipe, a large square bandage, some adhesive tape and a small, puissant looking scissors. Applying the wipe, I tried to flee a pain far worse than any alcohol or peroxide. But there was nowhere to go. I howled into my arm – hell, bang a drum, no one cared, not if the people around the corner were any indication. Then the bandage sent the pain off the charts. I bent over whimpering, but managed to get it taped down.

Marching off blindly, the pain gradually lessened three blocks on. I stopped to catch my breath and caught sight of myself in a store mirror and almost laughed, the look on my face. I might've –

I ripped the damn thing off. Christ, had I just dosed myself? Told to jab myself in the leg with a sharp-tipped umbrella, would I? No, no – you'll much prefer *this* goblet of claret, sir, not that one. Yikes! the wound looked like it had somehow almost closed, any poison coursing its way to my vitals.

I found a drug store and bought some rubbing alcohol and band-aids. What came next, Cat Wrangler's kooky, look-at-me red duct tape? She freaking had to sit down next to me on the LIRR. The alcohol barely registering, I almost dispensed with the band-aid, but then thought of riding a bus all evening – if I didn't soon morph into some swamp creature from my hand on up. I pocketed the slick little scissors, which looked like they cost ten bucks or more, having nothing like them in the Hovel's medicine cabinet. Alright, to the Greyhound, march!

Christ, it probably was poison, otherwise what was the point? Did I dare get stuck on a bus in Beltway traffic? Or should I just go check into a DC hospital and wait for someone to air-bubble my IV? Probably get better care from a bus driver, anyway. Throw a dart at the wall where pictures of numerous potential assailants hung, but what *message* to take from a very peculiar attack? 'Please, your bandage if you will, sir.' Like having a doc present to keep the detainee alive for more interrogation.

I walked and it felt good, even in the heat, to locomote upright on the earth. Pocketing a couple of band-aids, I donated the rubbing alcohol and the rest to the next homeless gathering. Glad of them, one guy confirmed the bus station dead ahead. *Alcohol*, right – a concept. Fall out on the damn bus one way or another. I crossed behind the beige, box-on-stilts convention center and kept going.

Hell, the place had potential. There was enough space in the poorer areas for all kinds of surprising things, car dealerships and parks, and there, for instance, another big, *grass* football field connected to a church a couple of blocks up from Union Station. You'd no more find that in Manhattan than a vineyard. And then, across a huge patch of fenced-in asphalt pretending to be a parking lot (not a car in sight), I saw the grey dog ready to gallop. No deli or anything nearby, they presumably had the crap I needed inside the bus station – all except a bottle. Should've snagged one blocks back when I had the chance. Well, just hope for some old man playing the harmonica, leading us all in train songs and passing some fine sippin' whiskey round the back of the bus.

1. "Talkback Live," CNN January, 14, 2000.

Chapter Fifty-Six

Leave the Driving to Me

And lookey there, a chance to join my very own Movement. DC dispensing with the usual four-man, full-employment deployment, one lonely cop was set up outside the bus station's single entrance, a scavenged, orange road construction barrel his table. Not that a flock of passengers was descending on him, but still. A wan fellow, this cop, his chin flowing into his neck below a pinched face, he didn't look any too happy beckoning over a substantial woman in tight red pants dropped off by an ancient, shock-sprung Buick Electra.

Damn. Washington's air starting to burn going down, I just wanted to collapse on a bus pointed north. No pressing agenda up in Herald Square the week before, I'd stood idly by condemning the folks lining up to get home. But approaching the DC Greyhound, like them, I was hankering to get somewhere. Maybe the cop was only doing black females that quarter-hour, and the civ-lib lottery would let me skate without betraying my Movement. Otherwise, folks in *Milwaukee* telling MoFos to shove it, punt the prevarication and Goddamn stand up. Thrust my wrists for the cuffs or declare myself irredeemably half-assed.

The cop fumbled with her suitcases as I wandered up, and he and the lady both swore as a bag slid off the orange barrel. What if I missed the New York bus by thirty-seconds, the post-Plunge next not for another three hours. Was I even safe on DC's streets that long? Hell with it – I veered towards the door. Without looking up, the cop said, "No, no. Sir! Behind her. There's been an Alert. Behind her, now!" He pointed as he groped her bags. Fussing with a zipper, he mumbled something, and she barked, "You want it open, you open it yourself, cop."

Nice! Then it hit: I had a small scissors *concealed* in my pocket. I regretted their loss, but headed to the trash basket a few yards off before the approaching trio of scruffy young Bulgarians – whatever – all with enormous packs, got ahead of me. Let them profit from my *Just Say No* once I disposed of my lethal weapon.

"Sir, I'm not telling you again – behind her! There's been chatter!"

"Chatter – what the hell is chatter?"

"Chatter is you shut up and get behind her."

"But I'm just – "

"But nothing. Once you … *present* on line, if you leave, that's an Indication. Which means a trip to lock-up. Now stay there or go downtown! Your choice, but believe me, I'm sick of this shit out here in this heat."

The woman turned with a look of exasperated solidarity. That's right, darling, what bus you catching. Such indignities visited upon us, you got any sippin' whiskey in one of those bags? Defeated by the zipper, he said, "You don't have any bad shit in here, do you Miss?"

"What do you think?" And she grabbed it off the barrel, picked up her other two and stormed off. Jesus, what about the e-mails in my pocket I'd forgotten worrying about the damn scissors? He looked after her working his mouth silently, then turned to me. Holding nothing to obediently place on his barrel, the realization dawned that I wasn't actually subject to a search.

"Cop, I don't have any bags, so there's nothing to search. Besides, you got no right to search me. I *refuse*! You got that? This boy says no! Like it says, I'm secure in my person that I got nothing on anyway. So, see ya!"

Thus my formal, stirring refusal, rhetoric for the ages spouted in a sea of asphalt, none but the offending cop to hear. But I'd gotten it out, my meaning and thus my conscience clear. Milwaukie, Oakland, Indianapolis, who knew where – grasp my hand across the miles.

"Look, see." I held my hands up clutching my fingers open and closed in a see-idiot-no-bags gesture.

"Wait a minute, what the fuck's that on your hand? Don't move." He was suddenly so agitated I didn't. The three 'Bulgarians' plowed up, all about twenty and laughing and goofing and suddenly quiet when they saw something was going down. Thumbing his micro-zap, he barked, "I said, what happened to your hand? We got Regs on that."

I cut it shaving your mother's snatch popped into my mouth as my teeth clamped shut. "Why? Uh – "

He found what he wanted. "Alright, forget the hand-wound Regs. This is you, even in a different shirt." He held his micro-zap up so I could admire a loving portrait of myself in the blue dress shirt I'd worn all over DC. "Don't move!"

He got all tangled up putting his pacifier away and reaching for what, a tazer? "Am I under arrest for changing my shirt, cop? Cause I've done nothing but get my hand cut by some weirdo. I'm the vic, not the perp, and I'm leaving."

I turned, and he shouted, "Don't move! That's an order from a sworn Homeland Protector."

Jesus, he'd turned bright red. And he brought up a big gun with a dull gleam and pointed it at my chest from ten feet away.

Fuck me. Should I run? No, rush him, maybe – more props than getting shot in the back. Getting blown away carrying no bag but obviously refusing a search would do the Movement more good than "Penn Tale,' however stirring I might eventually write it. As foreigners, were the Bulgarians more or less likely to witness truthfully?

"Not so funny now, is it, you big piece of shit." He waved his gun around with a little laugh.

Hell, Al and Elaine could foist their scoop off on some other intrepid scribbler; they probably already had. As for the SecDef vid, well, that had been screwed from the start, so keep looking, Everett, you'll find that greater fool. Rush the MoFo, the ultimate refusal? Too much was enough. Go ahead, man – do it! Nobody would care. I – I thought of Lois laughing at the top of the stairs. She'd care. And I stood very still.

The cop ordered the three Bulgarians with their bulging packs to get their asses into the bus station, go on, scram! The gun not wavering, he got his micro-zap back out and dialed. "Got him. Who do you think – Forbes! At the Greyhound. Of course I'm sure it's him, though he tried to get slick, changing his shirt. Get here quick. What – no! Not in front of the surveillance cameras. I told you, only if he makes it necessary. And no cash here.

Right, OK."

Cash – great. "Cop, I repeat: unless I'm under arrest, I'm free to go. I've got nothing to search, they're illegal anyway, and I refuse." A Goddamn comedian was I. Careful, cause he sure looked freaked. "Since I've done absolutely nothing, I can't be under arrest. Now, I'm turning and walking that way. If you'll just put your little – "

"Shut the fuck up! Get down, get down now!" And holding his gun far on the other side of his body, he darted around his barrel. "Get down. You're a known T-Symp who's already caused a discharge within the last thirty days. If I feel threatened, you're the one responsible! Nobody's gonna question a Protector on the front lines of the C. P. Crisis."

He pawed at my sore shoulder, then slowly brought the gun up and pointed it at my head. I dropped, and was still lying there minutes later with his boot on my back when a heavy vehicle squealed to a stop, and I found myself nose to toe with a pair of enormous, tasseled loafers, the fancy-pants cuffs breaking over them in a soft, rich wave.

"Right, Mr. Swyve, you take it from here, BEI. I'm going on break now. The department's gotten strict about having to take them on time. That's two-grand in cash, right? You'll call me like you promised when the paperwork's gone through?"

Whoever snarled, "How many times have I told you never, ever to use my name? Huh, Umbert? It happens again, there's going to be trouble. Now, you'll get your money, though it would have been a lot easier – *cleaner* – if we were calling for the meat wagon right now. A front-lines Hero under constant threat guarding mass transit, nobody would have questioned a forced discharge involving this scum. But I guess you didn't want that bonus we talked about."

Jesus, that voice sounded familiar.

Officer Umbert almost whimpered, "I got him for you fair and square, that's all I could manage."

"Fine, pussy. You'll get your money, just not soon. There's been a glitch, and my firm isn't fronting it anymore. Not for just turning him over and dumping the disposal on me. It'll have to come directly from the client, which'll take a while, that kind of paperwork, especially a new client. You sit tight and wait till you hear from me. Got that? Now get out of here before some stinking bus rider shows up and sees him with a *Protector* – give me a fucking break."

The boot lifted, and the familiar voice said, "Alright, Forbes, get up slow."

I did and tried not to flinch. And I had to laugh that Lurch was driving the same absurd, no-payload Grinder pickup that he'd stormed ThinkTanked in the day before. Umbert fled as far as the door to the bus station, but lingered there.

"Go ahead and laugh, if that's how you want to go out." He lunged, threw me around and latched a fierce grip on my head from behind, his hands locking in front. I dug in my heels and flailed wildly but, pulling me by my head, he started marching us around the back of his vehicle to the passenger seat. I swung my elbows, but he was too far back for anything solid. I scratched at his hands, then tried to stomp his feet and claw his face. He yelled, "Don't! Or I'll snap your neck in half. And then we won't get the chance for a proper goodbye."

He must've had muscles on his knuckles he was so damn strong. It felt like the time I snuck into Hofstra's gym as a fifteen-year-old and got in a pick-up game with some guys from their team cause they needed a fourth for one side, these grown men playing with just a whole other realm of strength when I tried to mix it up inside.

I stopped my useless grappling and tried to think as he shoved me around the back of his enormous vehicle. He ground my face into the side of it and then got the passenger door open with one hand, a coil of rope falling out at our feet.

I grabbed at the scissors in my pocket as he tried to shove me in, and got them and stabbed him in the back of the hand, lucky that he didn't flinch at the last second. Blow-back, baby! He swore and I stuck him again, harder. He flung his hand up and jumped back and tripped over the rope and went down. I kicked him twice hard in the ribs with the black work boot so scorned by the silver-fox gatekeeper at Hart and heard a very satisfying crack the second time. He made a noise like metal ripping and got to his knees but no further. Another big vehicle pulled up behind us.

Let some bus riders watch as I killed the bastard. That's right – *him*, not me! Fucking-A, this vic was taking no more. One for our side to the many thousands on yours, MoFos! So what I went to prison, I'd be a hero. Three hots and a cot, it had to be safer than out here. He tried to rise, but something inside staggered him. I drew back my leg and took a sec to aim for his temple. And a voice calm and unhurried enough to be telling me the 3:13 leaves from track six said, "Forbes, I wouldn't do that if I were you. A lot of cameras right here by the bus station."

Somebody screaming 'No!' would've whipped my leg faster. But a voice that languid, I had to turn and look. A big old bull cop was standing by a black spewer, a smallish gut over his wide belt, big head, big shoulders and a big gun in his hand, silver hair on top of a face that laughed when others turned away. Looking green but almost to his feet, Lurch held his hand to his heart where I'd kicked him. I brandished my weapon.

"Cummings, this faggot's mine!" he rasped. "Have a nice fucking day, cause this doesn't concern you."

Jesus – *Cummings*. Yeah, people feared him.

"The way it looks from here, you might be glad of a little police protection, Swyve. Forbes, you brute, you can't play nice?"

"I'm warning you Cummings, back off." The rasp grew stronger.

"It's Commander Cummings. And *you're* warning me?"

Lurch finally rose, and Cummings barked, "Swyve, you know what I think of you. Don't tempt me to have to protect a Homelander. Or are you so used to picking on defenseless small fry, you didn't hear the safety coming off?"

That'd give folks something to digest, a top DC-cop MoFo shooting another top MoFo as I looked on – prompted (sorta) by my better-late-than-never search refusal. Lurch stopped, and Cummings motioned him back with his gun, thank God. Two big, ugly men facing off, one slightly stooped with pain, blood dripping from his hand, the other happily astride his wicked world.

"So what'd you do, Cummings, have Homeland Control tickle you if this asshole's name was mentioned on any micro-zap in the District?"

"It's not rocket science. But what I want to know is the name of that DC cop who ran into the bus station. Some uniform thinks he can line his pockets without forking over my half? How much you pay him, Swyve, to call if bright boy here showed?"

"What cop? I didn't see anybody."

I piped up just to prove I retained the power of speech. "I think his name is Umbert, something like that."

"Thanks, Forbes. I didn't even know Umbert got his gun back. Well, he's pulling midnight foot-patrols in Anacostia starting tomorrow. Now let's get something straight, Swyve. I am not some Homeland tool you can push around. This is *my* town – I don't care what you private bastards think. Look at you, dressed like you're selling women's shoes! No wonder you let this, this … *amateur* kick your ass. Driving around in a pimp-mobile. You expect to get any real work done in a ride that loud? My town, you got that?"

"Yeah, for how long? Once ASPIC gets that new contract, you're cut off at the knees."

"Maybe you ASPIC whores aren't getting that contract. Winds shift, Swyve. Until you do, I thought we got things straight in that little sit-down we had last month, you, me and Miller. Your boss is not nearly as stupid as you like to think. Now it's time for you to leave – bye-bye."

Lurch winced at his dripping hand. "You got a handkerchief, Cummings?"

"A hanky, no. I've got a kit in my vehicle, but it's too far."

I looked at it fifteen feet away and grinned. Stabbing him, I must have gone past those two strata of skin. Lurch finally just held his hand up and used the back of his florid tie to staunch the bleeding.

"Look, Cummings. This T-symp's been messing with the MTA up in New York, and you know how deep ASPIC has its hand in them. Plus he's annoying the Army for fuck's sake, and now he's an *existential* threat to a new client of mine. It's time to solve this little problem once and for all. I didn't want to mention it, but an old friend of yours – Bettinger – wants him … solved just on general principles."

"He's no friend of mine. Get that clear right now," Cummings said.

I knew Bettinger wasn't sitting on his hands, me naming him like that. Go ahead, dude, throw yourself on the heap of MoFos after me. But – gotta pay your dues, Bettinger – you start at the bottom.

Cummings continued. "How you hold on to your job, Swyve, amazes me. You made $537-grand last year. Chump change to a dedicated public servant – especially since HeadFuck – but not bad. It ever occur to you if this big zero here just disappears, they'll make a martyr out of him for his miserable little 'Movement.' Which, believe me, is getting strangled in its crib, I don't care what those pansies in the Boston PD do."

"I thought Oakland was our biggest worry."

"Come on, Swyve – is Oakland still part of this country in any way that counts? Anyway, far better to keep him alive and keep him scared. Those cameras over there don't actually work, but some *bus* rider has no doubt seen him here with me. He's not some Null we can disappear. Leave him stumbling around, he'll mess up."

"Dudes, I appreciate the heartfelt consideration two such high-powered MoFos are giving my future. But I got a bus to catch."

Shut-up, they both barked, and Cummings said, "I'm not asking you, Swyve, I'm telling you. Since he exposed that moron, Whitaker – which isn't the worst thing in the world if it wakes somebody far above him the fuck up – he's off-limits. However long Whitaker stays a senior Calfer, this idiot is under my protection."

Wow, our story worked! Saving me from the likes of Lurch was a damn good return on any piece of journalism. I couldn't wait to tell Lois.

"I would've thought you Calfers smart enough to throw Whitaker out years ago," Lurch sneered.

"These are matters of faith. It's certainly not for someone who hasn't demonstrated that faith to judge. As to shithead here, all he's doing is sending out boring e-mails. Oh, he *gets* sent some interesting ones, as I told Miller this morning. Your boss was quite interested in one in particular in light of your new client. You didn't know we talked most mornings, did you, Swyve?"

Lurch muttered, "Miller better watch himself too."

"Fine, knock each other off. Meantime, Forbes's file is stalled, and I'm sick of the sight of him. Plus I gotta get out the welcome mat for the jack-ass Nepalese 'sneaking' into town tomorrow."

"So, *Commander*, with your great intel, you haven't heard that that slut up in New York who managed to worm her way into getting shot with him is planning a search-refusal. She's getting some douchebag at one of the New York stations to go along and stage it big and loud. I'm telling you, Current Permanent Crisis or not, shit-wipe here can smash the piggy bank."

Wow – Carole! You go, girl.

"Beauty and the Beast, so what. My new wife dragged me to see it with her stupid kid. It means nothing. I'm telling you, his case is stagnating with him playing tourist here. Miller and I agreed we needed to goose it along. Which I did. Did you even notice I gave his hand the new Raytheon marker it took them so damn long to roll out? But one thing I'll be very curious to learn is how Umbert got himself assigned here *alone*."

"Slipping, Cummings?"

"You want to think so. You still report to Miller, Swyve. So how about you climb back into that compensatory toy of yours and go waste some Homeland pencil-pusher's time. Go, I'm bored." He motioned with his gun.

"You're going down, Cummings. You had a good run, you public 'servants.' I know. I dot-link – that's why they pay me the big bucks. And I'll be the first to dance on your grave. As for you, Forbes, enjoy it while you can, cause that ain't long."

About to smear blood on his fancy pants fishing for his keys, he tried with his other hand across his body, gave up, got his pants bloody and roared off.

Chapter Fifty-Seven

Cummings' Tease

"Alright Forbes, let's go. We've created enough of a stir here. We'd go to Union Station, except with that cut I gave you, those ridiculous Regs on wounds to the hand'll foul you up. Why don't you have your own fucking vehicle – oh, I forgot, you're a *writer*. So go Chinese."

I stared at him as he motioned towards his vehicle till he gave his bone-in-the-throat laugh. "What, dummy? If I wanted something to happen to you, you'd be with Lurch right now. But thanks."

"For what, cop?"

"It's been bugging me for years who he looks like, and now I know. A handsome guy like me, you'd figure I'm a sweetheart. But I'm not, or haven't you heard. So get in the vehicle. Believe it or not, I got other shit to do today."

There were enough screens and gauges and pulsing lights and whiz-whats jammed in Cummings' spewer to fly the freaking Chinese moon mission. I pointed to one with the outline of a man as its screen saver, and he said, "That's a honey. Can download biometrics from nine different databases. All this crap is fine as far as it goes, but I still learn a hell of a lot more the old-fashioned way – someone tied to a chair."

As big as it was outside, the seats were damn cramped, the steering wheel scraping Cummings' modest gut. I found the control to move the seat back, but it already was. He laughed and said he'd ordered the special "Big-Man Package," not that you'd know it – yet another hollow marketing triumph. He said he was glad of the opportunity to talk "man to man."

"Long as only one of us has a gun, it ain't man to man. But go on."

"You really are a disagreeable little shit. I hand you my gun, you're still mine. Could you even *point* to the safety in under ten seconds, by which point I've damaged you maybe six different ways. Don't think you didn't get damn lucky with Lurch, though I'll be laughing for a while, driving up and finding the likes of you ready to bash his brains in. That kind of violence isn't in your current profile, so welcome to my world."

"You can only push a good man so far, Cummings. You MoFos'll learn that someday."

"For somebody living in a couple of rented rooms filled with cardboard boxes of crap nobody cares about, you act like you're swinging a big one. Speaking of which, heard from your wife lately?"

"I don't have a wife. The MoFos – you or not, doesn't matter – put the final nail in that coffin."

"That was out of New York. But the tape I heard, she wasn't bad for her first time. You didn't catch on till the conversation was half over. We should sic her on her Wall Street boyfriend, who's pretty damn shaky."

"What'd you want to talk about, cop? It wasn't my private life."

"Your *what*? See, you don't know how to play nice. No wonder the only thing remotely like a friend you got is that alcoholic, Ralph."

He plucked any string he wanted, then wrapped it round my neck. "Nothing to say – right. First thing you gotta know, Forbes, there's a rule in this town: you don't mess with Calfers. And if you don't know – assume he is. If someone is worth your time messing with at all, the way things are going, he's probably a Calfer."

"Like you and Whitaker."

"Parnell? Unless you got your man tied to a chair, who knows deep down what anyone believes. He's still thinking with his dick, a guy his age, I know that."

He blipped his siren, got a cab to move and rolled through a red light. I said, "And what about you? Do you believe in that shit?"

"Get real, Forbes. A high school grad doesn't rise from busting heads in Southeast to running over half of one of the country's most ... *lucrative* police departments by shoving my head up my ass. Go along to get along. A concept you might consider."

"So why do I care about any of this?"

He slammed on the brakes, stopped and stared hard. "You think I have to fill out one single sheet of paper to drop you into any holding tank in DC I want? Then a word from me to turn my criminals loose, by the time they're done, there's not enough of you left to scrape off the floor and mail to your parents in Mineola – in a regular envelope."

I stayed shut up.

"I'm a patient man, but I'm a little busy with these damn Nepalese," he said, rolling again. "Now, you care, because Whitaker's an idiot, but he *was* a useful idiot. And it doesn't look good if a National Guard private and some buffoon – what's with those shorts, man? – take out a major defense company."

Feigning hard, "What in the world are you talking about?"

"The Grinder – leave it alone. And how the hell did you get Whitaker's e-mails, anyway? … Fine, don't tell me, I don't give a shit. That's Whitaker's look-out. Though I am surprised Bettinger has lost it enough to fax you instructions. He was never the same after that blast concussion he got showing off over in We're-Fucked-istan 'mentoring' the T-scum who got him. Plus taking down the Grinder sets a bad precedent, too many of you Homelanders getting way too many ideas as it is. Look at your search-refusal bullshit spreading like ditch weed."

"You don't care about all them Boots, three-hundred a year, getting killed in unnecessary rollovers, not to mention all the wounded?"

"The Grinder's not that bad, you drive it right. Just have to know what you're doing, war or not. Gonna get some for the department. No payload, but them new ones with fake windows, drivers get the hell out of their way."

"Three-hundred deaths a year – fuck 'em?"

"Forbes, nobody questions Pentagon spending. Not before HeadFuck and certainly not now. The number of foreign replacement Boots we got signing up, that's just another line item on a budget. There's always plenty more brown boys who want to learn English with a flag on their shoulder. Besides, the rollovers are nothing compared to the real combat casualties, especially if they pull HeadFuck's strings the way I'm hearing on our next Sands."

"Always, *always* gotta be that next one, huh?"

"We're supposed to go back to making widgets? You think you Homelanders even remember how? But a little closer to home – "

"You mean something you actually care about."

"Watch it, mister. Now Swyve, amazingly enough, is a big-shot at ASPIC's DC office – you know about ASPIC? And they are getting way too damn greedy with this privatization campaign of theirs. He and his boss, Miller, weren't allowed into the Calfers, and normally we take anyone in jobs like that. So that should tell you something. Swyve complained that it was because we thought he was too ugly. If he wants to think the Calfers are like some Georgetown fraternity, let him."

"I don't know – he could probably carry a keg on each of those shoulders he's got."

"Shut up, Forbes. Anyway, he's getting a little too damn ambitious telling me what I can and cannot do in *my* town. There's two number twos in this department, I'm one of them, and the chief has a lot of … outside interests, let's call them. And now someone who couldn't even keep you under his thumb stuck in a hospital room is giving me orders? That little embarrassment, by the way, is another reason he wants you so bad. And that's before I spread news of his ass-whipping today."

"My heart bleeds for you, Cummings. There's not enough T money to go around? In DC of all places?"

"Ain't never enough. Till you learn that, you'll never have more than that one window you got. Or are you satisfied with that, a man your age? Still, I'll say this, you somehow keep feeding yourself into a buzz saw and coming out the other side. So what I'm telling you, wise guy, is you get any good shit on ASPIC, you run with it – big."

He drove a block, pointed out some skell scratching to get by on the corner as "a Null ripe for it." Then, "I see you can keep your mouth shut. Who knew? Or did I hit a nerve?"

"Keep talking, Cummings. Hasn't cost me anything yet."

He slammed on the brakes again – oh spare me. "Do you

have any idea who you're talking to or what these two hands have done the last year alone? How easy it'd be if not for the *possibilities* you represent."

"I'm not kissing your ass – I'm past that now. Aside from killing me, which I agree is contraindicated from a strategic point of view, you can't really marginalize me at this point, so – "

"You aren't so marginal anymore. Or haven't you heard? And just so you know, no file is ever truly closed. Maybe that's where you civilians get your myth about the Minders."

"You mean the Minders, as such, don't exist?"

"You'll never know, certainly not with – what do you people call it? – a Blue coming your way. But, as tight as we got our hands on the wheel, people like me were gonna hand it over to some new outfit out of thin air just cause HeadFuck is on top for a while? That's after it took thirty-seven years to get what I got? *Bold, Extolled, Impregnable* – my ass."

"Oh come on, Commandant, *BEI* is the only thing with the remotest whiff of humor he's done these whole three years."

"It's Commander. Like you didn't know."

"Sure, sure thing, copper, just keep driving."

"Do you even know if HeadFuck is still alive? When was the last time you saw him not in some controlled situation already behind a desk or a podium? Months ago, right? Remember the surgery on his throat, those 'polyps.' Your voice changes, OK. But that doesn't explain why this HeadFuck looks a little shorter than the first one. Or why when he's angry and yelling, this one looks like he's faking it. The first one, you knew it was real."

"Why the hell you telling me this, Cummings?"

"You civ-lib fruits think we play nice in the sandbox at my level? Maybe I'm telling you cause I'm a patriot – just like you, Byline Boy. Or maybe I just think things have gone just a little too far corporate when hyenas like Lurch start acting like it's their turn."

"So everyone turns to the dude in the nasty shorts to get their story out for $250 a pop."

"It'd be for a lot more than that, trust me. A lot more. But here's your bus. Listen, Forbes, like all bullies, Swyve's a coward. He

503

won't cross me for a couple of days. Plus Washington's top Calfer spoke to Whitaker last night and reined him in. You should make it back to Queens OK. After that, turn the buzz saw around."

"It's bolted to the table."

"So pick up the table, asshole, a big guy like you. The ASPIC story should be easy enough, you get your hands on the right stuff. As to the HeadFuck story we were just talking about – depending on how you do on ASPIC – contact is strictly me to you. And no, it won't be someone with a short leg. Now get out and try to keep your ass in one piece. Maybe make some money for a change."

****

Jesus, an editorial try-out before he handed me the big score. Maybe he'll have it all typed up just awaiting my name on top. Taking HeadFuck down, or his simulacrum – that'd get me *Morning Dyspepsia* for sure, they got the balls.

The guy behind the window in the shabby waiting room said the six-o'clock bus was sold out. I got a ticket for the eight o'clock and left to buy the kid's composition notebook that was all I could find and the treat of a four-dollar pen. I was saving money why? My whole arm felt weird, the poison no doubt working its way up. Back in the 'waiting room,' the shrill Chinese music stopped my pen. Despite the danger of showing myself on the street, I found a spot on a wall to wedge between two bushes and scribble more "Penn Tale."

Heck if Carole was joining – no, *leading* – the team, she could use "Penn's" support. Surely our louche strategy summit was in the offing. So I got to writing of Frankie and his gun, the heart of it I'd been shirking. And was happy with the effort when I wandered back around 7:30 to find the next bus late getting in and not leaving till at least nine. Hence a plate of squid in the world's most deserted Chinatown.

The bus driver sucked a cigarette down hard, then lit a new one off the first. On the verge of escape – though nobody had tried a drive-by yet – I silently egged him on, hoping his cluster of shiny gold pineapples by the door would keep me safe. But forget my gallery of assailants. The driver devoted most of his attention to his micro-zap, yelling into it while wheeling the groaning old bus through DC's twists and turns with two fingers. Woulda been darn ironic, getting squashed on a bus.

But we progressed till a mammoth delay at that tunnel in Baltimore cost over two hours. As we sat and inched and mostly sat, I got my window open to inquire of a young guy in some sleek Eurotrash convertible. He said Homeland Control was "testing a new T-enhancement at the other end." I asked why they were worried about something *leaving* the tunnel, and he said, "Are you questioning T-shit, BEI?"

"It's the wave of the future, dude – all aboard!"

He digested that, flipped me the bird and said, "That's obviously why you're hanging out the window of a *bus* begging for information." And he scooted into an opening in the far lane. By the time we finally crept through the tunnel, there was nothing to see.

I sat, scribbled, stewed and marveled that this baby seal to Statie's club less than two weeks before had been about to kill a man. Eventually I saw a clock reading 2:39 as we wound through Philly. Happy not to have succumbed to poison, I jammed my work under my thigh and clipped my fancy new pen to my styling new shirt. Everything else I carried was out of sight.

PART TEN

Epilogue

Wedged hard up against it, something droning away nearby, I'm either sprawled across two seats of a bus or been gobbled by a dragon, jammed between his ribs and fire-maker. I open my eyes: bus. Manhattan's towers visible through the murk, where had the night gone? Sleeping in my own bed come what may Thursday night was a prime reason to quit DC. Then I remember the pointless foul-up at the Baltimore tunnel, jamming the biggest road in the country. Just a reminder, folks, life can get shitty any way, any time the MoFos choose.

Christ, looping down and around into the Lincoln Tunnel, there he is again, HeadFuck looming up way too close on a giant billboard. Part of a new campaign, maybe, to compensate for him being so seldom on TV, or dead or whatever. A stylized portrait like in Virginia, all martial and resolute, but the BEI is in static red letters ten-feet high, not Virginia's flashing neon. Whether his sterner glare here is anything more than the man's natural reaction to being so close to Manhattan, I can't say.

Hey, *Lincoln* Tunnel, the skinflint bus company purchasing landing rights in midtown. Cool, less of a trek to Nick's. I soon find myself on a stool gazing out a big window on Broadway in the Fifties armed with a three-buck bacon-egg sandwich and coffee ($8.79 in DC, powdered eggs and grinning lout at the door included). Outside, a cute, punkish couple out-all-night draped all over each other stop to kiss and rub it in. Should I have taken one of those jobs over the years and *maybe* still be ensconced with Nicki? What, and miss all these thrills and spills, women in Milwaukie trying to smuggle bras through enemy lines? I mop egg with toast and, despite her betrayal, dread seeing her. I –

Holy crap, what happened to my hand? The hot, paper coffee cup working the band-aid off, I see the cut's morphed into an ugly, raised, purplish scar that looks awfully permanent.

A bright, garish, jagged crust now lodged on my palm, either wear a band-aid to draw the MoFo's attention or display getting Raytheoned. Or keep my fist permanently clenched – what the times demand, right on! As this spreads, little illegal shops will spring up behind rotting fences to get this shit burned off at great expense and worse pain. Will my new stigmata prove a problem presenting my license to the gatekeepers in Nicki's lobby, its significance having already dripped down to their bottom rung of the MoFo ladder?

Just go freaking get divorced way up high in 47-J. Her building a tall, jagged tooth, I can't quite make out its exact color. The lobby guy dials up my picture on a large screen to his right, one worth saving, yeah, from years ago, the sun *visibly* setting over my shoulder on the ferry. He mumbles, compares it to my even more ancient license photo and brings some suit out from in back to confer – a whole lot of rigmarole for simply ringing a tenant. I inform them only something crucial would have me there that time of morning, and wheedle enough they finally deign to call the Turncoat Wife to authorize access.

Nicki opens the door wearing a soignée dark blue robe I've certainly never seen, turns without a word and flips a switch to part some complicated drapes for a floor-to-ceiling of what would be vast stretches of Queens had the murk not drawn down after a mile or so. Impressed in spite of myself, I drink my full while she crosses to the far side of the room and flops on a big, fancy couch, not a word from either of us. Man, the tripartite Comb-Over Bridge (re-christened to honor his recent shuffling off and to dis RFK) looks odd curling the wrong way looking east from here, not Bumfuckville's west.

"Are you going to stand there with your back to me?"

And yup, right where it should be is Stap's roof, the back yard so enormous I catch a glimpse of weeds even at this angle.

I turn and take in the highly stylized living room with its purple chrome coffee table and complicated, uncomfortable chairs. One wall is alternating tiger stripes of shiny yellow and matte black. The red wall over by the dining nook is marred by a big bright, abstract excrescence of the sort Nick and I used to snicker at in galleries. The only old friend her grandmother's big oak armoire, it's all shivery and spare and a far, fancy cry from our once comfy crib.

Jesus, she's cut her hair, all that crowning glory reduced to a horrible, executrix-bob length just below her ears, and has she colored it some too? I voice surprise, and she shoots back, "You're right, it's ugly as sin. You ever think, genius, that thanks to you I have damn good reason not to want to look like myself, maybe try to avoid the leeches with their licensed whole-vids. Huh?"

Nothing to say to that, I'm saved by Otis running up to snaggle back and forth between my legs. We have a glorious reunion and – certain it was going to take a small crane to hoist me up from the depths of her weird chair – then he's on my lap, his machine going full blast.

"You watch sports now, or what's with the giganto TV?"

"I've barely turned it on. I watch our crappy little old one in the bedroom. It's for show – gotta have something anchoring the wall opposite the couch, and those dusty paintings we had just didn't look right."

"For show – like this whole freaking place. I mean, where are all your books?"

"The building doesn't let you move in with old books – mites or something. Anyway, you fallen down a hole, wherever the hell you were, I finally called Poopous last night, who was just a little too delighted to hear from me. He had no clue about you, but said some men have been sniffing around. He said this is the most fun he's had since the colonels, and then he tried to flirt about me catching the reference. Amazingly, he's not pissed at you, but you gotta watch your ass with the Mexicans. Two more got snatched."

Bottom of the heap, Mexican dudes. Speaking of Turd-Touch, there was a copy of yesterday's *Toast* on the gleaming coffee table, a giant block headline, "DISGRACED!" over probably the only unappealing photo of Carole extant. I point. "What she do?"

"Big, big scandal. Years before Fire-Dude, her nineteen-year-old boyfriend was busted with a joint in his pocket at a park in Queens when she was an innocent slip of a girl of seventeen. It was past the park's closing time, hence the search, though they were just sitting on a bench."

"And all along we thought she was like Jessica Rabbit: not bad, just drawn that way."

"She defended you as having done nothing wrong in Penn Station, and there's talk she's planning to refuse a search herself. So the knives come out. Speaking of which, you've never actually refused a search, have you, Mahatma?"

Sure, that counted, I'd told Officer Umbert to shove it *and* told him why. "Actually I have, yesterday to a cop at the bus station in Washington. But there was no one else around. It – "

"How convenient, no one else around. So what happened? I mean, how'd you end up here so bright and early the next morning? Which thrills me no end, by the way."

"A top cop intervened on my behalf – no joke! He sees the bigger picture."

"Like I believe any part of that. You know, I had it going pretty good up here for all of two months before you came flying over from *Queens* and crashing through that big window there uninvited. I was going to be the chief copywriter on by far the biggest account in the history of the agency, and now I'm probably getting fired today. If Ernesto doesn't fire me, it's only because he thinks my notoriety – which I did *nothing* to invite – might attract some bottom-feeding clients when all this dies down."

I didn't know she could get any angrier, but she does. "And all of this cause of you and some little abstract civ-lib principle that nobody gives a fuck about. Not anymore, not after years of HeadFuck – Minders Turn Elsewhere! I – "

"The Minders don't exist. They're just the latest boogeyman made up to keep us in line."

"Tell that to the Nulls that keep disappearing. So now all of a sudden you're Mr. Inside Knowledge, you with your recent 'scoop' on a *general* of all people trying to line – what the fuck is that?" she demanded, pointing.

"What – a spider crawl out of my shirt?"

"That. That disgusting mark on your hand. What the hell is that?"

509

"Oh that. Nothing. They cut me and got some goop in it, and now I guess I'm carrying this around." I felt no need to tell her my assailant handed me the goop and instructed me on its use.

"Nice. It'll go with those shorts of yours that you refused to let me throw out years ago. Like you're not already enough of a target without a signifier on your hand. You know this stupid 'Movement' of yours that some diehards are making a stink with: HeadFuck has won, and anyone with any sense accepts that. Maybe we might've challenged him in his first month or two, but the leopard was too clever to show his spots too qiuck. Now, forget about it. And as far I can tell, so what? If you have a decent job – hint, hint – so you're not a Null, and you mind your Ps & Qs, what's the difference? Nobody cares about the shit you worry about. So what if they watch everything we do? Enjoy! Most of it is boring. What, you still want to have sex outdoors at your age? I was a secretary a couple of years ago, and look at where I landed. Look at this Goddamn couch!" She was screaming.

"Nicki, it's awfully early for all this. Don't you care about your neighbors?"

"Those creeps? Even before you unleashed your disaster, they'd rather choke than say hello to you." She got loud again. "All my life I've wanted a one-hundred percent Carpathian leather couch. Now that I've got one I'm still paying for, it's gonna look damn nice in whatever hole I end up in back in Queens. Queens *again*, I can't fucking believe it! I'll be lucky to get another friggin' secretary job."

She sat there sobbing, which moved me not a whit. Down the road, I didn't want memories of what was mostly a good marriage permanently marred by the sheer uncertainty of what Cummings, of all scumbags, had said. How many poor fools decided to trust him right before he strapped them to a chair?

Nick at a weak moment, catch her by surprise so maybe she won't lie. "So keeping a grip on all this splendor here – these life-affirming *possessions* – entitled you to rat me out? Excused you spying on me on the phone Monday night on the train, spying for whatever MoFo got to you and said he'd put in a good word with Ernesto or the cops or whoever? Huh, Nicki, huh?"

Her sobs grind to a sudden halt. "What the fuck are you talking about now? You think this is some kind of game? No, this morning is about me telling you what's what and you leaving. Now – "

"Nicki! We've been married a long time, and you've always been a lousy liar. It was obvious Monday night on the phone, all that butter-wouldn't-melt 'Oh, I'm so interested in what brings you to Washington' crap. And mentioning the Harrisburg 'right downtown' about six times, and then, for all the dunces listening in, saying that *Sy-ri-ac* – remember? – is easy enough to spell. Huh, Nicki? Before you lie to me, know that I've got proof."

"What proof!" I keep staring. Then, quietly, "Alright, look, Mr. Reporter-Man. I wasn't spying, not for real. That schmuck – this was in a freaking F&F conference room, him, me and Ernesto late Monday afternoon – said they just 'wanted to be aware of your intentions so as to keep you safe given the controversy surrounding you.' Or some shit."

"Apparently nobody bothered to try to keep some clown from shooting at me in Stap's backyard."

"They lie so much, and even when they're not it's couched in such bullshit, it's hard to know. Anyway, what could I do?"

I put Otis down, haul myself up, pace towards that window and note with satisfaction the bleary outline of the not terribly far Manhattan Bridge. I whirl on her. "You could quit your damn job. Decide maybe you don't want to be part of convincing black kids to kill and get killed. Maybe, your one ride this damn merry-go-round, if you don't give a shit enough, you can spend it doing something a little better."

"Like you, you self-righteous prick? Right, quit a job *post-Plunge* that pays like mine does. Or did, rather, thanks to you! Now get out! Like you really had 'proof' – you liar. Go! You sleazed your way to what you wanted. Fine, we're *divorced*, you hear that? Face-to-face, so it's official. Tell Stapapoopous to sign for the papers if you're off on one of your self-involved, little save-the-world missions."

There it was, the pronouncement – the axe. However expected, still a fish in the chops. I sat back down and Otis immediately leaped up.

"Yeah, well, don't waste any money on a lawyer. I don't have any to fight over, and I don't want any of yours."

"Too late. I had to show Ernesto a letter from an attorney."

"Punt the lawyer and download a form. I'm telling you, I got no reason to fight it."

"No shit. Look, I've gotta go figure out what to wear to keep Ernesto from firing me today."

She looked awfully pathetic in her gorgeous robe there on her ridiculous couch. Guess there'd be no hug and kiss to commemorate the good times. "What the hell are you looking at?" she demanded.

"Nothing. Just looking at my wife one last time. We went in different directions – nothing to be done."

"Ya think, genius? Why the hell couldn't you just pay your half of the rent?"

"Nicki, I owed you exactly one-and-a-half-months. It wasn't like I wasn't hustling every day."

"Hustling to write all this crap nobody wants to hear, even if it is true. And you got so smug, with this damn look on your face, always challenging people about the '*Imperium*' – oooh! I couldn't even take you to F&F parties anymore."

"Then you started having so much fun you didn't care. You haven't exactly let any grass grow under your ass since we split, have you Nicki?"

"What the hell is that supposed to mean?"

"MoneyBags isn't your first, is he?"

"Wouldn't you like to know. But you want to hear something funny? I did everything Ernesto and that prick asked of me in that room at F&F. So I stupidly thought it was a one-time deal with you on the phone Monday night. But it's never enough. That bastard came back Wednesday afternoon and said I was such a natural, he needed just one more 'favor.' "

"Favor, huh?" What else had she freaking done, taken them out to Mineola to scare Mom and Pop into showing them my boyhood room?

"Ernesto was smart, he just walked me to the room and told me to go inside and do what the man said – men, cause there were two of them, the new one even more slippery and threatening than the first. Turns out there were a couple of things they wanted me to try to worm MoneyBags into discussing at dinner that night."

Christ, did Cummings know about this, or is the over-grasping MoFo mind just always chasing the next score? "Yeah?"

"They said don't worry, they already knew where we were eating, they'd take care of recording it and everything. Just get him to talk about a few specific financial issues. It'd be easy cause they were gonna put something in his drink."

"And what issues were those?"

"All this technical shit. I had trouble enough memorizing it for that evening. The Chinese and different 'tranches' and stuff. Plus were any of his clients shifting out of the dollar into that new currency all the South American countries united to have."

"He talked?"

"On and on, putty in my hands all night. The next morning, Ernesto said they were really happy with me, not that he said anything about me keeping my job. He said if MoneyBags and I broke up, they had some old fossil in mind for me to date."

"A regular pro, huh?"

"Fuck you if you think any of this has been easy.... I should get some of whatever they put in MoneyBags' drink cause he just got wind of your little anti-search campaign. His – "

"Not so little, Nicki."

"Un-huh. Anyway, his biggest T client is freaking out with it catching on some, and he went ballistic on me. Who knows – you working your magic in spades – no job probably and maybe no MoneyBags. Maybe I *should* turn clandestine."

"Jesus, I should sit on the thing, feel the wonder of it."

"You're not sitting on anything, whatever you're talking about."

"You're willing to do an awful lot for a stupid couch."

She gets up and flings the door open. Otis on in years, I pick him up for our likely last cuddle and almost lose it as he purrs and kneads his paws up towards my face as I rub his belly. I say "Well, see you later" and go to kiss her cheek, but she darts away. Nope, no hug, no kiss, a decade down the drain, not so much as a goodbye. No nothing, no mas. What the times demand. Maybe the younger, marriage-adverse Nulls are on to something.

****

Having cut it off, not the wind-in-her-hair girl I'd married. A week ago I still loved her. God, to think of how thrilled I was that she dropped into an e-mail that she missed me, a meaningless pearl before swine. More crushed than I'd counted on, my feet find their way through the blur of Central Park. You have to present photo ID to walk through even the free part of the zoo, so I hump up a hill and around.

Going down the steps at 5th and 59th to the train, I blunder into the newsstand and, holy mackerel, there in all her prim glory on the covers of both the *Chirp* and the *Toast* is Chilean Cassandra in a stately, summer-weight light blue suit sitting serenely on one of those weird canes with an attached round little seat. I buy a *Chirp*. She was sitting in the middle of Penn Station with about nine cops massed behind her looking miffed, all under the headline: "Aristocrat Says No!" At the bottom: "Chilean Mr. Big's Estranged Wife Snarls Penn Refusing Bag Search".

The two-page spread inside (which describes me as the "ethically and sartorially challenged, de facto founder of the No-Search Brigade") identifies my prickly friend as Magdalena Eloy-Heurte y Martinez. She was "acting suspicious" in Penn yesterday evening, drifting around carrying her cane-seat and a little valise filled with what turned out to be nothing but tangerines. She meandered in front of the LIRR search table long enough to be finally summoned forward for a search at 9:27 p.m., and then she loudly refused " 'based on centuries of American law.' " She also claimed diplomatic immunity for, though separated from Chile's foreign secretary for decades, they've never formally divorced.

Then Magdalena unfolded her seat and sat – and sat – and the cops were afraid to approach, such was the old lady's steely mien. They ended up having to close Penn Station *and* evacuate the office tower above for close to an hour – one heck of a gnarly, expensive stick in their spokes. Finally one of those guys in a Michelin Man suit waddled up, and she couldn't have been more gracious, offering all the cops tangerines. Being led away in handcuffs, she said her Demo made her feel decades younger,

" 'carrying me back to my days protesting the Disappeared in my country.' "

I'm a cog in a big wheel gaining speed downhill. Fine by me. Carole and Magdalena make damn better figureheads than the mope staggering around in the spotlight. Let me try to do my thing tightening the reins on ASPIC a bit; that'd be a good job of work. The *Warpath* article saving my bacon yesterday afternoon, here's hoping "Penn/Bellevue/ASPIC" provides some long-term protection.

Things moving fast, I need to google myself, find out what I missed boycotting the papers while in DC. Will I be allowed to sit and pound the keyboard, then (in a pair of long pants) go out and pound a few beers, wake up and repeat tomorrow, all with the cops having found explosive residue on the pack they'd exploded? Damn, should've read that copy of *It Can't Happen Here* when I had the chance.

Or maybe head to Indiana to be that big-time investigater comely Barbara is looking for. Ain't nobody hanging Everett on Turd-Touch, but at least get greased doing something real trying to bring justice to someone who'd have laughed at my 'abstractions' (screw you, Nicki). Maybe even learn dead Everett's daughter's name as a first step towards helping to raise her up.

* * * * * * * * * * * * * * *

I come sweating up the walk, no cops or reporters visible, Mr. Staphilopoulos on the porch smoking a nail, his new sports shirt untucked.

"Hey, what's cooking, good looking? Somebody die and leave you a new shirt?"

"Ha-ha. I need such a shirt. A regular *Penn* Station around here since you been gone. Lawyers, newsies, cops. All kinds of people. Your *father* comes by – very nice man. Why you such a problem to him? Everybody easier if I look like guy owns this big house."

So my magic has benefited Stap, anyway. "Anyone I want to know?"

"I get to her. But first I have to say sorry. No, first, you still this side of the dirt. That's good, cause no one knows. Some man shoots my garage and, bingo, no more you. So nice to see you. It hot in Washington? You were there, your story says. Then maybe, who knows, big shot flies to Rome, have veal for lunch."

"Stap, what are you talking about? I've been riding a bus and eating egg sandwiches – cheap. So what's going on?"

"I don't like saying sorry, so I talk nonsense. But there were four of them, four big toughs. I try to stop them, but they push me hard up against that post there. I thought they break my hip. And – "

"Who did? Someone messed with an old guy like you? Did you call the cops?"

"Cops? They say *they* cops – who knows, they don't leave names. Besides, me and cops not friendly right now, they always taking all the spots on the block."

"I'm sorry about your hip – you OK? What'd they want?"

"They wanted you, what do you think. But my hip, that's the thing. You get a broken hip my age, not so good. I got a little scared – not something I like saying. So I lie there on *my* porch, right there" he points "and don't stop them going up."

"Stap, Jesus, nobody expects you to, four men against one. They knew my rooms?"

"Must have, because later – I was behind my locked door when they go – your door was closed but unlocked. And it was locked the whole time you're gone, I make sure. I couldn't tell if they took anything. Your computer's still there on the table."

"I'll find out soon enough. I'm really sorry about your hip. I don't mean to be so high maintenance – you know, like a Ferrari."

"You? You mean like that Plymouth going all rust in my backyard. The hip, it's OK, an excuse to get drunk that night. But drunk mostly cause I feel bad I let them push me around. Fifteen years ago, *they* be the one getting pushed. What's that on your hand?"

The scar looks angry. "They cut me, Stap. So now I'm branded, like a cow. No big deal – privacy was a memory for me anyway."

"They scum. People are not going to take their shit anymore, you'll see. Oh, before I forget, some cop making all nicey-nice left this for you, him practically begging. Like an old man can't carry a piece of paper around in his pocket." He fishes out a crumpled envelope.

"It's the ones making nice that are really out to get you, Mr. Staphilopoulos."

Just a business card inside, from an MTA Detective Tiggert, with a scrawled note I read out loud: *Please call at your convenience – there's reason to talk.* "They're scared, Stap, at least the cops who shot me. They're trying to play nice. That's cause Carole – you know, the blonde who got shot with me – went on TV saying it was all their fault. You believe that?"

"She getting in bed with you – ha! – another mystery. Your regular mail is upstairs on your table. I figure best not leave downstairs for some curiosity-cat. You got at least three envelopes from lawyers – trouble-chasers."

"Yeah, well, I got ninety days to file notice of claim." I held up the card. "I'll call this bastard Monday, see what he has to say. Can't afford a lawyer right now, so maybe just take notes and say as little as possible myself."

"That's what everybody thinks – smarter than cops. Then they start talking nice and offering coffee and cigarettes. This one's already started."

"I don't smoke cigarettes. So please tell me nobody got killed at the bodega down on the corner."

"You gone, no one here to ask. Tuesday, I went there to find out about all the cops there Monday night. The sandwiches are horrible, especially the bread – that I know for years. So I bought one of those tall green beers of yours. Better than most American beer."

"Alright, Ballantine, great. What the hell happened?"

"You saved him, that man who broke my garage window he still owes me. Cause the NYPDs already in the store know train cops are after you, and they thought the man in suit, maybe he a train-cop detective. So they not shoot him. They standing there with guns out yelling at him to drop his gun. But he doesn't – *and* they still not shoot, you believe that? Then everybody's hero, the store guy, sneaks up and puts his mop handle over the man's neck and wrestles him down. So the cops jump on top."

"The counter guy did that, really?"

"Right. The counterman. The man by the cash – what you call it?"

"What? Register."

"Register, right – he not move. But the other guy jumps him, and now he's a hero. Illegal, from Egypt, but Commissioner Ted, that dick, says he take care of that. So you do something good for somebody."

"Me? I didn't do anything."

"Sure you do. Bring man with gun in there, and now Egypt gets his papers. So now what you do?"

"What, now?" He nods. "I'm going upstairs. I got something to write."

"You mean like Wednesday, when you hang that general. What's the matter, *colonel* not good enough for you?"

"He's only got one star."

"You know about that?"

"Tits in the Senate – good, like Greek beach. My friend with computer, the Turk printed it out, and we all read it Wednesday night here on porch. Big arguments over your show-off English words. Army has orgy almost? Like Greece in the old days. So, you go after HeadFuck next, that phony?"

"Nah." I stand there smiling, deflecting any editorial conference.

"OK. You keep quiet till it comes up on the Turk's computer. How come you don't get in the *Daily Chirp* I can go buy? But you got your own ways."

"Thanks, Stap. I sure appreciate all your help and support. I mean – "

"Sit on my balls, mister. My hip's OK, so the bad thing is yesterday she turns me into your mailman."

She? Divorce papers? What did it matter, though Nicki could've mentioned it. "Yeah, what, somebody send me a chocolate cake?"

"Cake – you mean brick. The one hit me when another looker shows up looking for you, all whispering and nervous. And this one was *young*, too. Pinch her anywhere, no fat. That one calls herself your 'wife,' she a looker too, especially in that yellow dress. You know her yellow dress?"

"I've seen it, Stap."

"She always getting stuck on my porch. I'll drive her home to New York next time. But she's at least the same planet as you, your age and hers. But this one yesterday – twenty-six, tops!"

Elaine? Should I thank the *Chirp* for printing my address? "Alright, I'll bite: she wants to bear me sons. Who the hell was she?"

"Wait, big shot. You in a hurry? I was screaming at cop parked all sloppy, taking *two* spots. So he plays with his siren again, remember? Then he goes. So I sit here waiting for it to cool down – ha! – and up this little looker-mouse shows. She asks for you. I'm surprised – she not a newsie, I can tell – so instead of saying 'who?' I say you not seen head or tail."

"This was yesterday?"

"Yesterday, yeah, like I tell you. Now shut up. She was sneaking, watching the house, and she says she likes the way I 'handle' that cop. Handle – that for broom. I just say what any New York American say about parking right on a crowded street."

"More Americans speaking up every day. But Stap, where's the mail she gave you – you're making me crazy."

"Good, all the people you make crazy, including Mexico upstairs. They even more mad at you, you should know. Anyway, come in."

He leads me into the house and into his big dark apartment, telling me as he goes, "It was ten last night, and I tried to tell her I drive her to the train. It's OK, she can trust an old guy like me. Or get her a car service, call a Greek friend, the only one come down here probably now – another of your magic tricks. But she says no, she has a car around the corner."

He ushers me in to a surprisingly spotless kitchen, spotless cause, looking around, I realize it's not used beyond the opening of jars. He reaches into his stove and takes out a manila envelope. "That's the safest place cause I never use it. Fire-proof. You see I put my own tape on right on top of hers. Nobody can say nothing!"

If it was from Elaine, man, the girl's motivated. Christ, could she possibly be in league with Cummings, him worrying about ASPIC encroaching and telling me a story on them's a piece of cake? Come on, dummy, *I* presented myself at Al's office on Monday – the contact was me to him. My landlord stood there clutching it maddeningly.

"Stap, did she say her name?"

"What, you crazy – no. She just said she hated to leave it, but she was going to have to trust me. I old enough to be her father's father, I had to stop myself yelling about trust, looker American girls think they shit flowers. But she says – and what this mean? I try to figure, it's worse than that vest-pocket veto you told me about. She says she has to leave your letter 'before things go bump in the night.' "

"Right. So, Stap, please give me the envelope, I gotta get upstairs." I force myself not to grab it from the old man.

"Sure, but what that mean, 'bump in the night?' "

"Nothing. It means before something gets her – before a ghost materializes out of nowhere and goes boo!"

"*Boo*? She said bump."

"Stap, Jesus, I'm gonna scream. It's just a phrase, you know, like 'coming round the mountain when they come.' "

He stares blankly, and another cliché is shockingly out of reach. "You know. Or – or 'the early bird catches the worm.' It means before the MoFos get her, like the ones that are after me."

"Who are MoFos?"

"Stap, the motherfuckers!"

"They come through me first. I don't give a shit, an old guy like me. This most fun I had since *before* the colonels. They not fun – not like the stupid Americans after you."

I tell myself to count to five before I grab it from him. He hands me the envelope, waiting for me to open it right there. I look at him all expectant, but wave it at him smiling and shake my head.

"Good, do your job right," he says.

"I'm trying. A lot of people are helping me."

"OK, a surprise, OK? September's rent doesn't count."

"What do you mean, it's not the first yet, not even close."

"Hey, boy, listen to what people say. A little birdie paid for you for September. So keep that in your pocket, you need it. What I going to spend it on? Maybe you buy a big ad, put it up next to the sign HeadFuck's got on the BQE with those words nobody knows what they mean. Why he say he can't get pregnant?"

"Jeeze, Stap. I don't know what to say – you sure? I mean...." My protest sputters quickly.

He grunts, then gets animated again. "These MoFos you call them, like sharks driving slow around the block – God help you, you beep. It take at least *five* of them to get past me now. Like I said, I don't care." He pulls up his shirttail and shows me a big knife in a sheath on a second belt.

"Mr. Staphilopoulos! What are you, crazy? Put that away – I don't even want to see it. They'll shoot you. Jesus, Stap!"

"Yeah, yeah. You be a good boy and go write your stories and save the world. And let me take care of this porch. *My* porch, OK, big-stuff."

I give him a hug and try but fail to browbeat him into putting the knife away. I just hope he realizes, all his talk of fun, there's a little more of it this side of the dirt.

****

Up four flights and behind my papier mache door, the Hovel doesn't look horribly awry. Maybe the cartons on the far side of the bed aren't stacked exactly as I'd left them – not that they wouldn't do me a solid stealing those old files. As for my computer, anything truly important was printed out and in those boxes.

Bump. Have to get to a pay phone and call them tonight, make sure Al and Elaine are OK, Al who (unlike me, Lou) does have a young, very dependent child. For of course the envelope is from them, not that they included a note. Two contracts, twenty pages in all. A sixteen-page, "Executive Summary" of ASPIC's contract to privatize the MTA's search program and a four-page employment contract for that deputy MTA police commish, Everidge.

Throw in their rote responses I'll get on Monday (the police union too), and there's more than enough on the ASPIC-MTA angle. And, yup, the phrase "$159-million per annum" leaps off the front page. Flipping through, there's additional appealing verbiage: "Dedicated T Protectors, the armaments ASPIC's operatives carry will be left to the Contractor's discretion." Plus, "Sworn Peace Officers, ASPIC's operatives retain full powers of arrest." I can hope there's something buried in the back about consultants. There'd be one or two women tops, and it might be cake identifying the MTA board member's wife. As to Everidge, he's pulling down a cool $315,000 per, plus numerous incentives for providing "operational oversight support" – i.e., being a figurehead. And, holy shit, look at this: they're contracting to do three million searches a year! That's like eight- or nine-thousand a day.

Very riki-tik. A day-and-a-half crunching words – there on the table where I'd left them are the notes squeezed from my pen mid-Stuffing – and get "Penn/Bellevue/ASPIC" the hell out. Then reach out to Carole and Magdalena to acknowledge their place at the Movement's helm and....

Hell, I should hole up here and just write the whole magilla up as a novel. With Stap's astonishing September dispensation, I still had October socked away. Screw reporting, it's a mug's game. Nobody'll believe the last two weeks, anyway, so just spin my web. *Two weeks*, yeah, going back to that night on the LIRR – Statie and Cat Wrangler, Boss Conductor and the Sergeant Major – that started it all (my shoulder was still sore, damnit) and ratchet it right up to coming home today. One month to write up one week and October to write the second, no problem. Come up with a catchy title, that's the tough part, and make a bundle provided I conjured up a good enough hook. Get it out for the Christmas rush.

There's a loud hammering at the door downstairs – probably not Everett, though he's the only one entitled to righteous anger. As to the rest, nothing but venal, money-grubbing, power-crazed MoFos. That's right, Can't Freaking Touch Me! not till I hit send on "Penn" Monday afternoon. You got that?

Shit, the SecDef whole-vid! Had the foursome who'd invaded the Hovel somehow missed it? Three-hundred uselessly dead troops a year! Was that the zen-nugget secret of not giving two shits about yourself, Everett, my man? That not giving them makes you care *more* because everything you have is tied up in the Cause?

Wafting up the stairwell, I hear Mr. Staphilopoulos yelling loud about a warrant, and his taxes and this and that. Keep the Goddamn knife hidden, Stap!

I grab at the door hiding the pipes under the sink, then reach up on the front wall to find the micro-zap right where I taped it months ago. I jab at the computer. Work damnit – I should have turned it on first – please don't let them have turned it into a doorstop.

OK, *Warpath* Joe, get ready! I fumble to download it as I hear Stap yelling even louder, obviously signaling me, "You think he's up there somewhere, OK, misters – you find him! You monkeys come in here pushing me in my own house! Fuck you, American shits think you own the world!"

I grab the two ASPIC contracts and the envelope and shove them in different files, down deep in different boxes in my bedroom. The best I can do, the Hovel not offering many more hiding places, really, than a hospital room. Ah, Maureen, my lovely!

What if they've gotten to Joe, Calfers shutting him down cause of the Whitaker piece? Stanley seems pretty damn *impregnable* – send it to them both, suspenders and a belt, tell 'em up top, and let them AP-UPI it. I hear tromping up and down the third floor, people yelling in Spanish. OK:

Friday
Dudes:
They're just about at the door! This whole-vid legit, trust me. Happened at Aberdeen testing ground, whatever it's called, late Spring/early Summer (by calendar). Run it – it's already cost one death. CK site, SandsCasualties.org. for stats on non-combat Grinder deaths, hundreds a year. Sommer Fri, who cares. Get it out now! Them SecDef legs – you'll see – it'll bounce. Sneding to you both, suspenders and belt. Use my name on top, may be all it's got left in it.

Part about them being on the stairs NOT a metaphor. No reply to queries likely at this end. Just run the fucker and then push search-refusals!!! The multitiudes after me, no idea who clawed way to top of heap, or I'd sic you both on them. ASPIC, maybe, a DC biggie of theirs named Swyve. Just a GUESS. Repeat: guess! Push search-refusals – tiny acorn, mighty oak.

Boots thank you, me too.

Dan (byline, Daniel)

And … and … there, sent! Hope the Turk spots it and shows Stap. He'll get a kick out of it.

Man, would've been good to get "Penn/Bellevue/ASPIC" loosed upon the world. Guess I'll have to leave a more cogent rationale for the No-Search Movement – hell, leave clearing the Barmy Bungler's name – to others. Could've skipped that baseball game to write, I suppose, but I still would've been waiting on Elaine's envelope. Besides, I'm glad to have seen the Roughnecks run rough-shod. I can think of that – along with Lois at the top of the stairs.

Will I ever see my stern, fish-out-of-water sweetheart again? And what of Maureen, my lustrous Crimson Colleen, stiffener of spines, my fellow refuse and resister, assuming she wasn't deported, or worse?

More to the point, who to summon here now to help kick some MoFo ass? Whoever is downstairs, ain't no singing telegram. Lois has all that unarmed combat training and might show with some weapons. But who knows what revolutionary, street-fighting shit Maureen might know. Hell, get 'em both (though they won't like each other), and maybe Lou and Lucy too, while I'm at it. And Mac might have a little extra tension to dispel, just a tad. Get Al up here. He's skinny, but he knows a lot. And kung-fu Delores, she's got some anger in her after Tuesday night. Zeke the orderly, maybe, to compare notes on the proper cracking of a MoFo rib and Aretha Franklin for provisions. Zafar to teach them a little history and Shandre to plain stare 'em down. Egypt the counterman, long as he brings his mop. Marko and Bethany to immortalize us all, and Joe to run their vid, Barbara to swear and tear her hair and Everett – sure, he's alive, just slightly DWI-delayed in Pennsylvania – to smite them righteously. Hell, Stanley too, in case Joe gets too medicinally fogged. Fielding Ablegar to overawe them, Judge Feingold to sentence them, Cat Wrangler to gouge their eyes out with her heels and Coney Island Enchantress to take their breath away. God, to think of the thrill just dancing with her – different times. Penn Station's National Guardsman to throw off their aim (and get a medic quick). No, no, no. Get Magdalena, she's done the most for the Movement so far – plus she's got diplomatic immunity – and Carole to exonerate everyone on our side. Pop to hit 'em in the knees with a lead pipe, and Mom so they'll choke gobbling her carrot cake. Creep up the stairs behind them, Stap, you'll know what to do. Otis, claw their faces! Hell, enough fluff. Just get the "fighting machine from the Third ID" and sit back and enjoy the show.

I'd heard precious few chimes at midnight – lately. Still, what larks!

Jesus, they're stomping up the last stairs. Maybe it's only the Minders with a Blue, whatever that means if anything. Just as long as it's not Lurch; I know damn well I'm not getting lucky with him again. I ignore my advice to Stap and root out the carving knife Nicki insisted I take for some reason. Now where –

THE END

525

Afterword

Like all real events, these occupy their own time, two weeks in a specific late August. The year is indicated here and there if you look, maybe do a little arithmetic. To ease calculation, the timeline is occasionally fudged. Divine when to add or subtract, when not.

Some liberties are taken: the Washington Nationals still play at Robert F. Kennedy Memorial Stadium, that old football mausoleum over by the river in Southeast, and certain car companies still own other car companies. As to Philadelphia Phillie Chase Utley and his record-tying World Series which I improperly ignore, I imagine he'll survive the slight.

The rest is true. The footnotes are real – follow the links. Also true is the hush-hush cremation of many hundreds of human remains to make way for the New Jersey Devils hockey arena in Newark. I've interviewed people involved for an article I somehow never wrote (my bad, *New York*). The New York Public Library did require patrons to create a photo ID for the privilege of perusing – not removing – books in its main reading room. Sen. Ben Nighthorse Campbell (R-CO) did call to sic me on a Jack Abramoff still riding high, and I blew it – badly. Humvee Egress Assistance Trainers were widely deployed by the U.S. Army. And Congressional Cemetery really is a members-only dog run. Dues as of this writing is $250 per annum ($200 in *Derail this Train Wreck*'s post-Plunge economy), and there's a waiting list.

Chapter Ten, "Moo!" is straight shoe-leather reporting, aside from a bit of dialogue at the end. Carrying my book-filled, East German Army knapsack, I did futilely parade myself before cops doing searches, did encounter a long line of uncomplaining New Yorkers up the stairs at Herald Square and an MTA officer recording the characteristics of those searched at Penn Station. For many months a real sign there curiously instructed us to call "MTA.PD." PATH train announcements did encourage riders to carry nothing at all.

In fact, the whole darn book is true, now or in a future rushing ever closer. All except the references to the Narrator and Nicki's slipshod lawyer, one Steve by name. My and my wife's real-life civil-rights attorney, Jeffrey A. Rothman, is a lion of the New York bar. After years of tenacious effort, he achieved a settlement with co-defendants Lincoln Center and the City of New York. In an article in the *New York Law Journal* "Applying the Constitution to Private Actors," Christopher Dunn of the New York Civil Liberties Union cited the federal lawsuit Jeff so ably shepherded as bolstering free-speech case law. http://www.nyclu.org/oped/column-applying-constitution-private-actors-new-york-law-journal *Derail*'s website features a 99-and-44/100ths straight account, "At the Behemoth's Beck and Call," of the whole nasty evening.

Footnotes

Links available at <u>Derailthistrainwreck.com</u>

Chapter Twenty-Seven
1. United States District Court, Southern District of New York. 1:05-cv-07331-NRB.
2. Civilian Complaint Review Board: CCRB Case Number 200408189.

Chapter Twenty-Eight
1. Daniel Forbes, "Prime-Time Propaganda" and "Propaganda for Dollars" *Salon.com.* <u>http://www.salon.com/news/feature/2000/01/13/drugs/index.html</u> and <u>http://www.salon.com/news/feature/2000/01/14/payola/index.html</u>.
2. Daniel Forbes, "The Drug War Gravy Train" *Salon.com.* <u>http://www.salon.com/news/feature/2000/03/31/magazines/index.html</u>
3. Daniel Forbes, "Reading, Writing and Propaganda" *Salon.com.* <u>http://www.salon.com/news/feature/2001/08/08/channel/index.html</u>
4. Daniel Forbes, "Missouri Cops Said Ashcroft Agreed to 'Look the Other Way' on Forfeiture Law": The Progressive Review. <u>http://prorev.com/bush4.htm</u>
5. Daniel Forbes, "Judy Miller's Partisan Baggage" *The Huffington Post.* <u>http://www.huffingtonpost.com/daniel-forbes/judy-millers-partisan-bag_b_5064.html</u>
6. Daniel Forbes, "Blair Talks Turkey" *DrugWar.com.* <u>http://www.mapinc.org/drugnews/v04/n000/a108.html</u>
7. Daniel Forbes, "Noted War Blogger Cops to Copying" *Wired.com.* <u>http://www.wired.com/politics/law/news/2003/04/58346?currentPage=all</u>
8. Daniel Forbes, "Bound by a Patient in a Chair, the Feds Call Local Cops for Help" *DrugWar.com.* <u>http://www.mapinc.org/drugnews/v02/n1684/a03.html</u>
9. Daniel Forbes, "New York Used City Vehicles, Extreme

Noise as Weapons Against Peaceful Protesters" *The Progressive Review*. http://nyc.indymedia.org/media/text/high-speed.txt

10. Daniel Forbes, "Did Russians Use Blog to Aid Iraq?" *The Progressive Review*. http://www.informationclearinghouse.info/article2951.htm

11. Daniel Forbes, "The Governor's Sub-rosa Plot to Subvert and Election in Ohio" The Institute for Policy Studies. http://www.fornits.com/anonanon/Forbes/ohio/ohio.pdf

12. Daniel Forbes, "White House And DEA Work to Defeat Michigan Drug Initiative" *DrugWar.com*. http://www.mapinc.org/drugnews/v02/n1636/a06.html?1163.

13. Daniel Forbes, "Fighting 'Cheech & Chong' Medicine" *Salon.com*. http://www.salon.com/news/feature/2000/07/27/ondcp/index.html

Chapter Thirty-Three

1. Robert Housman and Daniel Forbes, "White House Blasts Salon" *Salon.com*.
http://www.salon.com/news/feature/2000/04/20/housman/index.html

2.Richard Linnett, "Adages," *Advertising Age*. http://adage.com/adages/post?article_id=51978

3. Daniel Forbes, "New York Used City Vehicles, Extreme Noise As Weapons Against Peaceful Protesters" *The Progressive Review*. http://nyc.indymedia.org/media/text/high-speed.txt

4. Mark Jurkowitz, "Online Journalist Tangles with Feds Over Antidrug Ad Policy" *The Boston Globe*. http://www.mapinc.org/alert/0161.html

5. Daniel Forbes, "Open Letter: Daniel Forbes Responds to Richard Linnett," *ALTERNET* http://www.alternet.org/module/printversion/13365

Chapter Thirty-Four

1. David Kiley, *Getting the Bugs Out: The Rise, Fall, and Comeback of Volkswagen in America* Hoboken, NJ: Wiley, 2002.

2. David Kiley, *Driven: Inside BMW, the Most Admired Car Company in the World*. Hoboken, NJ: Wiley, 2004.

Chapter Forty-One

1. Daniel Forbes, "$226 Million in Govt Ads Helped Pave the Way for War" *Antiwar.com.* http://www.antiwar.com/forbes/?articleid=2679

Chapter Fifty-Five

1. "Talkback Live," CNN, January 14, 2000.

Afterword

1. Christopher Dunn, "Applying the Constitution to Private Actors" *New York Law Journal* http://www.nyclu.org/oped/column-applying-constitution-private-actors-new-york-law-journal

2. "At the Behemoth's Beck and Call" http://www.derailthistrainwreck.com

Acknowledgements

This journey of many steps would never have been completed without these folks generously prodding my feet: Warren P. & Edith J. Forbes, Will Forbes, Susan Forbes, Margaret Forbes, Kurt Andersen, Caton Gates, Robert Dolan, Stephen M. Feldman, Harry Kafka, David Kiley, Philip Harris, David Milton, Peter J. Nickitas, Jeffrey Rothman, Anastasios Sarikas, Melissa Vu, Laurie Wen, Miriam Zellnik and especially Herself.

8536176R0

Made in the USA
Charleston, SC
19 June 2011